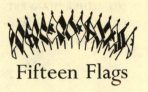

Fifteen Flags

Books by Ric Hardman

NO OTHER HARVEST
THE CHAPLAINS RAID
FIFTEEN FLAGS

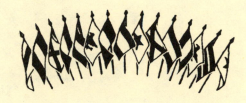

Fifteen Flags

by

RIC HARDMAN

LITTLE, BROWN AND COMPANY • BOSTON • TORONTO

C, 1

*For Kay, my wife, who always makes
long journeys seem short*

Cast of Characters

THE history of the American Siberian Expeditionary Force and of the Allied Intervention in Russia at the time of the Bolshevik Revolution is so little known that it might easily pass for fiction which, of course, it is not. American soldiers of the 27th Infantry Regiment *were* stationed near Lake Baikal in the center of Siberia and this, primarily, is their story. Episodes involving created characters are fictional within a narrative made as accurate as historical research permits. The following list of key characters will assist the reader in distinguishing historical figures and incidents from those created by the author wherever these are not clearly identified.

Actual Persons	*Characters*
OFFICERS AND MEN OF THE AMERICAN SIBERIAN EXPEDITIONARY FORCE	
Major General William S. Graves, commanding	Colonel Robert Spaeth, 27th Infantry Commanding
Colonel Oliver P. Robinson, Chief of Staff	Captain Hunkpapa Jack Carlisle, the Sioux
Lt. Colonel Robert L. Eichelberger, Assistant Chief of Staff	Lieutenant Ira C. Leverett, the Jew
Major David P. Barrows, Intelligence Officer	Major Taziola
Colonel Bugbee	Captain Bentham
	Captain Cloak
	Lieutenant Duke MacDougal
	Warrant Officer Duncan Ferber
	Lieutenant Ryan
	Joe Silverman, Interpreter
	Sergeants: Harry Austin
	Ed Baker
	Klagle

Actual Persons   *Characters*

OFFICERS AND MEN OF THE AMERICAN SIBERIAN
EXPEDITIONARY FORCE (*Continued*)

Corporal Blodgett
Privates: Carson
          Eisenbach
          Dixon
          Keever
          Crowe

WOMEN

Anna Vasilievna Timireva   Countess Tatiana Nojine, a Czech
                                      Maryenka Shulgin, a candy seller
                                      Mrs. Custer-Farquart
                                      Katya Massakow
                                      Masha, Sonia and Dunia

OFFICERS AND OFFICIALS OF THE KOLCHAK GOVERNMENT

Admiral Aleksandr V. Kolchak, Su-   General Bogoloff
  preme Ruler   Colonel Sipialef
Victor Pepelyaev, Premier   Captain Graetz
Loris Melikof   Lieutenants: Grachev
Generals: Dietrichs   Swerdloff
          Kappel   Potapov
          Sakharov   Soldiers and men:
          Denikin   Glubov
          Zankevich   Daddy Samson
          Rozanoff   Rodion
Cossack Atamans: Kolya
  Grigori Semenoff, Trans-Baikal Cos-   Karpov
    sacks   Timofeivitch
  Ivan Kalmykoff, Ussuri Cossacks   Anitsky, a waiter

OFFICERS OF THE CZECH LEGION

General Rudolf Gaida   Count Albert Nojine
General Syrovy   Colonel Dubrovski
Colonel Krakovetsky   Lieutenant Raul Markowitz

OFFICERS OF THE JAPANESE SIBERIAN
EXPEDITIONARY FORCE

General Kikuzo Otani   Major Subo Ikachi
General Narimoto Oi

Actual Persons	*Characters*

OFFICERS OF THE FRENCH MILITARY MISSION

General Pierre Janin, C.I.C.	Major Phillipot

OFFICERS OF THE BRITISH MILITARY MISSION

General Alfred W. Knox	Major Custer-Farquart
	Captain Fleming
	Captain Whyte

PARTISAN OFFICERS AND MEN

Generals: Marmatov	Timokhin
Yakovenko	Balashov
	Slavin
	Marrakof
	Berezkin
	Yakushef, the wolf hunter

ADDITIONAL AMERICANS

Newton D. Baker, Secretary of War
Roland S. Morris, Ambassador to Japan
Dr. Rudolf Teusler, American Red Cross
Admiral Austin M. Knight, U.S. Asiatic Fleet
Paul S. Reinsch, Minister to China
Ernest L. Harris, American Consul General, Irkutsk

Jud Conners, Russian Railway Service Corps
Dave Sawyer, Russian Railway Service Corps

BOOK ONE

The Aide-Mémoire

Men from fifteen nations attempt to halt the Red wave which swept over Russia from 1918 to 1920.

THE American general left the day coach at Kansas City. It was August 3, 1918, and unbearably hot. The general had been unable to sleep since boarding the train the day before at Palo Alto, California. He took a cab to the Baltimore Hotel and asked at the desk for Newton D. Baker, the Secretary of War.

Baker himself opened the door and pulled the general into the room as they shook hands. "General Graves," he said, "I haven't much time. I know you've wanted to go to France and I'm sorry to disappoint you, but if in the future you want to blame someone for putting you into this spot, I'm the one. I chose you, so don't blame General March."

General Graves' eyes had barely adjusted to the dim light in the room when Secretary Baker pulled an envelope from his pocket and thrust it into his hand. "This," he said, "contains the policy of the United States in Russia which you are to follow. Watch your step; you will be walking on eggs loaded with dynamite. God bless you and goodbye."

Baker picked up a small valise, apologized once more for his haste saying he had to catch a train, then he was gone.

General Graves dropped into a chair. He felt dizzy, turned around and a bit insulted. He opened the envelope carefully and read the document it contained: The Aide-Mémoire.

He read it once, then again.

The Aide-Mémoire was the result of President Wilson's very lonely thinking about the Russian business. "I have been sweating blood over the question what is right and feasible to do in Russia. It goes to pieces like quicksilver under my touch."

The document which the President had composed seemed to go to pieces as General Graves read it. He blamed this on his fatigue and the heat and skipped over it again trying to reconcile what appeared to be contradictions, or at least a kind of seesaw reasoning:

It is the clear and fixed judgment of the Government of the United States, arrived at after the repeated and very searching reconsiderations of the whole situation in Russia, that military intervention there would add to the present sad confusion in Russia rather than cure it, injure her rather than help her, and that it would be of no advantage in the prosecution of our main design, to win the war against Germany. It cannot, therefore, take part in such intervention or sanction it in principle. Military intervention would, in its judgment, be merely a method of making use of Russia, not a method of serving her. Her people could not profit by it, and their substance would be used to maintain foreign armies, not to reconstitute their own. Military action is admissible in Russia, as the Government of the United States sees the circumstances, only to help the Czechoslovaks consolidate their forces and get into successful cooperation with their Slavic kinsmen and to steady any efforts at self-government or self-defense in which the Russians themselves may be willing to accept assistance. Whether from Vladivostok or from Murmansk and Archangel, the only legitimate object for which American or Allied troops can be employed, it submits, is to guard military stores which may be subsequently needed by the Russian forces and to render such aid as may be acceptable to the Russians in the organization of their own self-defense. For helping the Czechoslovaks there is immediate necessity and sufficient justification. Recent developments have made it evident that that is in the interest of what the Russian people themselves desire, and the Government of the United States is glad to contribute the small force at its disposal for that purpose. . . .

But it owes it to frank counsel to say that it can go no further than these modest and experimental plans. It is not in a position, and has no expectation of being in a position, to take part in organized intervention in adequate force from either Vladivostok or Murmansk and Archangel. . . .

At the same time the Government of the United States wishes to say with the utmost cordiality and good will that none of the conclusions here stated is meant to wear the least color of criticism of what the other governments associated against Germany may think it is wise to undertake. It wishes in no way to embarrass their choices of policy. All that is intended here is a perfectly frank and definite statement of the policy which the United States feels obliged to adopt for herself and in the use of her own military forces. . . .

It hopes to carry out the plans for safeguarding the rear of the Czechoslovaks operating from Vladivostok in a way that will place it and keep it in close cooperation with a small military force like its own from Japan, and if necessary from the other Allies, and that will assure it of the cordial accord of all the Allied powers; and it proposes to ask all associated in this course of action to unite in assuring the people of Russia in the most public and solemn manner that none of the governments uniting in action either in Siberia or in northern Russia contemplates any interference of any kind with the political sovereignty of Russia, any intervention in her internal affairs, or any impairment of her territorial integrity, either now or hereafter, but that each of the associated powers has the single object of affording such aid as shall be acceptable, and only such aid as shall be acceptable, to the Russian people in their endeavor to regain control of their own affairs, their own territory, and their own destiny. . . .

General Graves folded the document. The on again, off again nature of it confused him and he decided to read it again when his mind was fresher. A second envelope contained an order from General Peyton C. March, the American Chief of Staff, stating that Major General William S. Graves had been appointed to command the American Expeditionary Force in Siberia.

On the same day, August 3, 1918, while General Graves considered these orders and wished that somewhere along the line someone had briefed him on conditions in Siberia, the British and the Japanese began to disembark troops at Vladivostok.

CHAPTER ONE

LIEUTENANT Hunkpapa Jack Carlisle, the Sioux, walked down Svetlandskaya Street with a peculiar rolling motion as though each leg forced to bear the weight of his body nearly collapsed before the other relieved it. With his infantryman's hat tipped forward against the indeterminate mist which hung in the air and his hands stuffed deep into the pockets of his coat, he gave an impression of drunken truculence or of a fighter fresh from a scrap in which he hadn't done too well. Occasionally he shook his head in disgust, scattering a shower of water beyond the shoulders of his coat, and those who saw his face stepped aside to let him pass. His nose, mashed a bit to the right, was a monument to old causes, his cheeks suspended by heavy cheekbones were pulled taut by the weight of his massive bronze jaw, and there was no white in his eyes. The iris was black and the pupil yellow, with the blood supply traced on the surface, and it was this blood map in his eyes which gave Carlisle the appearance of smoldering belligerence.

For weeks the clouds over Vladivostok had shed a cold drizzle which wasn't rain or snow but something between. It was a negative substance which didn't fall or drift, but hung in the air threatening to define itself as either rain or snow but always failing to do so. At night it froze, leaving a skin of ice on the bullet-pocked walls of the buildings, on the sidewalks and the streets; it diffused the lights of the city and the riding lights of the warships in the harbor and it muffled sound.

It was an intolerable mist and the population of Vladivostok, swollen six times its normal size by refugees and foreign troops, shuffled about in it contemplating their own uncertainties. The streets smelled of damp wool, damp leather and damp fur as the people coming out of their overcrowded quarters gathered in the streets to exchange current rumors in a dozen languages. Each morning they counted the warships in the frozen harbor to see if there had been any arrivals or departures and they gathered at the various legations watching who came out and who went in. But all these efforts failed to relieve the uneasiness which hung over the city like the clouds.

Newsboys trotting down the streets sold papers which turned soggy and disintegrated before they could be read, as though the indeterminate slop in the air was waging a war against the exchange of intelligence. Copies of the *Dalny Vostok* fell to pieces before the editorials could be absorbed. The news was as pulpy as the paper on which it was printed.

Carlisle turned toward the train station, but he had to wait at the corner for a cavalry patrol to pass. There were fourteen men in double file, two Czechs, two Serbs, two Japanese, two Americans, two Chinese on short fat horses, two Russians, and two Canadians. They were part of the International Brigade charged with keeping order in the city under the terms of the Allied protectorate, and the hoofs of their horses clattered irregularly on the brick street. The ponies snorted and tossed their heads as a streetcar passed, and the French captain at the head of the column sat very straight, looking morose as the water ran down his cheeks into his beard. The Chinese soldiers grinned at each other, their damp faces round and harmless. The Americans stared dully at the necks of their horses. The Japanese scowled down at the people who had stopped to watch them pass.

As he crossed the street Carlisle blundered into a girl coming in the opposite direction. He smiled apologetically and his face, so uniquely capable of expressing belligerence, was transformed by a look of almost comic good will. There was no subtlety in this change of expression, it just burst forth as though Carlisle had a limited stock of facial expressions, each of which was a grotesque overstatement of the emotion or reaction he intended to convey. The effect was so startling that the girl paused to stare after Carlisle before she moved on again.

When he came into the square Carlisle pushed his way through the crowd toward the kiosk near the station gate where he knew Sergeant Austin's girl, Maryenka, would be. He'd seen the girl and could understand Austin's infatuation. She was young, with a round, dark-eyed wholesome face which promised against all reason a settled existence with children by a fireside, things Austin yearned for, Carlisle supposed. Ordinarily he wouldn't care what Austin did about a girl, but the big coarse-faced sergeant was making a fool of himself over this one. He was making fools of both of them by insisting that Carlisle forward an application for marriage to their commanding officer, Colonel Spaeth. This Carlisle refused to do and consequently they couldn't be in the same room together without their fists bunching and an exchange of snarls behind every word they spoke to each other.

Carlisle hunched his shoulders against a sudden chill in the air and, looking around to account for it, saw that other people had also noticed the change. The quality of sound in the square had taken on a crispness which hadn't been there before, and a feeling of excitement ran through the place as everyone realized that the drizzling uncertainty which had hung over the city for so long had changed to snow. The moisture in the air was crystallizing and beginning to fall.

People held out their hands to catch the first flakes and an audible sigh of relief ran through the crowd. Carlisle too felt the relief; he saw the kiosk ahead, but still didn't know what he was going to say to the girl, or what effect anything he might say would have. It was, nevertheless, a question of company discipline and for some reason he felt the girl would understand. Given the facts she'd understand.

Two children ran by screaming shrilly and people stopped, their faces blank; then a train whistle began to blow short, continuous blasts. Suddenly everyone was running about calling back and forth.

Carlisle stopped at the kiosk where Austin's girl was arranging her goods on the counter. She wore a scarf over her hair and a heavy woolen sweater buttoned high around her neck. She looked at Carlisle, then her attention was taken by the shouting in the square. A crowd spilled out of the depot. Some people were dancing, others threw their hats in the air. A French major with blue eyes and freckles seized the lapels of Carlisle's coat and kissed him on the lips. He yelled something which Carlisle was too stunned to hear, then he burst into tears and ran toward Svetlandskaya Street, his greatcoat flapping and clods of dirty snow flying from his boots.

Carlisle wiped his lips on the back of his hand trying to erase the impact of the Frenchman's kiss. "What is it?" he asked the girl.

"The war is over," she said.

"Which war? What are they talking about?"

"The one in Europe," she said.

Across the square someone fired a Mauser and the girl looked toward the sound uneasily. Some of the street vendors began packing their goods. The two Serbs Carlisle had seen in the cavalry patrol galloped by on their dark, steaming horses, heading for their own quarters to spread the news, and the girl was smiling, apparently not yet aware that she had just lost Sergeant Austin.

The news ran through the square gathering strength and the church bells began to ring.

Carlisle took a pack of cigarettes from the counter and offered to pay, but the girl shook her head and said they were a gift because the war was over. He smiled in his abrupt, flashing manner and thanked her, but he left the money on the counter.

As he walked back through the crowded square all the bells of the city were ringing and Carlisle grinned thinking that Austin had been saved by the bell because now they'd be going home. The war was over and the big sergeant with his snub nose and flat blue eyes would come to his senses.

Two privates from his company, Dixon and Crowe, ran by and seeing him they skidded to a stop. "Hey, Lieutenant!" Crowe yelled. "The war is over!"

Carlisle nodded and they ran on trying to find someone who hadn't already heard the news and tell him before it was too late. They wanted to see the surprise on people's faces and laugh. It was a joke, a big joke for everyone. The war was over!

Carlisle passed a store-front café. The Chinese proprietor was standing in the doorway eating sunflower seeds from a paper cone while behind him a Victrola played "Bye-Bye, Blackbird."

"War's over," Carlisle said.

The Chinese shrugged and popped another palmful of seeds into his mouth. He didn't get it.

Before Carlisle left the square it occurred to him that no one had said who won the war. He knew, of course, but none of the fools running around the square seemed to give a damn. Carlisle thought someone ought to say it for the record, so he threw back his head and yelled: "The Americans won the war!"

Nobody paid any attention.

« 2 »

On the second floor of the Kunst and Albert department store Countess Tatiana Nojine was trying on a pair of gloves when the church bells began to ring. The clerk behind the counter, Sofia, a thin, pretty girl with bad teeth, looked around anxiously as customers and clerks dashed to the windows. The sounds of the bells, faintly muffled by the snow, rebounded from the slopes of Mount Klykov and from Tiger Hill and presently they were joined by the wail of sirens and horns from the ships in the harbor.

With her hand still halfway in a glove which was too small, Tatiana joined the others, expecting to see shells exploding in the streets below. The first thing she noticed was the snow on the iron railing beyond the window. The people around her were perfectly silent until a man rushed up from the floor below and yelled that the war was over. His voice seemed terribly loud and he stood in the vacated aisle with a stricken look on his face as though he had uttered a terrible obscenity. He repeated it again softly, more as a question than a statement of fact. "It is," he said plaintively, "the war is over."

Everyone rushed to the man. Their voices built to a crescendo and presently they were dancing and crying and the poor man who had brought the news was pushed and pulled about and required to repeat the good news over and over again.

Tatiana stayed by the window wondering if there was any truth in the story she'd heard as a child that noise can change the weather. The roar of Napoleon's cannon fire was supposed to have caused rain, so perhaps the bells of Vladivostok had changed the mist to snow. She tried to recall if this was something her father told her or something she'd read. She couldn't remember and this failure was more irritating to her than it might have been to someone else. Lately there had been many things she couldn't remember distinctly. The features of her husband's face were not as clear to her as she thought they had been a year ago. But she wasn't sure that a year ago they had been as clear to her as she now thought they might have been.

This trick of her memory annoyed her; it lost the recollection of recollections and it frightened her to think that soon it might lose the power of recollection entirely. She distrusted her memory, and as though to punish her lack of faith it frequently betrayed her. Tatiana's only defense against this was to make the present vivid, so now she studied the snow on the grill beyond the window, trying to record it indelibly with the bells and her feelings about the war being over. The snow reminded her of sleigh rides in Prague with Albert or her father. But during the four winter months of their marriage Albert had gone to Paris, where he'd learned to fly, so the ride she was remembering must have been with her father, who died when she was eleven — or was it twelve?

Tatiana sighed. Her past seemed to have been carried away like boats on the Vltava which as a child she'd watched from her bedroom window on the castle heights. From there she could see four of the bridges joining the old town and the new, cutting the broad river into almost equal sections of leisurely flowing time. She should have kept a diary or some account that would have enabled her to place her experiences in orderly progression. Heretofore she had depended on the bridges of Prague, but now through the raw, swift current of events memories often surfaced, such as the sleigh ride in the snow-clad park, and she was unable to identify the people in them, or place them surely in time, because she had come to depend so much on the bridges across the Vltava.

"I will begin a diary today," she thought. "November — what is the date? — 1918." And to position herself in time she recited her name, Tatiana Nojine, recalled her age, twenty-four, and reminded herself that her cousin, Raul Markowitz, was waiting on the street below.

Surely there was time enough yet to fill a respectable set of journals to which she could refer when, as now, she was in search of some incident she had forgotten. But the things one put into diaries were hardly ever what one wished to recall. Trivia always turned out to be more important than one expected and trivia were hard to record, like snow on the grillwork when the war was over.

Below her at the corner of Aleutskaya there was a great crowd. Soldiers in various national uniforms were running about, waving their arms and shouting as the bells continued to ring. A tram rounded the corner with people hanging out all the windows, and an American soldier was dancing on the roof.

An old woman dropped to her knees on the sidewalk and began to pray, bowing her forehead to the ground over and over again and blocking her ears against the wild sound of the bells.

Albert would be free.

This thought coming so late startled Tatiana. It should have been the first to occur to her — that now Albert could join her, that the war was over for him too. She laughed joyfully and turning from the window found the glove clerk at her side.

"Will madame take the gloves?"

Tatiana removed the glove from her hand and gave it to the girl. "I noticed how well they fit *you*," she said. "Won't you take them as a gift from me?"

The girl put the glove into the box with its mate. "You'll take them?" she asked again.

"No," Tatiana said, "they're for you, a souvenir of the Armistice. That way we'll both remember it, by the gloves, you see."

"Oh, madame, we aren't allowed," the girl began, but she broke off and cried out, "Isn't it wonderful! My brother Kolya was called three months ago and now he'll be coming home!"

"Who is he with?" Tatiana asked.

"Oh, the Whites, Countess, of course!" the girl said as though this explained a great deal. They were silent a moment, listening to the bells and the shouts of the people below.

"Surely it must be over now," Tatiana said quietly, then she went downstairs.

As she reached the ground floor an Italian officer caught Tatiana around the waist and danced her into the crowd. He was singing in a high, lyric voice with his head thrown back and his eyes half closed. He spun her around giddily several times, then he took her face in both his hands and kissed her on the lips. His dark eyes snapped with amusement at her surprised reaction and Tatiana, perfectly willing to fall under the spell of unreasoning gaiety, laughed too. The Italian threw his arms up, danced a few steps alone, then he ran down the aisle and caught another girl.

A young Czech lieutenant in French uniform with a red and white ribbon on his blouse and a patch in the shape of a Hussite cap on his sleeve caught Tatiana's hand and pulled her after him toward the street door. "We've lost our cab," he said. "The minute the bells began the fool driver galloped off down the street. I tried to get another, but I think we'd better walk."

The street noise was deafening. Several people, already drunk, were waving bottles and singing boisterously. Some of the ships in the harbor fired their guns, punctuating the clamor of bells with their blunt concussion.

Tatiana and the lieutenant were often separated by the crowd, but they called to each other and tried to cling together, laughing with all the others who were laughing around them. It was ridiculously childish and they knew it, but catching sight of someone who also knew it caused them to laugh all the more.

"What does it mean, Raul?" Tatiana called. "What will we do now?"

"It means a free Bohemia, Tatiana. We've liberated Czechoslovakia!"

"And we'll go home now to Prague?"

"I think so. Yes, I do."

When they reached the Aleksander Hotel their shoulders were covered with snow and their faces were shining.

"Raul, is there any way to reach Albert?" Tatiana called. "Surely he'd wire a greeting to us with such news as this, don't you think he would?"

Raul Markowitz scowled and nodded as they forced their way through the crowded lobby and went upstairs to the second floor, which was occupied by the Czechs. "If he could get through to us, yes, but communications will be overloaded with all this."

"I wonder what Albert will be thinking now."

"That's hard to know," Markowitz said.

In the Bay of the Golden Horn water taxis plied back and forth in lanes of broken ice, bearing guests recruited ashore for the shipboard festivities. Laughter rang over the bay and many of these guests, particularly the girls, already giddy with drink, had to be carried aboard. Two Russian ships, rusted and long inactive, were firing blank charges and the crews who inhabited the ships with their families were trying to decide what signals to raise for the occasion. Since the Treaty of Brest-Litovsk in March had ended hostilities between the Soviet Provisional Government and Germany the Russian sailors weren't sure they had any right to celebrate the Armistice, but it was their hope that a general cessation of fighting would carry over to the Red and White forces, so they banged away with their guns and when they hoisted their flags to the signal block the message was: Peace and Freedom.

Aboard the U.S.S. *Brooklyn,* flagship of the Asiatic Fleet, Admiral Knight was pleased that after the initial burst of enthusiasm his men had grown quiet. Down the line of anchored ships he saw H.M.S. *Suffolk* and the Japanese cruiser *Asahi.* They too were calm and the Admiral wondered if the Russians ashore were going to ring the bells all night. A signal officer came to the bridge wing and saluted. "General Graves has agreed to come aboard at once, sir."

"Thank you, Turner. Have the usual brought to my cabin, will you?"

The usual was a bottle of light sherry — the only thing General Graves permitted himself to drink even on historic occasions.

« 3 »

Colonel Robert Spaeth looked out the window at the crush of traffic along legation row; automobiles kept discharging passengers and driving off again and groups of men, some with swords, some with attaché cases, White Russian officers and Zemstvo officials stood about trying to guess which legation might hold the key to their future. A car with a Czech flag stopped at the French legation and the crowd drifted a few steps toward it, then another car stopping at the Japanese legation pulled them in another direction.

The volume of the bells had diminished and the street crowds had dispersed indoors out of the snow, but here and there bands of roving soldiers, Americans, Canadians, and British for the most part, hailed each other, then stood about trying to decide where they would go. The Japanese, he noticed, were apparently not celebrating.

Spaeth removed his steel-rimmed glasses and polished them on the sleeve of his blouse; a tall, spare man in his late forties he gave the impression of weary tolerance as though everything was a bit too much for him, but this was deceptive. As he replaced his glasses a young lieutenant with a muskrat cap perched cockily on his head burst into the room, which was crowded with staff and regimental officers waiting to see General Graves. "Home by Christmas!" the lieutenant cried and he looked around as though he expected everyone to shout hoorah. "The Whites are organizing one hell of a victory ball over at the Aleksander," he said.

Spaeth, irritated by the lieutenant's brashness, called him over.

"Home by Christmas." Among the American troops this phrase had followed the news of the Armistice so closely that one couldn't distinguish which had come first, the end of the war or the expectation of being home by Christmas.

The lieutenant removed his cap and joined Spaeth at the window. "Yes, sir? Waiting to see Graves?"

Spaeth scowled. "It's *General* Graves, Leverett," he said.

"That's right, sir, General Graves."

Leverett's head tipped slightly and his grin broadened. His black hair was damp and curly and there was an insolent, good-natured glint in his brown eyes. He was a kid, a sixty-day wonder who'd joined the regiment in September. Spaeth guessed him to be twenty-two or -three, old enough to behave if someone taught him how.

"Did I hear you say home by Christmas, Leverett?"

"That's what I hear, Colonel."

"I suppose you've spread that word through your platoon."

"No, sir, it was there ahead of me. Some of the men have already started to pack."

"Any idea what this might do to morale?"

"They're damned happy right now, sir, I can tell you that."

"Ever hear of occupation troops, Leverett?"

The lieutenant's eyes clouded slightly and the other officers in the room grew silent.

Spaeth realized he'd spoken too loudly. Annoyed with himself he turned his back on the room and crowded Leverett into the window bay.

"Think the A.E.F. is just going to throw down its weapons and fox-trot home?" he asked.

Alarmed by the Colonel's quiet intensity Leverett shook his head and he too lowered his voice. "Of course there'll be occupation troops in Germany, sir," he said, "but where's the enemy here?"

Colonel Spaeth poked his glasses up more firmly on the bridge of his nose. The gap between the question and his need to grope for an answer expressed the frustration which had dogged the American Siberian Expeditionary Force since it had landed. No one could name the enemy or clearly define the American objective in Siberia.

"You need an enemy, Leverett?" Spaeth asked drily. "All right, I'll volunteer. From now on when you're in doubt about the enemy remember me. You're in C Company under Carlisle as I recall — 2nd Platoon, right? And all of them doing their Christmas packing I have no doubt. Well, they probably need an enemy too. You're it. Who's your first sergeant?"

"Austin, sir."

"I don't suppose he's packing too."

"I don't know, sir."

"I do. He's not. Austin is a soldier. There'll be a lot of celebrating tonight."

"Yes, sir," Leverett said enthusiastically, "there's going to be a ball at the Aleksander Hotel. That's what I came to say, sir. All Allied officers have been invited. There wasn't time to print invitations, but an adjutant from Ivanov-Rinov's headquarters came to tell us, so I thought I'd better let everyone know. They're collecting flags all over town to decorate the place."

The lieutenant's expression was so engaging, so utterly innocent of military demeanor, that Colonel Spaeth nearly laughed. He was tempted to turn Leverett away with an affectionate swat on the shoulder, but for the sake of the other men in the room he couldn't do this.

"Leverett, I want you to select eight men of your platoon and report to the International Brigade barracks. There'll be a lot of drunks on the street. I want you to organize and lead an all-night roving patrol."

"Tonight, sir?" Leverett asked miserably.

"You'll pick the men yourself, at random. Don't delegate that job to Austin. Do you get my meaning?"

Leverett nodded. "Yes, sir."

"After this don't pass yourself off as Santa Claus. You're still in the army, worse luck. All right, get to it."

Leverett hesitated, trying to remember if it was proper to salute indoors, uncovered, or whether he was supposed to put his cap on first.

Spaeth turned his back on him. "Sorry you'll miss the ball," he said. He heard the door close and presently Leverett appeared on the street below with his head tucked down and his hands jammed into his coat pockets, his whole figure expressing a keen sense of injustice as he walked toward the American military barracks.

Spaeth watched him go wondering if it was possible to hold a citizen army together without an enemy. He began whistling tunelessly, or so he thought, but Captain Bentham, his intelligence officer, came to his side. "Nice tune, Colonel," he said.

"What's that?" Spaeth asked.

" 'Home, Sweet Home,' " Bentham said.

"Oh, Christ," Spaeth groaned. "Glad you stopped me."

"It's better than 'Jingle Bells,' " Bentham said.

"What's holding up this meeting?" Spaeth asked.

"It's been canceled," Bentham said. "Robinson just let us know."

"Canceled?"

"The General is going out to the *Brooklyn* to confer with Admiral Knight."

Spaeth nodded and followed the other officers downstairs.

When they reached the street Bentham asked if he was going to the party at the Aleksander.

"Sure, Charlie, why not? The war's over, isn't it?"

Bentham nodded glumly and they walked down the street toward their headquarters listening to the noisy crowd and to the clamoring bells.

"Home by Christmas," Bentham said.

"Like hell," Spaeth grumbled.

CHAPTER TWO

LEVERETT thought of asking for volunteers, but he knew the men had planned a party, so he called for a snap rifle inspection hoping to blame the selection of men on dirty rifles, trying to remain a good guy, but the men weren't fooled. Sergeant Austin held the formation in the quadrangle surrounded by the dirty two-story granite barracks which housed the regiment. It was still snowing, which made the inspection ludicrous, but Austin followed Leverett down the ranks checking off the names of the men whose rifles failed to pass inspection. None of the rifles would have passed inspection and everyone knew it; they were model 1909 Benet Mercie guns which the men had brought with them from the Philippines and were to be exchanged in the next few days for Springfields, which were more reliable in the cold. Each man Leverett picked smirked bitterly at the hypocrisy of the inspection but only one of them, Private Carson, a big shambling Texan, asked to see the dirt Leverett found in his rifle barrel.

"Shut up, Carson," Austin growled and Carson shut up.

Leverett didn't object to being a puppet officer; what he objected to was that the men expected him to play the army game. They wanted him to play lieutenant and resent him for it, but they'd resent him just as much if he refused to play, so there was no way around it.

When he'd picked the men Leverett turned the platoon over to Austin and crossed the quad to the company office. The men fell out and as he opened the door Leverett heard one of them call to Austin, "Hey, Sarge, whose notion was this? The Sioux or the Jew?"

Leverett shut the door and found the company clerk, Corporal Blodgett, staring at him, trying not to show he'd heard. Leverett smiled and nodded toward Carlisle's office. "Hunkpapa in?" he asked quietly.

Blodgett grinned and shook his head no.

"All right, ring the Japs. I want to talk to the O.D."

Blodgett got the number and handed the receiver to Leverett with a shrug. "You try," he said.

The man on the line spoke Japanese, then switched to pidgin Russian as Leverett tried to make himself understood by repeating "Officer of the Day" over and over again.

At last he got the "Ahhh!" of dawning comprehension followed by a spate of rapid Japanese, then another man came on. "Major Subo Ikachi," he said.

Leverett winked at Blodgett and made a face. "Lieutenant Ira C. Leverett, American Siberian Expeditionary Force, 27th Infantry, C Company, 2nd Platoon commanding," he said rapidly. "I have called to inform you, Major, that we will have an extra duty patrol on the streets tonight for the purpose of maintaining order, soothing drunks, rescuing fallen tarts and other errands of mercy such as may be required by the delirium occasioned by the news of the cessation of hostilities in the European theater of war."

Blodgett cackled and muffled the sound in his hand.

"You should report to the International Military Police Brigade, Lieutenant," Ikachi replied.

"I thought I'd go to the top, Major, to the senior military commander in the area, General Otani. How is he?"

Ikachi's voice was cool and precise. "I appreciate your courtesy, Lieutenant Leverett. The General is fine, but the International Brigade is coordinating all patrol activity in Vladivostok."

"Not the Japanese?"

"No."

"Hard to believe. They've been coordinating everything else since I've been here. Well, I expect you'll be going home now, Major, right along with the rest of us, back to the wife and hibachi. Leave Siberia to the Siberians, right?"

Ikachi hung up. Leverett raised his brows, twisted his lips into a surprised grin and gently replaced the receiver. "My, they do get huffy," he said to Blodgett.

"Think we'll be home by Christmas, Lieutenant?" Blodgett asked.

"That was the question that got me this patrol. I asked Colonel Spaeth."

"What did he say?"

"Go on patrol. That's what he said. And so I miss the victory hop. I'm Cinderella, Blodgett, without a fairy godmother or a punkin. While everyone else is dancing in the fabulous ballroom of the Aleksander Hotel, dancing, romancing, drinking and prancing, where will I be? Poor Ira C. Leverett, shavetail, reluctant participant in the complex animosities of the world, will be leading a dismal patrol through the dismal streets of this dismal town. I tell you, Blodgett, I'm a lover not a warrior, a builder not a destroyer. And I'm going to write my Mama, Papa, and sister Ruth in Oakland, California, and tell them how I'm suffering, and tell them to complain to the President and all their elected representatives with the view of returning our fighting men at once to their native shores. Meantime you call the Brigade and let them know about our roving patrol."

« 2 »

Ira carried the forty-five automatic in his coat pocket fingering the safety catch every once in a while to make sure it wouldn't fire and blow his big toe off. It was after midnight and the bells had stopped, but the town was still noisy with bands of revelers careering through the streets.

The patrol tramped along behind Ira with their noses tucked down in the collars of their greatcoats, the cold working through their wool puttees into their shins. Their duty so far had consisted of rousing drunks who had fallen asleep on the streets and were in danger of freezing.

Between watches they lay over at the International Brigade barracks near the depot in a big, gloomy room with cots for the men who wanted to sleep on them at the risk of picking up a stray louse left by a former occupant. Ira had written a couple of letters home while the other men dozed or played poker for inflated ruble notes which the Japanese had printed as occupation currency. They were nearly worthless but had a nice crackle which gave an illusion of value.

One unfinished letter to his sister Ruth was still in Ira's pocket as he led the patrol toward the waterfront, where stacks of rotting war matériel lay covered with rime. It had stopped snowing and the sky was beginning to clear with stars showing through the breaking clouds. Waves slapping the stone jetty made the men shudder and squirm deeper into their layers of clothing.

They turned back on their own tracks scuffed in the new snow and Ira smiled remembering that balmy day on the Stanford campus when he had read President Wilson's call to war with Germany, printed in a black-margined box on the front page of the *San Francisco Chronicle*.

The precise, heavily moralistic passages had no particular effect just then because his mind had been dulled by long hours spent trying to absorb great slabs of contract law from that library of decisions by dead men on dead causes. His friends and fellow students, however, had fallen under the spell of Wilson's ringing — or if not ringing, at least well reasoned — prose. Some of them were so moved that they announced their intention to enlist that very morning — a corollary of this decision, Ira suspected, being that they would thus avoid the June examinations which would undoubtedly leave many of them strewn by the wayside as scholastic casualties. The fervor to grab a gun and kill a Hun ran in inverse proportion to the student's standing in class; those threatened with the possibility of flunking out of law school looked to the war as a reprieve. Given a choice, they much preferred to risk having their heads blown off in six or eight months than fail their examination in two. Ira didn't quarrel with this: the instinct for self-preservation always takes account of the immediate threats and there is no romance, or glory, or public support for flunking examinations; he did, however, have some reservations about Wilson, a man who had already passed his latest exam by being elected in November on the slogan "He kept us out of war!"

In December, Wilson had attempted to mediate the war, pointing out that all the belligerents were making the same claims for the rightness of their cause and the same disclaimers of having any but the most altruistic intentions.

"If the contest must continue to proceed toward undefined ends by slow attrition until the one group of belligerents or the other is exhausted; if millions after millions of human lives must continue to be offered up until on the one side or the other there are no more to offer; if resentments must be kindled that can never cool and despairs engendered from which there can be no recovery, hopes of peace and of willing concert of free peoples will be rendered vain and idle."

This had been Wilson's position five months prior to his declaration of war. He had managed to quell the war hysteria which accompanied the sinking of the *Lusitania* in 1915 and to win with his slogan at the polls, but in April, for no self-evident reason, he issued his call.

Ira had continued to read law while the President and the press attempted to define those previously "undefined ends" of the war. At first the nation was fighting for American rights of neutrality on the seas, but this was flat and much too specific. In attempting to define that which is previously undefined it is necessary to arrive at an indefinite definition.

That we were fighting to make the world safe for democracy was closer to the mark, and by the time Ira had passed his exams in June there was a new caption on the war which resolved the contradiction of its being waged by a nation which had elected a President whose previous slogan had been that he kept us out of war; the war he had kept us out of was now — The War to End War!

This slogan had a fine ring to it. Hopes of peace and of willing concert of free peoples were no longer vain and idle. The millions after millions of human lives which would continue to be offered up until one side or the other had no more to offer were now patently being offered to end the war, in fact to end War. This was perfectly obvious to anyone. Not as obvious to Ira as it should have been, perhaps, but he attributed this to brain fag induced by long hours of cramming for the fateful exams.

To clear his mind he took a vacation. And not only to clear his mind, but to escape the attentions of his family, his mother Rose, father Jacob, sister Ruth and uncle Dave. There was a way they had of looking at him which very soon became unbearable. They seemed to be storing up pictures of their Ira. How he looked when he was twenty-one. What he did, what he said.

His mother, her kind Jewish heart already storing memories, looked after him too well. She hovered over him, fed him, insisted he have a good time. "Have a good time, Ira! Enjoy yourself! But be careful."

His father and Uncle Dave were frequently portentous as they read the evening headlines. Uncle Dave, a socialist, had added his name to a petition protesting the U.S. declaration of war. "I did it for you, Ira," he said. "For me too, but mostly for you."

Unable to bear all this family affection, riding as it did on the submerged theme that our Ira may not be with us long, Ira packed a bag and went up the coast to Mendocino. Before he left he confessed to Ruth that he would not be alone. Ruth was eighteen and they thought themselves emancipated.

"How old is she, Ira?" Ruth asked.

"Thirty-six."

"No, I mean it, seriously."

"Twenty-eight and she wants to do her bit for the boys. When you're ten years older maybe you can do the same."

Ruth pouted and Ira slapped her fanny. "You're not very nice," she said. "I don't blame you. I don't mean that. But I think someone in the family should at least know her name."

"I'm not the kind to kiss and tell. And damn it, Ruth, I don't like all this business. I'm not dead yet."

"Oh, Ira! How awful."

"Yes," he said, "it is."

But in Mendocino with his girl, Joy Bailey, who wasn't thirty-six or twenty-eight, but nineteen and rather silly, he found himself playing the we who are about to die salute you role. He'd rented a cabin with one of his law school chums, "Cruiser" O'Dell, whose reputation with girls had given him the name but who had enlisted in the Navy to preserve the tradition. The girls rented another cabin and for two weeks the foursome lived like married couples.

Joy Bailey made love with such patriotic devotion that Ira began to feel he would be betraying the flag if he didn't join up. The assumption everywhere was that all the fine young men would soon be marching off and elders of the Mendocino community smiled tolerantly at the fiction that these four young people were married.

All is fair in love and war but Ira tried to be honest and one night, lying beside Joy in the dark mosquito-infested cabin, he mentioned his reservations about Wilson's call to arms, to which she had responded by clutching him to her naked bosom and murmuring earnestly, "Oh, Ira, you've got to come back! You've just got to!"

Since he had not yet gone Ira was at a loss how to continue the discussion, so he let it ride. And toward the end of this two-week idyl he began to realize that he could not resist the pressures society had brought to bear, not viciously, not even consciously, but lovingly. He was being loved into going to war. Loved by his mother and father, by his sister and Uncle Dave and by Joy Bailey. They all loved him so much at the prospect of losing him that he was afraid that if he didn't leave they wouldn't love him at all. He knew for certain Joy Bailey wouldn't. She'd be busy loving someone else. But he hoped after this she'd have the decency to wait until the poor guy was in uniform.

On October 16, 1917, Ira joined the United States Army, that being the only army willing to contract for his services or approved by his loving friends and relations. This step removed a great weight from his conscience and although there were no celebrations in the city to mark the event (some neighbors thought his delay had already done harm to the Jews) Ira felt relieved. In fact he was ridiculously happy about joining the ridiculous Army which had, ridiculously enough, offered to send him to Officers' Training School because he had passed his law exams. This was the first tangible reward for his months of legal cramming. Of course his mother wailed; his father and Uncle Dave clapped him on the back and grew misty-eyed; Ruth kissed him and holding him at arm's length solemnly announced she was proud. "Oh, Ira, I'm so proud!"

He couldn't help laughing at himself and all of them, and this effervescent, sometimes idiotic mirth never left him. It wasn't cynicism or sarcasm, he was just terribly amused by the whole process and from that day on he decided to enjoy it.

At Officers' Training School he proved himself to be thoroughly capable, a bit irreverent, lacking those qualities of dogged earnestness so highly prized by the military, but a good fellow, highly esteemed by his classmates, and so he graduated with approximately three hundred other fresh shavetails and was assigned to the adjutant general's office at Camp Fremont, California. There he spent six months shuffling legal documents, checking procurement contracts and begging to be assigned to active service.

Joy Bailey, true to her commitment to death — or at least the prospect of death — before dishonor, refused to have any truck with a legal filing clerk even though he wore Uncle Sam's suit and broke Uncle Sam's bread. She wanted heroism in the hay, not procurement contractors. Then Ira got wind of a provisional force being organized for a General William S. Graves. Destination was top secret; the need for manpower was great and Ira volunteered as an infantry lieutenant. To his astonishment he was assigned as a replacement in the 27th Infantry. On August 14, 1918, he boarded the *Thomas* with forty-two other officers, including Major General Graves, and two thousand enlisted men taken from the 8th Division, part of a force of five thousand men being sent as replacements to the 27th and 31st Infantry, which were assumed to be in the Philippines. Under convoy of the U.S.S. *Oregon* and the gunboat *Vicksburg,* the transport sailed from San Francisco while Papa, Mama, Ruth and Uncle Dave waved lovingly from the pier.

Joy Bailey hadn't come to see him off.

And now walking through the dark, snow-mantled streets of Vladivostok with his forty-five nestled warm as a baked potato against his thigh Ira wondered how many other young men Joy Bailey had loved into the army since he'd joined. He smiled and guessed she'd supplied a full platoon, which meant that her contribution to the war effort was considerably greater than his. He wondered too what her thoughts might be on this eve of the Armistice, whether she worried that all the young men she had clutched to her passionate breast and implored to return might do so, or if she worried that they might not.

Ira chuckled softly, rather pleased now to be on patrol instead of carousing with the other officers. It gave him time to think and make plans. It was time to get one's feet planted in the starting blocks for the race which would begin when all the servicemen were spilled back into the booming American economy.

He led the patrol toward the railroad yard to check again on a trainload of Austrian prisoners of war who had been brought down from their prison camp at Krasnaya Rechka near Khabarovsk to be repatriated under terms of the Treaty of Brest-Litovsk. They had been living in the train for two weeks on a diet of Japanese rice and American corned beef, waiting for the ship which was to take them home, but now the defeat of their own countries, coming so quickly after the negotiated peace with Russia, left them stranded. They didn't know whether to celebrate the Armistice or give way to despair.

Their commander, an Austrian officer who had been a prisoner for two years, wore a threadbare blue greatcoat and a worn pair of cavalry boots and tried by his manner to convey a sense of his former elegance. At first he had refused Ira's offer of a pack of American cigarettes, but at last he accepted them — in the spirit of everlasting peace.

As they came down the steps into the yard, Ira could hear the Austrians singing, but a new train in the yard blocked his view of their cars. It was an armored train, the first Ira had seen, and as he picked his way over the tracks toward it he experienced the instinctive dread he had of reptiles and scale-armored land-roving insects and beasts. As a boy he had managed to control this unreasoning fear and when other children, particularly his sister Ruth, thrust a lizard or a centipede at him he didn't yell or run away but took the creature in his hand, and while holding it lectured himself, admonishing his fear and even managing a smile. He had learned to conceal the revulsion he felt, and now as he approached the long steel-plated train he shuddered and spoke a bit too loudly.

"That's a beauty," he said. "Look at that! Wonder where she's from?"

Private Dixon, closest to Leverett in the double file, looked up at the train. "Bronevik," he said.

"What's that?"

"Bronevik is what they call them," Dixon said. "I saw a couple up near Ushuman when we went after the Bolshies with the Japs. The Whites have a lot of them."

"Useless damned things if you ask me," Carson grumbled.

"Why's that, Carson?" Ira asked. "Why useless? Looks pretty lethal to me."

"Nothing but a rolling gun platform. Easy enough to stop it. Just take out the rails. They're slow as hell anyway," Carson said.

As they walked along the adjoining track toward the head of the bronevik Leverett lectured himself, but to him the bronevik was a huge sleeping centipede. Pale light came from the slits in its armor plate and he could hear murmuring voices and movement inside. It seemed to be watching, to be breathing; its black sides glistened and an occasional sigh escaped from the locomotive.

They came to a flatcar with a pedestal-mounted four-inch Krupp gun behind a shield. A soldier jumped up beside this gun and Leverett jerked the forty-five from his coat pocket. The soldier at the gun barked a challenge and swung his rifle up.

Carson glanced at Leverett, hesitated a moment, then called to the soldier. "Amerikanski. Amerikanski, you fathead!"

A rifle bolt snapped close to Ira's ear. "Take it easy, Dixon," he said.

The soldier on the flatcar stepped behind the gun shield and yelled in Russian alerting the rest of the train guard.

Ira started down the track again. He stuck the pistol back into his pocket; it was cold and his hands were clammy. He walked quickly wanting to get around the train to the Austrian prisoners, who had stopped singing. He heard the clatter of metal, gun ports being closed or opened, machine guns being run out or the Krupp gun turning on its mount; he didn't know; he just wanted to get away from the damned reptilian train.

They'd gone the length of two cars when a door ahead of them opened and a group of soldiers jumped to the ground and ducked out of the path of light left by the open door. One man stayed behind, a Mongolian or Tatar by the look of him, with bandoliers of ammunition across his chest and a big automatic pistol on his belt.

Ira stopped and his men stumbled up close around him. The Mongolian beckoned them forward. "Stay put, I'll go," Ira whispered and he walked toward the Mongolian thinking it would be just his luck to get shot on the day of the Armistice.

The Mongolian wore a short black Cossack blouse, black trousers and boots, and a big sheepskin hat on his head. He watched closely as Ira came forward and stopped just within the light. "American?" he asked.

There was a musical sneer in the Mongolian's voice which annoyed Ira, who nodded and said yes. "Whose train is this?" he asked.

"General Bogoloff's, out of Verkhne-Udinsk. Who are you?"

More reassured by the Mongolian's English than by anything else, Ira introduced himself. The Mongolian said his name was Sipialef and that he was General Bogoloff's train commander. He offered his hand. Ira shook it and the rest of the patrol came up to the edge of the light.

Sipialef barked an order and the soldiers who had taken positions in the darkness along the train eased their weapons down and came back to the door. There were ten of them, heavily armed.

Taken one by one they seemed to have been chosen for their vicious appearance and together they presented a terrible picture of Eastern depravity. One knew at a glance that there was no crime these men would not commit. They wore black Cossack uniforms, but each man was armed with weapons of his own preference, more like pirates than disciplined troops. They carried daggers, Mauser pistols, Krag-Jorgensen and Lebel rifles, but their main weapon was their fierce appearance. They stood beside the car in complete silence as though their tongues had been removed to prevent them from screaming when wounded.

Leverett shivered and Sipialef, aware of the impression his men had made, signaled to them and they hoisted themselves aboard the car without a word and the steel-sheathed door grated shut behind them.

Sipialef fell in beside Ira and they walked forward toward the engine. "This is the Invincible," Sipialef said. "We have four broneviks. The Invincible, the Scourge, the Czar, the Wolf. Here is the General's private car. White, you see."

They passed a machine gun car, one-inch plate with firing ports for eight guns; two more troop carriers and a flatcar for the General's automobile. Then they came to a gun tender and beyond it an armored car with a 4.7-inch naval gun mounted in a revolving turret. This car was particularly buglike and menacing with observation slits and ventilation tubes for the gun crew. Dirty ice clinging to the riveted plate had scaled off in places, making the car appear diseased, and there was a fringe of icicles at the base of the turret like the complicated, ugly mandibles of a parasitic insect.

The men in the patrol scuffling through the snow behind Ira and Sipialef were no longer interested in the bronevik, but Ira was still in the grip of his instinctive hatred of the thing.

At last they came to the engine, a big Class F Mallet twelve-wheeler, its customary lines squared off by iron plate. It too was painted white with the name Invincible blocked out in black Cyrillic letters along the side. Sipialef grinned waiting for Ira's reaction.

"Heavy," Ira said.

Sipialef was disappointed. "Powerful," he said. "Powerful."

"Slow," Ira said.

"Slow as hell," Carson said. "Come on, Lieutenant, let's go."

Sipialef drew himself up and tucked one thumb into his belt. "This is the best armored train between Chita and Irkutsk," he said. "In three great battles the enemy ran from it. It strikes fear into all the people. All the people."

"I could stop it with three sticks of dynamite," Carson said and he yawned against the back of his hand.

"Or a can opener," Dixon said and the men chuckled.

Sipialef was gravely insulted and his face seemed to swell, drawing his eyes nearly shut and pulling his mouth into a flat-lipped slit. He glared at Ira a moment. "Amerikanski Zhid!" he said, then he spat to the side with contempt and stalked away.

Ira found the men in his patrol staring at him as though they expected something. "What did he say?" he asked.

Carson glanced at Dixon uneasily, then Eisenbach spoke up. "He said 'Jew,' Lieutenant, only it was more like 'kike.' "

There was a flash in Ira's mind like a low-voltage short circuit; the shock was very mild and passed instantly but the men were waiting for him to react. He glanced after Sipialef. It was one of those fateful moments when something had to be proved. He started toward Sipialef, still uncertain, thinking the least he could do was swear after the man, but then he remembered the war was over. He stopped and turned to the patrol and feeling like a stupid comic on a burlesque stage he shrugged. "The war's over," he said.

"Yeah," Carson drawled, "home by Christmas."

Ira met Carson's eyes and recognized the taunting expression of racial bigotry, but he'd already lost Carson's respect, so it didn't seem to matter.

Ira forgot about the Austrians and led the patrol up the platform steps through the depot. But he'd left something behind; it was back there on the tracks, a small, stupid failure lying among his footprints in the snow.

Well, the war was over.

Ira smiled and shook this other thing out of his mind. In a few months' time they'd be scattered and the incident on the track would die of neglect, would die more quickly because it wasn't the kind of thing one could tell about as it would have been if he had slugged Sipialef. Yes, he'd done the right thing. Let them think what they wanted to think. In a month it wouldn't matter.

At the Brigade barracks Leverett checked in with the O.D. and another patrol went out. The men removed their coats and clustered around the stove and Leverett sat down alone at a table to finish his letter to Ruth.

CHAPTER THREE

LIEUTENANT Carlisle wouldn't have come to the celebration at the Aleksander Hotel if Colonel Spaeth hadn't insisted.

Carlisle had no wit, no small talk, and although he danced on demand he did so with such a driving sense of absorption that his partner was often filled with dismay, or if she was a person given to laughter she usually excused herself rather than be rude to his face. He would have preferred the quiet of his barracks room reviewing the company table of organization or correcting the company records, about which he was very meticulous, but Colonel Spaeth had insisted, so at ten o'clock Carlisle ran a brush through his cropped black hair, scowled at his heavy-lipped face in the mirror and left for the Aleksander.

The hotel was in pandemonium as Carlisle stood in the doorway to the ballroom removing his coat and glaring about with the judgmental reserve of a sober man who has come into a room crowded with drunks. Female laughter cascaded over the sound of an orchestra playing gypsy music. The room sparkled with jewels and decorations, saber hilts, epaulets, polished boots, painted mouths. In one corner a group of White Russian officers were tossing Allied officers into the air and catching them with a shout before they hit the floor. A Japanese colonel rose toward the ceiling, twisted catlike in the air and fell, the baubles on his uniform dangling and his saber clattering on the floor as he narrowly missed being dropped on his terrified face. The Russians captured an Italian and tossed him three times with three booming yells. When they set him up again he vomited helplessly on his boots.

Fifteen flags hung over the bandstand. Displayed in a single line they rippled in gusts of hysterical laughter: Imperial Russian, Lettish, Serbian, Czech, Polish, Rumanian, Italian; the American, the British, the French, the Belgian, the Canadian, the Chinese and two flags for the Japanese, in honor, one supposed, of General Otani, who was senior military commander in the area. One of these was the national flag, the other for the Japanese Imperial Marines.

Carlisle looked around for the American table and located it across the room, then he saw a girl seated alone at a small table in the corner. She was staring wistfully at an empty bottle and looked as though she were about to cry. Carlisle dropped his coat on a chair and sat down beside her. He wanted to get used to the party before he joined Colonel Spaeth and the others. "Speak English?" he asked the girl.

"No," she said and she smiled at the bottle. Her teeth were bad, but she was appealing in a dress of blue patterned silk with clumsy tucks in the waist to make it fit.

"Where you from?" Carlisle asked.

She turned the bottle around and read the Russian label, then she glanced at him sidelong through hazel eyes, blue-flecked and very drunk. "You're a Buryat," she said.

"No."

She gestured, palm up, her long white fingers limp as she swept his sleeve to the bar on his shoulder. She was genuinely puzzled.

"You with anyone?" he asked.

She continued to look at him, her smile broadening to reveal more missing teeth.

"My name is Carlisle."

She snickered. "Theda Bara," she said. "American."

"You with anyone?" he asked again.

She looked around the room, trying to remember. "He went," she said and she started to get up, but Carlisle dropped his hand on her shoulder and eased her down again.

"You all right?"

She mumbled in Russian. Her head was very loose and she seemed to want to kiss him, to kiss anyone. "I know you," she said.

There was a pleasant, slurred coarseness in her voice but she was too drunk to be of any use. Carlisle laid her down on the bench against the wall. She frowned up at him, giggled and promptly fell asleep. Carlisle took his coat from the chair; one of her arms was dangling and he put it across her chest, then he wrapped his coat around her so only the top of her head was showing. There was a line of clean white scalp where her hair was parted and Carlisle couldn't resist running his finger along it, then he smiled in his abrupt, simple way and crossed the room to the Colonel's table.

"Home for Christmas, Jack," Spaeth said. "I gave that shavetail of yours hell for saying that."

"I know, sir."

"Patrol duty."

"Yes, sir," Carlisle said and he sat down.

The officers who had been at the table had gone to the vast buffet at one side of the room. Colonel Spaeth's lank hair toppled down over one of the lenses of his glasses and he brushed it back; then, missing the other officers, he looked around for them. "Want something to eat, Jack?"

"No, sir. Can I get you anything?"

Colonel Spaeth shook his head. "I'm going to get out of here," he said. "Go write a letter to Peg and the kids and tear it up. Makes as much sense as anything we've been doing out here. Have a drink, Jack. You look stone sober. That one's vodka, this one's sake, Scotch, champagne and bourbon." The Colonel shoved an assortment of bottles across the table and gave Carlisle a glass. "The Whites made sure not to slight anyone's national preference in booze," he said. "Be nice to know where they got all this, not that it makes any difference now, I suppose."

Carlisle chose bourbon and poured himself a light drink. The Colonel raised his glass. "To the end of the war and the promise of concord ahead," he said.

"Any idea when we'll be leaving?" Carlisle asked.

The Colonel shook his head gloomily and scowled at his glass. "Sake is one hell of a lousy drink," he said.

The other officers returned to the table carrying plates laden with hors d'oeuvres; caviar, jellied salmon, meat pastries, salads, pickled cucumbers and herring. They greeted Carlisle with unusual warmth and sat down with an air of expectancy.

Colonel Spaeth fumbled in the breast pocket of his blouse and brought out a pair of captain's bars which he tossed across the table to Carlisle with a smile. "You probably have the distinction of being the only officer promoted on the day the war was over," he said. "It came through this afternoon."

Carlisle looked at the bars with blank amazement. The officers laughed and demanded a speech. Their noise attracted people at the nearby tables and presently there was a crowd standing around with glasses in their hands, some singing, others congratulating they knew not what.

"Come on, Hunkpapa, on your feet," Major Taziola demanded. "Speech!"

They beat the table, threatening to attract more attention, and to prevent this Carlisle rose clumsily. "Thank you," he said.

Everyone cheered.

"This means a lot to me."

They cheered again and applauded.

Carlisle tried to find something else to say, but they didn't care what he said or what he felt, they only wanted to cheer. They enjoyed his embarrassment and Carlisle realized how ridiculous it was for the promotion to have come at the end of the war, even more ridiculous to have taken it seriously, which is what he had done. It showed on his face and in his manner. He should have laughed. He should have made jokes, but he didn't know any jokes. Leverett would have managed it. Oh, yes, he would have had them howling.

Carlisle stood there paralyzed, with the blood pumping behind his eyes as the crowd continued to yell. "Speech! Speech!"

"Thank you, Colonel," he muttered.

Colonel Spaeth rose and took his arm. "Come on, Jack," he said. "I want to get out of here. Give me a hand."

He threw an arm across Carlisle's shoulder pretending to need more help than he actually did and laughter boomed and rippled behind them as they came into the hotel lobby, where Colonel Spaeth dropped his arm and straightened his blouse. "I didn't think it would go like that, Jack," he said.

Carlisle nodded and looked around. The lobby was full of people calling to each other, beckoning and signaling as though they were on the floor of a stock exchange.

Two German clerks at the reservations desk wore expressions of intransigent refusal. There were no rooms to be had. Vacancies, when they occurred, were filled in private transactions, the former occupant subleasing to the next, so even the clerks couldn't say who was currently in residence. The Russians, Czechs and Japanese held most of the rooms for themselves and their guests and it was common knowledge that no American had ever been invited above the second floor.

"Doesn't matter, Colonel," Carlisle said.

"Those bars have been overdue for years," Spaeth said. "Well, go on back to the party. I've got a car outside."

"I'll walk you out, sir."

They started through the lobby, but had to wait as a glittering procession descended the staircase and crossed to the ballroom. "Reinforcements," Spaeth said. "General Otani with Ivanov-Rinov, and General Gaida. There's Kalmykoff, the little blond one, and General Bogoloff from Verkhne-Udinsk."

But Carlisle's attention had been taken by a woman with dark hair and very fair skin who came down the stairs on the arm of a Czech officer. She wore a light green gown with a garnet necklace close around her neck. It was the necklace which had captured Carlisle's attention. His first impression was that her head had been severed but had not yet fallen from her body, that it was delicately balanced, so she had to walk carefully to prevent its toppling off and rolling down the stairs. It took him a moment to realize that the red line at her throat was a necklace and he was deeply relieved. But the brilliant, blood-colored garnets on her white throat made such an impact that he knew it was one of those inconsequential details he would never forget.

As he turned to watch her pass into the ballroom Colonel Spaeth tapped his shoulder. "Go on back, Jack," Spaeth said. "The party has just begun."

"It's late," Carlisle said and he followed the Colonel to the street.

Outside it was bitterly cold, but the snow had stopped. Colonel Spaeth tucked his hands into his armpits and went to his car at the curb. "Get in. I'll drive you back," he said.

"Hell, I left my coat and bars," Carlisle said. "I'll pick them up and walk. You go on."

"All right, Captain," Spaeth said.

Carlisle grinned. "That's a title, isn't it," he said, "one I can tack on my name when I retire."

"You're a damned royalist at heart, Jack," Spaeth said. "Get out of this before you freeze." He popped Carlisle on the shoulder, got into the car and drove off.

When Carlisle came into the ballroom the orchestra had been replaced by a Russian military band. The arrival of the high officers and their ladies had settled the crowd like oil on stormy waters. Several drunks were being helped out of the room and the revelers had returned to their tables. Theda Bara, wrapped in his coat, was still on the bench, facing the wall with her knees drawn up. He decided he'd wake her and if she had a room he'd take her home.

Carlisle went to the American table to retrieve his captain's bars; Captain Bentham, Captain Cloak and Major Taziola were still there but they were watching the new arrivals and didn't notice as he dropped the bars into his pocket, plucked a bottle of bourbon from the table and started back toward the girl.

He hadn't gone four steps when he saw the woman who had attracted him on the stairs. She was dancing with a very tall, elderly Russian general and one wing of her dark brown hair had fallen over her face. The general was not aware that one of his epaulets had entangled her hair and that she was trying to free herself. Carlisle stepped to the general's side and caught his epaulet. "You're tangled up here," he said. Carlisle thrust his bottle of bourbon into the general's hand and unfastened the epaulet but in doing this he disarranged the rest of the woman's hair, which fell down her shoulders in a glistening hazel cascade. She tried to catch it, then burst into laughter and fled toward the powder room with Carlisle behind her still clinging to the epaulet.

As the door to the ladies' room fell shut behind them Carlisle saw his stricken expression in the dressing table mirror.

"Please!" Carlisle said and to excuse his presence he held up the epaulet still tangled in her hair.

They were in a small room papered in a pink rose pattern. A door to one side stood ajar and Carlisle glanced toward it nervously. "I was afraid to drop it," he stammered. "Afraid it might tear your hair or pull your head off."

"Yes, I see," she said. "Thank you."

She sat down at the dressing table, took a comb from her bag and disengaged the epaulet, which she handed him. "It belongs to General Bogoloff," she said.

Carlisle nodded and backed to the door. "I'm sorry, ma'am."

"You're very kind, Lieutenant," she said, "but I don't lose my head so easily."

"Carlisle," he said, "Captain Carlisle." It was the first time he'd identified himself to anyone as a captain and he felt like an impostor. "I haven't got my bars on," he added.

She offered her hand over the back of the small gilded chair. "Countess Tatiana," she said. "Tatiana Nojine."

Carlisle took her hand, which he found surprisingly large, in his own. He didn't know what to do with it. Her gray eyes set very wide under straight dark brows had an expectant expression which alarmed him. Her face above the garnets was smooth and unpowdered and she was smiling, a bit perversely Carlisle thought. "I noticed you as I came down the stairs, Captain," she said.

The precise, musical seriousness of her voice drove Carlisle further into himself.

He released her hand. "I saw you too," he said bluntly. "On the stairs."

She waited, but seeing he wasn't going to say any more she turned to the mirror and began to do up her hair.

Their reflections in the mirror shocked Carlisle. He looked so awkward, so heavily, darkly ugly that he felt his presence there should have terrified her, but it terrified him. He didn't know how to leave, what to say to make leaving possible, and he was fascinated by her large white hands moving quickly as though each had a mind of its own. She met his eyes in the mirror. "Have you been in Vladivostok long, Captain?" she asked.

"Since August," he said. "With the 27th Regiment. C Company, 27th Regiment. I've been up the line at Spasskoi and Khabarovsk part of that time."

"I was also at Spasskoi for a time."

"I must have been at Khabarovsk," he said.

She held her hair with one hand and searched in her handbag with the other. Released from her attention Carlisle excused himself but as he reached the door she spoke again.

"My hair clips must have fallen to the floor," she said and she appealed to him.

"I'll go look," Carlisle said, but on an impulse he took his new captain's bars from his pocket. "Would these do?" he asked. "They have clasps."

Countess Tatiana looked at the bars on the palm of his hand and smiled. "Yes, but you should put those on and give me the others. Would that be permissible?"

Carlisle removed his silver bars. Tatiana clipped them into her hair, then stood up and helped Carlisle fasten his captain's bars. "Not many officers can have been promoted in the ladies' powder room," she said and she laughed, a clear-throated, rising sound which lifted Carlisle and made him laugh too. "From now on you are my Captain of the Powder Room," she said. "That sounds very warlike indeed!" and she took his arm.

When they reappeared Tatiana wore silver bars in her hair and Carlisle was a captain. There were shouts, glasses were raised and everyone crowded around begging Tatiana for a similar rise in rank. Carlisle offered General Bogoloff his epaulet, but the towering General, speaking in ponderous rolling English, refused to accept it until the Countess made him a field marshal.

"Very well, I'll keep it for a wand," Tatiana said and taking the epaulet from Carlisle she held it aloft. "Make way or I'll change you all to frogs and goats," she declared. "The Captain and I will dance."

Everyone bowed allowing them to pass and Carlisle moved toward the dance floor in a daze.

"That takes the cake," Captain Cloak said.

"Hunkpapa Jack Carlisle is about to do a war dance!" Bentham said.

Taziola shrugged comically. "Give a man a little rope," he said. "She belongs to the high command, rumor has it."

"You're up on all the rumors, aren't you, Taz," Bentham said.

"I'm not a communications officer for nothing."

Carlisle shuffled about the dance floor like a trained bear on a chain and couldn't remember having been so miserable. Tatiana smiled and Carlisle found her smile persuasive; it seemed to control his lips, so he smiled too. "Shall we finish this dance at least?" she asked.

"I was leaving," he said.

"If you have an engagement, of course," she said.

"No," he said quickly. "No, no."

"It won't be much longer now."

"I'm not much of a dancer."

"You are," she said and he believed her.

When the music ended a Czech officer came to Tatiana's side. He had her hair clips. "Oh, thank you, Raul," she said and with a gesture like the flight of a white bird she introduced the officer to Carlisle. "Lieutenant Markowitz, Captain Carlisle."

The Czech clicked his heels and bowed. "A pleasure, Captain," he said, but it wasn't.

"Yes," Carlisle said, then to his own complete surprise he bowed to the Countess. "Thank you very much, Countess Tatiana," he said and turning on his heel he marched to the door. The officers at the American table rose as one man and gave their imitation of an Indian war whoop, popping their hands over their mouths to flutter the sound. Carlisle glanced at them. They were all smiling. "Count another coup for the Sioux," Bentham called and he waved cheerily.

Carlisle, irritated by their coltish exuberance, remembered his coat and veered off to get it. Theda Bara was sitting up in the corner. "I was watchin' you," she said. "The Countess was in my store today. Her hands are big."

"Did you come alone?" Carlisle demanded.

"I make a decent living," she said and she scowled at him.

He was about to ask if he could take her home, but the war was over. "It's all over and no use starting anything," he thought to himself.

"I came with a gentleman," she said. "But I don't see him, do you?"

"I'd like my coat," he said.

"Oh!" she said. "I thought it was his." She rose and gave Carlisle his coat. Carlisle felt sorry for her, but the war was over, so he thanked the girl and left.

« 2 »

Sergeant Austin moving carefully to avoid disturbing Maryenka, got out of bed and pulled his greatcoat over his naked shoulders. The tiny room under the eaves of the building was cold but they'd used all the fuel the night before; it was the main extravagance of their private celebration, the warm fire, a bottle of whiskey and talk.

Austin snapped a stick match on his thumb and lit the stub end of a cigar he'd left on the table, then went to the dormer window. It was four-thirty. He'd have to leave soon to reach the barracks before reveille. He always gave himself a half-hour head start on the men.

From the window Austin could see the squat graystone depot which rose from the street like a gloomy fortress. Its streaked walls were damp as though springs inside them issued trickles of water which flowed down to the mixed brick and cobblestone square.

A trolley came along the street, its wheels clattering over the switches, sparks flashing blue-yellow from the trolley arm as it knocked ice from the overhead line.

The early light crept around the corners of the buildings and across the square where snow, trampled by many celebrant feet, lay in patches sealed by crusts of ice. A man in a tattered black coat with a muffler wrapped around his face stirred coals in a steel drum, heating water for a samovar as the first vendors came into the square looking cold and exhausted though the day had only begun.

Austin sat on the table and put his bare feet on a chair. He and Maryenka had spent most of the night reassuring each other and making love. She'd agreed to marry him. It was settled, and he was happy as he gazed out of the window into the market square where he'd met Maryenka so many times.

Now that the war was over he'd take her back to Detroit; he hadn't been there in years himself, but he'd take her back and show her the house in Hamtramck where he'd been born. He'd tell her the games he used to play on the block as a kid. Things he hadn't thought of in years would be new to her and because of that they'd all come back to him. Everything he'd thought or done had a value now because of Maryenka. Ordinary things delighted her. The way he snapped a match, the melodies he hummed, everything he told her. She laughed ingenuously and was a bit ashamed for being so easily entertained. "I'm silly," she would say. "I'm just dumb." At first he'd disagreed, but later as their love deepened he'd agree and she'd defend herself with a look of fierce determination. "That's permitted of me to say, but not you! Who knows English *and* Russian *and* some German too?"

"You do."

"And what do you know?"

"Nothing."

"And who is silly?"

"I am," he'd say and they'd hug each other.

From the train yard Austin heard a hiss of released steam followed by a clash of couplings. A train was moving out. The engine, chuffing deeply, spun its drive wheels on the cold tracks, then the cars began to roll, screeching over the switches until they reached the right of way. Austin could see the train as it emerged from the depot, just the top of it over the wall. Two brakemen on the roof of a car swung their arms against the cold and stood with their booted feet wide apart. The train engine was white with a Russian word on its side.

Austin watched as it picked up speed heading toward Khabarovsk. One of the armored cars was particularly ugly; it had been adapted from a tank car with a reinforced turret added to the stern, where the snout of a gun poked out. Two men were standing in a hatch at the top of this car, just their heads and shoulders showing. One of them had a full beard, nearly white; the other one, wearing a cap, waved at someone or at the whole city as the train rolled north. Austin smiled and waved remembering times in the Michigan countryside when he'd waved at the trains and all the passengers waved back at the kid on the fence whom they'd never see again.

Austin snubbed out his cigar and cursed himself for getting so damned tenderhearted, but he enjoyed it. He enjoyed thinking about things as long as she was there. Who in hell else could he tell what he thought? Not Carlisle. He couldn't tell Carlisle, for instance, that love was a sweet tooth. He doubted he'd even tell Maryenka, but crazy things came to his mind these days. Love was a sweet tooth. He met Maryenka because he liked candy. He'd been a candy hog from a kid, so that's how he met her. He'd stop at her kiosk a couple of times a week and pretty soon she came to expect him. "You are my best customer," she said one day. Those were the first words he remembered, spoken in precise book-taught English with the emphasis on the wrong syllables.

He'd been surprised. He really hadn't noticed her before. He smiled and supposed he wasn't her best customer, but that he was a regular one.

She didn't understand the difference, so he'd tried to explain that the word "best" had something to do with good, whereas "regular" meant often, or steady, but he lost himself in the explanation.

"You're not a bad customer, then," she said.

Austin allowed he wasn't and she decided he was a good man and therefore a good customer and insisted that she'd said it right in the first place. "You like cigars and candy," she said as though this proved her point. As though anyone who liked cigars and candy had to be good.

After this when he came to her kiosk Austin stayed to talk and their conversations took up more and more time, distracting Maryenka from her work, but if he mentioned this she always insisted he stay. "For my English," she'd say. "How can I do better, but talk it!"

She'd learned English from a self-taught political exile who lived in her village, Pashkova, east of Khabarovsk on the Amur. "A good old man," she said, "who was bad for the Czar. He was a socialist. He learned to read some English books and he taught me because my father was kind to him. He was learning German too, but he died and couldn't teach me. But I loved him."

One afternoon he asked if she would have dinner with him. "I was wondering, Miss Shulgin, if you'd have dinner with me."

She'd looked quite startled. "But no!" she said. "I am twenty-three years old! I was married a whole year to Petra Vassilyvitch Shulgin, who died of his heart. Now I'm to be a teacher, you see. When the schools open and everything is right again I will teach. English too. To the children."

It was such a rush of words that Austin hardly knew what to say. That she was a widow struck him as incredible. She was so young. "Do you have children?" he'd asked.

She seemed confused and looked around for something to busy herself with. "I stay open for the last train," she said.

"What if you missed it?"

"I don't know!"

"I'll buy everything on your counter, so you'll have nothing to sell."

This had annoyed her.

"I will not sell to you. You cannot make me do as you wish in that way."

"How then?"

"Why do you ask? You see me here as I am."

"Because I like you and candy and cigars."

Then she'd laughed and tucked her hands into the sleeves of her sweater. "But I should know your name."

"Austin. Sergeant Harry Austin."

"Ostein?"

"Ahstin. You make it sound Jewish."

"My father is Jewish too," she said. "So it's good."

He sighed. "All right, Ostein, then. Ostein. But will you come? Just to dinner. Dinner is all."

So she had come.

The armored train was gone from Austin's view, and the man with the samovar was selling tea. Newsboys came up from the depot with bundles of papers, the Khabarovsk, Chita and Irkutsk editions. Tomorrow he and Maryenka would be listed in the vital statistics column. Carlisle would hit the roof. Austin would have to explain to Colonel Spaeth, but that wouldn't be hard once they were married.

Austin dropped his feet to the cold floor and decided to get some coal before Maryenka woke up. He dressed, gazing fondly at her sleeping face. She was so young and warm and wise. There weren't enough names for her. Christ! He'd be calling her pet names if he didn't look out.

He closed the door quietly and went down the six flights of narrow board stairs which creaked ominously under his weight.

Outside the air bit deep into his lungs, jolting him more awake than he had been. He beat his arms together as the railway brakemen had done and jog-trotted across the square to where he knew wood and coal were sold. He made his purchases from an old woman wrapped in rags and sacking who looked more like an animated lump of coal than a human being. The chock of split wood was bound by a willow sapling, but the coal was loose and he'd forgotten to bring anything in which to carry it. The old woman shrugged at his plight. She had no sacks or baskets, just a little cartload of loose coal which she'd probably picked off the tracks. Austin removed his coat, put the coal inside, tied the arms together and ran back across the square with the wood under one arm and his coatload of coal in the other.

The six flights of stairs required three stops to readjust his bulky load and catch his breath. When he came into the room Maryenka was standing in the center of the floor with a look of panic on her face.

"Ostein!" she cried and she threw her arms around his neck. "I thought you were gone!"

The coal spilled out of his coat over the floor. He dropped the wood and took her in his arms. "I was, you fool."

"I see it, but I thought you'd gone forever! I was pacing about and pacing about. Waiting and waiting and then I knew you were gone forever."

"I was gone about two minutes."

"No! Hours and hours."

"Just down to the square for fuel."

"Yes, you said."

"No, I said you were a fool and you are."

Then she laughed. "Oh, I have such Russian ears! I can never learn! Never. Never! Fool, fuel! It's so hard!"

She helped him pick up the coal and Austin built a fire in the small cast-iron stove which had been made in St. Louis, Missouri.

"Now, you see," she said accusingly. "I don't know what to do away from you. I had good sense before, but it's gone. Look at your coat!"

She began to brush his coat, raising a cloud of coal dust which settled on her light flannel nightgown. The fire blazed and Austin shut the stove door. He took the coat and pushed Maryenka toward the bed. "Hop in until it's warm," he said. "It's time for me to go. Past time."

She resisted his pushing and frowned. "What would happen if you missed that — revelry?"

"Reveille," he said. "I've never missed it."

Maryenka nodded soberly, got into bed and sat there with the blankets pulled around her shoulders, watching him. Austin brushed his coat a couple of times, then looked around trying to remember if he'd left anything. He hadn't, but he didn't want to put his coat on. The fire was crackling nicely. He checked his watch again.

"I missed the last train," Maryenka said quietly. "Many last trains."

"Somebody has to take the roll. I suppose a lot of men will be sacked in drunk."

"Sacked in drunk?"

"Boozed up because of the celebration last night."

"And you have to go count them?"

"Somebody does."

She sighed pathetically and looked toward the stove. "And I should open the kiosk. Business will be good today."

Austin threw his coat on the floor and jumped into bed with his clothes on. Maryenka ducked under the blankets, but he caught and held her lecturing sternly. "We have no sense of decency, no sense of anything. Aren't you ashamed?"

Maryenka nodded, but her eyes sparkled.

"We have to get married today!"

"Tomorrow will do or one after," she said.

"Or the day after that?"

She frowned a bit and shook her head. "Not so many days. I will write my people, my father and mother and my brother Sasha, and I want to make a dress. Three days at most."

"All right," he said and he kissed her. "Tell them you're coming with me."

"Yes," she said.

"And for the rest we'll see what happens."

"Yes," she said, "we'll see. But you must never go away like you did. I was about to run out to find you."

"Here I am."

"Yes, but I was about to run out."

Then she turned her face away and to Austin's great consternation she began to cry. "I'm so silly!" she said brokenly. "Truly I am!"

CHAPTER FOUR

A WEEK after the Armistice, on November 18, Vice-Admiral Aleksandr Vasilievich Kolchak was declared Supreme Ruler of Russia in a coup d'état which overthrew the Omsk Directory.

The little admiral of the stern visage who only a few months before had been living a hand-to-mouth existence in a second-rate Tokyo hotel waiting for a break in his fortune was amazed to find himself acclaimed the savior of Russia. The enthusiastic throngs of Omsk roared their approval of him for no other reason than that he was Russian; not Czech, Japanese, British, French or American, but Russian! That his experience was exclusively naval, that he knew nothing of politics or of the economic conditions of Siberia, of finance or diplomacy, mattered not a bit because Kolchak was Russian.

Before the coup, Admiral Kolchak had served one month as Minister of War for the Directory and was never able to ascertain what forces were under his command or their effective strength, but he accepted the acclaim of the populace with solemn expressions and absolute faith that God would provide the answers to questions which his ministers and generals dared not ask.

Military maps showed the White forces to be advancing. It was better therefore to leave it so and wait for the day when these maps showed the Kolchak banner flying in Moscow and the nation saved.

The Americans who heard of the coup were indifferent. Omsk was far away, fifteen hundred miles beyond Lake Baikal, three thousand miles from Vladivostok, and the Americans were oriented toward Seattle and San Francisco. They were waiting for ships to carry them home. They watched the harbor and threshed rumors on the barracks floors, but as the days passed and there was no announcement about the ships nerves frayed, tempers flared and social activity increased.

Nurses of the Evacuation Hospital No. 17 gave a program dance in honor of the Canadian officers. Sixteen dances on the program, waltzes, one-steps and fox trots. Officers of the 31st Infantry exchanged a smoker with officers of the U.S.S. *Brooklyn*. The Gun Deck Minstrels sang. Officers and their ladies danced to "Ja Da," "For the Two of Us," "Indianola," and "Smiles." They sang "Dear Little Boy of Mine," "The Rose of No Man's Land" and "Everyone I Love Lives Down in Dixie." Almost every occasion ended with a mellow rendition of "Dosfidania."

But there was a terrible undercurrent no amount of booze or romance could erase. Someone said they wouldn't be home by Christmas — shipping shortage, new orders, they didn't know what, but someone said.

And they sang "When Alexander Takes His Ragtime Band to France" adding sotto voce "It'll get lost."

Most of the interventionist forces had officers' clubs in Vlad, but everyone gravitated to the Russian Club on the ground floor of the Aleksander Hotel. The Americans came hoping for a clue to their immediate future. The Russian Revolution, except in its broadest outline, was incomprehensible to them. They knew the Czar and his family had been killed and that some group known as the Bolsheviks or Maximalists had taken over. They weren't sure what Bolshevism or Maximalism was but generally they were inclined toward democratic forces and remembered that President Wilson had approved the change in the Russian regime. The assassination of the Romanovs didn't sit well with them on humanitarian grounds, the Romanov girls looked rather pretty, but monarchy was distasteful, except of course the British, which was different. But the names Lenin, Trotsky, Chicherin, Kolchak, Kalmykoff, Kornilov, Dutov were alien to them. There were too many actors on the stage, too many speeches and too many places. There was a front somewhere beyond remote Omsk near even more remote Samara where the Whites were fighting the Reds for something. At Murmansk and a place called Archangel British and American troops were also stuck in a situation not so different from their own. They knew also that an army of Czechoslovakians, whose country was not even on their maps, was dispersed across the Trans-Siberian Railroad, close to seventy thousand of them, whose plan had been to tranship from Vlad and join the Allies on the western front and fight against Germany. But the war was over! If the Czechs wanted to liberate their country from the Hapsburgs they had succeeded. Bravo the Czechs! They were democratic, also clean.

But for the most part the Americans couldn't piece it together. They listened, reported what they heard, studied the maps and were confused, and the question underlying their interest in Russian affairs was — where in hell are the ships?

Ira Leverett spent his time buying souvenirs and writing cheerful letters home. In this way he avoided much of the frustration other men were experiencing; in fact he avoided the other men in so far as possible.

Assuming the war which was waged to end all wars had been brought to a successful conclusion, then it was the only war Ira would have to talk about. In sum it had been rather inglorious, a bit disappointing as far as he was now concerned. Not the kind of thing one can make conversation about. It needed embellishment, so Ira spent his time gathering material which might have value in the future. A pair of Cossack sabers was one such acquisition. On the whole he felt very much like a tourist and would have enjoyed it thoroughly if Captain Carlisle hadn't been so tedious about the military end of things. He wrote his sister Ruth about Carlisle:

As I said he's a Sioux, or half a Sioux, which is a good deal less than half a Franc, ho, ho! They call him Hunkpapa, and they call us the Sioux and the Jew, which shows you that army wit is not better than mine. Worse!

Since joining Hunkpapa's company as second-in-command I think he's said seven words to me, four of which were, 'Don't get smart, brassbar!' That was when I was explaining to him how fouled up the army was, taking as an example the system whereby a first lieutenant wears a silver bar but a second lieutenant wears a gold bar and since gold is more valuable than silver, as anyone knows, the insignia should be reversed, or else Second Louies wearing gold should have the edge on lieutenants wearing silver. 'Don't get smart, brassbar' was his response to this undeniable logic. He's a terse fellow. Of the remaining seven words two I cannot pass on to your still, I trust, virginal ear. The third word is 'Brains!' which word, accompanied by a disgusted shake of his big head and packed with infinite loathing, is his usual response to any suggestion I might offer to improve the current condition of the company, which, until we received the happy news that the war is over, was fairly miserable in the spirits department. Now that we know we're coming home this has changed.

We're a short company, only a hundred and sixty-two men (military secret!), and one suggestion I made was that we rotate positions once a month so everyone would have a chance to be company commander or first sergeant before coming home. A broadening experience, you see, and it would keep the men alert. The Sioux growled that he for one had already been everything (he came up through the ranks, it seems) except a horse's ass, leaving a strong implication that I filled that vacancy nicely. My second suggestion was offered to alleviate homesickness. It was that we introduce a lottery for the purpose of financing cablegrams home. The lucky winners being able to communicate with any place in the United States. This didn't even draw a verbal rebuttal, but I got a look from the depths of Carlisle's carnelian eyes, which would have broken stone, a material I'm sure he thinks my head is made of.

Incidentally the Sioux, whose picture I enclose, snapped while he was earnestly paring his nails, was made a captain on the night of the Armistice. I like to think this was in response to my discourse on the metallurgy of insignia, that the War Department felt obligated to remove this particular source of my confusion (now if they'll just elucidate the derivation of the term 'shavetail,' which even a cursory examination of my posterior will convince them is not aptly applied to me, I will feel that I know enough about the army to last a lifetime) but the probability is that Carlisle had it coming. There are those who say he is an excellent officer. I agree entirely. As an officer he is an excellent example. I, on the other hand, am and shall remain a tourist.

So much for the military, now for the nasty gossip. Another installment in the serial romance of First Sergeant Harry Austin and his girl Maryenka.

Can an American soldier find love and true happiness with a little Siberian candy seller? Is difference in age an insurmountable barrier to married love? What will their parents say? What will the U.S. Government say? Read the next issue of Leverett's *Siberian Lovers' Gazette*.

Yes, they got married! In our last issue we saw heartless Lieutenant (now Captain) Carlisle threatening to tie poor little Maryenka Shulgin (now Austin) to the Trans-Siberian Railroad tracks to be diced like Harvard beets 'neath the wheels of an onrushing freight train rather than see his faithful friend commit his life to an alien. But!

Were the lovers deterred? Did they falter? Nay!

And now, dear reader, they are man and wife. And those whom the city officials of Vladivostok, be they Red or White, as the case may be (and who knows?), hath joined together in civil matrimony let no military tribunal put asunder.

I was a witness (a minor flaunting of Carlisle's injunction against such liaisons) but not best man, exactly, there wasn't one, but I did the best I could. Sergeant Austin requested my presence and my signature on the documents on the assumption, I suppose, that any officer's name made more official that which was at best dubious. Platoon Sergeant Baker also supported the marriage contract with his name. It was a double ring ceremony, plain gold bands with initials and the date scribed inside. To support her claims of legitimate existence Maryenka also brought two witnesses, a middle-aged post office official (her officer I suspect) and a young lady of decided Oriental derivation who lives in the same apartment building. The Oriental belle took a shine to Baker and they vanished soon after the wedding breakfast. The bride wore a russet-colored satin frock made by hand and a pair of high button black shoes which creaked as though they were borrowed, or new. Fortunately I had the foresight to provide myself with articles to satisfy the old quatrain: Something old, Some-

thing new, Something borrowed, Something blue. These provided the only
charm in what was otherwise a dreary ceremony, though the principals didn't
appear to be aware of this. Their eyes saw dimly through the rosy gauze of love.

We gathered in front of a sallow, somewhat nervous city functionary who
tied the knot, a record clerk or a judge or some petitioner off the street who
saw a chance to collect a fee by impersonation, and before he began to mumble
his dry marital incantation I bedecked Maryenka with the following items: an
old lapel watch, the kind dowager ladies pin on their heaving bosoms and can
see without tipping their heads; new earrings of Japanese pearls which I had
intended sending you (too bad); a 27th Infantry collar insignia which I "borrowed" from Carlisle, a pleasant irony to which the groom didn't respond
wholeheartedly, and a huge bouquet of incredibly blue hothouse iris which a
Chinese florist and herbalist coaxed out of the earth against all dictates of the
season by feeding them goldfish, or so he told me.

Having performed this ritual which I claimed would guarantee the marriage
permanence, joy, wealth, children and insure it against military interference,
the bride, I must say, was terribly pleased. She is pretty, rather blocky in the
Russian style, but nice. I think you'd call her refreshing. Isn't that what you
call your girl chums who are sweet and a bit too simple to bear?

We had pictures made afterward by an Oriental whose camera appeared to
be designed to dispatch its subjects to another world rather than to capture
their image in this. He used about four pounds of flash powder and when the
smoke cleared off we were all relieved to be alive. Unfortunately the plates
aren't developed yet, but I'll send you a print when I can. I'm sure we'll all have
the firing squad stare.

Until the picture arrives take a look at Sylvia Cowan, the one whose daddy
is the druggist down the street (I never touched her!). Maryenka Austin is
something like I remember Sylvia, same hair and eyes, but more friendly (or
Austin would never have gotten to know her, like I didn't get to know Sylvia
Cowan).

Now all that remains is to get the official reaction to this union. Anyone
getting married is supposed to have the commanding officer's approval prior
to the event, but I doubt not that in this case approval will be forthcoming.
After all a nation with victory in hand cannot very well deny the fruits thereof,
and I'm sure Maryenka Austin will make a very acceptable housewife in the
great American Midwest or wherever they choose to settle. Austin has decided
to leave the army and go straight, though Lord knows what he'll do since he's
been in it nearly all his life.

End of installment.

Will the newlyweds from such disparate backgrounds be able to accommodate to life in the new world? What will the neighbors say?

Don't miss the next issue!

Captain Carlisle, our defeated villain, has gone into a terrible sulk over the
affair. He looks at me accusingly and treats Austin with a cutting formality
one usually reserves for mutineers. I'm quite certain, however, that Austin
can take care of himself and, if anyone can do so, he can also take care of

Carlisle. So be it. Soon we'll all trace our ways back to loving arms at home, if not by Christ's birthday surely by George Washington's and what could be more fitting? No entangling foreign alliances, right? unless of course they are of a nuptial nature. (I have no plans.)

So dear Ruth, Mother, Dad and Uncle Dave, it only remains to say that I am healthy, buoyant, anxious to get home and regale you with other amusing events of this sojourn. Meantime I entrust you all to the care of Mom's ubiquitous chicken soup and enjoin you to enter my name as a candidate in all local elections and to inform as many attractive young ladies as you run across, including Sylvia Cowan, that Ira C. Leverett will soon be in their midst.

Ira finished his letter with a special line for each of the family, then with love he signed and sealed it.

But he was no longer buoyant. Writing home always left him depressed. It took a surprising amount of energy to link two such different worlds, more as time went on, and Ira wondered if there wasn't a point ahead when the effort would be too great, a point at which he could no longer hold the immediate world and the remembered one together in his mind.

He tapped the envelope on his fingertips and looked around his room, the privileged quarters of an officer, with a cot and a field desk and a big Russian stove in the corner stoked with coal each morning through a door which opened on the hall.

Details.

Austin's wedding had been depressing, in one of those terrible places with official notices on the walls and an oily board floor worn down to the nailheads by the feet of tax assessors and suppliants. The only color in the room had been the irises against Maryenka's russet breast. Russet and blue. Kolchak's colors were green and white and lately these banners had begun to appear. The pearl earrings had been a disaster. Too sophisticated.

Details!

Ira wondered how soon they'd fill his mind, coming stealthily to exclude everything else so his letters would seem alien and his mother would frown and ask, "But what does it mean? What is this word, these places, these people? Is this Ira?" And no one would be able to say.

He was lonely. That was the point.

Ira snorted and looked at the letter in his hand. He hadn't realized how simple it was — he wanted his Mama and Ruth and Uncle Dave and his Dad. He was homesick.

« 2 »

A few days prior to Admiral Kolchak's meteoric elevation the weather in Vladivostok turned mild. Thin remnants of snow vanished from the streets and sunlight pale as sherry weakened the ice in the harbor. The sky was clear, as though the elements were paying homage to victory, and there was a peace parade down Svetlandskaya Street and past the movie house on Soetlanslaya.

The streets were lined on both sides by spectators many of whom had marched themselves not many months before, carrying flags and signs protesting the disembarkation of foreign troops on Russian soil. Now they were passive, assuming that this parade was the last great show before the troops reembarked for their homelands.

French sailors from the gunboat *Kersaint* marched briskly down the street followed by Indo-China Tirailleurs commanded by French officers. The American 31st Infantry and units of the 27th then in Vladivostok made an impressive block of khaki competence and behind them came a Russian band and a battalion of Russian Stryelki under the command of General Ivanov-Rinov.

Chinese residents of Vladivostok, their hair braided in queues, watched their national soldiers and sailors pass. There was an Italian detachment wearing black plumes in their hats, Serbian officers, British sailors from H.M.S. *Suffolk,* the Canadians and, of course, the Czechs.

Marching on the flank of his company Carlisle caught sight of Leverett in the corner of his eye and wanted to boot him in the rump. Leverett was strolling; he was in step and his eyes were front, but still he was strolling. How any man could express such disinterest in a parade without actually breaching discipline was beyond Carlisle's comprehension, yet there it was, not ten feet away, ambulating civilianhood, with a college degree. Given three more months Carlisle swore he'd make a soldier of Leverett, but this evidently was not to be. But what did it matter?

Carlisle decided he envied Leverett's poise. Yes, that was it. The uncommon ease with which Leverett set himself apart from other men was a quality Carlisle yearned for since meeting Countess Tatiana and he resented Leverett for possessing it. Leverett had style, Carlisle had none.

"Pick it up, Leverett," he growled.

"Yes, sir!" Leverett responded smartly, but there wasn't enough sincerity in it to suit Carlisle.

Discipline had gone to hell. Since Leverett's arrival and Austin's marriage the whole damned company had just gone to hell, but this was his responsibility. The whole situation was slack. His mind wasn't on his work. He often thought of himself as the Captain of the Powder Room.

Now isn't that a hell of a thing for a soldier?
"Wipe that smirk off your face, Leverett."
"Yes, sir!"
It was a grand peace parade.

CHAPTER FIVE

ON December 6 it turned cold again and the staff and key liaison officers
attached to the American Siberian Expeditionary Force were again summoned to a meeting at General Graves' headquarters. They came in from
the street chafing their hands and stood about wriggling their toes against
the inner soles of their boots trying to warm their feet.

Outside a bitter wind came off the Bay of the Golden Horn where Allied
ships lay at anchor, the *Suffolk,* the *Asahi,* the big U.S.S. *Brooklyn* with its
four tall stacks braiding columns of pale smoke against the skyline.

Free ice driven by the wind piled up against the ships and would have
frozen there if work details armed with boat hooks hadn't shoved it off.
Sailors chipped salt ice from the decks, the cables and chains, their blue
hands fumbling tools as they fought it. To make the work tolerable some
pretended the ice was an enemy and hacked at it bravely, planning massive
assaults with hot water and defensive measures with canvas ice shields, but
in a few hours the ice was back. There was no victory to be had.

The entire population of Vladivostok was depressed.

The Armistice celebration seemed now to have been a distant event, but
its aftereffect, a terrible, sullen hangover, would not abate. If a smile was
seen on the face of a man in a bar or a club it was invariably an expression
of disillusionment, a mocking little smirk usually accompanied by a shake
of the head and a snort recognizing the folly of high expectations. Everyone was a bit ashamed of having been so ecstatic about the Armistice, but
at the same time all thought it to be a great injustice that they should feel
ashamed. Their celebration had been proper, indeed not to have celebrated
would have been impossible; but somehow, somewhere, someone had
tricked them and because no one could say who this was they were inclined
to be suspicious of everyone. So, throughout Vladivostok, there was an
atmosphere of guarded silence. No one wanted to commit himself again

and this was particularly true of the officers who had come to meet with General Graves.

They gathered in a conference room furnished with a long table, a blackboard, chairs, scratch-pads and pencils and studiously avoided mentioning what was uppermost in their minds. They nodded to each other, shook hands, lit cigarettes, pipes, cigars and put them out again. They took a great deal of time finding places for their fleece-lined coats, muskrat caps, gloves, mufflers, and removing their overshoes. Most of these officers had already discovered by one means or another that the command was scheduled to remain in Siberia, but until General Graves confirmed this they were honor bound not to discuss it.

Colonel Spaeth sat down near the head of the table across from Colonel Kirk, commander of the 31st Infantry, who smiled, then got absorbed in a game of tic-tac-toe on his note-pad. Other members of Graves' staff stood about the room staring at fixed points on the wall or the floor. Eichelberger, the Assistant Chief of Staff; Barrows, Intelligence; the Adjutant General, the Inspector General, Chief Quartermaster, Chief of Surgeons — these and the others on the staff were waiting for the General and trying to appear at ease.

Lieutenant Colonel Morrow, C.O. of the 1st Battalion, 27th Infantry, sat down beside Spaeth. A tall, loose-limbed Southerner with a perpetually mordant expression masking the humorous snap in his eyes, Morrow picked up a pencil and began to doodle on the pad at his place.

"Looks like us poor chickens are going to have to peck up the leavings," he said.

"How's the weather in Spasskoi, George?"

"Very sanitary. Freezes a corpse solid in half an hour. I just hope we get out before the thaw."

Spaeth nodded.

There were three liaison officers in the room, one from the Czechs, one from the British and one from the French. They stood in the doorway talking earnestly to two Americans representing the Russian Railway Service Corps and the Railway Advisory Commission. Morrow glanced toward them. "Preconference conference," he said. "Decisions always get made by the door on the way in or out. Nothing gets done at the table but doodling."

"How are your men, George?"

Morrow tossed his pencil down. "Same as yours I expect. When you send soldiers into a theater of war with orders to fight as little as possible, and if possible not at all, it takes the stuffing out of them. They feel stupid and they look stupid. You get my report on Krasnaya Rechka?"

"Yes."

"Dobbs has it. You know Dobbs, E Company. He came to me last week, poor guy. He'd done a good job on that detention camp, cleaned it up, got the Red Cross and Y.M.C.A. working, improved the food, handed out a clothing issue, then he came to ask me how many prisoners were supposed to be there. I told him two thousand and he said he had twenty-five hundred and that it was going up."

Spaeth sighed and Colonel Kirk, whose regiment had charge of a prison camp at Kraevski, shook his head wearily.

"The Russians outside were breaking into Dobbs' prison camp," Morrow said. "Now he posts a heavy night guard to keep them out and every morning at roll call he goes down the line looking for those who can't speak German or Hungarian, but the prisoners give lessons, so the break-ins learn enough to pass the test.

"Dobbs found a tunnel two blocks long under the fence. He closed it but they're still coming in faster than he can throw them out and I know he hates like hell doing it. We decided to hold the break-ins three days and feed them before they were tossed out again. That way they have a chance, but not much.

"When I left, Dobbs had three thousand and had given up trying to explain to his men that it was their duty to stop outsiders trying to break into the prison camp. How in hell do you explain that to an American soldier? 'Don't let the Russians break into our prison, boys, it's for Krauts and Magyars only.'" Morrow shook his head ruefully. "Upside down," he murmured. "Topsy damned turvy."

Lieutenant Colonel Olie Robinson, the Chief of Staff, came into the room followed by General Graves. The officers who were seated rose as Graves took his place at the head of the table. "Take your seats, gentlemen."

There was a rustle and scraping of chair legs but the General remained standing. His straight unsmiling lips and blocky jaw gave him the appearance of a fundamentalist minister, and a shock of light brown hair fell forward as he studied the notes he'd put on the table. His big expressive hands supported his weight as he bent over them with a nearsighted scowl as though he wasn't quite convinced by what he read.

In his previous post as Assistant Chief of the Army General Staff, Graves had earned a reputation as a thoroughly reliable administrator, but he lacked the dash usually sought for in field commanders. Graves was stable, long-suffering and uncompromisingly honest. He breathed heavily and the air whistling through his nose impelled the men around the table to match their breathing to his, so that each intake was followed by a uniform sigh which might have put them to sleep if the General hadn't cleared his throat.

"We'd better try to review the situation as it stands," he said. His deep, grating voice was inexpressibly weary. Fed up with the equivocal situation in which he found himself, he always started each conference with the dogged phrase: "We'd better try."

He raised his eyes to look along the table, skipping down the line of faces with a glint of recognition for each officer and sometimes a nod.

"As you may know, there's a new government at Omsk under an Admiral Kolchak who has been given the title Supreme Ruler of Russia." Graves dropped his eyes to his notes, which was a sufficient comment on the validity of this title. "This Kolchak government announces its intention of combining the currently scattered forces of opposition to the Lenin-Trotsky regime and mounting an assault on Kiev, Petrograd and Moscow. There is, accordingly, a front in formation along a line from the Caspian Sea to the city of Perm planning to link with forces now stationed at Archangel. Our current intelligence of the number of effectives, the armament and logistic support of these troops is unreliable. A large area of the Urals around Ekaterinburg seems to be held by Kolchak forces, also an area around Samara. There seems to be a number of cosmopolite regiments moving forward composed of Czechoslovakians, Serbs, Poles and Italians. There are two light Polish regiments under a Russian brigadier near Verkhne-Udinsk." Graves paused and looked up from his notes with a scowl. "I won't detail these to you, but statements issued from Omsk rise to figures close to a million men, including the Czech Legion, which is now being estimated at a hundred thousand."

He referred to his notes again, letting this fact register. "Of course these estimates will be refined by our intelligence as soon as possible," he said, then his voice assumed a heavier tone of authority. "Now, gentlemen, it is evident that the French and the British intend to support the Kolchak government. General Pierre Janin of France has been assigned as commander in chief of all Allied and Russian troops west of Lake Baikal, with the use of British troops to be approved by General Knox and of Canadians by General Elmsley."

A look of consternation passed down the table as the officers tried to justify this extraordinary chain of command. If Janin controlled the troops west of Baikal it was obvious that Kolchak's title was hollow indeed. It appeared he didn't command his own forces except east of Baikal, which was largely controlled by the Japanese and their Cossack atamans, Semenoff and Kalmykoff. It made no sense.

"The Japanese have given tacit approval of the Kolchak regime," Graves said, "but the position of the government of the United States remains unchanged, which is to say that we do not recognize anybody."

Graves paused again to let this sink in. It was a point which he emphasized on every occasion and one which brought down on him the scorn of every factionalist in Siberia. He was accused by all sides, by the French, the British, the Japanese, the Whites, Reds, and all shades between, of having secret predilections, preferences, political motives. He was abused in the press. He was watched. The U.S. State Department was suspicious of him, finding it impossible to believe that a military man would not sometime reveal an opinion not strictly within the area of his military competence, and if he had done so they would have been on him like a pack of wolves. Indeed they could not be restrained from snarling now, but his behavior thus far had been unimpeachable.

General Graves glanced at the Czech liaison officer, a young lieutenant whose French uniform bore no markings but the red and white Czech colors on his breast pocket. The Czech smiled, then looked down at the pad on which he was sketching a locomotive.

"As you know," Graves continued, "one function of our command as represented in the President's Aide-Mémoire was to aid the Czech echelons in their drive across Siberia to Vladivostok, from which point they were to be transshipped to the Allied western front and fight against Germany. Just why it was necessary for eight thousand Americans to aid seventy-two thousand well-armed Czechs, representing the only intact military force in Siberia at the time, we shall probably never know. I would, however, hazard that since the war is over their presence on the western front would be superfluous at this time. I would also hazard that since the Czechs have turned west to support the Kolchak front we will have a hard time assisting them."

It was so rare for Graves to exhibit irritation that the officers around the table were distinctly uncomfortable. They looked at the Czech, calmly drawing his locomotive, and wondered if General Graves considered the Czech decision to support Kolchak a betrayal of their original purpose. Interpretations clicked through their minds like the whirling symbols in a one-armed bandit; anti-Czech, anti-Kolchak, pro-Bolshevik? pro-Japan, pro-Directory, anti-Bolshevik? But there was no jackpot and they watched Graves waiting for him to deposit another coin. He turned a page of his notes.

"In this connection I quote from a memorandum issued by the President in response to General Janin's request for military support: 'It is the unqualified judgment of the military authorities of the United States that to attempt military activities west of the Urals is to attempt the impossible.' I believe that is perfectly clear," he said.

A sense of relief passed along the table, objectified in some cases by a circle or square drawn on note-pads to signify that at least the officers knew the outside boundary of future operations.

The Czech liaison man raised his pencil and Graves acknowledged him.

"With all due respect to your President, sir," the Czech said softly, "the Czech Legion, it may then be said, has done the impossible both west and east of the Urals. I enter this remark as an obligation to my comrades in arms as their representative here, not in criticism of your country's military policy. There is also, sir, a question as to how it can be that your government does not change its policy when all the circumstances under which it was made have changed."

General Graves' face colored slightly as he stood taller and faced the smiling Czech. "You may be sure, Lieutenant Markowitz, that the President is fully aware of and has a deep respect for the Czech Legion wherever they fight. He is also aware of the shifts in British and French policy, and of their military efforts against the Bolsheviks launched from Latvia, the Crimea, the Caucasus, Murmansk, Archangel and Omsk. That our policy has not changed would, I hope, be considered a stabilizing influence where no others are to be found, but if I have overlooked something please point it out. We came, as you know, to assist the Legion in its desire to join the Allies on the western front; we came also to protect military stores, the railroad and prisoners of war. If necessary I will state again that my directive prohibits interference in the internal politics of Russia. I intend to obey it. I hope you understand."

The directive was impossible and everyone knew it, but the subtle distinction between knowing an impossibility and admitting it was one which Graves intended to maintain. He called this "walking on eggs" and though he sometimes came down hard, as he had on the Czechs whose decision to turn back had been a disappointment, he rarely broke one.

Lieutenant Markowitz looked up at Graves affably. "If the General will permit," he said.

"Yes, of course," Graves said.

Markowitz' voice was reserved and pedantic and he tapped the table with his pencil to the rhythm of his speech.

"It is perhaps needless to review the Czech position in these matters," he said, "but with the Armistice one must take into account the altered circumstances. The purpose of the Czech force in being has been to insure the liberation of the Czechoslovakian state from the Hapsburg Austrian oppressor. In this we have been successful. It remains now to return our legion to its homeland. Obviously the most direct route is west, accepting whatever assistance we can find. In this case the White forces. It will be remembered that as early as June when our forces were in possession of Vladivostok the shipping we had anticipated to take us to the European front was not provided."

Markowitz shrugged slightly as though to dismiss the implicit criticism and went on. "We could not be expected, I think, to walk on the water. Our sole objective now is to get home with the smallest possible loss of life. We cannot, however, turn our backs on those who are willing to assist us, or those whose objectives, for a time, parallel our own. It is hoped however, that our wish to return to Czechoslovakia will not be considered political in its motivation."

The statement, charged once again with criticism of the American position, had been so neatly disarmed with its little joke about walking on the water that the French liaison officer turned his head slightly to approve Markowitz.

"Major Phillipot?" Graves asked sharply. "Is there anything definite from General Janin?"

Major Phillipot pursed his lips under a faintly red bristle mustache. "He is in Omsk, at present, sir," he said. "For the moment that is all we know."

The British liaison man, Captain Fleming, volunteered that General Knox, senior officer of the British Military Mission, was also in Omsk.

There was an extended silence as General Graves pretended to be sorting over his notes, but his expression made it clear he was about to make an announcement. Presently he looked up.

"Well, gentlemen, as many of you know, we'll be staying here for a time." Graves' voice was a bit louder than even he had anticipated and he lowered it slightly. "The reasons for my delay in telling you this may not be obvious, but nothing has been up to this point. I was hoping to get more clarification than I can offer you. We are to assist in protecting the railroad. I take that to mean we will protect our sectors against anyone who attempts to injure, destroy, or disrupt service over the tracks. Our task, assisted by the Railway Service Corps, will be to keep the Trans-Siberian operational. Colonel Robinson will pass out your orders and if you'll arrange the map, Wilson, we'll get on with it."

An adjutant unrolled a large map of Siberia with the Trans-Siberian, Amur, Ussuri and Chinese Eastern railroads blocked out in bold colors. Lieutenant Colonel Eichelberger, the Assistant Chief of Staff, took a pointer and ran it over a blue sector from Ussuri to Khabarovsk. "We're blue," he said. "The Japanese are designated in black; the Czechs, green; Chinese, white; Canadians, brown, and so forth."

"No Red?" Colonel Kirk asked and a chuckle ran along the table.

Eichelberger smiled broadly. "Not from this headquarters, Sam," he said. Then he pointed to the other blue sector, which lay between Verkhne-Udinsk and Lake Baikal. "As you can see, the 27th, which will take this sector, and the 31st on the Ussuri line are about half a continent away from each other."

"How did that happen?" Spaeth asked.

The representative of the Russian Railway Service Corps, Albert Cloyd, a short, intense-looking South Dakotan, wearing the uniform and simulated rank of an American colonel, volunteered an answer. "I think the Inter-Allied Railway Commission pulled those assignments out of a Japanese magician's hat," he said gruffly.

A casual glance at the map showed that Japanese units were predominant and that they controlled all the key points from Verkhne-Udinsk east including the vital junction points at Chita and Khabarovsk.

"Of course they've got ten times more troops here than we have," Cloyd said, "but there's nothing we can do about that now."

Cloyd stared dourly at the map as though he were about to continue. He was one of two hundred and fifty American railway engineers who had volunteered for service on the Trans-Siberian. Most of them were over the military age limit and had accepted commissions in this specially created service as their way of fighting the Central powers and out of their professional interest in railroading, but the bewildering military and political events since their arrival left many of them uneasy about their contribution to the rehabilitation of the Russian railway system. Some had asked to be relieved of their contract obligations to the Corps after Russia sued for peace with Germany, and Cloyd was one who believed that it was no accident that the 27th Infantry had been sent to the Trans-Baikal. American troops stationed in the geographical center of Siberia would settle all misgivings about the need for keeping the railroad operational. The railroad would be their only means of support and members of the Service Corps who had considered resigning would now feel obligated to stay on.

"Anything else, Colonel?" Eichelberger asked.

Cloyd sighed heavily. "No," he said. "No, that's all."

Colonel Spaeth looked at the folder Robinson had put down in front of him and thought of Peg, his wife. Her face appeared dimly on the manila cover, rose toward him, then grew blurred and was lost. This was going to be hard on her, very hard. Both the kids had colds. The weather was bad. The water heater had rusted out and Bobby Jr. was waiting for him to come home and fix the brake on his bicycle.

Spaeth opened the folder and glanced at the papers inside. Verkhne-Udinsk. He looked at the map Wilson had put on the blackboard and saw a sector in blue lying between Verkhne-Udinsk and Lake Baikal.

Colonel Robinson was describing the area, pointing out the bridges and military installations with the tip of a pencil. Seven thousand Japanese stationed east of the town. Prison camp at Beresovka. Important bridges across the Selenga River. Spaeth's attention drifted.

Peg's last letter had been bright and amusing as always, but she was losing a battle against deterioration. She said the house had begun to mutiny, that she often got up at night and walked around lecturing sternly, warning it of the harsh measures which would be taken when the C.O. returned. "I threatened a leaky water tap with a dishonorable discharge last night and then went down in the basement and cursed the furnace for ten minutes. Next morning at breakfast Bobby and Alice both solemnly declared they'd heard bad words coming out of the heat vents in their rooms. I told them the furnace was a 'bad customer' given to profanity and backdrafts of sooty smoke but that when you got home it would settle down. The same day Bobby swore an alarmingly bad word (which I'm sorry to say I learned from you, but never thought I'd utter) and his defense when I hopped on him for it was that he'd learned it from the furnace, which should have its mouth washed out with soap. Oh, hurry home and save me from the furnace!"

Spaeth smiled, but the big old house was a problem. When he was home he enjoyed taming the place, but it wasn't for a woman alone with two kids. Maybe she ought to sell and retreat to an apartment. They'd lose their home, but that was the army. Better to give the place up than have it fall apart.

Some of the wiring was bad.

He worried a lot about the wiring and had asked Peg to get someone to look at it, but he still had this fear of a short circuit starting a fire in the walls while Peg and the kids were asleep. He couldn't shake it. He'd write at once and insist that Peg move to an apartment. He didn't want her to spend another night in that house.

Robinson finished his briefing and asked if there were any questions. Spaeth had absorbed most of the information; the orders in his folder were complete. No one had any questions.

When the meeting adjourned the officers rose, all seriously preoccupied by adjustments which had to be made in their personal lives. The Czech, French and British liaison men were the first to leave. General Graves joined Robinson and Eichelberger at the map and gazed at it solemnly, then he asked Spaeth if he had a minute.

Spaeth, still obsessed by a vision of flames licking through his darkened house, followed General Graves. He checked his watch to estimate the time in American City near Tacoma, Washington, and wished to God he'd never bought the house. The county fire department was half an hour away.

General Graves sat down at his desk and motioned Spaeth to a chair. "Not as bad as all that, is it, Bob?" he asked.

"Thinking about Peg," Spaeth said.

"You're going to have it tough up there in Verkhne. I want you to know that."

"I know," Spaeth said.

General Graves sighed and leaned back in his chair. "Every possible effort is being made to have me relieved of this command, Bob," he said quietly. "The British and French have made strong representations in Washington to get me out. Consul General Harris at Omsk has been filing optimistic reports about the Kolchak government which are directly contrary to the findings of our military intelligence. Caldwell and MacGowan haven't accused me of being Lenin's disciple yet, but I expect they'll get around to it. I won't bore you with my problems. I'm getting paranoid.

"Yesterday I learned that Dr. Teusler told General Gaida I wouldn't dare refuse a request for support by American troops of any action the Czechs might take. When the director of the American Red Cross starts making policy statements for me you can see what I'm up against. Of course Teusler never loses an opportunity to point out that he's Mrs.

Wilson's cousin. His latest contribution to diplomacy has been to dispatch three hundred thousand union suits by rail to support the Kolchak government." Graves picked up a railroad bill of lading and let it drop back on his desk. "Union suits," he said wearily, then he took another paper from his desk and waited for Spaeth's full attention.

"There are a couple of things I want you to do, Colonel. First I want you to listen to the key sections of a proclamation to be posted in Russian at all stations, villages, and at all camps and guard posts which come within your sector." Graves put on his glasses and began to read slowly from the paper in his hand, selecting the paragraphs he wanted Spaeth to hear.

" 'Now, therefore, the Russian people are notified and advised, that in the performance of such duty, the sole object and purpose of the armed forces of the United States, on guard between the railroad points above stated, is to protect the railway property and insure the passage of passenger and freight trains through such sectors without obstruction or interruption.' "

General Graves looked up to be sure Spaeth understood this. Spaeth frowned, about to comment, but Graves shook his head and continued to read:

" 'Our aim is to be of real assistance to all Russians in protecting necessary traffic movements within the sectors on the railroad in Siberia assigned to us to safeguard. All will be equally benefited, and all shall be treated alike by our forces irrespective of persons, nationality, religion or politics.' "

Graves put the proclamation down and waited for Spaeth's reaction.

The proclamation was another testimonial of Graves' adamant refusal to exceed the scope of the orders issued him by President Wilson. Since the policy of the U.S. State Department seemed to be in direct conflict with that of the War Department, Graves had frequently requested clarification of his orders, but none had come.

Spaeth tried to reconcile the proclamation with the orders in his folder and found it impossible. "The railroad will come under Kolchak's control, I assume."

Graves smiled wryly. "That's a good assumption this week, Bob. Two months ago it would have been reading tea leaves. A few months ahead, who knows? Certain sectors are in fact controlled by Semenoff, Kalmykoff and the Japanese."

"Continued operation of the railroad works to Kolchak's benefit. Let me put it that way, then."

"Without it the Kolchak government wouldn't last a week," Graves said.

"Then we're supporting him."

"All right," Graves said quietly, "you've hit it. Now listen carefully. I hate to hamstring a commander, Bob, but I want you to get out of this thing clean. Every order you issue must be checked through me. I assume responsibility for whatever occurs here.

"I want the contents of that proclamation thoroughly understood by every man in your command and as of now I want you to drop such words as 'benefit,' 'support' and a few others in your vocabulary. Our duty is to keep the railroad operating, that's it. If the Czechs try to blow it up we stop them. If the Reds, the Whites, the Greens or anyone else tries to disrupt service we stop them. On the other hand anyone is entitled to passage on the line. Even the Bolshies."

"Impossible," Spaeth said.

Graves' head swung up. "Of course!" he snapped. "Of course it's impossible! But I am bound by my oath and by the Constitution of the United States not to commit an act of aggression. Now I've been told not once but a thousand times by every Allied officer who comes through this office that I'm too literal in these matters. All they want from me, they say, is an expression in their favor. If I'm not for them, I'm against them. Well, until I get clear-cut, unambiguous orders from the President and the War Department I am not for or against anyone.

"Now, Bob, to put it straight, if you can't hold that line, if you have any thought which may prejudice your ability to transmit this idea to the men in your command, I want to know about it. I'd rather relieve you now, Bob, without prejudice and with the greatest respect than put you in this situation. I'm sending someone back to confer with General March in Washington. You could handle that and I'd approve any request of yours for a transfer."

Spaeth glanced at his orders and thought of Peg alone in the house with the kids and the damned frayed wire snapping blue sparks in the wall. He stood up and offered General Graves his hand thinking, even as their fingers touched, that he was going to express his gratitude and accept the assignment to Washington. "I'll stand by you in this, sir," he said intending, he was sure, to add the words "in Washington," but to his astonishment they didn't come. "You want the 27th in position between Verkhne-Udinsk and Lake Baikal by March 10?" he asked.

"That should give you plenty of time."

"Yes, sir."

"Thanks, Bob," Graves said. "I hope you've got men in your command who can give you the kind of support you've just given me."

"I hope so too," Spaeth said.

CHAPTER SIX

THROUGH the generosity of Mrs. Stern of Menlo Park, California, twenty thousand crated oranges arrived at the American supply depot in Vladivostok with a request that they be distributed to the enlisted men of the American Siberian Expeditionary Force at Christmastime. These large, very orange oranges, each separately wrapped in a sheet of crimson tissue paper, were accordingly transported throughout the Maritime Province of Siberia. Some went to Harbin. Some went as far inland as Chita.

They traveled by rail, in boxcars pounding over the poorly graded track at an average speed of eight miles an hour in weather which often fell to twenty degrees below zero. There was pilferage, of course, and in the wake of one train or another it was sometimes possible to see a bearded Russian stationmaster turning a huge orange over and over in his mittened hand, marveling at its size. And if there were children at the station, as there nearly always were, the stationmaster would deliver a lecture to them about oranges which came from Africa and South America, but also from Odessa where the French had landed. Then he would peel the orange and share the sections out to the children, who were surprised by its sweet, tart flavor.

Some of the oranges came under attack by roving bandits or partisans who shot at trains as a matter of course, warming their hands on the barrels of their guns while the bullet-shattered oranges trickled juice which soon froze. Others got caught in the general mismanagement and confusion of the railroad and were shunted onto sidings where they froze, thawed, froze again and finally turned black with the passage of time.

But enough of Mrs. Stern's gift oranges survived the depredations of theft, gunfire and neglect to give each American soldier two at Christmastime, and what these shuddering men thought as they held the faraway oranges in their hands can hardly be imagined.

Sunkist, for Christ's sake!

Some peeled and ate them, others sucked out the juice, and those who didn't like oranges traded them for chocolate or cigarettes. On the whole the men were grateful for the oranges, but on the whole they wished they were home to buy their own and tended to suspect that if such exotic gifts were being forwarded to them it meant they would be in Siberia for a long, long time.

Christmas was miserable, oranges or not. In general the men were quiet, suffering the presence of their clumsily decorated Christmas trees and singing carols because the chaplains, the Red Cross, the Y.M.C.A. and the Knights of Columbus insisted with forced joviality that they do so. But when it was over the trees, gift wrappings and orange peels were burned, buried or stuffed away, and no one mentioned that Christmas had come or was gone.

The significant military event of the day was that Kolchak's northern army captured Perm.

« 2 »

Life for the men of C Company was considerably brightened by Maryenka Austin, who was a frequent visitor, and although the ratio of men to women was a hundred and sixty-one to one (Carlisle excluded himself) somehow she managed to create a sense of family. At Christmastime she was offered a hundred and sixty oranges and laughing delightedly, her face shining with joy, she refused these tenders of affection. "My goodness! What could I do with them? Please, you must not!" But she was forced to accept a dozen of Mrs. Stern's oranges.

There was a constant grin on Sergeant Austin's face which practically incapacitated him for military duty. If he bellowed at the men they smiled, indicating they loved Maryenka too, and Austin hadn't the heart to discipline them as he should have done. The whole company was in love with Maryenka, who treated them like children in a Russian classroom. She told them folk tales, taught them the Russian alphabet and Russian songs, and her classes grew, threatening to include the whole regiment as men from other companies drifted over to take part.

On the whole Colonel Spaeth approved Maryenka Austin's visits since these relieved the depression which had come over the men after his announcement that the regiment had been ordered to Verkhne-Udinsk.

Because of Maryenka the men had begun to take an active interest in their surroundings and very often, standing at his window at night, Spaeth heard them singing Russian songs and he was pleased by Austin's marriage. Maryenka was the daughter, mother and sister of the regiment and Spaeth shared the men's affection for her. She reminded him a bit of Peg just as she reminded each of the men of someone back home.

But Carlisle, who had no one back home, was reminded of Tatiana and for this reason Maryenka's presence was intolerable. He tried to concentrate on preparations being made for the move to Verkhne-Udinsk and spent hours with Captain Fish of the Engineers Corps going over data about the steel girder bridge which crossed the Selenga River in his sector. Fish, having found drawings of the bridge, expressed his concern about certain "ambiguities in the stresses" which the Corps intended to look into with all possible haste. There were six spans of two hundred and eighty feet and two of fifty-six for a total of one thousand seven hundred and ninety-two feet supported by stone pillars.

Carlisle examined these drawings and tried to decipher Russian topographical maps of the area, but all this activity did not conceal what was for him a terrible erosion of his will power. He couldn't get the woman out of his mind.

He hadn't seen Countess Tatiana since the night of the Armistice ball though he'd been several times to the Russian Club at the Aleksander hoping to pick up some information about her, but each time he went there it was against his will, for it violated his sense of duty.

He loaded himself with work that should have been handled by Leverett or the company sergeants. He went over every requisition form and every duty roster trying to drive the cameo image of Tatiana's face above the garnet necklace from his memory and sometimes he could be seen at his desk late at night, trembling. The skin over his cheekbones glistened and his broad face took on the polished glow of dark hardwood as he fought the temptation to go again to the Aleksander.

In these tense moments Carlisle was filled with impotent rage. It seemed to him that in every respect he was missing those qualities other men took for granted. Other men seemed whole to him; they seemed all of a piece with roots in the past which enabled them to act naturally, unselfconsciously. But for himself there was that gap in his heritage, that threatening fault in the rock formation of his character, which brought him close to hysteria whenever he ventured beyond the boundaries of strict duty.

This incapacitating hysteria swept over him on the night of the Armistice ball when Spaeth had presented him the promotion. He hadn't been able to speak easily as another man would have done. And later, dancing with Countess Tatiana it seemed to him that the two faces of his character were grinding against each other, slipping inexorably so that at any second one half of himself or the other would crash into the dark, unplumbed depths of his nature. This he feared above all things.

Other men, he was sure, did not live in such danger. He saw them as trees rooted deep in the earth, but he thought of himself as a faulty stone arch over a chasm. The only force he knew to support and strengthen that arch was his sense of duty.

Countess Tatiana fascinated him, but at night seated at his desk, poring laboriously over the company records, Carlisle had only to look at his hands to be reminded of this fault in himself.

His hands were too small for his wrists and he'd fractured them more than once by expecting them to bear the weight of a blow shot by his heavy arm. They were his father's hands; white hands, grafted to his body by the act which ultimately forced his father to marry his mother.

Yes, Corporal Hinky Carlisle, out for a good time in Montana, had laid the wrong Sioux. Alice Buckeye, a determined Indian girl, dragged Hinky into a military court and made him acknowledge their child, made him support her for seven long years off the reservation, made him "talk white" to his kid, made him write to his relations about his happy marriage, insisting they record the birth of Jackie Carlisle in their family Bibles.

She was a strong woman trying to make the transition between her world and the world to come, but Hinky Carlisle was too frail a vessel to carry her through. He took to booze and after seven years Sergeant Hinky Carlisle died, leaving mementos of the Indian wars; a cavalry sword, a Sharps carbine and a pair of worn leather gloves which on one occasion his son had slipped on to see how well they fitted.

They might have been made for him.

Sometimes women commented about his hands. Turning them over in their own they'd measure them against the blocky proportions of his arms and chest and look at him curiously, but something in his expression warned them not to ask. They said his hands were nice, or fine, or small, and a girl he'd lived with in Manila said she liked his hands best of all, but only when she was half asleep.

After the death of his father Carlisle and his mother returned to the reservation and lived a little better than most on a widow's pension, government allotments and what they could scratch out of the ground, but the fact which hung over their lives like a dreary cloud was that they were members of a dying race. Evidence of this was present every day in the poverty, squalor and hopelessness of reservation life. None of Hinky Carlisle's relatives, whose family Bibles supposedly bore witness to Jack Carlisle's existence, ever wrote, but Alice Buckeye Carlisle clung tenaciously to the idea that her short-legged, brown-bodied, massive-headed son had inalienable rights in the white world. She drove this idea into his mind and at last she drove him away.

In 1900 at the age of seventeen Carlisle joined the army as a scout. The following year he was transferred to the newly organized 27th Infantry Regiment, put aboard the army transport *Sheridan* and sent to the Philippines where for three years he fought to pacify the Moros. During the assault on Fort Binidayan he distinguished himself and was promoted to the rank of sergeant.

But this action, known as the Battle of Bayan, had more importance for Carlisle than for the average soldier. Up until this time the Moros had been characterized for him as ruthless guerrilla warriors whose Moslem religion drove them to acts of fanaticism and terror. They beheaded village chiefs and tortured their captives. By day the Moro villages looked peaceful enough, but at night one could not be sure that the men did not slip out to launch attacks on American positions. They fought an unconventional, cowardly war, striking suddenly with inferior weapons, the spear, the kris, the bolo and ancient pistols and rifles loaded with shot which left terrifying wounds in comparison with the almost surgical punctures inflicted by the high-velocity bullets sprayed into the jungles by American Gatling guns and rifles.

Up to the assault on Fort Binidayan Carlisle had behaved as well as any soldier in a campaign. He fired his rifle at figures which appeared distantly in the patches of sunlight with no thought as to whether they were men, women, children or animals. He cursed, sweated profusely and fought the jungle rot which attacked his boots, clothing and skin. In the common travail of soldiering he was accepted by his mates, who called him Sioux as he called them Tex, Dago or Red. The names sprang up and their derivation was incidental to the bonds of soldiering. He slogged along the jungle trails and upland roads and regarded the Moro villagers with soldierly contempt and distrust. They were frail primitives who faded quickly with age, and though some of the girls caught his attention he did not think of them as persons.

He served at Zamboanga, Malabang and Parang, accepting all he had been told, doing everything he was ordered to do, with his mind in a rather agreeable state of suspension.

Binidayan had changed this.

The baffling reluctance of the Moro minority to surrender themselves and their lands to the benevolence of America was causing agonies in Washington. Blowhard humanitarians, artists and scientists, none of whom were acquainted with the facts available only to the President and his closest advisers, were complaining loudly about the injustice and prolonged duration of the war. Politicians in their turn heaped scorn on the Department of the Army for not being able, with the massive technological advantage of weaponry and of manpower at their disposal, to quell a minor insurrection.

Old Indian fighters were plucked from the retirement list and thrust into the jungle.

The war was described as "a new kind" never heretofore fought by American troops.

It was claimed that the wily, unchristian, fanatical enemy had the advantage of jungle terrain and weather; they struck out of the night without warning, particularly in the rainy season to which they were as impervious as ducks while our boys were mired to the armpits in mud. After every engagement the enemy heartlessly removed their dead and wounded from the field of battle to give the illusion that our artillery and rifle fire had done no damage, that our mortars, howitzers and grenades had been ineffective.

There was little doubt that the enemy was both subhuman and demonic. In a state of crazed religious exaltation a Moro warrior brandishing his bolo could absorb a full clip of bullets from a forty-five automatic and continue his charge. They fought like snakes long after normal men would have been declared dead. There was no doubt about it.

But the Army, with these and many other weighty reasons to account for its laggard success, was nevertheless embarrassed and to relieve the pressures from home many commanders in the field used a device invented by an American army doctor to get the quick settlement America demanded. This was a humane form of torture, the water torture, which consisted of forcing a hose into a Moro's throat and funneling buckets of water into his stomach to flush out the desired military information. The elasticity of human tissue, particularly of Moro tissue, guaranteed that no permanent harm would come of this operation. One could even sit on the distended stomach, or jostle it with a boot to encourage the purge of information.

Prior to Binidayan Carlisle had witnessed such an interrogation on a sun-struck jungle plateau where two companies of the 27th Infantry were encamped. The existence of Fort Binidayan was known but its precise location was not, and this information was being flushed out of a naked young Moro staked on his back in the clearing. Two Filipino interpreters squatted beside his head holding the funnel in his mouth while Sergeant Converse, pouring water from a bucket, kept muttering, "Swallow, you bastard, or drown."

Seated in the shade of the trees around the clearing the men watched the Moro's belly rise. His limbs quivered and there was a puddle of watery excrement under his buttocks. His narrow chest heaved convulsively as he snatched for air, but the funnel in his throat prevented any loud sound.

No one liked it. There was a call to action in the pit of each soldier's stomach; each thought he should stand up and try to put a stop to the business, but none of them did so. Instead they hoped that the torture was harmless as it was purported to be and that the Moro would tell the location of Binidayan.

Carlisle hoped so too. Each time the funnel was removed and the Tagalog interpreters bent to question the prostrate, semiconscious Moro, Carlisle found himself praying they wouldn't have to start again.

Sergeant Converse put his foot on the Moro's belly and water welled up in his mouth, running into his ears and into his brown, glazed eyes staring blankly at the sky.

"He still breathing?" Converse asked and one of the interpreters nodded. "Jesus Christ!" Converse said. He dropped the bucket and walked over to Captain Scully, who was studying a field map of the area with tense, blind-eyed absorption.

From his place Carlisle couldn't hear Converse and the Captain but their glances toward the naked Moro and the sag of their shoulders told him the Moro had won. In his heart Carlisle was pleased and he scowled trying to discover what this meant and he saw that the other men were pleased too. There was in the worst of them some innate decency, a sense of justice which the Moro, pinioned in the center of the clearing, had attacked and overbalanced by his helpless passivity and suffering.

When Sergeant Converse told them to cut the Moro loose a dozen men ran to do so. They gathered around the vomiting Moro with tenderness in their eyes. They built a stretcher for him and wrapped him in blankets.

They couldn't do enough for him. Carlisle felt privileged to help carry the stretcher and as they moved into the jungle he wondered what it was that had changed their anger and contempt for all Moros into solicitude for this one.

He had no time to solve this riddle because ten minutes later they ran into Fort Binidayan. The first barrage of cannon fire came from a wall of green not twenty yards away on their flank.

Sergeant Converse and the soldier who was carrying the stretcher with Carlisle were killed instantly. Several men were severely wounded. The column broke and fled in panic. Carlisle was pulled down by the falling stretcher, and the waterlogged Moro sprawled on the ground beside him.

Carlisle yelled for help and his voice brought the fleeing men to their senses. They dropped to the ground and began at once to organize a firing line.

Carlisle and the Moro were caught between the American line and the stone parapets of Fort Binidayan, which could now be seen through its camouflage of jungle overgrowth. The massive stone fortress was defended by a large force of Moros armed with Spanish rifles and several batteries of brass cannon which poured scrap metal into all quarters of the surrounding jungle. The second company fell into the line, taking a share of the casualties, and the battle settled into a steady exchange of blind gunfire which only slackened at nightfall.

Carlisle found a sheltered place between two logs for himself and the Moro prisoner, who continued retching water and bile and finally nothing at all. He kept the Moro wrapped in blankets and was glad when he fell asleep.

Dawn was greeted by a hail of shrapnel from the Moro lantakas and shells from three howitzers which they had kept in reserve the previous day. This deception convinced Captain Scully that Binidayan had been reinforced during the night and he dispatched a message to division headquarters requesting additional support.

The men of Carlisle's company, crouching behind the shallow earthworks they'd flung up during the night, called across the fifty yards of intervening landscape to ask how he was.

"I'm all right," he yelled, "but hungry."

"How's the Moro?"

"He's fine too."

After this the gunfire picked up.

Carlisle and the Moro lay on their backs listening to the bullets from both sides sing over their heads. Sometimes the air close above them was torn by an angry sound and they could see a swarm of scrap metal and stones fired from the Moro brass cannon passing by. Some of these objects spun into the ground close to them and they pressed their bodies against the sheltering logs trying to make themselves small. Whenever their eyes met Carlisle smiled but the Moro was puzzled and sullen. He looked at Carlisle's mahogany-colored face, at his hands, at his smoky, yellow eyes trying to decide if he was a Filipino and if so of what tribe, Visayan, Tagalog, Ilokano, Pampangan. Carlisle knew he was being mistaken for an interpreter or a scout and he knew also that the racial and religious enmity between Moros and Filipinos was deep.

"Me American," he said to the Moro and smiling he nodded his head vigorously.

The Moro's expression did not change. "Me from U.S.A.," Carlisle said.

Something came into the Moro's eyes and they shifted away, leaving Carlisle with a feeling that he had been dismissed with contempt.

Toward noon there was a lull in the firing and Carlisle raised his head cautiously. The massive stone face of Fort Binidayan had been denuded of much of its green cover by bullets and mortar shells and looked all the more formidable. The Moros defending it could not be seen but the sporadic belch of their cannon and the bitterly snapping rifle fire whenever there was movement in the American lines attested to their watchful presence. Carlisle was trying to decide what to do when this was taken out of his hands by the Moro, who stood up, wrapped a blanket around his waist and began walking toward Binidayan.

Two shots were fired from the American lines, but there was a roar of protest from the men of Carlisle's company. "Hey, that's our Moro!" they yelled. "Cease fire! Cease fire, you bastards!" They were enraged.

Another shot came from the second company position, fired by someone who hadn't witnessed the torture and consequently didn't know that the man stalking across the field was "their" Moro.

Several men of Carlisle's company jumped up from the earthworks, cursing and brandishing their weapons in the direction from which this last shot had come. "You dirty sons of bitches!" one of them yelled. "Hold your fire, or I'll blow out your god-damned brains!"

Gunfire from both sides was suspended and the Moro with the blanket tight around his waist paused in the field to look back at Carlisle. He seemed very young, very frail, and there was a doubting expression in his eyes, but gradually this changed. He smiled and beckoned Carlisle to come. Carlisle got up and stepped over the log in the direction of the Moro, then he stopped stunned by the realization that he had been about to follow the Moro to Binidayan. It seemed the natural thing to do and a chill ran over the surface of his skin.

The Moro waited, still smiling, and Carlisle took another step toward him before his buddies began to yell.

"Come on, Sioux!" they yelled. "Run for it, Sioux! Come on! Come on!"

Carlisle turned and scampered toward his own lines in a panic. He tumbled over the raw earthworks and fell into the pit, where he lay gasping. The men laughed, pulled him to his feet and pounded his shoulders welcoming him back. He saw the Moro ascend the rock steps on the face of Binidayan and disappear into a portal. Then the firing from both sides recommenced.

Fort Binidayan held out for two more days until a battery of American artillery sent forward by Division began to reduce its resistance.

Carlisle fired at everything that moved on the shell-pocked stones of Binidayan. He was too filled with rage to sleep. The blood pulsed in his eyes, turning them carnelian, and the men of his company were in awe of the violence which flowed from his body like a magnetic field. He led a night patrol which succeeded in mining a section of the wall and the next day, when the charge was blown, Carlisle was up and running before the smoke cleared and the officers saw that the walls of Binidayan were unscathed. Carlisle charged the fort alone. After a moment the men of his company followed and then the second company joined the assault.

Carlisle climbed the face of Binidayan and dropped into the compound before his comrades could reach his side. He fought alone with unparalleled ferocity. The Moros surrounded him, but he clubbed them away with the butt of his rifle and carried his charge to the door of the Sultan of Bayan, who rushed forward swinging his glistening kris and was shot dead at Carlisle's feet by Americans who had topped the wall.

Binidayan fell. The vanquished Moros fled or died in suicidal bolo-brandishing attacks. Seventeen lantakas, three iron cannon and one brass howitzer were captured. There were forty-seven dead Moros left in the fort; among them was "their" Moro with a warm pistol in his fist.

After this the 27th Infantry returned to Columbus Barracks, Ohio, where it was reorganized and sent to Camp Columbia, Havana. In 1909 it returned again to the United States and Carlisle was commissioned as a second lieutenant. He made first lieutenant when the regiment was shipped back to Manila.

But the key experience of Carlisle's career was the moment in the field before Binidayan when he'd stepped toward the Moro who beckoned him. The details had faded but he knew well the temptation of that moment and he felt it again when he thought of Tatiana, who also tempted him to abandon the safety of his own lines.

Carlisle reproached himself for a fool. He tried to exhaust himself with work and drive Tatiana from his mind, but everything conspired against him. The captain insignia on his collar seemed at times to give him the right to call on her, at other times it only reminded him that her associates were counts and generals. Austin's marriage to Maryenka proved that unusual relationships were possible, but Maryenka was a little Russian candy hawker, not a countess.

Often he lay awake at night trying to place himself in the hierarchy of Tatiana's society, which he imagined to be a ladder of titles, wealth and privilege rising upward to queens and emperors, and he couldn't even approach the base, much less find a rung for himself. He resented his ignorance, his inarticulateness and lack of poise, and wished he could somehow acquire the easy charm and mannerisms of a kid like Leverett.

But at this thought he cursed and tossed over in his bed and swore once again to put Tatiana out of his mind.

CHAPTER SEVEN

PREPARATIONS for the transfer to Verkhne-Udinsk proceeded, but not without attendant aggravations. Since the 1st Battalion of the 27th was located at Khabarovsk and elements of the 2d were scattered along the Ussuri line at Kraevski and Spasskoi, Colonel Spaeth was frequently absent from Vladivostok. His plan had been to consolidate the regiment and transfer it from Khabarovsk as a unit, but railway officials claimed they were unable to provide enough coaches for a regiment; consequently the 27th was to be forwarded in sections as railway cars became available. Spaeth pointed out that regiments of Japanese and Czechs were often transferred over the line in unbroken units and asked why, if they could get trains, the Americans could not. He collected the serial numbers of railway coaches, vans and trucks standing idle at various sidings and requested that these be combined into trains for the 27th Regiment. None of his efforts were availing and he began to see that this refusal to provide enough rolling stock to carry the 27th to Verkhne-Udinsk as a single echelon was a power struggle in the highest inter-Allied councils.

The Japanese commandant at Khabarovsk, General Oi, promised to do what he could. Ataman Kalmykoff with six armored trains and innumerable coaches at his disposal sighed and shook his head helplessly. The British, the French and the Czechs all complained of the same treatment, but would not relinquish their coaches to the Americans, and the officials whose direct responsibility it was to make up the trains either defended their entrenched position with masses of paper work proving that all the coaches and trucks in the area were assigned, or pretended to be sublimely ignorant of the problem.

"But Colonel, it is factually impossible to commandeer so many first class coaches at one time," a bland Russian stationmaster said and throwing up his hands in a fine show of despair he groaned. "What's to be done? What is to be done!"

"Who said anything about first class coaches?"

The stationmaster looked at Spaeth feigning surprise and began combing his russet beard with his fingertips, and a crafty look came into his eyes.

"But surely the Americans would go first class," he said. "Be assured, Colonel, that not one of us had any other thought. Nothing for you but the best, of course."

Spaeth held his temper and explained for the tenth time that he did not expect better travel accommodations than other Allied forces, but that he wanted enough cars to hold the regiment together.

"But not teplushkas, Colonel! Not ordinary trucks for Americans!"

"Ordinary trucks will do!" Spaeth declared.

The stationmaster pursed his lips and shook his head wonderingly. "This changes everything," he said. "We've been on the wrong trail all the time. Let me see what I can do."

But, of course, there was nothing he could do except offer vacant space in trains which were already made up and would accommodate a platoon or a company, no more.

At last Spaeth gave it up. It seemed more important to get the 27th into position than to continue this fruitless haggling. The next day, having made this concession, he received a schedule of coaches and departure dates which appeared to have been made weeks in advance and he knew that he had been badgered into submission. He regretted it. He had failed his test in Asiatic bureaucracy and he was determined never to do so again.

Major Taziola, Captains Bentham and Cloak went to Verkhne-Udinsk with Headquarters Company on the last day of December, with the rest of the regiment scheduled to follow in sections over a period of two months. The more Spaeth thought about it the more he realized how disruptive this was, how damaging to morale and to the sense of organization. He condemned himself for this, but General Graves took it upon himself. "I tried, Bob, but I couldn't do anything. Our allies wanted to rub a little mud on my nose and they chose this way to do it. If the Japanese, British, French, Czechs and Russians can't agree about anything else they're shoulder to shoulder when it comes to dishing out humiliation to us. The Chinese, on the other hand, are cooperative." Graves smiled and sighed. "Not that they trust us, exactly, but they distrust us less than they do the others. I've arranged for some of our people to go out by way of Harbin over the Chinese Eastern to Chita and from there to Verkhne-Udinsk."

"That'll help, sir," Spaeth said.

"We've got to learn to appreciate small favors."

The weather in Vladivostok remained clear but cold and the sharpness in the air affected people according to their mood. To some it was zestful and invigorating, to others it was bitter. At the same time of day one could see a couple like Sergeant Austin and Maryenka swinging gaily down Svetlandskaya Street arm in arm with their coats thrown open and cheery smiles on their faces while others hunched along muffled to the ears and shivering.

People with Bolshevist tendencies were warmed by the news that the Red Army had occupied Riga and Kharkov. Those who supported Kolchak were similarly warmed by the parade of British-trained Russian Cadets going off to the front and by the text of the Prinkipo proposal with its tacit recognition of the Kolchak regime by Britain, France and the United States. Favorable news seemed to mitigate the temperature.

Austin and his wife were the happiest people in the whole of the Maritime Province. They smiled, they talked, they laughed, they kissed. They fed on the world and on one another trying to store up this wild happiness against the day of their temporary separation.

Maryenka had decided to return to her family in Pashkova until Austin could find a place for her in Verkhne-Udinsk. Her determination to follow him would permit no denial and Austin made none, only asking her to wait until he found them a safe and suitable place to live.

"Oh, safe and suitable!" she said scornfully. "A place with a roof, is all."

"And four walls at least."

"Oh, walls! Walls, walls, walls! I hate walls!" Then she laughed merrily, clutching her stomach and doubling half over in the street.

A Cossack officer passing by scowled ferociously at Austin, who returned this look with equal belligerence and would gladly have sent him sprawling, but Maryenka pulled him away.

They went to the cinema and three times a week Maryenka came to the barracks to teach her class in Russian, but these sessions were devoted more to laughter than to instruction. Maryenka tried earnestly to set a disciplined tone for the class and the men worked just as earnestly to subvert it. They shot spit wads at one another, made faces and told Maryenka outrageous lies about the United States which she believed until she saw the expression on Austin's face, whereupon she would look at the speaker and shaking her head reproachfully say, "Brother, it seems you have little regard for the truth."

This invariably brought roars of laughter and applause from the men, who'd made a game of trying to string her along, and a fad sped through the 27th Infantry so that men who had never met Maryenka could be seen shaking their heads solemnly and replying to a friend, "Brother, it seems you have little regard for the truth."

On one occasion Austin invited Leverett and Sergeant Baker to dinner, but Maryenka was self-conscious and quiet. She wore the russet dress in which she'd been married and the pearl earrings and lapel watch Ira had given her.

She'd prepared a fish and a goose and kept darting between the table and the stove in a great state of anxiety about the food until at last Austin rose, took her by the shoulders and forced her to sit down at the table. "Maryenka, relax," he said.

"But they are the first guests!"

"If they make you so nervous I'll throw them out."

"Ostein!"

"He's right," Ira said. "It's like my mother at Thanksgiving. She sits down, looks at the table and up she jumps to get something else from the kitchen. To watch her you'd think there were bedsprings on her chair. Up, down, up, down. The table is groaning. Turkey with oyster stuffing, candied yams, mashed potatoes, cranberry sauce, string beans, peas, carrots, pickled crabapples, a casserole of this, a casserole of that, but the minute her bottom touches the chair up she bounds to bring something she's forgotten. A dish of plum preserves, pickled watermelon rind, kumquats, then there are pies in the oven that have to be looked at, sauce to be made for this or that, so the whole meal goes by with her chair vacant and her plate untouched. It's the penance she exacts from the rest of us for all the work she's gone to preparing the feast."

Maryenka looked distressed and appealed to Austin. She was close to tears.

"Maryenka, what is it?"

"All we have is fish and goose," she said despairingly. "The stove is so small!"

Austin hoisted Maryenka in his powerful arms and whirled her around like a baby. She screamed and he kissed her resoundingly. "Maryenka, if you go on like this I'm going to throw *you* out." He carried her toward the window and she clung to his neck, laughing. When he put her down again Maryenka blushed crimson and spoke to Baker. "He's so strong," she said apologetically and Baker nodded over his glass of vodka.

The dinner was a great success. Steam frosted the windows of the little apartment high under the eaves of the building and when they'd finished the goose and the fish, with kasha, carrots, cheese, caviar and wine, they sat around the open door of the stove cracking sunflower seeds in their teeth and throwing the husks into the glowing coals.

"My father came to America from Kiev," Ira said.

"I didn't know that," Austin said.

"Never mentioned it. Never really thought about it."

"When was that?" Maryenka asked.

"I really don't know too much about it," Ira said and he frowned thoughtfully, wondering why. "I'll have to look into it. Both my father and my Uncle Dave were born in Russia."

The coal embers held their eyes and they talked drowsily until at last Sergeant Baker dozed off. He sat in his chair with one broad palm full of sunflower seeds and a single seed in the fingers of the other hand. This seed dropped to the floor and the others watched Baker, waiting for his head to fall. Baker sighed, his golden, nearly invisible eyebrows quivered, then his head toppled forward on his chest with a clopping sound as his teeth clacked together. He jerked his head up, startled, his pale gray eyes wide open. "That's right!" he said loudly as though he had been listening to the

conversation all along. The others laughed and Baker grinned. "About time
to go, don't you think, sir?"

Ira agreed. They got their coats and said good night.

"See you in the morning, Harry," Baker said.

"Right."

"The Sioux wants a full pack inspection and we're going to take a little
stroll to try out those new Shackleton boots."

"I know."

When Ira and Sergeant Baker reached the street the cold air made them
gasp and they hurried back to the barracks in silence, each filled with envy
of Sergeant Austin warm in his bed with Maryenka.

The next morning Ira rose an hour before reveille to prepare for the hike
which the Sioux had scheduled. He depended heavily on Austin to run the
platoon, but he felt obliged always to appear in front of the men with his
uniform and kit in perfect order with just a single distinguishing touch to
satisfy his vanity and express the fact that he was at heart a civilian.
Heretofore this distinguishing feature had been a pair of cordovan leather
riding boots which he wore in preference to the regulation lace boots issued
to officers. These were beautiful. They were handmade for him in San
Francisco and the leather had the deep look of fine old port wine and like
wine they changed color from black to brown to ruby depending on the
light. Ira put boot blocks into them every night and rubbed them down.
There was something about having pampered feet which made the common
annoyances tolerable. When Carlisle snapped an order at him, or grumbled
about the condition of the company, which he did constantly, Ira had only
to drop his eyes to the glowing toes of his boots to make it right. "I may be
a lousy soldier," he'd think, "but by God my feet are planted in style"; then
he'd smile in a way which he knew infuriated Carlisle and say, "I'll get
right on it, Captain. Glad you brought it up."

But this morning he was going to be deprived of his boots and he cursed
Sir Ernest Shackleton who'd designed the clumsy-looking arctic boot which
had been issued to C Company for protection against the freezing temperatures at Verkhne-Udinsk.

Ira was standing at the window of his room wondering how he was going
to get any psychic satisfaction from Shackleton's combination of canvas,
rubber, leather and felt when he saw Sergeant Austin come into the
compound. Austin was whistling softly and the sound rebounding from the
cold walls of the still silent building was clear and melodious. Then Carlisle

appeared; he seemed to have materialized out of the dim, gray morning light. Obviously he had been waiting for Austin.

" 'Morning, Sioux," Austin said.

"I've been waiting for you."

"I see you have. What's on your mind?"

"I don't want her here anymore, Sergeant," Carlisle said.

They were standing in the quadrangle on a cinder path over the ice-clad stones. Austin shook his head and frowned. "What's that?" he asked.

"I don't want her around the men."

"Maryenka?"

"It's bad for the men."

"They're all crazy about her!" Austin protested.

Carlisle nodded. "That's it," he said.

"What's it?" Austin demanded peevishly. "What in hell is 'it'?"

"She tells them too much," Carlisle said.

"About what! What are you talking about?"

"Just her presence here," Carlisle blurted. "Her just being here is bad. It's disturbing the men and I have to put an end to it. That's all!"

Austin scowled at Carlisle. "No," he said, "that's not all."

Carlisle's face darkened and his voice rose in the cold air. "I don't care what you do. I don't care about that, but she's not to come here anymore. Is that clear? If you don't understand, then telling you my reasons won't change it."

"Try," Austin shot back. "I'm not stupid."

They stood facing each other very close, bulky as grizzly bears in their coats with their fists clenched in their pockets. Each man stared directly into the other's face, unflinching.

"I've watched this company go downhill ever since she showed up here," Carlisle said.

"I've watched it go uphill."

"We've got a job to do."

"The work's getting done."

"Not the way I like it. I don't like their attitude."

Austin snorted. "There's something in this world called joy. That's what you don't like, Jack. You've never had it."

"I'm posting an order, Austin. If one woman gets in, what's to prevent every slut in Vlad from setting up shop in our barracks?"

"You're beginning to talk like an officer, Sioux," Austin said softly. "You know what you're saying doesn't make sense and you think it doesn't matter because you've got the bars, but you're talking to me, Hunkpapa. For three years you were in my platoon and no one stepped on your love life. You want a scrap, fine, you'll get it. But before you bust one of those lily-white hands of yours I'd like to know why. You jealous of me, or has that damned commission gone to your head?"

Carlisle pulled one fist from his coat pocket, but Austin struck him fast with the flat of his hand. The report of the blow rebounded in the confinement of the quad and Carlisle's head slewed to one side. He was stunned, but still on his feet.

"Feel better?" Austin asked.

Carlisle glared at him, fist cocked.

"The difference between us, Sioux, ain't that commission. The difference is that I love a woman and you love the Army."

Carlisle's blow glanced off Austin's forearm, struck him on the shoulder and sent him sprawling, sliding over the icy stones. When he stopped he was laughing. "Break it?" he yelled.

Carlisle shook his head, stuffed his fist in his pocket and went inside.

Austin stood up, shook himself, and still chuckling quietly he crossed the compound to the 2nd Platoon barracks.

Ira was amazed. He shook his head to be sure he hadn't imagined this scene, then reveille sounded thrusting him forward into the rigors of the day.

C Company marched six miles into the barren hills around Vladivostok and back again, arriving after nightfall, and the boots Shackleton had designed for service on the polar icecap were discovered to have one miraculous property: they made every mile seem like seven leagues. When C Company was dismissed the men fell to the ground and began stripping off the Shackletons rather than take the few remaining steps to their quarters in them.

"Mother Machree!" Private Crowe moaned.

"Ought to give these damned things to the enemy," Private Carson declared. "Knock the fight out of them in two days!"

Carlisle limped across the compound to the office and when Leverett came in he'd stripped off his Shackletons and was examining them dourly. "They're too hot, too heavy and the soles don't give any traction," he said.

"It's like walking on frying pans," Ira said.

"This is another one of Dunc Ferber's promotions," Carlisle said as he put on his regulation boots and laced them.

"Ferber?"

Carlisle looked up at Ira, scowling. "The regimental supply officer. Don't you know our table of organization yet, Leverett?"

"Oh, yes, Ferber!"

"How long have you been with us, Leverett?" Carlisle asked.

"Now let's see," Ira said thoughtfully, "it's going on six months the way I figure it."

Carlisle's ruddy eyes narrowed and he shook his head. "You haven't even arrived yet, Lieutenant. You aren't here. I'm still waiting for you to show up and I'm getting tired of waiting. When I first saw you I said to myself: 'There's a man who can memorize a table of organization in under six months. He has brains, competence, style, a college education. I'm lucky to have such a man assigned to this company.' Now tell me, Leverett: Did I fail to welcome you properly when you arrived here? Did my greeting lack warmth? Is there something missing to make you feel at home in this outfit?"

Ira was unsettled by Carlisle's biting sarcasm. He'd grown used to a blunt, unequivocal directness from the man, but this was something different. "No, sir," he said.

"Just level with me for once," Carlisle said. "We're going to be together for a while."

"I hadn't anticipated staying on after the war."

"That's too bad," Carlisle said. "Neither had I. Neither had the men in this company. But we are staying."

"I know."

"I don't know if you know or not. All I know is that you're bucking me and I thought I'd tell you one time that I don't like it."

"How am I bucking you, Captain?"

"If you have to ask, Leverett, you've got one hell of a lot more to learn than the table of organization." Carlisle stood up and tossed his Shackletons on the company desk. "In the morning call Dunc Ferber and tell him we're turning these boots back. Carson was right; they ought to issue them to the Bolsheviks."

At another time Ira would have pointed out that there was in this statement of Carlisle's an implication that the Bolsheviks were the enemy, which contradicted the American policy of neutrality. He could have launched into a marvelously embroidered speech on the theme, but on this occasion he kept his mouth shut. Perhaps for this reason he was rewarded with one of Carlisle's flashing, ingenuous smiles, which unsettled him nearly as much as the sarcasm had. "I'd like to get along with you, Leverett," Carlisle said. "I really would."

"I'd like to get along with you too, Captain," Ira replied.

Carlisle nodded and scowled down at the desk. "The Sioux and the Jew," he said. "We've got that going for us, or against us, I don't know which, but I know you can't kill a slogan. We're leaving next week by way of Harbin and the Chinese Eastern. There's a hell of a lot to do." He looked up then and offered Ira his hand. There was a carefully measured, probationary friendliness in his eyes as their hands met, then he left the office.

During the next few days Ira worked hard to merit Carlisle's respect. He was back in his cordovan boots again but they failed to give him the sense of detached superiority which once they had. There was too much catching up for him to do to qualify even minimally for Carlisle's esteem and surprisingly he found himself wanting this. He was, in fact, a bit afraid of the violence in Carlisle and he was puzzled by his flashes of unguarded, almost helpless simplicity. The Sioux was a riddle which Ira wanted to solve and the first step was to earn his confidence.

Ira packed the souvenirs he'd collected and sent them home with letters of explanation to the family: "This is a Siberian tiger pelt to be thrown over the baby grand as a conversation piece. I couldn't get the head, which is probably just as well. You can refer to it as a Tiger Rag. Ho. Ho. Also enclosed is a genuine Cossack hat complete with the skull and crossbones insignia of the Annenkoff Cossacks. Great for all occasions, particularly Hallowe'en. If you find any customers for this model I can have them made to order by a local Chinese hatter at three dollars a head, bald men pay no more."

He also asked to be enlightened about his father and Uncle Dave's hegira from Kiev to Oakland. "I only lately realized, after a conversation with Maryenka Austin, that I have in fact returned to the land of family nativity. My ignorance about this is woeful and somewhat embarrassing and I'd like to have it corrected as soon as possible."

Then one afternoon as he and Carlisle were making space allotments in the five railway coaches which had been assigned to the company a Czech motorcycle messenger came into the office. He wore a leather helmet, goggles, a black leather pilot's coat and gauntlets. "Captain Carlisle?" he asked.

"I'm Carlisle."

The messenger saluted, took a small envelope from the pouch on his shoulder and presented it to Carlisle. "I'm to wait for an answer, sir," he said.

Ira detected the fragrance of scented stationery as Carlisle opened the envelope. He saw Carlisle's face flush as he read the note and thrust it back into the envelope. He looked at the messenger sharply, then at Ira.

"Invitation?" Ira asked.

Carlisle nodded, put the envelope on the desk and stared at it. The messenger pulled his gauntlets up more firmly on his hands and shifted his weight from one foot to the other. "It requires an answer, sir," he said presently.

"Written?" Carlisle asked with a touch of panic in his voice. "A written answer?"

The messenger, perplexed by Carlisle's reaction, glanced at Ira. "You could telephone, sir," he said.

"Yes, I'll do that," Carlisle declared.

The messenger saluted again and went out. They heard his motorcycle catch, roar, then splutter out of the compound and down the street.

Carlisle scowled at the envelope and pushed it away from him across the desk. He turned his attention again to the diagram of the railway carriage, but the fragrant envelope seemed to have destroyed his ability to concentrate. "You finish this, Leverett," he said abruptly and he jammed the envelope into his pocket and left the office.

« 2 »

When Carlisle was admitted to the suite on the second floor of the Aleksander it seemed to him that he'd blundered onto a stage in the middle of a performance. All the actors stood, or sat around the room in various poses, the men wearing elegantly tailored uniforms, the ladies in gowns and jewels. For an awful moment Carlisle felt that it was up to him to supply the line of dialogue that would set the play in motion. A thousand pairs of eyes seemed to be staring at him expectantly and he wanted to flee, but the little servant in a white mess jacket who had opened the door and taken his coat ushered him into the room.

Carlisle shuffled forward, his face was blazing, blood hammering in his ears. He made for a vacant armchair and dropped into it as into a dugout. Then he saw the reason for the posed silence in the room. A young Rumanian soldier was at the piano playing Robert Schumann's "Arabeske." The notes rippled and flashed beneath his fingers, which seemed to be activated by electric shocks from the keys, and his thin, supple body shuddered with delicate intensity.

From where he sat Carlisle could not see Countess Tatiana but he tried to simulate one of the attitudes of elegance and sangfroid on exhibit in the room. Lieutenant Markowitz stood nearby with his hand resting negligently on the back of a damask chair. He was smoking a cigarette in an ebony holder, his eyes focused dreamily on the spiral of smoke as the music absorbed him. Other Czech, French and Russian officers nodded their appreciation smiling slightly or making sincere eyes at a particularly significant passage.

Carlisle knew nothing about music. They were cultured; he was not. They could discuss the pictures hanging on the walls. He could not. They'd all been in similar rooms and knew how to behave, so he watched them covertly and suffered as the music continued, effete, amusing and intricate as snowflakes.

Countess Tatiana's invitation crackled in Carlisle's breast pocket as he shifted his position trying to hide his hands, which looked exposed and naked on the arms of his chair. He folded them in his lap and sat bolt upright wondering if the Countess was watching him from some quarter of the room. She'd written him a note on the margin of the invitation: "Captain of the Powder Room — You are especially ordered to appear. T."

For two days Carlisle had struggled against his desire to see Tatiana again. He hadn't phoned or written a reply, saying to himself all the time that he wasn't going to go, but knowing very well he was. Then, at the last minute, using the fact that the company was scheduled to depart the very next day as an excuse, he went to the barber, had his black hair shorn close to his head and came to the Aleksander. He hadn't expected so many people. Her invitation had simply stated she would be "at home" between the hours of four and seven.

The music stopped. The pianist tossed his head back with a triumphant smile and bowed to the pattering applause.

Everyone began to speak and move about. Some came to the piano to congratulate the Rumanian, others fell into conversational groups, their voices cultured, their laughter mild.

Carlisle stood up and looked around. There were half a dozen women in the room, but Tatiana was not among them. It struck him then that he'd come to the wrong place, that presently someone would ask for his credentials. To avoid this Carlisle edged toward the hall, intending to leave, then he saw Tatiana coming toward him, her hand extended. "Good afternoon, Captain Carlisle," she said. "I am pleased."

The cool touch of her hand, the calm depths of her gray eyes lifted him out of himself. His words, the very tone of his voice seemed alien to him as he said, "I hope you will pardon me for not replying to your invitation, Countess, but until the very last moment I wasn't sure I could come."

"I knew you would come," she said.

"Yes?"

Tatiana slipped her hand from his and guided Carlisle into the room. "Yes, because I have your insignia and I made an ancient gypsy incantation over them which directed your steps to my door."

"I think you're right," Carlisle said.

"I would have returned them sooner, Captain, but some friends in my husband's squadron were at Spasskoi aerodrome and I spent the holidays with them."

"Oh, with your husband," Carlisle said.

"No. Albert wasn't able to come. They say he flew to Tsaritsyn with some dispatches for Denikin. I was disappointed, of course, but at least they say he's well."

Tatiana took his silver lieutenant's bars from a china bowl on a table and offered them to him.

Carlisle frowned. "I thought you'd keep them," he said.

Her eyebrows raised and she tipped her head. "Without your permission? Certainly not."

"You have my permission."

She smiled. "Thank you, but I don't think I have any use for them. And they must be of some value to you or to someone in your family as a keepsake."

"No," he said.

"But I have no intention of keeping them," she insisted. "How extraordinary!"

"They'd have a value to me if you did," Carlisle said.

This declaration came as a surprise to Carlisle. It was something he would have expected another man to say, one of those glib young college-bred officers he so thoroughly disliked. He backed half a step away from her and thought again of leaving.

"Please take them," Tatiana said and she tried to thrust the bars into his hand.

"I can't," Carlisle said.

"But why?" she asked, quite puzzled.

"Because people would accuse me of being an Indian giver," Carlisle said and he burst into an awful whickering laughter. It was nervous and womanish, but he couldn't stop. By the look on Tatiana's face Carlisle knew she'd never heard the expression "Indian giver," that this derogatory little phrase he'd turned so spitefully on himself hoping she'd overlook his lack of grace, his ugliness, was unfamiliar to her. She didn't understand the humor and he was braying like a fool.

Everyone turned to watch. One of the ladies produced a lorgnette. An officer beckoned one of the servants presumably to capture and expel the lunatic before he proved dangerous. The Rumanian was accompanying his laughter on the piano and Carlisle clenched his teeth and almost strangled with the effort to stop whinnying.

Tatiana appeared not to have noticed; she tucked her hand under his arm again. "I'll keep them then," she said. "Now come and meet the others."

Carlisle allowed himself to be led through the room. He was introduced and he responded. No one seemed to have noticed his outburst. No one at all. Incredible. They must have heard his braying, seen his expression of glazed hysteria, but they were cordial; his lapse appeared to have been stricken from the record.

"Would you like some tea, Captain?"

Carlisle nodded and she took him to the alcove with windows overlooking the street.

A Czech orderly brought them tea. The alcove was furnished with chairs, a round table and a small desk with photographs above it on the wall. There were potted ferns and rubber plants along the window sill filtering the afternoon sunlight. Across the room the Rumanian continued to play.

Tatiana put his bars on the desk. "Here is where I make my diary," she said. "Do you keep a diary, Captain?"

"No," he said, "I never have."

"I think one should, don't you? It gives form to events one tends to lose especially in times like these."

"Yes," he said. "That's true."

"You must have had a great many experiences which you probably can't remember."

"Nothing interesting," he said feeling boorish and incapable of conversation.

"Of course you have," she insisted, "but you've forgotten because you kept no diary. You really must begin. I began last month and I haven't missed a day, so you see I am an authority!" Then she laughed in her quick, breathtaking way and drew him closer to the desk. "Forgive me,

Captain, but you've already put several amusing pages in my diary which otherwise might have been blank. I'm trying to fill it quickly, you see, to compensate for the time I've lost." She indicated a picture on the wall. "Here is Albert, beside his aeroplane. You can't make out his face so well in that one, but the uniform is quite attractive."

Carlisle looked at the photograph as Tatiana continued talking about her husband in a dispassionate manner. In one picture she and Albert were together. Tatiana was seated, and the slender young man stood at her side. They were smiling fixedly, but Albert's gaze ran off beyond the frame of the picture while Tatiana's eyes were focused on the camera itself.

In every picture the Count had this stare of abstract intensity. It was an expression Carlisle equated with too much education, with disdain for routine and detail. It was an attitude shared by idealists who avoided the immediate situation by concentrating on an obscure future goal and this, to Carlisle, was a form of cowardice.

"You have the most ferocious scowl, Captain," Tatiana said. "Are you disapproving Albert or do you have a headache?"

"He's very handsome," Carlisle said.

Tatiana smiled. "Men always say he's handsome. I suppose he is, but what does a picture tell? Come and sit down. I want you to write in my book."

"Is that where you live?" Carlisle asked, indicating a photograph of a vast building surrounded by a park.

"No. That's the Hrădcany Palace. Our home is down the hill."

Carlisle sat at the table and Tatiana gave him a pen and a morocco-covered book open to a blank page. "Please write something," she said.

Carlisle stared at the book, which he imagined to be filled with poetry extemporized by other officers to whom she'd given it, clever testimonials to her beauty, charm and grace, pen and ink sketches of flowers, moonlit scenes, or caricatures with witty comments. His hands were clammy and he gripped the fountain pen, certain it was going to slip from his fingers. "I don't know what to write," he said.

"Anything you like, but you must sign it 'Captain of the Powder Room' so I'll be sure to remember."

"I'll have to think of something."

"Yes," she said and she sat down at her desk with her back to him. "I won't watch. I hate being watched when I'm trying to think. Albert hated autograph books even when we were small. He'd never sign them, which was considered impolite in those days, but he said they were sentimental. I haven't heard from him in three months. They say he's flying for General Denikin. He's never in one place long enough for my letters to reach him, so it's useless to write. I've almost decided to go home now that the war in Europe is over, but I'd like Albert's opinion. I'd thought of going by ship but now it may be best to go overland."

Carlisle began to write in his slow, painstaking manner. His handwriting was small but legible, trained to be so because of the military records he kept. He'd never see her again. This was the first thought he expressed. Then he paused to think what license, if any, this gave him.

"Are you done?"

"No."

She drank her tea and continued to talk as Carlisle's hand worked slowly across the page.

"Albert took me up once and it was quite exciting. Sometimes I'm jealous of his aeroplane. Isn't that ridiculous? But I am."

In a rush Carlisle tried to express the impression Tatiana had made on him. Using strings of words from a source never previously tapped he tried to compensate for his previous outburst of inane laughter. It was vital that she think well of him, that she understand:

"Dear Countess Tatiana," he began. "I leave tomorrow and will not see you again, but I take with me for always the memory of your face above the garnet necklace you wore on the night of the Armistice ball. No woman will ever again speak to me as directly as you did when you came down the stairs. I stared, and later when we met by the happy intercession of General Bogoloff's epaulet I was struck dumb, as I always am in your presence, by the simple marvel of your existence."

He signed it "Carlisle, Captain of the Powder Room." When he read what he had written he found that it horrified him. He contemplated tearing out the page but was afraid to do so. He stared at it as though it were a writ for his own execution, wondering if he could cross out a word or alter a phrase and make it right, but it was hopeless. He was a clumsy, presumptuous fool.

"Albert talks to his machine when he flies," Tatiana was saying. "He confessed this to me and was irritated when I said that talking to an aeroplane struck me as being more sentimental than autograph books and even a little dotty. He said all pilots talk to their aeroplanes, like people talk to horses. Do you talk to horses, Captain?"

Carlisle looked up and saw she'd turned to face him. "Yes, I think I have," he said.

Tatiana frowned. "I suppose I have too, but I'm quite certain I wouldn't talk to an aeroplane. Now that I think of it, men often talk to machines, to ships and automobiles, but I don't think women ever do. I wonder why."

"Men know machines and they don't answer back," Carlisle said.

"Oh, I'm interrupting you! Please finish. I'll be quiet."

"No. I'm finished," he said and with a sense of doom he closed the book and put it on the table with the pen.

"May I read it?" Tatiana asked.

Carlisle laid his hand on the book and shook his head.

"Does it matter so much?"

"Yes," he said, "it's foolish."

Tatiana was amused. "One always is in autograph books, which accounts for their charm. Important people very often write the most insipid, silly things in autograph books. It's a revelation to read them. 'Roses are red, violets are blue; I'm very pleased to have met you.' Yes, actually! That was written by a very somber Canadian, General Elmsley, just last week. He looked so fierce that when I read it I laughed half the morning and felt very fond of him with his roses and his violets. Come, I'll introduce you to him. He's been to Verkhne-Udinsk and can tell you something about it."

"Then you know I'm going."

"Oh, yes," she said. "Certainly."

"How?"

"Through my cousin, Raul Markowitz. You met him at the ball. He's the Czech liaison officer to General Graves' headquarters."

Carlisle nodded and was annoyed that she already knew something he had intended telling her. It robbed him of the one bit of conversation he'd had and made what he'd written in her book all the more foolish.

Tatiana watched him over the back of her chair with an amused glint in her eyes. Then she rose abruptly, took his hand and pulled him up. "I think you think I'm a spy!" she declared.

"No!" Carlisle said and he shook his head resolutely.

"I have access to all sorts of military information. You'd be astounded what people tell me."

Carlisle continued to shake his head, utterly confused.

"You don't think I could be a spy?"

"I don't know."

"I'm disappointed, then. I think that would be enjoyable. At least it would be of some use. The only thing I seem not to be able to find out is where Albert is and what he's doing. I'm always expecting him, you see. He could walk through that door any minute."

Carlisle glanced toward the door she'd indicated half expecting it to open and reveal Count Albert Nojine in his flying uniform with a swagger stick in his hand.

"Getting messages to Albert is like throwing bottles with notes into the ocean," she said. "It's terrible."

"Can't he be reached through the Allied Command?"

Her eyes clouded slightly and she looked away. "I know he's had some of my letters, but nothing comes back. I don't know why. I'm sure he loses track of time. But I'm anxious to know what he expects me to do."

There was a note of appeal in her voice and Carlisle wondered what she expected of him. Until now he hadn't sensed her desperation, hadn't seen that beneath her charm and frivolity she was trembling. This disconcerted him. Her gray eyes swept over his face and settled on his. He struggled for something to say and didn't find it.

"I'm sorry," she said.

"For what?"

"For imposing my troubles on you. It's a bad habit of mine. I'm selfish, you see, and think everyone should be concerned for my welfare."

"I am," he said.

She touched his arm as Lieutenant Markowitz came into the alcove. "You're very kind, Captain," Tatiana said.

"Colonel Jaubert is leaving, Tatiana," Markowitz said.

"Excuse me, I'm neglecting my other guests," Tatiana said. And bowing her head in a slight apology to Markowitz she hurried to the door where she bid goodbye to an austere-looking French colonel.

The Rumanian pianist had vanished. It was past six and dark outside. Markowitz offered Carlisle a cigarette, which he declined. "Would you care for a drink?"

"I have to go."

Markowitz studied the tip of his cigarette a moment, then looked directly at Carlisle. "You have been told about Captain Nojine, I think."

"I didn't know he was a captain."

Markowitz' face was smooth, the skin appeared to be poreless as china-ware, and his features were small but incisive. If there was a family resemblance to Tatiana it was in the auburn sheen of his hair. His eyes were dark and he had a tendency to flash them to punctuate his remarks, to look up piercingly to see if he had been understood, then down again at his drink or his cigarette as he went on speaking. He was handsome with a look of biting intelligence which Carlisle instinctively distrusted. "Yes, in the Czech Air Squadron," Markowitz said. "He always was a solitary man. No one knows where he is."

"The Countess spoke of his flying dispatches to Denikin."

"Telegraph connections between Omsk and southeast Russia are uninterrupted," Markowitz said and his eyes piniomed Carlisle's. "The Kolchak government can speak directly to Denikin at any time." Then he focused on the smoke of his cigarette once more. "There is what you might call a conspiracy among those who love Tatiana which is meant to protect her against the possibility that her husband is dead. People who know how dependent she has always been, how deeply she loved him, pretend to have seen Albert when actually they have not. Of course she prefers to believe these tales however farfetched they are. For my part, I believe he's dead."

"Has he been reported missing?" Carlisle asked.

"Nothing!" Markowitz said, his voice tense with annoyance. "Nothing! He's reported seen here and there. He flies about like a phantom and those who wish to ingratiate themselves with the Countess need only say they have run across him to win her attention. It's been this way for six months and she waits. She waits. She waits. I dislike it, of course. I disapprove, but what can be done? He may have been captured. He could turn up."

"I hope so," Carlisle said.

"Do you?" Markowitz asked quickly. "Do you indeed. Of course you don't know the man, but I thought you should be acquainted with the situation."

"Why?" Carlisle demanded.

Markowitz smiled in a way that irritated Carlisle intensely. "Because Tatiana has a penchant for unusual types," he said. "She collects them and confides too much in them. As a child she was always attracted to the hunched, the disabled, and blind. Gypsies fascinated her. She was head over heels for the exotic and skewed, believing, I suppose, that these had special insights, supernatural gifts and what not. Of course they adored her at once and tried to confirm her opinion of them. In a room of a hundred people Tatiana will unerringly pick out the most aberrant person with whom to associate."

"Me for instance," Carlisle said.

Markowitz looked up with feigned astonishment, then he laughed mirthlessly. "Don't misunderstand me, Captain! I intended no reflection on you, which is not to say you aren't unique. Ah, but now you've got me doubling back on myself. Please accept my apology. I was merely attempting to explain Tatiana's impulsiveness. She's under considerable tension."

"I see," Carlisle said.

Lieutenant Markowitz put out his cigarette. The bland smile remained on his lips as he tamped the butt in the ashtray and tucked the ebony cigarette holder into his breast pocket. "Have you been to China, Captain?"

"No."

"You'll see a good deal of it this trip. I hope you find it interesting."

Tatiana returned to the alcove and tucked her hand under Markowitz' arm. "What have you two been talking about, Raul?" she asked.

"The enigmas of China," Markowitz said.

Standing shoulder to shoulder Raul Markowitz and Tatiana were a picture of graciousness, beauty and elegance and Carlisle ached to be as they were. He wondered if they sensed his yearning, if they thought him common. His claim to their society was shabby indeed, a pair of captain's bars, and the accident during the Armistice ball. He'd assumed far too much on the basis of these and had made a fool of himself. "I must go," he said.

Tatiana appeared disappointed, but Markowitz shook his hand and walked him to the door. The servant had his coat ready as though his departure were long overdue. "I hope we'll meet again, Captain," Tatiana said.

Carlisle missed the armholes of his overcoat and fumbled for them awkwardly. He broke into a sweat, trying clumsily to get his fists into the sleeves of his overcoat, certain that he was never going to make it. He kept mumbling "Yes, I hope so," and "Thank you very much." The wrestling match with the overcoat seemed to go on interminably, but at last he got it on, snatched his hat and bolted out the door. "Goodbye, Countess," he said.

When he reached the street Carlisle stood against the wall to calm himself. Motor traffic in front of the hotel was heavy. The lights of the cars were diffused by a fog drifting in from the bay and people hurried along with only the tips of their noses showing between their mufflers and the caps on their bowed heads. An orchestra in the Russian Club was playing a czardas and the music spilled into the street whenever the hotel door opened.

Carlisle stuffed his hands into his coat pockets and joined the crowd. He grinned at his own stupidity, then remembering Tatiana's invitation still in his pocket he considered tearing it up. Her face appeared to him and he understood her expectant expression and the reason for her extraordinary beauty; she was a woman always on the verge of dashing into the arms of her lover. She held herself for this moment, groomed for it, poised and radiant for it with a passionate cry of happiness ready to burst forth the moment she saw him. Little wonder she was irresistible and that every man who saw her wished to be Count Albert Nojine.

Carlisle snorted. He was no count. He took her invitation from his blouse pocket, but the scented envelope acquired talismanic power in his hand and he couldn't bring himself to tear it up. He stared at the pale square and it reminded him of Tatiana's autograph book and of the tripe he'd written in it. He moaned aloud. "What slop!" he said. "What god-damned slop!" And he knew that that page with its multisyllabic protestations of what he thought passed as fine emotions would be like an old wound for the rest of his life. It would heal, yes, but consciousness of its existence would never pass away and just now it was raw. ". . . by the happy intercession of General Bogoloff's epaulet."

Carlisle ground his teeth together in mortification. He stuffed the envelope back into his pocket and hurried down the bitter street being sniped at by phrases of his own making. "I take with me for always the memory of your face." — "No woman will ever again speak to me as directly — "

Carlisle winced and twisted like a soldier running across an open field during an artillery barrage. The only saving thought was that tomorrow he would entrain for Harbin and be forever out of range of her gray eyes.

« 3 »

Lieutenant Markowitz put his arms around Tatiana's shoulders and they touched their foreheads together. "You seem tired," he said.

"Exhausted!"

The guests were gone but the room, though silent, seemed to be filled with lingering voices. Wisps of cigarette smoke hung in the air and all the furniture bore the uncooled imprint of its recent, crowded occupancy. Markowitz guided Tatiana to the sofa and she dropped into it, closed her eyes and massaged her temples with a rotating motion of her fingertips.

"I'll get you something," Markowitz said.

"How soon can we go, Raul? This is all so tedious. If we could get back to Omsk we'd be closer to Albert and closer to home."

"Omsk is chaos just now," Markowitz said and he returned to her with two stemmed glasses.

"Vladivostok is chaos."

"Yes, but without bandits racing through the streets shooting up the place."

Tatiana sipped her drink and made a face. "What is this?"

"Korean sherry," Markowitz said.

"You're not serious! It tastes like shellac."

"Perhaps they mixed the labels," Markowitz said.

"Would you get my book before you sit down?"

Markowitz went to the alcove and brought Tatiana's autograph book from the table. "The Koreans cannot make sherry," he declared.

Tatiana opened the autograph book to the last page and read it slowly. She frowned, sipped her sherry absentmindedly and made a distasteful face. "Awful!" she said.

"May I read it?"

Tatiana, lost in thought, let Markowitz read the page. "I agree," he said. "The man is a fool."

"I meant the sherry, or shellac, whichever it is, not Captain Carlisle."

Markowitz closed the book and put it aside. "Sentimental rubbish. I'm not surprised."

"I am. Autograph books are always full of sentimental rubbish, but I think this is different. I expected something stilted, you know, cold, formal, unrevealing."

"It's no secret he was taken with you," Markowitz said irritably. "Most men are."

"I find him interesting."

"You mean curious."

"Very well, what's wrong with that?"

"Only that I have never been a sufficient curiosity to attract you. My devotion has never been enough for you."

"Raul, please," Tatiana said wearily.

"You've always been helplessly attracted to human abnormality, Tatiana."

"He is not abnormal!"

Markowitz assumed an expression of restrained impatience; his voice was precise and icy. "He's an awkward half-breed American Indian. Anyone looking at him knows he's an odd customer. He was uncomfortable here. He didn't know how to behave and I think you enjoyed that. There's a streak of cruelty in you, Tatiana, which you won't admit."

"I'm going to Omsk at once."

"You won't find stranger types to collect there than here and it's ridiculous to expose yourself to the dangers of the trip until the railway has been secured."

"One of the officers at Spasskoi offered to fly me to Chita."

"Why didn't you go with him?" Markowitz asked calmly.

"I had no luggage."

Markowitz laughed, vastly amused. "Was he flying a boxcar, or what? No luggage!"

"Besides, I don't think he was serious."

Markowitz took Tatiana's free hand in his. "Is there any doubt as to my seriousness, Tatiana?" he asked. "Doesn't it sometimes occur to you that I am also a very peculiar man, freakish enough for your taste surely, freakish enough to have devoted my life from childhood to you and to have continued doing so long after other men would have given it up? Doesn't that variety of madness interest you?"

Tatiana withdrew her hand from his. "You know I love you, Raul," she said.

Markowitz' face set in a porcelain mask. "I've asked you not to say that, Tatiana. It's such a contemptible mockery."

"I'm married to Albert!"

Markowitz bounded up and turned on her, his eyes blazing. "And that too is a mockery!" he cried. "It always was! Face it, Tatiana, before it's too late! Albert is dead!"

"Raul!"

"If not actually dead he's most certainly dead to you. He hasn't written, or wired, and he could have done so. He knows you're here with me and I'm sure he derives a great deal of sadistic pleasure knowing what that does to me, supposing he is alive."

Tatiana rose and started to leave the room, but Markowitz caught her arm and pulled her around.

"Yes, to me," he continued through clenched teeth, "because I'm sure he knows how untouchable you are."

"Raul, my arm!"

"Is there some feeling there?" Markowitz demanded and he tightened his grip until she winced, and pushed his white face close to hers. "Cry out for once in your life, Tatiana! Let me hear an expression of pain at least."

"Albert is alive, Raul," Tatiana said steadily. "He may be a prisoner, but he is alive."

"You'll cling to that, won't you?"

"It's my duty."

Markowitz threw his head back and laughed harshly. "It's your pose, Tatiana! It's a damned, bloodless piece of statuary! Albert was fascinated by death; he drank death in his mother's milk and saw it in his father's calculating eyes. For a time you distracted him from it, Tatiana, as a mirror or a bright flower might have done, but you can be damned sure that Albert will never return to you. Saving Albert from his suicidal moods, his grand depressions, his damned portentous, ghostly melancholia and fits of gothic romanticism, all of which fascinated you because they were so strange, was perhaps a worthy occupation. It was a challenge in an otherwise useless and tedious existence, but it was never a marriage, Tatiana."

"You don't know that!"

"Yes I do," Markowitz said calmly, "and so do you."

"You're a beast, Raul!"

Markowitz nodded agreeably. "I am," he said. "As are we all. Beasts are flesh and blood and they acknowledge it, Tatiana. The thing I fear above all is that you'll never acknowledge your own flesh and blood, Tatiana, and I begin to see now how perfectly Albert guaranteed this. If he is dead you'll go on waiting for him. You'd be too proud to relinquish him to your competitor, Death, until at last it won't matter anymore, until you're old. Until I'm old."

"And you think he's done all this to spite you?"

Markowitz nodded. "I think so," he said. "I don't say I'm right, but I think so. My hatred of Albert and my envy are in proportion to my love for you. They're both very great, Tatiana. I'm stretched between them. Obsessed if you like. The argument between us can be stated simply: If Albert Nojine were alive, I would think of him as being dead; if he were dead, you would continue to think of him as alive."

"Stop this, Raul, before I despise you for it."

"That would be something, at least."

"I'm going to Omsk at the first opportunity."

Markowitz' face darkened; he opened his mouth to speak, then a startled expression came into his eyes and he laughed sharply. "I was about to say, 'You can go to the devil,' but that's exactly what you intend doing. He's a devil, Tatiana. That's the truth of it."

Markowitz stood for a moment struck by this thought, then he shook his head and left the room.

Tatiana took her autograph book to the desk in the alcove. She felt cold. Markowitz had chilled her. She looked at the picture of Albert beside his aeroplane. He was not satanic. Aristocratic, yes; aloof perhaps; but she remembered his tenderness also. Certainly there had been tenderness? Correctness always, but tenderness too. Or was this only her imagination?

She couldn't remember.

Tatiana clutched the autograph book to her breast and stared out the window into the mist-shrouded street below. The headlights of the automobiles blurred and expanded like iridescent jellyfish struggling in a milky sea. There were no hard shapes, no distinct lines. It was the substance of memories not to be relied upon, a drifting sea and she was much too exhausted to swim anymore. She took a deep breath and desperation came with it like a sharp pain. She gasped and tried to twist away. She was terribly frightened, alone, forgotten, going down into the confusion and the cold. She tried to call out, but there was a hard knot in her throat.

The autograph book fell to the floor and she kept thinking to herself, "Be calm, Tatiana, be calm." But her panic increased with every step until she reached the door to Markowitz' room and rapped on it.

"Raul?" she called and the broken sound of her own voice caused her to burst into tears and when the door was opened she fell into Markowitz' arms and clung to him like a terrified child.

CHAPTER EIGHT

IN his last letter from Vlad, Ira suggested that his family not think of him as being in Siberia with all its dreary associations: "Nay, let us rather consider winter sports in a lovely Alpine setting. Ice skating on Lake Baikal, snowshoeing and skiing by day and cheese fondue beside a roaring fire at night. As to the tiger pelt, don't worry, Mom. If you examine it closely I think you'll discover it to be an old cow hide with stripes skillfully painted by an unscrupulous dealer in curiosities. Authorities here assure me that the Siberian tiger is as extinct as the mastodon."

This letter filled with hollow cheerfulness was what they expected at home. And in return his mother sent letters commending his bravery and fortitude, saying how much he was missed, asking about the food, cautioning him to be careful and to have a good time. Ruth wrote newsy letters. Edie Samson O'Dell was pregnant and Cruiser had decided to make a career in the Navy. Sylvia Cowan married a Catholic and her father was so distraught that he mislabeled some prescriptions and nearly ruined his business. His father and Uncle Dave sent him newspaper clippings about sports and local politics.

But none of them told him their troubles. He would have liked a letter filled with the problems and complaints of family life. These, to a certain extent, were necessary to his recollection of them as real people. He missed his father's complaints that business was bad and his mother's references to Uncle Dave's socialistic tomfoolery. The irritations of that household were suddenly more precious to him than its cheerfulness. Ruth was fading fastest of all. Her letters were cheery and inconsequential, intended to make him smile or chuckle, and though they succeeded in this he read them with a certain bitterness. They'd loved him into the war and now it appeared it was his bounden duty to laugh himself to death.

His letters home were as amusing as he could make them, but they were false as hell. Lake Baikal wasn't St. Moritz just as a trench in France hadn't been Brooklyn Heights or Piccadilly Circus, but the idea was to pack up your troubles in the old kit bag and export humor to the home front.

Ira did his share.

« 2 »

On the day of their departure C Company mustered in the train station at seven a.m. At seven-ten they were told to stand at ease. At eight Carlisle sent Leverett to find out what happened to their train. At nine Sergeant Austin told the men to fall out but stay close. At ten Carlisle went to find Leverett.

The men sat down on the station platform resting against their packs, or against each other, smoking, dozing, grousing. Carson, Dixon and Crowe played rummy with a soiled pack of Red Cross cards.

"No Greaser can run a railroad," Carson drawled. "I knew we wouldn't be out on time."

"They ain't Greasers," Dixon said.

"Don't tell me I don't know Greasers," Carson grumbled. "I lived around Greasers all my life and I know. There's a Greaser." He nodded toward a swarthy Oriental in a railway uniform carrying a flat wooden signalman's paddle.

"That's a Chinese," Crowe said dubiously.

Carson shook his head in disgust and shuffled the cards. "Put a Mex hat and poncho on him and you got yourself a Greaser," he said. "Mañana. Mañana! They're all the same."

Sergeant Austin paced the edge of the platform wishing he could run upstairs and find Maryenka at her kiosk outside the station door, but she'd gone to Pashkova to be with her family until the company was settled, then she'd come to Verkhne-Udinsk or to one of the villages close by.

He'd put her on the train for Khabarovsk and watched it leave, waving, fighting the impulse to run along beside the train until he ran out of platform, regretting now he hadn't.

He wrote Maryenka every day, short optimistic letters promising to find a place for them to live at Verkhne and it was this place which filled Austin's mind as he tramped back and forth on the station platform puffing his cigar.

He visualized a cabin in a forest. The picture was so clear he was certain he'd seen it on a Christmas card. It was a night scene with a high round moon and a cabin in the trees with soft, harmless snow on the roof and two windows yellow from the fire inside. There was a rick of chopped wood on the porch and cords of wood piled along the side of the cabin to keep the fire glowing and there was a trail pressed in the snow to the door. He entered the picture along this trail, a big figure all coat and hat, a paper cutout figure with a tab through a cut-along-the-dotted-line, which could be moved from behind. He must have had a card like that as a kid. It wasn't the kind of thing he'd make up, but he liked it because Maryenka was waiting behind the door.

A train shunted backward through the marshaling yard toward their platform and Austin flipped his cigar away. Carlisle and Leverett came down the stairs, Carlisle scowling, Leverett talking and waving his arms defensively.

One hour later C Company, 2nd Battalion, 27th Infantry Regiment, was on its way to Harbin.

« 3 »

Major Subo Ikachi boarded the train at Pogranichnaya, the boundary station between Russia and Manchuria. His destination was Chita, where he was to assess the results of the Pan-Mongolian Congress, a political device suggested by the Japanese and convened by Ataman Semenoff in the hope of gathering broader support for his cause if the Kolchak government should fail.

Major Ikachi was small, not over five feet three, but well proportioned. He seemed to have been made with care, almost with precision and his face had a beauty most often seen in statuary. The bridge of his nose was fine, with a gentle arch starting just below his wide, dark eyes, and there was an amber shade to his skin which seemed to glow, not waxen but with a steady interior heat. He spoke three languages, his own, English and French, and of the three French was the one he preferred because it reminded him of the three happiest years of his life, spent at the École Militaire, intensely romantic years which changed the course of his life. He spoke French with a lingering, wistful intonation as though behind each word there was a host of associations. He was a Shintoist who approved all things French — French love, French style, French diplomacy. And like the French he thought Americans were ridiculous, but this adopted prejudice was one he hoped to eliminate or corroborate before he left the train at Chita.

Ikachi's importance in Japanese affairs far exceeded his military rank. He was a member of the Secret Society of the Black Dragon, a combination of Japanese industrialists, politicians and militarists whose influence on the course of the Japanese Empire could be rivaled only by that of Emperor Yoshihito himself. Members of this society and Ikachi in particular had been deeply impressed by *The Valor of Ignorance* by Homer Lea, a young hunchbacked American military theorist and self-styled General of the Chinese Militia. This book had recently been translated and given wide circulation in Japan. It outlined the conditions of rivalry between Japan and the United States for power in the Pacific and predicted a war between these two nations. Japanese strategy in this conflict, campaigns for the seizure of Hawaii and the Philippines and for the ultimate assault on Alaska and the coastal states, had been laid out in meticulous detail and the underlying assumption was that Japan would win this contest. But the book was published in 1909 before America's entry into the European war, with the consequent enlargement of its military establishment, and though the underlying principles of it were sound Ikachi was anxious to adjust them to current developments.

He had practically memorized Homer Lea's slim volume and knew as much about the geography and weather conditions of the coastal states as many of the Americans resident in them. He had fought the Russians in 1904. He'd seen Russia and China eliminated as Pacific powers and he dreamed of being in command of the Japanese column which would land at Bodega Bay while another landed at Santa Cruz for the combined attack on San Francisco. He was anxious to meet as many Americans as he could, to get a sense of their character and an opinion as to their military intentions now that the European war was over.

Americans intrigued Ikachi much more than the Cossack atamans and

White officers which it was his duty to play off against one another. This was a bit like juggling; it required coordination, but after a bit it got to be boring.

Grigori Mikhailovich Semenoff was not a likable young man, but his Savage Division, composed mainly of Mongols, controlled Chita, the junction of the Chinese Eastern and the Amur line, which meant that all rail traffic from Vladivostok and Khabarovsk to Omsk had to pass through his grasping hands. Ikachi's current mission was to inform Semenoff when to squeeze and when to release and also to make it clearly understood that if he should fail to be a responsive valve the Japanese government was capable of replacing him on very short notice.

Semenoff was senselessly cruel and vainglorious, with a penchant for self-bestowed titles: Duke of Mongolia, Ruler of Trans-Baikal. His men were required to sing his praises in formation:

> *Ataman Semenoff!*
> *Formidable avenger!*
> *Unyielding victor!*
> *Righteous pacifier!*

He was none of these things. He was a strutting cock, twenty-eight years old, with a pomaded cowlick and sliding green eyes who dressed himself in sable capes and morocco boots and enjoyed careering up and down the railroad in his armored trains spreading terror.

The other valve on the railroad was Ataman Kalmykoff who controlled Khabarovsk. Some thought him mad, others were charmed by him. On the whole Ikachi preferred him to Semenoff because he had moments of self-doubt; his sadism and brutality had a quality of helplessness about it as though he were striking out blindly in the dark. "I'm corrupt," he said to Ikachi one evening. "I'm thoroughly befouled," he said with a plaintive tone in his voice and wonder that was almost angelic in his eyes. "Kalmykoff is a tyrant," he said as if he could not believe it. Then he shrugged and sighed, saying "But what is a man to do?" as though all the options of life had been exhausted in his twenty-five years.

Kalmykoff was no problem to control and though Semenoff was much more powerful he too could be handled. There was no need for delicacy. The simple threat to replace Semenoff with Kalmykoff, or with Sipialef, who worked under General Bogoloff out of Verkhne-Udinsk, was enough to temper Semenoff's ambitions, or at least those of which Ikachi was aware.

Major Ikachi enjoyed rail travel. The heavy progress of a train through vast expanses of countryside was relaxing to him. He liked the dulling effect of train wheels over the rails and the thoughtfulness it brought to people's faces as they watched the scenery fall back along the windows.

Having traveled the road many times and in all seasons, he knew the country intimately and could interpolate fields of cabbages, sorghum and opium poppies on the hillsides of the Mulin Valley which were now winter-stricken, or fields of dark wheat among the timber stands of ash and elm along the Mutan River.

He was pleased to find some American commissioned and noncommissioned officers sharing the first class car. Hopefully this would give him an opportunity to correct some of his impressions about Americans, for he was always on guard against those imbalances of mind in himself which he regarded as flaws in the character of others.

The first class passenger cars on the Chinese Eastern were commodious and well-appointed, with nine compartments separated by sliding doors, and another sliding door opening to the aisle down one side. Each compartment had two berths crossways rather than parallel to the train yet with ample room to stretch out because the wider track base on the Russian road was translated into roomier passenger accommodations with a chair, a small table and a built-in couch.

There were two dining cars on the train, one for the American troops and one for passengers in the first class section. Ikachi, who knew the Chinese waiters, had arranged to have his table next to that of an American captain and his lieutenant so he could observe them more closely.

He was fascinated by the aggressive sweep and extravagance of American history. That any nation could have acquired so much of the world's territory and wealth in so short a period of time amazed him. Even more was he amazed by the Americans' professed innocence of an obvious historical truth, which was that the United States intended to dominate the world, both east and west. The few Americans he had come into contact with absolutely denied world ambitions or acquisitive designs and he had come to believe they were sincere in these denials. This was the paradox which intrigued him. They either laughed at or were insulted by his assertion that they were intent on world domination. The very idea surprised and aggrieved them just as Kalmykoff was surprised to discover himself a tyrant. But at least Kalmykoff admitted it; he saw what he was and was sometimes enraged, sometimes saddened by it.

Americans, on the other hand, were simply blind to the most obvious facts of life. To hear them talk one would think all their acquisitions of land and resources, wealth and power, had fallen upon them like an avalanche; that Alaska, Cuba, the Philippines, Hawaii, Texas, California and all the rest had been wished upon them as a penance for their good intentions.

Ambitions in the Far East? Certainly not! Ridiculous, they would claim. America has no designs in Asia. What an absurdity! Yet here they were, a well-outfitted infantry company headed for Harbin and then to Verkhne-Udinsk. The Americans were almost singlehandedly reequipping the Trans-Siberian Railroad at the cost of millions of dollars. The engine pulling the train was a huge American decapod assembled from parts shipped to Vladivostok and Subo Ikachi was under no illusion that the Americans, having established this bridgehead, would retire from it. There was no precedent in their history for such an assumption.

There still remained, however, their puzzling individual behavior. It was inscrutable. It seemed unlikely that each of them had been taught to dissimulate, yet they were all of one mind in any discussion of national aims. All they wanted to do was to go home, but they stayed. It was a puzzling national characteristic; the British did not have it, nor did the French.

Lately Ikachi had begun to think that the key to the paradox was the Americans' sense of humor; that what they did or intended to do was never explicit, but was always an inverse expression of what they said. He noticed, for instance, that American friends frequently cursed or hit each other when they met. Their affection was invariably stated in aggressive and competitive terms: "Harry, you old son of a bitch!" — "What do you mean 'old,' you bastard! I can still run circles around you!"

Having observed this behavior at train depots, Ikachi inferred that Americans could not be taken at face value. To win their regard one had to absorb their blows and curses and return them in kind, but always with a smile and a good deal of disarming laughter. On the other hand anything said in a courteous manner could not be trusted. He'd observed this at depots, too.

"Hello, John, glad to see you." A firm handshake and both men looked off, avoiding each other, uneasy and anxious to be away.

Yes, the mark of American sincerity was an insult and a rough clap on the back.

As a rule they had never honored a treaty or a commitment made to a race darker than themselves.

As a rule they steadfastly refused to believe that any other nation had a worthwhile sense of humor.

As a rule they believed themselves to be frank and honest to a fault, but Ikachi was certain they intended to insult, slap and laugh their way into the heartland of Asia.

He admired their temerity and disliked their manners.

Nevertheless Ikachi was anxious to understand American psychology, hoping it would help him foresee how large a hegemony the United States intended to have in Asia and whether or not Japan would be able to accommodate it. To this end he waited for his chance to meet the two American officers on the train.

Judging by their behavior, these two officers were the best of friends. They were extremely discourteous toward one another and made a display of their annoyance at having to be together. The captain grumbled at the lieutenant in a most uncivil way and the lieutenant frequently made sarcastic faces behind the captain's back for the amusement of the noncommissioned officers at the next table down. Taken at face value one would have concluded that the captain and the lieutenant disliked each other, but Ikachi was not misled.

Having made his observations, Ikachi decided the time had arrived to present himself. Coming from the washroom at the end of the car one afternoon he met the lieutenant in the aisle and bowed formally. "Lieutenant Leverett, I am Major Ikachi."

"Hello," the lieutenant said. "Glad to meet you," which meant, of course, that he was not happy at all, but annoyed and anxious to be off.

"If I am not mistaken we had a conversation in Vladivostok," Ikachi said and he smiled politely waiting for the lieutenant to confirm or deny this.

"Gosh, I don't remember," Ira said.

Ikachi nodded pleasantly and asked Ira if he and the captain would join him in a drink before dinner.

"I'll ask him," Ira said.

"Thank you very much."

"When?" Ira asked.

"Anytime," Ikachi said. "When it's convenient to the captain."

"Well, I'll ask him then."

"Thank you," Ikachi said again and bowing he stepped aside to allow Ira to pass, then he went to his compartment, ordered tea, whiskey and glasses from the steward and waited.

For Ikachi waiting was a pleasure, particularly on a train. Impatience was absent from his nature. He could be demanding and irritable toward subordinates, but never because they made him wait.

He sat in his chair facing the window with his hands resting lightly on his knees. They were approaching Irchentiantze with its hill of white marble where gangs of Chinese quarrymen labored to extract blocks of stone to be carved into statuary or sliced and polished for walls and floors of public buildings. Harbin was a hundred miles ahead, a cosmopolitan sprawl on the Sungari River with brothels catering to every taste, some in surroundings so exquisite one could not believe the women in them were real.

It occurred to him that while waiting he nearly always thought of women. Odd that this should be so, but no doubt it accounted in part for his enjoyment of it. He would select a woman in Harbin during the stop there.

Ikachi heard a tap and found Lieutenant Leverett standing in the doorway with a broad smile on his face. "Now, I remember! The night of the Armistice. I called General Otani and got you!"

Ikachi rose and was so encouraged by the lieutenant's hearty smile and boisterous tones that he tensed his muscles and was disappointed when the blow he had anticipated didn't follow. "Won't you sit down, Lieutenant," he said and he bowed toward a seat.

Ira sat down on the side couch, still grinning. "That was a stupid thing to do, but with the war over I was larking around. Funny I got you, isn't it?"

"I was attached to General Otani's staff and had the watch that night," Ikachi said.

"Yes, but odd we should run into each other, that's what I mean."

"I trust we shall yet run into each other with greater force," Ikachi said loudly. "Is your captain coming? If so I'll wait to pour a god-damned drink!"

"He's putting his blouse on," Ira said, a bit taken aback by Ikachi's hearty manner.

Carlisle had seen enough Japs in the Philippines to know that behind their smiling cordiality and formal manners they always had something up their sleeve. He'd never trusted them; they were notoriously silky and devious, never said what they thought and were always scheming. When he came in the Jap bowed and Carlisle stuck out his hand. "I'm Captain Carlisle," he said. "Glad to meet you."

"Major Subo Ikachi," Ikachi said and he shook hands.

"Going to be with us long, Major?"

"I'm going to Chita," Ikachi declared. "May I pour you old boys a drink?"

Carlisle scowled at Leverett and sat down. The drinks were strong, whiskey and water, but no ice. Carlisle sipped his while Leverett told how he'd met Ikachi on the phone.

"Have you seen much of this country, Captain?" Ikachi asked.

Carlisle shook his head. "I went as far as Ishim last August."

"Only the Maritime Province, then."

"That's right."

"You'll be able to renew your acquaintance with General Bogoloff. He's the military commander at Verkhne-Udinsk."

"I'm not acquainted with General Bogoloff," Carlisle said.

"I thought you were," Ikachi said. "I saw you with him and Countess Tatiana the night of the Armistice ball."

Carlisle glanced at Leverett, whose interest in the conversation had quickened. "Oh, yes," he said. "Bogoloff."

"I was on the point of helping the Countess myself, but you acted first," Ikachi said.

Carlisle nodded, but his face had gone dangerously sullen.

"I met Bogoloff's train commander," Ira said quickly. "Colonel Sipialef."

"I know him," Ikachi said.

Leverett told of his encounter with Sipialef at General Bogoloff's armored train, embellishing and editing the tale as he went along so that in the end it was thoroughly pointless. He left out Sipialef's contemptuous slur against the Jews and having done so was troubled again by a feeling of cowardice. Carlisle looked at him expectantly, waiting for him to conclude the story. "That's all," Ira said and he felt like a fool.

"You'll find General Bogoloff interesting," Ikachi said. "A Russian soldier of the old school. They taught us a great deal in 1905."

"You beat hell out of them," Carlisle said.

Ikachi smiled agreeably. The caustic bite in Carlisle's tone of voice led him to believe that they were about to cross into the area of boisterous hostility which was the American way of expressing cordial relations. He was anxious to get there and wracked his brain for a suitable rejoinder, one which indicated he was ready for the preliminary rough-and-tumble. "Well, old man," he said, "they called us the Yellow Peril and not so very long ago in America they were calling your people the Red Menace. If you'd had a few machine guns, there might be a redskin in the White House today," and laughing heartily he slapped Carlisle on the knee.

Carlisle's eyes popped with astonishment. He looked at the place on his knee where Ikachi had slapped it as though he'd been shot. His face went black and he gulped his drink preparing to pull the Jap out of his chair and send him sprawling. But before he could do so Ikachi snatched his glass.

"Bottoms up," Ikachi said. He stood up, drained his own glass and refilled both of them swaying slightly to the action of the train.

Carlisle half rose, then remembering Leverett he sat back again. "What the hell!" he said.

Ira, tense as a runner in the starting chocks, watched both men anxiously, ready to jump between them in an instant.

Ikachi was still chuckling as he handed Carlisle his glass. "Sure you can hold your booze, Sioux?" he asked.

"Where'd you get that, you bastard!"

Ikachi roared delightedly. "Hell, I'm not blind! I asked a couple of Americans about you in Vladivostok. I knew you were a redskin, but I didn't know the tribe. Come now, Captain, don't tell me you're sensitive about your aboriginal background."

"What about yours, you slanty son of a bitch!" Carlisle bellowed.

Ira leaped to his feet. Ikachi, certain that he'd broken into the charmed circle of American intimacy, was a bit unsettled by the lieutenant's alarmed expression. "The Sioux and the Jew," he said. "That's what they call you two, isn't it?"

"They'll be calling you bloody balls in about half a second," Carlisle roared. He set his drink aside and stood up.

"Take it easy, Captain," Ira said.

"Sure, take it easy," Ikachi echoed, but he sensed something was going awry.

Carlisle slung the door open, nearly shattering the glass, and Ikachi made a desperate effort to get back on a proper footing, but was unsure where he'd gone wrong. "Wait, Captain," he cried, "you and I have a great deal in common."

"Crap! That is pure crap!"

"No! All Indian roots are here in central Asia. My roots are here too."

"Crap!"

"Crap hell," Ikachi declared. "I'm Chinese, Ainu and Mongol, as near as I can tell. What's your mix?" Ikachi was about to pop Carlisle on the shoulder affectionately, but the gesture was so alien that he couldn't quite bring himself to complete it.

Carlisle glared at Ira. "One more word and I'm going to break his arm," he yelled, then he pushed Ikachi aside and lunged out into the corridor.

There was a prolonged silence.

"Jesus!" Ira mumbled presently.

Ikachi sank into his chair, brooding.

"You trying to get yourself killed, or what?" Ira asked.

Ikachi sighed and attempted an explanation but he could see it was hopeless. The lieutenant kept shaking his head in bewilderment. "Well, Major," he said at last, "the next time you try one of these sociological experiments don't pick the Sioux."

"Yes, I see. I hope you'll convey my apology."

Ira nodded, thanked Ikachi for the drink, and left, closing the door softly behind him.

Ikachi sat in his chair gazing out of the window solemnly. He finished the bottle, but the whiskey had no appreciable effect. There were still complexities of American psychology which he didn't understand. Perhaps it had something to do with the idiomatic language they used. He would study American slang. Perhaps the key was there. But he wasn't discouraged because he was sure that the future relationship of two great nations depended on just such matters. Then, as the night wore on, he burst into genuinely merry laughter thinking what a fool he'd been and how narrowly he'd missed having the bridge of his fine nose smashed.

CHAPTER NINE

THE military attaché of the American Consul in Harbin boarded the train at Ashikhe and came through the cars looking for Carlisle. A slim young first lieutenant affecting a swagger stick and a manner which clearly implied that he was destined to have an impact on the course of history, he smiled splendidly and shook hands. "MacDougal, here," he said. "I hope the trip hasn't been too dreary."

There was a flip British intonation in his speech which set Carlisle's teeth on edge and amused Leverett, who liked MacDougal at once. The lieutenant pulled a notecase from his blouse pocket and ticked off the arrangements which had been made. "You'll be here overnight. Red Cross accommodations for the men, I'm afraid. Cots, doughnuts, coffee and magazines, that sort of thing, in a building adjoining the station. They'd best feed before they leave the train. Breakfast will be given in the morning before they entrain. Consul Moser invites you to dinner, but if I may say so aside, you'll miss Harbin if you go. Up to you, of course. As a precaution I'd keep the men in close quarters. Harbin's reputation as the roughest city in the world is not exaggerated. I can tell tales to make the hackles rise."

Carlisle and Leverett excused themselves from dinner with Consul Moser, and MacDougal, a bit put off by Carlisle's lack of response to his charm, turned his attention to Ira, with whom he had more in common.

As their train approached Harbin the lights of the city began to come on, revealing a sprawl of squalid buildings on a flat dirt plain. It was an exceedingly ugly city with the skyline broken by factory chimneys erupting dark smoke. MacDougal told Ira it was the junction point where the Chinese Eastern met the Japanese Railway, which went south to Mukden, Dairen, Port Arthur and on to Peking. They slowed to a crawl in the marshaling yard, which was choked with battered freight cars, tenders and engines. Coal-blackened Chinese yardmen scuttled about, pulling switches. MacDougal called them coolies, whereupon Carlisle rose and left the compartment, to find Austin he said.

"Abrupt chap, isn't he," MacDougal said.

Ira grinned and nodded. "Abrupt as hell. But he runs deep."

"I suppose you'll be spending a lot of time with him."

"That's right."

"Bad luck," MacDougal said sympathetically. "In that case you could do with a bash."

"He'll want me to stay here."

"Hell, I bet I could tow you out on some pretext. Let me try."

"Fine," Ira said.

After a series of jolting switches, the train eased into the depot and was surrounded by a horde of babbling hawkers, porters, hotel runners and newsboys. The first class passengers detrained and fought their way through this crowd. Men and boys were eager to render any service, to shine shoes, carry bags, sell anything, and beyond these there were women whose approach, though more gentle, was just as insistent. MacDougal left to confer with Carlisle. Major Ikachi appeared on the platform supporting his officer's sword in one hand and wearing a huge boxlike pistol holster. The crowd made way and he passed through without a backward glance.

MacDougal returned to the compartment with a smile of accomplishment on his handsome face. "You're going to dinner with Consul Moser," he said.

"I thought we begged off. What did Carlisle say?"

"That I could have you, the implication being that if you missed the train he wouldn't mind."

"But you said dinner with Moser would be dull."

"Hell, Moser left this morning for Peking to talk with Consul General Reinsch."

"How could Carlisle and I have gone to dinner with him then?" Ira asked.

MacDougal sighed. "I invited you, but I touted you off, didn't I? That way the amenities and protocol have not been violated. You were invited, but refused. Come on, grab your coat and your pistol if it's handy."

Ira laughed. "You're worse than the Japs, MacDougal. What if we'd accepted?"

"Moser would have been taken ill. Women and diplomacy are the same the world over. Sad but true. Come on."

They left the train and trotted along the platform like two boys liberated from school.

Their first stop was a bar where MacDougal was known by the Spanish-looking headwaiter, who bowed continuously as he guided them to a private booth and produced a bottle of bourbon and two glasses without having appeared to leave them for an instant. MacDougal uncapped the bottle, filled the glasses and touched his to Ira's. "Here's to serious drinking," he said and they began talking. Their words tumbled over one another punctuated most frequently by the exclamation: "Oh Christ! I know what you mean!"

They were thrilled to have found each other; their eyes shone with parched eagerness to share the totality of their past lives, which proved to have been very similar.

MacDougal went to Yale. MacDougal studied law. MacDougal had a weekend with a home town girl. MacDougal was a Delta Kappa Epsilon.

"I'm a Jew."

"Oh, Christ! I know what you mean!"

They hardly heard each other but in twenty minutes they were intimate friends and knew the names of each other's sisters, fathers, mothers and brothers. MacDougal was called Duke and his brother, still at Yale, was Phil, the Pill.

"I call him Phil the Pill."

"Oh, Christ! I know what you mean."

They finished one bottle and ordered another with dinner, which seemed to have sprouted like mushrooms from the top of the table. They ate voraciously, chewing their food with their words and washing them both down with bourbon. They grew reflective and soul-probing.

"It's guys like us against the whole damned world, I say. Right, Ira?"

"Dead right, Duke."

"There's just too damned much protoplasm walkin' around on human legs. That's the whole problem. Too much!"

"You bet."

"Die like flies. Ought to keep their peckers in their pants. What kind of life is that?"

"Not much."

"And what in hell we supposed to do about it?" MacDougal growled belligerently. "Damned Reds revolting don't solve anything. Life is cheap; that's what I've learned, cheaper than candles. I'm lookin' out for number one, you can bet your ass on that. We shouldn't be here at all if you want my opinion, my honest opinion."

"You hit the nail on the head, Duke. We've been suckered again."

They grew sentimental, showed their snapshots, exchanged addresses and promised to write. Finally they lapsed into a satiated melancholy which called for more drinks and girls.

"Let'sh get out of here, Ira," MacDougal said carefully and he stood up very tall, his face set in an expression of extreme hauteur as though the world had just lowered itself beneath him.

They came out onto Sungara Prospect, an impacted dirt street with a line of light poles like big three-pronged hay forks against the night sky. "Take you to old town," MacDougal muttered and they stood together swaying while MacDougal looked for a horse cab. He yelled at one, but it was already occupied. "Have to look out for hunghutze. Keep your pishtol handy."

"What's hunghutshe?"

"Bandits. Chinese. Cutthroatsh."

"Thought they were cab drivers. There's one! Hey!"

They boarded the four-wheel cab and fell back on the cushioned seat. MacDougal gave the driver an address and they clopped off drawn by a woebegone nag which expressed its displeasure by emitting flatulent blasts of foul-smelling air in their direction.

Ira and the Duke were convulsed. They roared at each horsy fart and tears ran down their faces. "Look out — That was a beauty!"

Ira fell into the bottom of the carriage clinging to his sides, begging for relief. "Oh, God! Oh, God, Duke! Tell him to stop!"

"I can't! I can't! I don't speak horse, just a little Chinese, but I think the driver's fallen in with him!"

"Duke! Duke! Tell him to turn the horse around and pull us backward!"

They whickered, bleated and bellowed like two maniacs. Nothing had ever been or could ever again be as supremely, hysterically, roaring funny as their trip down Sungara Prospect behind the farting horse. It was classic. They were brothers.

"I say, old boy, is that bad hay or the national anthem?"

Ira threw up his arms and sank into his coat. "Stop it, Duke! Oh, God save me!"

MacDougal stood up and tapped the taciturn driver on the shoulder. "Tell me, good man, what's the compression ratio on your steed."

Ira blubbered helplessly and plugged his ears.

They left the cab and watched it vanish with mingled relief and regret, then Ira looked at the dark buildings along the narrow street and was distinctly uneasy. "Where are we, Duke?" he asked.

"Come on."

MacDougal led him through a wooden door in a wall and across a stone courtyard. They reached another door, MacDougal rapped on it with his swagger stick and Ira found himself in a room with a blue tile floor and a fountain. Potted plants and cages of canaries hung from the walls. The person who had admitted them seemed to have vanished, but then, near the door, Ira met the solemn brown gaze of an Oriental dwarf dressed in a gold brocade gown. This creature bowed and MacDougal led the way.

"Where are we, Duke?"

"Frat house," MacDougal mumbled. "They'll sober us up, clean us up, press your uniform, shine your shoes, shellac your cane, bathe, massage, shave, manicure, powder and perfume you. We'll catch a couple hours sleep and then go down to hear the Louisiana Trio. They go on at four in the morning."

Ira was nervous. He took a linen robe from an attendant and followed MacDougal into a room where they removed their clothes and put the robes on. Ira's fingers trembled as he tied the sash but he tried to imitate MacDougal's savoir-faire.

"Need a drink to start?" MacDougal asked with a grin.

Ira shook his head.

"You'll never have another experience like this in your life, so enjoy it."

"Where you going?" Ira asked with a touch of panic as MacDougal started out.

"You don't need me, chappy. Just relax."

"Do they speak English?"

"If you like. But the communication is to the senses, lad, not to the brain. I'll catch you in about four hours."

He was gone.

Ira looked around frantically. He felt MacDougal had deserted him and was contemplating this bitterly when two girls appeared in the door wearing linen kimonos like his. They were Eurasian types with oval faces and dark eyes, and their hair coiled high on their heads made them appear tall and slender. A chilling apprehension crept over Ira's skin but, led by their smiles and graceful gestures, he followed them down the corridor to a steam-filled room with a sunken tile bath in the center of the wooden floor.

"I need a drink," Ira said as the door shut behind him.

One of the girls, fifteen, sixteen, twenty years old, Ira couldn't guess, asked him what he wanted—Scotch, whiskey, sake?

Ira said Scotch and she left the room. The other girl went to a low massaging table and began to lay out an assortment of tools, single blade razors, combs, brushes, scissors, bottles, boxes and towels. She indicated the bath. "You get in, sir," she said.

Ira shrugged, dropped his robe and stepped down into the bath. The water was scalding, but he plunged in gasping and remembered his mother's oft-repeated admonition: "Have a good time, Ira. But be careful." At this he laughed and the girl looked at him from her place beside the bath and smiled.

"Now I know how a lobster feels," Ira said.

The girl didn't understand, but she nodded enthusiastically. Obviously her linguistic accomplishments were confined to simple requests.

The other girl appeared with his Scotch in a porcelain cup. Ira tossed it off and it took the strength out of him. He lay on his back supporting himself against the corner half afraid he would slip under and drown.

The girls stood above him, taking stock of the problem in a clinical manner, then they nodded as though they had reached a decision about the division of labor. One of them dropped her robe and came into the bath, wading through the waist-deep water to Ira's side. Her amber skin glistened in the steam as she took a brush and began to scrub him industriously.

For a time Ira allowed her to shove him about like a drugged sea lion. She scrubbed his ruddy genitals in the same dispassionate manner that she went after his toes, taking stock of each speck of him for future operations, but at last Ira had to assert himself. He seized and kissed her mashingly, her mouth sweet and astonished against his. The other girl began to reproach him from the edge of the bath in a language he assumed was Chinese. The girl in his arms giggled, her breasts and stomach palpitating against his until he let her pull away. "I am bath girl," she said. "Bath girl."

"Let me out of this damned hot broth!" Ira demanded and he climbed out of the water, his skin red and tender. He was sufficiently confused and annoyed to have forgotten his nakedness.

They both giggled, amused at his irritation. "We bath girls!"

They were friendly, but too damned familiar. All the sex had been parboiled out of Ira and he submitted to their combined efforts to dry him. They led him to the massaging table and pressed him down, but he resisted. "When I'm bare ass, everybody is bare ass," he said bluntly. "You take off that."

The girl still in her robe shrugged out of it unconcernedly, revealing a body stronger and more blocky than the first girl's; her dry skin was a curious hue of orange with veins radiating close to the surface from the tips of her breasts. She took a pair of scissors from the floor with a smooth, dipping motion, as though to defend herself, but her face was gentle as she pushed him over, face down on the table. They began to knead him, working down from the nape of his neck.

Ira let his eyes fall shut, absorbing pleasure which sank into him like water on desert sand. He heard the scissors working. They trimmed his hair, shaved his back, pared his toenails, manicured his fingernails. They poured rubbing alcohol in the pit of his back, sending a shudder up his spine as they rubbed him dry with it; then they oiled him, tugging at his arms, legs and fingers. It was heaven.

Ira lay on the table, limp and sweet as warm taffy but with a smug and secretive smile on his face, waiting for the tap which would indicate they'd done with his backside.

When they tugged to roll him over Ira kept his eyes shut, reached out and caught one of the girls, in the cradle of his arm, snatched her up on the table and kept right on rolling until she was under him. She struggled and pitched while the other slapped his fanny scolding earnestly.

"Get out of here," Ira said.

"You cannot! It is not allowed for us."

Ira was angry. He bounded off the table and caught the second girl, who backed away, struggling, and they both toppled into the bath sending water up the walls. Afraid of the heat Ira hauled her out onto the floor, where he proceeded to perform an act which in any other circumstances would have been defined as rape, and perhaps even in these was not far from it.

The girl accepted him with fatalistic enthusiasm, but at the same time the other girl began drying him with a large towel.

Ira swatted her away. "Later!" he roared.

The girl let the towel fall over them and retreated to the door, where she stood guard, an act of decency for which Ira was grateful.

In the limited privacy of the towel Ira consumed his acquiescent Eurasian. He fell in love with her lips, with her gilded eyes, with the rippling run of muscle under her amber skin. She was anxious and the two girls often spoke to each other, then the girl in his arms responded to him with a frantic urgency which he suspected was intended to get him off her and back onto the massaging table. The effect was as she expected. Ira fell over her gasping; and before he could recover, each of them took an arm and hauled him up.

This time they worked on his front side, washing, massaging, oiling, rubbing. Then they wrapped him in towels and told him to rest.

Ira fell into an untroubled sleep filled with velvet shadows which passed through one another in waves. He sensed the smile on his lips and the relaxed elasticity of his body as his consciousness rose to the surface, then sank easily down again. On one of the rising moments he heard subdued voices and water splashing. This seemed to continue for a very long time, causing him at last to open his eyes, whereupon he saw Major Subo Ikachi seated at the edge of the bath with his legs in the steaming water.

Ira sat up and rubbed his eyes. "What time is it?" he asked.

"Something past midnight," Ikachi said. "Are you going in or out?"

"Out, I think."

"Don't you know?"

"Out," Ira said.

"Is the Captain with you?"

"No, I came with a friend."

Ikachi barked an order in Japanese and one of the bath girls appeared with sake and porcelain cups on a tray. She smiled toward Ira demurely and he recognized her as the girl he'd taken under the towel.

"Will you join me?" Ikachi asked. He swung his legs out of the water;

the girl wrapped a huge towel around him and he remained seated cross-legged on the floor.

Ira slid from the table and sat down across from Ikachi. The girl poured the sake, then at a signal from Ikachi she left them, pausing at the door for a final smile, which Ira found annoying.

"The girls here are very pleasant," Ikachi said.

Ira nodded.

"They are immaculate."

Ira smiled at the strange use of the word.

"They see mankind as it is," Ikachi continued, "predatory, brutalizing, vicious; they see this side more frequently than anything else and they neutralize it for a time with love, is that not so? Every man is neutral in a house of prostituiton; would you agree, Lieutenant?"

"I hadn't given it a thought."

"Yes, we're all neutralized by love and death," Ikachi said and he took a sip of his sake and smacked his lips with satisfaction. "You and I, you see, are both neutrals here."

"As far as that goes I'm neutral outside too, Major," Ira said. "The American position in Siberia is one of neutrality."

Ikachi waved his hand dismissingly. "American positions," he said, "are one thing, the facts of human intercourse another, eh? A man does not choose neutrality, Lieutenant, he is neutralized. America is neither impotent nor a eunuch and when it makes claims of being so its purpose is to slip unchallenged into the harem. Let's speak frankly to one another here."

"Personally my aim is to get home with a whole skin," Ira said. "There's nothing I want here."

"You've made one conquest already, I think."

Ira frowned. "If you call laying one of these whores a conquest, so have you."

"I call it a conquest," Ikachi said soberly. "I respect these women. They teach me a great deal about life. Their love is not meek; it absorbs and pacifies the most aggressive lusts. The worst men in Harbin consort here, thieves, murderers, the worst types in the world, but here they are harmless. Oh, that's not to say there haven't been fights, but always on the way in, never on the way out. This says something, I think." Ikachi poured himself another cup of sake and tossed it off. "Asia is a woman, Lieutenant; it is many women and we good allies are in the waiting room. We're a bit suspicious of each other, yes? We're all flexing and posturing to conceal our impatience and boasting of our powers. We drink a little too much maybe, and maybe there's a fight, but in the end Asia will pacify us all. We'll take our satisfactions and go away until the next time."

"National policy is a hard on, that it?"

"Exactly!" Ikachi said and he laughed uproariously. "We understand each other."

Ikachi's merriment was so infectious that presently Ira was laughing too. It was so preposterously true. "There are one hell of a lot of limp cocks in Europe this year," he said.

"They'll be back."

"And what about the Bolsheviks?" Ira asked.

Ikachi's manner changed abruptly. He scowled. "They aim to do away with the whole business," he said. "They're internationalists. They are the common enemy. Our only disagreement is how best to stop them."

Ikachi outlined the current tactical situation in European Russia in hopeful terms. The Reds were encircled, threatened on every side and sure to collapse; the only crucial point was how the victorious forces were going to share the benefits of that collapse. "This, my friend, is what our quarrel is about."

Ira listened politely, but he was bored and anxious to get back to the train. He wondered where MacDougal was. "Are you going back to the train, Major?" he asked.

"I'll be more comfortable here," Ikachi said. "So would you be. They'll wake us in time."

Ira shook his head. "No, I'll find my friend and go back," he said.

"Good night, then."

They rose together and shook hands. "The girl will show you the way," Ikachi said.

It was two a.m. when he rejoined MacDougal.

"I hear you performed carnal acts with the bath girls," MacDougal proclaimed. "Bad form, old man. They'll want a rise in wages."

"I suppose you've got pictures to prove that allegation."

"Yes, my son, they'll be off in the morning mail, captioned for the home front: 'Our brave boys doing their duty on the Asian front. Buy Liberty Bonds.' "

"That'll sell a bundle."

"Raise enlistments too. Your patriotism is to be commended."

When they reached the street a cab was waiting. MacDougal gave the driver directions and they were on their way to see the trio Duke had mentioned, three American Negroes who sang minstrel songs and tap-danced.

"How'd you like the place?" MacDougal asked.

"Fine."

"I had a Red Cross train through here last week headed for Omsk. Twenty nurses, seven doctors, two men from the War Trade Board and three American missionaries from Japan. They were wild about it."

"Come on, Duke."

"Really! I took the men there for dinner. Went in with twelve, came out with four. The missionaries were missing."

"Listen, Duke, I think I'd better get back to the company. I'll drop you off and you head the driver toward the station for me."

"All right," MacDougal said.

They rode along in silence with the growing awareness that they'd said all they could say to each other, that their spasm of comradeship was over, that they wouldn't write each other, meet after the war or marry each other's sisters. At best they'd share a memory of the farting horse.

"They do a job on you there," MacDougal said.

"Yes, they do."

"I'll be off at the corner then, Ira."

The cab stopped and MacDougal jumped out. He shook Ira's hand. Ira thanked him and offered to pay his share, but the Duke grinned and shook his head. "Keep your pecker up," he called, then he was gone in the darkness and the cab jogged on toward the station.

Ira smiled. He'd been done a job on. Yes, indeed. His boots were polished. His uniform had been spot-cleaned and pressed, the buttons and brass bars shined. He'd been gone over with a thoroughness of which he was not totally aware until the skirmish at Siding 85 when he discovered that the cartridges in his forty-five had also been burnished to a fine golden glow.

« 2 »

C Company had been billeted in a drafty warehouse next to the marshaling yard which smelled of coal, machine oil, sour rice and rats.

The men slept on cots in their clothes. Those who had taken off their boots slept less fitfully than those who had not, but they all tossed and groaned and some stood up and tramped around with their blankets over their shoulders.

Sergeant Austin was awake, smoking a cigar and making a box for a necklace of Chinese coins he'd bought for Maryenka from one of the hawkers who had besieged the place. Each coin had a square hole in the center and although the hawker had kept chanting "Gold, gold, gold!" Austin supposed it was bronze or brass. He'd mail it to Pashkova in the morning and hope Maryenka would get it. He saw Ira come in and walk down the rows of cots looking for a vacancy.

"Over here, Lieutenant," Austin said quietly.

Ira sat down on the next cot, which Carlisle had occupied until he decided to go out and look at the engine repair shops.

"Where's the Captain?" Ira asked.

"Out learning how to be a locomotive mechanic," Austin said.

"That for Maryenka?"

Austin nodded.

"It'll look nice on her, Harry."

Austin was surprised. Occasionally Baker, Klagle or Carlisle called him Harry, but he'd grown used to being addressed less familiarly as Austin. "I hope so," he said.

"Suits her better than those earrings I gave her."

"She likes them."

"Really?"

"Why not?"

Ira shrugged. "Too sophisticated, I thought."

Austin nodded and stared at the necklace. "I'll mail it to her in the morning. No great loss if she doesn't get it."

"What time do we leave?"

"Eight."

Austin put the necklace in the cardboard box, wrapped it in paper and tied it carefully with string. He took a pencil from his pocket, licked the tip, then began to address the package, but paused, scowling thoughtfully. "She was married before, did you know that?"

"No."

"Yes, to a man named Shulgin. Petra something Shulgin. I can't remember. He was a political exile, some kind of radical who'd had a very hard time."

Austin completed addressing the package and showed the neatly printed Cyrillic lettering to Ira. "She taught me to write that much at least," he said, then he put the package into his coat pocket. "It's odd," he continued, "I have a feeling of gratitude toward Shulgin and he's dead. I don't think

Maryenka would have married me if she hadn't been married to Shulgin before."

"Why do you say that?"

Austin put out his cigar. "Oh, a lot of things. A girl who's been married before has different feelings about men. Shulgin was good to her and he was an outcast himself. Having married him she was able to marry me, which took courage. A lot of Russian girls have been beaten and disowned for associating with American soldiers. You've heard these stories."

"Yes."

"In Khabarovsk the Cossacks nearly flayed two girls to death with ramrods because they'd been seen on the street with Americans."

Ira nodded. "How did her husband die?"

"Rheumatic heart," Austin said, then he smiled at Ira in a puzzled way. "I thought I'd be jealous of him, you know, that I'd think of them being together like man and wife, but I never have. Instead I've got this feeling of obligation and gratitude as though I owed it to Shulgin to be as good to Maryenka as he had been. And he's dead."

"He must have been a good man."

"He had to have been because Maryenka married him," Austin said.

Ira smiled. "You're a good man too, Harry."

"Hell, I didn't mean it that way."

"I know."

But Austin was thoughtful once more. He lay back on the cot and pulled his coat around him. "While I was with her I didn't notice how I felt toward Shulgin. She was there full of life and I didn't really think about anything else. Now that I'm away from her I think of him frequently and he's been dead four years. Isn't that a hell of a thing?"

"Will she be coming to Verkhne-Udinsk?"

Austin grinned. "As soon as I find a place she'll be on the first train."

"It'll be good to her," Ira said.

"This'll surprise you, but Carlisle said the same thing."

"Yeah, that surprises me."

"The Sioux is full of surprises," Austin said, then he cocked his hat over his eyes and prepared to go to sleep.

« 3 »

THE train repair shops at Harbin worked around the clock to keep ahead of breakdowns and failures on the line. There were seventeen big engines on the floor in various stages of reconstruction as Carlisle walked through the massive shop pausing at the pits to watch the men at their work.

Welders' torches snapped and flashed, driving shadows up the walls and leaving the tart stink of fused metal in the air. The welders pushing their dark goggles back to examine their work revealed Kirghiz, Mongol or Chinese eyes in two grease-free circles on their faces.

There were forges whose heat carried by gusts of air came as a blessing. Drop hammers and lathes crashed and howled and the men were dwarfed by their tools, huge wrenches, levers and hammers, all scaled to the hands of giants.

An electric crane capable of hoisting a locomotive while its drive wheels were removed dangled massive tentacles of chain from the roof. Replacement parts lay about, nuts the size of a man's head, bolts the thickness of an arm, gaskets, driving rods, all in the proportions of a larger world.

Carlisle climbed in and out of engine cabs, gathering information until he was certain he could start a locomotive and stop it. In one cab he found a shattered pressure gauge, spent machine gun bullets, and a sticky substance on the floor which was blood, not grease.

Three of the engines had come under heavy-caliber machine-gun fire and were stripped down. Their exposed pipes were like atrophied intestines which surgeons with goggles and torches were patching deftly or cutting out.

This identification of the engines with living matter was natural to Carlisle; they were iron horses and as such elicited his affection. The workers attending them seemed to feel this too; their faces illuminated by the glare of forge and torch were intent and tender. There was no finicky small work to be done. It was all large, requiring the whole strength of a man.

Carlisle stopped at the round table and looked down into the pit wanting to lay his muscle to the work. The hot smells, the noise, the flame, the huge tools and big parts appealed to him. It was a man's place. There were no finger workers here, no pianists or watchmakers, no painters or poets, no fops, gallants or phrasemakers, no women.

The parts fitted together. Each had a function, an integrity, a beauty of its own, and when assembled they were a locomotive.

No woman had designed it or could appreciate it. No woman could see that from these pits, these fires, this painful noise there emerged a kind of life.

"— sensitive about your aboriginal background?"

Carlisle snorted contemptuously. The Jap had seen him with Tatiana. That one stupid indiscretion was destined, it seemed, to dog every step of his way. He had to kill it.

Her invitation was still in his pocket and still possessed of a power which stopped him from throwing it away.

Wakan.

Carlisle frowned and standing in the center of all that creative fire and noise he remembered the old fools of the tribe who had tried to impress the youngsters with their tricks; who walked on heated rocks and chanted dreams. Wakan.

Old medicine men with gray blind eyes calling for the past and fondling their magic bags. Wakan.

They would say there was magic in her note. Stupidity! Rattling, shield-shaking stupidity!

But why not take it now and drop it in the pit? Throw it in a blazing forge?

There were no women here.

The great crane whined as it passed overhead and Carlisle didn't move to take the note. His arms were heavy. He was tired. He walked back to the warehouse needing to sleep.

Wakan. Wakan! Old fools shuffling their feet on ceremonial floors. Dying.

In their taut brown guts they believed it all, but he believed none of it.

He was not superstitious. There was nothing supernatural about a locomotive, about steel and rails, ties, embankments, riveting hammers and fuel. Nothing.

When he wanted to destroy her note he would. But he would not be spooked into it.

What he needed was sleep.

CHAPTER TEN

THE train of fourteen cars crossed the Sungari River bridge on the next stage of its journey, five hundred and eighty miles west to Manchuria Station. Ira spent much of the time recording his impressions in a rambling letter to be mailed home when they reached Verkhne-Udinsk. He'd write a page or a paragraph and put it aside and sometimes he'd stare out the window at the frozen grass on the uninhabited plain and his thoughts, trailing back along the length of the train, grew diffuse and were lost like smoke from the engine. Occasionally he'd start and look around, wondering what he had been thinking about; then, having once more established contact with reality, with the train and the men around him, he would fall again into a smoky reverie.

They passed through Duitsinshan, Anda and Tsitsihar, the capital of Manchuria Province, and their thoughts trailed off. Clouds of them, and Ira smiled content in this company of train-bound dreamers.

To pass the time some of the men played poker. Sergeant Austin, Sergeant Baker, Sergeant Klagle and the other N.C.O.'s had a high stakes game the men often gathered to watch. In the evening Corporal Blodgett would bring out his banjo and a group would sing until Carlisle told them to pipe down.

They passed Barim, Bukhedu, Khingan, Yakeshi, Chzharomte, basaltic cliffs, stunted timber, up the valley of the frozen Yal River, through the pass in the Khingan Mountains, into a tunnel two miles long protected by Chinese troops in quilted uniforms, through rolling country, cattle country, Montana and Dakota country, the kind of country in which Carlisle had been born and spent his youth.

And this caught him, held his eye, made him remember and he blamed Ikachi for having planted the idea.

He wouldn't have made the comparison himself. Consciously, no, he would not have made it, but having been made it was inescapable.

Countless times each day the windows of the train flashed scenes which reminded Carlisle of reservation life. Wasteland. Isolated yurts. A figure on horseback bowed against the bite of the wind. Muffled children at small stations staring longingly at the train which represented a larger world. Dirty-faced, ruddy-complexioned kids living in Indian poverty on Indian ground, clinging to their ignorance, which was their only defense against desperation. Better not to know anything better exists than to know it and not have it. Yes, better, perhaps.

But the trains come, each one an assault on the defenses of ignorance, and by the time Carlisle was ten he knew he was especially poor and ignorant and ugly and dirty and that everyone of any consequence had made his way to heaven on earth by a route he would never discover.

Beg with your eyes, not your hands. Beseech but don't grovel. Pitch coins against the station wall. Fight like hell when you're crossed. Steal a little.

The boys drink when they can; the girls fuck when they're able and they all die young.

Carlisle got out on his mother's shoulders and hated her for it and hated himself for hating her. This old agony was deep, and because Ikachi had brought it up he hated Ikachi too.

The train stopped at every station to take on fuel and water. The men jumped out to stretch their legs, buy what they could and mail letters on the improbable chance of their reaching their destination with curious postmarks. The passengers in the third class cars ran to the tap which supplied hot water for their samovars and bought food from wizened Chinese peasant women — roast fowls and root vegetables from the winter cellars.

Carlisle watched the children and once he gave them money, feeling that his very presence betrayed them. And once he saw Major Ikachi observing him from the far end of the platform and he turned away abruptly.

Sensitive about your aboriginal background?

All Indian roots are here in central Asia.

And it was true, god damn it! It was true in the children's eyes, true in their hair, true in the snot on their faces.

Carlisle recognized kids on the platforms with whom he'd spent long, cold afternoons as a boy staring listlessly at the dirty station floor, trying to achieve the imaginative leap which would give them all something to do until the next train came.

And the kids recognized him as one of their people. They came to him and stood around speechless, marveling that one of their own could have risen so high. They whispered about him to each other. They scurried off and brought others to see him.

"You sure as hell have a way with kids, Captain," Leverett said to him once.

Carlisle nodded and tramped around trying to avoid their eyes. But they knew; those dark-eyed, ruddy-faced kids knew his blood and he wondered if one in ten thousand of them had a mother who would drum into them they were better than everyone else because their daddy had died a sergeant in the Army. A white sergeant, let's not forget that. Not one in ten thousand of these kids had a white sergeant daddy. Not yet anyway. Come back in ten years and he might run into himself on one of these platforms.

At Khailar, nearly a thousand miles from Vladivostok, Carlisle saw a town so like his own that he couldn't leave the train.

"You coming?" Leverett asked.

"No, you go on."

He sat alone with his back to the window, a fugitive from his youth.

In such a place his mother was buried. Mud walls, patchwork shanties, a wagon trail, thin sandy soil and sheep. It was the sheep at Khailar which brought his mother up to him out of her grave on that barren Montana hillside. She kept sheep and sent him the wool money. The only time she wrote was after shearing, and the only time he wrote was to say he received her letter and to send the money back.

DEAR CORPORAL JACK CARLISLE, U.S.A.,

The wool been in plenty this season. Held flock to one hundred with increase at lambing and sickness to account. Grass thin and water down, but on shares with C and X range doing fine. This extra cash on postal money order G 309657 to see your way ahead in the Army as your father would want.

write to me.

ALICE BUCKEYE CARLISLE

It wasn't extra money, it was all she had and it broke his heart when she sent it to him. To send the money back he had to make out a new money order in her name and he knew without being told that she showed these money orders to everyone on the reservation as evidence of his love. "Corporal Jack has sent me another money order. Well, he has no use for money. He puts it in my hand. This comes all the way from someplace — Cuba, it says there, I think. Well, that's a good way south of Mexico, they say. He's a fool with his money."

And those who knew the current price of a fleece and the size of Alice Buckeye's flock would nod and keep silent. Corporal Jack was a generous son.

She took his letters to the grave and there wasn't a word of affection in them. Not one.

And now he couldn't look out the window at Khailar because he knew his mother would be there. He clenched his fists and cursed his goddamned redskin superstition, but he was quivering and he felt his mother's eyes on his neck and knew she was framed in the window imploring him to turn around.

Leverett came down the corridor and stopped in the doorway. "You all right, Captain?" he asked.

Carlisle nodded.

"You're white as a sheet."

"Keep your god-damned mouth shut!"

Stunned, Leverett backed out of the compartment and closed the sliding door.

When the train began to move Carlisle shuddered as though he was being torn apart by horses. He stood up, breathing heavily, perspiration pouring down his face. He was all right. Sure. Sure.

But part of him remained forever at Khailar.

« 2 »

It was ten degrees below zero at Manchuria Station, but the air was so still one hardly noticed the cold. The ground was hard as concrete underfoot and ice had to be chipped from the pipes of the fortified water tower before the engine could take on a fresh supply for the boiler. A caravan of huge two-wheeled carts pulled by camels and laden with sacks of meal met the train. Chinese and Russian customs officials poked wire probes into the sacks before allowing them to be loaded and the caravan drivers remonstrated so shrilly that everyone was certain there was contraband hidden in the sacks. None was discovered.

The caravan drivers looked as savage and snappish as their camels; they stared at the American soldiers and conjectured about them openly and were not in the least intimidated. Sergeant Austin thought they looked like bandits and Ira agreed. The drivers had a way of leering which made him distinctly uncomfortable though he supposed it was their way of showing friendliness.

He returned to the train and twenty minutes later they crossed the Manchurian border into Russia. Ira recorded this fact in his letter to Ruth, then went back to studying a report made by the Railway Commission which Carlisle had given him by way of apology for his outburst at Khailar.

"Here, Leverett," he'd said, "read this. Sorry I blew up back there, but I thought my mother was in the window." He dropped the report in Ira's lap and left the compartment.

Carlisle's apology was more unsettling than the outburst which occasioned it. Since their interview with Ikachi, Ira had begun to notice the striking similarities between the Sioux and some of the people at the stations along the way but he hadn't realized how deeply this affected Carlisle. Heretofore Ira had thought of the Sioux as rock solid, unimaginative and entirely self-possessed. He had come to rely on Carlisle's stability, but now he was no longer sure of it.

He read on through the report: "The railroad in general shows signs of having been hastily built and the ballast of sand is insufficient to maintain good track alignment. This produces bad conditions of spreading or sagging particularly in the marshes and swamps of frozen muck or *fossil frost*. The earth to a depth of fifteen feet is a mixture of black silt and ice and when the ground cover is removed the sun frequently melts the ice, causing the earth to flow like pitch in a slow, glacier action."

Ira gazed out of the window and fell under the spell of the vast, memory-smearing Siberian expanse. They'd come more than a thousand miles from Vladivostok and he had begun to sense the glacier action in himself and in the subsurface character of the men around him. Ira was wondering if he had a sufficient ballast of sand to maintain good alignment when he was jolted forward out of his seat. He heard the hot screel of wheels on the rails and a popping sound. The train came to a buffeting stop, throwing him to his knees.

Sergeant Austin burst into the compartment. "Where's the Sioux?" he yelled.

Ira started to get up, but Austin dropped on him. The window shattered and pieces of glass fell over them.

"Come on, we've got some action!" Austin said and he scuttled out of the compartment and ran down the corridor crouched low.

Ira was still on his hands and knees, bewildered, cold. He wondered who in hell had broken the window. He raised his head and saw several figures on horseback ride by. He ducked. They had guns and were firing down the whole length of the train.

Even then it took Ira a moment to realize that the train had come under attack.

"Christ!" he moaned and he cut his hand on the glass as he scurried about trying to remember where he'd put his automatic.

His legs and arms were weak. He seemed incapable of moving except in slow motion. Everything was slow except his heart, which was threatening to shake loose in his ribs. He was shaking all over.

He found his forty-five and pulled the clip to see if it was loaded. The bullets had been polished! This struck him as wildly funny. He stood up, laughing, and ran out to find someone to show the polished bullets to.

He got to the door and jumped to the ground. There was gunfire everywhere and he saw a group of riders round the tail of the train and gallop toward him. He ducked under the train and crawled over the tracks to the other side.

C Company was sprawled along the embankment firing in both directions. The first person who caught Ira's attention was Major Ikachi, who was walking calmly toward a band of galloping men. In one hand he held his naked saber, flashing in the pale sunlight; in the other he had a huge automatic pistol which he raised, aimed and fired with incredible style.

The charging riders split around Ikachi, hiding him a moment, then passed on to reveal him again sighting along the straight of his arm and firing evenly spaced shots at the bandits with the calm detachment of a man on a pistol range.

There was a scream. Ira trotted along the embankment toward the sound. Private Saunders had been hit in the neck. Carlisle was there trying to hold the wound closed, blood welling up around his hands. Private Carson had also been hit and was trying to rise, cursing the Greasers, but his leg was broken and he kept falling over.

Ira saw Austin running toward him.

Ikachi was coming back. There was blood on his saber and a terrible splotch on his hip; he staggered, steadied himself with his saber and came on. Ira started out to help Ikachi, but Austin said something as he passed. "What?" Ira asked.

"They're coming around again!"

Ira saw the hunghutze and they struck him as picturesque. They rode bent low over their scrub Siberian ponies, strung out in a line like a frieze against the plain. One or two of them had round shields and sabers. Ira thought of the Mongol hordes. He was curious and his sense of danger had vanished. He heard the rifle fire. He saw Ikachi stop, brace himself with his saber and fire his automatic again. One of the hunghutze split off to attack Ikachi. Ira saw the upraised sword. Ikachi turned very slowly, it seemed, and fired again. The bandit's turbaned head flopped forward as though he had been struck from behind. He clutched his throat, veered away and fell backward on the rump of his horse, which galloped off dragging what appeared to be a bundle of loosely tied rags.

"They're taking off!" Austin yelled.

Ira looked toward Austin, who'd jumped up on the step of the train. Ira thought he was going inside, but Austin turned to watch the hunghutze ride away. There was a distant, lazy report. The expression on Austin's face went blank and a black smudge appeared over his right eye as though a blob of soot had fallen from the roof of the car. He made a gesture to brush this away, then he fell straight forward down the embankment and lay there, shuddering, face down.

Ira ran to Austin thinking to hold him still as one would do if a man were having an epileptic seizure, but he still had his forty-five in one hand and the clip of polished bullets in the other and blood from the cut on his hand had run over the clip. As he wiped this off, Ikachi hobbled to him. The Major glanced at the clip and there was a golden flash of comprehension in his almond eyes.

Ira jammed the bloody clip into his forty-five as though he were reloading it and Ikachi sat down against the cindered embankment with a low groan.

Ira saw Sergeant Baker kneeling beside Austin. "He's dead!"

Carlisle ran up and rolled Austin over, revealing the dark hole above his right eye. He glanced up at Ira. "Take some men and clear that barricade off the track."

"Yes, sir!"

Ira trotted forward with Sergeant Klagle and several men. It took them twenty minutes to clear the track. The train crew went forward to inspect the rails. Two had been loosened and the crew anchored them again with spiking mauls.

When he got back Carlisle and Baker had dressed Major Ikachi's hip wound and were about to lift him into the train.

"Give a hand here, Leverett," Carlisle barked. "This may hurt a bit, Major."

Ikachi's face was drawn and he still held his pistol in one hand. He gestured with it to indicate he didn't mind the pain.

"You're one hell of a god-damned soldier, Major," Carlisle said gruffly.

Ikachi smiled. "That much we have in common, Captain," he said.

They lifted Ikachi gently and maneuvered him up the stairs and down the corridor to his compartment where the berth was ready. As they laid him down the train began to move toward the next stop, at Dauria.

"What about Austin?" Ira asked.

"He's dead," Carlisle said. "Saunders is dead. And we've got five casualties."

"He mailed her a necklace from Harbin."

"What?"

"Harry. He bought his wife a necklace."

"That's too bad," Carlisle said. "See if any passengers were wounded and report to me."

"Yes, sir."

"Leverett?"

"Yes?"

"You'd better learn to step into Austin's shoes fast."

"I'll try."

Carlisle bobbed his head. "Now that he's gone you can't fake it anymore." Then he left, moving heavily against the sway of the train.

When Ira returned to the compartment where Austin had saved his life the cold air streaming through the shattered window stung his eyes. He stared at the blurred, fast-darkening plain and swallowed in gasps. "I'm not a coward," he whispered. "It was all too unreal." But the words torn from his lips by the wind seemed unreal and the unfired forty-five in his pocket was very real indeed.

CHAPTER ELEVEN

THE village of Pashkova, muffled in two inches of new snow, was perfectly quiet as dawn came. The single broad street running between the forty huts with their outbuildings was softened by snow so virginal that not even the village dogs had broken its surface. It absorbed the morning light and gave back a rose glow which gradually drove the shadows along the eastern eaves until they were hardly visible.

Over each habitation there was a transparent column of smoke rising from the huge stoves around which the villagers still slept, enjoying most of all these morning hours of enforced winter idleness. Then, as the consciousness of the day came, they slept defensively against its boredom, thinking perhaps of the spring work ahead and of the summer harvest. They longed to hibernate, but at last the women stirred. They left their warm places, feeling abused for having to be the first to rise and self-righteous for having done so. Without their rising nothing would be done and the day could not begin. They slipped on their footgear and looked through the frosted outer windowpanes at the fresh landscape beyond. Those whose men, in hiding from the levy officers, had come in to spend the night thought of the trails the men would leave as they returned to the hills and wondered if this would keep them over another night or maybe two. If so the snow was welcome; if not, it meant fresh trails to hide.

A few women stepped out into their yards for wood or water or to make their morning visits to the privy. Still dazed with sleep, they didn't speak to one another, but moved slowly, bundled against the chill morning air, taking comfort, however, in the figures moving about in other yards, other women similarly martyred while their husbands, lovers and brothers lay sloths abed. Coming back from their tasks they paused, however, to pass a morning greeting and to examine the white landscape.

The aspen and birch trees along the distant railroad bed were bushed out with snow which fell in puffs when the wind stirred the topmost branches. The women always looked this way, toward the railroad. It seemed natural to do so even though the scenic aspect lay the other direction toward the Little Khingan Mountains. So now they saw the riders come through the screening trees, fifty of them riding abreast, followed by another fifty several horse lengths behind. They rode toward the village at a slow trot, the hoofs of their horses popping through the snow raising a white wave which preceded their coming.

The women of the village, five of them in all, stood very still. None was willing to believe her own senses and each was afraid to look at her neighbor and find in her the corroboration of what they were seeing.

Having come so recently from sleep, they wished it to continue, for what they were seeing had often come to them as a terrible dream and now they were waiting for it to vanish, waiting to wake up, trying desperately to convince themselves they were still in that half-world where illusions played havoc with reality.

But the double line of Cossacks swept through the ruffling snow like a black scythe and while they were still three miles away the women heard their jingling gear and the creak of saddle leather. Only then did they realize what they had long feared was coming to pass, that for their sins had come the day of retribution.

They looked into one another's eyes and what they saw was even more terrifying than the Cossacks across the fields of snow. They each saw that the others were prepared to save themselves and their families by siding with the Cossack force. Those with men in the hills would point to those whose men were home and all of them would sacrifice the Jews. The undeniable presence of death robbed them of compassion and mercy.

Dunia Petrovna dropped the load of wood in her arms and ran inside to rouse Maryenka, Sasha and Abram Afimovitch. Her action sent the others scurrying and presently the whole village was filled with the sound of wailing women, weeping children, and men roaring to find what the excitement was about.

Several men rushed into the street, still pulling their trousers on.

Seeing the Cossacks now only two miles away they were staggered by the hopelessness of their situation. Some turned and ran barefooted toward the mountains yelling for their families to come, their only thought being to postpone the inevitable time when the Cossacks would be in their midst.

Others fell to their knees and began to pray. There were fewer than twenty able-bodied men in the village and of these only four had the presence of mind to formulate a plan. Among these four were Abram Afimovitch.

They stood together in the street watching the Cossacks. They had come to punish the village for failing to send its quota of recruits to join the Kolchak army. No doubt that is why they had come. The levy officers must have reported the villagers' resistance.

But until they arrived and bared their swords, until they actually began their bloody work, one could hope. But for what? One could only hope that some of the inhabitants of Pashkova would be spared. No doubt there was a bronevik concealed by the embankment near the Amur River. Its guns would be as indiscriminate as Cossack sabers.

"We must go meet them," Abram Afimovitch said quietly.

"Yes," agreed another man, still buttoning himself into his coat with sure-moving, unhurried fingers. "We must find what they're about."

This reference to the possibility that there could be any question of what they were about gave all four men courage and they set off down the road toward the Cossacks.

Dunia, Maryenka and Sasha came outside just as the four men started away. Dunia called to her husband, her voice high and wavering in the cold air, but he didn't look back. Sasha started to run after his father, but Maryenka caught him. He struggled briefly and she cuffed his face. "Come, we must find a place to hide."

Sasha looked around wondering how in all that untouched snow they could hide. He had trailed snow hares too often not to know how clearly marked their paths would be.

By now the villagers who had dared to hide their horses from the animal draft, not more than six in all, were trying to decide how they should be used. Women with infants refused to leave their other children behind; men torn by fear and by anger at having to make a choice raged at their families, bellowing senselessly while the horses stood by unmounted. Others tried to harness their beasts to sleighs, knowing even as they worked how senseless it was.

Maryenka decided to run to the river rather than toward the mountains which the mass of villagers had chosen. She pulled Sasha along, cutting obliquely in the direction of the Cossack flank hoping that when they began their charge it would carry them by and that she and Sasha and Dunia would be overlooked in the ensuing melee. She was congratulating herself on this decision when she saw that others had made a similar one and that small groups were scattering out of the village in all directions, running grotesquely through the light snow which showed them up like shadow figures against a sheet.

She and Sasha reached a shallow, snow-drifted ravine which hid them momentarily and the temptation was to burrow into the snow or to follow its course, but Maryenka knew it led toward the Cossack center and she pulled Sasha after her up the bank.

"But Mama's gone," he cried. "Mama's gone!"

Maryenka struggled to hold him and saw her mother running heavily toward the four men who had gone to meet the Cossacks. "Come, Sasha," she said.

"You don't care!" Sasha cried in horror and he wrenched his hand out of Maryenka's grasp. "You don't care," he screamed again and plunged back into the ravine before she could stop him.

Maryenka screamed his name and stood rooted to the spot, for in the distance she saw her father step forward and raise his hand. She couldn't hear his words, but knew in her heart that he had begun his usual greeting: "Ah, good brothers — "

From her position on the flank Maryenka could see both files distinctly. The Cossacks pulled their swords in a single whispered sigh and the pace of a hundred horses changed to a canter. The first rank of the scythe passed over her father leaving him on his knees. He rose clutching his head just as the second rank rode him down, sabers flashing.

A yell rose from the Cossacks as they spread out to envelop the people attempting to flee. Maryenka's mother was surrounded by four riders whose horses reared. Sabers flashed down like threshing flails and came up dripping.

Maryenka found herself running across the clean snow, expecting at any moment to hear hoofbeats behind her.

In the panic of her flight she lost all sense of physical being; she could only feel the weight of the sword and hear the slashing sound of it through the air, followed by the abrupt cessation as it swept into her flesh. She expected annihilation and after running nearly a mile she began to curse death for not having come.

She fell in a heap gasping for breath, her body contracted against the swift fall of the sword, and when again it didn't come she opened her eyes and found herself near a grove of trees. Afraid to rise she furrowed through the snow and lay in a hollow among the tree trunks.

They were killing her family! Now! Somewhere! This instant Sasha was dying. Her mother lay gasping. Her father. Oh, God! She moaned, biting mouthfuls of snow, feeling the saber cuts in her body and unable to die. Oh, God, come quick, but she could not die. They had all gone off and left her. She dug into the snow, scraping her face on the frozen earth, eating it, gasping. They had abandoned her and death was late in coming.

Golden circles with square holes. Windows to see through. Little frames dangling in the air, each with a picture in it. She saw the necklace with Austin's bloody face in all the windows and to stop herself from screaming aloud for deliverance she jammed her fingers into her mouth and bit them until the taste of blood came and vanished.

Gradually reality began to assert itself.

Maryenka raised her face from the snow and looked toward the village. One of the houses was on fire, raising a cloud of filthy smoke. The Cossacks were rallying around the fringes of the village, driving people toward it with the flats of their swords. Here and there the snow was marked with a dark bundle, the body of someone who had failed to escape the initial charge.

Maryenka was shaking terribly. She looked around the grove of trees, so remarkably silent that for a moment she was lulled into the belief that nothing had happened. She saw the tracks of some small animal in the powdery snow — a squirrel, she thought — and she wondered about its state of mind, wondered if her arrival in the grove had made it dash for refuge in one of the trees. She felt a sympathy for it which she longed to express. Poor, small, terrified creature. She wanted to hold it, to caress and comfort it.

Above her the branches of the trees shed their snow, which drifted down retaining a fan shape which collapsed when it touched the ground. The air was bright and so clear that it gave a feeling of suspended animation. In her mouth was the taste of blood and earth.

Maryenka looked once more toward the village. The slaughter continued. Another house was in flames and now the Cossacks had broken into patrols following those trails in the snow which did not stop at a sprawled body. Three riders were coming toward the ravine where she had lost Sasha.

Maryenka crawled through the grove on her hands and knees, but once beyond it she rose again and ran. If she could reach the river perhaps there was a chance. Perhaps they wouldn't follow. Perhaps there was bare ground somewhere along the river where they would lose her tracks, perhaps there was a break in the ice into which she could throw herself.

The golden circles from Harbin danced on the surface of her eyes. There was hope still, yes hope. There was a place. To live. There was one. For whom to live. In all the death. From Harbin. Still. Even yet. In all the horror. There was.

Half blinded by desperation Maryenka ran on. Stumbling through the glistening snow, she reached the railway embankment and plunged into the drift at the crest which dropped abruptly to the tracks below. At the top she lost her footing and fell, sliding down the slick face of the cut to the right of way, where she lay stunned, trying to catch her breath.

Her heart was racing and she couldn't see. She sat up, wiped her eyes on the sleeve of her coat and looked around to get her bearings. Down the track she saw an armored gun car, an ugly black turret with its gun pointed her way. The rest of the train was lost around the curve. Shocked to find the train so close, she couldn't move; the cannon seemed to be centered on her breast and she was certain it would move with her if she got up.

"Here's one flown our way."

Maryenka spun around and saw three men coming toward her along the tracks. She shrank against the embankment as they stopped in front of her. The youngest of the three, blond with a wispy mustache and wearing a sailor cap, dropped on his haunches. "Don't be frightened, little one," he said, smiling sweetly.

Maryenka looked across him at the other two. They were Cossacks, but unarmed. One had a terrible face, beardless, with a purple birthmark covering half his head. The other was huge, but old, with a steel-gray beard stained yellow with tobacco around his lips.

The blond reached out to touch her cheek and Maryenka struck his hand aside. "We're the gun crew," he said with a touch of hurt pride in his voice as though she should have known.

"Let me go, please."

"But there's no place to go," he said. "We'll look after you. Me and Rodion and Daddy Samson. Won't we look after her?"

Rodion, the man with the splotch on his face, grinned and the splotch shifted back on his head, turning purple.

Maryenka tried to rise, but the blond put his hand on her shoulder, pushing her down. "If you scream the whole train crew and all the troopers will be on to what we have here. If you run they'll find you soon enough and there'll be no saving you. In the troop cars they use girls up in a day. A hundred men, you see, all drunk. And they just throw what's left of you out the door into the snow."

"Kill me, then," Maryenka whispered.

"I have no wish to do so," the blond said. "You'd better come along before it's too late."

"Where?"

"To our gun car. It's comfortable there. We have some privacy."

Maryenka sprang up, but before she had taken two steps Rodion struck her and she fell on the ties between the tracks. They seized her and as Rodion and Daddy Samson carried her the blond bound a gag tightly over her mouth. "Until she learns it's for her own good," he said.

"Hurry, before the bastards take her away from us," Rodion growled.

Maryenka tried to remain unconscious. The instant she was aware of returning consciousness she willed herself into the blackness again. She had heard it was possible to kill oneself by willpower and she tried with all her heart to do so, but the horror of her experience pressed in around her. She saw her father cut down; she wondered what had happened to her mother and her brother. She began to weep, choking around the gag in her mouth.

Someone slapped her several times and looking up she saw the three men of the gun crew hovering over her. "Not so loud, sweetheart," the blond one said. "The Cossacks are coming back and they'll hear you. Then it'll be over. Wait until the train starts. Wait, wait a little."

They were holding her inside the gun turret. In the dim light through the observation slits she saw the gun itself, the iron racks for shells and the wheels for turning the turret. Outside she heard shouts and laughter and the hoofs of many horses on the roadbed. A hard-palmed hand squeezed her thigh and she tried to scream, but the gag prevented her.

"You wait a little too, Rodion," the blond said.

Maryenka struggled, but one of them threw a blanket over her head, suffocating her, and she lost consciousness.

When she came to herself again the train was in motion. She heard the grating rumble of the wheels beneath her and it was dark. She moved and found her clothing and boots were gone and that she had been wrapped in blankets and securely bound. She squirmed trying to free her hands to get at the gag in her mouth. She rolled over and sat up, bashing her head against some protruding object. The pain made her sick and she thought she was going to vomit into the gag and choke to death. She sat very still waiting for the sickness to pass, trying to assess her situation.

She thought of Austin. His face seemed to hover in the darkness before her. She remembered the comforting bulk of his body and the deep compassionate tones of his voice. "Hell, I've seen so much nothing surprises me anymore. Some of the worst people are the best. It's not what happens to people, most of which is pretty awful, but what they do that matters and why they do it. You're the first and only good thing ever happened to me. I've been dead all this time and didn't know it and if you leave me, Maryenka, I'll be dead again."

Her only reason to continue living was Austin. If she could reach him nothing else mattered.

Sometime later a hatch was opened and the old man, Daddy Samson, slid through carrying a lantern in one hand and balancing a bowl of hot soup in the other. Rodion and the blond one looked in at her, grinning and nodding vigorously. "She's wide awake, Daddy," the blond said, then he closed the hatch and fastened it from outside.

Daddy Samson hung the lantern on the breech lock of the cannon and looked down at her. "Soup," he said, "but you mustn't cry out. There's only one car between us and the first troop van. They'd make us suffer too, if they knew you were here."

A kindly tone in the old man's voice gave Maryenka hope that the gunners were seriously interested in her welfare. She watched Daddy Samson closely as he squatted on his haunches in front of her. His flat gray eyes under bushy brows were filled with innocent concern. He looked like many of the village uncles Maryenka had seen plodding about, mumbling to themselves or dozing by their fences in the sun. "You won't cry out?" he asked.

Maryenka shook her head.

Daddy Samson set the bowl of soup on the floor carefully, then he undid the knot which bound the gag in Maryenka's mouth and she spat it out. "Careful now, it's hot," he said and he held the bowl to her lips and tipped it.

Maryenka spluttered as the soup filled her mouth and spilled over her chin. It was hot and there was too much.

"Better do it yourself then," Daddy Samson said and setting the soup aside he untied the cords which held the blankets around her.

Maryenka caught a crackle of amusement in the old man's eyes as she clutched the blanket before it fell away. "You must feed yourself, you know. I have two daughters your age, Anna and Katya, both married now and one with a daughter of her own the last I heard. They live off the beaten track, praise be, in a little village up the Khilok River, but their men are away and who knows if they'll be coming back. They're living together now, I think, with a good house against the weather, keeping out of mischief. They're big, healthy girls able to work and manage and I've warned them often enough to stay out of the way, not to come into the towns or to the stations, to stay away from the tracks. You can see the reason for that."

Encouraged by the gentleness of Daddy Samson's voice Maryenka reached for the bowl of soup and the mere fact of doing something made her feel more at ease. The soup was warm and good and she was grateful for it. "Who's the other one?" she asked presently. "The one with the yellow hair."

The old man sat down with his back against the gun stanchion. "Glubov? — he's not so bad. He's our gun captain, does the aiming you see, while I load and pull the lanyard. Rodion puts the shells through the hatch from the ammunition compartment. Glubov can be handled if you don't anger him. Yes, he can. But you must be careful. He's romantic, all sorts of nonsense in his head, and he reads books and sometimes he's honored to play chess with Sipialef, Colonel Sipialef, our train commander. You'd never want to meet him. He'd make a spectacle with the likes of you. The kind no one would talk about after. No, not even the men in the troop cars would talk about it. Not even the worst of the lot."

Daddy Samson shook his head woefully and licked the stained hairs of his mustache.

"Where are we going?"

"To Chita first and then to Verkhne-Udinsk, I think."

Maryenka's heart jumped at the mention of Verkhne-Udinsk. She tried to keep her hand from trembling, but the old man wasn't watching her.

"It's up to the Colonel. He's out to annoy Ataman Semenoff, you see."

Maryenka shook her head, mystified, and Daddy Samson nodded, smiling sadly.

"They're at each other's throats all the time. Semenoff has an armored train called the Destroyer, armor a half inch thick backed by eighteen inches of concrete, ten machine guns, two one-pounders and two three-inch guns in turrets like this one. It has a reputation, the Destroyer has, greater even than the Invincible, some say. That's this train, the Invincible. Of course they don't say so where Colonel Sipialef could hear them say it. No, they don't."

Maryenka's hands trembled so violently that she had to put the soup bowl down. "Why," she whispered brokenly, "why did you attack Pashkova?"

Daddy Samson frowned. "Not me, darling," he said. "Sipialef. I just do my duty."

"But why?"

"To annoy Semenoff, you see. To show him that the Invincible can go anywhere. Semenoff has been making raids down the Selenga Valley, he's extended his power to Makaveyevo, Adrianovka, Borzya, all too far east of Chita to suit Sipialef's taste, so he comes west, you see, and makes these raids to give Semenoff something to think about. They're in a contest, you see, and Sipialef doesn't like Semenoff running his trains into the area around Verkhne-Udinsk."

Maryenka's eyes filled with tears and she saw the sabers flashing not in retribution, not to punish the village for its resistance to the demands of the levy officers for men and animals, but for this utterly senseless thing. Sasha dead. Her mother dead. Her father dead. Her neighbors all dead, or worse, because two men were contesting for power. It robbed them of all dignity. They were nothing, less even than pawns. Nothing.

She'd left her Chinese necklace hanging in the window where she could see it at night sifting the moonlight and framing the stars. It made her feel close to Austin.

No doubt some Cossack in the cars ahead had it now. She saw it clearly in his sword-calloused hand preceding her by several cars to Verkhne-Udinsk. If she lived to reach that place Austin too would be there.

How must she live to reach that place and what would she be? Maryenka brushed the tears from her eyes with a corner of the blanket. Useless tears. Useless as death. Death wasn't a protest; it was pointless. Pointless. Pointless.

Daddy Samson was watching her with a tender light in his gray eyes. "Are you warm now, dear?" he asked.

Maryenka nodded. "Thank you," she said.

"You've hurt your head, I see. Here, let me have a look." Daddy Samson pitched forward on his hands and knees and stared at the bump on Maryenka's head intently. His posture was so awkward and he took such a long time, doing nothing, that Maryenka turned her head and found a different, unmistakable hue in the old man's eyes. "Let me just kiss it, dear," he said.

Maryenka drew away, but the old man lunged and fell over her, bearing her down. He covered her mouth with one big hand. "Don't cry out," he warned. "We'll look after you."

Maryenka tried to bite, but her teeth found no hold on the hard palm pressing her head to the floor. She struggled under Daddy Samson's weight and he grew stern, lecturing her as though she were a naughty child. "Here, now! Have I come at you with whips or knives; have I beaten you? Here! Think where you are! If my own girls had been taken as you were I could only pray they would fall in with such good lads as you have. We'll keep a whole skin on your body if you behave. Otherwise we'll have our way all at once, then throw you forward to the Cossacks. A hundred of them, my dear, instead of three."

Maryenka lay still and after a moment the old man drew his hand away and gazed down, smiling into her eyes.

"You'll kill me after all," she said.

"No, no. We don't have the chances the others do, so we're not so wasteful, dear. We need a woman of our own and we'll look after you."

In her helplessness Maryenka didn't know what to do. She was certain of the horrors which lay in wait for her in the cars ahead and she knew what was expected of her where she was. Of two evils she chose the lesser one. What could she save by killing herself? Why did she feel this was the thing to do? It was defiant and self-respecting. It was proud. But was she of no use to anyone? Was all her life meaningless? One could suffer and stay alive or one could die. But who was left to care?

Maryenka didn't know. She was too exhausted and terrified to think. She rolled her head from side to side, gasping for breath, trying not to make any noise while the tears spilled from her eyes.

Daddy Samson, clucking tenderly, fussed about. "You're a good strong girl," he said. "Hush, hush. We're all clean, I vouch for that. Hush now."

As he drew the blanket away, Maryenka gasped brokenly and clenched her eyes shut, fixing her mind on the golden bangles of her Chinese necklace which had come with Austin's precious note from Harbin.

The bronevik Invincible moved ponderously along the Amur line west toward Chita. Like a satiated snake it squirmed over the uneven rails and spongy track bed, slowing in some places to five miles an hour, as though the effort of dragging itself onward was too exhausting. But where the rails were straight and there was enough sand ballast on the roadbed to keep it level, the train increased its speed to fifteen and sometimes twenty miles an hour, the big white Mallet engine tossing a mane of dark smoke against the sky. Behind it at irregular intervals beside the track, the train deposited dark bundles of digestive waste, bloody stools which steamed for a time in the freezing air, then grew cold and lay still for the next snow to conceal or for the preying birds and wolves to settle on. They were the last victims taken from the village of Pashkova.

It was a long train with twelve cars for horses alone and many flatcars where the Cossacks, weary of their own cramped quarters, could come to exercise themselves and watch the passing countryside. The first of these appeared at dawn.

Rubbing their bleary eyes, yawning and stamping their feet, they stepped to the edge of the flatcars to relieve themselves, gazing vacantly across the landscape.

As the day went by they shot at anything that moved, and cheered the marksman fortunate enough to hit a target, man, woman, child, horse or dog, it didn't matter to them. They were cold and bored.

There was a gun car near the center of the train coupled to a wagon-lit with the shades drawn where Colonel Sipialef lived and entertained himself. Those who had seen the interior of his car came away awed by the trophies it contained, a collection of inlaid swords, fine weapons of all sorts, rugs and furnishings stolen in countless raids.

The last car of the train, separated from the others by a single flatcar, was the turret car where Maryenka was being held. The cold gray barrel of its three-inch gun pointed back down the tracks with menacing directness. The forward hatch of the ammunition compartment which also served as living quarters for the crew opened onto the flatcar ahead.

As the day brightened Daddy Samson came through this hatch onto the flatcar with Rodion, who was complaining bitterly as he undid his trousers and pissed. "I see why Glubov wanted to be last," he said. "He's still with her."

"We drew straws," Daddy Samson said glumly.

"Glubov rigged it," Rodion said.

"No."

"The way he held them up was rigged," Rodion said doggedly.

Daddy Samson sat down dangling his legs over the edge of the car. "They're sleeping only," he said. "Like lovebirds all wrapped up. Would you believe it? There's a smile on her face as she sleeps. Who can know a woman?"

"She never smiled at me."

"Perhaps you didn't behave."

"She groaned and bit her lips and never looked at me. Am I such a beast? Is it my fault that God marked my face?"

"Let's not talk about it. The thing now is to keep the others from finding her."

"She'll have to do better by me or they'll find her quick enough," Rodion said and he hiked his trousers up and sat down beside the old man.

Daddy Samson looked at Rodion with a yellow glitter in his eyes. "My dear," he said softly, "if you did such a thing and deprived Glubov and me, what do you think?"

"She's cold."

"She's like a daughter to me, dear Rodion. So be good."

They sat in silence, waiting for Glubov to appear.

When a half-hour went by they grew tense, but were too proud to let this show. Rodion began whistling through his teeth and several times Daddy Samson was on the point of mentioning that the girl must be hungry, but he knew Rodion would see through this excuse, so he kept silent. He didn't know her name and he wondered if Rodion knew it. The thought that Rodion would know the girl's name when he did not filled Daddy Samson with sullen anger. He brooded, thinking perhaps he'd pitch Rodion off the train at the next bridge, then there would only be Glubov; but before he could carry this out several Cossacks came onto the flatcar.

Seeing the gunners, the Cossacks began boasting of their exploits during the night. They raised their voices over the sound of the rumbling wheels, clapped each other on the backs and grinned artificially as they relieved themselves. "Lord, I'm amazed to see you have something left to function with this morning, Bepla. — Not much, he has! — Enough to match you all! There's my sign in the snow! — Glad I'm not a gunner, poor lads, playing cards for cigarettes while we have all the fun."

Colonel Sipialef allowed the Cossacks to keep anything they caught or stole, except that he had the pick of the loot and of the prisoners. His gunners, however, were technical men and as such they didn't share in the spoils. They had to remain by the train at all times; their compensation for this was that they were rarely exposed to danger, their living quarters in the gun cars were private, and they were paid regularly at the rating of sergeants.

The Cossacks, while pretending to look down on the gunners, were actually jealous of their prerogatives and lost no opportunity to bully them. They came to the gunners' end of the car and continued their banter.

"You should have come knocking last night, Daddy Samson," one of them said. "We had a bit of leftover who might have pleased you."

"About your age," another Cossack grumbled sourly.

"That's all behind me, brothers," Daddy Samson said quietly. "All behind me."

"But you were a horse in your time, eh, Daddy?"

"Every man is a horse in his time," Daddy Samson said. "But the Lord in his wisdom turns our minds to other things as we approach the grave."

Rodion, offended by Daddy's Samson's pious tones, glared at him. "Like to what?" he asked.

"God's blessings," Daddy Samson said.

The Cossacks hollered with glee and accused Daddy Samson of various deficiencies, conjecturing which of the three old maids in the gunners' car served the other two, or if they all served each other turn about.

Rodion's patch turned a darker hue, nearly black, as he hunched his shoulders against the insults. "Pigs!" he muttered darkly. "Pigs!" And at last unable to bear any more he jumped to his feet and yelled at them. "Pigs! You're all pigs at the same trough. There's nothing to you. Nothing! You make me sick, the pack of you."

The Cossacks roared with delight and Rodion advanced on them with his fists clenched, the mark on his face flushing from red to purple to black and clearing again like an exposed heart on his cheek. The Cossacks retreated, laughing uproariously — pitying his celibacy. "Next time come knocking, Rodion! — We promise you a serving, eh, brothers! Something for poor Rodion."

"I wouldn't take it," Rodion bellowed. "I'm not such a pig as you. We have our own —" And realizing how close he had come to revealing the girl's presence in the turret Rodion choked and tears of rage came to his eyes.

The Cossacks, overjoyed at having brought Rodion to this state of stammering frustration, retired into their car and laughter at the gunner's expense spread through the whole train.

Daddy Samson had risen and was standing at the hatch of the ammunition compartment. He had taken a pistol from inside and was holding it gently in one huge paw. "You nearly did for yourself, brother," he said. "I'd shoot you in the belly, then Glubov, then the girl and myself before I'd let them come in here."

"Shoot yourself first, Daddy," Rodion said sullenly, "and the rest won't matter."

Glubov poked his head through the hatch. There was a sunny smile on his face which the other two gunners deeply resented. "Let's eat, boys," Glubov said. Then he looked over the landscape with dancing enthusiasm in his eyes. "Life has taken a turn," he said and he dropped back into the compartment and began rattling pots.

BOOK TWO

A Proposal for Peace

LATE in March, 1919, Premier Nicolai Lenin looked at the armies and nations arrayed against his fragile and encircled government and sought a way of extricating it from what appeared to be certain annihilation.

He drafted a proposal which he thought would satisfy the interests of all parties in the conflict and yet give him time enough to create a stable government in a small area around Moscow and Petrograd. In this proposal he offered an immediate armistice on all fronts, he promised to assume responsibility for all debts of the Russian Empire and to recognize the independence of the following anti-Bolshevik territories: Estonia, Latvia, Lithuania, Poland, Rumania, Bessarabia, the Crimea, the Caucasus, half the Ukraine, Georgia, Armenia, Azerbaijan, Finland, Murmansk-Archangel, the whole of the Urals, the whole of Siberia.

Never before had one government made such a generous offer of territories which were beyond its control.

The next question was to whom this proposal should be addressed. Woodrow Wilson seemed to be the most likely prospect. Wilson at this time was in Paris negotiating the terms of the Treaty of Versailles; therefore the proposal was sent to him with an expiration date, April 10, 1919.

The earth, moving along its sun orbit at approximately sixty-eight thousand miles an hour, did not slacken as this fateful day came. The surface rotation of the earth at Moscow continued steadily at a thousand miles an hour. On April 10 the sun appeared and vanished and there was no reply from Wilson.

Perhaps it was asking too much of one man to settle the affairs of three fifths of the globe, a man sixty-two years of age, suffering from headaches, neuritis, an enlarged prostate and the intractability of his allies.

At any rate there was no reply. Wilson gave Lenin's proposal to Colonel House, who filed and forgot it.

Lenin sighed and cinched his belt tighter by a notch.

The war in Russia continued.

CHAPTER TWELVE

AT Verkhne-Udinsk the weather was bitterly cold. The Selenga River was not completely frozen and slabs of ice along the banks frequently broke away and slashed into the racing current, making navigation hazardous. The dirt streets of the city had been shoveled and swept free of snow, which blanketed the countryside all around, but the summer ruts and potholes left by wagon wheels were frozen solid and it would have required jackhammers to remove them. Instead these had been filled with water, which froze, leaving a smooth though slippery surface.

Temperatures ranged down to twenty degrees below zero and people had a strong disinclination to venture outside. Overheated chimneys in overcrowded dwellings often caught fire, and instead of abandoning the building at once the occupants remained until the last possible minute to enjoy the heat.

Kolchak's Omsk government had been recognized by General Denikin in the south; by General Krasnov, Hetman of the Don Cossacks, and by General Filimonov, Ataman of the Kuban Cossacks. The first congress of the Communist International was being held in Moscow. Béla Kun had set up a soviet regime in Hungary. Chapayev's name was often in the news. Admiral Kolchak was planning his spring offensive. The value of currency had dropped by half. There was no salt to be had at any price.

Colonel Spaeth and his staff occupied a military barracks on the edge of town toward Beresovka. Militarily Verkhne-Udinsk was more than adequate. It ranked third after Omsk and Irkutsk in strategic importance and therefore was well supplied. Communications were good, with telephone connections to Chita and to Omsk. The railroad yard, foundries and shops were only excelled by those at Irkutsk. On the whole one could not find much to fault except the weather, which could be deceptively exhilarating. The native residents of the city were aware of this and conserved their energy, but the newly arrived Americans had to be warned against the buoyancy which overtook them in the clear, cold air. When he was outside Colonel Spaeth's most frequent comment to his personnel was: "Take it easy, soldier." A man could walk one mile, perhaps two, with a feeling of steadily increasing energy and then collapse, felled as though from behind by an exhaustion he hadn't even suspected. Ten of the fifty beds at Field Hospital No. 4 were already given over to such cases and a general order had been issued limiting the amount of work to be performed at temperatures below zero degrees.

For his own part Spaeth was bored, a fact which he tried to hide from his staff. Each morning he plastered what he hoped was a genial smile on his face and tried to keep it there all day, but the smile felt so false he'd grown a mustache on the theory, he supposed, that hair would conceal his deceit.

His home near Tacoma had not burned down. Peg had tamed the furnace and fixed Bobby's bike and he wished she hadn't done that. The one thing he'd wanted to do was to fix that bike. He'd sensed the bike waiting for him in the garage, needing his attention almost more than anyone else in the family needed it. The bike had played a big part in his dreams of their reunion. After the hugs, the kisses, the joyous tears, he'd grab Bobby's hand and say, "Well, old-timer, let's have a look at that lame bike of yours."

He wouldn't be able to do that now. By fixing the bike Peg had robbed him of his best homecoming line. He didn't have a substitute for it and he couldn't think of one.

The broken bike had been damned important. And the furnace was fixed too. If he didn't get home quick they'd have the whole place in tiptop shape.

"Don't fix anything more!" he wrote. "Save it for me. Break a few things and let me know about it. Verkhne is dull as dishwater and the only thing that keeps me going is to imagine the house is falling down. How in hell could you fix my furnace! I feel as though I'd lost an eccentric relative."

In her reply Peg said she'd always thought of him as a lover, not a fixer, and assured him that things were still falling apart at a great rate.

This made the smile under his new mustache a little more comfortable.

At his desk Spaeth glanced through the medical officer's weekly report. Three of the casualties suffered by C Company had been evacuated to Vlad. The total number of prophylactics given at the station located across from the Chinese market was, to date, three hundred and seven. At least the eight thousand registered prostitutes in Vladivostok had been confined to "Kopeck Hill," but here they had the run of the town. Spaeth intended to confer with General Bogoloff and the Japanese commandant, Major General Yoshie, about this situation.

Spaeth skipped over the frostbite and exhaustion cases and came to a note at the bottom of the report:

"Our associations with the Red Cross have been very pleasant. They have practically done nothing for the expedition. On the other hand we have furnished them with several thousand dollars' worth of medical supplies."

Spaeth grinned knowing General Graves would derive a small pleasure in having this comment forwarded to Dr. Teusler.

He countersigned the report and turned to the daily analysis of the effective strength of the regiment. As of this hour he had, with Headquarters, Headquarters Company, Supply Company, Machine Gun Company, Companies A, B, C, I, K, L and the Medical detachments, sixty-five officers and two thousand and forty-seven enlisted men to guard a railroad sector one hundred and two miles in length from Verkhne-Udinsk to Mysovaya on the shores of Lake Baikal.

A Military Police force of four officers and one hundred and twenty-five men guarded the railyards at Verkhne and from there the men were stationed along the line, at Mostovoi, Selengenska, Tataurovo, Verst 404, Posolskaya and at the various bridges and sidings to Mysovaya.

Most of the men on the line lived in Russian boxcars which had been requisitioned from Kolchak's Minister of Ways and Communications. These had been converted into bakery and kitchen cars, hospital and dental cars, delousing cars, latrine cars, tailor cars, barber cars. There were sixty-seven cars along the line, some occupied by as many as eleven men.

For the most part Spaeth was satisfied with the disposition of his command. Three things nagged at him specifically. The first was that the regiment had been brought up to strength by volunteers only recently arrived from the States who carried with them some of the ferment being expressed at home over the justification for having American troops stationed in Siberia. These men had been scattered through the command, and though it was personally distasteful to Spaeth he had asked that they be watched. The phrase he'd selected with reference to them was that they should be "brought along."

The second problem was that he found it nearly impossible to make sense out of the various military and civil authorities in and around Verkhne-Udinsk. Part of this he knew to be a language problem, but Mr.

Silverman, the American interpreter assigned to the 27th, was at an equal loss. One day it seemed that every officer behaved autonomously and his power was in direct ratio to the number of effective troops in his command. The next day all the military men were deferring to Mr. Nocolski, the mayor of Verkhne-Udinsk, who had no troops and very little common sense as far as Spaeth could tell. Major General Yoshie had three thousand Japanese troops garrisoned in the area. General Bogoloff had only eighteen hundred Russians, but he seemed to be high man on the ladder, perhaps because of his armored trains, which were potent symbols of power. Colonel Lvoff had three hundred Siberian Infantrymen and four hundred and fifty grubby-looking Cossacks and behaved as if he was answerable to no one. Then there was the assortment of commanders who drifted through Verkhne-Udinsk and seemed to take precedence over everyone else while they were in town. General Levitsky, commander of the Semenoff Buryat-Mongolian Brigade, was one of these. Lieutenant General Artemieff, commander of the 9th Siberian Division at Irkutsk, was another. General Myssura of the Zai-Baikal Rifle Brigade yet another. Colonel Krupski, Semenoff's aide in Verkhne-Udinsk, was universally deferred to, as was Colonel Ivashkevitz who held the title of military commandant for the city and very little else except for the quantities of vodka he consumed. Colonel Sipialef was another powerful figure, but Spaeth had given up trying to understand the lines of authority which ran through all these names and titles. He had turned the problem over to Major Taziola.

The third thing which nagged the Colonel was the death of Sergeant Austin and the effect this had had on the men who had known Maryenka. He had not realized himself how deeply attached he was to the Sergeant and his wife until the commemorative service held in the marshaling yard for Austin and Saunders, whose bodies had been returned to Vlad.

The regimental chaplain's brief eulogy had not been nearly as affecting as the idea that Maryenka Austin had yet to be informed of her husband's death. Lieutenant Leverett had written a compassionate letter to Maryenka in Pashkova, but this had been returned marked "Addressee unknown."

Spaeth didn't like this and he knew the men liked it less. Carlisle urged that the matter be settled. He'd called twice about it.

Spaeth sent for Major Taziola, an officer from the 53rd Telegraph Battalion who had been attached to the regiment for reasons which weren't quite clear.

General Graves' Chief of Staff, Olie Robinson, who'd made the assignment, was vague about the necessity of having a staff grade officer in charge of communications. He said Taziola was a good man and Spaeth had let it go, but lately he had come to believe that Taziola had a political function, or was connected with Army Intelligence. For this reason he found himself conferring more with Taziola than with Bentham or Cloak, because he wanted to keep his eye on the Major, who seemed to have surprisingly good connections all the way around.

Taziola was short, with a good-natured Italian face and the habit of cocking his head quizzically as though he'd just barely missed the point of what was said to him. This was annoying, but in all other respects Taz was a thoroughgoing officer who was almost invariably a step ahead of every request made of him. He was forty-four, a bit potbellied, with a cocky walk and a lot of gray in his crinkly hair.

"Yes, Colonel?"

"It's about that Pashkova business, Taz. I want to get it settled."

Taziola took a telegraph tape from his blouse pocket and put it on Spaeth's desk. "This just came through," he said.

Spaeth read the tape: "Pashkova burned out. Inhabitants dead or scattered. Investigation proceeds. Fillmore. A.R.C."

A feeling of bleakness settled in Spaeth's chest. He looked up at Taziola. "Anybody know about this?"

"The signal clerk."

"Keep it under wraps."

"I can do that."

"You have any theories, Taz?"

Taziola nodded. "My guess would be Bolshie partisans."

"I knew it would be," Spaeth said. "You're getting to be predictable, Major. Let's keep the guesswork under wraps too."

"Yes, sir."

"Let me know when anything new comes in. Just me, is that clear?"

Taziola cocked his head in his sparrowlike manner and smiled. "Perfectly," he said.

« 2 »

The only café of distinction in Verkhne-Udinsk was the Mulligan, which occupied two floors of a building facing the Selenga River. The upstairs rooms were reserved for private parties but by two a.m. divisions between private and public sectors broke down and people simply drifted about looking for new faces. The clientele was predominantly military, those with money to spend, and there was a large selection of women whose style of behavior was characterized by loud sardonic laughter covering reserves of bitterness which was stimulating because it was so honest.

The main downstairs room at Mulligan's seemed to have been decorated with the booty of several campaigns. None of the chairs or tables matched. The china and silverware, much of it very fine, was sure to have been taken from someone now dead, from a looted estate or a sacked town, and people dining often paused to gaze at a crested fork or a Sèvres dish wondering what histories these articles held and shivering sometimes at their thoughts of death and dispossession.

This consciousness of the war and of the uncertainties of life might have flagged if it had not been for Anitsky, the headwaiter. A Polish émigré with a wrinkled, incredibly comic face, Anitsky carried on a running monologue from table to table, room to room, language to language. He was small and bandy-legged, with terribly solemn eyes begging to be understood but which only increased the comic aspects of his face with its broad mouth and sharp, turned-up nose. Anitsky was the self-appointed conscience of the world; he dashed about seating people, signaling the waiters and talking in a high-pitched, stuttering voice. His hands fluttered continuously about his head as though he were plucking words from the air or swatting aside those which annoyed him. He was always in motion physically and verbally.

"Good sirs, good sirs, why must it be so? To what end? Let us behave ourselves! Be civilized. Dear God, the things I've seen! The mind won't permit it. And for what? What? Why can't we be good?"

With this particular question Anitsky always smiled hopefully as though expecting an answer.

"Is God not watching? Is there no decent way to settle these differences, and what are they? Who among you can put a name to your cause? The Red Army has occupied Kiev? Let them have Kiev. Bad luck to them! Let them have Transcaspia! Must we slaughter each other night and day? We could talk! Draw straws! Go home and live in peace. There is starvation, great starvation and typhus at Ekaterinoslav. Send blessings to them, send food and doctors. Isn't that better than bullets? Will we not stand one day at the feet of our Maker? And what will we say? Yes, yes, good sirs, what will we say to the Face of Our Lord? Ah, kind sirs, be good, be good against the holy day when our dear Lord will ask: 'What have you done?' "

The Mulligan was always crowded and because the windows were draped exhausted celebrants, pushing their way out through crowds of people coming in, frequently asked if it was night or day, snowing or dry. Kolchak officers in their white uniforms, shoulder straps and swords, or staff officers from one of the numerous nonexistent corps, were always gay, boastful and enthusiastic. There were Cossacks, Czechs, Japanese and a variety of foreign military attachés and, of course, the Americans.

Here General Bogoloff held court. He took all his meals at the Mulligan surrounded by his staff and guests. A huge, genial man of sixty and a magnificent host, he seemed to be a fixture of the place and his heavy voice provided a conversational bass scale to which Anitsky's was a hectic counterpoint, topped by the running laughter of the women.

Bogoloff loved to talk and those who were drunk sometimes thought he was to be seen in every corner of the room, his big figure bent over the upended ear of one of his cronies or that of a new officer he wanted to pump or brief. He whispered on these occasions, but his whisper was like coal pouring down a metal chute into a bunker. He talked to everyone all the time and was never dogmatic. He admitted his confusion, his ignorance, his willingness to learn, with such candor that people stood in line to educate him. Very often he laughed and throwing up his arms would rumble: "But, of course! I'm frightened to death. I want my Czar!" And this frank, almost childlike admission of dependency often brought tears to the eyes of those who also found that the assassination of their Czar had cut them adrift in a cruel and unsettled world.

Bogoloff was respected, in fact loved. He was so big, so clumsily benign, so willing to extend himself that people had for him the instinctive affection usually reserved for very large dogs, Saint Bernards, Newfoundlands, or bloodhounds. He didn't have the sleek, too highly bred and therefore suspect sophistication of a Borzoi or an Afghan.

Bogoloff could be trusted.

But among the colorful pack around Bogoloff, the flashy Dalmatians, haughty greyhounds, and posturing setters, there was the mastiff, Colonel Sipialef, who always stood a bit to one side, watching. And if Sipialef was not in attendance everyone knew something was afoot, some bloody business which usually came out a week or so later, a raid, a battle or a reprisal. Sipialef was distrusted and people sometimes wondered why Bogoloff put up with him. Of late Colonel Sipialef had been absent and people were waiting to see what his return would bring.

So, the Mulligan was the heart of Verkhne-Udinsk. It pumped night and day, music, song, dance, rumor, speculation, espionage, sex, gambling. And without that heart the city very likely would have died. One could not say it was a bad heart or a good heart. It was the only heart the city possessed and no one ever suggested improving city life by removing it. Preposterous! One had to live.

On Tuesday nights Colonel Spaeth and his staff officers were in the habit of playing poker at the Mulligan. This gave them a chance to hear the latest, which was a duty they owed the command and, although they didn't partake of the baser pleasures, they enjoyed the proximity of sin.

None of them ever missed a Tuesday night.

Anitsky always met them at the door and began his chant. Americans were particular favorites of Anitsky's because sometimes they actually listened to him. "Ah, kind sirs, good gentlemen, is there no peace to be had? Tell us, you who see it with stranger's eyes, are we visited with a curse of God? Are we chosen to consume each other for our sins and is there no one to intercede for us? I loved my gracious Czar, God cherish his soul, but must all our young men march to their doom until another Czar is found? Give us the Grand Duke, give us Wilson, but bring an end to this tragedy! This way, good sirs. I have a room upstairs."

And he led them up the staircase and down the hall of what probably had been a hotel. The doors to the rooms were screened from the passageway by strings of glass and wooden beads which clattered pleasantly as the waiters went in and out, and they could see into these rooms as they passed.

The use of narcotics was permitted in certain upstairs rooms which still had doors and raised a riot of imagination in the American mind. In contrast to the boisterousness and loud drunkenness of the people downstairs these rooms were quiet and therefore sinister.

Major Taziola always shuddered as he passed them and visualized supine white girls straddled by ravening Mongols, suffering indignities with never a word or a moan. Taziola rather enjoyed this picture, which gave a ruthless fillip to his poker game. The notion that a drugged girl was being raped in the next room took the sting out of the losses he suffered at the table. If he lost a large pot the raping Mongol in the next room was also a Bolshevik agent who advocated the nationalization of women.

Anitsky usually stayed ten minutes or so observing the game and inspecting the refreshments on the sideboard, cheese, sliced meats, bread and various hors d'oeuvres. The players had a rule never to drink anything but beer at the Mulligan, on the theory that they had to be careful what they said.

The game usually started with five officials and it went into the early hours of the morning. Sometimes General Bogoloff took a seat. He was in the habit of shuffling the cards interminably when it was his deal. Interminably! He shuffled them over and over as though he were washing his hands, meantime addressing the group on whatever was uppermost in his mind. Captain Cloak, who thought all talk should be outlawed at the table, was particularly aggrieved when Bogoloff got his hands on the cards. Once he timed Bogoloff, who shuffled the cards for twenty minutes while describing the battle tactics of General Kappel. On this occasion Cloak had all he could do to keep from yelling: "Deal! Deal, god damn it!"

On one particular Tuesday evening the game was proceeding with proper solemnity; Cloak was nicely ahead and Taziola losing steadily.

Lieutenant Leverett, who had come in from the camp at Tataurovo, made a fifth hand and a visiting captain named Simonsen made a sixth, leaving one seat open.

Having just thrown in a hand with a groan of disgust, Taziola offered the opinion that Anitsky was a spy.

"Oh, come on, Taz!" Cloak said. "Play cards."

"Nevertheless —"

"You keep that up, Taz, and we're going to lose a fine waiter," Bentham said.

"There are more important things."

"Your deal, Leverett," Cloak said.

Colonel Spaeth scowled across the table at Taziola, who lit his pipe. "I still say we have to be careful," Taz said.

"No one is suggesting we not be," Spaeth said. "But part of that caution is not to make judgments about matters which don't concern us."

"I'd say it was a matter of concern to us," Taziola said.

"Will you deal, Leverett?"

Spaeth smiled at Taziola cordially. "If you have evidence someone is going to interfere with the operation of rail travel, going to blow up a bridge, or steal tracks let me know, Taz. Otherwise let's not contribute to the rumor mill. Deal, Leverett."

These exchanges between Taziola and Colonel Spaeth had gotten to be familiar. Once a week or so Taziola threw out a suggestion as though to test Spaeth's current political position and when Spaeth replied, as he invariably did, that it was none of their business Taziola appeared to be satisfied. But he made no secret of the fact that he thought American neutrality was absurd.

Leverett's down card was a three of diamonds, his next was a seven of clubs, so he folded and continued to deal to the others as the betting progressed.

After the establishment of headquarters at Tataurovo, life in C Company had taken on a routine which had compensations. The first of these was Ira's discovery that such practical matters as carpentry, laying barbed wire or organizing the defense perimeter for a bridge were things he could do as well as the next man, that book larnin' hadn't incapacitated him for the pleasures of physical labor.

Twenty wooden freight cars, or teplushkas, had been issued the company when it reached Verkhne-Udinsk. For each car there was a kit consisting of one stove, four window frames, two cases of glass, three bundles of sheet iron, stove pipe, asbestos, nails and three hundred pieces of lumber.

Each squad was responsible for outfitting its teplushka, and the men turned to like boys building clubhouses. Ira's best hours had been spent working side by side with Carlisle on the car which was to serve as company headquarters. They planned the interior and constructed it, working for hours with the silence broken only by the sound of hammer and saw.

The layout for each car was standard. There was a round iron stove in a sandbox in the center of the floor; sliding wooden doors on each side and a sliding wooden window forty by fifteen inches in each upper corner. They installed two bunks and a table at one side of the car and built an office at the other. The first time Carlisle bent a nail and cursed Ira took heart. The Sioux was not infallible. When a board Ira sawed came out an inch short, Carlisle forgave him with a shrug and sawed another board, which came out only half an inch short, whereupon Ira grinned and sawed a third board, which fitted. Being officers they were obliged to conceal the defects of their workmanship from the men and this conspiracy of rank also drew them together.

The men were proud of their teplushkas but had to be discouraged from painting the exteriors of the cars as the Czechs did. Carlisle limited decoration to a one-line slogan on the door of each car: Carlisle's Caterwaulers — Kolder than Kelsey's — Belly Acres — Old Soldiers' Home — The Arkansas Traveler — twenty assorted expressions of primitive wit and the longing for home. The door of their car read: H.Q. C Company. Jack Carlisle, Capt. U. S. A. Cmdg. Lt. Ira C. Leverett. Exec.

When C Company was reinforced three more lieutenants had been added to the roster. Ira had not thought he would continue second-in-command

and was extraordinarily pleased when Carlisle had ordered him to stencil the door of their teplushka with himself named as executive officer. To show his appreciation Ira packed his splendid cordovan boots away and never wore them again. From Supply he drew a pair of used boots as nearly like Carlisle's as he could find.

If Carlisle noticed the change he never said a word, but Ira had come to understand that their growing friendship was more often characterized by the Sioux's silence than by anything he said.

C Company was stationed along the line between Mostovoi and Posol-skaya with the 1st Platoon detached for guard duty at Beresovka. Head-quarters was set at Tataurova, with Carlisle, Leverett and fifty-eight enlisted men. The 2nd Platoon was at Selenga. The 3rd at Posolskaya. The 4th was at Mostovoi, fifteen miles out of Verkhne.

The reason Ira had come to Verkhne on this occasion was to turn over twelve hundred dollars the men had collected for Maryenka Austin and to tell Colonel Spaeth why he thought his first letter to Maryenka had not been delivered. Major Taziola had been in the Colonel's office at the time.

"You see, sir, I addressed the letter to Maryenka Austin at Pashkova and I remember now a conversation with Austin when he sent Maryenka a package from Harbin. I'll bet anything he addressed it to Maryenka Shulgin or to her parents."

"Why would he do that?" Taziola had asked.

"Because she wouldn't have been known there as Austin. She'd been married before to a man in Pashkova named Shulgin."

"Do you know her parents' name?" Spaeth asked.

"No, I don't."

Taziola pursued the question to a point which exasperated Ira. It seemed so obvious to him.

He didn't know if Maryenka's parents knew of her marriage. Yes, it might have been kept from them. Marriages between Russian girls and American soldiers were sometimes unpopular. She might have been discriminated against.

"By whom?" Taziola asked sharply.

"How do I know? Girls have been beaten for less."

"Who told you that?"

"Austin did."

"And who was Shulgin?"

"An exile. He's dead."

Major Taziola's head cocked over. "An exile," he said and he looked at Colonel Spaeth significantly.

"All I want to do is send another letter!" Ira declared.

Colonel Spaeth nodded sympathetically. "We have your first one back, so I'll have Silverman send it out again. The name was Shulgin?"

Ira nodded. Colonel Spaeth had made a note of the name, then he'd invited Ira to join them at the Mulligan.

But now, as he passed the deal, Ira caught an expression on Taziola's face which he remembered from the meeting, a look which conveyed the idea that Taz had snapped his teeth into something and had no intention of letting go. What this was Ira didn't know, but it made him uneasy.

Bentham dealt another hand. Ira caught a pair of kings in which he had no faith.

He drew three cards and found a third king, which caused a flutter of excitement in the vicinity of his belt buckle, but after three stiff raises he lost the hand to Bentham, who held a jack high straight.

"That does it for me," Ira said and he stood up.

"You're a good loser, Ira," Bentham said. "Stick around."

Ira grinned. "I'm beginning to think I'm on your charity list, Captain."

"You and Cloak," Bentham said.

"Deal, Taz!" Cloak said.

As Ira came through the beaded hanging into the hallway Anitsky fell in beside him and began chattering. "The waste, the terrible waste of life, my good sir. Appalling, senseless, continual. Do we turn our backs on such things? Do we come away unscarred? I have dreams, sir, terrible! Sleep is torture to me."

"That's right, Anitsky. Is Masha downstairs?"

"She was when I came up, sir."

Ira started down, but Anitsky caught his sleeve on the first landing and glanced around to see if they were observed. "Excuse me, sir."

Ira was a bit annoyed by Anitsky's secretive manner. "Yes?"

"Colonel Sipialef is here tonight."

"So?"

Anitsky looked more confused and hesitant. "You asked after Masha and he'll be with her tonight. Sometimes our guests don't know these things. I speak to avoid unpleasantness, you see. The Colonel has had bad luck with his train. All shot up. Several men killed. At such times men are easily provoked."

"Thank you, Anitsky."

Ira had just reached the main floor when he was hailed again, this time by Captain Simonsen, who came down the stairs two at a time. "Leverett, is it?" Simonsen said and he pulled up short and thrust out his hand.

"Yes," Ira said and shook the hand, which remained passive and cold in his own.

"I'm Captain Simonsen. Jewish Relief Administration?"

The question, or statement, confused Ira. "What about it?"

"You're Jewish, so am I."

"What's this all about?"

A gilded look crossed Simonsen's eyes and his mouth turned down defensively. "You are Jewish," he said.

"I didn't say I wasn't! I'm also a lawyer, a lieutenant and a cocksman in inverse order of importance. You're a captain, ergo I salute you."

Simonsen touched the bars on his collar self-consciously. "Oh, that," he said. "Don't mind that. It's a simulated rank. It's the only way we can get things done over here. We have to have authority to act or no one would listen to us."

"Who in hell is us?"

"The Jewish Relief Administration!" Simonsen said. "We're investigating the pogroms, the massacres, the anti-Semitic activities in Russia, trying to alleviate the conditions of our suffering people. You know about Kishenev of course, and it's our duty to bring to the attention of the world other even more grave racial crimes. I'm making a report on the anti-Semitism incipient in the Russian character. I'd like your help."

"My help?"

"Yes, any little thing. Anecdotal, personal. Whatever you think might be of value, add color to a report. You've been around."

"Which color do you intend to add?" Ira asked wryly. "In my company all the men call me the Jew — oh, not to my face, you understand."

"They don't!" Simonsen declared and his jaw dropped.

"We have an Indian in the outfit and they call him Hunkpapa Jack or the Sioux."

"Oh, well, that's out of my area. What I want is material on the Russian attitudes," Simonsen said and he waggled his hand and frowned at it with grave intellectual concern. "I've got a chance of getting something into *Harper's.*"

Ira nodded gravely. He pondered for a moment, then smiled radiantly. "Captain Simonsen," he said, "I wonder if you'd accept a suggestion."

"Yes, of course," Simonsen said with a glow of expectancy.

"Go fuck yourself!"

Ira turned on his heel and stalked through the crowded room to the bar. He wished he'd punched the phony damned captain on the snout. First there was Taziola, then the three kings had let him down, then Anitsky warning him about Sipialef, and it was all topped off by Simonsen. That bastard!

But even this wasn't all. For some reason he'd been reminded of his failure to support the action at Siding 85 and his consequent guilt about Austin's death. And having thought of this he thought of Ikachi, about whom he'd had no intention of thinking. It was damned frustrating.

Ikachi had been taken from the train at Dauria eight miles from where the attack had occurred. The town was the site of a prison camp with medical facilities and Ikachi required immediate treatment. Carson and the other American wounded were treated by a doctor on the train until they reached the hospital at Verkhne-Udinsk.

Ira sat down at the bar and ordered vodka, which came in a frosted glass. It warmed his throat as it went down and he turned his attention to Masha, the Rumanian gypsy woman who was Sipialef's mistress. She was singing moodily to the accompaniment of two balalaikas. No one appeared to be listening, but Masha always sang for herself, gazing off into the upper corners of the room. Her voice was pliant and sorrowful and she sat on a stool with one knee pulled up and held in her interlocked hands. There was a streak of white in her loose dark hair and two of the more attractive girls at the Mulligan, Dunia and Sonia, were her daughters.

Ira saw Sipialef across the room and they recognized each other. This was acknowledged on Sipialef's side by a disdainful smirk. After this they occasionally locked eyes and Sipialef invariably broke off with a shrug which Ira chose to interpret as a victory for himself.

This was ridiculous, but it bolstered Ira's self-esteem. He saw General Bogoloff at a nearby table whispering jovially to a pair of Czechs, one of whom Ira thought he'd seen before in Vlad.

He tried to concentrate on the Czechs, but his mind took a course of its own and he remembered Carlisle's grudging admiration of Ikachi's bravery at Siding 85.

"A man shows what he is under fire," Carlisle had said.

"I thought you didn't like him."

"Who I like or don't like doesn't matter. He attacked those Chinks singlehanded. He stood straight up to them."

Ira had two more drinks and felt better, or at least he felt less, which was better.

Masha was singing sadly and Ira hummed the melody, then Anitsky appeared at his side. "Sir," he said, "there's a gentleman here asking about Captain Carlisle."

Ira looked at Anitsky slowly. "Tell me, Anitsky," he said, "how do you know I know Carlisle?"

"It's my duty, sir," Anitsky said with a tremulous smile. "I try to bring people together. There's so much separation these days. I try to draw people closer and to do that you must know them."

Ira sighed. "Where's the gentleman?" he asked.

Anitsky bowed and Ira followed him to General Bogoloff's table, where he was introduced to one of the Czechs. "Lieutenant Markowitz, this is Lieutenant Leverett, who knows the captain you were inquiring after."

The Czech rose and shook hands. "Won't you join us?" he asked.

The other Czech got up, offered Ira his chair and went to find another.

Ira hesitated, then sat down. "I can't stay long," he said.

General Bogoloff gestured and a waiter appeared with another frosted vodka for Ira.

"I am reminded that your captain and I met in Vladivostok," Bogoloff said.

Ira now remembered that he'd seen Markowitz at the Russian Club in Vlad. "Is that right, sir?" he said.

"You must have seen *me* there also, at the ball. But no! You were entertaining my train commander, Sipialef, that evening." General Bogoloff tipped back in his chair and roared with laughter, then he told everyone at the table the story of Ira's encounter with Sipialef.

To Ira's astonishment the story, as Sipialef must have told it to Bogoloff, bore no more resemblance to the truth than the account he had given Carlisle and Ikachi.

As General Bogoloff told it, Ira had insisted on searching the train and Sipialef called out the Cossacks to prevent this. The Americans surrounded the train and there would have been a fight if Sipialef hadn't reminded Ira of the Armistice.

"And a good thing too," Bogoloff concluded. "But think! He'd forgotten the Armistice!"

Everyone laughed, including Ira, who was so pleased by this colored version of the story that he could have kissed Bogoloff on both cheeks.

Masha began singing a wild, gypsy song and presently there were three Cossacks dancing in the center of the floor.

Ira was happy. A wave of delirium swept over him. All the people at the table were his friends. General Bogoloff was a mountain of good will. Lieutenant Markowitz was charming. Dunia, the younger of Masha's daughters, came to the table and they made room for her to sit beside him.

"Are you stationed here now, Lieutenant?" Ira asked.

"No, I'm on my way to Omsk," Markowitz said. "I leave tomorrow."

"Sorry to hear that."

"I am also sorry," Dunia said with an inconsequential smile. Unlike her mother she was thin and fair, with the short attention span and abstracted gaze of a narcotics addict. She rested her hand on Ira's shoulder and forgot it.

"How is Captain Carlisle?" Markowitz asked.

"Fine."

"My cousin asked that she be remembered to him," Markowitz said.

"Your cousin?"

"Countess Tatiana. Perhaps he mentioned her to you."

"No, he hasn't."

Markowitz shrugged slightly. "It doesn't matter, I think. But she did ask me to convey her regards if the opportunity came."

"I'll tell him then."

"Yes, thank you."

Markowitz lit a cigarette. Bogoloff was telling how Countess Tatiana had changed Carlisle to a captain in the ladies' powder room. Dunia's hand on Ira's shoulder squeezed gently and relaxed, squeezed and relaxed in a most provocative way. Ira was drunk and happy. "In the powder room?" he asked.

"My cousin calls him the Captain of the Powder Room," Markowitz said.

Ira hooted. "Captain of the Powder Room! No wonder Carlisle didn't tell me about it."

"He's an impulsive man," Markowitz said quietly.

"Carlisle? You don't know him."

"A little," Markowitz said and he smiled in an infuriatingly superior manner.

A quick, pent-up belligerence brought a scowl to Ira's face. He shook

Dunia's hand off his shoulder and turned to Markowitz squarely. "What do you mean by that?" he asked.

"That I know him a little," Markowitz replied easily but there was a belittling tone in his voice to which Ira objected and he was going to fight. This came to him as a complete surprise, but Ira knew it was inevitable. He only wanted to get the proper groundwork done before he jerked the supercilious Czech to his feet and hit him. He was going to do what Austin would have done. "You'd better explain," he said.

"I shouldn't have mentioned it. Please accept my apology."

Ira rose, irritated because his anger was slipping away. "You said he was impulsive!"

Markowitz looked up coolly. "Men are often impulsive where women are concerned, Lieutenant. Please forgive me. I shouldn't have mentioned it." He puffed his cigarette and exhaled a smoke ring.

Whether blown by accident or design it was the smoke ring that triggered Ira. It was so casually done, so perfectly circular, so contemptuous that Ira leaned over the table and hit Markowitz on the bridge of the nose with his fist.

Markowitz fell backward out of his chair. There were screams, the clatter of glasses and plates as people bounded up.

Markowitz' nose gushed blood. He was snatching wildly at the pistol in his holster. The Cossacks who had been dancing leaped on Ira, pinioned his arms and rushed him toward the door. He saw the pistol in Markowitz' hand. He heard the shot and everyone in the room dropped to the floor.

The Cossacks pushed him out the door into the street and yelled, motioning him to run. Ira stood there, cold sober, trying to decide what to do. Anitsky rushed out and gave Ira his coat. "Hurry, sir! He's gone mad!"

Ira put his coat on and pulled the forty-five out of his pocket. "Tell him I'm out here," he said, feeling like a fool.

Anitsky saw the pistol and ran around the building howling lamentations. The Cossacks dove back inside and Ira stood there in the frozen street shivering, but ready to fire all those polished bullets at his adversary.

Captain Cloak appeared in the door. "Jesus Christ, Ira!"

"Tell him I'm out here," Ira said again.

"You drunk, or what the hell?" Cloak asked. "That god-damned shot went right through the center of our table. Blew poker chips all over the room. I had a two pair, kings high!"

Ira began to laugh. His knees buckled and if Cloak hadn't caught him he would have fallen. "Oh, Christ, Ben," he said. "Those kings would have lost. I had three and they let me down!" He couldn't stop laughing and he didn't know what he was laughing about except that Cloak was mad as hell and there was a man inside who wanted to kill him.

"You'd better get the hell out of here, Ira," Cloak said.

"Not me, god damn it," Ira declared. "Not me."

Colonel Spaeth came out looking frosty as hell. "Spill it, Leverett!" he demanded.

"Well, sir — "

"Pull yourself together! Stand up!"

Cloak let go his arm and Ira came to attention. Spaeth snatched the forty-five out of his hand, removed the clip and handed the automatic to Cloak. "You'd better have a good story, Lieutenant."

"He insulted Captain Carlisle," Ira said.

"That's sweet," Spaeth said acidly.

"I had to do it."

Major Taziola and Captain Bentham joined the circle around Ira. Taziola glanced at Spaeth and shook his head.

"What's the Czech say?" Spaeth asked.

"He said it was a misunderstanding. To forget it."

"Like hell, " Ira blurted. "Like hell it was."

"I don't intend to forget it, Leverett!" Spaeth said. "Don't worry about that. I intend to remember it for a long time. Now you get the hell out of here while I try to straighten this mess up. Cloak, see that he gets on a train. Taziola, phone Carlisle and tell him he's got a damned fool on his hands. Bentham, let's see what we can do."

They went back inside leaving Ira with Cloak, who looked at him and grinned. "You plan to make a career in the army, Leverett?"

Ira shook his head.

"That's good. Let's go."

They walked down the ice-clad street toward the station and Ira's one consoling thought was that he'd gotten rid of his clip of polished bullets. When they reached the yard, Ira recognized Sipialef's armored train standing much as he had first seen it in the yards at Vlad, but the engine and the metal-sheathed trucks had been badly mauled by shellfire and the gun car at the tail of the train had been blown open. There was a gaping hole in the rear plates and the gun turret sat askew on its bed.

If anything the train was more abhorrent to him than it had been. He tried to appear nonchalant, to put on a good face, but the train made him think of an insect rotting.

"You going to be sick?" Cloak asked.

"Yes," Ira said and he was, terribly, all over the boots which he had hoped would look like Carlisle's.

CHAPTER THIRTEEN

CARLISLE tramped along the bank of the ice-filled Selenga River listening for the morning local from Verkhne-Udinsk. He'd received a call from Major Taziola about a gun fight or brawl at the Mulligan involving Leverett. Taziola's story, as he was the first to admit, was incomplete. All the facts weren't in, but with Taziola the facts were never in. When they did come in they were usually Taziola's facts, to which Carlisle often took exception. On the whole he was amazed that Ira could have been in a brawl, much less a gun fight. Taziola hadn't told him the cause of the fracas, saying it had not, as yet, been determined. The "as yet" was a typical Taziola reservation which annoyed Carlisle, for whom drunk was drunk, fight was fight, and it was no man's damned business to look into the motivations.

But it was not Taziola's call which brought Carlisle out of bed; he had been up as usual to witness the dawn.

It was a particularly cold hour with frost standing on the girders of the bridge over which the train would come. It was the hour of profound stillness when all shapes seemed to contract inward generating the energy necessary to cast their shadows outward with the sun.

It was still dark, but Carlisle sensed that moment of visual explosion which always came like the blink of an eye. In one moment the world was taut, then there was an expansion of the senses. The sound of ice chunks bumping in the current, the sound of the wind, of a footfall on frozen ground, were all better defined and more apparent in the light, as though one heard them with the eyes. And the light speeding over the snow-clad hills brought a tingling sensation to the ears, as though it could be heard, and in that moment the guards on the bridge frequently rubbed their ears with their mittened hands wondering if they had been frostbitten.

The world gathered weight with the advent of light. Ice clinging to the footings of the bridge broke under the impact of it. There was a fresh smell of sound which bit the nostrils for just an instant, then was lost. Kinetic senses changed abruptly and men abroad at that moment often stumbled.

It was a time when sleepers tossed over in their beds and knew the light had come.

Carlisle was well acquainted with these phenomena. It was his custom to be up and outside to catch the dawn. He'd done this for as long as he could remember and he knew to within five or ten the number of times he had missed a sunrise, not above a hundred times in close to forty years. But here, in this country, there was a difference.

Most of his army life had been spent in the south and the southwest in Texas, Cuba, or the Philippines, in temperate or tropical zones where the warmth made him a stranger to his youth. This was no longer so. In Siberia he was carried back inevitably to times he had put out of mind.

Carlisle stopped beside the river near the bridge. Above him the guards, aware of his presence, spent less time warming themselves beside the oil-drum stoves stationed on the stone pillars which supported the six-span bridge, and walked their posts from span to span, their boots hard on the planked trestle. Then the rhythmic beat which announced the approaching train joined the dark rushing sound of the water and something floated up in Carlisle's mind sharp as broken ice:

> *Ateyapi kin*
> *Maka owancya*
> *Lowan nisipe-lo*
> *Heya-po,*
> *Heya-po,*
> *Oyakapo — he!*

"Thus the father sayeth/ Lo, he now commandeth/ All on earth to sing/ to sing now. Thus he hath spoken/ Thus he hath spoken/ Tell afar his message."

Carlisle looked up from the river, cold to the bone.

The song was one his mother had sung.

For years it had been dormant in his mind, until the power of the cold brought it out. And now with a shudder he remembered it all.

After his father's death they'd lived on the Rosebud Reservation with his mother's brother, Henry Buckeye, a member of the Sioux police. It was the time of the ghost dancing, of the Indian Messiah, of the Massacre at Wounded Knee where over two hundred men, women and children were shot down at point-blank range by Hotchkiss guns. Three days later their torn, frozen bodies were buried in a common trench. Henry Buckeye was one of these; he believed, as his sister had believed, that there could be a spiritual link between opposing cultures: a Red Messiah.

Carlisle had been ten years old.

After this he and his mother returned to Montana. She raised sheep and men visited their ramshackle house which was so much like those at Khailar.

Seven years later two hundred and sixty-six men were killed in an explosion in Havana harbor and those deaths opened doors for Carlisle which the deaths at Wounded Knee had closed for his mother. The recruiting officer neglected to ask whether Jack Carlisle, half-breed, was a citizen or a ward of the government, so he joined the army.

Carlisle remembered the *Maine,* but until now he had forgotten his mother's song: "Lo, he now commandeth/ All on earth to sing."

The train came over the bridge, moving slowly, leaving hollow bellies of sound beneath the spans as it passed from pillar to pillar. It stopped at the end of the bridge and a dark figure dropped from the cab, then waved the engineer on.

Carlisle waited until the train moved off, then he went up the bank.

Leverett turned, surprised by Carlisle's sudden appearance, and saluted. "Your prisoner, sir," he said.

"What's it all about?"

"Didn't they tell you?"

"Taziola said you'd got into a brawl at the Mulligan." There was a hint of approval in Carlisle's voice and Ira moved closer to see his expression. "That all?"

"He said someone fired a shot that blew their poker pot all to hell."

"Cloak had two pair, kings up."

Carlisle laughed, his breath crackling in the cold air. "No wonder they were mad. You fire the shot?"

"No."

"Well?"

"It was a Czech named Markowitz."

Carlisle's mouth remained open as though he was about to speak, but instead he made a quick erasing gesture with the flat of his hand and looked away. With his hand still raised he turned slowly, watching the hills, listening intently.

The light had come.

Leverett saw it too. Suddenly it was there. Evergreen trees appeared on the white hills. Space sprang out between the steel girders of the bridge. They could feel the presence of the mountains and the great cold expanse of Lake Baikal. They heard the train going toward Posolskaya. The guards were perfectly still and alert.

Then it passed. It was daylight. There were pale shadows. Sound and sight blurred together. Another day.

Carlisle walked back toward their camp of ten cars on the siding near the settlement of Tataurovo where the spur line branched off and ran down the Selenga Valley to Kiakhta. His hand was still raised in a hushing sign, but after a few steps he put it in his coat pocket.

Leverett trotted after him. "You want to hear about it?" he asked.

Carlisle increased his pace and shook his head.

"He had a message for you, then he made a remark."

Carlisle went up the wooden steps to their car and threw the sliding door open with a crash.

Ira followed him inside and closed the door. "Captain of the Powder Room," he said. "That's a good one."

Carlisle stood with his back to Ira and his head pulled down between his shoulders.

"I guess Markowitz and that cousin of his draw a lot of water. I wish I'd seen her."

Carlisle spun around, his face black, his eyes filled with blood. "You're all alike! All of you, all alike!"

The expression on Ira's face was set by a freezing shock which ran up his spine.

"Talk!" Carlisle roared. "That's all you god-damned people do is talk. You can't leave anything alone. The whole god-damned world is your business." He stripped off his coat and threw it on the bunk, his chest heaving, his breath short with anger.

"She sent you her regards."

"Shut up!"

"All right."

Ira took off his coat and hung it up.

The only sound in the car was their coarse breathing, which was charged with violence. For a time they engaged in a contest to see which of them would be the first to speak, then Carlisle went to the stove and made a great noise stoking it with coal.

"All right, what did he say?"

"That you were impulsive."

"That why you hit him?"

Ira nodded.

Carlisle swung away from the stove and paced back and forth. "You shouldn't have mixed in. It was none of your business. When are you going to learn that?"

"What is my business, Captain?" Ira asked levelly.

"To protect this section of the railroad and to stay neutral. You're not supposed to fight the Czechs, god damn it!"

Ira smiled. "I hadn't realized this came under General Graves' proclamation. How does that go? 'All will be equally benefited, and all shall be treated alike by our forces irrespective of persons, nationality, religion or politics.' That leaves out a lot, doesn't it?"

"What's that mean?"

"That there are some things a man can't be neutral about, that's all."

"You can be neutral about anything if you have a sense of duty."

Ira snorted and looked at Carlisle, his anger rising again. "It's ridiculous!" he declared. "Some things you can't be neutral about. Friendship, for instance. People have feelings."

"In the army they don't count."

"Your feelings for Austin don't count? What about Maryenka? You've got feelings, Sioux."

"They don't count," Carlisle said.

"And that woman in Vlad, the Countess or whatever she is. No feelings there, right?"

"Nothing that counts!" Carlisle retorted but he was trembling and his fists were clenched hard as rocks.

Ira frowned and shook his head slowly. "I'm not going to be your punching bag, Captain. I'll be a friend if that doesn't violate your sense of duty, but I'm not going to swap punches with you like Austin used to do."

"He tell you that?"

"No, I saw it. Austin wouldn't have told me."

"He was a damned fool!" Carlisle said explosively. "A god-damned fool!"

They glared at each other, both tense, both balanced on a high wire of anger; then Ira drew a deep breath. "You can't hit Austin anymore, Sioux. He's gone."

Carlisle bent in the middle. His breath came out in an awful sigh and his face went gray. He stumbled to the door, threw it back with a wood-splintering crash and jumped to the ground; then he slung the door shut with a crushing sweep of his arm, but it bounced back, leaving an opening through which Ira could see him walking toward the river clawing at his breast with both hands as though he were wounded.

At the edge of the river Carlisle took an envelope from his breast pocket and ripped it to shreds with every bit of his strength, over and over as though he were throttling a human being. When he could tear it no more he cast the bits into the river.

They fell like snowflakes, gently.

Ira watched overawed. He'd witnessed a murder. This he knew. He didn't know who or what had been killed, but the intent was unmistakable.

Carlisle stood still, face taut, staring fixedly into the flat sky over the hills. A few bits of the paper had fallen on the shoulders of his blouse and he seemed to be waiting for the wind to cleanse him.

Ira stepped to the door and closed it.

« 2 »

Lieutenant Markowitz, his customary elegance destroyed by several layers of adhesive tape across his nose, looked out the window as his train crossed the bridge at Tataurovo and saw the American encampment.

Several soldiers waved at the passing train and Markowitz, sure that he saw Carlisle in the doorway of one teplushka, pulled back from the window. He smiled at his timidity and this hurt his nose and annoyed him. The camp was gone in an instant.

He supposed he could thank Tatiana for a broken nose. She took such drivel to heart. Clumsy drivel at that: "No woman will ever again speak as directly to me as you did —"

Markowitz snorted and winced. An Indian love call couched in second-hand prose.

Impulsive? It was mawkish!

Tatiana, of course, had grown misty-eyed.

She was beautiful, yes, but unrestrained. Entirely unrestrained. She would probably have broken his nose herself if he'd given her the chance. Appointments in Samara. Bastard!

Markowitz lit a cigarette and relaxed blowing smoke rings, watching the irregular smoke shapes broaden, warp and disappear. It was embarrassing. Americans have no sense of propriety. The code duello was precise in such matters. He should have killed the Jew.

Markowitz sighed and watched his smoke rings vanish.

Relations between the Kolchak government and the Czechs had taken a turn for the worse. The Admiral, surrounded by bumbling incompetents, didn't know whom to believe. He expected too much from the Czechs and distrusted them.

Markowitz put his cigarette out. He was weary. All the Czechs were weary. They wanted one last offensive to carry them home. Home!

Markowitz closed his eyes and listening to the beat of the wheels on the track he remembered a quatrain from Žižka's battle song:

> *Long the Czechs have said*
> *And have proven*
> *That under a good lord*
> *There is good riding.*

But of all the lords from which to choose — Kolchak, Janin, Knox, Cecek, the Japanese, English, Russian or French — Markowitz could not say which was good.

He tossed in his seat trying to relieve a pain like a stitch in his chest and he cursed under his breath.

Under a good lord there is good riding.

A contemptuous smirk turned one corner of his lips and Markowitz shook his head.

Under a good lord.

He was not a good lord then and the riding had been bad. Tatiana was a pane of glass, cool, clean, transparent, not there.

Markowitz groaned. His throat seemed to be filled with ashes. He'd accused her of being shallow, substanceless. "You're all surface, Tatiana! You're cold."

"I'm not afraid anymore, Raul."

The train wheels hammered in his head and the window stared at him. It was aloof. It was dispassionate, separating him from the life beyond it as Tatiana had always done.

He'd spent his life on glass. Others saw through it. He only saw the glass, was dazzled by it, cherished it, yearned from childhood to possess it and had discovered at last the impossibility of ever doing so.

Markowitz shut his eyes and turned his face from the window. He had never known how much glass there was in the world until it began to mock him. There was no escape from it, except in death. Even with his eyes closed he sensed the observing presence of glass. Having seen glass and understood it one could never forget it; one would have to have been blind from birth to avoid the knowledge of glass. Death was the only transparency through which he could step.

Markowitz drew a sharp breath and opened his eyes. A sheet of light stung tears into them.

His heart was racing. He was death-bent, like Albert.

He had stopped at Verkne-Udinsk on the chance of meeting Carlisle, intending to provoke him and be killed. There was no other reason to have stopped there. He was out to obliterate glass.

"Albert, for the love of God!" he said aloud.

Markowitz took a pill to steady himself and waited for the narcotic to take effect. Presently he sighed and closed his eyes and through the glass of memory lodged and shimmering in his brain saw the big house in Malástrana, the baroque house with sculptures by Brokoff where Albert Nojine lived. They had come from school and were in Albert's room. He saw the black paper circle pasted to the ceiling over Albert's desk and asked what it was.

"That," Albert said, "represents eternity," and he smiled in his coldly formal way. Then he sat down at his desk and arranged three mirrors so the black spot was reflected in each of them; took a revolver from his desk drawer and put the barrel into his mouth.

Horror-stricken, Markowitz could not move.

Gazing into the mirrors which reflected black eternity on the ceiling, Albert pressed the trigger slowly until the firing pin snapped on the empty chamber.

He'd taken the pistol from his mouth and looked up at the black circle as though expecting to see a bullet hole in it. "Would I have hit the mark?" he asked. "Do you think I would have hit it?"

Markowitz gripped the arm of his seat experiencing again the terror of that moment, not when the trigger snapped, but when Albert had asked if he would have hit the mark. At the time he had been speechless.

"I want your opinion about the accuracy of my aim."

"But suicide!" Markowitz had gasped.

"About that I do not want your opinion. You're a fool."

From this instant their relationship had matured into one of glacial formality. Albert would not permit anything else. He did not trust anything else. Love was in his opinion invariably self-serving and weak. Hatred and anger were unreasonable. All emotions, all feelings were simply stupid and were to be observed dispassionately through the accurately ground lens of contempt.

Those who did not know Albert well were fascinated by his brilliance, chilled by his coldness and finally put off by his affectations. The contempt he engendered in others for himself was always less than his own for them and this was exemplified by the black circle and by the pistol and mirrors which he always carried with him.

"Since we're told that one must have an object in life I've chosen mine with great care, Raul. I intend to perfect my aim, without the advantage of a test firing, as you can see, until I know, with the same deep certitude of those who believe in God, that I will put a bullet through my brain and into the dead center of this black circle.

"It's faith, you see. It's religion and intelligence all in one packet. I have a goal, a reason for being. I have a ritual of three mirrors, a pistol and a black crepe circle, religious symbols every bit as good as anyone else's."

Albert Nojine.

Yes.

Markowitz' head fell forward and he was smiling. The train bore him onward on dark circles of eternity clattering over rails of glass. Yes, death was certain; therefore taking aim at eternity was an act of faith.

Yes.

Markowitz' palm rested against the shuddering window glass. Yes, the surface of her skin was as impersonal as glass and on an invisible plane in his mind there was a black circle.

« 3 »

During the early days of her captivity while the heavy train beat its way toward Chita, Maryenka made a journey of her own. She could not tell whether the physical immediacy of almost constant assault drove the despair from her body or whether it vanished of its own accord. She had no time to dwell on the death of her family or to think about what the future might hold. She was too intimately occupied with the gun crew.

Certain that her life hung by a slender thread, she was willing to throw it away at any moment and this gave her powers she had not expected.

She wasted no time condemning herself for the choice she had made. It was a narrow one. But she knew there was a point beyond which she would not allow herself to be debased.

She was not even sure where this was, but it gave her a small reserve which she nurtured and gradually broadened.

She insisted from the first that she not be treated as an animal. She had no power to enforce this demand except the men's desire for her and she used this and increased it steadily.

She demanded soap, which they had, and warm water to bathe and she asked that her clothing be returned to her. Rodion, to whom she had made this request, refused, but later she heard a furious argument in the ammunition compartment and that night Glubov came to her with a gift of her clothing. Her undergarments had been washed and clumsily pressed, her boots had been polished and her skirt painstakingly brushed. Glubov delivered a set speech as he presented these to her while the others listened from the open hatch.

Rodion had polished the boots, Daddy Samson had cleaned her skirt and shawl, Glubov had done the rest. She thanked them all and they smiled, but after Rodion and Daddy Samson shut the hatch Glubov whispered to her that the whole thing had been his idea.

As the days wore on the thing which troubled Maryenka most, and which she frequently pondered, was that she did not despise them. Rodion's behavior often frightened and disgusted her. Never, as often as she had felt the weight of his dank scrotum against her inner thigh, had she been able to think of him as other than a brute gulping beast. But she came at last to pity even Rodion, perhaps more so than the other two, and this astonished her, this conversion of one feeling to another.

She could not resist them on pain of death; this much Rodion made clear and the other two, using Rodion's explicit threats to keep her in fear of her life, pretended to sympathize with her. Maryenka did not give herself, they took her and it was in the taking that she discovered the secret possibilities of sin.

One evening when locked in Glubov's arms she sensed his face hovering above her own and in that moment, tempted to join Glubov's ardor, she thought of Austin.

Instantly she knew the grave danger of faithlessness. Her eyes flashed open and Glubov, stricken by the expression in them, stopped making love to her. "Are you hurt?" he asked.

"No," she said.

But Glubov could not continue, for he too had sensed the danger she had passed into. He pulled up his trousers and covered her with the blanket. "Can you tell me?" he asked.

Maryenka shook her head.

"I'll go then."

"Thank you," she said.

And in that way Maryenka came to know that sin is in the imagination, in the refusal to confront reality. She had been tempted to pretend Glubov was Austin. In this she could have been momentarily successful; having been successful with Glubov she could have included Daddy Samson and even Rodion, which would have been a grievous crime against Austin, but one which she would never have had to confess.

This crime would have lain in her heart, a coiled secret, and it would have gradually poisoned her existence.

But the intimacy and revealing power of the sexual act was binding in many ways and these she had to face honestly.

Her body did respond. Her mind was often filled with dark, pleasurable thoughts even in the arms of bristle-bellied, groaning Rodion. She had to confront these men as they were and not escape by thinking of Austin.

Of Petra?

Maryenka shuddered. How vile! Dear Petra who made love to her so sweetly, apologizing because he was so frail. Petra Shulgin had always been more a child to her than a man. A respected child and she could not think of him. It was Austin who made love to her as a man, but she must not think of him. No, her eyes hereafter would remain open, staring into the eyes of Glubov, Rodion and Daddy Samson as they came to her. She would see them clearly, attempt to understand them, and she would not commit the crime of counterfeiting passion on Austin's image.

The three gunners noticed the change in Maryenka at once and were challenged by it. They grew silent and puzzled and a peculiar tension developed among them.

Rodion was angered by her steadfast gaze. "Shut your eyes, you slut. It's indecent!"

"No, I will not."

Rodion thereafter shut his own and was more gentle.

They began to think of ways to please Maryenka.

To relieve the forbidding interior of the gun turret they tried to furnish and decorate it. They brought a pallet and made a crude bed between the wall and the gun with canvas. They draped the gun slits to keep out the cold and when she complained of the darkness they worked feverishly removing one of the plates at the back of the turret to make her a window, which they covered with a sheet of isinglass. They found pictures and an ikon. They made her a chair from a packing crate. They bartered with the Cossacks for loot which they thought would please her. In short the gunners made a nest and the gun turret began to resemble the interior of a Tatar's yurt.

They scheduled the time each man spent with her but Glubov, being the gun captain, preempted the nights.

In the mornings Daddy Samson came with her breakfast, bread, tea, bacon and an egg. He would sit down against the wall and watch as she ate, claiming he only wanted to talk. He talked a great deal about his wife, who had died of cholera, and he talked about his daughters. He was fond of them and his eyes grew misty as he recalled their childhood; how they dashed to him when he came home from work; how they thought he was the biggest man in the world until he took them to a carnival in Khabarovsk where they saw a man half a head taller than he was. This broke their hearts. "I never felt so small as when they looked up at that man," he said.

Daddy Samson always said he only wanted to talk, but in the end he'd kiss her "for Katya and Anna." Then he'd bring her to the bed and whether he succeeded in making love or not he was invariably ashamed and left her saying he'd control himself next time. "You're a fine girl, Maryenka," he'd say. "Next time I'll remember." And he'd go out, crestfallen and angry with himself.

Maryenka never answered if they reproached themselves. About this she maintained a strict silence. She didn't condemn them or forgive them. She just met their eyes with an exacting tolerance and waited.

Then one day near Chita the alarm bells rang and the train came to a jolting halt. There were shouts and the sound of gunfire and Rodion leaped up from Maryenka on the bed, snatched his trousers hanging from the breech of the cannon and stumbled toward the hatch.

Glubov appeared. "God!" he cried. "Get that plate back on! Samson!"

They heard the machine guns firing and the clatter of horses hoofs.

Samson brought the steel plate they'd removed to make a window and began to bolt it back in place.

"Maryenka, get out," Glubov yelled. "Rodion, don't stand there, bring the shells!"

Maryenka followed Rodion through the hatch into the ammunition compartment. She sat down and slipped into her boots and skirt while Glubov tore into the furnishings of the turret trying to free the gun for action. He cursed and flailed about hysterically, tore the drapes down and kicked wildly at the bed tied to the gun.

Rodion passed the first shell, which Samson fumbled into the breech of the fouled gun.

Glubov got his headset on and reported the gun ready to fire although it was still pointed back along the tracks. He worked furiously to elevate it, but Maryenka's shirtwaist, hanging on the wheel, snarled the gears.

Daddy Samson was beside himself. "Her shirtwaist!" he cried. "You're tearing it!"

"Damn the shirtwaist," Glubov roared. "Get it out," and he began tearing at the material and trying to reverse crank.

Daddy Samson picked up Maryenka's blanket from the floor and started to hang it up, but Glubov slapped it out of his hands. "I'm tidying up," Daddy Samson said with an injured expression.

"Load the gun, you ass!"

"It is loaded," Daddy Samson said indignantly. "I'm ready to fire it."

"I have to aim it!"

"Aim it then."

Glubov made another effort to do so, but the gun was hopelessly jammed. "Fire!" he yelled.

Daddy Samson hesitated, the gun was still pointed straight back along the track.

"Fire," Glubov raged. "I said fire!"

Daddy Samson pulled the lanyard and the recoiling gun tore the bed apart. The pictures and the ikon fell off the wall and the plate Daddy Samson had tried to replace also fell to the floor.

Glubov roared commands trying to get the turret turned and the gun on target. Rodion passed the shells while Daddy Samson fought through the debris to load the gun. They got the turret turning, then it jammed. They continued firing irregularly and through the missing back plate Maryenka could see the bleak, snow-clad landscape, with guns flashing from a dark line of trees.

Machine gun fire began to rake the train. It came in gusts, sweeping along the sides of their car and passing on. She heard horses screaming and knew that some of them had been hit. The train began to move.

The noise was awful and Maryenka, still naked to the waist, shuddered. Smoke and the smell of explosives filled the compartment. The train picked up speed and the sound of machine gun fire diminished. The forward gun stopped firing and after one more shot their gun too fell silent.

The turret turned so that the entry hatch came into alignment with the ammunition compartment and Glubov jumped out. He was not less excited than he had been at the start of the engagement. "Cover yourself, woman, for the love of God!"

"I have nothing!"

Maryenka glanced into the turret and through the opening where the plate was missing saw Cossacks galloping after the train. They were still under fire and the machine guns peeled riders from their horses like corn shucked off a cob.

"Get her something, Rodion, you idiot! Samson, clear that out in there! Everything out! The Colonel is going to have us flayed. We lost our Cossacks and he'll blame us!"

"Who attacked us?" Daddy Samson asked.

"I don't know, you fool! I'll tell the Colonel we took a hit to excuse our failure. Hurry."

"A hit," Rodion said dumbly.

Daddy Samson was wadding blankets and drapes and debris and forcing it out through the open place in the turret.

Glubov looked at Maryenka again in exasperation. He tore a locker open and tossed her a man's blouse. "Here, put this on." Then as the thought occurred to him he took a pair of trousers too. "And these. Out of that skirt and into these and find a way to hide your hair. Our only chance is to disappear."

As she put on these clothes, Rodion came to the hatch door and held up the ikon. "Do you want this, Maryenka?" he asked. "It's pretty."

Glubov, who had taken several hand grenades from the ammunition locker, turned to Rodion in fury. "You damned fool, you're dead and don't know it! Sipialef will decorate a fence post with that ugly red-splotched face of yours —"

"Don't," Maryenka said quietly.

Both men looked at her. It was the first word of defense she had uttered in anyone's behalf. She turned away to finish dressing, confused herself that she had said anything.

Glubov went into the turret and ordered Samson and Rodion to remove the shells which hadn't been fired. He told them to get out, put the grenades on the floor, then plunged through the hatch, slammed the door behind him and motioned them down.

There were four explosions. A piece of shrapnel tore through the hatch, spent itself on the roof of the car and fell on Rodion's naked back. He yelped and leaped up. Yellow smoke issued around the edges of the hatch. Glubov opened it and jumped inside. As the smoke cleared he and Samson surveyed the damage wrought by the grenades.

"It's all done now," Rodion said.

Glubov shook his head. "It won't work. The Colonel's not such a fool that he won't know how this was done. We'll have to jump for it, boys."

"It was a pretty place," Rodion said sadly.

Glubov glared at him. Samson looked bewildered. "How will we get on without papers?" he asked. "How'll we live?"

"Minute by minute, old man," Glubov said. "Better gather what you think you'll need and drop off."

The three men set about equipping themselves. They packed food and took their weapons and ammunition.

"Better slide off the back in case there are some men on the car ahead," Glubov said.

Samson nodded and went into the turret. Rodion followed but stopped at the hatch. "What about Maryenka?" he asked.

"I'll look after her," Glubov said.

"Why not us all?"

Glubov raised his pistol and fired. The shot hit Rodion in the neck and threw him down. He thrashed, half rose, then fell under the gun. Glubov fired again and killed him.

Daddy Samson gasped, threw his pack and rifle through the hole left by the vacant plate, then dove after them head first. His big body was too large to go through at once and he struggled, panic-ridden, expecting to take a bullet along his spine.

Maryenka put her hand on Glubov's pistol and pressed it down and they saw Daddy Samson fall to the track behind the train. He lay there for a time, then he rose and hobbled back along the ties to recover his pack and rifle.

"We'll wait a bit," Glubov said.

"What can we do?"

"Join the partisans," Glubov said. "There's nothing else for it."

CHAPTER FOURTEEN

HAVING established his headquarters at Tataurovo and given specific orders to his men never to venture beyond camp without permission and then only in pairs and armed, Carlisle made an exception of himself and set out alone to explore the area on both sides of the track which it was his responsibility to protect. Although he pretended these reconnoitering trips were of a military nature the pleasure he took in them sometimes made him a bit guilty, particularly as he had outfitted himself with a pair of Norwegian skis and a fine shotgun purchased secondhand in Verkhne-Udinsk.

When he returned he nearly always had a bag of snow grouse, or rabbit for the pot, but Leverett never referred to these excursions as hunting trips or asked to go along. He sensed Carlisle's need to be alone and as they grew closer he began to understand Carlisle's feeling for the country, to understand that it was the country of Carlisle's youth.

To make these trips conform to his sense of duty Carlisle made copious notes, maps and sketches of all the countryside bordering the track: "At this point the railroad leaves the valley of the Briana River and enters that of the Uda. The Uda River flows through a comparatively uninhabited valley to Verkhne-Udinsk. The bridge which crosses the Uda to the north bank is three hundred and fifty feet long, supported by stone pillars laid in watertight compartments."

These entries written in a surprisingly fine hand were revised and refined but the notebook, which had begun as a dry testament of useful or at least exacting topographical observations and engineering data, took on another character.

This change occurred with the entry: "I met the wolf hunter." It was the first time Carlisle had used a personal pronoun and thereafter Leverett noticed that the notebook, which had previously been put with other company records, was no longer left out where he, or anyone else, could read it and he knew that Carlisle had begun writing a diary.

Carlisle had seen wolf tracks many times, never a wolf, but on the morning of the day he began his diary he'd come upon the half-devoured carcass of a horse in a circle of wolf tracks in a broad field of snow. The only way for it to have come there was to have been brought on a sledge. There were no hoofprints, so Carlisle concluded it was a bait horse set out by a hunter to attract the wolves.

He was about ten miles east of Tataurovo and could see the frozen surface of the Briana River in the distance. It was very still; the white landscape was relieved here and there by hazel thickets, some alder and Siberian fir trees, and by clumps of berrybrush, which, bowed under its heavy mantle of snow, made ideal lairs for all manner of wild life including wolves.

He stood very still in all that white stillness with the uneasy feeling that he was being observed. The sun, a misty, flat silver disc, had barely cleared the mountains and gave light but no heat, and it too seemed to observe his stillness.

The light was harsh to his eye, but the shadows it cast were pale, as though they had been bleached. Carlisle was very apprehensive, straining his senses, but all he heard was the working of his own body, his heart, his lungs, an unsettling gurgle in his belly.

He unslung his shotgun, removed the shells he kept ready for light game, and loaded it with the heavier shot he carried on the chance of seeing a deer. When he snapped the shotgun closed it rang sharply metallic in the cold air, causing him to look up to see what effect this announcement of his presence might have had, and he saw a movement, or rather the cessation of a movement, among some fir trees up a slope, two hundred yards away on his left flank.

He loosened the flap of the holster on his forty-five and headed toward the place, wary but relieved. There was a slight drop to the base of the slope and he gathered speed, his skis crackling through the fresh morning crust of the snow. Then, as he started up, a figure appeared above him, a man with a huge coil of red-flagged rope on his back.

Carlisle stopped and looked at this man, so perfectly silent, whose appearance had the effect of coming face to face with an unexpected mirror. Their meeting was a shock and they shared one expression which was a perfect statement of their mutual astonishment. It was not that they looked so much alike, though their similarity was striking; it was that merely by his existence each spoke directly to the other. They knew each other, and were sure of a deep previous awareness of the other's existence, as though they were brothers meeting after a prolonged separation.

The man with the rope on his back was the first to speak — more, it seemed, to reassert his own identity than to introduce himself. "Yakushef," he said.

"Carlisle," Carlisle said.

For another moment they stared, looking now for those features which distinguished them from each other, and finding these they were reassured and they smiled.

"Yakushef," the hunter said once more and this time he tapped his chest.

Carlisle nodded, repeated his own name and also touched his chest, whereupon Yakushef moved on down the slope uncoiling the length of rope behind him, leaving it on the snow. He worked purposefully and Carlisle watched trying to guess what Yakushef was up to.

The rope had blood-red streamers of cloth attached to it a yard apart and these, lying against the snow, gave the white landscape an appearance of gaiety. In some places Yakushef draped the flagged rope over the brush so the streamers were suspended three feet above the snow, and when he reached the end, about a hundred and fifty yards, he worked his way back, cutting saplings to support the rope where it touched the ground.

This done he passed Carlisle without a word, went into the grove of trees and reappeared with another coil of flagged rope, and proceeded as before. Carlisle cut saplings and followed Yakushef, fixing the rope above the snow as he had done. They worked in absolute silence until the pale sun was high overhead and in this time they had made a circle of rope almost a mile in circumference with a narrow gap which opened toward the carcass of the horse.

The hundreds of red flags rippling in the air reminded Carlisle of the garnet necklace on Tatiana Nojine's white neck when he had first seen her at the ball in Vladivostok and he stood for a moment puzzling about the line of flags and about why his thoughts so often turned to this woman whom he had made such a determined effort to dismiss from his mind.

Yakushef beckoned and they went to a light basket sledge which contained the hunter's gear, his shotgun, a few small traps and his food. He offered Carlisle a drink from a clay bottle which contained a jolting vodka that brought tears to Carlisle's eyes and a grin to Yakushef's face. He brought two steaming baked potatoes out of a wolfskin pouch and offered one to Carlisle, who took it and from his own pack shared a thermos of hot coffee and two baked-ham sandwiches. Yakushef reacted to the coffee as Carlisle had to the vodka, but he relished the ham and the cigarettes, taking one to smoke and another to put behind his ear.

There was on the whole a curious reserve between them; they avoided looking directly at each other, as though afraid of becoming entangled again in that confusion of identity which had occurred at their first encounter. But they studied each other on the sly, each trying to describe this thing which was between them and thus put it to rest.

Yakushef was forty-five, his mother was an Evenki from the Kureika River district who had married a Ukrainian, a Siberiak, one of those men who had come east to settle the virgin taiga. In his early years Yakushef had lived the nomadic existence of his people, following the reindeer, his home a birchbark wigwam. After the death of his mother he came south along the Yenisei River to the Angara, and then east to Irkutsk and finally to the village of Onokoi where he now lived with his Buryat wife and two sons making his living as a hunter.

His father, typically, had abandoned the Evenkis shortly after Yakushef's birth and though he bore the man's name he wouldn't have recognized him, but sometimes he wondered if there weren't other Yakushefs in the world, half brothers or sisters of his who, if they met, might recognize in each other's features their common father. He was sure Carlisle was not one of these and that he was not an Evenki, but there was, all the same, this startling sense of kinship.

For his part Carlisle realized that what they shared was a common Indian heritage. He didn't know the tribe, or the circumstances of Yakushef's life, but he knew the features, the broad dark face with its prominent nose, black piercing eyes, the straight heavy black hair; but it wasn't until Yakushef began to explain the significance of the broken circle of red flags in the snow that Carlisle made the connection to his own family.

Yakushef bore a strong resemblance to Henry Buckeye, Carlisle's uncle, who had taught him to hunt in the Dakota winter. The similarity was not in his features but in his gestures, posture and in the hunter's patience expressed by his hands and his eyes.

Yakushef drew a diagram of the flags which nearly encircled a thicket of brush in which he planted the print of a wolf with five single marks, indicating a pack. He traced a line from this thicket to the bait horse and indicated that the wolves traveled from their lair to the horse to feed and back again to sleep. Occasionally he spoke, more to himself than to Carlisle, as though the words were more important as magic than for the information they conveyed. Henry Buckeye spoke in just the same way and Carlisle nodded, feeling himself a boy again, being tutored by a man with an instinct for hunting deep in his bones.

Carlisle understood that circle of flagged rope would contain the wolves and that beaters would arrive to drive them out of the thicket toward the gap near the bait horse. Where the beaters would come from and why the wolves would not jump the rope once they were alarmed he did not know.

Yakushef lit his second cigarette and settled down against the sledge. Occasionally he took a sip of vodka, but he gave no further recognition to Carlisle's presence and Carlisle, remembering long hours of silent waiting beside deer trails with his uncle, felt closer to this man than to any he could remember. It was the deep, silent kinship of those who wait in sparsely timbered snow country, listening with all their being to nothing, letting their half-shut eyes fill with details of the landscape until all of it is thoroughly known.

Slowly the area began to populate itself with creatures which had been there before, unnoticed. A martin came up from the frozen Briana and disappeared into a hummock of snow. A pair of deer passed along the crest of the far hillside. A black crow settled on the bait horse and probed the frozen carcass for a hold with its beak. Smaller birds and rodents caused silent flurries of snow in the branches of the trees. And gradually the two men began to sense the presence of the five wolves sleeping in the thicket circled by the flags.

In the late afternoon Yakushef rose and beckoned Carlisle to follow. The beaters had arrived; they were Yakushef's sons, although Carlisle didn't know this until after the shoot. He saw them approaching on horseback, down the shallow white hill toward the circle of red flags. He followed Yakushef to the gap in the circle and took his place beside a stumpy fir where the line began.

Yakushef crossed the gap and knelt beside a bush. He patted a place in the snow and laid out his shotgun shells, four of them, and two for the barrels of his ancient shotgun, six shots for five wolves, and Carlisle wondered if the man had really intended to take the whole pack alone, and knew he was stupid to wonder.

He checked his own shotgun to be sure he'd loaded the heavy gauge shells; he had only six others that would do anything to a wolf and he wondered where to put them to have them in easy reach. His coat pocket seemed deep and far away, so he stuck two in his belt loop and four into a crevice of the tree trunk at his side and he was still happy about the weight of the forty-five on his hip.

He had just settled this when he heard the beaters yelling half a mile away beyond the thicket. Their voices, clear and piercing in the cold air, broke and soared in a staccato chant, *Aie, chak, chak, chaka,* which was accompanied by a whistling sound.

Carlisle tensed, waiting for the wolves, expecting them to charge out of the thicket and head for the gap at full speed. He was wrong about this, for when the wolves did emerge from the thicket they came one at a time and stood looking about, taking stock of their situation. Their attitude of deliberation was more menacing than a precipitous charge could possibly have been. Three of them were huge, with broad ruffed heads and long heavy jaws; the other two were as large as any wolf Carlisle remembered having seen in Dakota.

He glanced toward Yakushef, who was watching the pack with a glint of approval in his black eyes. The beaters continued to yell and now one of them appeared riding well outside the line of red-flagged rope, waving something which appeared to be a ratchet noisemaker. The wolves, apparently unharried by this sound, began to move toward the gap. They paused now and again and one of the pack would lope off to explore, but coming to the line of rope, it would stop and return to the pack. They seemed to be exchanging intelligence, planning an action as they came slowly toward the gap along the trail they had traveled between the bait horse and their thicket.

Their size seemed to increase disproportionately to their exhibition of calm intelligence, but they would not cross the barrier of red flags. Each of the pack approached the flags at one time or another but they turned back as though the line was insurmountable, whereas they each could have jumped a solid barrier three times as high.

Carlisle was strongly impressed and as the wolves drew closer he found himself wishing one of them would jump and make an exit for the others, not because he was afraid to face them, but because he didn't like their intelligence being foiled by such a flimsy barrier. It made him feel the wolf in himself, his own artificially circumscribed existence, his refusal to step beyond flagged lines toward the people who were important to him, toward worlds of freedom he sensed but dared not venture toward. And as the wolves drew closer their wariness angered him because it was too self-protective and timid within the limits of the red-flagged taboo. They were incapable of crossing the flags, so they were going to be slaughtered, and as they drew into firing range Carlisle felt no pity for them. Escape had been possible every step of the way, but they refused it.

He sighted his shotgun on the large wolf nearest him, and saw in the corner of his eye that Yakushef too had raised his gun. He decided not to pull a trigger until Yakushef fired, and tracked his chosen wolf over the gold bead sight between the barrels of his gun noting the gray fleck in its yellow eyes, the tossing, alert nervousness of its head. The afternoon breeze had freshened and coming from behind his wolf it raised the shag of fur around its neck and Carlisle realized by the direction of the wind how wisely Yakushef had chosen his site. The black nostrils of his wolf quivered intensely as though probing for a moment just ahead which it could not smell. Its mouth was shut and dry. It stopped not twenty feet away and its shallow eyes settled on Carlisle, who almost felt the imprint of his dim outline on those wild irises.

He heard Yakushef's gun, a deep crashing report, followed by an enraged howl, and the snow behind his wolf was churned by heavy shot. As his wolf leaped Carlisle fired and saw the black swarm of pellets catch the wolf in the hindquarters and bowels rather than forward as he had planned. He raised his gun and fired at the second wolf now racing toward the gap; it went down, rolling side over side, then came to its feet and fell.

Carlisle broke his gun to reload and saw the first wolf he'd shot roweling toward him through the snow, its fangs snapping over a terrible pained roar.

Fumbling for the cartridges in his belt Carlisle backed away from the tree and to the left toward the rope. He heard two more quick reports and dimly realized that after his first shot Yakushef had reloaded his gun, leaving one shell in the barrel.

While keeping his eyes on the wolf which had turned to follow him, dragging its bloody hindquarters, Carlisle got the shells into his gun. He was beyond the rope now, with the wolf on the other side, all its savage hatred focused on getting to the man.

Carlisle raised his shotgun, but to his astonishment the wolf stopped at the flags. It was not six feet away, roaring, snapping furiously at Carlisle over the red flags on the rope, but it would not cross. The wolf swung its huge head from side to side seeking even in its death throes a way to get around the rope and reach Carlisle, but the strength went out of it and it lay down groveling and gnashing and before Carlisle could fire it died.

Carlisle lowered his shotgun. He experienced a singing moment of complete unreality and the luster passing from the eyes of the wolf seemed to transmit their final message to him.

When he looked up, Yakushef and his sons were retrieving the fallen wolves. Between them they had killed the pack of five.

One boy began to skin the wolves as Yakushef came to Carlisle with the other, a lad of twenty with strong Mongolian features and a vast grin which narrowed his eyes to slits of merriment. Yakushef offered Carlisle another drink from his bottle of vodka and Carlisle took it, pleased now by the jolt it gave him. He had to get back to Tataurovo. It was late and he had ten miles to go.

Yakushef indicated the wolf and asked by signs if Carlisle wanted the pelt. Carlisle did not. He tapped his chest and gestured toward his camp. "Tataurovo," he said.

Yakushef made a gesture with the flat of his hand toward his village, exactly the same gesture Henry Buckeye would have used. "Onokoi," he said.

They nodded and parted as brothers.

Carlisle slung his shotgun, took the shells he'd put in the tree, and left with only an hour of light to guide him. The snow, perfectly white around the tips of his skis, fell off to gray and darkness was beginning to block in the areas among the trees. On the far side of the field Carlisle stopped to look back at Yakushef and his sons. One of the boys was recovering the rope, coiling it into the sledge as he went along, and the flags which had been so brilliant were now almost black against the snow.

He reached camp after dark.

"I was beginning to worry," Leverett said as he came in.

Carlisle removed his coat and boots and sat down near the stove, exhausted. "I met a wolf hunter, Yakushef," he said. "We shot five wolves between us. A whole pack."

Leverett poured him a mug of coffee and Carlisle talked about Yakushef and the wolves. He even told Leverett his feeling of kinship for the hunter and how this related to his maternal uncle, Henry Buckeye. It was the first time he'd spoken so intimately of his background to anyone. But he didn't tell Leverett about ringing the wolves with the flags and how they died failing to cross this line. This was still too fresh in his mind, too incredible. He wanted to discover its meaning for himself. It was not a common thing.

Thereafter whenever Yakushef ringed a pack of wolves he sent one of his sons to Tataurovo with an invitation for Carlisle to join the shoot. Sometimes it took weeks to locate a pack, lay the bait and accustom the wolves to travel to it from their lair without suspecting a trap. They were extraordinarily intelligent and wary and would never touch a bait until the winter crows had picked at it, signifying there was no human taint.

When he could not go Carlisle sent gifts of shotgun shells to Yakushef, but he went as often as he could, trying to discover for himself the mystery of the wolves' behavior, always hoping that one wolf coming to that red line would know how flimsy it was and jump across it to freedom. On each occasion when he saw a wolf scout toward the line and pause to study it Carlisle was held in suspense while in his mind he urged the beast: "Go over. Go over!" And on each occasion he felt a keen disappointment when the wolf turned back to the pack.

When they reached the gap Carlisle killed them expertly and with a certain disdain.

Yakushef didn't share Carlisle's expectation that a wolf would breach the magic line, and although he too killed them expertly he did so with undiminished respect.

This was the great difference between the two men.

During this time the wolves and the ring assumed such importance for Carlisle that they invaded and confused his dreams. In them he often saw the railroad, the Amur line, the Trans-Siberian and the Chinese Eastern, from Verkhne-Udinsk to Chita, to Khabarovsk, to Vladivostok and back again, as a great loop around the wolves, or again it was a garnet necklace in the snow with interior lights dazzling his yellow eyes as he circled around, but could not cross. The faces of Yakushef, Leverett, Austin and Tatiana appeared in these dreams, no other, and once the slightly acid odor of wolf was so sharp in his dream that he woke up trembling.

Ordinarily Carlisle dismissed his dreams, but these he carried with him and some found their way into his notebook written in a hand which appeared to be guided not by Carlisle but by the dreams themselves. The calligraphy was so distinct that Carlisle wished to discover whose it was. And once this hand wrote across the page of a diagram of his latest hunt with Yakushef: "We must break out."

And Carlisle remembered that the clan of his uncle, Henry Buckeye, carried the sign of the wolf.

« 2 »

The axis of the earth tipped once more and somewhere in the Trans-Baikal a ruff of snow slipped from the boughs of a Siberian cedar and fell unheard to the base of the tree.

The Siberiak hunters, always close observers of the seasons, watched the inevitable change which meant so much to their daily occupations. An icicle clinging to the eaves of a hut, thawing by day, freezing by night, told the omul fishermen of Lake Baikal when to mend their nets and caulk their boats. Fur trappers could tell the thickness of an ermine pelt by the sound of the snow crust breaking under their feet and farmers, watching the sky, knew when the wild seeds would begin to stir and when the earth would turn under the blade of a plow.

Slowly the long days thawed more than the nights could freeze and the intense cold was beaten back with cannonades of breaking ice on the lakes and rivers and roaring avalanches in the mountains until at last General Winter had to conduct his forays entirely under the cover of darkness. He was, however, never defeated, because he held the earth two feet below the surface in his grip.

But spring was due to come. It was inevitable and those men who considered themselves allied with the forces of the season were certain of victory over the Bolsheviks. The position of the world on its axis favored them, inevitably. Opinion of all the capitals of the world favored them, inevitably. Military authorities planned an Allied summer in all Russia, inevitably. No power on earth could change the coming season.

The Bolsheviks, surrounded in the heartland of European Russia, were isolated, blockaded, bankrupt, unrecognized, war-weary, demoralized and outnumbered.

In the north from Murmansk to Archangel an army of forty thousand — Russians, British, Canadians, French and Americans — prepared to move south and close the gap between themselves and the Kolchak armies advancing from the east. On the western front from Reval to Odessa armies of Rumanians, Poles, Germans, Letts and Estonians, almost two hundred thousand men, prepared to attack Petrograd and Moscow. To the south the French 30th and 156th Divisions and the Greek 2nd and 13th Division, plus twelve thousand volunteers and elements of the French Navy, held a line from Odessa to Sevastopol linking with the Volunteer Armies of the Don of eighty thousand men holding the front from the Sea of Azov to the Caspian. General Dutov with fifty thousand men would close the gap between Kolchak and the Armies of the Don. There was money, matériel, manpower. God and the powers of March were aligned against the Bolsheviks, whose defeat was — inevitable.

M. Pinchon, the French Minister of Foreign Affairs, made an estimate of troops in Siberia supporting the Kolchak government, directly or indirectly: "Czechs, 55,000. Poles, 12,000. Serbians, 4,000. Italians, 2,000. British, 1,600. French, 760. Japanese, 28,000. Americans, 7,500. Canadians 4,000. (White) Russians, 100,000."

In some cases M. Pinchon's estimates were conservative; the Japanese, for instance, had close to seventy thousand troops in Siberia and the French had not so many as stated. But excusing M. Pinchon's natural inclination to exaggerate his country's contribution to the expected victory, it is safe to say that two hundred thousand troops faced the Bolsheviks on the eastern front, so the total encirclement added up to a force more than adequate to the season.

Russian bonds issued to guarantee French loans to the Czar traded briskly once more on the Bourse. British and American transportation and manufacturing tycoons were making gentlemen's agreements about the division of Russian markets—the Japanese were willing to be moderate; they would settle for the Maritime Province and a few concessions — and since commerce follows the flag one could assume, from the number of flags alone, that Mother Russia was due for an unprecedented commercial renaissance.

Within the circle of flags the Bolsheviks were surprised each day to find themselves still in power, and to stay there they labored mightily, sowing confusion around the clock. They distributed confusion by speech and by proclamation, by publication of laws, edicts, slogans, condemnations, accusations, by meetings, meetings, meetings, congresses, conventions, talk, talk, talk. Each statement drew seventeen rebuttals, and each rebuttal drew surrebuttals too numerous to count. Lenin alone chewed forests to pulp. Members of opposition parties plugged their ears and went underground, where, like worms, they enriched the soil for more confusion to root. To all except a few madmen, a few fanatics, a few men too preoccupied with the daily struggle to see it, defeat of the Bolsheviks was inevitable. The forces of March made it so.

The earth was tipped on its axis and days in the northern hemisphere were long.

Soon General Yudenich and his White Guards would enter Petrograd.

Which general would capture Moscow was the subject of an international sweepstakes, but General Denikin, only four hundred miles south of Moscow with his Volunteer Armies of the Don, was strongly favored.

But in the Trans-Baikal where the cedar and pine trees shed their mantling show; and all across the Siberian plateau, in the taiga, and on the plains, the Russian peasant who in most cases could not read or write or name the passing flags watched the signs of spring and knew the time to work had come; and when armies with alien flags, speaking alien tongues, put themselves between the peasant and his labor, battle lines were drawn which no politician had taken into account.

CHAPTER FIFTEEN

As the weather grew mild the Americans in their camps got mud in exchange for snow. Roads and footpaths around the company bivouac areas and in the adjacent villages turned overnight into a dark, energy-sapping mud and everyone wished to God it would freeze again because, of the two enemies snow and mud, they much preferred the snow, which was cleaner.

The spring thaw was an unwarranted catastrophe. Around the camp cars mud was two feet thick and the men made duckboards to support themselves, miles of duckboards which the mud consumed. They hauled stone and railroad ties to make foundations for their paths and cursed the mud, scraped it from their boots, shoveled it out of their cars, flaked it off their clothing and their skins, but the supply of fresh mud was inexhaustible. Wherever a foot, wheel or hoof touched the earth it bruised and exuded water which promptly turned to mud.

Armies, gathered for the spring offensive, bogged down and waited for the mud to harden so they could move again. Train traffic slowed as ties and rails slipped and warped along the thawing embankments.

There was no escape from the mud, not in the cities, the villages or in the vast taiga which thawed slowly, leaving black pools on the frozen subsurface.

Carlisle gave up hunting. Yakushef and his sons slept through the muddy season. The ice broke on Lake Baikal and was flushed away on the swollen Angara River, pulverizing itself in the rocky gorges with a tumultuous roar.

To keep up with the weather damage to the roadbed in the American sector Colonel Spaeth doubled the frequency of his track patrols. Armed with rifles, spiking mauls, crowbars and all the tools necessary for making temporary repairs, these men could be seen tramping along, heads down, looking for loose rails, damaged ties and clogged culverts. From Tataurovo two patrols went out each morning; one went east toward Mostovoi, the other went west to the siding at Talovka.

Ira enjoyed these patrols and led one himself whenever he could. In the morning, before they left, each man chipped in a dollar and guessed how many loose spikes they'd have to drive, closest guess took the money. This wager kept them alert, but sometimes there was an argument about whether or not a spike was loose enough to need driving and Ira was the judge, not because he was an officer, but because he didn't have any money in the pool. The number of loose spikes increased steadily with the thaw. Sometimes they'd drive or replace fifty of them in seven miles and the men, having walked the section so often, could tell with their feet how much the ties had shifted.

"This track is going to sink out of sight if they don't get some sand under it," Private Eisenbach said one day.

"I wouldn't miss it none," Keever said.

They were marching toward Talovka through a driving rain every other drop of which was close to being ice. They came to a place where there were four loose spikes in a row and the men with spiking mauls began to drive them while the others stood around in a half circle with their backs to the wind.

"This makes thirty-six already," Eisenbach said.

"Thirty-four," Miller said.

"Thirty-six," Harris said. "Who's got the right count?"

"The Lieutenant," Eisenbach said.

"I make it thirty-four with these," Ira said.

"What the Lieutenant says goes," Eisenbach said and he shrugged.

Ira smiled and walked up the track. He'd gained the confidence of the men, which was in part due to Markowitz. The story of their altercation at the Mulligan had raced through the command and the men were particularly delighted about the shot which had gone through the poker table around which the brass had been gathered. They saw Ira in a new light. Underneath his mild exterior he was a fire-eater; why, he would have killed the poor Czech if they hadn't stopped him. Those who had witnessed Ira's encounter with Sipialef in Vlad reinterpreted the incident, saying Sipialef was lucky he hadn't pushed any further because the Lieutenant was tough.

The men drove the last two spikes and continued up the track. Ira shuddered in the icy rain and glanced up wishing the dark clouds would pass and let the sun break through.

The "Duel at the Mulligan," as it was known, had earned Ira a stinging letter of reprimand from Colonel Spaeth which had gone into his service record: "This officer is deficient in those qualities of good judgment and self-restraint necessary for line duty. On rare occasions these qualities may be acquired through experience, but until they are thoroughly proven, I recommend he be assigned to administrative tasks."

Administrative tasks!

The matter was never mentioned again, not by Carlisle, or Colonel Spaeth, or any of the officers who might have had access to the letter, but Ira found himself trying to exhibit those qualities of good judgment and self-restraint which the Colonel felt to be necessary for line duty. The reprimand had been a direct invitation for Leverett to request a transfer. Why he hadn't done so was something of a mystery. To punish himself? To prove himself? Perhaps, in part, but the basic reason, the one which surprised him, was that he had grown fond of Carlisle and the men of the company.

"Better have a look here, sir," Keever called from behind.

Ira went back to a culvert which drained a small creek into the river on the opposite side of the track. It was clogged with mud and the walls, made of stacked ties, were about to collapse.

"A couple of you men with shovels try to clear this out," Ira said.

Two men sloshed into the heavy, half-frozen mud and began to open a passage. Ira made a note to report the condition of the culvert and was about to go up to the track again when one of the men digging let out a sighing whistle. "There's a man here, sir," he said.

They freed the body with their shovels and pulled it out. It had been a huge man; the freezing and thawing had blackened his flesh, but his eyes were open and though milky with decomposition they appeared to be staring at the flat gray sky. He had a massive gray beard now limp and plastered to his cheeks. There was a deep gash behind his ear. He wore a soggy uniform, but his black, horny feet were bare and he appeared to be about sixty years of age.

"He must have crawled in there," Keever whispered.

Ira removed his coat and dropped it over the old man to keep the hard rain out of his naked eyes.

"You'll be cold, sir," Eisenbach said.

Ira nodded.

"Shall we bury him, or what?" Corporal Turnley asked.

Ira looked around. He didn't know. Administrative questions came to mind. Death certificates, wills to probate, heirs to notify. Search his pockets for identification? Ira supposed this must be done. He was already very wet and cold, but he dropped on one knee beside the body and turned back the coat. Pushing his fingers into the wet pockets he turned them out and found nothing but mud. He covered the body again and stood up. "Find a high spot and we'll bury him," he said.

The men scattered, looking for a suitable place, and Ira went up the embankment to the track, thinking as he did so that it was unusual not to find papers. Most soldiers had them and Ira concluded that the bearded old man was a deserter or perhaps a partisan.

"How about here, sir?" Corporal Turnley called. He was standing on a mound of earth several yards back from the track. Ira nodded. "That'll do," he said.

The men began digging easily at first, but then they hit the permafrost. They attacked this with a shovel-nosed pickax and scraped it out, but the work was hard and depressing.

Ira told those who weren't digging to find rocks for a cairn, then beckoned Eisenbach and went to the body.

They stood together beside the lump under the coat and Ira looked at Eisenbach hopefully. "Do you remember anything about the burial service?" he asked.

"No, sir," Eisenbach said, "I've never been to one."

"Do you remember any prayers that would be right?"

Eisenbach frowned and shook his head. "Just say the Lord's Prayer or something. This man has no relatives here, sir. It's not like there was anyone to console."

Eisenbach kept glancing toward the men on the hill as though he was ashamed to be seen talking over the body. His furtive manner reminded Ira of the time he and Ruth had smuggled a Christmas tree into the house as a symbol of their religious emancipation. Of course his mother had discovered the decorated tree.

"Pagans!" she cried and that evening there had been a trial during which he and Ruth were prosecuted by their mother. Uncle Dave was counsel for the defense and their father the judge. Their right to the tree was saved by Uncle Dave on a plea of innocence, faddism and insanity and they were allowed to have the tree on the condition that they never let the neighbors see it. Thereafter they had a tree each year in his room or in Ruth's and for them the hidden tree came to symbolize all that was meaningful in the holiday season.

The men on the hill had stopped digging and were waiting. Ira glanced at Eisenbach. "All right," he said, "help me carry him up."

They rolled the body in the coat and lugged it to the grave, which was only three feet deep.

"It'll have to be deeper," Ira said.

"We'll be here all day, sir," Turnley said. "That ground is frozen hard as hell."

"Then we'll be here all day!" Ira retorted and snatching a shovel from Keever he jumped into the shallow grave, but the frozen ground turned the shovel under his foot. He took a pick and socked it into the earth, which cut like heavy tar. Having committed himself Ira couldn't stop and he hacked at the frozen ground determinedly for fifteen minutes, then Eisenbach jumped into the grave and removed his coat. "Here, sir, take this. I'll warm up on the pick."

Ira pulled the coat around his shoulders and stepped out. After this the men traded off and in two hours they had a grave five feet deep in the icebound earth.

"Shall we leave him in your coat, sir?" Turnley asked.

Ira nodded. "Yes," he said.

Miller and Harris got into the grave and lowered the body, then scrambled out, their faces white.

Something had to be said. They didn't know the man in Ira's coat, but something had to be said and they all looked at Ira waiting for him to say it.

Ira was cold; he wanted to get it over with and he remembered his Bar Mitzvah.

He remembered facing the congregation; his new suit itched and his hands trembled as he traced the lines of Hebrew which he had memorized to read from the Torah. Everyone was looking at him. Uncle Dave nodded to give him confidence. His father's face was stern and proud. His mother threatened tears and Ruth was annoyed by the hypocrisy because she knew Ira couldn't read Hebrew but was only pretending to do so for the occasion. He saw the scroll before him. The Hebrew characters appeared and Ira thought to repeat what he had memorized then, but the first words took him by surprise and came from somewhere deeper.

"El moley rahamim shohen bamromim, hamtzeh menuhoh nehonoh tahas kanfey hashhinoh, bemaalos k'doshim ut'horim kezohar korokeea mazhirim, es nishmas —"

And here he faltered because he didn't know the name, but Eisenbach joined him and together they carried the memorial prayer for the departed to its conclusion.

When they'd finished Ira nodded and two men with the shovels began to fill the grave. The first earth to hit the corpse gave back a hollow sound and Keever drew a shuddering breath. Ira handed Eisenbach his coat.

"No, sir, you keep it."

"No."

"I'll swap off with Harris or Keever if I get cold. You keep this one and the rest of us will switch around."

It made sense and Ira didn't care to argue.

"You did fine, sir," Eisenbach said quietly. "They liked it."

Ira stared down the tracks and realized that the guiding voice of this prayer had been his Uncle Dave's and that the person to whom it was dedicated was Zelda, Uncle David's wife. Ira had never seen this woman, but there was a faded tintype in his uncle's room and often as a boy, just as he was falling asleep, he'd heard his uncle's voice through the wall of their adjoining rooms: "El moley rahamim —"

The grave was filled with muddy earth and the men piled the stones they had gathered on top of it.

"We'll mark it on the next patrol," Ira said. "Let's go."

They returned to the track and continued on to Talovka siding. They'd forgotten their wager about the spikes and though they found several more to drive no one asked for a count.

On the way back to Tataurovo Ira noticed that it wasn't just Harris and

Keever loaning their coats to Eisenbach; the whole patrol was involved. One man, then another, would remove his coat and hand it to the man who'd been walking without one.

Ten minutes later the sun came out. There were buds on the larch and alder trees. The cinder-strewn, smoke-stained patches of ice along the tracks began to melt and a train came toward them heading for Irkutsk, one of the big fast freights. They stepped aside, felt the engine heat and winced at the wild clatter of the wheels as it passed, then they went on, one man among them always without a coat.

This sharing of coats had somehow become an act of communion. No one spoke of it, but they all felt close to each other as they passed the coats down the line and Ira, not wanting to be left out, gave the coat he was wearing to the man behind when his turn came and so the exchange was completed as they approached their camp.

When Ira came into the teplushka Carlisle looked up from his place at the desk. "Where's your coat?" he asked.

Ira warmed his hands over the stove and told Carlisle how he'd used his coat to bury the dead man.

"You'll have to requisition another one," Carlisle said.

"I suppose so."

"Until then use mine," Carlisle said. "I've got a lined field jacket."

"Thanks, I will," Ira said and he was tempted to tell Carlisle about the communion of the coats, but it was the kind of thing which, more often than not, lost its meaning in the telling, but thereafter when he thought about it Ira included Carlisle among those who had shared their coats that day.

« 2 »

Colonel Spaeth popped Carlisle on the shoulder as he came into the office and motioned him to a chair. "That old engine is yours," he said.

Carlisle's face lit up in one of his enormous grins and Spaeth laughed. "You look like a kid who got his first toy train for Christmas."

"I was a kid who never got one," Carlisle said and frowned abruptly.

"Neither did I," Spaeth said and he sat down on the edge of his desk. "They'll haul it down to you next week. The Railway Service Corps says you're nuts, but they'll loan you whatever tools you need."

"It'll give the men something to do," Carlisle said.

"They need something to do?"

"The engine will come in handy," Carlisle said.

Spaeth nodded, picked up his glasses and studied them for a time. "If it'll help morale I'm for it," he said. "We have a problem that's going to affect morale. A tough one. You know the men took up a collection for Mrs. Austin."

"Yes. Leverett handled it."

"I just learned that Pashkova was sacked. Everyone there is gone. Maryenka too."

Carlisle frowned and shook his head. "Who did it?"

Spaeth tossed his glasses on the desk and stood up. "That's the first question, isn't it? It was mine, but I thought I'd see if it was yours too. It's the logical question, I suppose."

"I'd like to know," Carlisle said.

"Why?"

"She was Austin's wife. What other reason would there be?"

"I know she was Austin's wife."

"You still haven't told me who did it."

"I may not. I've been sitting on this thing for days, Jack, trying to decide what to do, and I'd like your advice. It appears she's dead."

"How did you find that out?"

"From Intelligence. I'd like to keep this hushed up, but the men who contributed money to the fund are entitled to have it back. The point is what do we tell them?"

"Tell them the truth."

"Noble," Spaeth said tersely. "You can guess how they're going to feel about it."

"They'll want to get back at someone, but that's the price."

"Price of what?" Spaeth asked.

"Of getting involved — in a personal way."

"How else do you get involved?" Spaeth asked.

"You know what I mean, Colonel."

"I'm not sure I do."

"If Austin hadn't gotten involved none of this would have happened. That girl would still be in Vladivostok. A mess like this always starts because someone gets involved. The trick is to avoid getting involved."

Spaeth looked at Carlisle in a puzzled way and sighed. "You know, Jack, for the first time in my life I'm in a situation where truth and duty are incompatible. I suppose it's a common thing, but it's damned uncomfortable for me. I guess this is what the men in the State Department call statesmanship. I'm not going to tell you the truth about Pashkova, but at least I can tell you, in strict confidence, that I'm lying to you."

"Why?"

"To keep you from getting involved. That's the trick, isn't it? You'd only be angry and you wouldn't be able to do anything about it. I'd have to see to that. So, I'll send a letter of explanation when I return the money your men collected and that'll be the last word on this whole subject. Is that understood?"

"Yes, sir," Carlisle said.

"All right. The main reason I called you in, Jack, is that I want you to go with me to Omsk. General Graves and Ambassador Morris are going up to have a look at Kolchak and I think you're the logical man to survey the line between here and Irkutsk. If things go wrong, that information could be vital. The only question I have is about Leverett."

"What about him, Colonel?"

"You'll be gone for a week or so. Should I put someone in charge of your company or can Leverett handle it?"

Carlisle said that Leverett could.

Spaeth looked dubious. "I'd be a hell of a lot happier if Austin were there."

"So would I, but Klagle and Baker are good men and Leverett can handle it."

"I wish I could be as sure about that as you are."

"I'm sure."

"All right, Sioux. It's your company. I'll let you know when to be ready."

Spaeth walked Carlisle to the door. "Leverett's proving out, is he?" he asked once more.

"Well enough," Carlisle said.

"All right, then."

« 3 »

The regimental supply officer, Warrant Officer Duncan Ferber, or Old Dunc as he was known, was not satisfied with Leverett's form requesting a new trench coat. No, he wasn't satisfied at all.

For close to twenty years W.O. Dunc Ferber had been guarding government property from the unscrupulous, the crafty, the prodigal demands of soldiers who thought, because they ate government bread and drew government pay, that government-issued articles of apparel and equipment came unaccounted for from a horn of plenty.

To combat this opinion Dunc Ferber squeezed every article he issued through the tip of the horn and nothing spilled from the open end. He knew where every piece of equipment he had issued was supposed to be and how long it would wear and he could tell to within five percent how many men would find holes in their socks on any given day.

A wool trench coat — lost? Impossible! An officer might lose an eye, a leg, an arm; he could have his head blown off, but his coat would be salvageable. A little brushing, patching and dry cleaning and usually it would be good as new. Dunc had reissued coats whose former occupants had embraced grenades and the stitches hardly showed. It wasn't a matter of penuriousness with Dunc, give him a pair of worn-out boots and he'd issue a new or reconditioned pair to replace them without a quibble, but certain things were supposed to share the life expectancy of the man to whom they had been issued.

Leverett's crime wasn't that he'd lost a coat so much as that he was still alive and asking for another. Dunc had another; he had several others, among them the coat he had issued to Sergeant Austin which was a perfect case in point.

The Sergeant was dead, but his coat was still serving the country. Here, on the other hand, was a living man whose coat had deserted.

It set Dunc's teeth on edge.

He couldn't recall having issued a second trench coat to one man. Not once. It was an unprecedented case.

Dunc examined the requisition form closely. Leverett, Ira C. 2nd Lt. C Company. The name tugged at Dunc's memory. He squinched his eyes and tapped his teeth with his knuckles, making a wooden sound in his head. Leverett, Levite, black marketeer. Ferber's pendulous ears reddened. The name was unsavory. His dark brows fell together and from his small office in the warehouse he looked toward the chicken wire enclosure which protected his stacks of supplies. Then he remembered the Mulligan affair. "Ah!" he sighed. "Of course!"

Dunc stood up and paced around his office pleased with himself for having put his finger on it. Leverett was exactly the kind of man who'd attempt to cheat the government of a trench coat. Probably lost his in a drunken orgy or swapped it for narcotics. Dunc sat down and got Major Taziola on the phone. Taz would know. Taz knew everything.

"Yes?"

"Major Taziola, this Dunc Ferber, at Supply."

"Yes, Dunc?"

"You know a Lieutenant Leverett in C Company?"

"I know him, sure."

"I've got a requisition from him. He wants a trench coat."

"I'll tell him to pray for warm weather. Last month I wanted some wire and I haven't got it yet."

"The wire came in, which is one reason I called you, Major."

"Then why tell me about a trench coat?"

"The point is that unless Leverett can prove his was lost in the line of duty it has to come out of his clothing allowance."

"When do I get the wire?"

"You can pick it up any time, Major."

"I'll send someone over right away."

"That's a lot of wire, Major," Dunc said anxiously. "I think we should keep some reserve."

"Look, Dunc, I'm responsible for communications. Every time one of these Russian yahoos wants a dog leash, or something to tether a horse, they cut our wire. You go out and collect it from them if you want, I haven't got the time. I've decided the thing to do is to hang some well-marked coils of wire along our active lines and hope they'll take that instead of disrupting our field phones."

"But you'd be giving away government property!" Dunc protested and he began to shake.

"Tough, Dunc. Take it up with the Colonel."

"Major! If that's what you're going to use it for, rope is cheaper."

"All right, give me rope."

"We need it!"

"Then I'll take the wire."

Dunc swung his head from side to side. His stores were being plundered of rope, wire and coats. It was a bad day.

"Leverett was responsible for that mess at the Mulligan, wasn't he, Major?"

"That's right."

"What I want to know, Major, is how in hell does a man lose a trench coat?"

"Ask Leverett."

"I plan to. I just wanted to get a line on him. If there'd been some kind of action, a skirmish or something, I'd understand it. There hasn't been anything like that, has there, Major?"

Taziola was annoyed. "No, Dunc," he said. "There hasn't."

"All right, Major. Your wire is here."

"Thanks," Taziola said.

Dunc Ferber left his desk and walked through the warehouse to the rack where the trench coats were stored. Three coats were hanging up; the rest were in mothproof cartons. Leverett wanted a medium size but Dunc sure as hell wasn't going to break out a new coat for the man who'd lost his old one. He checked the size of the three on the rack. One was small; it had belonged to Saunders, who was killed in the skirmish at Siding 85. Good thing they hadn't had time to get their coats on. The second was also small; it had belonged to a man in F Company who'd broken his leg in four places and was sent back to Vlad on a hospital train. The third was large, Sergeant Austin's coat.

Dunc caught the sleeve of this brave coat and vowed not to issue it lightly. "Not by a damn sight!" he said. And with this resolve fresh in his mind, and the fierce protectiveness of an outraged mother in his heart, he marched back to his office and found Captain Carlisle waiting for him.

"What can we do for you, Captain?" Dunc asked.

"I stopped by for Leverett's coat."

Dunc was displeased. He didn't want this matter handled by proxy. "There are a few details I need for my files," he said and he pulled Ira's requisition form out of a pigeonhole in his desk. "What happened to the coat?"

"He used it."

"Used it? I can't put 'used it' in the *Consumed* column, Captain. Your man hasn't completed the form correctly. He didn't turn in a coat to be salvaged. I can't make out a stock record on what he gave me. He signed an affidavit here: 'I do solemnly swear that the article of public property shown above was lost, in the manner stated, while in the public service.' Is that correct?"

"Sure, it is," Carlisle said, irritably.

"He didn't state the manner in which it was lost, so it can't be correct, can it? How did he lose the coat?"

"He buried it."

"He did what!"

"He used it to bury a dead man found by the tracks near Talovka. You'll find a report on that in Captain Bentham's office."

"His coat?"

"It was the only thing he had."

"He buried a man in his coat!"

"That's what I said."

"Well, by God, that's the damndest thing I ever heard!"

"You want him to go dig it up again?" Carlisle demanded.

"I am sure as hell not going to issue another coat for such a stupid reason as that. You bet I'm not."

"I'd call burying a dead man a public service, wouldn't you?"

"Not in a government-issued overcoat, I wouldn't. No, sir!"

"Well, that's just too damned bad."

"He's irresponsible," Dunc wailed. "I've heard of using a blanket, a shelter half, but a coat? Never! Who did he bury?"

"I don't know. Some Russian."

"You mean it's not even an American buried in that coat?"

"No, it's not even an American!" Carlisle retorted. "We usually bury Americans in coffins, Dunc. Now get me a coat and shut up!"

"You'll have to sign for it," Dunc said and he shoved the form at Carlisle, who scrawled his signature on it.

"This doesn't end here," Dunc said.

"I'll bet not," Carlisle said.

"I'm held accountable for all these things, ya know."

"I know."

"You'd be surprised at some of the stuff people get away with."

"All right, Dunc, get the coat. We'll take good care of it."

"You'd better. It belonged to Austin."

Dunc rose and went into the warehouse and returned with the coat, which he offered to Carlisle. "Well? You want it or not?"

"You're a real bastard, Dunc," Carlisle said, but he took the coat and left.

« 4 »

When Carlisle came into their car at Tataurovo, Ira smiled. "You got my coat," he said.

Carlisle tossed Ira the coat. "Yeah, I got it," he said.

Ira tried the coat on. The sleeves covered his hands and the skirt almost touched the floor. He laughed and danced a couple of steps. "What is this, Dunc Ferber's revenge? It makes me look like a damned ape!"

"If you don't want it I'll keep it," Carlisle said.

"Yours wouldn't fit any better," Ira said and he took off the coat and held it up to see if he could move the buttons and shorten the sleeves.

Suddenly the coat was snatched from his hands and he found Carlisle glowering at him.

"Take care of this one! Understand?"

"All right, Sioux," Ira said evenly. "All right now."

Carlisle gripped the coat hard in both fists, his heavy face tense, as though he were about to tear the coat apart; instead he thrust it back at Ira. "Take care of it," he growled.

"You said that once."

"Sometimes once isn't enough for you, Leverett. To give orders you have to learn how to take them. You'd better learn fast because the Colonel wants me to go with him to Omsk, which means you'll be in command while I'm gone."

"Oh," Ira said.

"I told him you could handle it."

"Thank you."

Carlisle nodded and sat down at the company desk and took out his diary.

Ira wanted to express his gratitude for the confidence Carlisle had shown in him, but he couldn't bring it out. "When will you be going?" he asked.

"End of the month sometime. It's up to General Graves."

"He going too?"

"Yes."

"How long will you be gone?"

"I'm not sure."

"Well," Ira said lamely, "Don't worry about things here."

"I won't," Carlisle said and he smiled generously. "That Dunc Ferber is one damned fool. He really got under my skin. Sorry I took it out on you."

"That's all right, Sioux," Ira said. "I'll take good care of the coat."

CHAPTER SIXTEEN

WHEN Carlisle's switching engine with its rusty tender was hauled in from Verkhne-Udinsk and left on the siding near the Headquarters car all the men turned out to have a look.

Carlisle tramped around it, trying to conceal his pleasure. He slapped the boiler plates and bent down to squint through the wheels at the underbelly.

Ira looked at the thing in consternation, wanting to ask what Carlisle had in mind, but the affectionate expressions on the faces of the men told him that the company had acquired a mascot.

Sergeant Baker's round, jowly face was cocked over; he had one eye closed and his lips were pursed in appraisal close to a kiss.

Sergeant Klagle was frowning profoundly as he estimated how the reconstruction job was going to be done.

Carlisle hopped up into the cab and pulled a lever. It came off in his hand and the men roared.

"Well, Captain, at least her wheels are round," Sergeant Klagle yelled.

"That's right, Klagle," Carlisle said. "And that's a start."

The men began work immediately. During their off-duty hours they stripped the engine and carried the parts to their cars, where they polished and oiled them. They divided the engine like a beef on a butcher's chart and each squad chose a section to work on.

The engine had been made in Japan, altered in China, refurbished in Manchuria and abandoned in Siberia. There were English parts, French parts, Italian and American parts. It was undoubtedly the most mongrelized locomotive on wheels.

Carlisle supervised the work with a maternal concern, cautioning Baker and Klagle against working too fast. "Take it easy," he growled. "Take it easy. Rome wasn't built in a day. We're going to destroy her god-damned character."

Then one morning at formation Carlisle read Colonel Spaeth's letter about the massacre at Pashkova. He read it quickly and without emphasis.

When the men were dismissed they stood about in consternation trying to understand what they'd heard. Those who hadn't been paying attention asked the others to explain it.

"Pashkova? What's that about Pashkova?"

"He said we was to get our money back from Blodgett."

"The money we sent to Maryenka? How come?"

"That's what he said."

"To Maryenka?"

"That's right."

Ira was shocked by the news and even more by Carlisle's dispassionate delivery of it. He glanced at the men gathered in groups on the mud-packed field. "You should say something to them," he said.

"The Colonel's letter says all that's necessary."

"Half of them didn't hear it! I didn't hear half of it myself."

"I'll post it," Carlisle said and he started back to their car.

"You should have given them time; held a special formation. Something!"

"It's got to be routine," Carlisle said.

"Routine!"

"Routine," Carlisle said bluntly. But as he started up the steps one of the men on the field suggested they name their locomotive Maryenka. "That's it!" another yelled. "The Maryenka!"

Carlisle turned to Ira. "Put a stop to that," he demanded.

"To what?"

"That talk about naming the engine Maryenka. Put a stop to it!"

"How can I do that? What's wrong with it?"

Carlisle stepped down and shoved his face close to Ira's. "Do it!" he spat. "Do it now and do it fast! Don't ask how or why. Do it for once in your god-damned life!" and he shoved Ira toward the men.

Ira signaled Baker and Klagle. They trotted over and came to attention in front of him. "Put a stop to that Maryenka business," Ira said. "That's an order."

Klagle and Baker exchanged a glance, then nodded. "Yes, sir," Baker said. Ira returned their salute and watched the sergeants approach the men from two directions like sheep dogs.

"What stupid jackass decided to name that broken-down engine Maryenka?" Baker bawled. "That is the dumbest thing I ever heard. Austin would turn over in his grave!"

Klagle shook his head from side to side. "Jesus, you jawbone bastards are dumb, real dumb! All right, let's get to chow. Come on, move!"

The men bunched up like an unwilling flock and headed for the kitchen car. They mumbled, lowed and baaed, looking concerned, not at all sure their suggestion hadn't been a good one. They queued up for chow and didn't talk much, but there was a sense of undischarged obligation in the air.

Ira went into the car and sat down at the small table where he and Carlisle shared their meals. "Klagle and Baker took care of it," he said.

Carlisle nodded.

"I'd like to see the Colonel's letter."

"On the desk."

Ira read the letter, which had about as much feeling as a notice of a public auction. Only two phrases, "regrets to inform" and "wish to commend the generosity of those who contributed to the fund," made any concession to the deep attachment the men had for Maryenka Austin. Otherwise it was coldly official. "Intelligence reports that Maryenka Austin is believed to have been killed during a partisan massacre at the village of Pashkova."

Ira put the letter down wondering what horrors that sentence concealed. "About the same time Austin was killed," he said.

"Yes," Carlisle said.

Ira tried to eat, but he was filled with indignation. "I feel damned rotten about it," he said.

"We all do," Carlisle said, but he continued to eat, unperturbed.

"What do you think about it?" Ira asked.

"I think it's finished! When a person is gone, he's gone!"

"I meant Maryenka," Ira said.

"I know what you meant!" Carlisle declared. "I know how the men felt about her. I'm not stupid. I know how you felt about her, but she's gone. We can't do anything about it, I don't want a lot of useless sentiment. It's bad for the men."

"Why don't you just say you're sorry as hell she died?"

"What difference would that make?"

Ira shrugged. "All right, but I owe Austin more than an intelligence report which states that his wife is 'believed to have been killed.' "

"Since when did you owe Austin anything? I knew him for fifteen years before you came along!"

"I was at his wedding."

"Damned white of you. She might be alive in Vlad if you hadn't been."

Ira bounded to his feet, his fists clenched, an angry retort on his lips, but he heard footsteps and Corporal Blodgett came in.

"You'll have to figure out a fair way to divide that money, Corporal," Carlisle said. "It's in the drawer."

"That's been taken care of, Captain," Blodgett said. "The men took a vote and donated the money to the engine fund. They want to buy the parts with it. They decided at breakfast."

"Were Klagle and Baker there?" Carlisle asked.

"Yes, sir."

"All right, I suppose that's the way to handle it," Carlisle grumbled. "Make out a ledger sheet for the engine fund, Blodgett."

The little switch engine with its double camel hump and 2-6-0 wheel arrangement weighed about forty tons. In a week its boiler, undercarriage and cab had been painted glossy black and trimmed in red. An American flag was painted on the cab roof and two more decorated the sides. If human affection could improve the performance of a steam engine, this one had to be the best of its class. The only thing it lacked was a name.

Pipes for the boiler had been scavenged from a wrecked Mikado located in Chita. Sergeant Baker had taken a crew of four men to disembowel this ninety-seven-ton monster and returned not only with pipes but with fittings, gauges and lubricating valves all made by the American Locomotive Company. At last the great day came.

The men had cut wood and stored it under their cots to dry and now these offerings were stacked on the embankment to be fed into the firebox. All attention was focused on the steam pressure gauge waiting for it to reach two hundred, which was assumed to be the optimum pressure for the engine. Carlisle, Klagle and Baker were in the cab adjusting the blower, heater, blowback, atomizer and tank heater valves.

Private Carson, back from the hospital, walked around the engine shaking his head and muttering: "Well, I'll be god-damned. It's a real son of a bitch of a locomotive. Look at that big damned bell!"

The big damned bell was one of the best purchases made from the engine fund. Corporal Blodgett had spotted the bell in a junk yard at Verkhne-Udinsk. It was part of a carillon made in Germany and was embossed with a fierce-looking eagle holding a Greek Orthodox cross in its claw. It weighed over two hundred pounds and when struck gave a mellow low C boom of such solemnity that Blodgett found it irresistible. He campaigned for the purchase of the bell over Carlisle's strenuous objection. He brought it down from Verkhne on consignment and set it up near the engine for the men's approval. He polished it to a soft golden glow and rang it to announce meals and formations and in three days the men got so accustomed to hearing the bell that they elected to buy it for their engine.

Sergeant Klagle delivered this news to Carlisle, who called for Blodgett. "I'm not turning this engine into a rolling church steeple, Blodgett! What the hell is the idea?"

"A locomotive has to have a bell, sir," Blodgett replied meekly.

"All right, a bell. But that thing is two and a half feet high!"

"Oh, you measured it, sir," Blodgett said.

"Of course I measured it! Why shouldn't I measure it?"

"I suppose you measured it to see how we could mount it on the engine, sir. The bell committee made this plan for your approval." Blodgett took a drawing from his pocket and gave to Carlisle.

"Bell committee? What bell committee?"

"The committee that wants the bell. I have their signatures here, sir."

Blodgett offered a petition, but Carlisle waved it away in disgust. "All right, Blodgett, rig the bell, but I won't forget this. You bet not."

"Thank you, sir," Blodgett said and the bell was mounted ahead of the forward boiler hump.

"That's sure one hell of a dingdong bell," Carson said. "Ring it for us, Captain."

Carlisle pulled the lanyard and the glorious bell rang deeply. It was a big sound for such a small engine; it had dignity and importance and the men grinned.

Carson wagged his head. "Oh," he said, "that is a bell!"

"Ninety pounds and going up," Klagle reported.

The men cheered.

Ira joined Carlisle in the cab. He looked at the dials, handles and valves. "Sure you know how to handle this thing, Captain?" he asked.

Carlisle nodded but his brow was beaded with moisture.

The men cheered every degree of reported pressure and passed more wood up to Baker.

The steam pressure needle continued to hover at a hundred and fifty. Klagle and Carlisle made adjustments trying to bring it up, but they built more pressure in themselves than they did in the engine.

"I'm going to try her," Carlisle said at last. He eased a lever back and the locomotive shuddered. There was a great clanking, tearing racket of protest, then the engine began to move. Carlisle gaped at Leverett, who yelled: "Hey, we're moving! This thing is moving!"

The men cheered as the locomotive with steam pouring from its boiler rumbled down the track. The drive shafts lurched, balked and lurched, forcing the wheels around half a circle at a time, then the action settled into a hesitant rhythm and the engine picked up speed.

"You better stop," Leverett said.

"I'm trying to," Carlisle bellowed.

Klagle jumped from the cab and sprinted toward the jack switch and threw it open just in time to shunt them onto the main track.

"Christ!" Carlisle roared. "The eastbound is due through here in five minutes!"

Baker began pulling wood out of the firebox, trying to drop the pressure.

"Throw the damned thing in reverse."

"I'm trying to!"

The sandbox dropped open, strewing sand under the wheels, the big bell was ringing dolorously, but suddenly the engine shuddered and pitched backward.

The men on the track scattered as the engine came at them in reverse.

"Jump!" Baker yelled.

"I'm yellow," Ira said. "Jump yourself!"

Carlisle reversed the engine again but this time an agonizing sigh escaped from it, clouds of steam inundated the cab, and the wheels locked. It slid backward another four feet, shuddering and complaining, then it stopped and stood panting, steaming and snorting.

Carlisle, Baker and Leverett, expecting the engine to blow up, abandoned the cab and dove over the embankment.

"She's a real snorter!" Klagle yelled. "A real snorter!"

The men were delighted. The Snorter! The name was adopted by acclaim.

The boiler pressure never rose above a hundred and fifty and the Snorter's maximum speed varied between ten and sixteen miles an hour, but this was enough. The men weren't interested in efficiency, they wanted character. They painted the Snorter's name on the cab in both English and Russian and as she went down the tracks snorting and grumbling, with the great booming bell announcing her presence, the men were proud. They converted the tender into a gay but lethal vehicle with swivels to mount machine guns and a stack mount for one of their thirty-seven-millimeter cannons; it became, in fact, a small armored car.

During this time the massacre at Pashkova and Maryenka Austin appeared to have been forgotten. No one mentioned her name and Ira assumed that Maryenka's place in the affections of the men had been filled by the Snorter.

The men spoke of the engine as "her" and did everything they could to please it, as though this clanking mass of machinery were capable of returning their devotion.

The Snorter dominated camp life at Tataurovo. In the morning the men were awakened by the sound of its bell and the first sight of their engine standing so gaily on the siding invariably brought smiles to their sleepy faces. The bell summoned them to formations and to meals and the last sound they heard after taps was the Snorter's bell ringing the end of another day.

Ira was no less fond of the Snorter than the other men, but the engine was a reproach to him for not having pursued his inquiry into the Pashkova affair.

The Snorter had greedily consumed the money intended for Maryenka and more. It demanded constant attention and was temperamental as a diva. For an inanimate machine it displayed a wide range of emotions not the least of which was coquetry. Fear that a quick frost might burst its pipes made it necessary to establish an extra guard detail, known as the Snorter Watch, whose duty it was to keep the firebox glowing. In the dead of night the Snorter would often sigh peevishly and half the men in the company would wake up like mothers of new infants and lie still, trying to interpret what that sigh had meant.

A week before Carlisle's departure for Omsk, the Snorter was particularly grumbly and soulful and the men on the Snorter Watch, Carson and Eisenbach, were anxious as parents with a colicky kid.

"What the hell's wrong with her?" Eisenbach asked.

"She knows the old man is leaving for Omsk," Carson said.

"Ah, come on, Carson."

"Hell, yeah, she does."

"Think we ought to wake Klagle up?"

"Naw, let her moan. My Ma said that sometimes a woman just has to let down."

At four in the morning Ira sat up out of a sound sleep with a vision of the Snorter falling apart plate by plate until there was nothing left but a heap of bolts, wheels, pipes and metal. He listened intently, but all he heard was the river.

"You awake?" he whispered after five minutes of suspenseful waiting.

"Yeah," Carlisle said.

"You hear that?"

"What?"

"I don't know."

Carlisle got up, went to the stove and stirred the fire. "I can't sleep for a damn," he said.

"Keyed up about going to Omsk?"

"I suppose."

"Only natural. She sure is making a racket tonight."

"Yeah. I'll go have a look."

Ira lit a cigarette and Carlisle got dressed.

"You'd think that engine was human," Ira said.

"Yeah," Carlisle said fondly. "She almost is."

"Bringing that engine in was a damned smart way to handle the whole thing."

"What whole thing?"

"Maryenka Austin. Pashkova. All that."

Carlisle buttoned the shirt, his movements picked out of the darkness by the glow of the stove. "I asked for that engine before I knew about Pashkova."

"You didn't tell me that."

"You think I'd bring a whole damned locomotive down here because there was a massacre at Pashkova? Sometimes you baffle me, Leverett."

"The fact is that it distracted the men."

"The fact is that it gave them something to do other than jaw. You keep them busy too. I don't care how you do it, but keep them busy and don't for Christ's sake bring up Pashkova again. That's water over the dam. There are some things I ought not to have to tell you and that's one of them. These men need something to do, not something to think about. Too much thinking makes trouble."

"All right, I'll stop it."

"I'm waiting for you to start," Carlisle said and he laughed abruptly. "No, what I mean is that the way you think is too damned complicated. Keep it simple, Leverett. It doesn't take a brain trust to run this company. Just keep them busy and don't let them get worried about things that don't concern them."

"Like Pashkova and Maryenka?"

"Exactly. The way you talk you'd think they built the Snorter because of her."

"They did."

"Oh, for Christ's sake!" Carlisle said disgustedly. "Go back to sleep. It's a steam engine, not a woman. None of us have been out here that long!" And putting on his coat he went out, sliding the door closed behind him.

Outside it was dark and the sound of the river dividing turbulently around the caissons of the bridge was fresh and cool. The ground underfoot was firm and there was the smell of new growth in the air, a smell of awakening green.

Carlisle walked to the Snorter intending to go aboard and check the stand-by pressure on the boiler, but the bell, glowing softly, caught his attention and suddenly he knew why he had objected so strongly to it. It wasn't the size or the shape which troubled him, it was the tone. It was the heavy tone of the Armistice bells at Vladivostok and reminded him of Tatiana. He thought of her each time it rang and hadn't really known until now.

The Snorter groaned and a jet of steam issued from its drive piston.

"You're still a locomotive," Carlisle grumbled and he went to the cab, where he found Sergeant Klagle.

"You too, Captain?" Klagle said.

"What's wrong with her, Klagle?"

"Some of the boys say she's complaining because you're going to Omsk. She's a jealous old bitch, if you ask me. Either that or she needs her pipes flushed."

Carlisle glanced at the temperature gauge and tapped the blowback valve with his knuckles.

"Wish I was going with you."

"Why?"

The question was snappish and Klagle shrugged. "Like to see it, is all."

"You and Baker have plenty to see to right here. I don't want any surprises when I get back and I'm depending on you and Baker to see that I don't get any. Keep things tight for me, understand?"

Klagle nodded. "Right, Captain. It'll all be here when you get back."

Carlisle grinned flashingly. "I know that, Klagle. Just be damned sure."

Klagle nodded. "Don't worry, Captain."

"I plan not to," Carlisle said, then he jumped from the cab and walked toward the bridge waiting for the magical dawn.

CHAPTER SEVENTEEN

WITH few exceptions the early advances made by the Kolchak armies were successful and there was an exuberance in foreign capitals. Newspaper headlines accompanied by diagrams of the front announced each victory in unshakable prose which gathered force and momentum as Kolchak's right flank pushed toward General Ironside's troops in north Russia and his left flank approached the Armies of the Don in the south. Political cartoonists drew wild-eyed commissars and bearded, bomb-toting Bolsheviks being strangled by the noose of Freedom, Justice and Equality.

Kolchak troops captured Buzuluk, Uralsk, Nikolsk and Yershov. Samara and Saratov were within grasp. Two Red battalions deserted to the White side.

Ufa fell. Sterlitamak fell.

Newsprint was jubilant.

Lines of White troops marching over the spring plains with their bayoneted rifles waving like wind-blown grass felt invincible as the Reds retired and retired and retired.

The unfenced plains and high plateaus of Siberia were in blossom. Clusters of asters, pinks, gentians and violets decorated the roadside, and regiments of dusty men marched from color to color choosing blue, pink, or yellow for their milestones as they tramped toward the horizon which cheated them hour by hour.

In Moscow, Omsk, Archangel and Astrakhan politicians and generals studied maps for an overview of the strategic situation. Colorful pins representing Army Corps, Armies, Regiments and Battalions pleased them as much as the asters, buttercups and wild iris pleased the sweat-drenched marching soldiers.

Encouraged by the military successes in March and April the great powers extended de facto recognition to the Kolchak government. On the maps Kolchak's front centered on Kazan, less than five hundred miles from Moscow.

The front looked formidable in pins and President Wilson, bending to the pressures of his State Department, agreed to recognize Kolchak if he would hold free, secret, democratic elections, grant independence to Poland and Finland, and acknowledge the Russian national debt. The Kolchak government responded favorably, though its pledges were not as generous as Lenin's peace proposal, and Senator Lodge's admonition that the United States should remove its troops from Russia because they were too many to be sacrificed wantonly and too few to be effective was lost in the halls of Congress.

In view of the changed circumstances General Graves expected his orders to be modified. But to his repeated requests for clarification the War Department replied that his original orders were to be carried out. This, of course, was absurd.

Neutrality.

Elements of the American 339th Infantry had already engaged the 2nd Moscow, the 96th Saratov, and the 2nd Kazan regiments of the Soviet Army in the north at Bolshie Ozerki.

There was no neutrality, but for the sake of the men in his command Graves tried to conceal the bitter conflict between the State Department, the War Department and the President.

A lesser man forced to live in this state of schizophrenia would have given in to despair, but Graves followed his original orders with grim determination.

He knew very well that his career could not survive such a swirl of cross-purposes, that no doubt he would be condemned by all sides, but in a way this released some of his tensions. He was able to smile a bit more often at himself and to take a deeper interest in the men around him. When he was ordered to accompany Roland S. Morris, the American Ambassador to Japan, to Omsk for the purpose of assessing the Kolchak government he actually laughed and called Robinson and Eichelberger into his office.

"Well, they've tied me to the stake, piled the fagots around my feet — that's not necessarily a reference to State, if either of you gentlemen are keeping diaries — and now they want me to light the fire. I'm going to Omsk to evaluate Kolchak's military situation, while Ambassador Morris looks into the politics. Evidently they're still nervous about granting the Kolchak regime full recognition."

Robinson and Eichelberger kept their opinions to themselves and Graves appreciated their restraint. Everyone at American Headquarters had begun to see the wisdom of Ambassador to Russia David Rowland Francis' axiom that all the truth all the time was always dangerous. It was a comforting maxim in circumstances where no one knew any of the truth any of the time.

"This reminds me of a story General Otani told me," Graves said. "When Otani was a young lieutenant he was assigned as orderly to General Grant while Grant was in Japan. Military etiquette in the Japanese Army requires that an officer unsheath his sword while on active duty. Otani decided being an orderly to Grant was active duty, so he reported in full dress uniform with his sword in hand. After two days of sight-seeing Grant finally said to him, 'Young man, you had better put that thing in the scabbard, you might stick someone with it.'"

Robinson and Eichelberger looked puzzled and Graves laughed. "While I'm gone don't stick anybody, that's all I meant. Wire Spaeth and say I'll pick him up in Verkhne-Udinsk. Meantime keep your swords sheathed and your powder wet. We're still neutral."

« 2 »

There were not more than twenty families in the settlement at Tataurovo. They made a sketchy living cutting ties for the railroad, fishing the Selenga River and tending their gardens. Carlisle refused to let his men associate with the villagers, but the presence of the American camp across the bridge had had its impact. Tataurovoan girls delivering fresh eggs and vegetables which Carlisle had arranged to purchase made it known how much they pined for their young men away at the front. They giggled and whispered to one another, dark eyes flashing beneath their head scarves, as they delivered their baskets of produce to the commissary car. Strong, blocky creatures, they exuded an animal warmth which was irresistible and there were meetings, of course.

No one from the American camp was allowed to cross the bridge to Tataurovo at night. But half a mile upstream there was a place where the river divided around a rocky buttress which could be reached from both sides by raft. The trip was not without its risks, but the rewards for those who made it were compensatory. The method was as ancient as Neolithic man's quest for security from attack by the saber-toothed tiger. A raft, tied to a tree upstream, was swung into the current and by means of poles and paddles brought to the island. To regain the bank the crew simply hauled themselves back on the rope. Those who made the trip usually arrived soaked to the waist, but garments had no utility once the company was met, so the clothing was hung up to dry beside a sheltered fire.

In the center of the island there was a sandy depression surrounded by rocks and natural caves with petroglyphs etched in the stones, stick men and animals, stars, rivers and fish. An aura of prehistory hung over the place, of primitive rites and long shadows in the firelight; and the river, rumbling along the stone flanks of the island, brushed language away. Those who came there went back to the time of signs; they warmed themselves at fire, made love in the caves and sat about listening to the river with the rose glow of the embers on their naked bodies. Some brought blankets, some brought furs, some brought food and drink, but mostly they brought their bodies and their silent minds. Under the spell of the place they fell into a primitive trance which was sometimes expressed in a slow dance of such self-contained exuberance that it blurred their vision and seemed to scorch the stars.

No one knew who these fortunates were, not in the village or in the camp. And the participants themselves gave no clue, spoke not a word to each other or to anyone else. There was no boasting. Coming back from the island they came back millions of years and what had happened there was so true that only silence could express it.

But, alas, there was a snake in Eden.

One morning the Cossacks, called up by Kolchak's levy officers, began to arrive at Tataurovo, which had been chosen as a point from which they would entrain for the front.

They came from their distant villages on horseback and in carts, whole families of them, in a long caravan winding down the Selenga Valley. Because there was a shortage of horses many were afoot, trudging along in the dust raised by those who rode ahead. Cossack veterans of old campaigns led the column. Warriors sixty years of age and more, they sat straight on their wiry Siberian ponies; their hooded eyes were fierce and their beards had been trimmed close to their faces, showing patches of black or brown left from their youth.

Their faded uniforms and battered arms, their scars and their pride impressed everyone who saw them pass and most of all Carlisle, who had seen men like these before. After Sitting Bull had been killed by the Indian police Carlisle had seen a thousand Ogallalas file into the Pine Ridge agency and the old men at the head of that column were just as stern and proud as these old Cossacks.

The Cossack women made camp in the flats beyond Tataurovo and began roasting a whole ox which two venerable Cossacks slaughtered with their sabers. The priests, having accompanied the Cossacks from their villages, went about bestowing blessings on the young men and being paid in vodka. There were challenges to feats of horsemanship, wrestling matches and gambling, and in the space of half a day the environs of Tataurovo rang with noise of the Cossack celebration.

For this occasion Carlisle allowed his men to cross the bridge. He organized a military police patrol and issued stern warnings but there was a shade of leniency in his manner and the men knew they could let themselves go and they did so wholeheartedly.

On the afternoon of the first day Ira joined Carlisle at the edge of a field where a line of willow stakes had been driven into the ground at ten-yard intervals. A grizzled Cossack rode from this line to the far end, where he whirled his horse, drew his saber and with a shout that cracked his voice galloped back. The saber, glinting in his fist, seemed to act of its own accord lopping six-inch sections from each stake with a side stroke which would have caught a man somewhere between the ear and the collarbone. At the end of the line he spun his horse and galloped back using a chopping stroke. The stakes popped under the blade and the severed section barely touched the ground before the next one was cut with a sixty-degree slash which would open a man from the base of his neck to his heart.

Ira set his jaw as the old Cossack came back a third time. He did not see the skill, the grace, the poetic coordination of horse and rider; instead he saw the stakes as human figures and he winced as the Cossack, bent low over the saddle, swung a backhand stroke as he passed each stake and cut it down at the kidney level.

The men and boys standing along the line cheered and whistled. Carlisle was applauding.

The Cossack came to a stop, turned in the saddle and saw one of the stakes still standing. He brandished his saber and yelled threateningly at it. The stake appeared to wilt, then it fell tearing away a strip of bark. The Cossacks roared but the old rider grumbled disapprovingly and sheathed his saber, saying by every action that he wasn't as good as he had been.

"By God, he's great!" Carlisle exclaimed. "I've got to try it myself."

"You go ahead."

"What's wrong with you, Ira?"

"Just trying to hang on to my neutrality," Ira said.

"I don't know what the hell you're talking about."

"Heard about Ekaterinburg? One of Kolchak's Cossack atamans killed three thousand Jews as his contribution to the war effort."

Carlisle's expression tightened into a blank, hard-jawed stare. "Where in hell is Ekaterinburg?" he asked.

"That's where the Czar and his family were killed," Ira said quietly. "So?"

"So, you asked. It's five hundred miles beyond Omsk."

"Well, for Christ's sake!" Carlisle said disgustedly. "What has Ekaterinburg got to do with this?"

"You go on," Ira said. "Get yourself a horse and sword. I'm going back."

On the center span of the bridge Ira stopped to look down at the Selenga. The water swirling around the caissons made air bubbles like galaxies which came from nothing and were swept away in the current. Each was different, an infinite variety of whirling galaxies. Ira spat into the center of one and watched as it broke away from the caisson and vanished downstream.

It was a warm day. The sun through the trees along the riverbank brought a rich smell of moist earth. There were new leaves on the alders, and the sword fern was beginning to unfurl. He heard the Cossacks and the horses, felt the warm movement of all those people on the field around their tents, the busy women, the children, the dogs.

A moment of total awareness took Ira by surprise; in all that motion, the river, the people, the birds, the fleeting sunlight, there was a point of arrest as though time itself had stopped.

Ira stood at the bridge railing with his head raised and was so unaccountably joyful that he almost laughed aloud. Then it was gone and Ira looked around as though it were something that could be seen, a large bubble of contentment which had formed around him for an instant before it floated off downriver.

He walked on across the bridge slapping the wooden rail with the palm of his hand and smiling foolishly.

At the end of the bridge he turned upriver along the bank, trying to hold this feeling of irresponsible, feminine joyousness, half ashamed of it, but ready to scamper along the riverbank like an exuberant kid. He wasn't thinking of anyone. No one had made him happy. There was no circumstance to account for it. He caught the branch of a hazel bush and looked at the full buds tipped with green; he brushed it against his cheek. "I'm happy because the leaves are coming," he thought and thus he explained it away.

Ahead he saw Carson seated on a stone gazing at the river, chewing a stalk of grass. He fed the stalk through his teeth, spat the half-masticated wad into the water with an angry jerk of his head, and cut another stalk with his sheath knife.

Ira sat down beside Carson, who jumped slightly, startled because the sound of the river had concealed Ira's approach.

"Oh, howdy, Lieutenant."

"How's the leg, Carson?" Ira asked.

"No trouble," Carson said and he looked upriver to the place where it divided around the island. "Not so pretty to look at, maybe, but it gets me around. You bet on that."

"Have you seen the Cossacks ride?"

"Not me," Carson said. "I don't mix with them Greasers. They got their place, I got mine, and that's all right. In my time I seen plenty of trouble come from mixing, you bet, but some of these boys can't be told. They're just too dirt dumb to be told. Let a Greaser get a holt on you anyway he can and there's sure trouble. They got a million ways to sneak in on you and it's either you club them on the head when they cross the line or you're one of them. That's all there is about it, nothin' more. But there's nothin' sadder or worse than a White Greaser. You can't trust them, by God, for a minute. They'll say one thing to your face and do another after dark. If you don't know who they are you're in sad trouble. I'd rather be in a pinch with a Greaser at my side and know what to expect of him than to be in the same pinch with a White Greaser who might stab you in the back out of the blue."

Carson kept chewing grass, spitting green and glaring upriver at the island. "I didn't think watching a bunch of Cossacks ride would be called mixing," Ira said.

"There's a lot more to that than meets the eye," Carson declared and he fixed Ira with a knowing look and nodded his head sagely. "You'll see what I mean. I aim to fix them bastards' wagon and I done it. I'll be right there at the bridge toting 'em up as they go by. Wouldn't surprise me none if one of them didn't shoot me in the leg from behind back there at Siding 85. That's the way they do. Just when you're gettin' the upper hand on their Greaser buddies they bushwhack you and hardly know theirselves why they did it. A kind of craziness gets into their blood to the point they don't know what side they're on. Them are the ones you got to know about when the trouble comes."

"Carson, I don't know what in hell you're talking about," Ira said.

Carson pursed his lips and stared hard at the river. "You'll see," he said. "Them mixin' bastards are goin' to get theirselves one surprise tonight. That's all I can say about it, Lieutenant, 'cause I sure ain't one to shoot my mouth off without the facts. I ain't no god-damned squealer either. Sure as hell no one is ever goin' to say old Carson blabbed. What I done was my duty as I saw it and that's all I'm goin' to say." Carson spat a final time and stood up. "And if push comes to shove, Lieutenant, I just wouldn't mention this talk to anyone 'cause I just never had it with you at all."

Carson sheathed his knife and plunged off through the brush, headed back to camp.

« 3 »

Yakushef and his two sons were going to the front with the Cossacks because their horses had been drafted. Government remount officers scouring Trans-Baikal took anything that could carry a man or a load and the boys, seeing their horses had to go to the front, went too; and Yakushef, seeing his sons go because of the horses, volunteered to go himself, and for this Yakushef's wife cursed the horses and swore she would have killed them if she had known they would lead her men to war.

She wasn't a Cossack woman and consequently she had no sense about such things.

When he returned to the car Carlisle's mood was one of intense excitement. He'd been sabering willow stakes and racing Cossack ponies half the afternoon and he came back only to change his clothes. "Yakushef is going with them," he said to Ira.

"He's not a Cossack, is he?"

Carlisle told Ira about the Yakushef horses.

"That's a lousy reason to go to war," Ira said.

"You don't have any feeling for horses," Carlisle growled. "They raised those horses. They're damned good horses."

"I suppose it's as good a reason as any when you come right down to it," Ira said.

"Come over later," Carlisle said. "It's a hell of a crowd."

"I may do that," Ira said but he ate his dinner alone and reread Ruth's latest letters. These seemed to change each time he read them, to say more and say it differently, which was disconcerting. She wrote in black ink, solid, unmistakable words, but still the meaning changed, or he changed from one reading to the next, so a letter three weeks old seemed almost entirely new.

"We've been keeping company for nearly a month. Tuesday was our anniversary as a matter of fact. I know you'll laugh but to me before Herb Kalish is like B.C. where all the dates go backwards and are such a muddle. I can't believe from one time I see him to the next that he'll be there and he says it's the same for him, so we're both just impossible to everyone else. It's awful, but nice, and the big fright is that it'll just come to an end. Of course Mother thinks he'll never amount to anything because he's selling motion pictures. I just grit my teeth when she talks about him.

"I feel silly writing all this to you, but what else is there? I wish there was something I could do like whisk you home on a magic carpet. When I look at the picture of you and Sergeant Austin and Maryenka on my desk I'm almost frightened. They look so happy in the picture (you look silly, but nice, as always) and now he's gone. The picture makes me feel awfully helpless."

Ira folded the letter feeling helpless himself. Ruth didn't come through anymore. She went on for pages in other letters about Herb Kalish, an ex-doughboy who'd come back from Europe to get in on the ground floor of something called motion picture distribution which sounded like a seamy racket to Ira and he disapproved.

At home the war seemed to have been over a hundred years. All the doughboys were distributing goods and the girls were distributing themselves. Hot commerce, hot love, hotcha.

The best letter he'd received had come, after all, from his Uncle Dave. He'd had it a month and it brought him the closest feeling of home, so for this reason he read it once again:

DEAR NEPHEW IRA,

I was happy to get a special letter from you. I thought it was special anyway since I hear mostly of you through Ruth who shares all your letters with the family. I talked it over with Jake to get his opinion and we had a good argument over the details, which accounts for my delay in answering you, but since I'm writing the letter I've got the last word. Jake can write his version anyhow he wants.

Your father and my wife (your Aunt Zelda who you never knew) and I came out of Russia through Turkey in '79, then to England where your Papa met and married your mother, then to New York in '91 and finally to Oakland in '95 where you were born a year later. Since you're interested in the Russian part of it I'll skip the rest.

P.S. Ruth is acting as editor-in-chief on this letter which I've had to copy over and correct three times and this is the last! Unless I let her read over it again, which I won't, so forgive the errs to writers cramp.

The story is we came from Kiev. If so I don't recall it for I remember having been born and raised in Faztov, one of three brothers, though we did get to Kiev for one year and I think Jake must have told Rose he'd come from Kiev as part of his Jewish brag when he was courting her in England and doesn't now want to admit the lie. But Kiev, or Faztov, ghetto is ghetto. In '77 I was conscripted to do my five years and your old man, though only sixteen at the time, volunteered for service to escape it, escape the ghetto, that is, which should give you an idea of what ghetto life was if a youngster chose to shoulder a big Russian Krenk rifle and march off with strangers rather than stay in it.

It was dull and poor as hell and we were always under the thumb of the Kagal, the Jewish consistorium, and those bastards ground their own to bloody dust. Jews grinding Jews day and night, night and day. If you got a thought in your head that wasn't orthodox they made life impossible and I mean that. Your grandfather Hershel was a luft-mensh, one of those poor devils who rose with the sun and looked out at the weary street and wondered how he would avoid starvation another day. He made a living out of the air, as they say. It's a hard occupation to teach and there was lots of competition. He scurried about all day long, picking up bits and pieces, trading this for that, scavenging, selling, commissioning and somehow wracking a living out of pins and needles. Us kids never knew how he did it, all we knew was that we wouldn't be able to so the army was one way out. The only regret I had when I left was that Zelda Weiner who lived in the next house hadn't wept with the others.

In '78 Russia declared war on the Turks and Jake and I found ourselves in Caucasia supporting the siege of Kars which was being conducted by a Russian, Loris Melikov, who neglected his left flank, Jake says right, and Mukhtar Pasha drove us from the field and back to the Araxes valley. We stayed there from June until October when the Grand Duke Michael assumed command and we began marching about fighting Turks in places I no longer recall and which don't appear on many maps. Your father and I were with the baggage train most of the time and the cossacks never wasted words on two Zhid kids. When they wanted something we learned to pull in our necks and run for it and take a half hearted slap of a quirt as thanks and a blessing.

If we hadn't been together there were times when I think we would have thrown in the sponge. As it was we kept going by fighting each other almost continuously. Jake can't now remember, nor can I, how we hit on this device, but it worked then and still does to some extent. The troopers in our outfit kept us alive to see which of us would kill the other. We gave them entertainment. They made book on which of us would flatten the other before the day had passed.

At night we nursed our bruises and secretly, I think, complimented ourselves for having learned how to make a living out of the air as our father had done before us. Two Zhid kids accommodating the world by making fighting cocks of themselves.

A hell of a thing.

When the war came to an end your dad and I had earned a leave. The thought of returning to Faztov didn't appeal to either of us so we fought about that. Then a letter came from Zelda from Nikolayev where she'd gone into service in the house of a wealthy Russian Jew, Moiseyevich, a real exploiter.

I decided to go there and Jake tagged along, though he says it was the other way around and we've always fought about that.

Zelda Weiner was a beautiful person and in my opinion you and all of us can thank her for the life we've had. About this I don't think Jake would disagree. When we reached Nikolayev she'd already made plans for leaving Russia. She was sixteen years old. The idea of leaving Russia had never occured to Jacob or me until Zelda told us her plans in the Moiseyevich kitchen at which we began to compete with each other to carry them out.

A kind of wildness took hold of us, a frenzy to get away. We needed money for passage to Constantinople and for this we appealed to Moiseyevich who promptly informed the police of our intentions.

Looking back I can't say I blame him entirely. The appearance of two unknown soldiers intending to desert the army and carry one of his kitchen maids off to Constantinople must have struck him as shoddy business. The local police took us in, checked our leave papers, and since we weren't due back to our unit they simply ordered us out of town.

I was outraged, of course, and so was Jake. We returned to the Moiseyevich house, bound, gagged and robbed the old man and fled with Zelda to Odessa. There we shed our uniforms, bought forged papers and took a steamer to Constantinople.

You can guess the panic we were in, expecting any moment to be apprehended and shot on the spot. Zelda kept her wits about her and we managed to get through, but in Constantinople our money ran out, Moiseyevich's money, that is. I'm sure he never reported the theft to the police or we would never have gotten as far as Odessa and years later, from England, we returned the money we'd stolen from him with a letter of apology. The bank draft was cashed, but we never got a reply.

Constantinople I remember for its stench. We joined the Jewish community. Zelda and I got married and the three of us set up house, three penniless kids under nineteen. It seems strange even to me, now, but at the time it wasn't unusual. Life expectancy wasn't much. People died old at forty, or they didn't seem to die at all. Your father went to work hauling stone for the Galata quay and I took a job in a plant which processed dog manure for a product used to soften leather for ladies gloves. By this occupation I earned remission of all my past and future sins — shoveling dog crap into bins to be "purified." One of the great advances of science was the elimination of the need for this product, but even today I automatically think of Turkish dog manure when I see a woman wearing gloves.

(Ruth didn't believe this part, but Jake told her it was true and she laughed like hell.)

We were in Constantinople two years saving every penny we could. I worked myself up from dog shit to the slaughter houses where I stripped the hides off horses, sheep and goats, processing the guts, bone and hair. I had just elevated myself into the horn department when Zelda announced that we had enough money saved to get to England.

We arrived in Southampton broke and in reaction to my experiences in Constantinople I decided to go into the cleaning business which Jake and I have been in ever since as you know.

We were in England ten years when Zelda died and I didn't want to stay there anymore. By this time your father and mother were married so we came to New York and the rest is what you know.

As for being a Jew in Russia what can I say? Now is not then. We suffered as much from our own people as from those who cursed us, at least that's how I remember it. There were government restrictions, expulsions, relocations, taxes, conscriptions. The Khapers chased your grandfather through the woods to drag him into the army, but the term of service then was twenty-five years, I think, so we're lucky he escaped. But the Kagal and the Rabbinate, acting as intermediaries between us and the Russian community, administered these harsh laws and for that we hated them, at least Hershel Leverett's family did, which is why we aren't very strong for those old traditions today. The kheders and yeshivas, zadiks and rabbis wanted to shackle our minds and our resentment of them made us rebellious.

For me Zelda was the only person I ever knew who brought beauty to the ritual of Jewish life and for her alone I respected it. She was a cucumber to me. There was the fresh, sweet greenness of the cucumber about her to me. If you ever meet a girl with the breath of a cucumber, marry her. I would come home from heaps of dog dung or the bowels of rotting goats and her presence would cleanse me. I smell cucumbers when I pray or when I say her name and if someone slices a cucumber where I am I think of Zelda. Some men compare their women to fruit and melons, my Zelda was a cucumber, always green and fresh to me for which I thank God. For me the cucumber is a sacred thing.

So now the old Jewish life is being swept away, or so I read. The Pale is gone, old traditions breaking down, the people scattering. Injustices against the Jews will continue I have no doubt. I think we covet these a little bit, like salt. But enough is enough.

The pogroms I've read about are beyond anything I recall and I believe the hope of the Jews lies with Marx and Engels. A man of the Kolchak type has anti-Semitism in his blood and bone, maybe through no fault of his own, but it's there.

As for relatives which you might find in Russia, the answer is no. The last of our immediate family died in Faztov. Jake and I tried to entice them out, but they wouldn't come because they'd scraped enough money together to start a dry goods business which promised to do well and give them more security than they had ever known. Your uncle Aaron died in 1906, unmarried and old at forty-two.

So, Ira, what more can I say? I wish you were home is all. Old men are foolish with their advice and I have none to give though my desire is to send you comfort. I know you and love you, my only boy in fact. You have a good heart, follow it and what happens happens.

Love from us all and from me, your uncle,

Dave

Ira folded the letter carefully and returned it to the leather case in which he kept all the letters he received wondering, as always, if it was going to be large enough to hold those yet to come.

He sat for a time staring at the surface of the table. The car was very still, only the fire whispering in the stove. He thought again of Simonsen who'd approached him at the Mulligan, of his angry reaction to him. Simonsen the professional Semite, the artificial captain toting up his massacres and anecdotes for a tidy little article in *Harper's*. God, he'd been disgusted, but his own reaction to the Cossacks was a Simonsen reaction. "Heard about Ekaterinburg? — Killed three thousand Jews!"

Was it possible for a Jew to be neutral about Jews?

Was a secret Christmas tree an effective antidote for his Uncle David's prayers? Evidently not. When they buried the old man on the hillside he had not been inspired to sing "O Come, All Ye Faithful," or to recite the Lord's Prayer, no, El Moley Rahamim had welled up from within.

To date he had been a living neutral. A neutral Jew, a neutral pagan, a neutral intellectual. He had a neutral overview, neutral ambitions and above all he had been neutral at Siding 85 where he showed what he was under fire. A neutral.

Ira snorted contemptuously and went out into the freedom of the night.

The air was crisp but still filled with the warm smells of the afternoon.

Across the river the Cossacks were singing, their voices blurred by the water and the sighing trees. Ira crossed the bridge and found Carson on the main span staring into the darkness on the upstream side.

"Evening, Carson, what do you have there?"

Carson came to attention. "Sergeant Klagle told me to clean it, sir," he said. "Nice night, isn't it, sir."

A Very pistol dangled in Carson's hand. Ira asked to see it.

"It's pretty oily, sir," Carson said and he wiped it industriously with a rag before he gave it to Ira.

"How many do we have?"

"Four, sir. Sergeant Klagle told me to clean them all."

"We should test-fire them sometime," Ira said. He returned the signal pistol to Carson and crossed the bridge on the double-planked walk beside the tracks.

Ira found Carlisle seated among the Cossacks around the main fire. His appearance in that company reminded Ira of tribal chiefs he'd seen on railroad calendars, their faces bronzed, their eyes focused on vanished freedoms and vanished glories. Yakushef, wearing a shaggy wolf pelt jerkin with a ruffed collar, was seated next to Carlisle and they were all listening raptly to a singer whose voice soared out of the darkness in a high melodic wail full of savage melancholy.

Ira went to Carlisle and squatted beside him. "What is this?" he asked. "A forum on the Russian Jewish question or a branch meeting of the Siberian Klan?"

Carlisle looked around and scowled. "What's eating you?"

"Mosquitoes."

"Sit down and listen," Carlisle said and he moved to make a place for Ira.

"What's he singing?"

"I don't know the words."

"But you get the message, right? — Farewell, dear one, I'm off to war, keep faith till I return. Put a candle in the window while I kill and burn."

Carlisle turned back to the fire, his shoulders hunched against Ira's presence.

"I wonder how many of these old buggers were at Kishinev," Ira said. "They had one hell of a pogrom there."

Yakushef glanced at Ira in a puzzled manner.

"You leaving the wolves to your wife, Yak?" Ira asked.

"That's enough," Carlisle said quietly.

"Don't you get it, Sioux? Ordinarily you'd say: 'You leaving your wife to the wolves?' But that's not a joke out here, is it."

There was a rose glare in Carlisle's eyes. "What's eating you?" he demanded again.

Ira smiled and shrugged. "These poor untutored folk might get the idea we Americans are on their side if we continue accepting their hospitality."

"They're leaving tomorrow."

"Not with your blessings, I trust."

Carlisle stood up, moving awkwardly as though he were drunk. He made a sign to Yakushef, then lumbered away, looking back to see if Ira was following.

"Come on, Ira," he said heavily.

They walked to the bridge and when they reached the first span Carlisle caught Ira's arm and pulled him to a stop. His voice was heavy with anger. "Don't get smart with me again, Leverett. I don't like your wit. It stinks. Just say what you have to say and say it plain. You've been talking all day like you had a bellyache."

"I don't like Cossacks."

"That is a crying shame," Carlisle said, then he thrust Ira away and moved on. There was a loud pop and a star flare blossomed over the river, flooding it with harsh light.

"That's Carson," Ira yelled.

Another shell burst overhead.

Carlisle pointed into the river where two rafts, pitching wildly in the rough current, shot toward the bridge. A dozen shrieking Tataurovoan girls were clinging to one raft and the same number of American soldiers were trying to control the other.

A crowd of Cossacks, villagers and men from the company ran to the bridge and the riverbank. Some tried to toss lines to the rafts as they bumped over the rocks. Then the flares guttered out.

"Swim for it!" a voice yelled.

Another flare shot up from the bank and Carson appeared. "I seen you, Baker!" he yelled. "I seen you too, Eisenbach, you dirty mixers!"

The girls, seeing the people gathered on the bridge and along the river, dove into the water.

"I see you, Harris," Carson howled. "And Turnley! Keever! I seen you too!"

A stout woman from the village dragged one of the girls out of the water and began to beat her, the wet clothes making a cold slapping sound under the flat of her hand. Two girls ducked under the water and swam downstream intending to get away, but a group of women on the bank followed them, yelling threats and curses. Some of the girls reached the shallows and stood there weeping shamefacedly.

One soldier, it was Keever, swam to a girl in the deepest part of the basin and they clung to each other as the third flare hit the river and sizzled out.

Carlisle groaned and pulled Ira across the bridge. As they reached the other side another flare popped overhead and they saw Carson standing at the edge of the river with Blodgett, Stauffer and Miller all yelling the names of the men in the water.

"When it goes out follow me," Carlisle whispered. "Shove as many of our men as you can into the water."

"Shove them in?"

"You heard me, god damn it!"

When the flare went out Carlisle and Ira charged. Carson yelped as he was boosted into the river from behind. Ira shouldered Blodgett, who fell into the current with a screech. Between them Carlisle and Ira knocked half a dozen men into the water, then they ran back to the bridge. By now the pandemonium was general. More Cossacks arrived bearing torches.

Carson stood up to his neck in the water bellowing. "Get them mixers, get all of them!"

But the mixers, both male and female, had taken things into their own hands. Girls in the process of being beaten pulled their assailants into the water. Some of the more drunken Cossacks leaped from the bridge with flaming brands in their hands and in a few minutes the pond around the caissons was filled with men and women, laughing and chasing one another through the cold water.

Tataurovoan mothers, seeing a chance to save their daughters' reputations, joined the public dunking while swearing to tan their daughters' rumps in the privacy of home. A contingent of Cossacks arrived on horseback and splashed into the river, where most of them were unhorsed.

"Find Klagle and call a formation," Carlisle said to Ira.

At the formation ten minutes later more than half the men in the company were drenched and shivering. Carlisle asked for an explanation but no one spoke. Carson, looking like a wet scarecrow, glowered at those men he had seen on the raft, but since he was as wet as they were he didn't say a word.

Carlisle scanned the formation scowling ferociously. "From now on all personnel is restricted to this bank of the river," he growled. "Dismissed!"

The formation broke and the men dashed to their cars for dry clothes. Carlisle and Ira went inside and stood together with their backs to the stove.

"Wonder how long that's been going on," Carlisle asked.

"You can't beat human nature," Ira said.

Carlisle's mouth set in a stubborn line. "You can," he said, "if you keep your mind on it." Then he smiled, abruptly, surprisingly, and laughed. "Oh, Christ!" he said. "What the hell!"

« 4 »

The next morning the Cossacks entrained for the front and General Bogoloff arrived in an armored train to see them off. The ragged formation of inadequately equipped Cossacks stood at attention beside their horses while General Bogoloff, massive in his Czarist uniform, delivered a theatrical harangue. Colonel Sipialef stood nearby flicking his trouser legs with a quirt, his eyes narrow as the machine gun slits in the armored wagons.

Carlisle and Leverett attended this ceremony, but they had difficulty understanding it without an interpreter. The old General's emotionalism seemed excessive. Leverett detected a glittering disdain in Sipialef's eyes; he seemed to strain like a borzoi on a leash anxious to be off on a course of his own. When the General had finished his speech Sipialef stepped forward and offered him a handkerchief with a gesture of almost slavish deference.

General Bogoloff mopped his face, and Sipialef, his voice tauntingly musical, extended the General's invitation that Carlisle and Leverett join them for a toast in the General's private car, and his eyes slid past Leverett without recognition.

Some Cossacks were still drunk from the night before and the first of these to ride toward the waiting freight cars spurred his horse to a gallop, thundered up the incline planks and vaulted, horse and rider, through the open door at the other side of the car.

This feat of horsemanship brought howls of delight from the Cossacks and many tried to duplicate it. They galloped up the planks and the horses, discovering the drop too late, often balked in midair and came down stiff-legged, shuddering with shock while their riders spurred them to make another attempt. Some horses tossed their riders, or shied into the ends of the cars. For a time it looked as though the Cossacks were trying to break their legs to avoid getting it worse at the front, but finally the senior members got the rest under control and the loading went ahead in an orderly manner.

Cossack women passed food up to their men, then stood back, dry-eyed, but with painful expressions on their mouths and their hands clutched hard to their heaving bosoms.

Leverett watched one of Yakushef's sons lead his horse up the planks into a car, urging it tenderly, trying to calm it. "Eh, Kulubai," he said. "Eh, eh, Kulubai."

Carlisle and Yakushef shook hands, then Yakushef seized Carlisle and kissed him soundly on both cheeks and boarded the nearest car.

Carlisle came to Ira, his cheeks blazing.

"Yakushef bite you?" Ira asked.

"He'll do more fighting in the next few months than you'll ever see," Carlisle said.

"Sorry."

"All right, let's get it over with Bogoloff."

When they came into General Bogoloff's car they found the Cossack elders had been invited too. They stood in a line, caps in hand, clearly out of their depth as Bogoloff filled their glasses with vodka and said a private word to each of them.

The old Cossacks tossed off their vodka, then backed out the door bowing, bumping into one another and expressing their gratitude. Once outside they gave a rousing cheer, then hurried to their train, which almost immediately cleared the siding headed toward Omsk.

General Bogoloff smiled indulgently and poured Carlisle and Leverett a drink. "These poor chaps hardly know what it's about," he said. "They're thoroughly confused, but they'll fight like demons."

"Why not let the Russian people decide for themselves?" Ira asked.

Bogoloff turned to Ira, genuinely confused. "Decide what?" he asked.

"What government they want," Ira said. "Who they want to rule."

Bogoloff tried to retain the look of gravity on his long, saber-scarred face. "That's the very point," he began patiently, then he burst into laughter and looking merry as a Christmas figure shook all over. "That's the point," he bellowed, "but when are they going to decide? The Russian people run about, back and forth, up and down, squawking like chickens in the barnyard, trampling each other — and how do you make them decide until they're too exhausted to do anything else?"

"One thing you can do is to stop frightening them," Ira said.

"They frighten me!" Bogoloff replied. "They frighten me half to death! There is no order, no reason, no sense in it at all. We give them choices, what else can we do but that, and if they're too foolish, too hysterical to see the options, how can they settle down? Force is the only answer. Force, force, force until they come to their senses."

"Have an election," Ira said.

Bogoloff snorted contemptuously, his merriment gone. "God will elect," he said, "and until He does, let the people drop to their knees and pray. Some say the peasant dreams of having the land. Who in God's name has ever had it but the peasant? Yet they revolt on all sides against one group then another, raging about, spilling their own blood, pillaging, looting, burning, doing everything but tilling the soil. Don't you think they rule themselves? Do you imagine the Czar, bless his memory, ever ruled without their consent? You Americans! I lose patience. What in God's name do you think we're doing here but trying to settle the people so they can once again rule themselves. Now they demand punishment! They demand it with every voice, with every action, and do you think those demands are easily met; that one man takes pleasure in punishing another; that we are all sadists?"

To Ira's astonishment tears had appeared in Bogoloff's eyes, crocodile tears he had no doubt or tears of self-pity.

"You dislike me," Bogoloff said after a moment. "I see it is so." And he sighed heavily as though weighed down by a great injustice. "If you knew my country perhaps that would not be so, but so is so."

Ira nodded. "Yes," he said, "so is so." And he was struck by this phrase because it was so much like one his Uncle Dave would have used.

General Bogoloff turned to Carlisle and offered him a ride to Verkhne-Udinsk. "You're leaving this afternoon for Omsk," he said.

Carlisle was surprised that Bogoloff knew this.

"Colonel Spaeth informed me," Bogoloff continued. "He thinks a great deal of you, Captain."

"And I of him," Carlisle answered.

Bogoloff sipped his vodka and smiled. "You'll have a chance then to renew your acquaintance with Countess Tatiana and perhaps to do me a service. The vixen kept my epaulet. She's something of a collector of mementos, but I was attached to that pair. They were given to me by Grand Duke Michael."

"She'll be in Omsk?" Carlisle blurted. "In Omsk?"

"She wrote me to say so. Tatiana is my niece, you see. My sister Olga married her father, Speraski. As a child in happier days she was often in our home in St. Petersburg."

"You know her husband then," Carlisle said.

Bogoloff frowned and shook his head. "No, I do not."

Carlisle looked around in confusion as though he'd misplaced some-thing. He thanked Bogoloff hastily for his offer of a ride to Verkhne-Udinsk, but declined it saying he had to pack. He shook Bogoloff's hand, then Sipialef's, and was about to shake Ira's too before he realized it. "Come on, Leverett," he grumbled and he left the car.

From the door of their teplushka Ira and Carlisle watched Bogoloff's train switch off the siding and grind its way back toward Verkhne-Udinsk.

"She must have passed through without stopping at Verkhne," Ira said.

"She?"

"Your countess."

Carlisle's eyes narrowed and his jaw took on a granite look.

"If she stopped, Bogoloff could have recovered his epaulet. She must have gone through shortly after Markowitz did."

Carlisle turned slowly and Ira was dismayed by the molten look in his eyes. When he spoke his voice came up from the depths like lava. "Lever-ett," he said. "This is my company. It's the only thing I care about in this world, do I make myself clear? The only thing! And by God, if you mess it up don't be here when I get back!"

That afternoon Carlisle stood at the bridge waiting for his train and Ira watched from the steps of their car. They hadn't spoken since Carlisle's angry admonition; they'd been avoiding each other.

Ira heard the train coming, slackening speed as it approached the bridge. He saw Carlisle tense, ready to swing aboard, but as he did so he raised his arm and one of his great, world-forgiving, white grins flashed across his face. "Good luck, Ira!" he yelled.

Ira jumped to the ground and ran toward the train, waving. "Same to you, Captain," he yelled. "Take it easy!"

Carlisle hung onto the side bar of the carriage and waved to his men who'd gathered to see him off. They called after him and Blodgett was ringing the bell on the Snorter as Carlisle was carried out of sight.

CHAPTER EIGHTEEN

MOVING heavily through the night behind two engines and protected by an armored car with a guard detail of British troops, the American diplomatic train stopped frequently to pick up new envoys, liaison men and represen-tatives of various governments, so that by the time it headed into the last stage of its journey it carried in capsule all the complexities, uncertainties and conflicts of interest which bedeviled the vast land through which it traveled.

Carlisle had come aboard at Tataurovo. Major Subo Ikachi, extending the courtesies of the Japanese government, boarded the train at Irkutsk. General Janin and General Knox had their representatives on board, as did the Serbs and the Czechs, the Italians and the Canadians. There was much talk, much champagne, much fine cuisine, but not the slightest clue why the American Ambassador to Japan and the American General from Vladivostok were so far from their customary posts. The assumption was that something very big was in the making.

On the whole Ambassador Morris and General Graves kept to themselves. They didn't discuss their separate missions with each other or with anyone else largely because they would have been hard pressed themselves to define what these were. To pass the tedious hours and avoid leading conversations they played poker each afternoon with a few selected officers and in this way had gotten to know each other.

Ambassador Morris, a small, mild-mannered, intelligent man, admired President Wilson and had been close to him since their Princeton days. He conceived it his principal duty as a diplomat to reduce Presidential tensions, so he tried to synthesize the complexities of any given situation in a way that would give the President a valid choice. Consequently he viewed Siberian politics with detachment in order to get an overall view and the train, carrying as it did so many elements of the Siberian struggle, was a useful introductory experience for him. He listened closely to incidental snatches of conversation; noticed the tensions among the Allied officers and began to shape his recommendations even before the train reached Omsk. He sensed that a rejection of the Kolchak regime at this time would topple the government; therefore the alternatives which remained were prompt recognition by the United States, or a diplomatic delaying action until such time as the coalition which Kolchak represented began to show conclusive results. Morris was not sure which he would recommend, but his tendency always was to advise caution.

Carlisle and Colonel Spaeth shared a compartment and in the evenings, watching the light fade from the broad Siberian sky, they frequently talked with the quiet intimacy of men made aware of their own finitude. Relaxed by the measured sound of the wheels over the rails Spaeth often spoke of his wife Peg and their kids. "You ought to get married, Sioux," he said one time. "Have you been?"

"I've never tried it."

"Women make good sense."

"Some do."

"Peg is damned patient. She finds it hard to explain to the kids why I'm still out here. Bobby has taken to slaughtering Bolsheviks in the backyard with his toy rifle, but Peg wants him to get back to cowboys and Indians."

"That's better," Carlisle said.

"He always takes the Indian side if it's any comfort to you."

"We need all the help we can get."

Spaeth laughed. "Have you talked with Major Ikachi? He caught me in the corridor yesterday and told me how well you handled the situation at Siding 85. He's a fan of yours."

"He's all right himself, but I don't know what he's up to."

"Maybe nothing."

"The Japs are in heavy with Kalmykoff and Semenoff and I wouldn't be surprised if Sipialef wasn't their man too. It makes me nervous."

"It makes us all nervous, Jack. It makes General Graves nervous as hell, but there's damned little he can do about it just now. Damned little any of us can do about it. My guess is that the Japs would just as soon see Kolchak go down the drain. They're interested in concessions in Manchuria and the Maritime Province and a strong government in Siberia, Kolchak's or any other, would be inimical to those interests."

"So our real reason for being here is to counter the Japs."

Spaeth nodded. "You've put your finger on it, Jack."

"We still calling it neutrality?"

"That's what we call it."

The next afternoon General Graves invited Spaeth into his private compartment for a drink. "Well, Bob," he asked, "what are you picking up?"

"Bits and pieces, General. Nothing you haven't heard, I'm sure."

Graves stood at the window for a moment frowning at the passing landscape, then he sat down across from Spaeth. "I think Morris is right," he said. "With the British and French jumping up and down to support Kolchak and Ambassador Francis promising to smash the Bolsheviks given fifty thousand troops, what can Morris say? The art of diplomacy is saying what people have to hear, not what they want to hear, necessarily, but what they have to hear. He'll recommend support to avoid trouble with the British and the French, and if Kolchak falls, then we're all in it together."

"Like three men in a tub," Spaeth said.

"A leaky one at best."

"I just hope we all bail out together."

General Graves shrugged and settled more comfortably in his chair. "All right, Bob, let's discuss what you're going to do if there is a collapse. Your command is the farthest west and if the dam busts there's going to be a log jam from Baikal to Vlad. We've got American personnel clear to Omsk, hospital and Red Cross people, railroad technicians and engineers all across the line. They've got to be brought out and there'll be a lot of others who'll face firing squads if they don't cross the Chinese border."

"How much notice do you suppose we'd have?"

"Your job on this trip is to tell me how much you're going to need. I want you to be prepared for it. Thoroughly prepared. If Kolchak falls every six-bit Cossack ataman with loyal troops or an armored train will try to slice himself a piece of Siberia and who knows what might occur on the Chinese Eastern?"

"Any idea when it might come?"

"The collapse?"

"Orders to pull out."

Graves' congenial manner changed abruptly. He shook his head. "They're making noises in Congress. I'd say a year, but your guess is as good as mine. Right now your command is in the dead center of a political Sargasso Sea. What would your immediate situation be if Kolchak fell?"

"You seem to think it'll go that way," Spaeth said.

Graves' neck stiffened and his big face set hard. "You know, Bob, I get awfully damned tired of being interpreted. I don't know anything more tiresome. I haven't said anything for the last year that somebody hasn't tried to guess what I meant. The problem is that I always say what I mean and I always talk about what I'm talking about. I don't talk about one thing and mean another. I don't make riddles or do I? I sometimes wonder myself. I get the feeling all the time that the words coming out of my mouth are something else than what I intended to say. That's a terrible thing, Bob. I was asking about your situation. I wasn't prejudging Kolchak's. A good troop commander has to be prepared for every eventuality or am I wrong?"

"No, sir."

"It's damned tiresome," Graves said and he sighed. "Now suppose we talk about what we were talking about."

Graves stared at the window as Spaeth outlined his plans for the withdrawal of American and Allied personnel. "What if the Trans-Baikal tunnels are gone?" he asked abruptly.

"If the lake is open we can ferry people from Baikal to Posolskaya and pick them up. If it's frozen we'll organize sleigh transport for those who need it. The rest would have to walk. But the Czech defense of the tunnels seems adequate."

"Yes, but what if they were blown?"

Spaeth was disturbed. "What interest would the Czechs have in destroying the tunnels?"

"The Czech Legion is a curious article, Bob. I think we'd be foolish to depend on them if the going got hard. They've been fighting one hell of a long time and they want to go home. The Czech state is an accomplished fact, it has been since October last year, and that's what they wanted from the beginning. There are some ambitious Czech leaders, but what about the rank and file? There are a lot of socialists among them, Reds if you like. There's a case to be made that their original pledge to the Russian government could adhere to the present Bolshevik regime, particularly if Kolchak collapses. In that case it could be to their interest to align with the Bolsheviks in exchange for a guarantee of amnesty. Part of that arrangement could be to block Kolchak's escape. Kolchak has possession of the Russian State gold reserves, about three hundred million dollars in gold bullion. The Reds will want that and one practical way to stop Kolchak would be to destroy the Trans-Baikal tunnels."

Spaeth nodded considerately. "I'll put Carlisle on it right away."

"You'd better plan to have someone at Irkutsk to see our people through. I'll send you a list of personnel for whom we are responsible. Now, what about Bogoloff?"

"He's living in the past as far as I can tell."

"And Sipialef?"

"He's power-hungry, but so far he's been running under Bogoloff's wing. You've seen my report on Pashkova."

"Yes," Graves said, "and I've seen orders written by Kolchak's generals that you wouldn't believe. We get atrocity reports and appeals for intercession continually. All I can do is refer them to the inter-Allied command, which shunts them around until the next set of atrocity reports buries them. In one case five hundred Cossacks deserted Kalmykoff and surrendered themselves to Colonel Morrow for protection. I referred that one to the Japanese, who of course denied they had any influence with Kalmykoff and advised I return the mutineers to him. Poor Morrow still has them in a detention camp. We sent an investigating team out to Pashkova, did I tell you? Nothing left but a few charred timbers. How did your men take it?"

"I didn't tell them the connection between Pashkova and Sipialef."

General Graves looked troubled. "That'll come out," he said.

"When it does I'll have to deal with it."

Graves remained silent for a time, then he checked his watch and stood up. "Time for the game," he said. "You going to take a hand?"

"I've got some homework to do," Spaeth said. "I'll put Carlisle in touch with the Russian garrison at Irkutsk and turn him around at Omsk. We'll get right on this, General."

"Oh, give the man a chance to enjoy himself, Bob. The Kolchak regime should last for a while — now don't interpret that remark! I take a long view of history."

Spaeth laughed and they saw Major Ikachi passing down the corridor toward Ambassador Morris' compartment for the poker game.

Subo Ikachi's charm for Ambassador Morris was that he did not dissemble, but seemed himself to be frankly confused by Siberian politics. Some of his statements were so candid that they might have been considered simple-minded if it were not for the fact that Ikachi was a superb poker player.

As they waited for the other players to arrive Morris speculated about the reception they would have at Omsk. He hoped it would be informal, but he supposed the Russian love of protocol would make a round of dinners and military reviews inevitable.

"The British will not overlook the occasion," Ikachi said.

"No reason to assume the British will be calling all the shots," General Graves said.

Ikachi frowned as though searching his memory. "The Admiral was forwarded by the British as I recall."

This bland assertion caused General Graves to smile. "That's right, Major," he said. "They bundled him up in Tokyo and shipped him in C.O.D. as you know full well."

"I expect it's in the British tradition to pick an admiral for such a position," Ikachi said.

"Yes," Graves said, "and in the Japanese tradition to pick men like Semenoff and Kalmykoff."

It was a stinging retort, quite beyond the niceties of diplomatic expression, and Ambassador Morris looked uneasy.

Ikachi, not a bit ruffled, nodded pleasantly. "Desperate situations often call for desperate measures, General Graves. The slaughter of Cadets at Chapultepec; General Sherman's march to the sea; the water tortures on

Samar, the extermination of the Sioux, Nez Percé and the Cheyenne. American examples are not lost to history, General. Mine is an awakening nation and we're more than willing to carry our share of the white man's burden." Ikachi smiled affably and took a cigarette.

"I'm not happy about the instances you mention," Graves said. "But my observation has been that the ordinary Japanese soldier doesn't appear to have any respect for the individual and I blame this on the attitude of their officers."

"Attitudes are often hard to transmit, Colonel," Ikachi said. "Mine, for instance, are almost exclusively artistic."

"I don't know what that means," Graves responded.

"Yes, it's hard to transmit," Ikachi said. "I'm interested in the form of things, in their balance and tension, in the way they manage to describe something which is always just out of touch." Major Ikachi raised one hand lightly. "I abhor violence. Truly I do. I hope my country will come to emulate yours in many ways. I can think of nothing better. Your history fills me with wonder. I think it fills the hearts of most Japanese with burning envy. Imagine, gentlemen, how it affects us to see that in less than a hundred and fifty years, a period of time which could almost be spanned by two consecutive lives of seventy years, your country by waging almost continual warfare has secured for itself practical control of two fifths of the world."

General Graves' head jerked up and he scowled.

"The history of the occupation of your primary land base, of the annihilation and dispersal of the native populations, is in itself a classic example of acquisitive drive. The annexation of Mexican territories, Texas, New Mexico, California, was truly gargantuan. The liquidation of the Hudson Bay Company in the Pacific Northwestern territories, the force applied to the Canadian border — fifty-four forty or fight, wasn't that the expression? — the purchase of Alaska, the acquisition of the Spanish colonies, the Philippines, Puerto Rico, the occupation of Panama, Honduras! There's no end of it, gentlemen, and here you are ready to partition China right along with everyone else and very anxious about Japanese designs in Manchuria.

"Gentlemen, for centuries Japan was no larger than your original thirteen colonies, but your good Admiral Perry insisted that we wake up, so we have awakened. Now if you want to talk with me about massacres, atrocities, brutality, the behavior of common soldiers, I'm quite prepared to do so. But I feel very sure that I have more material to draw upon considering your history than you will have considering the history of the Imperial Japanese Army, which only came into existence in 1872."

There was a prolonged silence, then Ambassador Morris grinned and passed a bottle of Scotch to Ikachi. "Have a drink, Major?" he asked.

"Thank you, I will," Ikachi said.

Two other officers, Major Custer-Farquart representing General Knox and a Czech colonel representing General Pierre Janin, came into the compartment. Ambassador Morris spread the cards and they drew for the first deal. General Graves won with a ten of diamonds.

"We should reach Omsk by four, don't you think?" Morris asked.

General Graves, his face clouded by a heavy frown, checked his watch. "Yes," he said, "that's what I've been given to understand."

The hip wound Major Ikachi had sustained at Siding 85 left him with a slight limp and this evidence of their shared experience plus the close confines of the train made it inevitable that he and Carlisle meet again. For a time it appeared as though each was waiting for the other to speak first; then one afternoon, approaching each other in the corridor, they spoke simultaneously, laughed and shook hands.

"How is Lieutenant Leverett?" Ikachi asked.

"Fine," Carlisle said.

"He's still with you then."

"Yes, he has my company while I'm away."

"Ah yes," Ikachi said, but there was something veiled in his expression which put Carlisle off.

"He's a good man," Carlisle said.

"I'm sure he is," Ikachi said.

"He is."

They fell silent and were uncomfortable as they grew aware of the train wheels rumbling beneath them and of the creak and rattle of the carriage.

"I spent part of an evening with the Lieutenant in Harbin," Ikachi said.

"I didn't know that."

"Yes," Ikachi said. "He impressed me as being a clever man."

"Clever?"

"Intelligent, affable, the administrative type."

Carlisle scowled. "Glad to see you again, Major," he said and he continued along the corridor and they didn't speak again until the train reached Omsk when they bade each other a formal goodbye.

Carlisle found Ikachi's remarks upsetting, particularly the reference to administration. It was coincidental, perhaps, but Ikachi appeared to share Colonel Spaeth's opinion of Leverett as expressed in his letter of reprimand: "I recommend that he be assigned to administrative tasks."

Carlisle had gone against this recommendation and for what reasons?

Personal involvement?

Certainly not.

Leverett, the college boy, had nowhere near the claim to his friendship that Austin had had. Oh, he liked Ira well enough, Carlisle supposed, but why? He wasn't half the soldier Austin had been. They had nothing in common, but here Carlisle stumbled, unwillingly, into the partial truth of the matter.

Since he had been made a captain, since meeting Tatiana, since his enforced association with Allied officers of undisputable style and refinement, he had wanted to change himself and Ira was his tutor.

Everything he had taught Ira Leverett about soldiering had been exchanged for the opportunity to absorb Ira's manners, Ira's vocabulary, Ira's attitudes about many things which had not been important before. Now they were. They were very important indeed.

The narrowness of his army life had become intolerable and without thinking about it he had taken Ira as the model by which to correct his gracelessness and lack of style. Carlisle realized that this defense of Ira's competence to handle the company was a payment on his obligation and had nothing to do with common sense or duty. He regretted this and was anxious about it.

As they left the train at Omsk, Carlisle fell in beside Colonel Spaeth and cleared his throat self-consciously. "I'd like to get back to my company as soon as I can, Colonel," he said.

"Hell, Jack, we've only arrived."

"Just the same."

Spaeth was puzzled. "Anything wrong?" he asked.

Carlisle scowled and shook his head. "Nothing specifically, sir," he said. "These diplomatic things are usually a bore and I've got a job to do."

Spaeth glanced at Carlisle. The statement that diplomatic things were usually a bore was so alien to Carlisle's normal way of speaking that Spaeth thought he was being funny, but the expression on Carlisle's face was profoundly serious.

"General Graves wants a complement of American officers with him, Jack. You're one of them. Bored or not, you'll stay until the General tells me you're no longer needed here."

"Yes, sir," Carlisle said.

CHAPTER NINETEEN

ADMIRAL Kolchak, well aware of the importance of Ambassador Morris' visit, took pains to have some heavy guns drawn up in the form of English-speaking ladies of charm and wit to assist in putting the American party at ease. He knew that his precise, rather icy personality did not go down well with Americans and hoped that by creating an artificial society things might go more smoothly.

His mistress, Anna Vasilievna Timireva, was sent to Irkutsk on a visit for, though her relationship to the Supreme Ruler was accepted by the British and the French, the Americans with their provincial morality might find her presence in Omsk a cause for scandal. One never knew about Americans. They would not understand, for instance, how Admiral Kolchak could remain on friendly terms with Rear-Admiral Timirev, the senior Russian naval officer in Vladivostok who was, incidentally, Anna Vasilievna's husband, or how he could speak fondly of his wife currently residing in Paris. Kolchak was fond of both women, but in the present circumstances Anna Vasilievna was more useful than his wife, who tended to be a bit hysterical. Timireva was calm. She warmed his bed and body. They were friends of long standing and her husband had served under Kolchak in the Baltic Fleet. She was in her middle thirties, dark, placid, handsome and unassuming, and though he knew how vital the United States was to the interests of his government Kolchak resented having to deprive himself of her. But being a true statesman, he made the sacrifice and agreed to accept Mrs. Edna Custer-Farquart as official hostess during the American stay. A great man could do no less.

Mrs. Custer-Farquart, whose name caused considerable merriment among the American officers, Red Cross personnel and nurses stationed at Omsk, was herself an American married to a British major on General Knox's staff. A southern lady of massive proportion with money from a bathroom fixtures concern established by her father, she had insisted on coming to Omsk for the season, to do good works shoulder to shoulder with her valiant husband.

Mrs. Custer-Farquart spoke of her marriage as a "jointure" of two great cultures, which made it seem as though she and her husband had been plumbed together rather than consecrated in holy matrimony. She referred to herself as a cultured but earthy person. "I'm cultured, but earthy," she said, "cultured, but earthy. The kids have grown up and floated away, but damned if I'll sit on my can."

To avoid this fate she had come to Omsk to observe the ebb, flux and flow of revolutionary politics. The word "Bolshevism" set her teeth on edge. "Sounds like something that happens inside one of Papa's toilets" was her evaluation of this particular movement. She didn't like the Mensheviks either, for about the same reason. She had a tendency to judge everything by its sound and to make broad generalizations on a scale of obscure plumbing tones. "I have an unerring ear," she said. "Perfect political pitch."

Kolchak sounded like a good man to her, all business, no nonsense. Graves sounded somber and dedicated. Surprisingly she was more often right than wrong, but people who knew this peculiarity of hers invariably wondered why she had married Custer-Farquart. What passions had this combination of sounds aroused in her virginal inner ear? What mad dreams? The man himself was innocuous, one of those sandy Englishmen who appear always on the verge of falling asleep, so people made desperate efforts to save him the embarrassment of having done so by talking to him more than they ordinarily would have. Major Custer-Farquart was of the English squire class, a Somerset man with an estate, whose interests were confined to horses, hounds, foxes, guns, cards, sherry and, perhaps, his wife.

Be that as it may, Mrs. Custer-Farquart was a force, one of those well-connected women with relatives in Congress and other places of high finance. She was anti-Bolshevik, pro-Kolchak and determined to make the winds of Washington blow favorably toward Omsk. She had already done much to encourage a syndicate of New York financiers to advance Kolchak a loan of five million dollars to buy two hundred and sixty thousand rifles which had been made in the United States for the Kerensky government but not shipped when that government fell. She had induced Kolchak to secure this loan with gold bullion deposited in Hong Kong and just prior to the arrival of Graves and Morris had received the happy news that these rifles were due to be shipped to Siberia in August.

Mrs. Custer-Farquart, silly or not, was a person who got results and for this Kolchak admired her. It was not illogical, therefore, that she was his hostess for the reception to be held at Stavka Headquarters for the American Ambassador.

To avoid a premature confrontation of Morris and Kolchak which might stumble into the realities of the current situation, as, for instance, that the Kolchak front was weakening, that Cheliabinsk seemed about to fall to the Reds, who had already occupied Ashkhabad and refused to be budged from Perm, Mrs. Custer-Farquart, who knew the value of clutter, glitter and noise, insisted that the initial reception be as large as possible.

The fact that neither Ambassador Morris nor Admiral Kolchak would attend this swarming reception made not the slightest difference. Their emissaries would be there, and a subsequent meeting might or might not be arranged as a result. The purpose of the reception was threefold: to honor the American Ambassador (who remained in his private railroad car that evening), to provide a setting in which the envoys of the powers represented could make their arrangements, and to show that a brilliant, calm, self-confident society could amuse itself knowing that the Supreme Ruler in his eyrie had the future of Russia firmly in control.

The reception line was long and calculatedly benumbing with generals and cabinet ministers and their ladies smiling cordially and making mental notes of who could conceivably be meaningful in future events. There were probably a dozen such men among the four hundred guests. None of them were certain who the others were, but as evening wore on they would gravitate or be guided to each other; they would smell each other out.

Colonel Spaeth and Captain Carlisle were assumed to be members of the influential group. Major Subo Ikachi was included. General Graves did not attend these preliminaries, of course, and General Dietrichs, currently Kolchak's Chief of Staff, was not present. The social-political-military sniffing about was left to the lesser dogs.

Loris Melikof, Kolchak's chief diplomatic adviser, made mental notes as to whom he should invite to an "informal" supper following the reception, hoping fervently that he did not overlook one of the important dozen. His chances of doing so were slight because most of the guests were chaff and he had twenty men to invite, which left him a margin for error of eight. The ladies would simply be chosen for their charm.

Melikof, a bespectacled, rather portly fuss-budget in his late sixties, had a boundless, almost feminine, interest in gossip and petty intrigue. As a young man, after having gained some notoriety in the Turkish wars, he abandoned the military for a diplomatic career. He was multilingual, knew the limitations of his talents, and his bumbling, unambitious charm was always welcome in court circles. The revolution failed to excite him until he was forced out of Moscow by the Bolsheviks. Eventually he came into Kolchak's service, where his former associations and vast memory for names proved invaluable.

Melikof shook hands with those who passed down the line, introducing them facilely, and the pressure of his fingers measured their importance with incredible exactitude. Experience had taught him when in doubt that a little added pressure was good insurance, so it was that Colonel Spaeth and Captain Carlisle were the recipients of one of his more hearty handshakes as he passed them on to Victor Pepelyaev, Kolchak's Minister of the Interior, whose brother Anatol was a general in the Kolchak army.

When the reception line dissolved, Mrs. Custer-Farquart, smiling brilliantly, launched herself into the crowd determined not to let her party flag or go flat, but to keep it fluffy as an omelet. No one could overlook her presence. She wore a lavender evening dress with pearls and a diamond brooch at her throat and flourished a wicked-looking feather boa fastened to her right shoulder by a large enamel pin bearing the crest of the Custer-Farquarts.

Her husband, the Major, stood in the corner sipping sherry with a bemused expression as he watched his wife shuttling from one group to another igniting conversational fires. Guests who saw her coming, mostly the chaff, flared into laughter, hoping to ward her off, for they'd noticed she didn't stop where things appeared bright, but circled away, ever watchful, armed with a set of "topics" with which to fuel those poor souls who were being treasonably quiet.

Attacking one such group on the flank she cried: "This epidemic of spotted typhus is just too dreadful, don't you agree? I've taken a vow never to sit in an upholstered chair. It simply isn't safe. We must find a way to defeat these lice."

To another: "They tell me Samara had a lovely theater before the Bolsheviks came. Now they won't allow Chekov, not that I approved of him thoroughly, did you?"

And another: "My President, Woodrow Wilson, is domestically sound, but he hasn't the British sense of history to guide him; therefore we have an obligation to see him through these troubled times, as you know."

"Of course you have yet to meet our Ambassador to Japan, Roly Morris, who is very well connected. A cousin of mine has known him for years! I'm sure these troop reviews and parades will tire him to death, but how else can one make policy in the world as it is?"

To avoid these "topics" the guests assumed a defensive brilliance, seizing any subject at all and worrying it to death rather than have Mrs. Custer-Farquart in their midst.

Countess Tatiana had come with Colonel Dubrovski, who'd once been an employee of her father's. She was standing next to a British major, a pudgy man with light blue eyes who looked at her and nodded toward Mrs. Custer-Farquart. "Marvelous woman," he said.

"Yes," Tatiana said. "Who is she?"

"My wife of thirty years," the Major said. "Mrs. Custer-Farquart. Her father established a business on the alimentary canal and it has been going great guns for half a century. She's going to open a British branch."

"How very enterprising she is," Tatiana said stifling a giggle.

"American know-how," the Major said and he tapped his nose solemnly. "They do very well in heavy industry and the rest of it, but their genius is for the cosmetic values. They're great for covering up, making things silent, smooth, easily forgotten. Great plumbing, great morticians, fine packages, all the rest of it. Cosmetic values, you see? Better than the French. I've made a life study, had to. Got two boys and a girl from a cabbage leaf."

Tatiana laughed aloud, which pleased the Major immensely. He chortled and offered to fetch her a drink, but Tatiana said her escort, Colonel Dubrovski, was on that mission. Looking around for him Tatiana saw Mrs. Custer-Farquart rise out of the center of one chattering group and catch poor Dubrovski as he made his way from the bar with a glass in each hand. Perhaps she had mistaken Dubrovski's concentration on the drinks for petulance, a quality she could not tolerate, or his clumsy manner may have caused her to question his credentials. In any case she caught his arm and smiling broadly demanded that he explain the Czechs to her. "I do find it so confusing, really!" she cried. "They've had every chance to leave through Archangel or Vladivostok, but here they are and here they remain, fighting this way and that. Only last March they could have gone home by way of the Kara Sea. That marvelous Norwegian, Jonas whoever, you know who I mean, had it all arranged with Elsa Brandstrom of the Swedish Red Cross. Churchill dished the scheme, but I don't see why they didn't go without British agreement. It is difficult to understand, but I love the Czechs, love them for being so loyal to our Admiral."

Colonel Dubrovski, taken completely off guard, undertook to explain the activities of the Czech Legion and soon was hopelessly involved in a conversation with several people; and Mrs. Custer-Farquart, her mission accomplished, took the extra drink from his hand and moved on.

Major Custer-Farquart shared Tatiana's enjoyment of this spectacle.

That such a woman could exercise power over those in the room for even the shortest period of time struck at the foundations of history. That she could play a role, however limited, in the destinies of nations and of people was incredible.

"The best thing to do," Major Custer-Farquart said, "is to get comfortably intoxicated and stand aside. Given an opportunity my wife could rule the world. She appreciates the madness of it. She knows the illogicalness of it. Her conclusions are usually right. Her way of reaching them is a mystery. Reads history by names of the participants. Uncanny!"

Colonel Dubrovski extricated himself from the group into which he had been trapped and brought Tatiana her drink. "I don't understand it," he said shaking his head soulfully. "That mad woman absolutely swamped me with talk!"

The Major chortled and Tatiana tried to relocate Mrs. Custer-Farquart in the crowd. She saw Loris Melikof across the room, wearing a particularly pained expression; then she heard Mrs. Custer-Farquart's strident voice. "He will be our savior! Can there be any doubt of it? Jack Johnson was an insult to southern womanhood and Jess Willard was no better, but Dempsey! Give us Dempsey!"

Melikof was trembling. He looked around wildly, wondering if the British, French or the Americans had injected a new procurator general into the already confused situation. "Dempsey," he murmured, "Dempsey?" and he rushed off to find someone who could tell him who Dempsey was, intending to add this person to the supper list.

Spaeth and Carlisle had been on the point of leaving when they were taken under Mrs. Custer-Farquart's raking fire. Why she had attacked them with the topic of boxing they did not understand. But having stunned them with her opening declaration, Mrs. Custer-Farquart looked around for Melikof who had vanished. "But he was there just this instant! You must meet Loris Melikof, or have you? Budgy had the most charming things to say about you both."

"Budgy?" Spaeth asked.

"My husband. He rode in on the train with you. Major Custer-Farquart."

"Oh, yes! Budgy!" Spaeth said glancing at Carlisle, whose face had taken on a look of graven stone. "Allow me to introduce Captain Carlisle. This is Budgy's wife, Jack."

Carlisle mumbled an acknowledgment under his breath and spiked

Colonel Spaeth out of the corner of one eye. "We were about to leave, Madam," he said.

"But no!" Mrs. Custer-Farquart declared. "I don't know where Melikof has gotten to, that divine man, but there's General Rozanoff. You must talk to Rozanoff. He's commander of the Siberian Militia and has designed new uniforms. Very colorful. The sketches have gone to New York with an order for fifty thousand. I'm sure they'll do a great deal toward stabilizing the situation. The problem is morale and I'm convinced, as Rozanoff is, that a soldier dressed in an ill-fitting, drab uniform is no match for one who is wearing something smart and colorful. Fashion and ritual still have their place on the battlefield, which is something the Reds seem to have forgotten."

"The Hessians were dressed very well during our Revolution, but they lost," Spaeth said.

"That's not the same!" Mrs. Custer-Farquart protested. "Not the same at all!"

"You can stay if you like, Colonel," Carlisle said. "I've got a lot to do."

Just then Loris Melikof, having discovered Dempsey was an American boxer, not a general or a statesman, came through the crowd, introduced himself and invited Colonel Spaeth and Carlisle to his "intimate little supper" and at that moment Carlisle saw Tatiana.

She was across the room gazing at him with an expression of warm amusement in her deep gray eyes. A brutish-looking Czech colonel was beside her and the thought flashed through Carlisle's mind that this was her husband and just as quickly he denied it. The man wasn't good enough!

He heard Colonel Spaeth decline Melikof's urgent invitation as Tatiana came toward them.

"We'll stay," Carlisle said.

Spaeth looked at him, surprised. "It's up to Jack," he said.

Loris Melikof and Mrs. Custer-Farquart turned their persuasive powers on Carlisle, whose attention was concentrated on Tatiana moving effortlessly toward him in a long russet-colored gown like a bronze flame. Once again her head was set off, this time by a necklace of pearls which looped round and round, then fell over her bosom.

Mrs. Custer-Farquart's importuning face thrust up toward him and she was clinging to his arm. "Yes!" Carlisle said and Tatiana extended her hand.

"Captain of the Powder Room," she said.

With a sigh and a smile of almost idiotic simplicity Carlisle took her hand and, bowing, kissed it. Then with masterful aplomb he introduced Tatiana to the others. His manner was so elegant that Spaeth was dumfounded.

Melikof, whose sense of situation was flawless, promptly invited Countess Tatiana and her escort Dubrovski to his supper, thus insuring the presence of both Carlisle and the Colonel.

Mrs. Custer-Farquart smiled at Melikof and patted his arm. "There you are, Loris," she said. Then, having made this connection, she excused herself and assaulted another group with one of her "topics." This time, for some inexplicable reason, it was Paul Reinsch, the United States Minister to China.

"Reinsch!" she cried. "He's a marvel. I like a man who moves with dispatch. He opens the door, goes in, does his business without any fuss and the door remains open! Reinsch! Reinsch! The perfect man for China. And the door to China must remain open. It's the only way to air the place out!"

Tatiana caught Carlisle's arm laughing helplessly and in a moment Carlisle too was roaring like breakers over a reef.

"Now this is the kind of party it should be!" Mrs. Custer-Farquart declared.

« 2 »

The seating arrangement for Loris Melikof's intimate little supper put Tatiana across the table from Carlisle. She was seated between Major Ikachi and Colonel Spaeth and for a time Carlisle strained to hear bits of their conversation. He felt alert and vital and the pleasure of being able to see her was exquisite. Everything she did seemed perfect, the way she lifted her glass, her firm white hand, the flashing wine, her profile.

He envied Ikachi, who seemed to have captivated Tatiana. She turned more often to him than to Spaeth and smiled frequently.

The brilliant array of silver, chinaware and glass dazzled Carlisle. He was aware of the lady on his left, but had failed to catch her name. She spoke Russian and French, which Carlisle could not understand. Beyond her was Colonel Dubrovski, who spoke English, and as the meal began Carlisle detected a slight hesitation on the Colonel's part in selecting the proper fork, which showed that he too was unused to such affairs and this recommended him to Carlisle.

Loris Melikof sat at one end of the table, Mrs. Custer-Farquart at the other, and between them they monitored the conversation. Within five minutes they had excluded Carlisle and Dubrovski from the select circle of the truly influential. They had reservations about Colonel Spaeth. Major Ikachi was definitely in, as was the French attaché. A recently arrived British trade unionist, the Czech General Syrovy, and several other military men were included and Melikof was satisfied that of the four hundred guests he had gotten his bag of twelve influential men.

For Carlisle the supper was a succession of images and thoughts, all chaotic. Tatiana's reason for coming to Omsk was to be with her husband. Had she found him? If so, who was Dubrovski? The lady on his left inquired of Dubrovski if Carlisle was from South America. Dubrovski conveyed the question. "No, North America," Carlisle said.

"Are you stationed in Omsk?" Dubrovski asked.

"No, I'll be returning soon to Verkhne-Udinsk," Carlisle said and he wondered desperately if he would be able to see Tatiana again before he left.

After supper the men retired for cigars and brandy to a small drawing room decorated for Melikof in the Empire style.

"Well, Jack," Spaeth said, "you're full of surprises. The Countess seems to know more about you than I do."

Carlisle shrugged. "When in Rome," he said and flashed one of his overwhelming grins.

"Is her title Austrian or Bohemian?" Spaeth asked.

"I'm no authority on titles."

"Not yet," Spaeth said dryly.

"But Colonel Dubrovski might help, he knows her husband."

"Oh yes, I know Count Albert," Dubrovski said. "He flies about like a will-o'-the-wisp up in the air all the time, and never visits her. If I had a wife like his, wild horses couldn't keep me from her. Not wild horses, lions, or all the beasts in the jungle, but Nojine appears to have forgotten he's married! What better proof of madness could there be? The title? Why, it's Bohemian. Nojine's father was a director of foundries; the kind of man, you know, who always lands on his feet. He and Speraski, that's Tatiana's family name, you see, were friends, old friends. It was a family merger, you might say." Dubrovski, his heavy, good-natured face flushed with port, brandished one of Melikof's ceremonial cigars and talked on about himself.

He had been a lathe operator in one of the Speraski plants and a reserve sergeant in the Austrian Army. After mobilization he deserted to the Russians along with vast numbers of other Czechs who had no use for the

Hapsburg Empire. In the Czech Legion he rose rapidly and was now chief of the Czech Railroad Corps and proud of it. "Who would have thought Emil Dubrovski would be a colonel? Me, Dubrovski, dipping crackers in caviar? Well, I hope my wife, God bless her, has kept my dinner pail on the shelf, for who knows where it will end? A man can't be a colonel forever. There's still work to be done."

Dubrovski's one regret was that he didn't have what gentlemen called reserve. Asked a question he simply blurted out all he knew and was pleased to be listened to. He knew this was bad, but the worst of it was that he didn't know what to keep mum about. He sensed now that he was talking too freely and sighed. "Well, it's a topsy-turvy world, gentlemen, and that's the truth. What I am, I am; what I have been, I have been and I'll fill my grave with the rest of them."

Carlisle liked Dubrovski immensely because he had known Tatiana as a young girl and because he was clumsy and out of his class. He was about to tell Dubrovski his own background when he remembered General Bogoloff's epaulet. "Say! General Bogoloff asked me to pick up his epaulet!"

Colonel Spaeth was startled. "What in hell are you talking about, Sioux?" he demanded.

Carlisle explained about the epaulet, Tatiana's hair and the episode in the powder room, all in a rush. "I've got to do this before I go back, Colonel," he declared. "I promised General Bogoloff."

Spaeth was amused. "I can see this is a matter of great military importance," he said. "Why, it's your duty!"

"Of course!" Carlisle said. "That epaulet was given to Bogoloff by Grand Duke something or other." Then he laughed boomingly, because Bogoloff's epaulet was indeed a magic wand turning frogs to princes and raising officers in grade.

CHAPTER TWENTY

On the same morning that a military review was scheduled for the American visitors at Omsk, Kolchak's forces made another thrust toward much contested Cheliabinsk.

Among the fresh troops brought up for this assault was a company of ragged men who had made the long spring march across the blossoming plains of Siberia without having encountered the enemy. Young Kolya, whose sister was a glove clerk at the Kunst and Albert department store in Vladivostok, and his two older, more seasoned comrades, Timofeivitch and Karpov, were members of this company and like foot soldiers everywhere they did not know, could not possibly trace, the interaction of events which brought them to their current position.

To have been told that a three-hour informal supper in Omsk with champagne so cold that splinters of ice appeared in the glasses, with restegai of salmon, cotolettes de Kiev, kulibyaki, bliny, pelmeni and a dessert of pineapple jelly whipped in champagne and topped with fruit, had something to do with the assault on Cheliabinsk may have made their mouths water, but they would not have believed it.

The connection between caviar and combat was one they could not possibly have made, though they might have agreed with Admiral Kolchak's statement when he heard a report on the results of that same supper: "We need victories, Melikof, not suppers!"

This much at least would have made sense to them, but how these words from the lips of a small, dark, intense man with the sallow, brooding quality of Napoleon had reached into their lives would once again have eluded them. The ill-conceived scramble of military orders which followed this simple utterance was befuddling enough for commanders in the field; a soldier would have thrown up his hands in dismay and fallen asleep.

The orders they eventually did receive were simple: Attack Cheliabinsk.

They had been told that their company was in the second line of advance, and given this assurance they rose early and tramped off hoping those ahead of them would make quick work of the whole business and that they would come to a peaceful billet in the town with all its excitements.

By nine o'clock Kolya was marching through the broad field of volunteer wheat with the other members of his company spread out comfortingly on either side. The wheat had not been sown, but had sprung up from the unharvested yield of the previous year, so there were bare patches where the seed had not taken root, and the stalks were of different lengths. Those having made a late start were still green and unformed, but much of the wheat was breast high and fully ripe.

At times Kolya, looking to one side or the other to make sure he hadn't gotten beyond the line of advance, could only see the heads and shoulders of his comrades. Timofeivitch had a sprig of green wheat in his horse-yellow teeth, masticating it contentedly, and beyond him Karpov tramped along with his rifle slung over his shoulder muzzle down, as though he were coming into the bivouac.

Kolya carried his own rifle at the ready, in both hands, quartering his breast and he felt a bit foolish about this for they were not in the first line of advance, which meant they'd hear firing from the troops ahead long before they themselves came into action.

To excuse his appearance of nervous readiness Kolya pretended to use the butt of his rifle to clear a path through the wheat; he clubbed it aside, which took more energy than he wanted to expend, particularly after the long march to the edge of the field, but he was too embarrassed now to sling his rifle as Karpov had done.

The rifle grew heavy and warm in his sweating hands, but he was determined not to surrender and carry it in a more comfortable manner. This contest of his willpower against the weight of the rifle for the sake of not losing face among his comrades began to assume more importance than the battle which lay ahead. At one point he realized that none of the men flanking him cared how he was handling his rifle; he could have been dragging it by the butt for all the attention the others paid and Kolya was tempted then to give in. But he argued that it was not for their sakes that he was marching along as he was, but for his own. Having assumed this stance he would not give it up and a sense of pride, indeed of superiority over his mates who clumped along every which way, gave him a new infusion of strength. He straightened his back, gripped his rifle more firmly, and marched on with a triumphant smile on his shining face quite sure that in the eyes of the world he was the only soldier in the company who gave the appearance of bravery and self-confidence.

He could see himself as a poster soldier with hay-colored hair, a healthy, smiling face, deeply tanned and an encouraging smile for all those young adventurers who would follow in his footsteps. He knew that his sister, Sofia, would be proud.

They came to a place where the field sloped down and in the distance, beyond the heads of wheat, they could see Cheliabinsk, peaceful and innocent in the bright morning sun. A flock of blackbirds, alarmed by the soldiers' coming, rose, complaining raucously, and settled further on to feed once more. An order to halt came down the line. Timofeivitch sat down at once and was lost to sight. Karpov looked toward Kolya, shrugged and yawned against the back of his fist threatening to swallow it whole.

Kolya looked back up the hill and saw a group of officers; some were studying Cheliabinsk through binoculars, others stood around with their hands in their pockets in a most unmilitary manner. Kolya was ashamed of them; he brought his rifle down smartly with the butt just beside his worn right boot and stood at attention facing Cheliabinsk as though he were on parade; then, grinning at his own stupidity, he muttered "Fall out" to himself and sat down in the wheat with the others.

The blackbirds rose again. There was a crumpling sound and a turbulence in the warm morning air followed by an explosion and a geyser of debris at the edge of the city. Kolya glanced toward Timofeivitch.

"Our guns, testing," Timofeivitch said and he plucked another stalk of wheat and stuck it into his mouth.

Kolya watched the blackbirds jump out of the wheat at every shell and he wondered how it was they could hear the report of the cannon before it came to him. Then he decided they rose to the shell beating overhead rather than to the sound of the gun firing. But presently the birds gave up their feeding and flew away without a sound, skimming low over the field, toward the east.

"Maybe the Reds are gone," Timofeivitch said after a bit.

Kolya nodded with a slight scowl as though he disapproved.

Karpov, lying flat on his back, had begun to snore. Kolya gestured at him and grinned.

"Wish I could," Timofeivitch said. "I can't sleep all night before a battle."

"You did last night," Kolya said.

Timofeivitch looked surprised. "Did I?" he asked. "Did I indeed. Well, I think I never do, which is all the same. It leaves me weary in the morning." Then he smiled at Kolya, who had not yet been under fire. "They must have retired," he said, "or by now they would have come back at us with their guns. The Germans used to start right up."

Kolya, irritated at having revealed his uneasiness, watched the town. The shells fell irregularly, probing one section then another. The explosions, muffled by distance, seemed harmless and the geysers of smoke, after the first dirty gold eruptions, rose lazily and hung in the air suspended for a moment before they shed their heavier particles and began to collapse.

Kolya amused himself by counting the seconds during which these columns, having reached their full height, remained intact. Sometimes he got to seven or eight, sometimes only to five, and he wondered if this could be caused by the caliber of the shells being fired. This deduction gave him a feeling of military expertise and he was about to make the assertion to

Timofeivitch that he could distinguish the guns in this fashion, but the other man spoke first.

"The people down there have lost their breakfasts," Timofeivitch said.

Until this Kolya had not thought of people being there. Suddenly he had a vision of a table and a great splash of porridge and blood and after this each explosion was a mass of intermingling crockery, furniture, human parts, eggs, bread, and tea. He shuddered and looked to see if Timofeivitch had noticed, but Timofeivitch was chewing his stalk of wheat and staring drowsily toward the town.

Kolya stopped counting the explosions and found himself beginning to hope for the sake of the troops ahead that the Reds had gone.

After a while an order came to move on and Timofeivitch poked Karpov awake with his boot. "Come on," he said, "we're going."

Karpov sat up and shook his big, flat-featured head and one could see the present situation fill his eyes. "I dreamed of my wife," he said. "She was hanging out laundry by the river. Now isn't that one hell of a dream to have? She was hanging my britches on the line with a warm breeze filling the legs. You'd think a man would dream of being drunk or in bed at a time like this and here am I dreaming of the laundry, and her back was turned to me at that."

They all got up and started down the hill. Kolya carried his rifle as he had done before and he noticed that several others were doing the same though the town was still a great distance off. Only Karpov carried his rifle slung muzzle down as though he had no intention of using it.

They left the shelter of the wheat field and crossed a road. An officer rode down in front of them on a chestnut horse which insisted on trying to crop grass whenever it stopped. This irritated the officer, who kept pulling its head up. He was more intent on the horse's bad behavior than he was on the troops and Kolya wondered if he too was worried about cutting a good figure. He wondered if all of them, except Karpov, weren't more anxious about how they appeared to each other than they were about the attack on Cheliabinsk. He took comfort in this possibility, in fact he found it amusing and was about to make a joke about this to Timofeivitch when the sound of rifle fire stopped him.

The officer ahead of them dismounted and sent his horse to the rear, then he trotted toward the sound in a crouched position, struggling to pull his pistol from its holster.

The line of troops faltered and Kolya looked around in confusion. He couldn't tell from the sound who was firing, but it seemed very close.

Karpov had dropped forward on his hands and knees and was struggling in a most undignified manner to get his rifle unslung. Kolya despised him for this and was surprised at his own flash of anger. Why should he care how ridiculous Karpov looked?

The firing increased, filled in now by the steady beat of a machine gun, and the air around Kolya's head seemed alive. Timofeivitch had also fallen forward and was sliding along the ground toward a stone with his lips pulled back from his teeth, which were still locked on a stalk of wheat.

Kolya heard the even closer pop of rifle fire from his own line and realized that the men were firing blind at something in front of them. That this could be so filled Kolya with a terrible sense of outrage. He stood rooted to the place where he had stopped, perfectly erect, with his rifle clenched in his fists, shaking with indignation.

They could not have come upon the enemy! This simply could not be so because they were not in the first line of advance! If they had come upon the enemy, then their officers had lied to them. Other possibilities flashed through his mind — they were firing at their own forces; they were firing at nothing at all; a few Reds, one or two, had infiltrated the first lines of advance — but even so the officers had lied to them.

Kolya had expected a warning, much gunfire and shouting before he himself was engaged in battle. Like the others he had hoped the first lines of advance would win the battle and that he would march in to share the triumph, but here he had been tricked. They were fighting all around him! There were bullets in the air!

Kolya sat down hard, so hard that for a moment his breath was gone. He looked at the rifle in his hands and the sun gleaming off the barrel hurt his eyes. He thought of his sister Sofia who had always been so fair. She never lied, not even about the smallest things, and she was always hurt when he lied to her about things which were none of her business, like who he'd been to see and what they'd done. He regretted this now and was shocked to find himself thinking of it at such a time.

It was all wrong, but he tried to pull the bolt of his rifle, for even if they had lied he would fire.

Then to his horror Kolya saw blood gushing from a place above his belt and below his ribs. He felt no pain, but he couldn't breathe at all. He couldn't hear a thing. Using his rifle for support he pushed himself up and looked around for someone to help him, for someone to say it was all right, that it could be fixed. He looked back toward the field of volunteer wheat from which such help would come and he started toward it, but at the first step he was struck again from behind.

He fell face down with his rifle straight beside him, as though he had fainted on parade, and he thought to himself with whimpering tenderness and regret: "Kolya, my dear, oh Kolya, you are dead."

« 2 »

The military review staged for General Graves, Ambassador Morris and key Allied officers was held in the huge dusty square in front of the Stavka building. General Knox, Chief of the British Military Mission, supplied the band which played "Colonel Bogey's March" as two regiments of Kolchak's Siberian Rifles formed up and stood in docile ranks.

From his place on the reviewing stand General Graves scanned their faces and knew he would not commit these troops to battle. There was a terrible fatalism about them, a terrible recognition and acceptance of their role as bullet catchers. They stood massed in the hot sun wearing long winter coats, the bayonets fixed to their rifles sticking up beside their faces like billing spikes. Their legs, wrapped in wool, looked solid, but they wore a variety of shoes and boots none of which seemed to fit.

Graves suspected that the coats had been issued to conceal the shoddy uniforms underneath. He suspected that the rifles had never been sighted by the men who held them and that their ammunition pouches were empty. Worst of all, he suspected that they were not committed to anything, not even to life itself, and this appalled him. They wore the same apathetic expression Graves remembered having seen on the faces of cattle entering the slaughter chutes at the Chicago stockyards.

Several detachments of Cossacks had been brought in to add color to the spectacle and some of these flying pennants on their ten-foot lances were quite impressive as they executed tight cavalry formations, but a single well-placed machine gun would have scattered them. Among these were the Semipalatinsk Cossacks under Ataman Annenkoff whose fame thus far rested on the massacre of several thousand Jews at Ekaterinburg. They wore a skull and crossbones insignia in their karakul caps and exhibited a sneering contempt for the foot soldier whom they probably would herd to the front within the next month, sabering those who hesitated, as an example to the others.

Graves was depressed. Omsk had no charm for him. It was an overgrown Siberian village swollen six times its normal size by an influx of refugees. Beyond the river Irtysh which encircled the city there was nothing but an endless brown, wind-blown plain, empty except for a few horseshoe-shaped clusters of Tatar vurts. He disliked the landscape; he found nothing to appreciate.

Facing these ranks of blank-eyed troops brought forcibly to him that decisions of state are always countersigned in blood. The Whites had failed to capture Cheliabinsk and although the front was five hundred miles away this was not far enough as Siberian distance was reckoned. Both Graves and Spaeth agreed that without a miracle Kolchak could not hold out for another six months.

Not a mile from their present place on the reviewing stand was a train-load of wounded Kolchak soldiers. They lay in their crowded wooden cars untended. Graves and Spaeth had come upon them while walking along the track, discussing the previous evening's reception. The wounded men had cried out for help, for water, for relief of any kind, and the two officers, sickened by their own helplessness, could only turn away and lodge a complaint with the first White officer they came across. They found him in a park, a colonel in a beautifully tailored uniform with a woman on his arm. When he understood their complaint the colonel shrugged eloquently and begged them in courteous French not to bring such unpleasant matters to the attention of the lady.

Graves had sent a note to General Dietrichs but had no reply and every reason to believe that the wounded were still on the train crawling over each other blindly like the maggots which infested their wounds. Perhaps the doors of the cars had been shut to spare the sensibilities of the ladies.

As far as Graves had been able to discover, Kolchak's military situation with the possible exception of those units commanded and heavily reinforced by Czechs was chaotic. Omsk was crowded with old guard Russian saber enthusiasts, generals of army corps and staff officers who, when questioned about the deposition of their troops, gave vague answers and relied heavily on language barriers to conceal the fact that they had no troops at all. One of these had recently taken over a sector vacated by the Czech Legion; he drew rations and salaries for ninety thousand men, but a subsequent inspection found only four thousand men in the area, twenty-five hundred of whom were officers and subalterns with no experience in dealing with common soldiers, whom they despised.

Graves intended to inspect the front, for if Omsk was the show grounds of the Kolchak regime, then he had little hope of finding anything better further on and he was deeply concerned for the safety of American personnel.

"My guess," he commented wryly to Spaeth, "is that Dr. Teusler's one hundred thousand union suits have walked over to the Reds."

"How long do you think this will last, General?" Spaeth asked.

"Until the roof falls in, I suppose."

Graves looked at his program, printed in four languages to commemorate the occasion.

Two regiments of Siberian Rifles were to receive their colors, which had to be sanctified prior to their presentation. An altar had been set up on the square for a military mass and a mitered, impressively robed Russian priest, surrounded by acolytes bearing crucifixes and censers, was chanting in a ponderous, rumbling voice. He sprinkled the banners and flags with holy water and scattered drops to the four quarters of the compass. His measured gestures were more sacrificial than encouraging, as though death was a blessing, and the troops with the glazed look of condemned men in their eyes appeared to be grateful for this attention.

Admiral Kolchak himself presented the banners to the regimental commanders. Taking them from the hands of the priest he walked across the parade ground and presented each banner, kneeling and bowing his head as it changed hands. The officer receiving the banner also kneeled, and to General Graves it seemed that they were passing death warrants rather than battle flags.

When at last this ceremony was over the dignitaries were invited to inspect the troops. Ambassador Morris, General Graves and the rest of the reviewing party left the stand and began the tedious march down the files of troops.

A wind had come up and was blowing quantities of dust from the plains. It settled on the brows and shoulders of the sweltering troops, who squinted and blinked their eyes as the reviewing party passed. Most of them were new recruits and wore their uniforms with the same shuddering resistance a wild horse exhibits when his back is touched by a saddle blanket, and the pale dust powdering their faces seemed to be interring them prematurely.

Some of the young boys smiled pathetically, like orphans clinging to the hope that something in their manner would save them from unloved oblivion, that an officer in the reviewing party, for instance, would say: "Ah, there's a fine, intelligent chap. Have him report to me. We'll find a place for him."

Of course this did not happen. The smiles withered and there were instances in which tears mingling with perspiration made trails along the dusty cheeks.

Ambassador Morris and Admiral Kolchak walked side by side, surrounded by functionaries of the various interested Allies, but they hardly spoke a word to each other. Kolchak's demeanor was cold. Torn by spells of intestinal disorder, by mental depressions mounting to paranoia, plagued by fraud, rapacity, and deceit, he trusted no one except his valet, Kiselov, who, as it turned out, was a Bolshevik spy.

Kolchak believed, even while trying to encourage American recognition, that the American presence in Siberia was doing incalculable harm. He was, by class, typically anti-Semitic and characterized the American soldiers in Siberia as the dregs of the New York and Chicago ghettos, Jews of the lowest type for whom Bolshevism had a strong attraction. Though he hardly said a word to Morris or to Graves, his attitude of hostility and suspicion was impossible to conceal.

For his part Ambassador Morris had already reached a decision. He would report that the Omsk government was in urgent need of twenty-five thousand American soldiers and a loan of two hundred millions if it was to survive. This would relieve President Wilson of having to make a decision since it was a foregone conclusion that Congress would never approve such a loan.

When the review was over Ambassador Morris and Admiral Kolchak shook hands, nodded affably and through their interpreters wished each other well.

They did not meet again.

Loris Melikof was distraught, but there was nothing he could have done or could now do. That same afternoon Ambassador Morris listened to his entreaties for aid and promised to recommend them. Melikof could not quarrel with this, but he felt quicksand under his feet and paced about his office, searching for a new approach before the Ambassador returned to Japan. That he failed to find it was intolerable. Somehow his intimate supper had miscarried. He reproached himself and flogged his brain, but the barrier of the Ambassador's cordial agreement to recommend Melikof's proposals could not be overcome. When he reported this to Kolchak the Admiral's bloodless, saturnine face twisted with contempt.

"Sovereignty for uniforms again, eh, Melikof?" he cried. And he launched into one of his harangues. Gesticulating wildly, his eyes burning, he backed Melikof around the room practically shouting into his face. "The British gave us uniforms and a dozen generals. Where are the uniforms now, Melikof? The Bolsheviks thank the British for them! Yes, those uniforms deserted with our men inside them! Those uniforms got up and walked over to the Bolshevik side with our poor, protesting men trapped inside them. Is that it, Melikof? You think American uniforms won't run to the Bolsheviks if British uniforms only walk? I will not trade sovereignty for shoes that only walk east. I will not trade it for rifles. I shall fight alone and get all I need from captured enemy stores! If they won't help me without strings attached, then tell them to leave me alone! This is still Russia! This is Russia's war, not the foreigners'."

"We have allies —"

"Allies!" Kolchak shouted and he turned away, shaking with indignation. "Allies! I tolerate them. I tolerate Czech presumption, Czech requisitioning, tampering, interfering. The Czech Legion is contaminated, Melikof! Contaminated like an honest girl confined to a brothel. Let's not fool ourselves, Melikof. If we depend on the Czech Legion this front of ours will collapse. Their army is as rotten as ours was on the eve of the revolution and mark my words, Melikof, some day Czechoslovakia will go all the way down to Bolshevism. What have they been doing here? Black-marketeering! Gathering riches in an impoverished land. We cannot tolerate their sinister presence much longer, Melikof. We must rely on Russians! Somehow they must be brought to our banner. And quickly. Quickly!"

In the silence which ensued both men could be heard breathing heavily, then Kolchak came to Melikof and seized his hand. There were tears in the Admiral's eyes which he tried to shake away. "Melikof! Ah, Melikof, forgive me. I'm exhausted. Do what you can. Do whatever you can, my dear Melikof. I'm weary unto death. Send Kiselov to me. I need a bit of peace. Time to think. God has called us to this. God's will be done."

Melikof, weeping freely himself, left the room and finding Kiselov waiting in the corridor begged him to give the Supreme Ruler some peace.

Kiselov, small and dark, with a simple-minded smile and the manner of a barber, bowed solemnly and taking his bag went into Kolchak's suite.

CHAPTER TWENTY-ONE

Mrs. Custer-Farquart's manner during the grand reception had been the object of considerable ridicule among the ladies present. They gossiped about her among themselves and slyly mimicked her behavior, but those whose escorts or husbands were important enough to find themselves guests at Melikof's intimate supper soon had cause to regret this. When the men had withdrawn for cigars and brandy the ladies went to another room and they were certain that Mrs. Custer-Farquart was going to make them pay for every insinuating comment they had exchanged at her expense.

She stood in the doorway twitching her feather boa like a whip and scanning the ladies as though listing them in the order of the gravity of their offense to her. The pleasant smile on Mrs. Custer-Farquart's face struck fear into the hearts of those who felt themselves guilty and they began chattering, hoping thereby to avoid Mrs. Custer-Farquart's initial assault. But Tatiana, who rarely chattered in any event, was standing by the window wondering how soon Dubrovski would come for her when Mrs. Custer-Farquart swept through the room, seized her right hand and began to examine it as though it were a plucked capon she'd taken from a poulterer's counter.

"What beautiful hands you have," she declared. "I noticed at once. Whatever do you do?"

Tatiana was so taken aback she didn't know what to reply. Do? Do? The question seemed to have no validity. At last she explained that she was married to a Czech flyer.

"Yes, yes, I know," Mrs. Custer-Farquart said. "I know, but what do *you* do?"

"Why, I'm waiting for him," Tatiana said with a slight frown.

"You wait. Ah, yes, I see. You wait. They also serve who only stand and wait. Is that it, my dear?"

"Why yes, in a way, I suppose that's true."

"In what way?" Mrs. Custer-Farquart asked and she met Tatiana's eyes as though she were seriously interested in her answer.

Tatiana was intensely uncomfortable. She had no answer and resented the woman for trying to catch her up.

There was a profound silence as the ladies waited for Tatiana's reply, all of them deeply relieved to have escaped this catechism.

"Surely you do something," Mrs. Custer-Farquart insisted and she rolled Tatiana's hand in both of her own as though reading it for the answer. "You play the piano, or sew, write letters, or perhaps you drive a car! We all have talents or capacities which are hardly ever used. Don't you agree, ladies?"

Mrs. Custer-Farquart addressed this question to the whole room, and the ladies responded most agreeably that they did, indeed, agree. At this Mrs. Custer-Farquart dropped Tatiana's hand, turned to the full group and before the ladies had time to think they found themselves being enlisted in the Volunteer Nurses Corps.

Their expressions of amazement and confusion at having been so perfectly ambushed brought laughter bubbling to Tatiana's lips. The poor women, certain that Tatiana was the sacrificial victim, had fallen into Mrs. Custer-Farquart's trap. "Oh, yes," they had chorused, "we all have talents and capacities which are hardly ever used!"

Mrs. Custer-Farquart descended on them like a Saracen. Dismissing their feeble excuses of other more pressing duties she dragooned them into adding their names to the volunteers list and they did so helplessly, hoping that at some future date they could beg off, but knowing already they would never succeed in doing so while Mrs. Custer-Farquart remained in Omsk.

Some of the women looked at Tatiana accusingly as though she'd purposely decoyed them into this situation, so Tatiana signed the roster with a flourish, assuming, as many of the other women had done, that it would have no immediate consequences. In this they were wrong.

Having gathered their signatures Mrs. Custer-Farquart announced that they would assemble at nine a.m. the following morning at the depot to attend the sick and wounded soldiers there. "General Dietrichs himself brought this deplorable situation to my attention and asked what could be done about it. 'Why,' I said, 'the ladies of Omsk will manage it!' And we will! We most certainly will! If that madman Trotsky, a diarrhetic by the sound of his name, has a regiment of women in uniform we can raise a regiment of nurses. You ladies are the first to join and I'm sure you're all as proud of yourselves as I am proud of you."

The ladies were thunderstruck.

Mrs. Custer-Farquart gave them precise instructions about what to bring and what to wear and the ladies, with sinking hearts, realized that there was no way out of Mrs. Custer-Farquart's Volunteer Nurses Corps short of illness, death, or immediate flight.

Of the twenty ladies thus enlisted Tatiana and twelve others showed up the following morning and were greeted by the indomitable Mrs. Custer-Farquart, who wore a gray twill suit with a Red Cross armband.

"Good morning, ladies," she said brightly. "Today we are going to see more human misery, pain and helplessness than we will probably ever see again in our lifetimes. Some of you will be made sick by it. I hope all of you will last the day."

There were six hundred wounded men on the train with only two staff doctors and four trained nurses to attend them. Mrs. Custer-Farquart, with her hands on her broad hips, looked down the line of cars and when asked by one of the volunteers what they should do she raised one arm and shook it over her head. "We scrub!" she declared. And that was her battle cry. "Scrub! Scrub!"

With hot water taken from the station tank the volunteers washed bandages, clothes, blankets and men. Mrs. Custer-Farquart brought kerosene to attack the head and body lice. She commandeered a boxcar, made it airtight and began fumigating clothes with a concoction of burning sulphur, naphtha and kerosene. Her energy was boundless. Her willpower was overwhelming. By the end of the day she had plucked forty soldiers on leave off the streets and put them to work. A group of Russian officers happening by were browbeaten into service as orderlies but they sped off the minute Mrs. Custer-Farquart's back was turned and she swore to hound them to the ends of the earth. "I'll recognize them," she said. "I'll see them again and I'll see them in hell!"

Tatiana's admiration for Mrs. Custer-Farquart grew with each passing hour. She was exhausted and bespattered; her skirts were soaked through, but she continued to work with an intense, almost blind concentration. Tatiana hardened herself to the sufferings of the men on the train. There were too many of them. She had to treat them as objects, as wounded sheep or hurt animals because there was no time for compassion. A young Cossack blinded by a head wound kept calling for his horse which had been shot from under him. Often he jumped up and had to be restrained.

"Kulubai! Kulubai!" he called.

At first the other wounded men thought this was his brother, but it was his horse.

Tatiana touched his arm and told him to sit down and her voice attracted him, though he could not see. "Who are you?" he asked.

"A friend. A nurse."

"Where are you from?"

"Prague."

"Where are we then?"

"Omsk," she said, "and we're looking after you."

"I can't see."

"No, they've bandaged your head."

Tatiana moved on, but thinking she was still nearby the young Cossack told her he was from Onokoi.

As she continued her work Tatiana listened to the men talking among themselves and the war became a reality for her.

"They sent a battalion from Omsk to Ischin, a hundred and eighty miles. When it arrived there were only a hundred men left; the rest of them deserted. By dark there were only forty-three and the commandant locked them up to keep them from getting away."

"Two companies went over from our sector and the next morning we found them facing us."

Tatiana thought of Albert, who was more unreal to her now than he had ever been. Whenever she thought of him she frowned, trying to remember, trying to hold him, trying to convince herself that he would come and that the world of her girlhood would be real again. Until that time she would work hard. She would keep her share of their special world until Albert returned and found her to be his perfect counterpart, still gay, still captivating, and they would go back again to rooms filled with crystal and candlelight and brilliant people.

Tatiana looked at the wounded men around her. Flesh and blood. She pushed a fallen lock of hair away from her eyes and caught sight of her large, pale hand. The fingertips were shriveled from having been in hot water so long. Her bare forearms were dirty. Her back ached and her legs were trembling. "He will come," she said aloud and Mrs. Custer-Farquart appeared in front of her.

"You've had enough for today, Tatiana," she said. "One stiff medicinal drink, then home you go."

She poured the drink into the cap of a silver flask taken from her bag and gave it to Tatiana. "Knock it back, girl," she said.

Tatiana took the drink. It was brandy and helped immensely.

"How would you like to be second-in-command of this outfit?" Mrs. Custer-Farquart asked. "We're going to have to recruit more women and organize the other cities."

"I'd be honored," Tatiana said and her new-found respect for Mrs. Custer-Farquart was such that she meant this sincerely.

Mrs. Custer-Farquart smiled a bit grimly. "You've got it," she said. "Now run along."

Although she was exhausted Tatiana chose to walk to her hotel. She could sleep an hour before meeting Colonel Dubrovski and Captain Carlisle for dinner. Dubrovski's note said the Captain wanted to recover her uncle's epaulet, but Tatiana was certain the Captain was in love with her. Men fell in love so easily that it was almost tedious. She couldn't remember all the men who'd fallen in love with her. There was Raul, of course, poor Raul who simply didn't understand anything and who very probably hated her now. And there were, let's see, Rudi and Valerian and oh so many and they were all so helplessly ordinary about it. Only Albert had challenged her and she knew that by his refusal to write, or wire, or come to Omsk to visit he was asserting his right to be entirely independent of her and this very assertion was the measure of her hold on him. She was too proud to weaken that hold by begging him to come. Albert abhorred dependent people. "Except for our sex we're equals, Tatiana, and that is how it must be. We complement one another, but we must each stand alone. I can't have it any other way."

They surrendered nothing to each other and at the time Tatiana, jealous of her own independence, had accepted these terms. But lately she had begun to think there was something childish and perverse in such an agreement, that it was a way of arresting growth in a presumed state of perfection. Certainly she and Albert thought they were perfect together. They had never displeased each other and if the war hadn't separated them there would have been no strain on their relationship.

Yes, the war made it very hard. She must not give in to the war, that was the point. Albert expected her to rise above it and she would.

Tatiana walked slowly along the street crowded with uniformed men and was glad she'd accepted Mrs. Custer-Farquart's offer to be second-in-command of the Volunteer Nurses Corps. It gave her a role at least equal to Albert's in the war, which was what she needed, after all — a role, something to do. She'd write Albert a casual note about it and perhaps when he knew she wasn't simply waiting about uselessly for him he'd find it easier to come to Omsk.

All the same it was cruel of him not to write, but then she had known he was cruel because he was brilliant, just as she was often cruel because she was beautiful. It wasn't their intention to hurt others less brilliant or beautiful, it just happened that way and it was ignoble of her to assume that Albert intended hurting her. He expected her to be self-sufficient until they were together again and so she would be.

There had never been the slightest doubt in Tatiana's mind that she was beautiful. From childhood this had been a given fact of her existence and therefore of little consequence. Men were attracted to her and had been from the time she was eleven years old, which neither puzzled nor alarmed her. Sexuality was something all human beings had in common and it was therefore common. To make a mystery of it was foolish.

Albert alone had not been impressed by her beauty. "We are ridiculously made, Tatiana, and that's all of it, but I expect we're two of the best examples of intelligent protoplasm life has evolved, so we'll go together and see what comes of it."

What most often came was a kind of mutual sadness.

Ideas of purity and sexual fidelity struck Albert as the utterest rot. "There's nothing pure about peasant sweat and rutting. You're free to do as you like about these temporary satisfactions. Purity is in the mind and there we must keep faith. We live in a fragile society and it's up to us to hold it together."

It was in society that they expressed their love for one another, not in bed. There was a passion in Albert's insistence on perfect manners and ideal settings. And after a particularly successful party they frequently made love for hours trying to recapture its satisfactions. But this was impossible and one night Albert had acknowledged it.

"I've concluded, Tatiana, that it's quite impossible to wrest more out of copulation than is in fact there. You please my body, which, in a way, I rather resent, but there it is. Turn over and let me have a look at you. Dear God, it's laughable. We are really ludicrous creatures! Here we've been tumbling over each other like cannibals for above an hour trying to achieve who knows what heavenly transports when the fact is we are in heaven. Prague is heaven. You and I understand and illuminate that heaven. What more can we expect?"

"I love it."

"And so do I."

She could not remember ever saying to Albert that she loved him or that he had ever said he loved her. But this wasn't important, for together they loved and were embraced by society.

Tatiana arrived at the hotel and went upstairs to her room, which was depressingly small and had probably been the maid's pantry in better times. The floor space was almost entirely taken up by Tatiana's luggage. A single window looked down into the debris-strewn yard at the back of the hotel, and to avoid this prospect Tatiana kept the shutters closed; consequently the air was stale and the room was dark. Tatiana removed her coat and lay down on the narrow couch to nap before dinner. Raul had been right about the discomforts of Omsk.

Poor Raul. He seemed to think because they'd slept together in Vladivostok on that one occasion when she'd felt her world crumbling that he had captured her for a prize, as though she were a ship and he a successful boarding party. Her attempts to explain had enraged him. He interpreted everything she said as contempt for himself. When he threatened to tell

Albert she begged him not to be so excitable, and when she told him that she would tell Albert herself if she thought it would interest him Raul had slapped her face.

She had never been struck before in her life. And now, lying on the couch, she touched her cheek at the memory of that stinging blow. She had not realized until then how important sex was to some men. And as she dozed off she wondered if Albert's indifference to it wasn't due to something more than pride.

« 2 »

After the review of Kolchak's troops Colonel Spaeth had received permission to send Carlisle back to Tataurovo, but Carlisle was not as pleased with this news as Spaeth had expected him to be. He was to stop at Irkutsk, introduce himself to the Russian garrison there, then continue around the southern end of Lake Baikal on the old post road to estimate what traffic it would bear in event the Trans-Baikal tunnels between Irkutsk and Verkhne-Udinsk were blocked.

The two men were in the compartment of the train which had served as their living quarters while in Omsk, discussing how to proceed if orders came for a pull-out. The Colonel had explained that General Graves wanted a full report of conditions in Irkutsk and along the trakt by the time he returned to Vladivostok and Carlisle was making notes, but he wasn't as attentive as usual, which annoyed Spaeth.

"Are you listening to me at all, Sioux?" he demanded irritably.

"I'm taking notes."

"Damn it, man, don't take notes! Just listen. If Semenoff cuts the track east of Verkhne before we can withdraw, I intend to march the regiment overland up the Selenga Valley via the caravan trail to Urga, then across the Gobi to Kalgan and Peking. Anything you can learn about those routes would be helpful too."

"That would be quite a hike."

"General Graves thought so too, but he approved the plan," Spaeth said. "You see anything wrong with it?"

"No, sir."

"All right, you leave tomorrow."

Carlisle looked up from his note-pad with a scowl. "Tomorrow?"

"Anything wrong with that? I thought you were anxious to get back."

Carlisle nodded, but the scowl remained on his face.

"Take all the time you need in Irkutsk and learn what you can about the

Baikal ferries too, but be careful not to intimate anything about an American pull-out."

"Yes, sir," Carlisle said.

"That about does it."

Carlisle closed his note-pad and put it in his pocket.

"You worried about something, Jack?" Spaeth asked.

"No," Carlisle said. He stood up and glanced at his watch. "I'd better be on my way."

"You going to dinner?"

"I'm meeting Colonel Dubrovski at the station and we're going to dinner with Countess Tatiana."

"Oh, yes. Bogoloff's epaulet."

"That's right, sir."

"I hope you get it."

"I will."

"You can pick up a rail pass at the station," Spaeth said. "I'll see you off in the morning."

It was nearly dark as Carlisle crossed the railyard to the station. The sidings were crowded with coaches and boxcars which had been commandeered by various military and civil authorities and were being held in reserve for future emergencies. These were guarded by contingents of troops instructed not to let the cars be taken from them and there was a constant wrangling between the guards and the railway personnel trying to make up trains and clear traffic through the yard. There was a brisk black market in rolling stock and profiteers with railway cars at their disposal made fortunes leasing them at exorbitant rates. By and large the railway men themselves were honest and worked diligently to keep the railroad operational despite the corruption which bedeviled it, and Carlisle had more respect for the Russian railroad workers than any other group he had seen. The yard workers, engineers, firemen and brakemen, wearing massive beards to protect their faces against the cold, went about their tasks with a kind of resigned efficiency which made Carlisle think of them as Kodiak bears.

The interior of the station was dimly lit and packed with humanity waiting for space on the trains. Families of refugees who had been living in the station for weeks seemed not to know where they were from or where they were going. They sat about on the floor surrounded by bundles, their faces expressionless, their silence oppressive. Now and again they moved, but they were like heavy statues of warm clay. Even the children were silent and the infants, if they cried, did so in a subdued, apologetic manner.

Carlisle went to the ticket window, where he was to meet Colonel Dubrovski, who had agreed to help him shop for a gift for Tatiana. The idea of giving her something had struck Carlisle with the force of absolute necessity; he could hardly explain this compulsion to himself, but since having thought of it he had been preoccupied by a terrible indecision. What could he give her after all? He knew ladies accepted flowers and candy, but even supposing these were to be had they were perishable and he wanted his gift to be permanent, something she would treasure. But he simply didn't know what would be suitable and he was depending on Dubrovski's advice.

Dubrovski, however, was nowhere in sight and as Carlisle waited his agitation increased. Had he misunderstood? Perhaps they were to meet at the hotel. This might be his last opportunity to see her. He checked his watch and tried to calm himself. Dubrovski might have been detained.

On the walls around the ticket window there were hundreds of hand-written notices, some too faded to read, others buried by those on top. Carlisle was scowling at these, wondering if he should go to the hotel, when Dubrovski appeared at his side. "Reading the notices, I see."

"I can't read them," Carlisle said, grinning with relief.

Dubrovski pinned one of the notes with his blunt mechanic's finger. "Nearly all the same," he said. " 'Dear Yosha, I have gone on by echelon No. B.S. 410, 22 November. I will wait with the children at Sokhondo, Baikal Prospect, 12. Love S.' "

Dubrovski shook his head sadly. "Like castaways they leave notes wherever they stop, always hoping they'll be found, always afraid to sign their full name for fear of being bothered. Sometimes I wonder how many Yoshas or Ivans hurry to a reunion in some village or town only to find the wrong T, P, or S."

"About the shopping," Carlisle said.

"Ah, yes," Dubrovski said and he looked around the station. "There are sellers here, you can be sure. Half these refugees have trinkets stored away in their bundles in hopes of meeting just such a buyer as yourself."

Carlisle rejected the thought of buying something which had been used. There would be other spirits on the article, other ghostly associations which might contend with his. "No," he said. "No, it must be something new. I can't give her any old thing."

Dubrovski was troubled by Carlisle's vehemence. "You'd be surprised what can turn up in a railroad station," he said. "Let me inquire."

Carlisle caught Dubrovski's arm. "We've got to go to a shop!" he declared. "It must be new!"

"That can be expensive."

"That's not the point! Not the point at all."

Dubrovski shrugged eloquently. "It's your money," he said.

They found a jewelry shop near the hotel and Carlisle hovered over the articles displayed by an obsequious young Russian clerk and suspected darkly that all of them were secondhand. What indecision! Carlisle was immobilized. "Help me, Dubrovski," he said. "What do you think?"

Dubrovski selected a gold pillbox.

"Such a little thing as that?"

Dubrovski's brow furrowed. "Well, I don't know," he said. "I don't know what's correct. It's difficult. She's married, after all. A countess too, so I don't think you can give her anything very grand. This would be something she might carry, you see. Then she may have a dozen of the kind already. Then too I don't know what your feeling about it is."

"My feeling?"

"Why, a man gives presents for various reasons. It's not her name day. You haven't told me what your reason might be. And I'm not the one to advise in such matters anyway."

Carlisle examined the pillbox closely. It was plain gold and it looked new. He couldn't remember having seen Tatiana take a pill, but women kept such things about their person and he'd like the thought of her having it with her all the time.

"The man will engrave it at once, you see," Dubrovski said.

"How would it be engraved?"

"Well, I don't know. That's for you to say."

Carlisle was agonized by this second decision. Her initials? His? Nothing? He was in torment and Dubrovski watched him sympathetically. "Where did you meet her?" he asked.

"That's it!" Carlisle exclaimed and he had the jeweler engrave it *Vladivostok. November 11, 1918.*

As this was being done Carlisle thanked Dubrovski effusively and Dubrovski laughed. "You're mad, Captain. I believe you're in love with her like everyone else."

Carlisle flushed black and his eyes took on a hue of burnished brass.

Dubrovski stepped back in alarm. "Excuse me," he said. "I didn't mean —"

"Yes," Carlisle said and the clerk, equally alarmed, assured Carlisle once more that the gold pillbox was entirely new, then he wrapped it very prettily in saffron tissue.

By now it was dark. There was a cold, dry wind and the taste of grit in the air and as they went on toward the hotel Carlisle wondered how to tell Dubrovski, without insulting him, that he would like to be alone with Tatiana. He considered several ways of saying this, but he was obligated to Dubrovski and fond of him and wished the suggestion would somehow come from Dubrovski first. "This is my last night in Omsk," he said.

"So? I didn't know that," Dubrovski said.

"Yes, I'm leaving tomorrow for Irkutsk."

"You should have told me sooner. We could have made a farewell party of it. As it is there'll only be a few."

"A few!"

"Major Ikachi, Custer-Farquart and some of my comrades. We'll make a party of it all the same," Dubrovski said. "We have a table and I'll ask some others to join us."

"I don't want a party!" Carlisle protested and halted at the door of the hotel, but Dubrovski caught his arm and pulled him inside.

The hotel lobby was filled with the sound of voices and laughter and Carlisle was miserable as he followed Dubrovski through the crowd. A party! All day he'd been imagining a quiet supper with not even Dubrovski there, but now he realized what a fool he'd been. Why should she want to be alone with him when she was always surrounded by clever people? What claim did he have to her attention? Carlisle crushed the tissue-wrapped package in his sweating palm and cursed himself. He couldn't give her such a ridiculous thing in front of a lot of people.

"I've changed my mind about giving her this thing," he said to Dubrovski, but his voice was lost in the babble of the crowd.

"What?" Dubrovski asked. "Ah, there they are," and he towed Carlisle through the lobby to where Tatiana stood surrounded by several officers including Ikachi and Major Custer-Farquart. She had General Bogoloff's epaulet in her hand and her laughter rose above the sound of the other voices.

Major Ikachi was standing beside her with his white-gloved hand on the sharkskin hilt of his saber. "Your laughter is like brush strokes on silk, Countess," he said.

"Do you paint laughter then, Major?" Tatiana asked.

"I hadn't thought of the possibility until I heard you, but now I think it could be done. One could paint on silk the pattern, you understand, the quality of your laughter. One might do a whole series entitled portraits of laughter," Ikachi said, "joyous laughter, bitter laughter, social laughter."

"What an interesting idea!" Tatiana said.

Hearing this Carlisle stopped short; a feeling of inferiority swept over him and he fixed Major Ikachi with a belligerent glare. He crushed the tissue-wrapped package in his hand, trying to conceal it. He couldn't give it to her in the presence of all these officers who were competing with each other to be charming. He'd rather face a firing squad. Dubrovski had gone ahead and after greeting Tatiana he announced that Carlisle was leaving Omsk in the morning.

There was a murmur of feigned regret from the officers and Tatiana came toward him with her hand extended. "Is this true, Captain?" she asked.

"Yes," Carlisle said bluntly. And in order to take her hand he had to change the crushed package from his right hand to his left. The tissue paper was damp with perspiration and wadded around the pillbox. Carlisle wished he'd dropped it on the floor and kicked it aside.

"I was under the impression you'd be here much longer," she said.

"No, I'm going back in the morning."

"We'll be sorry to lose your company," she said.

"That's the way it is," Carlisle said. "I just came for the General's epaulet."

"Oh," she said, "of course," and she gave the epaulet to him.

Carlisle knew she was hurt by his abrupt manner and in a desperate attempt to make up for this he thrust the damp package into her hand. "Here," he said. "This is for you."

Tatiana looked at the miserable object in the palm of her hand. "For me?"

Carlisle wanted to bolt, but the other officers had gathered around and he was hemmed in. His face flamed and he tried to speak. "It's a — it's a thing — for you."

"Open it, Countess," Dubrovski boomed.

Tatiana stripped the soggy tissue from the pillbox and to Carlisle it was like having his skin torn off bit by bit. He tried to edge away. He was in a panic, waiting for a chance to run.

The pillbox was finally revealed and the officers commented appropriately. Carlisle rammed General Bogoloff's epaulet into the side pocket of his coat and wished he could crawl in after it. He cast Dubrovski a look of desperation, then calculated the distance between himself and the street door.

"Look on the back of it, Countess," Dubrovski said. "See how it's inscribed."

Tatiana turned the pillbox over. "How thoughtful of you, Captain," she said, but the inscription on the back was covered by a piece of tissue and she couldn't read it.

"Here, let me, Countess," Dubrovski said and he took the pillbox and polished it on the sleeve of his coat. "There now," he said and he returned the pillbox to her.

Tatiana read the inscription and smiled. "What a lovely way to commemorate the Armistice," she said showing the inscription to the officers beside her. Carlisle backed away in an agony of embarrassment; his eyes were stinging and he couldn't hear properly. Dubrovski was laughing, gesturing toward the dining room and suggesting they all go inside and propose a toast to Carlisle on the eve of his departure.

Major Custer-Farquart roared into Carlisle's ear: "Righto! A toast. Several toasts!"

Tatiana looked as though she expected him to offer his arm and lead the way. Dubrovski was nodding and winking at him about the success of their mutual purchase.

"I have to go," Carlisle declared. "Excuse me."

Dubrovski's face froze in an expression of comic astonishment and Carlisle bowled his way through the lobby toward the door. He heard Tatiana's surprised voice call his name but he sped on, nearly knocking two men off their feet as he crushed through the door.

On the street Carlisle turned around three times like a disoriented dog, then jammed his hands into his pockets and set off toward the river. Until this moment he had never known how cowardice could overwhelm a man. The contempt he'd always felt for men who didn't behave well under fire was turned against himself. They cowered in the face of bullets; he ran from repartee.

General Bogoloff's epaulet in his coat pocket beat on his thigh like a gavel reminding him with each step what a presumptuous fool he was to imagine he could cross the line into the society Countess Tatiana represented. He could no more do so than a wolf could jump Yakushef's flagged rope in the snow.

Carlisle turned onto the esplanade which fronted the Irtysh River. Dark figures passed him talking softly, their voices filled with the anxiety of the times. The street lamps cast a pale glow over the water and Carlisle tramped along trying to throw off the awful weight of his despair, imagining that even now he was being laughed at and discussed in the lobby of the hotel and that by morning there wouldn't be a soul in Omsk who wouldn't know what a fool he'd made of himself.

He'd gone perhaps fifty yards when he heard his name called and Dubrovski caught his arm from behind and pulled him around. "Captain, are you ill or what?" he cried.

"I'm all right," Carlisle said. "I have to go."

"But the dinner, my God! You said tomorrow!"

"My plans have changed."

"You're mad!" Dubrovski declared and he hung on to Carlisle's arm and towed him back down the esplanade. "You're worse than a Czech! Up, down, sideways all at once."

Carlisle hung back, but Dubrovski wouldn't release his hold. "Where are you taking me?" he demanded. "I won't go back!"

Then he saw Tatiana near one of the lights. She came forward quickly with an expression of sympathetic concern in her large gray eyes. "Is he all right, Emil?" she asked.

"Gone mad, I think."

"Have you gone mad, Captain?" Tatiana asked.

"I'm leaving," Carlisle said.

"Instantly?" she asked.

Carlisle nodded.

"We could walk you to the depot," she said.

"I don't go until morning," Carlisle confessed.

"Well then, we can talk," she said putting her hand under his arm.

"Gone absolutely mad," Dubrovski complained.

"Emil, go tell the others to start," Tatiana said. "Captain Carlisle and I will join you."

Dubrovski hesitated a moment, shrugged and started off. "Mad," he grumbled. "Absolutely!"

They walked along under the street lamps and the warmth of Tatiana's hand under his arm had a gentling effect on Carlisle, but they passed three lamps before he was able to speak and then it took all his courage. "I meant to ask about your husband, Countess," he said. "I hope he's all right."

"They say he's at Taiga now," she said. "It's doubtful he'll come to Omsk after all."

"That's too bad," he said.

"He can't leave the front, of course."

"No."

Again Carlisle struggled for something to say, but Tatiana didn't seem to mind his silence, which put him even more at ease. "Your friend, Markowitz, was in Verkhne-Udinsk."

"Yes, my uncle wrote me he'd stopped there. Raul is on General Gaida's staff now, somewhere near Perm, I believe. Have you seen my uncle?"

"Yes, when the Cossacks left I saw him. Several weeks ago. He was well. I didn't know he was your uncle."

"I could have introduced him to you in Vladivostok, but you have this habit of plunging off without a word."

"I apologize. I'm a fool."

She smiled and for the first time that evening Carlisle looked at her without being half blinded by embarrassment. She was wearing a fur coat with a high collar and there was a dark shawl pulled close around her face. Her eyes, caught in the lamplight, seemed very large and warm. "You're certainly different," she said. "But I like that."

"There's nothing much I can do about it."

"Why would you want to?"

"I'd like to be — to be more acceptable, I guess."

Tatiana laughed and hugged his arm just a bit. "You're entirely acceptable, Captain," she said. "Everything you do is unexpected and that's refreshing. Now you must come to dinner. I've worked all day and I'm famished. Please."

Carlisle stopped and shook his head resolutely. The thought of facing the others again was too much. "No," he said. "I can't."

She frowned. "But you'll at least walk me to the hotel. Or am I to be abandoned here?"

"Of course," he said and they went on toward the hotel together.

"You'll see my uncle when you return?"

"Yes, to give him the epaulet."

"I'm pleased now that I kept it," Tatiana said. "As a child I always hid things from him, objects, you know. His pipe, his stick. It was a game we played. He'd roar around the house cursing the servants while I giggled. He always threatened to hang Lizaveta, the housekeeper, for stealing things, then I'd save her life by bringing whatever he was looking for. I was fond of Lizaveta."

"She was lucky."

"Lizaveta? Oh, heavens, he wouldn't have hanged her! It was just a game, like with the epaulet."

"Lucky that you were fond of her," Carlisle said.

"You would have been too," Tatiana said.

"I can't imagine your kind of life," he said. "I've tried, but I can't do it."

"Why would you want to?"

"Because it's so different, I suppose. I was raised on an Indian reservation."

"I know nothing about that."

"It wasn't much," he said in a way that crushed any curiosity she might have expressed.

As they approached the hotel, Tatiana sensed his resistance increasing; each step they took toward the place added to it. He seemed to hunch down and withdraw into himself, and to spare him this tension Tatiana stopped some distance from the door and turned to face him. "You needn't come in if you don't wish to," she said.

A flashing smile of relief crossed Carlisle's face, then died abruptly. "It's not that I don't want to. I can't," he said.

She sought his eyes trying to discover the meaning of this statement and she found in them a look of naked adoration. Ordinarily she would have looked away; she would have made some inconsequential remark about the moon, the river, the weather and turned her eyes away. She had always been a close observer of people, of their mannerisms, their peculiarities, but she could not recall having looked so intensely into the eyes of another human being, not Albert, not Raul, not anyone.

She was terrified in a way which compelled her not to break this contact. To do so would have been a great failure of courage and yet it seemed indecent to stare so unabashedly at the devotion in his eyes.

She wondered what Carlisle saw in her own, if he knew how much she wanted to be seen as she was at this moment. For some reason she assumed he had this ability and she welcomed it.

For his part Carlisle, after the initial moment of terror, believed that he had been found entirely worthy in Tatiana's eyes. She did not turn away but poured light and warmth through his body and into his very soul. He felt taken out of himself and transformed into something finer than he could have imagined.

They could not have said how long they stood thus locked in each other's eyes. A minute of such unflinching exchange was more to them than a lifetime of casual glances, or momentary meetings of the eye which were hastily excused and disregarded. They seemed to have learned more about each other in this time, however brief, than any amount of self-confession could reveal. And when the moment came when they had nothing left to offer each other in this way they recognized it by common consent.

Carlisle pulled Tatiana into his arms. "It's all right," he said. "I'll go now."

"I know," she said.

"I'll never forget you."

"I'll always remember you too."

The words were so inadequate they regretted having said them. They stayed pressed in each other's arms for a moment longer, wishing they could avoid the awkwardness of parting. Then Tatiana pulled away and Carlisle released her. She didn't meet his eyes again but murmured goodbye and hurried on toward the hotel entrance.

Carlisle watched her out of sight, then walked slowly back to the rail-yard to pack for his journey to Irkutsk.

CHAPTER TWENTY-TWO

LIKE whales attacked by sharks the summer clouds dangled strips of torn flesh from their undersides and shed black clots of rain. In some places it soaked the earth leaving others perfectly dry, and in one place a labor battalion marching along under the watchful eyes of their White guards passed within a foot of a wall of rain and some of the recruited laborers held their hands into the water, which ran down their sleeves to their shoulders, but their feet were dry, raising puffs of dust.

Old men and boys, they had been conscripted to repair the railroad, to realign the tracks, plant new ties and add ballast to the crumbling bed. The old men were fatalistic, the boys were simply frightened. They walked in a hopeless shuffling manner, like tired draft animals, unsure of their master, unsure what was expected of them, but willing for the sake of peace to please.

Two young boys, twelve years old, no more, from a village on the river Khilok had tried to escape the levy officers by throwing themselves into the water. As the current bore them away the soldiers debated whether or not to shoot them. The villagers, lining the bank, implored them to be merciful and at last the soldiers went away.

The boys, Yurii and Alexei, were fished from the water, dried, fondled and treated as heroes. But the next day the levy officers returned and took them.

They marched along, one dark, one fair, both frightened and trying not to show it. The guards had been told of their attempted escape and the boys, sure they were marked for some terrible fate, would have liked to hold hands but they dared not even do this.

Yurii wore a castoff pair of felt boots which were much too big for him, coming nearly to his knees. They had belonged to his brother who was away at the front, and though they had grown uncomfortable after so long a walk Yurii was compensated for this by a sense that his brother was near. He clung to the idea that nothing terrible could happen to him as long as he wore his brother's boots and this made him the braver of the two boys, not by nature, but because of his brother's boots.

Often as they marched along Yurii spoke softly to Alexei, who was three months older and larger too. "It's going to be all right, Alexei," Yurii said. "It's an adventure and they won't keep us long."

And Alexei, miserable enough without having to put up with Yurii's encouragement, would nod and try to pretend it was an adventure. "If they'd asked me I would have volunteered," he said once. "They shouldn't run at a fellow like that, with guns."

A big White guard, half Tatar by the looks of him, tramped along on the flank of the column a few paces behind the boys. He wore a shapeless army coat which nearly touched the ground, and the rifle slung over his shoulder with a rusty bayonet affixed to its muzzle was taller by half than each of the boys. His presence behind them made their necks itch and sometimes they glanced back anxiously, to be sure the guard hadn't unlimbered his rifle to shoot them.

Noticing this the guard moved up beside the boys, who shrank in his presence. His big, flat face was dark and sparsely bearded and there was an evil crackle in his eyes which peered out beneath the shag of hair under his fur cap. "You're the boys who tried to escape us," he said.

Yurii and Alexei nodded dismally.

"Our work is near the Briana," he said.

Again the boys nodded.

"Been there?" the guard asked and his gruff voice eased a bit and looking at them he seemed to smile.

"No, Uncle," Yurii said, speaking first because of his brother's boots.

"Ah," the guard said. "Well, there'll be someone to look after you."

"What will we be doing there, Uncle?" Alexei asked.

"Pushing dirt," the guard replied. "Pushing dirt, laying rails. Think you can drive a railroad spike?"

"I don't know, Uncle," Yurii said. "I've never tried."

"Boys your size can do it if they're clever. I have a boy your size. I'll show you how it's done."

Alexei and Yurii glanced at each other somewhat relieved because the guard had a clever boy their size, a possibility which had never occurred to them, and because he was going to show them how to drive railway spikes, a craft in which they suddenly found themselves more than willing to excel.

The labor battalion moved on, some two hundred old men and boys, under the watchful eyes of twenty weary guards who would much have preferred another kind of duty. They came to the railroad tracks and headed east toward a siding where a train of five freight cars waited to pick them up.

Above them the dark, torn clouds trying to escape the ravages of the wind shed their moisture, which fell in heavy columns like sand ballast being jettisoned by passing ships.

« 2 »

From their hiding places on the slopes above the siding the partisans watched the labor battalion approach. The partisan leader, Timokhin, counted the White guards; there were ten at the train and twenty with the laborers, which made his force and theirs almost evenly matched. Timokhin passed the word to his men to fire on the train guards first, which would alert the labor conscripts and give them time to scatter. Then he settled down against a stone, waiting for the proper moment to give the signal.

A big man, over forty, wearing a sheepskin jacket fastened by a broad leather cartridge belt, Timokhin's face and all his body bore scars of a beating he had received while in prison at Dauria. He had been thrown into this prison for having mutinied against Ataman Semenoff, whose brutalities he could no longer stomach. Forty others had been imprisoned with him, members of the company which had refused Semenoff's orders. They were all scheduled for execution and for this they had beaten Timokhin half to death.

His own comrades.

They beat him because it was at his suggestion they had refused to attack and plunder a sleeping village.

So be it, but this was a thing Timokhin could not forget. His own comrades.

They had beaten him with ramrods supplied by the prison guards, flaying his face as well as his body, each man intent, it seemed, on striking the blow which would blind, maim, or kill — on the theory, he now supposed, that by killing him they would save themselves. But this was not the case.

As it came to pass they saved him, but not themselves, for when the time of their execution arrived the men of his company were marched away, but Timokhin was such a mass of raw, foul-smelling wounds no one believed he would live and to avoid having to carry him the guards left him behind.

To save a bullet, some of them said. That he might suffer to his last breath, said others, but they simply didn't want to soil themselves by touching him.

Later he heard that some of the men who'd beaten him cried out to be forgiven.

As the machine gun traversed their ranks, at knee level, many cried out: "Timokhin, forgive us!" Then the machine gun chopped into them again at belly level and they were left to die.

After this the prisoners rallied around Timokhin, marveling each day that he lived, and wondering if he would forgive the dead comrades who had beaten him.

He had not done so. No.

When he saw his lacerated eyelids, his cut mouth and his body denuded in so many places of muscle that only scar tissue covered the bone, Timokhin cursed them, cursed God and cursed the world.

The prisoners were shocked at his blasphemy and terrified by his appearance. He was Lazarus to them and many believed he could not die again. They also believed he had received the gift of prophecy. His voice, formerly a common baritone, had been changed by the beating to a hollow, rasping bass which seemed to emanate from a point above and behind his head as though it was speaking also to him.

The prisoners listened, awed by everything Timokhin said, and they concealed his condition from the guards saying that he was suffering unmercifully and would soon die. Instead Timokhin grew strong under their care and when it was no longer possible to fool the guards, when they grew suspicious of a man in his condition taking so long to die, Timokhin told the prisoners to say he was dead, for by then he was aware of the effect of his voice and of the hold he had over the men.

He chose six of the strongest prisoners to bear his naked body to the burial plot which was beyond the walls of the prison. Four guards accompanied them and when they reached the burial plot the prisoners laid Timokhin's lacerated body on the ground and began to dig his grave. As their shovels bit into the earth Timokhin spoke. "You too will die," he said and he sat up staring at the stricken guards. The sepulchral tone of his voice seemed to hang in the air and the guards, all their superstitions awakened, their eyes starting in their sockets, were felled by the prisoners' shovels.

Timokhin stripped one guard and dressed himself while the others gathered the weapons, then they all made off over the fields.

The prison alarm was sounded, but the troops sent out to give chase were careful not to find anyone. They were most of all anxious not to find Timokhin, for they truly believed that he had risen from the dead.

Timokhin watched the labor conscripts come down the track toward the siding, estimating the moment to give his men the signal; Timokhin the prophet; he who could not die.

Of the six men who had made their escape with him only three were still alive, Slavin, Balashov and Marrakof. Others hearing of him had joined the band, which never numbered more than thirty. Timokhin would have no more.

The latest recruit was Glubov, the blond gunner. Glubov who was in love with a girl who, he said, had to be watched.

Timokhin saw Glubov down the hillside crouched behind a boulder with his rifle.

Glubov wanted machine guns; he wanted artillery, but most of all he wanted Maryenka to love and forgive him. She was silent; she was patient. She cooked and served his meals and when there was a raid she stayed behind with the camp guards, whom Glubov threatened to kill slowly if they so much as looked at her. He often recited how slowly he would kill anyone who bothered her, slowly, slowly, as though he had someone in mind.

The labor conscripts came along the tracks walking submissively, heads down, counting the ties, and Timokhin was proud to be the instrument of their release.

He raised his hand.

Covered with mottled red scar tissue Timokhin's hand was like a flame and the men sighted their guns on the train guards below, waiting for a flick of Timokhin's wrist. When it came, thirty shots spat from the hillside.

The inaccuracy of rifle fire always amazed Timokhin. Of ten rail guards exposed on the siding only six went down. One might have supposed that these six were the only ones that had been fired upon, but this wasn't so. The men always tolled off their targets when they had the advantage of surprise. But sometimes Timokhin suspected that his men, or any man, given the chance to shoot another in cold blood from an ambush failed, more often than not, to do so; that some innate decency prevented him from sighting accurately, that the first shots were always a warning.

The probability was that five of the men on the ground had been hit by accident. Timokhin was sure he had killed the man he'd fired at, but there was no time to ponder this because the guards, having taken cover behind the train, were firing back.

On the roadbed the labor conscripts broke and scattered in all directions while their guards, momentarily confused, bunched together shouting contradictory instructions. Timokhin directed his men to fire at these guards and presently the air bristled with the sound of rifles.

Yurii and Alexei lay face down in a culvert beside the railway embankment while bullets flew overhead; some of these, striking stones, were spent and wailed off end over end. A heavy figure dropped into the culvert beside them. It was their guard, the one with a boy their size.

He cursed and fumbled with his rifle and the boys, hearing a loud explosion, realized that he was firing. He had already been hit in the neck but he didn't appear to notice and the boys wondered if they should call his attention to the wound or not. There was blood coming through a hole in the collar of the guard's coat. His face was gray, but he cursed and fired toward the hill, fumbling in his pockets for more cartridges when he needed them.

Once he glanced at the boys, saw their round, frightened eyes and grinned. "We'll drive them off," he said. "Don't worry. We'll be on our way again soon enough."

« 3 »

At Tataurovo Ira was among the first to hear the rifle fire. He stepped to the door of his car and listened for a moment, then he buckled on his forty-five and ran toward the Snorter. "Let's have a look," he called and by the time he had the engine rolling Klagle, Baker, and fifteen men had swung aboard with their rifles, helmets, two BAR's and a machine gun. Ira shoved the throttle forward and the Snorter got up to her cruising speed.

"What do you think it is?" Ira asked Baker.

"A disturbance," Baker replied.

For days the men had been picking up Bolshevik propaganda leaflets in their sector. Printed in English they were either tossed from passing trains or scattered over the area by Bolshevik agents at night.

You soldiers are fighting on the side of the employers against us, the working people of Russia. All this talk about intervention to "save" Russia amounts to this, that the capitalists of your countries are trying to take back from us what we won from their fellow capitalists in Russia. Can't you realize that this is the same war that you have been carrying on in America against the master class? You hold the rifles, you work the guns to shoot us with, and you are playing the contemptible part of scab. Comrades! Don't do it!

When the men on patrol picked up these leaflets and read them they laughed in a contemptuous way, but the leaflets made them a good deal more wary than they had previously been.

Do you realize that the principal reason the British-American financiers have sent you to fight us is because we were sensible enough and courageous enough to repudiate the war debts of the bloody, corrupt old Czar?

"Hell, we're not fighting anyone, and that's the god-damned trouble," Carson said.

Major Taziola ordered Ira to send samples of all leaflets to Headquarters and to burn the rest. He asked what effect they had had on the men and Ira said no one took them seriously.

"Don't be too damned sure about that, Leverett. Keep your eyes open. This is direct subversion."

"I know what it is."

"If you hear anything funny let me know."

"What's funny, Major?"

"Don't be funny!"

Ira had laughed, but the continuing appearance of the leaflets set everyone on edge and when they heard the rifle fire down the line it was almost with a sense of relief that they headed toward it.

The Snorter was seething and panting like an angry dragon. Sergeant Klagle went to the forward buffers to act as lookout while the men battened down to do battle. They adjusted the sandbags around the edge of the tender to make firing ports, strapped on their helmets and checked their rifles.

"How far do you think they are?" Ira asked.

"Five or six miles the way it sounded," Baker replied.

Ira checked his watch. They'd be into the "disturbance" in fifteen minutes if Baker was right about the distance.

Ira leaned out the cab window trying to see ahead through the steam. He'd forgotten his helmet, but he didn't care. He was looking forward to a fight. This was his chance to remove the stigma of Colonel Spaeth's reprimand and to relieve his sense of guilt for failing to support the action at Siding 85. With the steam blowing black in his face and the Snorter's bell booming of its own accord as the little engine rocked over the track Ira thought of Austin and it was as though the sergeant were watching over him. "I'll make it up to you, Harry," he thought. "This time I'll show them what a man can do under fire. We'll see who's an administrator."

Ira tried to nurse more speed out of the Snorter and he yelled to Baker over the racket of hammering wheels. "I'll stop short, Baker, and take half the men forward on foot. You bring the Snorter up when it's needed."

"Right!" Baker said.

And Ira grinned because he knew it was god-damned right.

Yurii and Alexei heard a sound like bread dough being slapped down on a baking board and their guard, who had been firing with slow deliberation, fell back into a sitting posture clutching his head, and his rifle clattered on the stones. He looked at the terrified boys, blood trickling warm between his blunt, dirty fingers. His mouth worked into a smile and nodding as though to dispel their fears he mumbled softly, "Don't mind, little ones."

He closed his eyes and the boys thought he had fallen asleep, then he toppled over.

Yurii and Alexei looked at each other to see what feelings they shared at this and something in their eyes, perhaps a mistaken interpretation by both of them, ignited their courage.

They'd grown used to the sound of bullets flying overhead and the guard in the culvert with them had become their friend. They looked toward the hill from which the attack had come, angry at those who were there and no longer afraid.

Yurii seized the guard's rifle. Alexei beckoned and jumping up the two boys left the culvert, more to escape the presence of the body there than for any other reason. They ran half crouched along the track and this apparently fearless action inspired some of the other boys, who began to cheer. Two or three of these took weapons from other guards who had fallen and presently there were twenty boys galloping heedlessly down the tracks, cheering like fools. Those with rifles waved them aloft to encourage the labor conscripts, and the remaining White guards joined the attack.

Timokhin was astounded to see the conscripts he had come to release fighting their way back into captivity. But this was so. In their ignorance the captives had joined their captors in a fight to regain their captivity.

The shouting boys, having dismissed the danger of the bullets, had in fact dismissed the bullets themselves. No one was shooting at them. Timokhin's men had stopped firing and were looking toward him for instructions.

Glubov left his place behind the rock and scampered up the hill, but he was hit and thrown forward on his face. He continued to crawl toward Timokhin, drawing fire from the guards below.

Timokhin pulled him to safety.

Glubov had been struck in the chest but was not yet aware of it. "The fools!" he cried.

Timokhin nodded and signaled his men to retire.

"I'm hit!" Glubov said. "I thought I stumbled." He touched his chest and looked at the blood which covered his hand as though surprised by its color.

Timokhin's men left their places one by one and crawled toward the crest of the hill, squirming between the rocks to avoid the heavy fire.

The advent of death startled Glubov. He didn't know how to respond. His jaw dropped open and he stared at Timokhin offering his blood-covered hand in evidence. Tears filled his eyes because it was so unjust, so ridiculous. He tried to speak, but Timokhin reached toward him with his fiery hand and brushed his eyes shut, gently. At this Glubov fell back with a fatal sigh.

Timokhin waited an instant for death to seal the man, then he rose and walked over the hill.

The sound of gunfire had come to a stop as Ira rose and ran across the trestle bridge with Sergeant Klagle and three other men behind him. He trotted toward the curving cut in the low hill ahead, matching his stride to the ties, feeling light and charmed, very sure that nothing bad could happen.

He beckoned the others with the forty-five in his hand, pleased by the strength of the gesture. He felt like a kid, bubbling with inner laughter, playing hide-and-go-seek.

The cut was about ten yards long, a bad place to be caught, and Ira put on a burst of speed. He came out the other side and saw the mass of charging figures. Instantly he dropped to one knee and fired several times.

Sergeant Klagle sprawled on the tracks beside him and ripped off a full clip from his BAR.

Ira yelled at one of the men to get the Snorter, and waited until he saw him running low, back toward the trestle bridge.

When he looked ahead again the track was empty. He fired another shot, but it was the only sound in the still air.

He looked at Klagle, whose face was terrible.

"I think they're ours," Klagle said.

Three soldiers, they were Whites, stood up and came forward with their hands over their heads. Their faces were grave and from behind them rose the wails of the grievously wounded.

When the Snorter reached the scene Sergeant Baker found Ira standing beside the dead bodies of two boys, his forty-five dangling in his hand, a look of curious abstraction on his face.

"I would have made the same mistake," Baker said.

Ira looked at Baker and smiled. "Any doubt about that?" he asked.

"Klagle said they came charging at you."

"Labor conscripts trying to escape, kids and old men."

"If they hadn't tried to escape —" Baker said, then he shrugged and moved away to help with the wounded.

Ira pulled the clip from his forty-five. One of the bullets polished for him in the whore house at Harbin still remained. Colonel Spaeth had returned the weapon with his letter of reprimand — "deficient in those qualities of good judgment." Ira removed his last bullet from the clip and dropped it.

The ragged clouds looked cold, like armor plate torn by shellfire. It began raining, a sudden downpour of heavy drops which exploded when they hit the earth.

Ira walked toward the bullet-marked boxcars. He was benumbed and miserable.

Klagle nodded toward a body beside one of the cars, a blond man with blood drying on the front of his leather jacket. "Partisans," Klagle said. "They just brought him down from the hill."

Ira nodded.

"They tried to ambush this column," Klagle said.

Ira looked up the hill where the partisans had been. "They might have shot me," he thought. "They might have shot those boys."

"They really chopped things up," Klagle said.

Ira dropped his forty-five into its holster. "Any casualties?"

"No."

"Better get some guards on our flanks," Ira said.

"You're all right," Klagle said and he tapped Ira's arm and smiled.

Rain swept down from the hill and the men scurried for cover. The labor conscripts ran to the boxcars and shoved or pulled each other inside. Two conscripts carrying a body between them ran to the last car and rolled it inside, face down, arms flopping uselessly, then they jumped up beside it and the White guards locked them in.

Ira went to the Snorter and rang the bell. It was over. An incident. Closed.

"They'll think twice before they hit this section of the line again," Baker said. "Probably put a stop to those damned leaflets too."

« 4 »

That night seated by his campfire in the Kharmoni Mountains, his nearly lidless eyes glazed by the firelight, Timokhin raised his hand and let it fall in a gesture of resignation. There was a heavy sigh in the air over Timokhin's head and the men looked toward their leader, expectantly. "They will not be free," Timokhin said gravely. "They want what they have always known."

Timokhin remained as he was, staring at the flames, and the men thought he was going to say more, but he stood up and there was another swooping sigh as though an owl had spread its wings to arrest its flight.

The men returned to their work, cleaning their rifles, sharpening knives or patching their clothing, and Timokhin went to the place where Glubov's woman was kept.

She rose as Timokhin came toward her. She was weary and long past knowing fear. Timokhin motioned her to be seated and sat down nearby himself. "He is dead, you see."

"Yes," Maryenka said.

"We won't be able to keep you then."

"Oh," she said.

"There's no one here to look after you and they'd all begin to growl," Timokhin said and he shrugged apologetically.

"Well then, I'll go."

"I have a friend in Verkhne-Udinsk. He's a Pole and a fool, but he's good to stray creatures. He has a small place outside town and might keep you there until you find what you must do."

"Are we close to Verkhne-Udinsk then?" Maryenka asked.

"It's not so far."

Timokhin noticed Maryenka's thoughtful expression. He admired her fortitude and had always been courteous, but he knew nothing about her except what Glubov had been willing to tell him. As he understood it Glubov had saved Maryenka from the Cossacks at Pashkova and had protected her until an opportunity came for them to escape. Glubov rarely spoke of this and when he did so he was uneasy and there were questions raised by his story which Timokhin let pass.

When they stumbled into Timokhin's encampment the girl had spoken for both of them while Glubov trembled. She seemed to have reached that point in life which Timokhin understood perfectly well, the point at which death is of little consequence and existence, moment by moment, is a sad surprise. Timokhin sensed this bond between himself and Maryenka and wondered what had brought her to it so young.

"I'll take you myself to Anitsky," he said.

"I'll go alone."

"You wouldn't know the way. I'll see you're safely there."

"You could be captured."

"And?"

Maryenka looked at Timokhin, who smiled slightly and shrugged.

"I wouldn't want to be the cause of such a thing," she said quietly.

"I'll take you all the same," Timokhin said. "There are worse things than being captured, eh?" He met her eyes and nodded. "We know this to be so, I think."

He touched her shoulder and Maryenka shuddered terribly but she didn't draw away.

"Yes," Timokhin said, "yes, yes." Then he dropped his hand and returned to the fire, where he sat staring into the embers wondering again why it was men refused their freedom. This caused him to doubt his purpose, to seek another way, to wonder if he should have forgiven the comrades who had beaten him.

CHAPTER TWENTY-THREE

IRA always felt a keen sense of displacement when he walked along the uneven dusty streets or on the double-planked sidewalks in the residential areas of Verkhne-Udinsk. The small, unpainted log houses with their fretwork porches, window boxes and colorful plots of garden reminded him of quiet mining towns in the Sierras, of Downieville, Chinese Camp, or Mariposa. But the atmosphere of Verkhne was charged with Asiatic violence, war and common murder. The small, unexpected things surprised him more than the exotic. The fact that he could buy Faber 2B pencils in any general store, that there was an automat at the railroad station, that one could buy carbonated water in siphons, Eau de Cologne at the pharmacy; and in one Chinese variety store there was an iron cock which crowed and laid a chocolate egg for a kopeck. These things upset his preconceptions about geography. One ought not to be able to buy a hot roast beef sandwich in the center of the Asian mainland, cans of Dutch and French sardines had no right to appear on the grocery shelves, and a Philharmonic Society? It was incredible, but all these things were there.

In a city of twenty thousand there was no sewage or water system, so Chinese water carriers hauled their barrel carts up from the Selenga or the Uda, which came together near the town, and claimed their water had been brought from fresh mountain springs.

Shallow draft steamers, paddle-wheelers and side-wheelers with tall black smokestacks, the same kind of boats Ira had seen on the Sacramento, hauled freight and troops up and down the river.

Big brown, double-humped camels with slings on their backs often padded down the streets, their large heads raised haughtily above their Chinese masters. They came in caravans from Kalgan in China via Urga and Kiakhta to meet the Trans-Siberian Railroad and the inland waterways. One camel had two crates of Campbell's Soup on its back. Campbell's Soup from Kalgan, China, to Verkhne-Udinsk? Where was the profit? Cans of opium labeled as soup — cans of gold? Endless speculation.

There was a brewery in the town, a tallow and candle factory, several tanneries, a steam flour mill, an oil refinery, and countless shoddy little industries busily doing something connected with the war, making boxes, clothing, blankets or tents.

Everyone was busy and at night the main streets were lit by a string of seventy-five-watt bulbs manufactured in the United States for the lamps of Asia.

After dark one had to be wary of thieves who were also busy and would garrote a victim even in a dense crowd. The local citizens hired guards to patrol the residential areas at night and kept dogs chained at their gates, so it was better to walk in the middle of the street after dark. One could follow the progress of a citizen down a side street by the snarling yap of the dogs and by the sound of their rattling chains.

Ira usually spend his leave in Verkhne alone. He could sit for hours on the bank of the Selenga watching the river traffic, listening to the boatmen and the soldiers singing. Their songs and the strains of the balalaika induced in him a state of Oblomovian torpor. He had begun to pick up conversational Russian and was trying to read Dostoevski in the original, and often when he came to Verkhne he'd buy pancakes, sour cream, cold cuts and cheese from the vendors in the park, and with his book and a bottle of wine a whole warm afternoon would go by without a word to anyone.

Ira had not been to Verkhne since the appearance of the propaganda leaflets and the skirmish with the partisans but one afternoon he received a call from Major Taziola asking him to come to Headquarters.

"What's up, Taz? I hate to leave."

"Anything wrong out there?"

"Nothing wrong. I just don't like to be away while Carlisle is. It leaves the company without —"

"You've got Klagle and Baker. This is important. We're going to do a little counterpropaganda of our own and I'd like your opinion."

"We could handle that over the phone."

"No, I don't think so. If you're uncertain about Baker or Klagle I can arrange for a reliable officer to be there while you're away."

Taziola's peremptory manner irritated Ira. He said there was no need to send an officer down and took the afternoon local, which put him in Verkhne at five o'clock.

"What do you think of it all, Ira?"

"What do I think of what all, Taz?"

Taziola tossed up his hands. "The whole damn shooting match. The Reds, the Whites. The revolution."

"Hell. What do you think of it all?"

Taziola smiled and sat forward. They were in the communications office and Taziola's desk was fitted out in the best executive style. He had an Out Box and an In Box, a miniature Cossack saber for a letter opener, a black onyx pen and pencil holder with his name and rank inlaid in brass letters. There was a big blotter on the desk and a picture of his wife framed in filigreed silver. Ira hadn't noticed all these things before, but now they caught his attention. He knew Taz was an electrical engineer who had an important job waiting for him in the personnel department of General Electric; he'd heard that Taz was a vice-president, but for the first time he wondered what in hell such a man was doing out here.

Taz picked up the miniature saber and ran his thumb along the blade. "It's a mess," he said seriously, "but I can tell you one thing: I've learned a hell of a lot."

"You live and learn," Ira said. "If we stay out here much longer I'll be able to try cases in the Russian Supreme Court."

"Think they'll have one?"

"They'll have something."

"Even if the Reds win? Think they'll have a system of jurisprudence then?"

"Every society has laws, Taz. Even the most primitive."

Taziola smiled and nodded. "The Reds are primitive," he said. "Marx is hogwash. It won't work. It'll never work because it's unnatural."

"I thoroughly approve of nature," Ira said.

"Do you?" Taziola said as though he'd scored a point. "I wondered about that."

"About what?" Ira asked, annoyed.

"About whether you approved of the natural order of things."

"If you're talking about the military order of things I'm inclined to believe it's crap," Ira said.

Taziola chuckled and tossed the paper cutter down on the blotter. "I'm inclined to agree with you, but don't let it get around. One nihilist in this outfit is enough."

Ira was put off. He wasn't a nihilist; he wasn't even sure Taziola knew the meaning of the word, but he didn't want to pursue the discussion because he'd begun to feel like an applicant for a job, nervous but eager to please. He almost regretted having fallen into the habit of calling Major Taziola Taz as though they were on intimate terms.

There were certain protections in military formality which he hadn't previously considered important. "Where'd you get the paper cutter, Major?" he asked. "It's very handsome."

"At Beresovka, the prisoner of war camp. Have you been over there?"

"No."

"I'll take you. We can eat dinner, shop, gamble, anything you want."

"I thought it was a prisoner of war camp."

"It is, but there's a world over there you should see, Ira. It might teach you a few things. It did me. Marx is crap and Darwin was right."

"I thought you said this was important."

"It is. We're meeting a couple of officers out there. One of them is pretty sure the leaflets we've been picking up come from Beresovka."

"A prison?"

"That's why you've got to see it. We're going to try and frame language that will rebut those damned Reds. Have you seen this? The British put it out to their troops in North Russia when they had the same problem."

Taziola passed a proclamation over the desk and Ira read it:

There seems to be among the troops a very indistinct idea of what we are fighting for here in North Russia. This can be explained in a few words. We are up against Bolshevism, which means anarchy pure and simple. Look at Russia at the present moment. The power is in the hands of a few men, mostly Jews, who have succeeded in bringing the country to such a state that order is nonexistent. Bolshevism has grown upon the uneducated masses to such an extent that Russia is disintegrated and helpless; therefore we have come to help her get rid of the disease that is eating her up. We are not here to conquer Russia, but we want to help her and see her a great power. When order is restored here, we shall clear out, but only when we have attained our objective and that is the restoration of Russia.

Ira put the proclamation on Taziola's desk without comment. He was experiencing an almost incandescent rage and wondered if this showed in his face. He tried to repress it, to hold it down, to let it pass, but Taziola was waiting for his response. Ira just stared at him.

"Well, what do you think?" Taziola asked.

"I think I'll go back to the company, Taz," Ira said and he stood up.

"But you've had experience!" Taziola protested. "Your men have read the leaflets and they've actually engaged the Bolsheviks. I want your opinion, Ira."

"This isn't my line."

"Damn it! I don't care if it's your line or not. We've got to take a concerted action against this thing."

"Who has to?"

"We all do. Sipialef approached me with this suggestion. I didn't go to him."

"Sipialef?"

"And the British. Captain Whyte, the British military attaché here. You know him."

"No, I don't."

"Well, you'll meet him tonight then."

"Who else knows about this? Does Colonel Spaeth?"

"It's only a proposal, Leverett. He'll pass on it when we have something to offer."

"You're sure he'll pass on it?"

"He will or he won't. We're just trying to formulate a rough draft. Something to give the troops. You're a lawyer. You've got a gift of language. All I want is the benefit of your advice."

"My advice is to forget it."

"For Christ's sake! They'll go ahead without us. I just want to make it acceptable and useful for our men too. What's wrong with that? What got your back up anyway?"

"The reference to the Jews for one thing."

Taziola spun the proclamation around and searched through it. "Where is that? What do you mean? Oh, for Christ's sake, we can scratch that out. I didn't even remember it."

Taziola picked up a pencil and scratched through the words "mostly Jews." "Anything else you think should come out?" he asked.

"If Bolshevism is anarchy pure and simple and the Bolsheviks have rendered Russia helpless, why in hell is Kolchak having such a hard time getting his troops to Moscow? One might suppose he's hitting some organized resistance."

Taziola smiled and tipped back in his chair. "Now you're being legalistic," he said.

"Oh? I thought I was just using common sense."

"Think common sense will appeal to our men?"

"I think so."

"Come along and tell that to Sipialef and Whyte. They'll listen to you because you know the men. They consider me a desk polisher and I think it's damned important that whatever goes out sets the right tone. We don't want our men laughing at our own propaganda do we — or at that of our allies?"

"I think we ought to leave it alone, Taz. That's my opinion."

"All right, fine. Tell them that. They're going to put something out by the end of the week and if we can't stop them at least we can help set the right tone."

"Colonel Spaeth won't be back by then."

"Yes, I was hoping we could get them to hold off until the Colonel returns," Taziola said.

"On that basis I'll go."

"Fine!" Taziola exclaimed. "Good enough! I knew you'd want a hand in this thing. I've got a car downstairs. Come on. We'll have time to look around before the others show up."

It was almost dark as they headed for Beresovka in an army Ford with Taziola at the wheel. Ira was deeply annoyed and felt that he'd been manipulated.

"By the way, have you heard about Anitsky?" Taziola asked.

"What about him?"

"I thought Cloak might have told you."

"No."

"Well, it's not important," Taziola said.

The Ford shuddered over the split log road and Taziola concentrated on his driving, but there was a cock sparrow expression in his eyes which provoked Ira.

"All right, Taz, what about Anitsky?"

Taziola grinned. "I suppose there's no harm in it," he said.

"In what?" Ira demanded. "What in hell are we talking about?"

"You're jumping out of your skin, Ira."

"All right, I am. It's damned aggravating. If you're going to say something say it; if you're not, don't. What's all the pussyfooting about?"

"Part of the technique, my boy," Taz answered. "Part of the technique."

"What technique, for Christ's sake?"

"You ever have anything to do with Anitsky?"

"To do with him? He's a waiter at the Mulligan. That's all I know."

"A damned smart one."

"Oh, sure, he's head of the Bolshie secret service in your book. I'd forgotten."

"You ever mention Sergeant Austin to him?"

"What is this? The third degree?"

"He knows a lot about Austin."

"What makes you think so? He knows a lot about a lot of things, Taz."

"Then why did he ask Cloak about Austin? If he knew so much, why would he ask?"

"Ask what?"

"He wanted to know if Austin was dead. How do you account for that?"

"How do you?"

"I'm not sure yet," Taziola said. "But we're keeping our eyes on him. Even Bentham thinks Anitsky's interest in us is unusual."

"You think he's an agent," Ira said.

"Darn right he is. If I was headwaiter at the Mulligan I'd be an agent too."

Ira laughed. Taziola's manner was outrageously solemn and the proposition that any headwaiter at the Mulligan would be a spy was particularly funny because it was so true. Anitsky probably expected tips for information he gathered, but he was too loquacious and bumbling to be a decent espionage agent. "Hell, the man is a compulsive chatterbox, Taz. Even the Bolsheviks would have more common sense than to engage him as a spy."

"Just be careful when you're around him," Taziola grumbled.

"Yes, I will be," Ira said gravely and after another fit of laughter he subsided and apologized to Taziola for being rude. "I'm sure you're right to be cautious, Taz," he said. "But it's all damned foolish when you come right down to it."

"I don't see it that way."

"No, I suppose you don't."

"I thought your attitude might have changed since your brush with the Reds."

"If you read my report you'll find that our brush was with labor conscripts and their guards."

"The Reds precipitated it!"

"Yes, all right. I made that clear too, but I don't see what relevance it has to my attitude."

Major Taziola grinned and shook his head. "These damned leaflets have us all snapping at each other," he said. "Let's forget it."

"Let's," Ira said.

Beresovka Prison was a large complex of brick and wooden barracks capable of housing twenty-five thousand men. Located in a heavily wooded section of hills the two-story brick barracks on one side of the camp were occupied by Czech Legionnaires and by units of Semenoff's Siberian Wolf Brigade. Half a mile from these a series of wooden buildings had been given over to Hungarian, Austrian, German and Polish prisoners of war, many of whom had been there since 1915.

Taziola parked the car and led the way to the prison gate, which stood wide open. A board fence surrounded the place but this was falling down and no effort had been made to repair it. There were two armed guards at the gate, a Czech and one other, whose uniform was unidentifiable. They glanced at passes and motioned people in or out with no apparent concern for security. The Czech yawned and lit his pipe, but seeing Taziola he drew himself up and saluted with a splendid grin of recognition. "Welcome, Major," he said.

Taziola saluted the guard and grinned at Ira as they entered the compound. "I'm known as a big spender," he said.

"Those the only guards?" Ira asked.

"They have twelve now, but they're trying to hire more."

"Who's trying to hire more?" Ira asked.

Taziola laughed and clapped Ira on the back. "Why, the prisoners! The camp council hires the guards. Come on, let's have a drink."

Ira followed Taziola through the dark compound which was teeming with humanity. Now and again a barracks door would open and a fan of light would catch faces of the people around them, some were gaunt, holloweyed and listless, others were as cheerful as burghers. Ira stayed close to Taziola, who made several turns, then came to a door and thrust it open. "In here," he said.

Ira found himself in a small tastefully appointed bistro with a bar, three musicians, and two waiters, who bowed and ushered them to a table.

Taziola was pleased at Ira's astonishment; he ordered rye, or Scotch if Ira preferred. Ira said rye would do and Taziola asked the waiter what was playing at the Hungarian Officers' Theater.

The Lawyer, by Molnár.

The Germans had a very saucy musical and the Poles were doing something original which the papers said was dreary and the author had challenged the critic to a duel. Two of the most popular actresses, disgusted by rivalry for their attentions, had taken up with each other, causing a scandal, but they were playing to packed houses now.

The waiter, a small, bald, refined-looking man with an obsequious twitch at the corner of his mouth, completed his recitation, accepted a tip and went to a group of Czech officers at another table.

"That's Colonel Nagy," Taziola said. "Student of philology, peer of Hungary, captured in 1914 near Lublin. At one time he was the camp commandant, but now he makes a capable if somewhat garrulous waiter, as you see."

"Does he own this place?"

"No, he's just a waiter. That's how he played his hand the second time around. This place and two others are owned by a Hungarian private up from the ranks. If I see him later on I'll point him out. His name is Luka."

They had two drinks, then went through another door into a main section of the barracks which had been divided into small stalls. The room was illuminated by kerosene lanterns and the center aisle was crowded with shoppers, mostly White Russian, Czech and Japanese soldiers, but here and there an American or Canadian.

"One of the market places," Taziola said. "Prison handicrafts. You'll be amazed at the variety. I'll show you where to get a letter opener like mine."

They passed stalls with inlaid wooden boxes, leather goods, sandals and slippers, picture frames, metalwork, embroidery, woolen knitwear, shoe polish, mirrors, shaving kits, flasks, and came to one containing the little sabers. They were about four inches long, all alike from hilt to scabbard. Ira picked one up and pulled the blade and a figure from the depths of the stall came forward and stood waiting. When Ira looked up he saw an officer with the faded red tabs and gold flashing of a Hungarian lieutenant on his collar. He wore threadbare red trousers, boots and an ornate Hussar helmet.

Standing in the shadows which hid his face he looked like a dusty mannequin in a museum of military uniforms from an age when cavalrymen in glorious colors charged over green meadows to clash with enemy cannoneers.

Ira asked how much the saber was and the officer stepped forward. One ear and half of his face was gone. The flesh had healed like suet, but his back teeth showed where his cheek had been cleft away.

Taziola mentioned a figure and Ira thrust the money into the Hussar's hand and hurried on.

"One of the early ones," Taziola said. "He caught that saber near Bachmach. They say he was handsome. Now he makes sabers."

The horror of the camp didn't appear to affect Taziola. They went through other crowded barracks, a food market, a clothing market, hardware, furniture. There was even a bank issuing notes which were exchangeable in town. Dozens of small industries had sprung up, manufacturing anything which could be sold. "They've contracted to produce mess kits for the Czechs," Taziola said. "They make water cans, buckets, hand tools. The one thing they aren't allowed to do is repair weapons, but they'd be damned good at that too. If you want a uniform made, there are tailors here who can do the job overnight. They'll design and make a ball gown of Chinese silk for your sister that you couldn't touch at home. I can show you fur coats that you'll never see again, beautiful things, sable, kolinsky, ermine. And they've done all this from nothing, don't you see?"

"If they've turned all these barracks into shops, factories and warehouses, where in hell do they live?" Ira asked.

"Those who can't afford a room live in the earth barracks. The laboring class. You've got to see the design of this thing to appreciate it. You're looking at the people and missing the point, Leverett. Come on."

Taziola pulled a flashlight from his coat pocket and Ira followed him outside. They came to a mound of earth and went down a slanting incline and through a heavy board door. "Back to the beginnings of man," Taziola said quietly. "To the caves where the whole damned struggle started."

They were in a large room, perhaps sixty feet by twenty, which had been dug seven feet into the earth. The dirt taken from this excavation had been piled around the edge to make the walls ten feet high, with joists supporting a peaked roof of crude lumber covered with dirt. There were three rows of planks raised above the floor on wooden frames, which served as common berths. A stove and two dim petroleum lamps gave the only light and heat. The air was foul and men dressed in rags lay on the plank racks like corpses. Several of them turned their faces; their eyes were open but dreadfully blank.

"They don't see after sunset," Taziola whispered.

"What do you mean?"

"It's called nyctalopia. One of the diseases of undernourishment, like scurvy."

"Let's get out."

Once again they were in the great dark compound. Ira took a deep breath and looked up at the stars. There were people all around, brushing past each other in the dark. Ira wanted to leave, but his Virgil, Taziola, would not let him go. "Come on," he said. "We've got to meet Sipialef and Whyte at the German Theater."

"What a lousy place this is!"

"Of course it's depressing," Taziola said enthusiastically, "it's depressing as hell. But look what it says! For years these men have been the victims of indifference and cruelty. Their numbers have been thinned by every known disease, smallpox, diphtheria, typhoid, cholera, you name it. They've been driven to the extreme. Detention psychosis. Madness. Things you wouldn't believe. Gradually they lost every semblance of dignity. Their military organization disintegrated until at last they were nothing but brutes trying to live. And out of that horrible condition what did they create? It's not a Marxist economy, my friend, no indeed. It's laissez faire capitalism!"

Five minutes later they were seated in a velvet-curtained box in a small theater. The predominant colors were red, gold and green. No labor had been spared to perfect it. Hundreds of mirrors on the ceiling reflected candlelight; the proscenium was done in plaster Florentine, vines with clustered grapes, lilies, tulips, roses, and in the corners edelweiss. The stage came forward beyond the heavy green curtain and rose slightly in the shape of a golden coronet which hid the footlights.

Ira looked across the table at Taziola, who was studying the dinner menu in smug contentment. "Holy Christ, Taz," he said. "Is that the point?"

"You'd be pretty hard pressed to make another. This is how society evolves."

"And at this point the evolution stops."

Taziola smiled. "It grows," he said, "but it doesn't change. And that's why the Bolshies are wrong. They're unnatural."

"And what about those poor beggars underground?"

"Sympathize with them?"

"Don't you?"

"I know they'd be dead if it weren't for men like Luka and the others who pulled themselves together and made this place a going concern. The Red Cross and the Y.M.C.A. weren't capable of looking after the prisoners. Over two million of them in Siberia alone! The Russian government made an effort before it collapsed, a token effort, but finally the prisoners had to look after themselves. Some did well, others not so well. Some found work on the farms outside and made babies for the peasant women whose men were away at war. Some escaped across the borders into China. Some with technical skills were put to work on the railroad. There's no end to the things they did, but those who remained in the camps and still survive have handled it like this. Ah, there's Luka, in the box across the way."

The man Taziola pointed out wore a long sable cape fastened by a bast cord and under this a tight blue blouse with silver piping tucked into cream-colored riding breeches. He carried a swagger stick and there was a brilliantly costumed woman on his arm. She wasn't young, but she was very attentive. Luka seated her and the two men who had accompanied them withdrew and closed the curtains of the box.

Luka sat down beside the woman; he was very pale, with a chunky baker's body, light hair and the harsh features of a busy man.

"I've ordered the goulash," Taziola said. "It's very good. Lamb, pork and beef on rice. We'll have a bottle of wine and coffee. How does that sound?"

"Fine," Ira said, but he wasn't hungry and he had begun to dislike Taziola intensely. "What's being done for them now?" he asked.

"For who?"

"The men underground."

"They're given work and there's a minimal food allotment, but it has to be augmented. There is some charity and an effort is being made to improve medical facilities. The chances are that most of them will live to be repatriated and they'll go back to their old life. Some of them down there in the earth barracks will resume their posts in business or government, perhaps very important ones, who knows? And Luka will go back to being a journeyman baker. But now that the Hapsburgs have been broken and things have been shaken up there'll be changes. Luka will probably rise again and another poor devil will sink. Survival of the fittest, right? Depends on one's ability to adapt to circumstances."

"Who's the woman with him?" Ira asked.

"Captain Rydel, a Pole; he made a great hit in *Liebelei* by Schnitzler last month. Ah, here come Sipialef and Whyte."

The two officers came into the box and Taziola introduced them.

There was a look of gilded recognition in Sipialef's eyes as he shook Ira's hand; whether this was a trick of lights or a flash of residual contempt from their encounter at Vladivostok Ira did not know. Neither of them admitted having met before, but their hostility was so obvious that Taziola was a bit taken aback. "Colonel Sipialef has been put in charge of subversion in the area," he said. "Captain Whyte is naturally interested; he's the British attaché in Verkhne."

"I would have thought the Japanese and Czechs might have a representative here too," Ira said and he shook Whyte's hand.

Captain Whyte, about Ira's age, with a wispy mustache which failed to conceal two protruding teeth, pursed his lips and nodded solemnly. When he spoke he raised both hands in front of his mouth in a gesture of cupped prayer and talked through his fingers. "Well, you see, Lieutenant Leverett," he said in a voice which rang with brassy intelligence, "the Japanese and the Czechs haven't been on the receiving end of this yet. It's been pretty largely confined to the American sector, which, of course, causes one to speculate."

"About what, Captain?"

"About what's in the minds of those who are circulating the stuff," Captain Whyte said.

"And about its origin," Sipialef said.

"The inference being that since it shows up in our sector someone there could be originating it?" Ira asked.

Captain Whyte whickered through his fingers and blinked his joyless eyes. "Not at all, my dear Leverett," he cried. "We're further along than that, Lord knows. Colonel Sipialef has already located the press they're using, right here at Beresovka."

"Then close it down," Ira said.

"I want the people, not the press," Sipialef said.

"The Colonel has that end of it well under control," Taziola said.

"I'm sure of it."

"I hear everything that goes on in Beresovka," Sipialef said. "Arrests will be made at the right time."

Ira turned to Taziola, his patience gone, his disgust with the whole affair too bitter to conceal any longer. "Taz, what in hell did you rope me into this for? I'm leaving. Colonel Spaeth would spit nails if he knew what was going on here."

"You're upset."

"Yeah, a little bit. Just a little."

"All right," Taziola said. "Sorry I brought you out."

"Can I pick up a ride at the gate?"

"I'll take you back."

Ira stood up, trying very hard to remain cordial. "If it's all the same I'll go alone."

Taziola shrugged. "All right," he said. "You can pick up a droshky outside."

"I'll see you around," Ira said.

Taziola smiled. "You think the Reds are going to win this thing, don't you, Leverett."

"I don't know."

"I do. Even if they beat the Whites they'll lose because Marxian economics and human nature don't mix."

"You might say the same about Christianity, Major."

"You think the Bolshies are Christian?"

"They sure as hell aren't Jewish," Ira said. He put on his coat and stuffed his fists into the pockets and left.

Outside Ira eased his anger by muttering curses at Taziola. He wondered what the hazel-eyed little pope's-toe-kissing bastard was up to. He didn't know and he didn't like it.

He lost his way trying to find the gate, then he saw the light ahead, a lantern where the guards stood — the hired guards, Luka's guards, the bankers' and warehousemen's, the pimps' and tarts' guards.

A terrible feeling of remorse swept over Ira, not only for the heaps of men in the earth barracks, but for himself and for Taziola too. They were both enamored of systems. For Taziola it was economics, for him it was something called jurisprudence. His concern for the men in the earth barracks was as abstract as Taziola's appreciation of the economic system which had sprung up in the camp. It touched no person. His shock at seeing the hack-faced Hussar had nothing to do with compassion; he had only wanted to get away, to pay the man and spare himself. Most of his life had been like this, a flight from feeling.

A few days ago he'd killed a boy, dead, on the tracks. Just a kid in big boots. He had been stunned; his face, his whole body had expressed regret and sorrow, not for the life of the boy, but for the nasty trick fate had played him. If the same bullet had ripped the life out of a big, healthy muzhik partisan he would have still expressed his regret, yes, but tempered by pride because warfare was a system which approved such a thing. The system didn't quite allow for killing a boy and it was this deficiency in the system which he had regretted, not the death of the boy.

The Czech guard at the gate recognized him and Ira asked for a droshky. The guard motioned him to wait under the lantern and went off.

Ira watched the people coming in and out of the prison camp. Soldiers, townsfolk, peasants, women of who knows what repute, merchants coming to stock up on imitation Faber 2B pencils and chocolate eggs for the iron cock. He watched them closely for a sign, a flickering recognition of his existence, a little acknowledgment. He wanted the passers-by to smile forgivingly and to say with their tender eyes: "We know how it is, brother.

Accidents will happen. It's God's will. The boy was in the wrong place. We're sorry for you, brother, so don't punish yourself."

But they all seemed to lower their eyes and avoid him.

Ira sought the faces of the crowd for a pair of eyes, any eyes, to meet his own however briefly. He singled out a curiously familiar figure of a woman approaching the gate and watched her hopefully. She wore a shawl which half covered her head and as she came into the light she looked at him. Her eyes grew wide, then she ran past him into the compound.

"Maryenka!"

Ira ran calling her name at the top of his voice, thrusting people aside in his effort to find her in the darkness.

He ran, stumbling through the massed bodies, turning this way and that, trying to get a glimpse of her again. Twice he accosted women who screeched in terror. He paused, wondering to whom he could appeal for help. He thought of Taziola and tried to find the barracks building which housed the German Theater. He asked directions, lost his way, continued to shout for Maryenka, then at last he found the theater and dashed into the box occupied by Taziola, Sipialef and Whyte. His frenzied expression brought them to their feet.

"Taz! I've just seen Maryenka!"

Taziola's expression was one of total confusion.

"Maryenka Austin! I just saw her at the gate. She's not dead!"

"Calm down, for God's sake."

"We've got to find her!"

"Now wait a minute," Taz said judiciously. "Did she see you?"

"Of course she did! We weren't two feet apart."

"Then how did you lose her?"

"She ran away! Into the compound. It was dark."

"Why did she do that?" Taz asked.

"Do what?"

"Run away!"

This stopped Ira. He looked at Sipialef and Whyte standing at the table with their dinner napkins clutched in their hands. A musical number began on the stage. Luka and his captain were no longer in the box across the way.

"I don't know," Ira said.

"Come out for a minute," Taziola said. He took Ira's arm firmly and excused himself to Sipialef and Whyte. Captain Whyte tapped his lips with his napkin and resumed his seat. "Certainly," he said.

Sipialef was scowling, his eyes bare slits in his masked face. "If you describe this person I could locate her for you," he said.

Ira resisted Taziola's attempt to pull him into the corridor. "Her name is Maryenka Austin," he said to Sipialef. "She married one of our sergeants. We thought she'd been killed at Pashkova, but I've just seen her!"

Sipialef nodded and sat down. "I'll do what I can," he said.

Taziola let go of Ira's arm and looked at him with a hard, accusing glare. "It couldn't have been Mrs. Austin," he said. "She wouldn't have run from you. It was someone who looked like her."

"No," Ira insisted. "It was Maryenka."

"Ira, you're stirred up. Any number of women might have looked like her in that light. If Mrs. Austin was alive she'd have every reason to get in touch with us. Isn't that right? Well, isn't it?"

"I know what I saw," Ira said, but he was already unsure of himself. He had been agitated. The light was bad and he could think of no reason for Maryenka to have run from him.

"The fact is that you haven't seen one damned thing straight since you came into this place," Taziola declared. "You need a good night's sleep. Sorry I insisted that you come."

The curt tone of dismissal in Taziola's voice caused Ira's face to blaze with indignation. "I know what I saw, Major," he said and he left without another word.

For a moment Major Taziola stared at the curtain through which Ira had gone; he seemed to be gathering his thoughts, then he sighed heavily and returned to the table with a cordial smile. "The Lieutenant has been under a great deal of pressure," he said. "I hadn't realized how much."

"This woman he speaks of was married to one of your sergeants?" Sipialef asked.

"We've established beyond doubt that she's dead, Colonel. The matter is closed."

"Yet he sees her."

"Someone like her. He mistook another person for her."

"Is he often like this?" Captain Whyte asked.

"All of us imagine things at times, isn't that so, Captain?"

"Yes, perhaps," Colonel Sipialef said and they finished their meal in contemplative silence while the chorus on the stage sang parodies of German beer hall airs.

Ira walked back to the gate where the Czech guard had a droshky but thought he'd lost his customer. Ira tipped him and stepped aboard. The driver clouted his horse and the vehicle headed for Verkhne-Udinsk at a slow trot.

Why had she run? Why that look of terror?

Had he forgotten what she looked like?

No. It was Maryenka.

"You know it was," Ira said aloud, then he nodded and settled back listening to the horse hoofs on the wooden road. He shut his eyes and saw Maryenka's startled face again. He was not mistaken.

Her avoidance of him had been purposeful. She had recognized and run from him.

He had been meaning to look into the Pashkova affair. Yes, his intentions had been good. His intentions at Siding 85 and during the partisan attack had been good, but the result in both cases was death. She must have recognized his good intentions and fled from them as she would have from a murderer.

Ira sighed and wondered how he would expiate his good intentions. To find her was a beginning, at least.

Carlisle had warned him against prying into the Pashkova affair. Well, to hell with Carlisle.

It was Maryenka. He was sure of it. She was alive.

CHAPTER TWENTY-FOUR

BECAUSE of the great numbers of prisoners exiled to Siberia it had been a long-standing practice of the authorities to pay a reward for the recapture of those who attempted to escape and native huntsmen, particularly the Buryats, Yakuts and Mongols, were always hopeful of finding such a prize to augment their scanty income.

Escaping prisoners unlike animal quarry, a bear or a wolf, were usually exhausted and fell into the arms of their captors babbling with relief at having been rescued from death by starvation or exposure. But since the reward was paid for delivery dead or alive the dispassionate hunter had to decide if his prey was strong enough to make the return journey under his own power, or if it would be simpler to haul him in dead. Even while expressing their gratitude for being saved many prisoners had seen a calculating look in the hunter's eyes, and before their horror could register their throats were cut and they were hung up by the heels to drain like any other animal.

To discourage desertions the Kolchak government extended this old system of rewards to include soldiers who could not produce the proper documents, tickets of leave, or travel orders. One hundred rubles were paid for each officer and fifty for each enlisted man recaptured dead or alive.

This was intended primarily as a psychological deterrent to desertion and much was made of the lone hunters who lurked in the woods waiting to pounce on their hapless human prey, but the effect of this was not as desired. Deserters either went over to the enemy, whose propaganda guaranteed their safety, or they left the front in groups large enough to fight off those who might attack them.

Nevertheless traffic in recaptured prisoners and deserters increased appreciably. Word spread through the forests and borderlands and the hunters, unaware of inflation or of the dubious value of Kolchak currency, did not hesitate to stalk and capture any man traveling alone. Of course these hunters could not read and in the early months some of them, after having packed a soldier's corpse for miles to a military post, found themselves charged with murder because their captive had legitimate papers. It did not take many reverses of this kind before the hunters learned to destroy all documents a soldier carried and in no case to bring a captive in alive so he might give testimony. The military authorities were thus confronted with a situation of paying rewards on the prima facie evidence of a corpse in remnants of a soldier's uniform or of abandoning the system altogether.

To have asked the hunters to wait for verification of the soldier's identity would have scared them off and in any case there were no adequate military records. So the officials were in something of a quandary. Recognizing the impossibility of policing the backlands and alarmed by the increasing desertion factor the Kolchak authorities decided to pay the posted rewards without questions. Thus they established a more vicious traffic than even they intended, for now all a hunter had to produce to collect his reward was a male corpse in a uniform, preferably an officer's uniform.

Some of the more sophisticated hunters found they could buy ragged secondhand uniforms very cheaply since deserters of all ranks were anxious to exchange these for civilian garb. A hunter could buy a used captain's blouse for six or seven rubles, then all he needed was a body to clear a profit; and soon the military found themselves paying rewards on some very unlikely subjects, old men dressed as coronets, youngsters with the insignia of full colonels, and even on some bodies which had obviously been exhumed.

Examples were made of a few hunters who violated all common sense as, for instance, one who tried to pass off an old woman as a corporal. He was given fifty lashes instead of fifty rubles and two weeks later was himself delivered in the uniform of a major.

The authorities tried to prevent these hunters from hunting on the city streets and after several arrests managed to drive them back into the forests, but the traffic between them and the secondhand clothing dealers was maintained and it was common knowledge that most hunters carried a uniform as part of their equipment.

What this meant, of course, was that no one was safe traveling alone and when Carlisle announced his intention of returning to Verkhne-Udinsk by cart the Russian officers garrisoned at Irkutsk tried to discourage him. Captain Swerdloff was particularly vehement.

"You're a fool, sir! An absolute fool. What's to be gained by it?"

"I want to see the trakt," Carlisle said.

Swerdloff smacked his head. "The trakt," he cried. "The trakt is a road! There's nothing to see. We can give you a complete description of it. Your obstinancy is astounding. The whole Zai-Baikal area is infested with partisans, Bolsheviks, hunters. I haven't heard of one person making that journey alone." Swerdloff looked around at the other officers, who confirmed this assertion.

"I haven't heard of anyone foolish enough to try," Potapov said. "There's a hunter rumored to work the southern tip of Baikal who stacks his corpses and sells them in wholesale lots at twenty-five rubles apiece; the purchasers supply the uniforms and make delivery. A nice business, eh? You don't want to go through there, my friend. You'd end up a hundred ruble corpse. Imagine our shock at such a thing. If you must go we'll give you a detachment of cavalry."

Carlisle shook his head. "No," he said. "I'll wire you from Verkhne-Udinsk." He started to leave but Lieutenant Grachev caught his arm.

"I'll go with you then," Grachev said earnestly. "Or I'll follow you, so it's not just your life that's risked, but mine also."

The warmth of this declaration confused Carlisle. There was something demanding and petulant about it which disturbed him, yet he liked Grachev and knew he would do as he said.

Potapov laughed and clapped his hands. "There, you've done it, Grachev! Now he'll accept the cavalry or we may lose our darling."

Grachev's face went crimson behind his frothy golden beard but he said nothing and he released Carlisle's arm.

"We may get a chance at this hunter who haunts the rim of the lake," Swerdloff said. "Time someone put a stop to him, but we've never had an excuse. They say the other hunters are terrified of him, won't go near his hunting ground except to barter for corpses with shotgun shells."

Since his arrival at Irkutsk, Carlisle had been the object of special attention by members of the Russian-English Club composed of officers of the Third Siberian Army Corps. Their garrison was located in barracks two miles west of the town at Volnie Gorodoff, but while Carlisle was in town the club members congregated at the Hotel Metropole, a two-story wood and log structure with balconies, peaks and ells near the intersection of Bolshava and Amurskaya streets.

Irkutsk, with a population of a hundred and forty thousand, was saved from being utterly squalid by the Angara River which cut through it like the letter S, giving a pleasant view from the two large public squares. The massive Irkutsk Cathedral rose above the one-story wooden houses and this, with the public theater, the city museum and the observatory located on the river gave the city a skyline without which it would have been monotonously flat and depressing.

The Angara River was very swift and a pontoon bridge connected the main part of the city, on the eastern bank, with the western suburb called Glaskov where the train station and yards were located. In the winter, when the Angara froze, the bridge was detached and swung against the east bank and the crossing from the city to the railroad station was made over the ice.

These were the details Carlisle had come to learn and which he recorded in his notebook. The military importance of Irkutsk did not escape him; it guarded the western entrance of the narrow Baikal neck extending eastward to Verkhne-Udinsk and could unquestionably stop the flow of traffic by road, train, or river in either direction, east or west.

Carlisle had been surprised by the cordiality of his reception by the Russian officers of the garrison. That they were currently superfluous — the Army was staging maneuvers in the mountains east of the city and there were too many officers for the men — did not wholly account for their friendliness.

Carlisle was pleased to find that these men did not regard him as a curiosity, a bronze, hard-faced, half-caste American Indian who happened to be a captain, and he found himself being more open with them than with any group he could remember. Of course there were moments of doubt when he wondered if they hadn't received orders from Omsk to entertain him, to learn what he was up to, perhaps, but he was circumspect about his mission, and his friends asked no questions and treated him with disarming candor.

Sometimes he felt like an absolute dandy, foppish and ridiculous, then he laughed, startlingly, for no apparent reason and the Russians he was with laughed too.

Swerdloff was gazing at him with a lazy smile on his lips and Grachev, having recovered his composure after Potapov's allusion to his effeminate appearance, was also waiting for Carlisle's response.

Fat Potapov returned from the hotel bar and announced he'd ordered drinks all around to celebrate their intention to sweep the southern tip of Baikal with a cavalry action of unprecedented glory.

Carlisle knew he was being coerced with the kindest intentions, but he didn't want his trip encumbered by cavalry, by Grachev's tender enthusiasms, or by Swerdloff dashing off after an unknown hunter who, if he had any brains, would spot the cavalry coming for miles. He wanted to be alone, whatever the risk, to make his own assessment of the roads and trails. Also it was necessary to conceal the nature of his mission. If they came along he couldn't make notes and examine the area without rousing their curiosity. But most of all he wanted time to think about Tatiana.

"I've heard it said he has no hands," Swerdloff was saying, "just stumps at the wrist, but that he manages to load and fire his gun with deadly accuracy. The Buryats swear he's a monster and have abandoned the whole southern rim of the lake to him, like to a rogue tiger or a bear."

"Then it's settled, Captain," Grachev said. "When will you leave? Swerdloff will arrange the escort and we'll all come along."

"I'll be at least three days here," Carlisle said.

"Excellent," Swerdloff declared. "By then I'll have everything in order. Depend on it."

But that same night Carlisle made his own arrangements. The light two-wheeled cart he hired had a wattle body like a large basket, big enough to hold him and his equipment, sleeping bag, extra robes, food and weapons. He chose a stalwart Siberian pony, tossed a supply of hay into the cart to cushion his ride and feed the beast, and at midnight he crossed the pontoon bridge over the Angara and set his course for Lake Baikal.

He felt free and enormously exhilarated. He wanted to sing and would have done so if he had known an appropriate song, but when the lights of Irkutsk fell behind he stopped and removed the bell from the wooden yoke over the pony's neck, then he went on with only the sound of the hoofs weighed against the silence.

"Tatiana." He said her name aloud. "I'm a fool," he said and he kept repeating this over and over, a fool, a fool, to the steady sound of the pony hoofs on the road. But fool or not, he was childishly happy, a bit ashamed to be behaving like a colt in a green field, but wanting also to make this wildness last. He hugged himself, laughed aloud and urged his pony to a trot. "Oh, you bastard," he said lovingly. And the pony as though affronted by these words broke into a choppy canter throwing clods of earth from his unshod hoofs as they sped down the Angara Valley toward Baikal.

Carlisle reached the lake before dawn and stopped on a hill to rest his pony and stretch his legs. The vast inland sea, surrounded by mountains, was shrouded by a heavy gray-brown mist which began to rise at the first appearance of the sun, and gradually the lake was revealed. It was perfectly still, with a secondary wisp of evaporation lying on its surface like silky fur. The dark columns and vaulting buttresses of mist were suddenly replaced by shafts of sunlight which struck down hard and brazed dazzling spots on the lake surface and then, having breached the mist, the light swept over the lake like a razor, leaving it clean-shaven, smooth and silent.

Overawed by the change, Carlisle laid one hand on the warm neck of his pony. A breeze touched his cheek. The lake awakened with a sigh and waves began splashing among the rocks along the shore. Two sleek-headed, fresh-water seals popped to the surface and looked toward the horse and man, then swam to one of the meadows of waterweed which spotted the lake.

Carlisle boarded his cart and drove on to the town of Baikal, where he spent an hour making notes on the docking facilities and the passenger capacities of the Baikal ferries; then he turned southward for his journey around the end of the lake on the trakt.

He let the pony set its own pace and recorded his observations, but the stubby pencil was frequently idle in his hand. Often he came back with a start and thought: "Christ! Someone may have to depend on these notes. What am I thinking of?"

The sun-soaked wattle basket rocked gently between the light wheels raising a trail of dust which obscured the road behind him and he thought about Tatiana, not by name but as a tension in which he was suspended, a sling held at one end by the hope that she thought well of him and at the other by the fear that she did not think of him at all. But as the morning wore on he filled several pages in his notebook with topographical sketches, trying as he did so to interpolate what the landscape would be in wintertime.

The red earth road skirted the lake, passing through a forest of pine which gave way in places to a view of a bay or a rocky island thrust up from the water like a crumbling castle. There was no traffic and squirrels or sometimes a deer, caught in a shaft of sunlight, stood motionless watching him pass with timid curiosity.

A breeze through the pine needles carried their fragrance and the blue lake flashing among the tree trunks had a hypnotic effect so that twice Carlisle found himself dozing. He fought sleep, warning himself that the famed carcass hunter of Baikal could slip up on him and cut his throat in an instant, but he was amused rather than alerted. Tales of this kind were always exaggerated by garrison troops who had no better way to improve their time. Still, it would not do to sleep, so he often walked along beside his pony.

At noon Carlisle found a narrow road leading south, and assuming it would intersect the railroad he left the trakt and after an hour came to a point where he could see the first of the Baikal tunnels below. He paused here to feed himself and his pony and study the tunnels, which were cored in solid granite. The stonework was massive and he judged it would take an expert demolition team to block them. He considered this problem with mild interest as he ate, estimating how much explosive he would call for if given the task.

He heard a train laboring down the line from the east and waited for it to appear. It came slowly, snuffling through the tunnels, an evil-looking armored train flying the green and white Kolchak pennant. Its wheels scraped and grated and a number of troops were sprawled on the roofs of the wagons taking the sun. Carlisle guessed they were part of the Third Siberian Army Corps returning to Irkutsk after their maneuvers.

As the train entered another tunnel the men who were standing dropped down, but one of them, clowning for the benefit of the others, ran along, jumping from car to car, waving his arms frantically and cackling like an hysterical hen. At the last minute he threw himself flat and was swallowed by the tunnel with a look of mock horror on his face.

Carlisle laughed. He admired the big loose-limbed Russian soldiers who, for all their lack of smartness, equipment and training, had a quality of endurance which only needed good leadership to translate it into victories. They were patient, good-humored and hard-working. It took a great amount of abuse to discourage them, but their officers at the front had succeeded in doing so, judging from the numbers of deserters reported to be roving the backlands.

Carlisle packed up, returned to the trakt and set off at a fast pace. There was wind now from the lake, which had darkened and grown choppy, and there were caves of deep shade on both sides of the road. Carlisle slapped his pony to a run. The wattle basket in which he sat cross-legged and hunched down swayed dangerously as the wheels clattered over rocky stream beds which intersected the road.

He could not remember having been alone for years. He'd always been surrounded by men, living a communal existence, always in pairs, he and Austin, or in squads, platoons, companies. Barracks life, bivouac life, whore house life, but all of it shared.

The pony galloped down the road with the cart, careening on one wheel then another, but after perhaps a mile of this Carlisle pulled up, wondering what it was he had been running from. His aloneness? How foolish! He sat in the cart, listening intently. What was it?

He searched the shadows among the trees and his scalp tingled. A mood of dark uneasiness came over him and he thought of Austin.

He couldn't account for this. The man was dead.

He heard a sound.

A horseman appeared ahead of him!

Carlisle's heart was hammering and there was a wildness in his mind, a horror of seeing Austin riding toward him. He saw the rider through the mottled shadows, through the bars of light and shadow which obscured his features; then with a joyous shout he galloped forward and dismounted with a graceful swing of his smoothly booted leg.

It was Lieutenant Grachev.

Carlisle drew a sharp breath of relief.

Grachev stood a moment beside his horse with an anonymous, tender smile on his face. "I'd given you up, Captain," he said reproachfully. Then he stepped forward and offered his hand, which Carlisle took. "Have you been hiding from me? I picked up your trail at Baikal and rode like the wind until I was convinced you could not have covered such a distance as I had done. So I had turned back, but here you are and I'm delighted. Have you been hiding then, or what?"

Grachev's light blue eyes played over Carlisle's face brushing the features for an answer to his question and Carlisle, still a bit stunned, clapped his other hand over Grachev's and shook it gratefully. "I turned off," he said, "to look at some of the tunnels."

"You didn't think I'd follow as I said I would?"

Again there was a mixture of taunting amusement and petulance in the question. Carlisle shook his head and released Grachev's hand. "I wasn't thinking about it," he said.

"What were you thinking about that carried you away without a word to anyone? And you deceived us into the bargain. Poor Swerdloff will be upset when he discovers we've flown."

"I was anxious to get back," Carlisle said lamely.

"In spite of the danger?"

"It looks peaceful enough to me," Carlisle said gesturing to the silent forest around them.

"I, for one, am relieved not to have to spend the night alone. I expect you think that's timid? Well, so it is. I've raced my horse all day and the poor beast is played out. Just as I saw you I was about to dismount and lead him though I'm exhausted myself. You've run me a terrible chase, Captain."

"I didn't intend to."

"All the same," Grachev said and he looked around with a heavy sigh. "I could do with some rest. We should find a place to put in for the night."

"I'd planned to travel through."

"But no!" Grachev protested. "I'm done in and so is my horse. Here, yours is lathered too! I think you were trying to outdistance me. You knew I'd follow, isn't that so?"

Carlisle shook his head, at a loss to explain why he'd raced his pony.

Grachev's eyes darkened and he drew himself up with a look of injured pride. "Well, if you're not pleased to see me, of course," he said and he took his horse by the bridle and made as if to start walking down the road.

"But I am!" Carlisle cried and he was alarmed by the intensity of his own voice.

Grachev returned at once with a quick, forgiving look in his beautiful eyes.

"You might have said so."

"You've come a long way for no reason," Carlisle said gruffly.

Grachev shook his head and smiled as though he were admonishing a child. "Reasons are no good in any case. It's an adventure. If you insist on poking on through the night, at least invite me into the cart. That way one can stay awake while the other sleeps and we can switch horses if need be."

Grachev's smooth, gentle face seemed to grow pale in the lengthening shadows as though a rebuff at this point would kill him. He was frightened and defensive, but so was Carlisle. "All right, let's go," he said roughly.

With this invitation Grachev's whole manner changed. He tethered his horse to the rear of the cart and bounded in with Carlisle, who pressed over to make room. Grachev seemed completely refreshed and lively. He sat in the bulging wattle basket struggling with his boots and talking in a breathless way. "What extraordinary luck it is after all," he said. "We could have missed each other hundreds of places. My feet are blazing! These boots belonged to Potapov's brother and they're too large, so no matter how I wrap my feet they slide and blister. But he'd done so well by the leather I couldn't resist them. Not every leather takes such a sheen and they're dry enough as far as I know. There! Lord, I feel as though I'd come out of prison!"

Grachev tucked his boots down in front of the cart and stretched his legs, which shivered like the flesh of a nervous horse. "What luck it is!" he exclaimed again. "My God, the air is sweet at dusk. Have you any wine? I drank my last at Baikal and was in such a race I neglected to get more. I'm thirsty as a nomad. Whatever you have will do — and if you have nothing, that'll do too, we'll touch the lake again in a verst or so."

Carlisle drove on and produced a pint bottle of vodka from which Grachev took three strong swallows, coughing and laughing together. "You'll have to talk to keep me awake. I expected wine. I'll doze off at once, I swear. Tell me about America. I dream of it. I'd give an arm to go there and I know nothing about it. Tell me about the cities, about New York. I dream about New York every morning. I'm a stranger to myself each morning because I've come from the streets of New York. My neck hurts from looking up at all the buildings. My ears are filled with English, the sound of automobile horns, machinery, subway trams and the crowds. You've been there of course and can tell me about it. I read every scrap I get, but it's not the same. One day, I swear, I'll fall asleep and live the rest of my life in New York. You must tell me."

Grachev lay back comfortably; his charm and indolent, catlike grace made Carlisle uneasy. The relationships between Russian men confused him; they kissed each other, walked arm in arm, held hands, confided their tenderest thoughts to one another and it was possible that Grachev's behavior was in this tradition. Instinct told Carlisle this was not so, but he was unsure. He had never been to New York, but to avoid another, perhaps more leading subject, he pretended he had been and as the last light faded from the sky Carlisle gave his impressions of a place to which neither he nor Grachev had been.

New York as Carlisle imagined it was not the New York of Grachev's dreams. It was a harsh place inhabited by big businessmen, bankers, lawyers and politicians who controlled the rest of the country through deceit and chicanery. Carlisle's native resentment of city people poured out and he pictured New York as a vicious conglomeration of bloodsuckers in a hell of brick and concrete which they'd thrown up to protect themselves from those whom they'd swindled. All the women were cheap and grasping, the men fat and avaricious, and it was no place for a decent man to live.

After a bit Grachev stirred. "What happened to you there?" he asked.

"Nothing," Carlisle said.

"Something terrible, I think."

"No."

"I've never heard of a New York like this."

"That's how it is."

"You must have had a disappointment, a tragedy."

Carlisle edged away, but there was no room in the small basket for their bodies without touching.

"It sounds to me like a love gone bad," Grachev said.

"No," Carlisle said bluntly.

"I hate Petrograd and all who occupy Petrograd for the same reason. When I think of Petrograd I long to put it to the torch. All my shame is there and I want to burn it out. Either that or go to New York."

"You won't find much there."

"It won't be the same for me as for you."

"What happened to you in Petrograd?" Carlisle asked.

Grachev sighed. He'd removed his cap and his fine, light hair stood up in the breeze. His head was cradled in one arm resting on the edge of the basket and his eyes seemed to capture all the light of the stars and of the pale half-moon which had risen above the trees. He smiled in his frighteningly tender, indefinable way. "Ah," he said, "in Petrograd I was in love. The universe was too small to encompass it. How two beings unknown to each other can strike such fire, can make such hell, such paradise, of a look exchanged between them in a crowded place I can't explain. But we know it. Before it happens we know it will happen and of five hundred people in a theater, or the street or at a ball one pair of eyes will leap out. One's heart stops with astonishment; the people vanish and two souls are exchanged."

Grachev paused and shifted his position to see Carlisle more clearly. "I believe love is an exchange of souls," he said earnestly. "Yes, I believe that. You feel the beauty of the other person too intimately for it to have anything to do with the senses. It's from inside, this experience. It springs up, a fresh existence, new attitudes, new insights, new pleasures, new fears. You experience the loved one by looking into yourself, a paradox I know and one I can't explain, but I know how it was in my case.

"Of course there's terror in this. It comes of being afraid that the soul you've exchanged, your own, now in the possession of another, won't bear scrutiny. What horror! One trembles, feels a poor miserable thing, and each day that passes without rejection is a miracle. And gradually one begins to take confidence in the value of one's own soul, and love becomes a reassurance, for if another is willing to keep one's soul it can't be such an awful thing. Not as bad as one thought it to be. But terrible things can happen. One is that you begin to long for your own soul, which has proven not to have been so bad after all, and you grow jealous of the person who possesses it. The other is that there are certain promiscuous people who, having examined one soul superficially, will exchange it for yet another. That, of course, is the most perfidious thing one person can do to another."

Grachev was silent and the cart moved on steadily through the darkness. The following horse trotted along obediently, the sound of his hoofs intermeshed with those of the pony ahead, so two riders seemed to be traveling the road side by side. A streak of moon on the lake gave light through the tree trunks on Carlisle's side but the darkness was intense on the other.

"What do you think of this?" Grachev asked presently.

"Which of these things happened to you?" Carlisle asked.

"I was betrayed," Grachev said sorrowfully. "I was left with the soul of a promiscuous girl and condemned for the rest of my life to search for my own."

This was so bizarre, so extenuating and yet so explicit that Carlisle turned to Grachev with a cutting remark on his lips, but there was such an imploring look in Grachev's eyes that Carlisle was seized by a vertigo which left him weightless, spinning through the blue night of Grachev's eyes where he saw the girl who had taken Grachev's soul, saw clearly the thoughtless tender smile on her lovely face, saw she was faithless, saw that what Grachev had told him was true.

"So you see," Grachev said quietly.

"No," Carlisle said and he drew himself away stiffly once again as Grachev adjusted his position in the cart. "I don't see," he said.

Grachev laid his head back on the edge of the basket and staring into the dark sky spoke dreamily as the cart jogged on through the forest.

He'd met the girl, Nelya, at a ball in Petrograd. Her father, a count, close to the court and very rich, had plans for his daughter's marriage of which she did not approve. With a glance she had awakened Grachev's love. She was beautiful, no more than a child, alternately playful and grave, innocent, charming.

Within a month they had exchanged vows and given their souls into each other's keeping. Grachev gave his trembling for its unworthiness but Nelya bestowed her soul with the calm assurance that it could not fail to please him. For days thereafter Grachev stayed in bed, afraid to move for fear of crushing the fragile soul which she had imparted to him.

When at last he rose again he walked carefully, talked softly and was gentle. His person was easily offended. He avoided his rough comrades, foul language, low boisterous places, because he did not wish to besmirch Nelya's delicate soul. His comrades noticed the change and joked about it. "Grachev is in love," they said. But of course they were mistaken. Love was in Grachev. He cherished himself only because he was the repository of Nelya's soul; he groomed and clothed himself elegantly for this reason alone, to be worthy of her soul.

For nearly a year he was happy, focused inward, glorying in that which he secretly contained.

But one afternoon as they sat by a pond on her father's estate Grachev detected a curious unfamiliarity in Nelya. At first he couldn't account for this; then in her eyes, which for him had become the windows to his own soul, he saw another's.

At once he was filled with terror. His soul was no longer present in her. "Nelya! What have you done?" he cried.

"Illyusha, forgive me, I was dissatisfied."

"But what has become of my soul?" Grachev cried. "Where is it now?"

"I exchanged it for another," she said wistfully.

"Nelya! You can't have done such a thing!"

"I've found a lover," she said, "I'm sorry."

"But you can't satisfy him!" Grachev protested. "My soul won't please him and it's mine, not your own, which you've exchanged!"

And she smiled in a way which Grachev had never been able to understand.

Carlisle looked at Grachev, who had broken off, and found him smiling in his peculiarly mocking yet infinitely tender way.

"This is her smile, you see," Grachev said. "She left me this smile and her inconstant feminine soul. These are all I have."

He drew a breath and sighed. "Imagine what it is to live this way. To be misunderstood, rejected, to be always searching for the soul you gave away. I've found that most people don't know their own souls, can't recognize them in themselves and therefore couldn't recognize them in another. They exchange souls as easily as hats and don't know from one week to the next if they contain the soul of a woman or a man or if they have one at all, for this is possible too.

"I've never given up the pursuit of mine, though with the war I lost track of it. Nelya's lover gave it to a wealthy Russian woman. When I approached her for it she turned me away with the same accusation her lover had used when I approached him. So you see, I'm regarded by all alike as something unnatural — which, I suppose, is true for who, in these times, can understand a person in search of his soul?"

Carlisle shook his head to dispel the persuasive urgency of Grachev's gentle voice. It was all madness; Grachev's way of justifying his effeminacy, but among the Sioux —

Carlisle frowned darkly and continued shaking his head like a bear brought to bay by a pack of dogs, but among the Dakota tribes the shamans captured the spirits even of beasts, and the spirits of men frequently patrolled the night searching for rest. His objection to buying a secondhand gift for Tatiana was that it would be contaminated by the spirit of its previous owner. Her note which he'd carried for so long in his breast pocket had been so powerfully charged with her spirit that it had nearly driven him mad. And how else could he account for the difference in himself since leaving Omsk except that he and Tatiana had exchanged something during their last few moments together? But all these were matters for the old bone-rattling shamans of his youth which he had abjured. He would not go back to that. No, he refused to be driven back to the primitive superstitions of his Indian youth.

Grachev sat up and put one hand on Carlisle's forearm. "When I first saw you in Irkutsk you had the stamp of a person who would understand. I'm very sensitive to this; it shows in the eyes. Am I mistaken?"

Carlisle did not answer but Grachev accepted his silence for acquiescence and lay back in the cart with a sigh. "Then you do believe me. You understand. My God, what a relief! In this world of exchanging souls I wait hoping to recapture mine. The chance is slight, but I wait all the same and when I see a person such as yourself I approach him. You understand, don't you, my dear Carlisle? You must! I approach with terrible fear. I approach with Nelya's soul to exchange for that of another, any other! I have no pride, you see."

Grachev's voice broke. There were tears in his eyes and he was trembling uncontrollably. "Take Nelya from me," he said beseechingly. "I'll do anything, anything at all because you have the power to relieve me of her. She's consuming me, Captain! I see it. I feel it! Each day she conquers a little more of me and soon I'll have nothing left to call my own. My very heartbeat has changed, Captain! But if you would be so strong as to take her, for a short time only, just until you found someone else to whom you could give her, it would be my salvation, Captain. Do you understand!"

Carlisle wanted to leap headlong from the cart. He wanted to strike Grachev's face glowing white so close to his own, the breath of it on his cheek, burning — the eyes of it, through which he saw the soul of Nelya, glacial and imploring. He believed it, all of it, believed the carved bone soul catchers of the shamans, believed the chanting incantations of the shadow dancers around the licking flames, believed in the spirits of rocks and trees, beasts and men, believed in his own soul and in the exchange of it.

Terror gripped him and a whimper rising in his throat through ages of raw longing burst forth in a wild cry which shattered the forest silence: "No! No, damn you! I won't be involved!"

The startled pony reared in the traces and began to gallop. Grachev's smooth face broke; his eyes went out, dark as extinguished lamps; then, as Carlisle brought the pony under control, he smiled graciously and they traveled on in silence.

For some time Carlisle had been troubled by a line which ran from tree to tree on his side of the cart. This caught the corner of his eye and he began to watch for it against the silver lake, a line through the trees, appearing again and again, and just when he knew what it was three men popped out on the road.

Caught in the moonlight they stood motionless straining all their senses. They seemed about to run when a deafening flash of sound and fire and a rage of heavy lead slashed from the darkness and cut them down.

One man rose from the tangled mass of bodies with a blind scream and staggered down the road hands upraised, his fingers clutching the air straining to be eyes.

Carlisle jerked the pony around and Grachev leaped from the cart.

A second blast caught the staggering man at close range and flesh-clotted pellets passing through his body clattered off through the trees.

Carlisle called for Grachev but got no answer.

The barrels of the gun rang sweetly as it closed on new shells. One of the downed men groaned in recognition of his death and Carlisle jumped from the cart warning Grachev not to move.

He drew his forty-five and crouching in the dark tried to locate the hunter.

Running feet! He turned toward the sound, but a black rising motion off to his right swung him around and he fired, arm tense against the kick of the pistol. Between the first and second shots, between the flash and smell of these two thundering shots, a horrible doubt filled Carlisle's mind. The object at which he had fired was gone. Was it Grachev? Then he heard bells and Grachev's cries of pain.

Carlisle ran to the voice and found Grachev trying to free himself from a set of barbed gang hooks attached to the rope which had trapped him. Carlisle slapped him to silence, but every move to free the hooks caused the cart bells on the line to ring. Alternating with the hooks and bells there were small red flags.

Expecting any second to hear an explosion and feel the hot impact of heavy shotgun pellets, Carlisle cut Grachev free and warned him again not to move, then he went stealthily back toward the object at which he had fired.

He found the man at the base of a hollow stump, sprawled there, still breathing and then, as Carlisle listened, not at all. He struck a light, turned the body over and was not surprised to recognize his wolf-hunting comrade; he had known the mellow sound of Yakushef's shotgun. But it was not the same Yakushef to whom he'd said goodbye at Tataurovo. One of his arms was gone at the elbow and his face, though unscarred, was arrested in an expression of blasted hopes and bitter desolation.

The match went out and Carlisle struck another as Grachev came through the trees.

Seeing the body Grachev sighed.

"I knew him," Carlisle said.

"What a pity it is," Grachev said quietly, and looking at Carlisle in the guttering light of the match he smiled Nelya's mysterious smile once more. "As miserable as this man was, I would gladly have exchanged Nelya's female soul for his. You see, my dear Carlisle, there is nothing I would not do to have the soul of a man."

The second match went out and in the darkness Carlisle felt a burning kiss, then Grachev hurried to the trakt, untethered his horse and rode off in the direction of Baikal.

For the remainder of the night Carlisle stayed beside Yakushef's body. He made a small fire, brought his cart from the trakt, and with his sleeping bag and robes around him he thought of the world of exchanging souls, of Yakushef's in flight, of Grachev's irretrievably lost, and of his own. He had not thought of it before. Indeed he had refused it recognition, but now he trembled because so much of his nature wanted to extinguish his Indian soul.

At dawn he went to the road and dragged the three men Yakushef had killed to a hollow place among the trees and covered them with earth. They were soldiers of the Third Siberian Army Corps who must have deserted the train he had seen the previous day.

He gathered the rope Yakushef had strung through the forest with its hooks, flags and bells. It made a great loop like the one he had used to circle the wolves, but a man, blundering into it, would draw Yakushef to him like a spider.

Taking in this rope brought forcibly to him the times he'd spent hunting wolves with Yakushef and his sons. He was so shaken by this recollection that he stopped with the rope over his shoulder and the bells jingled, tauntingly. Through the trees he could see the gray sheen of Lake Baikal. The ground at his feet was padded thick with pine needles and the sound of a train carried to him through the morning silence.

He looked around, feeling alone, all his instincts telling him to get back to the only thing he knew — back to his company, back to the safety of the pack.

Carlisle went to the cart, rolled Yakushef's broken body onto it and drove to the lake, where he found a place to bury the rope and the man. He did this quickly, unceremoniously, then he boarded the cart, snapped his pony to a gallop and sped on around the tip of the lake toward Murinskaya, where he could catch the train for Tataurovo.

CHAPTER TWENTY-FIVE

WITHIN three days of her arrival at Anitsky's cabin near the outskirts of Verkhne-Udinsk two facts struck Maryenka. The first was that she was pregnant. The second was that her husband, Sergeant Austin, was dead.

She had been seated by the stove considering the implications of her pregnancy when Anitsky returned from the city to tell her about Austin.

"I am sorry, my dear," he said quietly and began at once to prepare tea.

"Please, are you sure?" she asked.

"I knew before. But I made another inquiry."

"And you're sure," Maryenka said dully.

"I spoke to an American captain," Anitsky said. "Your sergeant was killed near Duaria by bandits before his company reached Verkhne-Udinsk."

"Ah," Maryenka said and this ragged syllable was her last complaint, for the facts of birth and death coming so close upon one another coalesced into a single conviction which was that the child in her womb was Austin's and for this reason alone it was her duty to live.

No other reason would have sufficed. Had she not been pregnant Maryenka would have killed herself.

As it was she experienced a searing fusion of mind and body into a fierce dedication to life, not only to her own, but also to that remnant of Austin's life which she bore.

The child was his. This was the cardinal principle of her continued existence. Her assertion that the child was Austin's, that it had to be his, was made incontrovertible by his death, for if there was a God, if there was compassion or justice, if there were compensations for suffering and loss, if love itself had any meaning, then the child was his. This she believed.

"You're smiling, my dear," Anitsky said as he offered her a glass of tea, and indeed she was. He had been prepared for tears, wailing, hysteria, but her calm smile unnerved him completely.

"I have his child," she said simply and she took the glass firmly.

"Ah, I see!" Anitsky cried. "I see. I see. I see!" and he whirled around so relieved that he actually danced a few steps. "Oh, I thought you'd gone mad! You had the beauty of madness on you. Extraordinary! Angels are mad, you see. All mad! All beautiful. They glow and fly about, carry on. Mad, you see! You were an angel and I was paralyzed, dear God, with terror! But motherhood! There's madness too, eh? What a world for infants! What a world, but they come! Complete madness. Overwhelming! New mothers and angels!"

Anitsky bustled about chattering continually. He was so lively and made so little sense that Maryenka was quite charmed by him. Ordinarily he slept in the morning after coming home from the Mulligan, but this morning he sensed Maryenka's need for company, and having a listener in the cabin was a new experience for him. He set the table and they ate a meal near the window, which framed a pleasant view of the Uda River. A path led from the porch through a grove of trees to the bank where one could sit and watch the steamers pass. The grass was high and there were dandelions and buttercups in it. Anitsky opened a pot of caviar taken from the Mulligan larder and spread it on his bread.

"Good waiters never starve, eh? New ones get the scraps, old ones take a share and the headwaiter lives like a prince. You'll be no trouble to keep, you see. They'll say 'Anitsky is trying to make himself fat,' and they'll wonder how it is I don't succeed. No one visits here, so you won't be bothered. You'll eat better than General Bogoloff's guests and rest as much as you like. Timokhin was right to bring you, though he's a crazy devil in every other way. Ah, now don't take offense. Timokhin has qualities I'll not deny. I knew him as a boy, wild to fight, like a fish in swift water, always moving, striking out, jumping upstream to what? God knows. But he was a marvel to watch. Flashing, you see. Exuberant."

Anitsky shuddered, took a swallow of tea and glanced toward the trees by the river.

"My heart stopped when he came out of the woods there. But for his eyes I wouldn't have known him. What things we do. What terrible things."

Maryenka said nothing. She ate generously, aware that she was enjoying the food, and this simple thing came as a surprise to her. She studied the piece of dark bread in her hand as though it could give reasons for her sense of returning life. The cadence of Anitsky's voice, the abrupt changes in his manner, one moment gay and inconsequential, the next filled with sorrow and dark questions, ran under her consciousness, supporting it like an idle boat on a warm sea. She didn't need to respond. Anitsky's voice and the bread in her hand were reasons enough to live. These and the child. Yes, Austin's child.

The first few days passed easily enough. At night Maryenka was alone in the stout log cabin, but she felt perfectly secure. The only precaution Anitsky advised was that she not light a lantern after dark in case some drunken marauders came out from town. She probably wouldn't have done so in any case. The warm glow through the oven grate gave enough light to satisfy her and in the evening after Anitsky went to work she often sat in the corner by the stove in languid contentment listening to the river and the boats and the small creatures in the yard beyond the door. These hours were as close to thoughtlessness as any she had known. Hours of sweet, blank existence which often phased into slumber.

In the mornings when Anitsky returned they ate together and then, after having chattered himself drowsy, Anitsky would sleep and she would walk along the river.

They were peaceful days. But gradually Maryenka's native industriousness asserted itself. She began to clean, to cook and to sew and Anitsky objected to this with unconcealed delight.

"Here, what's this! Diamonds in my windowpanes! I saw them flashing like heliographs from the edge of town. The steamer captains are rubbing their eyes and grounding their boats on sand bars. A dozen paddle-wheelers driven ashore by dazzled pilots. Why, it's a menace to navigation, these windows! And my shirts washed again! Are shirts so easy to come by that we wash the life out of them every other day? A little care, my dear! Unless I smudge my clothes a bit before going to work they'll suspect Anitsky has a woman in his house. They've noticed the changes already. 'Fine stitching,' Chukar says to me last night while he's passing with a loaded tray. 'Fine stitching in your britches, Anitsky,' and he gives me a smirk that deserved a mop in the face. 'I have a Singer sewing machine,' says I and now of course I'll have to buy one."

"What nonsense is that," Maryenka said.

"Nonsense, is it? Nonsense indeed! Chukar is a regular ferret. If he sees a lumpy stitch again you can be sure he'll ask what happened to my Singer and there'll be no end of it. You should have known to sew big, clumsy, uneven stitches, but now the damage is done."

Then Anitsky laughed and said he was lying. "My tongue is always ahead of my brain. Some day I'll have it tended to. Timokhin told me long ago: 'Anitsky, some day you'd better have your tongue tended to.' Some boys had been pounding the life out of me for the joy of it and because I'd accused one of them of stealing my pencil box, which, as it turned out, he had not done. Timokhin arrived and thrashed the lot and then thrashed me for refusing to fight the boy and when I was half senseless, but still babbling steady as a waterfall, he said: 'Anitsky, some day you'd better have your tongue tended to.' I never forgot it. Never had it tended to and Timokhin never stopped fighting. There's no wisdom in us. None. What we were we are and will be on the way to heaven. God save us all."

Amused and reassured by Anitsky's harmless chatter Maryenka found her interest in the world beginning to expand. For the first time since Timokhin had brought her to Anitsky she considered her appearance and tried to see herself in the little mirror Anitsky used for shaving, but she was so upset by the expression in her eyes that she burst into tears. Until she saw her own face she hadn't realized how deeply hurt she had been. She gave way completely and wept the whole morning out of pity for the face she had seen, out of pity for her reflected self. When it was over she felt stronger, but she didn't look in the mirror again.

That evening as they sat on the porch watching the river traffic Maryenka asked Anitsky if there would be work for her in Verkhne-Udinsk.

"Is it so bad for you here, then?" he asked, dismayed.

"I must manage for myself," she said.

"Well then," and he sighed heavily, "you should go to the Americans."

That she could or should do this had not occurred to Maryenka. Her instinct was to look after herself. "What would I say to them?" she asked.

"Tell them who you are."

"Maryenka."

"And Austin too, no?"

"Yes, Austin too."

"Well then, they have lots of money. They'll look after you. I know they collected money to be sent you when your husband was killed. I heard them talking about it. Colonel Sipialef himself added to the fund."

A shudder ran over Maryenka's body and hatred flashed in her eyes at the sound of Sipialef's name. Anitsky was shocked by her expression. Timokhin had told him about Glubov, not about Maryenka's captivity, but her terrible expression was enough for him to guess that she had lost more at Pashkova than even Timokhin knew.

"He is here then," Maryenka said presently.

"He's often at the Mulligan. Last night he was there."

"Sipialef?" she asked wonderingly.

Anitsky was uneasy. The look in her eyes had vanished too quickly.

She gazed at the river with her hands in her lap, then she folded them as though she had come to a decision. "The Americans and Sipialef are together at your restaurant? They eat together?"

"They're all fighting the Bolsheviks."

Maryenka shook her head and turned to Anitsky making an effort to understand this. "At Pashkova there were none."

"I don't know," Anitsky said nervously. "I don't know about such things."

"The Americans and Whites fought against Timokhin when he tried to free labor conscripts. He told me this."

"Timokhin always fights."

Maryenka was about to come to Timokhin's defense, but instead she stood up and walked to the edge of the porch. It was past time for Anitsky to have gone to work and she wished he would go.

Presently Anitsky went inside and returned with his coat. "Shall I tell the Americans then?" he asked quietly.

"Not yet. I'd rather look after myself until I can make up my mind," she said.

"But what's to consider?" Anitsky asked with a perplexed shrug. "They're rich! They can provide. There'll be a pension, undoubtedly. If you worked in town one of the Americans who knew you before would be certain to recognize you. What can you be thinking of?"

"Not just at once, please," Maryenka said earnestly. "Give me a day or so and I'll be off your hands."

Anitsky stepped back affronted and his hands fanned the air around his ears as though he were slapping hornets. "Is that what you think then? That I want to be rid of you! Have I complained, been stingy, made demands? Why, here now, you've filled my house, made it worth coming home to and you think I'd push you out? I was tempted not to tell you about the Americans, you see. Yes, tempted to make up other stories to keep you here, for I would keep you if I could, you see. There, I'm being honest. You're no burden to me. Money? I have money and what good is it to me? There in the settle is a fine collection of money, Kerensky rubles, Japanese rubles, Kolchak rubles, Russian, French, American money, given to me as tips, all dumped there in the settle. Lift up the seat and take your pick. Buy tickets to Vladivostok, to Omsk, to Petrograd if you wish. Bless my soul! I've found no use for it. I buy no food and few clothes. Take handfuls of it! Fill a stocking! I have as much use of money as I would have of two heads. Better two heads, for if one got chopped I'd have another to go by, but where does money buy a head? Take it all if you like.

I have no secrets from you. I'll do what you wish. I spoke of the Americans because I thought you'd want to know and you scold me for it."

Tears came to his eyes and he brushed them away indignantly.

Maryenka threw her arms around Anitsky and hugged him. "Oh," she cried. "Forgive me, please!"

Anitsky grew calm and sighed. "I'm an old fool," he said.

"No. I'm the fool."

Anitsky smiled. "Well then, we're fools together. Now let me be off."

He kissed her on both cheeks and went down the steps, but paused, looking back anxiously. "And you'll be here, then?" he asked.

"Oh, yes," she said.

"In the settle, if it's a comfort to you," he said, then he hurried off to town.

Nothing more was said about her leaving. Anitsky counted each day Maryenka remained as a blessing and she did her best to repay his kindness by seeming to be content. But she was not. One persistent dream disturbed her exceedingly.

In this dream she saw herself pressing through a crowd toward a table where Colonel Sipialef sat. She had a revolver in her hand. At the edge of the table she raised it and fired repeatedly into Sipialef's blank face and each shot made a feature where none had been before. The lump of white flesh at which she aimed exploded eyes, nose and mouth which combined an expression of utter contempt. The eyes particularly were unsurprised and contemptuous, staring at her as though she did not exist. When she could fire no more Sipialef laughed and thick blood spilled from his mouth and flowed across the tablecloth toward her and she backed away in horror as his laughter swelled into a wild roar which woke her up.

This dream was recurrent and Maryenka busied herself in a hundred small ways to keep from thinking of it. She argued it was not her place to do such a thing, but the dead of Pashkova, her father, her mother, her brother Sashenka, all cried out to be avenged. But Maryenka was restrained by her child. She could contemplate sacrificing her own life to kill Sipialef, but Austin's child? No, that she could not do.

But with this dream there came again a gnawing doubt as to whose child she was carrying. There was Glubov, Daddy Samson, Rodion, and she was often filled with bitterness at the thought that the Cossacks who had captured and raped her may have spared Sipialef's life. If she had been certain the child was fathered by one of the Cossack gunners her life would no longer be so important, indeed she would have spent it gladly to kill

Sipialef, but she was torn between this hatred and her love for Austin. Time and again she wondered if she was deluding herself. Her only defense against the awful dream was the assertion that her child was Austin's. She prayed a hundred times each day that this was so, but the doubt persisted and so did the dream.

Out of all this there came one thing. She would not go to the Americans. If it was true, as Anitsky said, that they were allied with such men as Sipialef she would not compromise herself so much as to ask their help. Since Austin's death they were no longer a part of her life and it was better so, better not to rake up old things.

After several days of this mental turmoil Maryenka decided she would have to find work or she would lose her mind. So one evening after Anitsky had gone to the Mulligan she took some money from the settle where Anitsky deposited his nightly tips. She left a receipt for this, pulled a shawl over her head and went to Verkhne-Udinsk.

She had nothing more in mind than to reconnoiter the place and she did so keeping in the shadows to avoid the soldiers who roved the streets in packs. Twice she was approached by women who offered her a place in one of the houses of prostitution and one of these, irritated by her refusal, made a crude gesture. "Go to Beresovka then if it's drudgery you're after."

"And what is Beresovka, please?" Maryenka asked.

The woman laughed. "They'll find a use for you there and leave your legs alone. That's where all the sewers drain."

Maryenka nodded courteously and the woman, struck by her manner, caught her arm. "If you're serious there's a way," she said quickly. "Some of the prisoners there aren't half bad. They make things, but need someone to sell for them. Anyone can go in, but only the important prisoners can come out. There's one I know of, an Austrian, Muller, who makes ladies' undergarments, silk and lace, quite the finest to be had, but he's ashamed to sell them himself. He was a captain. A bit odd, as who might not be after four years, but talented. He needs someone to peddle his things. The girl who did it before is in my house now. You should see her in the things Muller made! She's a fat thing, but marvelous in Muller's pantaloons. Go to Muller and say Glushenka sent you. It's honorable and there's a good trade waiting. I was tempted myself."

"What turned you away from it?" Maryenka asked cautiously.

"I have a Jap lover who promises to take me to Khabarovsk. Lies, of course. But I'm used to men, you see, and Muller has nothing in that way to offer. He won't look at a woman. Can't bear it. But he makes these things, perfectly stitched, snug, revealing here and there, you see. Each garment is a work of art. All the best whores have them. You could triple the price and sell them all and Muller would never know. He's odd, you see, works in a little cell by candlelight with his back to the world. All he wants is to buy more silk, lace, thread and elastic. Trust me, I've put you on to a fine thing."

"I'll consider it," Maryenka said.

The big, fleshy-faced whore wagged her finger under Maryenka's nose and scolded. "You'd better be quick. An opportunity like this doesn't go begging. There's a lot of wear and tear and those tarts over at the Mulligan will begin nosing about if they don't get new things to replace the old. They throw money away, they do, and give special orders too. You'd do best to get out to Beresovka at once. Muller is his name. Ask for the panty man. They make a joke of it, poor devil. They say he was married to a lovely woman and was a great philanderer too and that he works from memories of all the innocent creatures he disrobed. Stylish they must have been, that I will say, and I suppose it serves him right. Works right around the clock, Masha says. Masha is the girl who was with him last. Fat Masha, but he knows me too and trusts me. Tell him Glushenka sent you. I used to gather torn things after some ·of the debauches. Oh, what times! You can't imagine! I'd sell them back to him to remake, but now I've got my Jap. Tell any driver where you want to go. Do you have the fare?"

"Yes," Maryenka said.

"Then you're on your way," the woman said and smiling she patted Maryenka's cheek and left without even having asked her name.

Maryenka returned to Anitsky's wondering what to do. She believed the opportunity was real, but selling undergarments to whores was the next thing to being one. Long after she was in bed she lay awake trying to decide what to do. Only the most menial tasks seemed honorable, scrubbing floors, tilling fields, tending cattle, but even these could be questioned. Would she scrub floors at the Mulligan where Sipialef and the Cossacks walked but not sell undergarments to their whores? Would she sew uniforms in a factory for the White armies who in turn conscripted the peasants from the villages?

She thought far into the night about this but reached no conclusion.

In the morning when Anitsky came from work Maryenka had his breakfast waiting. He dropped his tips in the settle box, saw her receipt there and sat down at the table without referring to it. He took a Czarist ruble note of large denomination from his pocket and studied it so earnestly that Maryenka asked if something was wrong.

"Do you know an American major, Taziola?" Anitsky asked and his voice betrayed more nervousness than even he had been aware of.

"No," Maryenka said and she sat down across from him. "I don't know him by that name, but perhaps if you describe him."

Anitsky shook his head. "It doesn't matter then."

"But what is it?"

"He's onto me some way," Anitsky said miserably.

"Onto you? What do you mean onto you?"

"He gave me this bill when he left last night. 'Let's be careful where that one turns up, Anitsky,' he said. 'I know the numbers of it. They'll be exchangeable at par value again one day.'"

"Yes?"

"He's onto me for something, don't you see?"

"He was joking."

Anitsky tore the banknote in half, then shredded it as he spoke. "No. I've seen the look. I watch from the balcony often and I can tell from one week to the next what man will rise or fall and who may disappear. There's always a look exchanged near General Bogoloff's table. I've seen it pass, but tonight I turned around and there I found it in this major's eyes. He was staring at me from behind, you see. I turned pale and he smiled. Save me from such smiles! I trembled and it's worse because I don't know what I've done. But there's a look abroad in these times that tells the end of a man."

"You're imagining this, dear," Maryenka said. "Of course you are!"

"I know! I know! I know!" Anitsky insisted. "I pride myself on knowing such things. A headwaiter knows looks! A glance, a nod, a beckon, a shade in the eye. All these things I know. I must know them! I know from the change in a man's eye when he is going to have a cigarette. How else would I have the lighter ready? I can tell by the iris, by the pupil, by the tuck of the brow if a man approves his first sip of the wine. This is my training. And this applies to strangers, so don't I know this other look in the eyes of a man I've served so long? I know it! Of course I know it."

"But why?"

"Dear God in heaven, yes! Why? 'You're quiet lately, Anitsky,' he says to me. And like a thunderclap it comes to me that he is right. I've been quiet! And what could I say? 'I've been thinking sir,' I could say. 'And

what about?' he'd say. That's the sort he is. 'What about, my dear Anitsky?' And I couldn't tell him. No.

"What have I been thinking? Why, I've been thinking how nice it is she
is there. Now she's asleep. The cabin is warm. Tomorrow she'll smile and
speak. Oh, yes! Yes! She'll speak and I'll listen!

"So you see these are the things I've been thinking all the time you've
been here. Why, I've had thoughts some of which shame me, dear God, but
which are not to be shared at all. Before you came I had no thoughts, none.
Whatever popped into my head was shoveled out to the world. Chatter,
chatter. Meaningless. Foolish, wholesale chatter without a thought to hold
back or disguise, or to be ashamed of. Nothing holy. Nothing vile. Nothing.
Nothing!

" 'You're quiet lately, Anitsky,' he says. 'Yes, sir,' I say. Then he gives
me this and another look as he leaves."

Anitsky flung the shreds of the ruble note away and sighed despondently.
"Chukar notices stitches. This one notices silence."

"Because of me, then," Maryenka said.

"No, no!" Anitsky cried. "Because I have thoughts and can't chatter like
a fool! Because there's talk to come home to now where none was before.
Because I'm not so lonely."

"Ah," Maryenka said.

They ate in silence and Maryenka knew how much she had upset
Anitsky's life and that she would continue doing so as long as she remained. Her hesitation about applying to Captain Muller vanished and she
decided to go to Beresovka that evening.

"We must leave!" Anitsky declared suddenly. "Absolutely! It's far the
safest thing to do. Yes! To Vladivostok. Why not? What's to keep me here?
I have money. You've taken some, I see, and you're welcome to it. We
could travel together and be much safer." Anitsky bounded to his feet
excitedly and began to pace about weaving plans in the air with his hands.
'I could get tickets quietly, you see, and arrange for papers. I have connections. A day or so and we'd be out of it. Dear God, the thought had never
occurred to me. Why, I could open a café! You and I, in Vladivostok!
There's nothing to keep us here. Nothing at all and I have the money. I'm
sure there must be enough!"

Anitsky dropped on his knees beside the settle and began pulling coins
and bank notes out of it by the handful, trying frantically to arrange them
by denominations and count them as he continued to talk. He was nearly
hysterical and laughed nervously as a pile of coins toppled over. "Why,

here now! We can go as we please! There'll be excuses to be made, of course. Illness. There it is! A sudden illness has caught me. I know a doctor who will say as much for me, eh? Why, I'm free as a bird! Take warning and fly, eh? Ah, my dear, help me count it! The prospect has made me giddy. My hands are trembling. Vladivostok! Vladivostok! Why, from there one could go to Japan! To the world!"

Maryenka knelt beside Anitsky and helped him count the money. His hands were trembling and he babbled at an accelerating rate until the words stumbled over one another. He wanted to go at once and make preparations for their departure. Others had done it. The means to do it was here at their knees. Why had he never thought of it before?

"But there was no reason. I had no one, you see. There was only myself. But now it's as though I had a family to consider. You're my salvation. Yes! I'm risen from the dead. I feel young and hopeful. Oh, but please, don't misunderstand, my dear. We'll go together as father and daughter. Oh, yes, as father and daughter. But of course, what else?" And then Anitsky broke into tears.

Maryenka didn't know what to do. "What is it?" she asked. "Please what has happened?"

"Life has passed me by," Anitsky moaned and with tears streaming down his face he got up and went to his bed, where he threw himself face down, weeping.

Maryenka returned the money to the settle and went to him. "You're very tired," she said quietly. "All this can be explained. There's no reason for you to leave in haste. If you want to go to Vladivostok you can and I will go too as your true friend. You've been very kind to me, but let's not talk about it any more."

"And you would come to Vladivostok?" Anitsky asked plaintively.

Maryenka smiled and bending down she kissed Anitsky on the cheek as she would kiss a small child. "Yes, of course," she said.

That night when Anitsky left the cabin for work he was calm. "One must be deliberate and wise," he said and he winked and touched his lips with his fingertips. "Caution is necessary. Tonight I'll chatter like hornets at the American major if he comes. We must allay suspicion and move swiftly. Ah, what times! What times we'll have!"

He was filled with plans and inner excitement and when he was gone Maryenka took a cab to Beresovka.

The cab driver appeared to be in no hurry but jogged along at the side of the road allowing the faster traffic to overtake and pass them. Maryenka contained her impatience as long as she could but at last she asked how much longer it would be to Beresovka and the driver, who had been dozing, sat up and clucked his horse.

"It's not far now," he said. "You haven't been to Beresovka before this, I think."

"No, I have not," Maryenka said firmly.

"And what takes you there, if you don't mind?"

"I have business with an officer there."

The driver turned in his seat and looked down at Maryenka. He was a big man with a heavy beard and one bad eye which shone like a moon in his black face. "An officer, you say. I'm pleased you make such a point of that. It keeps me in my place, you can be sure."

"That wasn't my intention," Maryenka said. "It just happens to be so."

"Well, there are those who throw 'officer' in a man's face and expect him to knuckle his brow and bare his back to the knout."

"I don't care for such people myself."

The driver looked at Maryenka closely. "Is that so now?" he said challengingly. "So I suppose you'll report me to the authorities."

Maryenka, unnerved, glanced around to see if there was another cab nearby. "Why would I do such a thing? What would I say?"

"One thing is as good as another. The result is always the same." The driver made a pistol of his hand, pointed it at his temple and made a popping sound with his tongue, then he laughed uproariously and urged his horse to a trot. "The times are changing, my lady. I'm long past trying to keep up with it, so do as you like. Nothing surprises me anymore."

"Is it true that one can just walk into this prison?" Maryenka asked.

"The guards might examine your papers."

"And if they've been lost?"

"You have nothing? No receipt, no application?"

"I only arrived a short while ago and I've been ill."

The driver's voice seemed more friendly. "Ah, yes," he said. "Well, give the guard a few rubles and he'll never see you. Shall I wait, or will you be long?"

"I can't be certain," Maryenka said.

"So, if I'm here and see you come out I'll hail you," the driver said.

"Thank you."

"There, I'm not such a bad fellow after all. You made it safe and sound."

The driver stopped near the gate and Maryenka tipped him generously. "For that I'll wait an hour," he said. "Hurry now, there's your chance. One guard is coming this way for a cab. I'll hold him up. If the other one stops you, slip him a ruble."

Maryenka joined a crowd going toward the gate and had almost passed through when she saw Lieutenant Leverett, who had been Austin's witness at the wedding. Without thinking she fled into the dark compound.

Maryenka could not account for her fear, but she ran from Ira as she had run from the Cossacks who had sacked Pashkova. When she could run no longer she pressed herself against the wall of a building and waited until she could breathe calmly again.

He had seen her. She heard him calling. He would report it to the authorities and they would search for her. She must act quickly.

She looked around to get her bearings, then asked a man passing by if he knew the prisoner Captain Muller.

"Who?"

"Muller. An Austrian."

"The panty man?"

"I believe so."

"Barrack C," the man said with an unpleasant snicker. "Need a few things, do you?"

Maryenka hurried on, hugging the darkness.

Presently she sensed she was being followed and when she turned again she saw the dark bulk of a man close behind her.

"You're Glubov's woman," he said.

He was one of Timokhin's partisan band, the man named Slavin. His long, narrow face looked hawkish and intense, but a smile crossed his lips like a whip cut and he raised his hand to ease her fear.

"It's all right," he said. "I'm Slavin. I thought it was you. What brought you here?"

Maryenka drew a deep breath to regain her composure. "I'm on my way to Barrack C," she said.

"Barrack C? I'll show you. It's back this way."

Maryenka hesitated and Slavin smiled disarmingly. "Come along, we're all in the same kettle. Timokhin will be glad to hear how you're getting on. He's fond of you, which is a rare thing. Come on, sister. Timokhin would cut my throat if I misled you."

"You're still with him, then?"

"A few of us have come down to buy goods. Marrakof is somewhere with the others. I was to meet them at the gate, but I saw you."

Maryenka fell in beside Slavin and he guided her through the crowd. "And how is Timokhin?" she asked.

"They're pressing him a bit just now. Anyone who knew his whereabouts could make a good thing of it."

"I wish him well."

"Do you, then?" Slavin said and he stooped a bit to see Maryenka's eyes. "Yes, I see you do."

"He was kind to me," Maryenka said.

"Anitsky has treated you well?"

"Very well."

"There were some who thought you shouldn't have been let go. Marrakof for one. They swore you'd inform to the Whites."

"No."

Slavin nodded. "Timokhin said as much and he knows things that are beyond us. But even so he can't know everything."

"Do you come here often?" Maryenka asked.

Slavin glanced at Maryenka guardedly. "As often as is useful to us. We hear now that Colonel Sipialef has been given the task of searching us out. We hear this, but we don't hear enough. It makes us lay awake at night."

Slavin stopped near a low building and said it was Barrack C. Maryenka thanked him and was about to leave but a thought came and she spoke it without consideration. "If I heard something or learned something useful to Timokhin, how could I make it known to him?"

Slavin tucked his chin down on his breast and frowned. He seemed to be studying his feet intently and Maryenka began to wonder if he'd heard her question. "And what might you hear?" he asked.

"I don't know."

"But something, eh? Through Anitsky who works at the Mulligan where the officers go?"

"I hadn't thought of that."

"How else would you hear something? Who else do you know?"

"No one," Maryenka said.

"Well then?"

"Perhaps through Anitsky," she said.

"Is he reliable?"

Slavin looked at Maryenka closely and she wished she hadn't spoken. "I can't say. I don't know."

"He's an old fool!"

Maryenka flushed and shook her head, but she couldn't deny Slavin's charge. "Thank you for showing me the way. Carry my respects to Timokhin. He's a good man."

She turned and went toward the dark building, but Slavin caught her arm. "I come to Beresovka each week at this time," he said quickly. "I'll look for you by the gate; come there if you have information. So I've put my life in your hands, you see. Well then, be kind to it."

And he was gone before Maryenka could reply.

She stood alone in the darkness wondering to what she had committed herself; then she started to enter the building, but all at once she saw that this step too was part of the net of circumstances into which she was being drawn. Captain Muller's articles of apparel would bring her into contact with the women at the Mulligan and these in turn could lead her to Sipialef.

An expression of horror crossed her face as she saw her dream fulfilled. The heavy bullets smashed into Sipialef's featureless head and his blood washed toward her over the table.

She was going to kill him in spite of everything. They would seize her. They would execute her and with her the child.

Maryenka stood with her hand on the door handle knowing that if she pulled it open her fate was sealed. Tears filled her eyes and she saw again the snow-clad fields around Pashkova, saw the Cossack line, saw her father raise his arms and fall beneath the saber. She felt the presence of life in her womb, but she pulled open the door and went inside.

CHAPTER TWENTY-SIX

COLONEL Spaeth returned to his headquarters at Verkhne-Udinsk while Carlisle was still at Irkutsk. Nothing he had seen or heard at Omsk improved his opinion of the Kolchak government and his feelings about this annoyed him. The prospect of holding the regiment at Verkhne through the long Siberian winter was an unpleasant one, but General Graves had given no indication that the American forces would be withdrawn until events made this imperative and Colonel Spaeth found himself wishing that

Kolchak's government would collapse before the temperature began to drop.

He knew this wish violated his pledge of neutrality and that there were those, Taziola among them, who would suspect him of Bolshevik sympathies if they knew of it. He could not, however, dig the idea out of his mind.

Thoughts of his wife Peg and the kids having to wait another year for his return were unendurable, making him doubt his own perseverance, so altogether Spaeth was in a black mood as he entered his office and called his staff for a report of events during his absence.

Bentham had been raised in grade to major and Spaeth congratulated him perfunctorily. "It's about time, Charlie," he said. Then to Cloak: "They'll catch up to you one day too, Ben. All right, let's hear it."

He sat at his desk barely listening, tapping his spectacles against the palm of his hand, frowning darkly. Bentham and Cloak rattled on; everything was in good shape as Spaeth had known it would be, but he was waiting for a soft spot, waiting for any excuse to come down hard. He was going to do it; he knew he was going to do it and was angry at himself for feeling he had to reassert his authority in just this way. He was going to trim this outfit up. By God, yes! If they were going to be stuck in Verkhne, then by Christ they were going to stick hard. He was going to take up all the slack right now.

Spaeth was so absorbed in the dynamics of his own anger, in the self-feeding unjustifiability of it, that it took him a moment to realize that Bentham and Cloak had concluded their reports.

"That all?" he demanded, scowling furiously because he'd run out of something to grab. "Do you mean to tell me that's all you've got?"

Bentham and Cloak looked at each other, intimidated and confused by Spaeth's irritation.

"What in hell's been going on here?" Spaeth grumbled and he got to his feet and began to pace about. "I've been gone almost two weeks!"

"How were things in Omsk?" Bentham asked.

"Charlie, I'm not interested in Omsk at the moment," Spaeth replied.

"There's one item we should discuss," Taziola said.

"Ah!" Spaeth said and his anger was poised for this item, whatever it was. "What's that, Taz?"

"Leverett thinks he saw Maryenka Austin in the prison camp at Beresovka."

"He what!"

"He's convinced he saw her there and he's been looking for her."

Spaeth spun on Bentham. "Why didn't you tell me about this, Charlie?"

Bentham bridled slightly and scowled at Taziola. "Taz said Leverett had given the idea up — the idea that he'd seen her. Taz said Leverett was confused."

"I was mistaken. He's still looking."

"All right, let's hear it," Spaeth said. "All of it, Taz. Who, what, when, where and why."

Taziola began his story confidently enough, but every word seemed to feed Spaeth's anger. "What do you mean you met with Sipialef!"

"About the propaganda leaflets —"

"At Beresovka! Since when have my staff officers been conducting meetings out there?"

"It wasn't a meeting, Colonel —"

"Then what in god-damned hell was it!" Spaeth demanded. "First it was a meeting, now it isn't! Why was Whyte there? Never mind! Cloak, get Leverett up here at once!"

Captain Cloak bobbed his head and picked up the phone to call Tataurovo.

"Sipialef thinks those leaflets originate at Beresovka."

"I don't give a damn about that, Taz! I want to know about this Austin business."

"It's like I told you, Colonel."

"You haven't told me anything, yet!"

"Leverett thought he saw her at the gate and came back to ask for help finding her."

"Was he drunk or what?"

"I'm not sure about that, sir."

"Well, were you drunk? You say you were with him. Get it straight, Taz!"

"I wasn't drunk."

"I have Lieutenant Leverett on the phone, sir," Cloak said.

"Tell him to report here."

"Now, Colonel?"

"Yes, now! I want him now. Not tomorrow, not yesterday, now!"

Cloak ducked his head and spoke into the phone.

Spaeth turned on Bentham. "Charlie, I want you to send an officer down to take over C Company until Carlisle gets back."

"Yes, sir."

"Cloak, tell Leverett to report with his gear packed."

"He's off the line, sir."

"Well, ring him back! Tell him to pack up!"

Cloak rang Tataurovo again.

"Bentham, make out a transfer for Leverett. I'm sending him back to Vlad."

"Yes, sir. Right away."

"Taziola, I want a written report of this incident and I want it today. In fact I want it before Leverett gets here, so you haven't much time."

Taziola nodded and Bentham looked up from the regimental roster. "I can send Lieutenant Ryan to take C Company," Bentham said. "He's a steady man."

"Ryan will do. Get him down there at once."

Taziola and Bentham left the office. Cloak was still on the phone. "That's right, Ira," he said. "Packed and ready to move. No, I can't tell you that. All right."

Cloak hung up. "He'll come in on the Snorter, Colonel."

"Good, tell Bentham he can send Ryan back on it."

Cloak hurried out, closing the door quietly.

Colonel Spaeth sat down at his desk. He was relieved of his anger but a little ashamed of himself for having vented it so harshly. As he considered the implications of Taziola's story he was pleased by his instantaneous decision to transfer Leverett. This proved his judgment under stress was not impaired. Leverett had to go. He should have transferred Leverett after the Mulligan affair. He shouldn't have listened to Carlisle.

His temper began to rise again because he was sitting there justifying himself. "God damn it!" he grumbled. "What an unholy mess."

If Maryenka Austin was alive there could be hell to pay. Particularly if the truth about the Pashkova massacre came out. He wondered if Leverett had kept his mouth shut about this, but remembering his brash "Home by Christmas!" in Vlad, Spaeth groaned.

He picked up a pen and tried to write a note to Peg but his hand was so unsteady that every word expressed his anxiety. He rang for his clerk. "Sergeant, I want everything we've got on Pashkova and on Sergeant Austin and I want Lieutenant Ira Leverett's service record in here on the double."

"Yes, sir!"

"And get Mr. Silverman for me."

"Right away, sir."

While waiting for Silverman Colonel Spaeth leafed through reports on Pashkova.

"You sent for me, Colonel?"

Mr. Silverman stood in the doorway, smiling tentatively. Obviously he'd been told that the old man was on the warpath and he wanted to avoid being tomahawked. Silverman was thirty, studious and intense. He was one of four civilian interpreters attached to the expedition and had proved himself invaluable to Spaeth.

"Come in, Joe. The heat's off."

Joe Silverman grinned and dropped into the chair in front of Spaeth's desk. He was a big man, built like a tackle, was a Yale graduate and like Spaeth had a wife and two kids at home.

"What are the papers saying, Joe?"

"In a word, the Bolsheviks are doomed."

"I'd like to bet against that."

"General Denikin has occupied Kiev. Predictions in the White press put him in Moscow in sixty days. The noose looks to be tightening fast. How was your trip to Omsk?"

"Disheartening."

Silverman nodded. "I thought as much. Ambassador Morris' report to Washington must have been gloomy."

"How so?"

"The United States has officially refused to participate in the Allied blockade of southern Russia. That splits us away from Britain and France and indicates to me, at least, that we won't recognize the Kolchak regime. Clemenceau and Lloyd George must be spitting nails, but if they can't get Wilson to join them in a blockade I'd say this whole show is about to crumble."

"I didn't know about the blockade."

"It just came through this morning."

"Well, that makes the trip to Omsk seem more worthwhile."

Silverman smiled softly. "Neutrality, Colonel," he said. "Neutrality."

Spaeth scowled ominously and Silverman's smile vanished. "You're the best tea leaf reader in this outfit, Joe, with the possible exception of Taziola, but I don't want a lot of conjecture just now. I most particularly do not want it. There's too damned much gossip around here as it is. Have you read those propaganda leaflets our men have been picking up?"

"Yes, sir."

"Well?"

Silverman shrugged heavily. "Standard stuff."

"How do you combat it?"

"Ignore it."

"Have you picked up anything more on the Pashkova affair?"

"No, sir."

"What's new on the local scene?"

"Colonel Ivashkevitz seems to have been taken down a peg. Sipialef has moved in over him. The Japanese Brigade commander at Beresovka is being rotated home."

"Bogoloff?"

"Hale and hearty as usual."

"I like that man and I can't tell why."

"He's papa to us all."

"Maybe you're right."

"What did you have in mind, Colonel?"

"What?"

"You sent for me."

Spaeth removed his glasses, wondering as he did so if other people noticed how often he used them as a prop. They seemed now to express his uneasiness, to glitter and distort the objects caught in the lenses. He wanted to break them and to avoid doing so put them on the desk and was annoyed because his hands suddenly felt naked. "Have you heard anything about Maryenka Austin?"

"A rumor," Silverman said.

"Yes?"

"That she was seen at Beresovka."

"From Taziola, or who?"

"I heard it in the men's can at the Mulligan, Colonel."

Spaeth sighed. "That's all I wanted to know."

Silverman hoisted himself out of the chair.

"Did you believe it?" Spaeth asked.

Silverman smiled. "I ignore everything I hear in the men's can, Colonel. When I go in there I attempt to suspend most of my sensory apparatus."

"But you didn't hear it from Taz."

"No, sir. I don't think so. The voice was British and my back was turned."

"Captain Whyte?"

"It could have been. But there are more leaks in the men's can at the Mulligan than I care to look into."

Spaeth chuckled courteously. "All right, Joe," he said.

When Silverman was gone Spaeth's glasses, catching the pale light from the window at his back, appeared to be grinning at him. He poked them to knock the light out of the lenses.

Gossip! If it had gotten to the men's room at the Mulligan it had for damned sure spread through the regiment.

His mistake from the first was that he had tolerated Leverett.

There it was.

Peg thought of him as being an unprejudiced man. She thought so largely because of Carlisle. But damn it, Carlisle was a good officer. The Sioux and the Jew and Silverman too.

He'd tolerated Leverett to please Peg.

"Now isn't that one hell of a thing!" Spaeth said aloud and he smacked the desk with the flat of his hand. "One hell of a lousy thing!"

« 2 »

Sergeant Baker and Private Dixon operated the Snorter on the run from Tataurovo to Verkhne and Ira rode the tender with his duffel bag for a back rest and his foot locker for a seat. There was no doubt in his mind that Colonel Spaeth intended to transfer him. Captain Cloak's muffled but imperative tone indicated as much and Ira's feelings about this were a mixture of self-righteousness and indifference. He'd failed in so many ways that nothing seemed to matter anymore, but at the same time he felt that another man in the same circumstances wouldn't have done any better.

It had embarrassed him to have his gear put aboard the Snorter. The men didn't know whether to bid him goodbye or not and consequently fell into a foot-shuffling, awkward, mumbling ritual like a mating dance of one-legged birds. "See you around, Lieutenant," Sergeant Klagle had called as the Snorter began to roll and Baker had rung the Snorter's bell in response.

He rang it now again as the Snorter groped through the switching yard and came to a stop on a siding near the station.

"I'll help you get your stuff to the platform, sir," he said.

Ira dropped his duffel bag to the ground while Baker and Dixon hoisted the foot locker between them and set it down.

"Stand by the Snorter, Dixon," Ira said. "Baker and I can handle this."

"Yes, sir," Dixon said. Then he saluted. "Well, sir, I guess this is it. Goodbye, sir."

Ira returned the salute a bit surprised by the regret in Dixon's eyes. "I guess so, Dixon."

"It won't be the same," Dixon said, then he swung back aboard the Snorter.

As they approached the station platform an American lieutenant chopped toward them over the tracks. "Your name Leverett?" he called.

"Right."

The lieutenant was short, wiry and pugnacious. He glanced at Ira coolly. "I'm Ryan," he said. "They just shot me out to take C Company until the C.O. returns."

"This is Sergeant Baker," Ira said.

Baker saluted awkwardly, still holding one end of Ira's foot locker in his left hand.

"There's a car waiting for you on the street, Lieutenant," Ryan said. "As soon as you get back to the train, Baker, we'll move out."

"Right, sir."

Ryan nodded in a clipped way and went to the Snorter.

"A ramrod," Baker said as they went through the depot to the street.

"Do you know him?"

"I know the type."

A Mitchell touring car was waiting. The driver helped Baker strap Ira's foot locker to the luggage rack. Ira tossed his duffel bag inside and offered Baker his hand. "Good luck, Ed."

"Same to you, sir."

"If I don't get back say goodbye to Carlisle for me. Tell him I'll drop him a line."

"You bet," Baker said.

"So long," Ira said and he got into the back seat of the Mitchell.

Baker closed the door and the driver, a young corporal, got in.

"Headquarters, sir?" he asked.

"Ryan told you where to take me," Ira said.

"Right, sir," the corporal said.

Ira sank back as the driver made a wide turn in the center of the street. He felt drowsy. It was over. He knew well enough that his current difficulty had come about because he'd seen Maryenka at Beresovka. He'd made an issue of it and he could blame himself for that. He shouldn't have blurted it out to Taziola as he'd done. He should have handled it in his own way.

A motorcycle with an empty sidecar passed by and squirmed through the crowd at the intersection. Ira watched it for a moment and the realization that he probably wouldn't see such street scenes again made everything exotic. He'd grown accustomed to Siberia, to the mixture of European,

Slavic and Asiatic faces, to the sounds and smells, to the currents of violence and fear and to the deep, enduring patience of these people. But now he sat forward eager to absorb these last scenes because he was on his way out.

A Cossack belted into a fleece-lined coat with a ragged hem brushing his boots stalked through the crowd with only his set mouth and straight nose visible between the black shag of his fur collar and the brow of his cap. Skirted Chinese with their hands hidden in the sleeves of their robes, Evenkis, Buryats, Tatars, sashed, jacketed, booted, fur-hatted, all seemed to brush him fleetingly with their eyes, to take notice of and discount his presence. A clutch of Japanese soldiers on leave, jovial as marionettes, their puttee-bound legs taut as sausages, crossed in front of the car and Ira was reminded of Major Ikachi's statement that Asia was a woman.

Ira thought this was so. Asia waited as women wait. Asia was passionate, violent, fecund and nonaggressive in the Western sense. Asia absorbed.

He was on his way out, passion spent, docile. He searched the crowd for women's faces. Most were bowed, hidden in head scarves. The gravity of earth tugged at their blockily clad bodies and they were drawn in protectively upon themselves.

One figure, moving more quickly than the others, with a bundle clutched like a baby in her arms, caught Ira's attention. As though torn by indecision she stopped, retraced her steps, then went on again more swiftly and in turning she revealed her face.

Ira bolted up. "Driver, stop the car!"

"What?"

"I said stop the car!"

Ira swung the car door open but, instead of stopping, the driver accelerated, throwing Ira back into the seat.

"You damned fool! I said stop!"

"My orders were to take you —"

"You bastard! Stop it."

But the Mitchell raced on, rear door flapping while the driver hunched over the wheel, face white, expecting to be struck from behind by the officer he'd been ordered to deliver at once to Headquarters.

« 3 »

After waiting ten minutes Ira was admitted to Colonel Spaeth's office. Major Taziola's presence caused him to hesitate, then he crossed swiftly to Spaeth's desk and spoke without saluting. "I've seen her, just now in broad daylight. On the way here. Maryenka Austin, but the damned driver wouldn't stop or I could have brought her."

Spaeth rose, his face dark. "Snap to, Leverett!"

"But, Colonel, I swear —"

"Get hold of yourself, Lieutenant," Taziola said.

"I'll handle this, Taz!"

Ira came to attention and saluted.

"I'm sending you back to Vlad," Spaeth said.

"I don't care about that, sir. You've got to believe —"

"Shut up!"

Spaeth's voice cracked icily. Ira glanced at Taziola. Somebody closed the door to the outer office.

"Who have you told about seeing Maryenka?" Spaeth demanded.

"Who? Major Taziola —"

"Who in your company?"

"Sergeants Baker and Klagle. I wanted the men to be on the lookout for her when they came to town."

Spaeth sat down wearily. "How fast can we get him out, Taz?"

"The first train to Vlad goes in the morning."

"You'll be on that train, Lieutenant. That's all."

Ira stood there.

"You're dismissed, Lieutenant," Spaeth said.

Ira was astounded. He'd expected this to happen up to the moment he'd seen Maryenka on the street. "But sir, you don't understand!"

Colonel Spaeth closed his eyes. "Leverett," he said with great forbearance, "let's suppose I do understand. Let's just suppose that there is something I understand about all this which you don't and let it go at that."

Spaeth opened his eyes and smiled with a genuine effort at cordiality.

"But Colonel, I don't understand!"

"That's right, Leverett. *You* don't. Now if you'll do me the courtesy to withdraw I'd appreciate it. Or we can confine you to quarters, even lock you up. I've got a lot of options, Lieutenant, but I'd prefer not to exercise them. I believe you've seen Mrs. Austin and we'll do everything we can to locate her, but that's not your bailiwick is it?"

"I thought you didn't believe me."

"Yes, I do."

Ira looked at Taziola again, still confused. "All right, then," he said.

Colonel Spaeth stood up. "I'm glad we could strike a bargain satisfactory to both parties, Lieutenant," he said. "Goodbye."

Blood rushed to Ira's face. He was angry, ashamed and utterly powerless. He saluted smartly, turned on his heel and left the office.

Spaeth sat down again. "I've read your report, Taz," he said. "I don't much like it."

"I did the best I could in the time."

"Well, yes, I suppose," Spaeth said easily. "Sit down." He picked up the phone on his desk. "Ring Major Bentham for me," he said. "This'll only take a minute, Taz — Hello, Charlie, how many military policemen do we have in town at the moment? All right, locate Leverett before he leaves the building. I think he has a picture of Maryenka Austin taken at her wedding. Get it from him, issue a description of her to the whole contingent and initiate a search. She's been seen here in Verkhne. Yes, right here. Leverett saw her on the street. I want action on this fast, understood? O.K., Charlie."

Spaeth hung up. "Do you have a cigarette, Taz? I left mine."

Taziola fumbled in his blouse pocket and brought out a pack of cigarettes. Spaeth took one and tamped it on his desk. Taziola produced a lighter, but Spaeth shook his head and smiled. "I'm cutting down," he said. "This morning I caught myself fiddling with my glasses to avoid smoking. So I thought I'd try fiddling with a cigarette to avoid fiddling with my glasses."

Taziola returned the lighter to his pocket. "Makes sense," he said.

"As much as anything else, I suppose," Spaeth said. "You know, Taz, the Red Army is a curious article. They have such a shortage of experienced officers that they've been forced to use former Czarist officers in staff and command positions. I understand that almost half the Bolshevik forces have Monarchist officers."

"Yes, but they've Bolshie commissars watching every move they make. The commissars make the final decisions."

"What do you think of that system, Taz?"

Taziola cocked his head warily. "The system of military commissars?" he asked.

"Yes, Taz."

"Well," Taziola said, "what else can they do?"

"It must make for a lot of inefficiency and confusion, wouldn't you think?"

"They seem to be doing all right."

"So you like the system."

"Of course I don't *like* it," Taziola declared.

"Neither do I," Spaeth said quietly. "Not at all."

Colonel Spaeth continued to tamp his cigarette, then he took a match from his pocket and lit it. "There's something I'd like you to do for me, Taz," he said.

"Certainly."

"Request a transfer to Vlad."

Major Taziola's head popped up straight and a look of amazement came to his face.

"This outfit doesn't need a political commissar," Spaeth said.

"Now wait a minute, Colonel!"

"No, I don't think so, Taz. Not a minute. You stepped way out of line dealing with Sipialef while I was away. You went around Bentham and over me."

"We had dinner!"

"All right, I don't like your choice of dinner companions. There's no sense arguing about it, Taz. We don't get along. I don't want to go through the winter with you. Go back to Vlad and be comfortable."

"Like hell I will! How does that make me look?"

"Don't bump heads with me, Taz," Spaeth said ominously.

"You've got to have a reason — an official reason."

"I'll think one up and wire General Graves. Perhaps I'll suggest you'd be more suitably placed as a military liaison man to the State Department. You agree with their aims in this area and I think General Graves will get my point."

"The State Department happens to be right. The Bolsheviks must be stopped!"

"When the President of the United States issues an order to that effect I'll do my damnedest to obey it, Taz. Until that time I don't want a meddler on my staff."

Major Taziola stood up and his head wagged several times before he could speak. "You don't, you can't see what's going on right here, right under your nose," he stammered. "Leverett's a Red sympathizer, mark my words! I spotted him right off. I'm not so sure about Silverman either."

"That'll do, Taz!"

"No, by God! Maryenka Austin is a Bolshie. She was married to one, I checked that out. Shulgin was a socialist. And if she survived the massacre at Pashovka it's proof that she sides with the partisans. She married Austin to spy on this outfit. It's all clear to anyone who wants to look."

"I want you out of here the day after tomorrow, Taz. The day after Leverett leaves."

"You can't railroad me."

Spaeth laughed at the expression. "You're a damned fool, Taz." He picked up the telephone and asked for Major Bentham. "Charlie? I'm relieving Major Taziola. No, there's no particular reason, Charlie, I'm just being capricious. That's right. And I want to get on the wire with General Graves. I'll want you there too. Let me know when he can be reached."

"I intend to make a full report of this, Colonel," Taziola said when Spaeth hung up.

"That's your privilege, Taz."

"You should never have permitted Austin to marry that girl."

"I wish I shared your omniscience, but I don't."

Spaeth stood up once more and Taziola cocked his head worriedly. "Well, I'll put in for a transfer," he said at last.

"Under the circumstances that would be the gentlemanly thing to do. Thank you for the cigarette, Taz."

Half an hour later when Major Bentham came into the office he found Spaeth at his desk staring soberly at his spectacles. He looked up from them and smiled. "Sorry I barked at you this morning, Charlie. It's been an unraveling day."

"That's all right."

"I wish to hell it was over."

"We can get through to the General in ten minutes."

"Have you heard from Carlisle?"

"He telegraphed from Murinskaya to say he'd reach his headquarters tonight and would report here in the morning."

"That's a bright spot. Did Leverett have the picture?"

"Yes. The photo section is making an enlargement. They'll get copies out tonight."

Spaeth sighed heavily, then looked up at Bentham. "Charlie, did it ever occur to you that Maryenka Austin might be a Red agent?"

"Taz mentioned the possibility."

"He mentions all the possibilities, doesn't he."

"Yes, sir, he does."

Colonel Spaeth pushed himself up and went down the hall to the code room. "The trouble with this job, Charlie," he said, "is that no one is going to transfer me out of it."

« 4 »

After delivering Maryenka Austin's wedding photograph to Bentham's office Ira returned to his temporary billet in Headquarters barracks and wrote a letter home. He mentioned his transfer to Vladivostok but not the reason for it, and the letter, so burdened by unexpressed resentment, struck him as false from start to finish and he put it away.

It was almost dinnertime, so he took his coat and reported to the officer of the day.

"I'm going into town for dinner," he said.

The O.D., a lieutenant named Rice, looked up at him. "Leverett?" he asked.

"That's right."

"Your train leaves at 0800."

"I'll be on it."

"Where can you be reached, in case?"

"The Mulligan, I suppose."

The O.D. made a note on his clipboard. "O.K.," he said.

It was already dark and there was a crisp wind off the river. Ira put on his oversized enlisted man's coat and turned the collar up around his ears and thought about home.

Perhaps he'd locate his office in San Francisco, somewhere on the fringes of Chinatown where from his window he could see Oriental and Caucasian faces. He'd become a defender of the poor, take up unpopular causes, be a people's attorney. No corporate law for him. No more neutrality. His Uncle Dave would be proud.

He walked to the docks along the Uda River and caught himself trying to see the face of every woman he passed. Major Bentham had assured him that if Maryenka was in Verkhne-Udinsk she'd be found.

There were unusual numbers of American military policemen on the streets, patrolling in pairs, but they didn't appear alert enough to satisfy Ira. He stopped one pair, who saluted when he exposed his insignia, and asked if they had received orders to be on the lookout for Maryenka.

"Oh, yeah," one of them said. "But the description we got ain't much help. They all look the same to me."

"You'll get a picture of her."

"What was she supposed to have done?" the other asked.

"She married one of our sergeants."

"Is that a crime?"

"No, he's dead."

"She kill him?"

"No, she's his widow," Ira said irritably. "Where have you been? Maryenka Austin."

"Oh, yeah. I heard about that. It happened before we got here, sir. We came in with the replacements."

"Well, if you see her, bring her in."

"Why don't she come in herself?"

"I don't know," Ira said.

He stopped at a bar and had one drink, which depressed him. A pale Eurasian girl whose tightly ringletted black hair smelled scorched dropped one hand on his knee and drew the red bow of her mouth at him. Ira gave her a ten ruble note and left, headed for the Mulligan, intending to get drunk while listening to Masha's mournful gypsy songs.

CHAPTER TWENTY-SEVEN

MARYENKA was in a state of euphoria; it was all going so well, so easily, in such a preordained way that she felt no apprehension and hardly any need to act. The loaded Nagan revolver which she'd purchased with Anitsky's money lay concealed in the undergarments she was showing Dunia and it didn't seem to matter whether the weapon was seen or not.

Anitsky, pleading illness, had stayed home agonizing over the final preparations for their departure to Vladivostok in the morning. He hadn't even objected when she told him she was going to town to sell some things she no longer needed. What things had she to sell, after all, and why hadn't he questioned her?

It went so easily.

She had been admitted without question to the second-floor apartment which Masha, Sonia and Dunia occupied in the Mulligan. She had shown them Muller's latest creations and drank tea while the women modeled the garments and wrangled about who should have what.

The waiter had come to inform Masha that Colonel Sipialef was waiting for her below. Sonia had dressed quickly and accompanied her mother downstairs.

It was all going so easily.

Dunia came from the bedroom wearing a black chemise which accentuated her chalky skin. She gazed for a time at the door as though there were a mirror on it, but there was not. "It's too large," she said at last.

"I can mark it and Muller will take it in," Maryenka said.

"Does he do that now?"

"Yes."

Dunia drew a languid discontented breath. "I'm too thin," she sighed. "I'm getting thinner all the time."

Maryenka smiled agreeably. "It's the fashion now," she said.

"You're new, aren't you?" Dunia asked narrowing her colorless eyes. "Have you been here before?"

"Yes, I'm new," Maryenka said and she felt no impatience or sense of jeopardy. Sipialef was downstairs. She could hear the musicians and Masha singing.

"What happened to the other girl? She was a great fat thing, wasn't she?"

"I believe she was."

"Black is wrong for me, I think."

Dunia went to the center table where there was a lamp with a beaded amber shade. She looked down into the light, which tinted her face yellow, and rattled the fringing beads idly with one long finger. "Do you have morphine?" she asked.

"No."

"We're out just now. It's tiresome."

"Would you like to try something else?"

Dunia looked around with catlike suddenness and saw Maryenka unfolding a pink chemise. "No," she said. "I'll keep this and trade with Sonia. She has no taste. She's a slut. I dislike her. What's your name?"

"Maryenka."

Dunia went to an upholstered armchair and dropped into it, stiffening her legs and letting her arms dangle to the floor.

"Show me something," she said. "Model for me. The fat one always modeled for me."

"Oh, I can't do that," Maryenka said calmly.

"She often kissed me," Dunia said.

"I have another appointment."

"Men are pigs."

"You'll keep the black one then?"

Dunia closed her eyes and nodded her head. "But you'll have to wait for mother to pay. I have no money."

"I'll come back then."

"As you like," Dunia said and she began to roll her head against the cushioned back of the chair.

Maryenka gathered the garments from the floor and placed them unhurriedly in her basket. She arranged the Nagan where it could be reached, then went to the door. So easily, easily. As she left she looked back at Dunia, who was staring at the ceiling in a puzzled manner.

Maryenka went down the hall. Her head was so light that she seemed to float, to be pulled upward by it. She had no sense of walking. At the first landing she stopped to get her bearings.

Through clouds of smoke she saw the people below moving slowly like shadow figures in a dream. Officers leaning toward their companions seemed about to lose their balance and fall soundlessly to the floor. Masha was singing; her face looked blue and the words shaped by her wide mouth were lost.

Maryenka searched the room and near General Bogoloff's crowded table she saw Colonel Sipialef with Sonia. Anitsky himself had pointed him out to her from a picture in the newspaper taken during a troop review. He was turned away, so Maryenka couldn't see his features, but she knew these would appear when she fired the revolver.

She took the Nagan from her basket and concealed it in a black silk bodice. Some officers passed her going downstairs and their laughter trailed up in spirals like the smoke.

Maryenka left the basket on the landing and followed them down. The heavy revolver in her hand drew her on with a will of its own and when she reached the main floor Maryenka paused again.

The room was filled with dark shapes and blurred sound. A match flared and caught her attention. She moved toward it. The revolver rose upward and she caught it with both hands to keep it from flying away. She thought this strange, that the heavy pistol should be acting like a bird in flight. The bodice which had concealed it slipped away and the naked revolver swung around and pulled her along almost stumbling behind it. Someone nearby called out, then she saw Sipialef rise and turn in her direction. She fired at his dark blank face, then she closed her eyes against the nightmare and fired four more times in quick succession.

Over the shots there were screams and the sound of toppling chairs. Maryenka felt herself struck from behind and she was dragged away.

Men were yelling. "Bogoloff! The General!"

She felt a rush of cold air. She was being pummeled and torn at. She didn't care. She let her body go slack and a jarring blow slewed her head around. She was thrown upward like a sack, then rushed along head down, arms dangling.

She opened her eyes and saw she was being carried, then she was thrown down brutally on the floor of a cab and a figure fell in over her. "Go!" a voice demanded. "Go or I'll blow out your brains!"

The cab was in motion, hoofs hard on the brick-paved street. She tried to get up, but a hand forced her down by the neck.

"Turn here!"

The cab swayed.

"Slow up!"

She was pulled from the cab by a man brandishing a pistol. "Go! Go on!"

The cab ran on and Maryenka was pushed into an alleyway.

"Here, quickly! Put this on!"

She felt the coat around her shoulders and clutched at it as she was pulled along. She ran clumsily, trying to avoid tripping over the skirt of the huge coat. She was pressed into a dark doorway and held there.

"Maryenka, it's Ira. Ira Leverett. I'll get you out, but you've got to help. Are you hurt?"

She couldn't see his face, but felt the urgency of his breath against her ear. She shook her head.

"Stay here. Don't move!"

Ira ran through the alley to the other street hoping to find a military police patrol. People were running toward the Mulligan. In seconds he knew they'd be swarming back through the streets searching for Maryenka. He had to get her to Headquarters.

There was no cab, no phone, no sign of Americans.

Ira ran back to Maryenka and gave her his hat. "Tuck your hair under this," he said. "Pull that coat up around you and let's go. We'll have to chance it."

Maryenka did as she was told, pleased that her escape had been arranged in this fashion. She hadn't even considered how she was to get away after she'd fired the pistol, but this too was being done for her. So incredibly easily.

"Have I killed him, do you think?"

"My God, I don't know. It happened so fast!"

"He massacred my people at Pashkova."

"Who?"

"Sipialef. They attacked from an armored train."

Ira tried to take this in, but her dispassionate voice made it hard to grasp. Sipialef, Sipialef, the name ran through his mind. He was in a panic. "Do you know about Harry?" he asked.

"Yes, I have his child," she said and she smiled.

"Sipialef," he said.

"I've killed him," she said.

Ira stopped. The street was vacant. "They'll be swarming around the Mulligan," he thought. "What will the Americans do with her?"

He didn't know.

"Come on," he said, "I'll try to get you to my company at Tataurovo."

He took her hand and started off.

"Must we run?" she asked.

"I suppose you're right."

They came to the intersection and there, as though waiting for them, stood a muzhik's two-wheeled cart and pony.

"There, you see," Maryenka said and she got in and took the reins in hand.

As they started away a man ran out from between two buildings, pulling up his trousers and bellowing. The pony quickened its pace as though anxious to leave its master behind.

The gesticulating man ran after them, then fell heavily in the middle of the road, kicking wildly at the trousers which entangled his legs, his bare buttocks pale in the overhead light of the street.

Sergeant Baker, shaken roughly out of a sound sleep, sat up and found Sergeant Klagle at his side.

"Wake up, Ed, and listen to me."

"What the hell!"

"You awake?"

"God damn you, Klagle!"

"Lieutenant Leverett is outside. He has Maryenka with him."

"Maryenka Austin?"

"Meet us by the Snorter," Klagle said. "Hurry up."

By the time Baker had dressed and reached the Snorter a crowd of men were gathered around it, talking in subdued voices. They made way for Baker, who saw Maryenka in the cab drinking something hot from a cup.

There was an ugly bruise on her face, but she seemed calm and smiled in recognition of him.

Baker nodded to her and spoke to Klagle. "Where's Ryan?"

"Asleep."

"He won't be long. You back for good, Lieutenant?"

"I'm due out in the morning, but we've got to protect her. She took a shot at Colonel Sipialef."

Baker looked at Klagle incredulously.

"Colonel Sipialef and his boys are the ones that sacked Pashkova," Leverett said. "She lost her whole family there."

"Oh, Christ," Baker said. He looked at the men around the Snorter and had no doubt they'd protect Maryenka. "We'd better tell Ryan," he said to Klagle.

There was a mumble of dissent.

"You people button up," Baker said harshly. "No one is going to make trouble for Mrs. Austin."

"You're damned right," Private Dixon said.

"Find her a place to be comfortable instead of mouthing off," Klagle said.

A dozen hands were extended to help Maryenka down.

Eisenbach paused at Ira's shoulder. "We'll put her to bed and get a medic to look at that bruise. Don't worry about anything."

"Fine, Eisenbach," Ira said. "Come on Klagle, we'd better see Ryan."

Lieutenant Ryan bounded out of bed with his pants on and his forty-five dangling in one fist. "What the hell is up!" he demanded; then seeing Ira between Baker and Klagle he asked what he was doing there. "You've been relieved, Leverett," he said.

Ira, Baker and Klagle began to explain the situation but Lieutenant Ryan found it incomprehensible. "All right, stow it, stow it! Who did she shoot?"

"She fired at Sipialef," Ira said. "She may have got him. I don't know."

"Well, we'd better find out," Ryan said and he stepped to the phone.

Ira blocked his move. "What if she killed him?"

"That's what I intend to find out. Step aside!"

"Wait a minute. I want to talk this over."

"Talk it over with Headquarters, Leverett," Ryan declared and he reached for the field phone.

Ira pulled the wires.

Ryan's automatic came up and his eyes narrowed. "Repair that phone, Baker," he said.

"I think we should talk it over, sir," Baker said.

"That's an order!"

Baker nodded. "While I repair the phone," he amended. He pulled the field phone down and asked Klagle if he had a knife to strip the wires.

Klagle shook his head.

"In my locker," Ryan said.

Ira stepped toward Ryan, caught the automatic and pressed it down. He struck Ryan smoothly with his free fist. The sound of the shot filled the car as Ryan dropped to his knees and Ira stepped back with the automatic which he'd wrenched from Ryan's grip.

"Oh, Jesus!" Klagle whispered.

"Fix the phone, Baker," Ira said.

There was a clamor at the door and several men burst in. "Move them out of here, Klagle," Leverett ordered.

"I don't go for this, Lieutenant," Klagle said.

"You don't have to go for it. Do as I say."

Klagle went out with the men and shut the door after him. Ryan got to his feet, glaring.

"Don't make a speech, Ryan," Ira said. "Go lie down."

Ryan went to his bed and sat on it. "This is a mutiny, Baker," he said. "Don't follow his orders."

"He's under duress, Ryan," Ira declared. "Now you shut up. Take notes if you like, but shut up!"

Baker replaced the wires in the field phone and put it on the table. Ira kept the forty-five aimed at him, but they both knew this was a matter of form. "Ring Headquarters."

Baker did so and Ira took the receiver. "Hello, Rice? What in hell is all the excitement in town?"

"Somebody just assassinated General Bogoloff," the O.D. replied.

"Bogoloff!"

"That's right, who's this?"

"You're sure it was Bogoloff?"

"That's right. Who is this?"

Ira rang off and looked at Baker. "Bogoloff," he said hollowly. "She killed him."

« 2 »

It was close to midnight as Carlisle's train approached the bridge at Tataurovo and he found his spirits rising at the thought of being back in the security of his company.

To avoid thinking of Tatiana, Grachev and Yakushef he concentrated on his notes, neatly recorded observations of the topography and roads over which he had passed.

"Lake Baikal is approximately four hundred miles in length and varies from eighteen to fifty miles in width. The surrounding mountains rise to five thousand feet and are abundantly forested though the trees are not of great size being principally fir, pine and Siberian cedar. The lake begins to freeze in November, but is rarely covered with ice before the first half of December. A thick covering of ice lasts four and a half months, during which time the lake can be traversed, but the danger of this travel is increased by cracks three to six feet in width caused by shifting ice and often concealed beneath an unbroken covering of snow.

"Currently operable lake steamers are the *Strelka, Iakoo, Alexander Neoski, Sibirisk,* and *Nikolai.* Reports are that these are in need of overhaul, which would be advisable in event of obstruction of the Trans-Baikal tunnels."

He had gathered this information painstakingly and the rhythmic flow with which he was able to organize it now pleased him, but sometimes he stumbled into a distracting phrase.

"One icebreaker, the *Angara,* was disabled by Czechs."

He clenched his pen and steadied his notebook against the roll of the train.

"The *Angara* was disabled by the Czechs —"

He thought of Tatiana and looked out the window for landmarks to see how close he was to Tataurovo. Talovka siding. Soon now.

Carlisle closed his notebook, gathered his gear and went forward, through the cars.

"I have not been disabled," he thought. "I have not been disabled by the Czechs."

This thought was picked up by the wheels of the train and drummed back at him.

I have not been disabled.

Not by the Czechs.

Not been disabled.

Not by the Czechs. Not by the Czechs. Not been disabled.

Carlisle rammed his way through the crowded cars, stepping over sleeping humanity packed in the aisles with their bundles of food, clothing and blankets. There were snoring men and whimpering children, fat-breasted women with their mouths agape. Dull-eyed, they pulled their legs up to make room for him to pass.

In the first car he found the conductor asleep and shook him awake. "Tataurovo," he roared.

The conductor jumped up, quivering. Then he touched his cap and went forward to speak to the engineer.

Carlisle shouldered his pack, took his sleeping bag in one hand and hung on the step ready to drop off when the train crossed the bridge and slowed down. Beneath him the wheels were loud:

Disabled! By Czechs! Disabled! By Czechs!

Disabled! By Czechs! Disabled! By Czechs!

He saw the Tataurovo bridge ahead and then the engineer blew the whistle.

"Tat-iana!" it wailed.

Carlisle listened to the hollow sound as they passed over the river, then as the train slowed he jumped.

He hit the ground off stride and fell hard down the cinder embankment where he lay for a moment stunned as the train went on. When he stood up the first thing he noticed was the unusual activity around the camp cars. There was a crowd of men at the Snorter babbling excitedly and there were no guards on the bridge.

Carlisle squared his aching shoulders and walked toward the Snorter. No one saw him approach.

"What in hell is going on here?" Carlisle demanded and the men backed away, smiles wilting on their cabbage faces as silence fell.

Someone was hammering on the door of the H.Q. car.

"Where's Leverett?" Carlisle bawled and Ira jumped from the Snorter with a naked forty-five in his hand.

"Hello, Carlisle," he said.

"Put that damned automatic away," Carlisle said. "Klagle, call these men to order."

"We'd better talk, Sioux," Ira said quietly.

"Who's that hammering?"

"That's Lieutenant Ryan, sir," Baker said.

"Let me explain," Ira said.

Carlisle's eyes flashed red over the automatic, then with great deliberation he raised one hand and struck Ira a swipe across the face with his open palm. The impact spun Ira around and sent him sprawling at the base of the Snorter's main drive wheel.

Carlisle stepped forward and plucked the automatic from Ira's limp hand. As he did so a woman dropped from the cab of the Snorter and helped Ira to a sitting position.

"I'm all right, Maryenka," Ira said and he shook his head trying to clear it.

Maryenka looked up at Carlisle with a bewildered expression. Her sudden appearance took him by complete surprise. "What the hell is she doing here?"

Baker came to him. "Captain," he said, "it's Mrs. Austin."

"I can see that!"

"There's been some trouble."

"Bring Leverett to me," Carlisle said and he went to his car. He found the door jammed shut from the outside with a wedge. He pulled this out and was met on the threshold by Lieutenant Ryan. Carlisle grabbed Ryan by the belt, shoved him back into the car.

"I'm Ryan, Lieutenant Ryan! Leverett's relief!"

"Get your shirt on and shut up!"

"The whole company —"

"You're under arrest, you bastard!" Carlisle roared.

"Me!"

"Shut up!"

Sergeant Baker appeared in the door.

"Confine this man," Carlisle said.

Ryan pulled on his shirt, whimpering and raging in turns.

"Get him out, Baker!"

Carlisle reached for the field phone but it was gone. Klagle appeared supporting Leverett on his shoulder. "He's stunned, sir."

"Put him over there," Carlisle said, indicating a chair near the stove. "Get him a drink."

Baker reappeared. "Ryan's in the mess car. Should I post a —"

"Shut the door," Carlisle demanded. "I don't care where he is. Now spill it. Fast!"

As he listened to Klagle and Baker, Carlisle knew that the worst fear of his life had come true: that all the lines of order, duty, discipline and loyalty had become hopelessly entangled.

"Bogoloff!" he cried. "Why Bogoloff?" And he thought of the epaulet Tatiana had given him. "Her uncle!" he thought and he glared at Ira.

"She meant to kill Sipialef," Ira said and he told about the massacre at Pashkova. "We've got to get her away, Sioux. She's got friends in the hills."

"What friends?"

"Never mind that."

"Like hell! Baker, get me in touch with Headquarters. Klagle, order the men to fall in."

Ira rose unsteadily. "I won't let you send her back to Verkhne, Sioux," he said.

Carlisle's face blackened. *"You* won't!"

"Colonel Spaeth might turn her over to the Whites. He wouldn't want to, but he'd be on the spot. And with the story she has to tell I don't think she'd live a week."

"Get going, Baker!"

Baker stepped to the door but hesitated, looking hopefully toward Ira.

"The men won't let you send her back, Sioux," Ira said.

"This is my company," Carlisle roared.

"I'm taking her to Mysovaya on the Snorter. There's not much time."

"You're under arrest, you son of a bitch! You're not going anywhere."

"Captain," Klagle implored.

"Shut up, Klagle!"

"I'm going with her," Ira said.

"That's desertion!"

"Maybe."

"Captain," Baker said quietly. "She's pregnant. The kid will be Austin's."

"Let her go, Captain," Klagle begged.

Ira stepped to the door and threw it back.

"You can pick up the Snorter in Mysovaya," he said, then he dropped to the ground and walked toward the engine and the men parted to let him pass.

Carlisle tried to yell a command. His throat pumped convulsively and the blood in his eyes blinded him. He stepped forward, but his knee gave out and he pitched against the door, trying to close it. Baker helped him shut the door and they waited in tense silence.

The Snorter groaned and began to move. They heard the clash of its wheels on the switches to the main track, then the vacant sound of it on the bridge over the Selenga.

Carlisle stood with his back against the door listening to his authority vanish with the Snorter. He should have stopped it, or he should have ordered Ira to take it and go, but all he'd done was bluster. Sergeants Baker and Klagle were staring at him compassionately. Klagle opened his mouth to speak, but Carlisle silenced him with a gesture and sat down on the chair beside the stove.

They heard the Snorter's bell in the distance, but they couldn't hear the engine anymore. The men outside were talking quietly. Carlisle thought about fixing the phone. He could call ahead to one of the guard stations and have the Snorter stopped, but the realization that he did not want to risk giving an order came into his mind sharp as an obsidian arrow.

"Shall I have one of the men get your gear, Captain?" Baker asked.

"It's near the bridge," Carlisle said.

"I'll get our phone repaired right away, Captain," Klagle said.

"Fine."

"What about Lieutenant Ryan, sir?" Baker asked.

"Tell him to report to Regimental Headquarters in the morning."

"Do you want to see him?"

"No."

The sergeants left, sliding the door closed behind them, and presently Carlisle heard them bawling orders at the men.

Corporal Blodgett came with his pack and sleeping bag. "Welcome back, Captain," he said and he was about to say something more, but the look on Carlisle's face made him swallow the words and leave quickly.

Carlisle stared at the pack which contained his notes and Bogoloff's epaulet. At the height of the emergency he'd thought of Tatiana. When nothing on earth should have distracted him from the dangerous situation in the company he'd thought how stricken she would be at the news of her uncle's death and from that moment he had been incapable of decisive action. Even now he couldn't think what he should have done.

Sergeant Klagle came in with the field phone. "I'll have this hooked up in a second, Captain," he said.

Carlisle nodded, picked up his field pack and dropped it beside the cot. "You sure Bogoloff is dead, Klagle?"

"Leverett got it from the O.D. at Headquarters," Klagle said. "Shall I check, Captain?"

"I suppose you'd better," Carlisle said, then he lay down and closed his eyes.

« 3 »

Maryenka was not aware she had killed General Bogoloff. That the shots intended for Sipialef could have been so wild never occurred to her. She sat on the engineer's seat, bundled in Ira's coat, with the cool air rushing past her calm face and her feet warmed by the firebox.

It had all been done so easily.

Her American friends had saved her. Timokhin and his men would welcome her and in time, perhaps, she could get to Vladivostok, find Anitsky, have her child and be at peace.

So easily.

With one hand on the throttle Ira strained to see the track picked out by the yellow beam of the Snorter's lamp. He was afraid of meeting an oncoming train. He was afraid the American guards at Verst 404, at Selenga, or at the Kramatche River bridge might have received orders to stop them. His anxiety drew taut as a wire in the wind and Maryenka's trancelike repose, her belief that nothing could go wrong, brought it to the snapping point.

"How long will it take us to reach Mysovaya?" she called to him over the sound of the engine.

"Two hours, if we make it."

"That's fine," she said.

"How can we get in touch with your friends?"

"The people will know how to do it. You needn't worry. You can leave me at Mysovaya and go back."

"I can't go back," Ira yelled. "How in hell can I go back until I know you're safe! Sipialef will have the whole White Army looking for you!"

The tension in Ira's voice attracted Maryenka before his words registered. She had been pondering the significance of her escape, which seemed to have been ordained by God, and had reached the conclusion that it was God's will that Austin's child not be killed. She believed that the death of Sipialef and her escape were confirmation that the child was Austin's. How could it be otherwise? All doubts as to the paternity of her child seemed to have been swept away and she was smiling calmly when Ira spoke. "But I killed him, didn't I?" she asked.

Ira shook his head. "No. You killed General Bogoloff."

Maryenka's expression made Ira regret having spoken. Her eyes widened and seemed to explode with horror. She clutched her stomach and bent forward moaning, brokenly.

Ira caught her in one arm and drew her close. "It's all right, Maryenka," he said. "You'll be safe."

She shook her head and tears flowed from her eyes. "No. No!" she groaned for she had been thrown back into a hell of uncertainty which she believed was retribution for the crime she had committed. "I can't go on," she said. "I can't!"

"You must!"

"Yes, I know! I know, I know!" Maryenka cried.

Ira held Maryenka as the engine hurtled into the darkness, its great bell tolling now and again. Ira did not know the facts of Maryenka's captivity nor the significance to her of failing to kill Sipialef. He tried to console her and at last she stopped weeping.

"There," he said, "it's going to be all right."

"Yes," she said determinedly. "Yes. I have Harry's child to consider."

"That's right," Ira said. "Now you're talking sense."

The little engine passed on and the humming rails grew silent in its wake. The Siberian darkness closed behind it and there was a chill in the air. Soon there would be snow, and ice would sheathe the rivers. The glacial pace of human wisdom, never affected by the season, did not slow or quicken and the wolves sought their winter lairs.

BOOK THREE

The Hearing

THE House Committee on Military Affairs was called to order by the Honorable Julius Kahn of California, on Monday September 15, 1919, to consider a resolution by the Honorable William E. Mason, a Representative in Congress from the State of Illinois, that it be the expression of Congress to the President of the United States that American troops be removed from Siberia.

It was a bewildering and often acrimonious session with the Secretary of War, Newton D. Baker, present to defend the powers of the presidency.

Representative Mason stated his case succinctly:

MR. MASON: It is contended that the action of Congress, if it should pass such a resolution as is proposed, would be without precedent; but it would meet a condition and a situation that has been created by the Executive, which is also without precedent. It is the first time, so far as I know, when our troops have been sent into a country to take part in a civil war when we were not at war with that country. The war in Russia is between the Kolchak and the Soviet governments, a conflict in which we have no possible interest. Some of us may sympathize with one side and some with the other, but as American citizens we can have no possible interest in the outcome of the struggle between those two forces.

At the hearing before the Committee on Foreign Relations the other day I asked the Secretary of War — this hearing was an open session — why we had our troops there. He said they were there to guard the railroad. I asked him whose railroad it is. He said it belongs to the railroad company. I asked him how much money had been put in there by the President, and my recollection is that either he or one of the other witnesses said he did not know whether the President had put any money in there. But according to a report which has been presented to the committee on expenditures of the State Department, the President has put in there $5,000,000 or $10,000,000 to rehabilitate that railroad. The Secretary of War said they are not taking part in the fighting between the Kolchaks and the Soviets. But upon further questioning he said — and I presume his testimony has been printed by this time — that they were neutral. I said, "If that is so, are you not selling arms and ammunition to Admiral Kolchak, a man who is engaged in a war over there?" He said that they were, that they had a right to sell arms or ammunition, or what we would call contraband of war, to anyone.

MR. JAMES (of Michigan): If they are not taking part in the fighting on one side or the other, why are the American soldiers being held there?

MR. MASON: I asked him that. He said he had not heard of any battle they were engaged in. But we lost in the Archangel sector 480 men, and we have lost quite a number of others up there. My fear is, and the fear of my constituents who are relatives of those men is, that those two factions of the Russian people may get together, and if they do they are liable to wipe out the American troops. We have 8,000 men in Siberia. If Kolchak settles with the Soviets — and the indications are that it is a mere matter of money with him — they may combine their forces and wipe out our men.

The Secretary of War said they were selling guns to Kolchak and taking the notes of a private citizen in payment. I said, "Is that not an act of war, furnishing contraband of war to one side in a civil war?"

Of course, the Secretary of War was there to protect the Executive branch of government, so his answers to Representative Mason had been evasive. He didn't know to whom the railway belonged except to the railroad company. He wasn't sure if the President put any money into the Trans-Siberian Railroad when clearly he had. He had not heard of any battle, but four hundred and eighty American soldiers had been lost in the Archangel sector. The American troops were neutral, but the United States was selling arms to Kolchak.

The question of what constituted an act of war, however, drew voluminous testimony from Chairman Kahn in support of the President's right to do as he alone determined "even though his acts and omissions be fraught with political consequences of the most pre-eminent importance."

One authority for this position was Von Holst's *International Law,* to which Representative Mason commented: "That is a great German writer."

Thereupon Secretary of War Baker took the stand and delivered a lengthy justification of the President's position with respect to the American presence in Siberia. He recapitulated the history of the intervention and of the Czech involvement in it, citing statistics and incident and when at last he concluded Chairman Kahn once again dipped his oar on behalf of the administration:

THE CHAIRMAN: I think General March stated to the committee the other day that they are guarding the railroad, and the railroad is necessary, as I now recall his testimony, to send food and supplies to the starving peoples in eastern Russia.

SECRETARY BAKER: Undoubtedly it is used for that purpose.

MR. FULLER (*of Massachusetts*): Those reasons are all bunk, in my opinion. Those are not reasons. Why should not we know the truth?

THE CHAIRMAN: I am simply stating what the testimony before the committee is.

MR. FULLER: It takes a long time to answer the simple question why the American troops are in Russia.

SECRETARY BAKER: I think I ought to be permitted to express deep regret that my answers irritated the gentlemen so. I have tried to be explicit.

MR. FULLER: It does not irritate me at all. I asked a plain question. I have listened to the Secretary's story, but I do not get an answer.

SECRETARY BAKER: Unfortunately, that is not my fault.

Undoubtedly it was not Baker's fault. The fault lay in the necessity of Baker having to duck, obfuscate and confuse the intent of the questions asked him.

MR. ANTHONY (*of Kansas*): Would not withdrawal of American troops from Siberia now be tantamount to giving aid and assistance to the Bolshevist government?

SECRETARY BAKER: Mr. Anthony, I can not answer that; I do not know.

MR. ANTHONY: It would leave the Kolchak government without material, moral, and physical support which we are now giving them by our presence there, would it not?

SECRETARY BAKER: Yes, if our presence is a moral or physical support, and it is at least a physical support in that it keeps the railroad open.

Realizing he'd stubbed his toe, Baker immediately asked to put into the record a statement of the present forces in Siberia, because he had information later than that which he had when he testified before the Committee on Foreign Affairs. Granted permission to do this by Chairman Kahn, the Secretary read lists of figures "based upon knowledge of the organizations which are present, but without accurate knowledge of the strength of the organizations." This tactic of accurately reciting inaccurate statistics was effective in preventing Representative Anthony from pursuing his line of questioning.

The hearing stumbled ahead and exhausted itself in a final series of exchanges between Representatives McKenzie of Illinois, Sanford of New York, Hull of Iowa, and the Secretary of War:

MR. MCKENZIE: Do you think it would be unwise to provide that the President of the United States should not order an expedition into another country without first having the authority of Congress?

SECRETARY BAKER: Yes, I think so; I think that would be very unwise.

MR. MCKENZIE: You think it would be wise to leave that power in the hands of the President of the United States? Then if he desires to involve us in war with a neighboring country without Congress having taken any action, he could do so.

SECRETARY BAKER: Yes; I think so.

MR. SANFORD: The remedy in that case would be by impeachment?

SECRETARY BAKER: By impeachment or refusal of reelection.

MR. HULL: Do you think it would be wrong for us, representing as we do the people, and presuming the people want us to do it, to express an opinion in regard to a matter like this?

SECRETARY BAKER: Mr. Hull, the expression of an opinion upon a subject which lies in the power of somebody else is a very doubtful course.

So the power of the President, as Commander in Chief of the Armed Forces, to engage the people of the United States in a war without the advice or consent of Congress remained intact. Mr. Mason's resolution, which was simply intended to offer an opinion, was put aside.

Ten days later, President Woodrow Wilson, the lone possessor of the power to commit the United States to war, collapsed aboard his train after delivering an oration in Pueblo, Colorado, in which he compared the men in the United States Army to crusaders — "going forth to prove the might of justice and right, and all the world accepted them as crusaders, and their transcendent achievement has made all the world believe in America as it believes in no other nation organized in the modern world."

The President returned to the White House, where he was stricken by thrombosis in the right side of his brain which left him a paralyzed, bitter and querulous invalid. If for any reason he had taken it in mind to reinforce the American troops in Siberia and start a crusade against Bolshevism he would have found support at home and abroad and Congress would have been powerless to stop him. As it was, his attempts to force Congress to approve his League of Nations were more fanciful than practical and the fate of the American Siberian Expeditionary Force was left by default to a coterie of the President's close associates presided over by his second wife, Edith Bolling Wilson, who instituted what she called "a workable system of handling matters of state," and whose cousin and childhood playmate, Dr. Rudolf Teusler, had been such a long time in Siberia with the Red Cross.

CHAPTER TWENTY-EIGHT

A TATTERED backdrop of gunmetal clouds lay over the hills around Puget Sound and on the Seattle waterfront, swept by a dismal October rain, longshoremen snugged into their work gloves and made ready to load fifty boxcars of crated sewing machines aboard the government-chartered ship *Delight.*

Fifty carloads of sewing machines, destination Vladivostok.

That's a lot of sewing machines.

The seagulls wheeled overhead and squawked and the *Delight,* riding high, with her cargo hatches open, waited.

Fifty boxcars of sewing machines.

The longshoremen watched the first car being shunted out on the dock and wondered how many sewing machines it contained and wondered who in hell in Vladivostok was going to do all that sewing.

It was dispiriting. The gray rain seeping into their work shirt collars was dispiriting and there was in their bones an as yet unspecified reluctance to handle this cargo.

Sewing machines for Siberia? Civil war going on, ain't there? In Siberia?

Yeah.

The boxcar door was opened and a pallet board laid down. Four men climbed into the car and began to worry the first crate toward the door.

Heavy son of a bitch.

Take it easy!

Hold it!

The crate fell to the dock and burst open to reveal not bobbins or shuttles, but rifles manufactured by the Remington Arms Company, part of the shipment Mrs. Custer-Farquart had been instrumental in procuring for the Kolchak government.

They did not fare as well as Mrs. Stern's Christmas oranges.

The longshoremen stuffed their hands in their jacket pockets and walked off the dock. The union announced that its members would not move the hot cargo and that any dock which attempted to do so would be put under permanent boycott.

The *Delight* swallowed Seattle rain through its open hatches and pumped it out the bilges. The seagulls settled on its king posts and tucked their beaks under their wings.

The rifles did not move.

If this expression of reluctance to engage in the internal conflicts of a foreign country had been an isolated example perhaps the Bolsheviks would not have broken through the armies which encircled Moscow; International Harvester, Parke, Davis and Company, Westinghouse Electric, New York Air Brake and a host of other American companies would not have had to write off their vast investments in Russia; but the reluctance was not isolated, it was general in a world gut-tired of war and already disillusioned by the peace.

Formerly impassioned enemies had been too quick in their avowals of common interest and recent allies had divided bitterly over previously concealed conflicts of interest, so the longshoremen in Seattle, Washington, jammed their hands into their damp jacket pockets and walked off the job. French sailors at Odessa, terrified by their own audacity, mutinied rather than continue fighting the Reds. British troops and Americans, serving under British officers at Archangel and Murmansk, had already proved to be balky when ordered to advance against Red Army forces.

There was a terrible reluctance in the air.

Investment counselors shuddered and began to advise clients to unload or sell short certain stocks which not three months before had been on the rise.

And on the fronts in Russia and Siberia this reluctance expressed itself in hundreds of ways. A rifle or a piece of artillery sighted a few yards short of the target made the usual noise when fired but did no harm and the soldiers in the line were quick to discover the spirit of their opponents' marksmanship. On some fronts men blazed away for days with a fine show of fury for their officers and a great expense of ammunition, but no appreciable military result.

The meaning of this activity was clear to the soldiers of both sides: we must follow orders or risk courts-martial, but we intend you no harm unless you press an attack. And attacks when pressed by raving staff officers on lathered horses frequently turned into mass desertions leaving the officers goggle-eyed as whole sectors were stripped of their defenses. To avoid this the officers themselves grew reluctant, counseling each other to let well enough alone, to wait and see.

Armies of men fumbled and bumped against each other like clumsy millstones. There were brisk, irritable engagements for supplies and the shelter of one city or another, snarling battles for a chance to lie down in peace, but it was apparent to everyone that victory was going to fall spiritless and exhausted to the side which was the least reluctant.

Generals and statesmen were confounded because their traditional vocabularies, their appeals to patriotism, idealism, self-sacrifice and glory, were not specifics against the infection of reluctance. Fresh troops going into the line were just as reluctant as those who had been there for months. Even more so.

The Reds are going to nationalize your women, boys!

What?

They're going to nationalize your women!

How's that work?

Why, they'll nationalize them!

Good luck to the sons of bitches.

The White officers, tools of the capitalist exploiters, have committed unspeakable atrocities on their captives.

Unspeakable?

Mutilations!

You don't say.

Castration!

A lot of good it does me out here. I'm going to freeze it off if this keeps up.

Listlessness, inertia and reluctance fell over all fronts. The armies plodded about waiting for chaos to release them. The temperature dropped. The vast, swampy taiga froze and there was the smell of snow on the wind.

Then, with an ominous groan, like that which precedes the crack in the face of a glacier, the Kolchak front began to crumble. General Dutov's army evaporated. A Ukrainian brigade under General Gaida strolled over to the Reds. The First Siberian Army under General Anatol Pepelyaev lost its will to fight even reluctantly and fell back to regroup around Tomsk while the Second and Third Armies delayed the lethargic Red advance.

General Janin, in command of the Czechs reinforced by small detachments of Poles, Italians, Rumanians, Serbs and Balts, kept a diary of the current situation and his trusted Russian chauffeur, a Bolshevik spy, sent photostats of the entries to Trotsky by courier.

"The Czechs and Russians must be kept apart. Retreat is inevitable. Lines will crumble and hardly re-form. French prestige must suffer from our responsibility for a worm-eaten organization. Treason from all quarters is certain. Czech morale is low; but they have control of some communications plants, services; they even have ambulances. The Russians have nothing."

Encouraged by such information and more of the kind supplied by Admiral Kolchak's valet, Kiselov, Trotsky enhanced his reputation as a military genius while his troops headed for Omsk like cattle coming in from the fields at dusk hopeful of finding fodder and warmth in the barn.

Then General Janin received a telegram from Marshal Ferdinand Foch which announced the cessation of French support of the Kolchak regime:

"The Czechoslovak Army in Siberia shall not engage in battle; the armies of the Entente and those of America, to whom they are tied by feelings of solidarity, have abandoned intervention; they will henceforth limit themselves to passive defense and methodical retreat."

The concentration for repatriation would center on Irkutsk.

Informed of this decision Admiral Kolchak caught his stomach in a Napoleonic gesture. "I shall lead my own men in combat!" he cried. He had the ulcer, but he did not have the troops.

Trotsky smiled.

« 2 »

In September, 1919, the British began their withdrawal from Siberia. The first contingents leaving Omsk marched slowly through the wind-blown flurries of new snow and boarded railroad coaches for the long journey to Vladivostok. Men of the Middlesex Regimental Band stowed their bulky instrument cases on shelves and under the seats. In other cars the Hampshires stamped their feet and chafed their cold hands. The whole expedition had been a damned, bloody useless bore and some politician's head ought to roll.

A bloody eff up if yer ask me!

'Oos askin'?

We're pullin' out on Arky too, I 'ear.

Arky your arse!

Major and Mrs. Custer-Farquart shared their compartment with Tatiana, who was going with them as far as Irkutsk, where she intended to set up receiving stations for the wounded from the expected defense of Omsk.

Mrs. Custer-Farquart, however, had no illusions about saving Russia from Bolshevism. As their train began to move she watched the gloomy city of Omsk retire behind its screen of snow. "Down the drain," she said. "Aleksandr V. Kolchak, down the drain." There was a throaty note of plumbingful sorrow in her voice and two more words bobbed to the surface of her political toilet and remained floating there. "Trotsky. Bolshevism."

Tatiana, grown accustomed to Mrs. Custer-Farquart's scatological analogies, smiled. It all meant one thing to her: home to Prague at last.

Colonel Dubrovski was requisitioning trains for the Czech evacuation. The French military mission had asked the Czechs to turn over their aircraft to be crated and sent by train to Vladivostok. Albert was grounded. Raul had wired to tell her so. Dubrovski had promised to let her know which echelon Albert would be attached to and she would be able to choose a setting for their reunion. It was a great relief to know that she would not be taken by surprise. She still had some decent dresses and her jewels. She would collect some clever people in Irkutsk and be ready when Albert came, ready to re-create their very special life together.

Mrs. Custer-Farquart patted Tatiana's hand. "You really should come out with us, Tatiana," she said. "Oughtn't she to, Budgy?"

Major Custer-Farquart, already half asleep, looked up with an accommodating smile. "Yes, yes, Edna, my dear," he said.

"That husband of yours," Mrs. Custer-Farquart said, "that husband of yours is a mop."

"Yes, my dear."

"Oh, go back to sleep, Budgy!"

"Yes, Edna."

"Well, he is a mop!"

"I don't know what you mean," Tatiana said.

"I'm sure I don't know either, except that I dislike mops. They usually mean that something messy has gone wrong and that's how I think of your husband."

Tatiana was amused. "As something messy gone wrong?"

Mrs. Custer-Farquart nodded resolutely. "Exactly. I'm never sure what I mean until someone tells me, but I'm nearly always right."

"You'd change your mind if you knew Albert," Tatiana said.

"I hope I would, but if you can't meet him I can't. It's all too preposterously evasive. If I can come clear out here from my cousin Lydia's house in Savannah and find Budgy —"

"Yes, my dear."

"I see no reason why your husband couldn't have spent some time with you. A man who chooses duty over beauty was improperly toilet trained."

Major Custer-Farquart's head bobbed. "Yes, yes."

Tatiana suppressed a giggle, but Mrs. Custer-Farquart's expression was grave as she launched into one of her "topics," explaining how much important research was being done in this area, that toilet training and character formation went hand in hand. "I confess that as a girl I was always a bit ashamed to say that our family was in bathroom fixtures. I tried to pretend it was something else, but Papa insisted on putting our name right on the bowl for all to see. 'The world's work is nothing to be ashamed of, Edna,' he said. And psychologists are proving him to have been right in the end. Character building is what it's about, after all. I've interested myself in a number of things, politics, art and Budgy, but Papa was right. Shoemaker, stick to thy last."

Outside the snow thickened and began to cake the windows of the train. Men of the Hampshire Regiment settled down to their cards and curses and in idle moments wondered what was happening to the poor devils out in such weather as this.

The lights of the train came on, flickering dimly as the current pulsed from the faulty generator, and Major Subo Ikachi came through the train searching the compartments until he found the one occupied by Tatiana and the Custer-Farquarts. He was about to enter, but seeing the sleeping Major he touched a finger to his lips and waved, indicating he would visit them later.

"He'll be on your heels in Irkutsk," Mrs. Custer-Farquart said.

"I find him charming."

"Ikachi," Mrs. Custer-Farquart said disdainfully. "He's a French-fried Japanese who gives me the hiccups and makes me sneeze."

Tatiana burst into laughter, the melodious, soaring, unself-conscious laughter of untroubled times, and Mrs. Custer-Farquart, caught up by it, laughed too.

"What? What!"

"Oh, for heaven's sake, Budgy, go back to sleep.

« 3 »

Lord of the World, God of Creation,
Give us Thy blessing through our prayer;
Give peace of heart to us, O Master,
This hour of utmost dread to bear.

And on the threshold of the grave
Breathe power divine into our clay
That we, Thy children, may find strength
In meekness for our foes to pray.

Among General Mikhail Konstantinovich Dietrichs' effects was this poem written on a scrap of paper found in Ipatiev's house at Ekaterinburg where, on the night of July 16–17, 1918, Czar Nicholas II, the Czaritza Alexandra, the Czarevitch Alexis and the four Grand Duchesses, Olga, Tatiana, Marie and Anastasia, were shot to death by their guards. Little Alexis was fourteen years old and ill, the Grand Duchesses ranged in age from twenty-three to seventeen and the poem was in the handwriting of Olga, the eldest of the four daughters.

When the Whites took Ekaterinburg an extensive investigation was made into the assassination of the Czar and his family. Three of the guards at the Ipatiev house, Yakimov, Proskuriakov and Medvedev, were captured and questioned and the disused mine shafts in the forest near Koptiaki disgorged their grisly contents which were cataloged and packed in three suitcases and a wooden box.

These suitcases and this box were in General Dietrichs' possession when he arrived in Omsk and began to consider the problem of its defense. He tried to deliver them to Loris Melikof, who, when he heard what they contained, threw up his hands in horror.

"For the love of God, General!" Melikof cried. "The Supreme Ruler must not know they are here! He's depressed enough as it is. This would drive him insane. You must swear to keep this a secret, above all else."

Among the relics of the Imperial massacre were fragments of bone, human fat from the logs where the bodies had been burned, swatches of hair, an amputated finger which experts identified as the Empress's right ring finger, charred jewelry, the buckle of the Czarevitch's belt, scraps of clothing and shoes, bits of bloodstained carpet and spent bullets.

The poem, a copy of which General Dietrichs kept in his breast pocket, haunted him most particularly:

And on the threshold of the grave
Breathe power divine into our clay

Melikof's reaction to the presence of these relics upset the General. He had been appointed commander in chief of the Kolchak forces and it was his intention to defend Omsk, but to do so with the troops at his disposal required a miracle. Such miracles were possible if one had faith, but General Dietrichs' faith had been shaken by Melikof's reaction to the relics. The physical factors alone were insurmountable. There were grave shortages of food, fuel, clothing and ammunition. Typhus was rampant and frostbite was taking almost as great a toll. Along the railway there were fuel shortages, pumps and switches froze, and the armies falling back on Omsk were demoralized, as was the civilian population. It was hopeless.

General Dietrichs sighed and issued orders that preparations be made at once for an orderly retreat to Irkutsk.

When Admiral Kolchak was informed of this he was at his desk gazing blindly at the latest effusions of his ministers, many of whom were finding vital business which required their presence east of Omsk. He looked up at Melikof and waved his hand listlessly. "Inform General Dietrichs that he has been relieved by General — whom would you suggest?"

"Sakharov is outside," Melikof replied.

"Yes, Sakharov will do. — That he has been relieved by General Sakharov, who will proceed with the defense of Omsk."

When Melikof had gone Admiral Kolchak pressed his head against the tall damask back of his chair and closed his eyes.

The young, rather pretty woman seated in a shadowy corner of the room watched him closely. "Be calm, my dear," she said.

"Ah, Timireva!"

"God will keep you."

"Humankind. There is so much of it, Timireva! I'm not a sentimentalist. I can't mourn casualty statistics. I don't see their faces. I don't know their names, or their pain, or their sorrow. In all this war, this disease, this natural disaster, I seek a meaning and there is none."

"My dear Aleksandr."

"No, none. Historians will come and make reason where none existed, but here there are no historians, only events. You must go on the next train."

"No, I will not."

Kolchak opened his eyes and sought the woman in her corner. "Go to Sofia in Paris. She will be kind and she can provide."

"I have no doubt your wife would be kind, Aleksandr, but I will not leave you now."

"It will be terrible here."

"It is my life, Aleksandr."

Kolchak sighed and began once more to read and initial the reports of his ministers, accepting a share of their corruption with each scratch of the pen as though in expiation of his failure.

And while the Supreme Ruler of Russia sat at his desk the Red forces shuffled toward Omsk. Some of the men, asleep on their feet, woke with a start and were surprised to find themselves in the army. They looked at their comrades, grinned and shook their heads in disbelief. How can a man sleep and march? But down the line other men's heads bobbed and came up with a jerk and in that instant they had had a faraway dream which left them with the same look of astonishment on their faces. Cavalrymen fell forward on the necks of their horses, their arms dangling toward the snow as they beheld visions of a thousand common pleasures which were so remote that they could not be recalled in a waking state.

They were marching on Omsk. Well, that surely will be the end of it. We'll take Omsk and go home. They agreed, yes, and their eyes probed the cold landscape ahead, but it too was part of a dream. Such was their state of exhaustion that many of them could not tell the difference between sleep and reality, but their feet and their horses' feet plodded on, leaving footprints like initials in the snow.

CHAPTER TWENTY-NINE

AT the death of General Bogoloff, Colonel Sipialef assumed command of the military district of Verkhne-Udinsk and unleashed an unprecedented reign of terror. He had been struck once in the shoulder by the fusillade of shots intended for him; the other four bullets had thwacked into General Bogoloff seated at the table behind Sipialef's, killing him in the midst of one of his jovial discourses by driving his St. George's Cross into his heart, as the autopsy showed.

Released from Bogoloff's restraining influence Sipialef's activities were ruthless and unabated. His secret police and their informers produced lists of names and mass arrests occurred in the dead of night. The picture of Maryenka Austin intended for the American military police was billboarded with an offer of ten thousand rubles for information as to her whereabouts. Dunia, Sonia and Masha disappeared without a ripple. A night raid on the prison at Beresovka left forty corpses, among them Captain Muller draped in bloody scraps of silk. Newspapers blazoned the story of a vast Bolshevik conspiracy. Anitsky was arrested.

Prominent citizens searched their memories for utterances which might be construed as political and many decided to leave town. The fools among them applied for railroad tickets and were courteously escorted to a special train by Sipialef's transport agents. To Chita? Why, certainly, sir! But they found themselves on the branch line which had been started to connect Peking with the Trans-Siberian and which ended abruptly twenty miles south of Kiakhta close to the Chinese border.

Mongolian caravanists coming to Verkhne-Udinsk over the Gobi began to tell stories of bodies exposed to the weather where these tracks stopped, of hearing machine guns firing in the night and shrieks of agony. They took to avoiding the place.

Sipialef's headquarters issued a statement by an unknown surgeon general with statistics about the ravages of typhus, plague, cholera and the associated diseases of malnutrition. There were a hundred and sixty thousand cases of spotted typhus between Omsk and Irkutsk and the claim was made that Kiakhta was being used as a common burial ground in an effort to protect the living from the contagions of the dead. The statistics were undoubtedly correct, but they did not account for the machine guns or the cries of despair.

Colonel Spaeth received a formal note from Sipialef's headquarters accusing American military personnel of having conspired in the assassination of General Bogoloff. "And our informants, in sworn testimony, do affirm that an American officer present at the scene assisted the assassin, Maryenka Shulgin Austin, recent consort of an American Sergeant, to escape."

Spaeth encoded this to General Graves with the facts concerning Ira Leverett's involvement.

Major Taziola, wearing an expression of smug vindication, could not resist calling on Spaeth before leaving for Vlad. "My only regret," he said, "is that I didn't have time to finish my report before the facts corroborated it. Now it would seem that I was using hindsight rather than foresight."

"Too bad, Taz," Colonel Spaeth said tightly.

"Yes, it is. It makes one wonder how many others there have been who interpreted conditions correctly and who, if they had been heeded, might have altered the course of events."

"I expect you'd have put Leverett under arrest."

"I would certainly have confined him to quarters," Taziola said righteously.

"Any other suggestions?"

"In view of occurrences at Tataurovo I'd transfer C Company back to Vlad and bring the ringleaders to trial."

"I'm the only ringleader in this command, Taz. If you hadn't forgotten that, things might have been different."

"There are no mitigating circumstances in a mutiny, Colonel."

Colonel Spaeth caught one corner of his mustache and gave it a vicious twist. "That'll be all, Major," he said.

Major Taziola cocked his head and smiled slightly. "Goodbye, Colonel," he said. "Good luck."

"Goodbye, Taz."

Ten minutes later Major Bentham came in with a message from General Graves: Spaeth. Amexforces, Verkhne-Udinsk. Your 2239 filed. Ignore it. Initiate Code 3. Graves.

"Carlisle here?" Spaeth asked.

"He's been waiting all morning," Bentham said.

Spaeth read the message from General Graves once more, then tucked it under the blotter on his desk. "Send him in, Charlie," he said.

Carlisle, looking haggard, with a spent expression in his reddened eyes, came in stiffly.

"Close the door, Sioux," Spaeth said. "Sit down and relax."

Carlisle closed the door, marched across the room and came to attention.

"No, god damn it! Sit down. Sit down for Christ's sake!"

Carlisle groped for the chair and sat.

Spaeth snatched at some papers on his desk and pretended to read them. Carlisle's appearance of shattered self-confidence was a distinct shock. They'd been on the phone to each other repeatedly, but Spaeth thought it best to let Carlisle handle affairs at Tataurovo while he and the Allied military commanders in the area tried to temper Colonel Sipialef's excesses. He'd been working around the clock with no appreciable result, but assumed Carlisle to be the same granite hard soldier he'd come so much to rely upon. Now he felt as though he'd made a mistake. Spaeth put the papers aside and tipped back in his chair trying to keep his manner easy. "I talked to Ryan yesterday," he said. "He's a good man. For now, we're carrying Leverett A.W.O.L. and we'll continue to do so until something else develops. I told Ryan that I take full responsibility for everything that happened at Tataurovo and that if circumstances arose necessitating a statement from me I would side with those who protected Mrs. Austin. Ryan understood perfectly and I've detached him to Chita as our liaison man with the Railway Service Corps. — How are things at Tataurovo, Jack?"

"In hand, sir."

Spaeth nearly repeated this statement as a question: In hand? But he caught at his mustache again, thinking as he did so that he was developing a new nervous gesture. From spectacle tapping, to cigarette tamping, back to spectacle joggling, and now this. He decided to shave his mustache off and go back to smoking. "Good," he said. "I'm glad to hear that. It's no easy thing, Jack. For most of the men those propaganda leaflets were their first contact with the ideological content of the Russian civil war. It's damned disturbing for them. I'll admit I've been remiss in not doing more on that side of things, but damned if I'm sure I understand it myself. And we're neutral, that's the point. How in hell can you say anything if you're neutral?"

"I don't know, Colonel."

"But your sector is in good shape."

"Klagle and Baker have the Headquarters Platoon in control. The rest of the company wasn't in it."

"I see," Spaeth said. And what he saw clearly was that Carlisle could no longer be effective as the commander of C Company.

Mitigating circumstances in a mutiny? It was such a narrow line. When in April, 1916, I Company of the American 339th Infantry at Archangel had refused to advance against the Bolshevik front there had been mitigating circumstances aplenty. They were under British officers whose policy in Russia was not shared by the Americans. They had been inducted to fight the Germans and the war with Germany had been over for six months. They'd suffered through a harsh winter. Casualties in the area had been heavy and no one could explain to them why they were expected to fight. The White Russian troops commanded by General Miller had deserted in droves, leaving the American flanks exposed, so the behavior of the men of I Company was nothing more than plain common sense until the word "mutiny" was applied to it.

Colonel Spaeth was not going to let that word be applied in this situation.

The membrane of command was so fragile that Spaeth always marveled that it was not more frequently ruptured. He knew, however, that in this case it had been, he could see the wound in Carlisle's eyes.

He took General Graves' wire from under his blotter and gave it to Carlisle. "Jack," he said, "I called you in to take on a job of vital importance. I'm sorry I can't ask your preference in the matter. That's from General Graves."

Carlisle took the wire, read it and learned nothing.

"It's the reference to Code 3 that concerns you; it refers to our preparations for withdrawal. The British and French have started their evacuation of Omsk. Our people there are coming out with them. I want you to go to Irkutsk and organize transportation for all American personnel in the area. That includes the Red Cross, Y.M.C.A., Knights of Columbus, our hospital personnel, the Railway Service Corps and our consular staffs."

"Has the word come then, officially?"

"I want to be ready for it."

Carlisle frowned and returned the wire to Spaeth's desk. "That's a tour guide's job, Colonel," he said quietly.

"It's your job. I want you on the first train for Irkutsk."

"Who takes the company?"

"I haven't decided. Charlie will have your orders this afternoon. You'd better phone down and have your gear packed. By the way, did you get the Snorter back?"

Carlisle nodded and stood up. He was hurting, clearly. "Yes, it was on the siding at Mysovaya."

"Nobody saw them?"

"Nobody fool enough to say so if they did."

"I think he'll come in, Jack."

Carlisle's eyes flashed up and met Spaeth's. "He wrecked that company! Just tore it apart!"

Colonel Spaeth winced at the bitterness and looked away. "Ask Charlie to come in here, will you?"

When the door closed behind Carlisle, Colonel Spaeth found himself tugging at his mustache again. He'd lost a good officer and he knew it. It was a casualty no one could explain; there were too many factors, too many unknowns. Men change under pressure; some warp, some break, some are hardened by it. Spaeth wasn't certain which had happened to Carlisle, but he knew better than to keep him on at Tataurovo where he would be exposed to the rankling memories of what Lieutenant Ryan had characterized as a mutiny. Perhaps it was, but Spaeth's sympathy was with the men and with Ira. Had he been there at the time he would have seen to it that Maryenka Austin got safely away. Yes, he hoped she was safe. He liked to think she was, just as he liked to think Peg and the kids were safe.

He was sorry Carlisle had taken it so hard, but for a reason which he had not suspected until now. Carlisle had been shaken and if this could happen to Carlisle it could happen to Bentham, or Cloak, or to any of them, including himself. Yes, it could happen to any of them.

« 2 »

On the eve of General Bogoloff's assassination Anitsky had already been in a state of panic over preparations for leaving with Maryenka. He had scurried about packing his money and clothing in a bag, fretting himself, turning circles of consternation in the middle of the floor like a dog about to lie down, jabbering "Yes, yes," to himself over and over again as he remembered and promptly forgot something he had been about to do. One of these "Yes, yeses," had been in response to Maryenka's announcement that she had to go to town and sell something. Ten minutes later, when he noticed her absence, Anitsky was quite alarmed. For a staggering instant he couldn't remember her name; then, with a clutching gesture, he snatched it out of the air and cried "Maryenka!"

He stood in the center of the cabin floor; his much lined nose-ridden face elongated in a look of peculiar abstraction. "To sell something? To sell what, dear God?"

He looked around as though to discover what was missing that she could possibly sell. He seemed to recollect her having a bundle in her arms when she left. A basket. Yes, a basket.

"A basket," he said aloud. "A basket?"

He hadn't noticed this basket before.

A hundred conjectures raced through his mind. He unpacked his own bag and packed it up again, wondering why.

"Anitsky," he said and the sound of his own voice caused him to tremble. He listened breathless to the dying tones of it. "You're terrified," he whispered.

For a long time he remained motionless trying to discover the source of his terror. He decided to have a glass of tea and prepared it stealthily to keep from making a sound. He tiptoed with it to the table and sat down, quaking as the chair creaked beneath him. The rattle of the spoon on the edge of his glass crashed against his nerves.

"What is it about?" he wondered and the thoughts in his head were noisy. The words seemed to clatter together. He sat very still, listening intently to avoid his clattering thoughts.

The thought "What is it?" squeaked painfully under the sill of his mind and he closed his eyes tightly to hold the others out.

The black silence expanded around him.

The taut back of his neck grew cold.

He folded his hands together and bowed his head and the tea in his glass grew cold.

Outside it was cold.

He sensed the river freezing.

Then with a frenzied cry Anitsky bounded up, overturning the table and chair. The noise of their falling drove him out of the cabin. He snatched his bag and ran, leaving the door swinging on its hinges behind him. At the black edge of the Uda River he recoiled.

"My dear man," he gasped, "what possesses you? Calm yourself, sweetheart." And he stood on the riverbank panting for breath. "Be calm," he thought, "be calm. Think pleasant thoughts."

Gradually his breathing grew regular and he walked along the river bank toward town thinking of a summer visit to the Buryat Lamasery near a pass in the mountains around the Selenga Valley known as the Shamar Daban.

There, in cloister buildings on the shore of a small, blue lake, dwelt forty priests of the ancient Buryat faith. The day of his visit had been warm. He'd gone to them on horseback and when he dismounted his horse had walked to the edge of the lake to drink. The priests, dressed in curious waist-length jackets and robes, with nimble faces and placid eyes had greeted him courteously and they had watched his horse with longing. It was a good horse, they said. It was a horse to conjure with.

They spread a cloth beside the lake and brought him kumiss, tea and cheese. They asked about his background. He told them his father was Polish. Poland they knew, oh yes, Warsaw. Constantinople they knew and Prague. Oh, yes, all of this had at one time been controlled by their Buryat-Mongol forebears who had conquered most of the European and Asiatic world. Yes, they knew but their eyes followed the movements of his horse, which he had hired at a stable in Verkhne-Udinsk. At last he was given to understand that they would like to buy this horse of his. Anitsky had been surprised; it wasn't much of a horse after all, but they were earnest in their desire to buy it from him. When he explained that it was not his to sell, but belonged to the stable manager in Verkhne-Udinsk, they grew silent but continued observing the horse up to the moment he left.

Anitsky chuckled recalling the stable manager's rage. "You blockhead!

Why didn't you say you were going there? Every Buryat in the region will be after this horse. I won't be able to rent it out again. They'll plague my customers to buy him and plague me too."

"Why so?"

"Because they've taken sight on it; they've selected it! They sacrifice horses at certain times! They drink horse blood. They're known as the People of the Horse! You've lost me a horse, Anitsky!"

"So, sell it to them."

"Yes, and they'll look to me for more. They'll think I'm a special provider of sacrificial horses! They'll plague me! You've ruined my business, Anitsky!"

And so it was.

Six months later the stable manager sold out to escape the watchful eyes of the Buryats. He moved to Vladivostok where he prospered as a restaurateur, and in gratitude to Anitsky for this unexpected rise in fortune he had written to say that Anitsky would always have a job in Vladivostok if he should come.

Anitsky stopped. "Why, that's exactly what I shall do!" he said aloud and was astounded that this old recollection should have brought him around to his present circumstances. He had entirely forgotten the man. "Pankratov," he said. "Sergei Vladimirovitch Pankratov. Why, I shall write to him at once! At once!"

He looked around to get his bearings and at that moment a mob of howling people spilled out of the Mulligan. Unconsciously he had traced his usual steps to work. He saw Maryenka borne aloft. She was thrown down and dragged, then a man lifted her and ran.

There were shouts: "Murder!" "Assassin!" "Traitors!"

Anitsky stood paralyzed with his bag in his hand. A burly Cossack ran up and grabbed him roughly by the collar. "Did you see them?" he roared.

Anitsky couldn't reply.

"Who are you?"

"Sergei Vladimirovitch Pankratov."

"Stay where you are," the Cossack bellowed and he ran down the street, brandishing a machine pistol in one hand.

Anitsky stood rooted to the spot. "My God," he thought, "dear God in heaven, I've given the wrong name!" Then he dropped his bag and ran.

"There goes one of them!" a voice shouted and the mob at the door of the Mulligan, using his flight as an excuse, scattered in all directions.

Many chased Anitsky, particularly those anxious to escape in the direction he had taken, so they could drop off at their homes and apartments and hide.

Anitsky, buoyant with fear, fled down the dark residential streets. Watchdogs, wild on the ends of their clashing chains, barked and snapped at him. The thinning mob came on in his wake, led by members of Colonel Sipialef's Cossack police.

The name Pankratov hammered in Anitsky's oxygen-starved brain. Pankratov, Pankratov! Why had he done it? Pankratov!

At last Anitsky's strength gave out and he collapsed in a heap. The nearest pursuer fell over him. The next man reached down and jerked Anitsky up and shook him like a snake. "Who are you?"

"My name," Anitsky bleated, in the voice of the smallest child, "is Anitsky and I am very frightened."

He felt a metallic blow crush the side of his cheek and as he lost consciousness another heavy voice said:

"Save him! Save him, damn you, or we'll never hear the end of it!"

CHAPTER THIRTY

TIMOKHIN and his men were encamped in caves on the northeastern shore of Baikal near the Svyatoi Nos Peninsula. Far down the lake they could see the elongated hilly island of Olkhon encircled by a skin of dangerous ice which slowly grew thicker and one day would bear the weight of military patrols sent by the Whites to drive the partisans out of the mountains.

In a recent skirmish with one such patrol Timokhin had been struck in the chest by a bullet. The men saw him hit, saw him stagger, then straighten up and turn as if watching the flight of the bullet which had passed through his body. There was a hole in the back of his sheepskin jacket where the bullet had come out. Balashov and Slavin had rushed to support him, but Timokhin glared at them so ferociously, as though their offer of assistance was an affront to his dignity, that they fell back.

When the White patrol had been driven off, the only concession Timokhin made to his wound was to ride rather than walk to their caves. He never referred to the wound and the men dared not do so. If he dressed it he did so at night when no one saw.

This incident increased the reverence in which Timokhin was held by his men. Those who had recently joined the band to replace casualties regarded him with religious awe and tales of the man who could not die were whispered around all the humble stoves and campfires of the Trans-Baikal and Timokhin with only thirty men at his disposal became the most powerful single figure in all that region.

How this power was to be used was the question.

With the collapse of the Kolchak front, partisan bands were beginning to coalesce into larger units which were in turn gathered into two great partisan armies, one under Kravchenko, the other under Marmatov. Representations had come from both of these men offering Timokhin regimental commands to join them and Marrakof was particularly anxious that he accept. "But see here," he urged, "we are assured of winning!"

"If one is assured of winning, to fight is meaningless."

"They have artillery and trucks! They even print their own newspaper!"

"Do you read newspapers then, Marrakof?"

And the men laughed because none of them could read. But the problem remained and Marrakof was truculent. "If we do not join them," he said, "they will think of us as enemies."

And this was so.

Timokhin knew it to be so because Marmatov had already sent a message which did not request, but demanded, an answer to his offer. "We cannot afford doubtful men on our flank."

Kravchenko also asked for an immediate decision and Balashov began to side with Marrakof, arguing that further delay was unnecessary and dangerous, but Timokhin silenced both men with a wave of his scarred red hand saying he would decide in his own good time.

Because he had survived after having been struck in the chest by a bullet which would have killed any ordinary man, an awful question had entered Timokhin's mind; it occupied him night and day, both waking and sleeping, and incapacitated him for making decisions. Was it true, he wondered? Was it true, as they all believed, that he could not die?

Timokhin had no fear of death, but he had never believed it could not touch him. He'd allowed the story of his invincibility to spread because it gave him power over the minds of the people and commanded the loyalty and obedience of his men. But the wound in his chest which had not healed and had not killed him caused Timokhin to wonder if he had been condemned to eternal life on this earth. He considered this day and night and found it so dreadful a prospect that he asked what sins he had committed to merit such punishment.

Eternal life on this earth? What should one do? How could one act? What is the meaning of life without end?

Such questions made the decisions of which partisan army he should join irrelevant. The entire civil war was irrelevant if one was condemned to live forever. Those who could die could choose, but Timokhin had no choice.

Very often he sat up the whole night staring into the embers of the campfire through his lidless eyes and the men, increasingly disturbed by his lack of leadership, grew restive.

Balashov appealed to him again for a decision and Slavin added his voice to the others. "Something must be done," he said. "Shall it be Kravchenko or Marmatov?"

Their urgency puzzled Timokhin. He looked into their eyes trying to understand it. They did not seem to know that for him there could be no urgency, no matters of life and death. If they believed he could not die, how could they expect him to decide for them? "It doesn't matter," he said.

"But we must decide," Marrakof insisted.

"Decide then," Timokhin said.

The men looked at each other trying to guess who among them preferred Kravchenko to Marmatov, but they sensed the band would split unless Timokhin made the decision for them.

"We'll wait," Slavin said.

Then one afternoon Balashov returned from a trip to Mysovaya with the news that General Bogoloff had been assassinated and that two fugitives had been seen in the village. "They're hiding in a boat shed near the lake," he said. "An American and a girl. It's Glubov's Maryenka."

For the first time in days Timokhin took interest. "Are you sure, Balashov?" he asked.

"The town is alive with soldiers."

"Are you sure it's Glubov's Maryenka?"

"That's who they're searching for."

"Will the people hide them?"

"Yes, until you decide what's to be done," Balashov declared.

Timokhin beckoned for Slavin. "Bring her to me," he said.

"And the American?" Slavin asked.

"Let Maryenka decide, but be quick," Timokhin said and the anxiety in his voice brought smiles of relief because Timokhin had become their leader again and the men who had known Maryenka blessed her for the look of interest in Timokhin's eyes. He needed a woman, yes, that was it. They should have guessed as much, for they were all women-starved, but

Timokhin more than the others, for he never went to Mysovaya or to Verkhne-Udinsk.

« 2 »

Maryenka and Ira had abandoned the Snorter on a siding short of Mysovaya and skirted the village seeking a place to hide before daylight came. They were emotionally exhausted and chilled to the bone with only Ira's coat and one blanket between them. The village dogs barked as they passed, the sound carrying far out over the lake, and they were sure everyone in the village was alerted to their presence and that they would be apprehended momentarily, but just at daybreak they slipped into a boat shed near the lake and lay down in the bottom of one of the boats sheltered there. The advent of the light was awful, for it seemed to them to cast giant shadows of their crimes across the buildings and streets of Mysovaya for all the waking villagers to see.

Ah! What's this? Here's the black shadow of a murderess on the street. And there over the rooftops the shadow of a deserter. Let's find the place from which these shadows are cast and apprehend the criminals.

Ira and Maryenka lay perfectly still, listening for the approach of villagers armed with shotguns, axes and hayforks. Their eyes were wide open, focused upward on the shadows of their crimes towering over the roof of the shed, looming monuments of black basalt which would have been invisible at night.

The slightest sound sent a shudder through their bodies. The bark of a dog, nearby voices, a passing footfall turned their minds to cold stone. But at last the imagined monuments diminished and the shadows receded. No one was coming for them and they closed their eyes.

Ira dreamed he was conducting his own defense before a military tribunal but his impassioned plea for exoneration went badly askew as the features of the chairman became more distinct. He watched this stern officer's face closely as he tried to match eloquent gestures to his ringing statements: "I love my country deeply as any native son!" — His hand was left in the air waggling and ineffective. — "But in the circumstances I would not have it said that Americans were callous, were wanting in human feeling, did not revere life, liberty and the pursuit of happiness!" — Both hands were flung out before his face, fingers separated like bars in a jail window beyond which he could see the face of his judge, whose eyes had taken on a hurt look. — "Gentlemen, put yourselves in my place. Ask what you would have done! Search your own hearts and I know you will vote to acquit!"

He stood there head bowed trying to fetch tears into his eyes and one word shot out of the silence: "Guilty!"

He looked up and to his horror saw his mother in the officer's uniform. Her mouth was bruised with emotion, but her eyes flamed with the indignation of betrayal. "You don't love me," she cried. "She's no good! A thousand years hard labor to you!"

His father and Uncle Dave jumped up from their chairs and tried to calm the chairman, but she thrust them away, her bemedaled bosom heaving, tears streaming from her eyes. "He tears my heart to pieces! You don't know the pain of a mother's heart. Guilty! Guilty!"

Ruth fell into his arms and they wept together. "Ruth," he moaned. "Ruth. Ruth."

He woke up and found himself clinging to Maryenka in the bottom of the boat and his dream vanished even as he tried to remember it. The shed was almost dark. They'd slept the whole day.

Maryenka sat up. She was still wearing Ira's oversized coat and they had the blanket over them. She looked around dazedly. "I think it's begun to snow," she said.

They both listened and there was a thickened silence in the air outside. "Yes."

Maryenka threw the blanket back and struggled out of the coat. "If I go quickly the snow will cover my tracks."

"Go where!"

"I'll make some inquiries in town."

"You'll come back?"

"Yes."

She got out of the boat, but Ira caught her hand. "You're not coming back," he accused.

"What are you thinking of?"

"You aren't!'

Maryenka disengaged her hand. "You must go to your people," she said. "If you go now it would not be so bad for you."

"Not until I've seen you safe," he said.

She looked at him sternly. "Then you'll go?" she asked.

"Yes."

Maryenka promised to return in an hour. Ira put the blanket around her shoulders and watched from the door until her figure was lost in the falling snow. When he could no longer see her his apprehensions became unbearable. He paced about the low-ceilinged shed, knocking his head against the crossbeams, as night fell.

A few more days wouldn't add appreciably to the charges against him. Once Maryenka was safe he could walk in voluntarily and face up to them. What could the charges be, after all: absent without leave, complicity in Bogoloff's death, aiding the escape of a fugitive, refusal to obey orders, mutiny? They could bring a long list if they wanted to do it. Because of Bogoloff's death and his connection with it the American authorities might have to make an example of him, but even a harsh sentence in the field could be suspended when it was reviewed at home, away from the political pressures. Looked at soberly his position wasn't as bad as it had seemed to be the night before.

As a matter of fact it would be an interesting trial. It would bring to light Sipialef's connection with the Pashkova massacre and force the American authorities to extend their protection to Maryenka. The important thing was to keep her alive and safe. The next thing was to get their story out to the American press so public opinion could be brought into play.

"Cossack allies slaughter villagers!"

"Leverett says American policy wrong!"

Ira found himself growing excited at the prospect. It was the kind of case on which a man could make an international reputation! It had all the ingredients of great drama. He'd fight it himself, but not for himself, for Maryenka, the woman wronged, pregnant wife of a soldier who'd given his life for his country. Christ! He'd kill them with it. All he had to do was get to the press, get a letter out to his Uncle Dave, who'd know how to handle it. He'd tear the god-damned Army apart with it! What efforts had they made to find and protect Maryenka? Damned little. He'd make them swallow hot pokers over that!

Ira smacked a fist into the palm of his hand, savoring the prospect, imagining how he was going to pillory Major Taziola when he got him on the stand:

Can you tell us, Major, the circumstances under which you first learned of the possibility that Mrs. Austin was in Verkhne-Udinsk?

You told me you'd seen her at Beresovka.

At the Beresovka prisoner of war camp, is that correct?

Yes.

Was anyone else present on that occasion?

Captain Whyte, a British officer.

Anyone else?

Colonel Sipialef.

The same Colonel Sipialef who conducted the massacre at Pashkova?

I didn't know about that at the time. None of us did.

Upon hearing Mrs. Austin had been seen, or was reported to have been seen, what efforts did you make to locate her?

Well, I wasn't sure she had been seen. I hadn't seen her!

You believed the information was false?

I didn't know!

You made no effort to find out?

Taziola would squirm. He'd make all of them squirm like hell!

Ira stopped beside a boat and struck a match. "My God," he thought, "I'm raving!"

He'd forgotten Maryenka, forgotten the passage of time, forgotten everything but his plan to capitalize on Maryenka's tragedy and Austin's death.

He sat down on the gunnel of the boat, weary and filled with distrust of himself. He was behaving like a child. The match burned out and he dropped it.

"One thing at a time," he said aloud. "Take things as they come, one at a time."

He went to the door of the shed and opened it a crack to watch for Maryenka. It was dark and the snow had thickened. It had already covered the tracks she'd made on leaving and would quickly cover the tracks she made coming back — If she came back.

Ira shuddered and found himself praying for Maryenka's return. All his life he'd been loved or indulged, now he needed someone to rely on him, to trust him. Without this he would always be a boy, intelligent, entertaining, successful no doubt, but a boy.

How long had she been gone? They might have captured her and he would never know if she had intended coming back or not; if she had trusted him or not.

The tension in Ira drew out to the snapping point, then he saw a figure dark through the veiling snow. He snatched his overcoat and ran out to bring Maryenka to the shed. His heart bounded. She'd come back! She was coming back!

He felt overjoyed, safe and strong. The new snow popped under his feet and the dark figure toward which he was running grew larger. He called her name once, then in a final rush Ira swept Maryenka into his arms, nearly toppling both of them into the snow. "Here you are!" he said, his dark eyes dancing with relief.

Maryenka looked at him in a startled way, then she too smiled. "What did you think, then?" she asked. "I said I'd be back."

"It was important to me," he said.

"I've brought some food. I'm to wait in the boat shed for Slavin."

"Who's Slavin?"

"One of Timokhin's men. They know we're here. All the villagers know we're here. They'll help you back to Tataurovo and I'll go on."

She hurried him to the shed and closed the door. From under her blanket she produced a candle and matches. "It doesn't matter about the light," she said. "The patrols have been decoyed south by two men supposed to be us. They're all against Kolchak and the Whites, so we're safe. My description is posted all over the village, but no one would turn me in."

Maryenka put the candle on the floor and opened the bundle. There was fish, bread and a bottle of vodka. Ira ate greedily; he was famished, but he couldn't tell if the vodka or the fact that they were safe warmed him more.

"I'm going with you, Maryenka," he said.

"But no! You promised to go back."

"When you're safe. A few more days won't matter to me. I don't know Slavin and I won't leave until I'm sure you're all right. Besides, you can't stay in the hills forever, there's Harry's baby to consider."

"You know about the baby?" Maryenka asked and she seemed frightened. "How do you know?"

"You told me last night."

"About the baby?"

"Yes."

Maryenka rose and went to the door of the shed. She couldn't remember having said anything about the child. Had she told him about her captivity, or her gnawing doubt that the child was Austin's? She looked at Ira from the shadows and found him gazing at her worriedly.

"What is it, Maryenka?" he asked.

"I'd forgotten you knew," she said.

"That's why I'm coming with you. I've got to know where you'll be, then I can go back and make plans to get you out, to Chita or Vladivostok, where you'll be looked after. Do you think I'd let Harry's kid be born in some godforsaken hut in the mountains? I owe him more than that. I owe him my life as a matter of fact."

Ira described how Austin had thrown him to the floor of the train during the attack at Siding 85 just as the volley of bullets shattered the window where he had been sitting. He told her of Austin's bravery and how he had been killed, but when he reached this part he stopped, for there were tears in Maryenka's eyes and she sank to her knees like a crushed thing and fell forward moaning.

Ira caught Maryenka in his arms. At first he thought she was ill; he couldn't understand what she was saying because she spoke in Russian and her sobbing blurred the words, but at last she composed herself and moved out of his arms. "You have no reason to come with me," she said.

"But I just gave you my reason. Harry was my friend!"

"It's not his child," Maryenka said painfully and seeing the look of incredulity in Ira's eyes she sat with her back against the shed door and told him about her captivity aboard Sipialef's train and how she reached Anitsky at Verkhne-Udinsk.

As he listened Ira remembered Maryenka's wedding, how she'd looked in her russet dress with his hothouse iris clutched in one arm, how her eyes sparkled with adoration when Austin had kissed her; he remembered the sound of Harry's voice in Harbin as he wrapped the coin necklace to send Maryenka in Pashkova and he remembered Sipialef beside the Invincible at the marshaling yard in Vladivostok, and with all this he was filled with a sullen fury.

"— And I'd hoped, for just a moment, when you said you know about the baby, that Harry might have told you," Maryenka concluded. "He couldn't have known, of course, but all the same — I've never had a child, you see."

"It's Harry's," Ira said resolutely. "And I'm coming with you because that's so, and if you weren't pregnant right now I'd turn you over my knee and paddle you for not coming to me the minute you arrived in Verkhne-Udinsk and for running away from me that night at Beresovka. The only reason I'm not going to paddle you is that it might upset Harry's kid, but when he's born his mother is also going to get a swat on the fanny."

Maryenka was so taken aback by Ira's vehemence and yet so reassured by his insistence that the child was Austin's that she didn't know what to say and Ira gave her no chance to reply.

"I'm going with you and that's all there is to that! I was best man at your wedding and Harry's best friend. Slavin and Timokhin, whoever they are, will just damned well have to put up with me until I can arrange to get you to a place where Harry's kid deserves to be born. And you can bet your life when Colonel Spaeth hears about this he'll turn the regiment out and tear Sipialef and his god-damned armored trains to pieces. That son of a bitch will wish he was dead. How soon do you expect this Slavin to turn up here?"

"I'm not sure," Maryenka said humbly.

"When he gets here you just tell him I'm coming along! You tell him, by God, that I'm godfather to your kid because that's who I am from now on out and you don't have anything to say about it. Why in hell didn't you come and get me to shoot Sipialef for you? I'd have enjoyed it. You could have been killed or hurt. Are you sure you're all right?"

Maryenka nodded.

"That dirty son of a bitch," Ira blustered and he took a long pull on the bottle of vodka. He felt very brave and domineering and he was pleased to have overwhelmed Maryenka's fears. She was gazing at him wonderingly, depending on him as she would have depended on Austin, and Ira wasn't going to let her down.

"I don't want any argument," he said.

"But you'll go back soon? As soon as you've seen how it is with Timokhin?"

"Of course! Didn't I say so? I'm going back to take care of Sipialef and then the whole 27th Regiment will escort you to the best American hospital in Siberia with flags flying and bands playing and General Graves himself will confer American citizenship on Harry Austin's kid and President Wilson will send you a telegram of congratulations."

Maryenka smiled, then she giggled. "You're a fool, like Harry," she said.

"There's always a supply of fools," Ira said and he offered Maryenka some bread, then he wrapped the blanket around their shoulders and they watched the candle flame dance in the drafty air of the shed as they waited for Slavin.

« 3 »

Within forty-eight hours of his appointment as C.I.C. for the defense of Omsk, General Sakharov was forced to concede that General Dietrichs' appraisal of the military situation had been correct and that evacuation was the only advisable course of action.

Though it was already November the Irtysh River had not yet frozen, which meant that Kolchak's main forces would not be able to march across, but would have to make a stand with their backs to the river. The civilian population had no intention of supporting the defense; those who had been drafted to dig earthworks on the outskirts of the city vanished the minute their guards' backs were turned. The case was hopeless and when General Sakharov reported this to Admiral Kolchak the Supreme Ruler bowed his head.

"You understand, of course, General, that once the order to evacuate is given, once this government is in flight, it means the end."

"We can regroup and defend Irkutsk, your excellency."

"Irkutsk is not Moscow, General," Kolchak said. "Do you understand the implications of this move?"

Sakharov nodded solemnly.

"And there is no other way?"

"We cannot defend Omsk, your excellency."

Admiral Kolchak remained silent for a time gazing at the snowfall beyond the windows of his office. "The collapse of a government, even a bad government, is a terrible thing, General. It takes so many of the innocent down with it."

The Supreme Ruler continued to gaze out the window. He'd asked his Prime Minister, Vologodsky, to attempt negotiations for a surrender and been told that the Red advance was so inexorable that such negotiations were not possible. He'd replaced Vologodsky with Victor Pepelyaev, formerly the Minister of Interior, and received the same reply. Juggling ministers and generals was obviously no longer going to bring even temporary relief. His government was finished.

General Sakharov cleared his throat and Kolchak looked at him absent-mindedly. "Yes?"

"The plans for evacuation must be set in motion, your excellency."

Kolchak could not bring himself to speak the words which would bring the end of his regime and General Sakharov did not force him to it, but turned on his heel and left the room.

When he returned to his headquarters Sakharov began working around the clock to accomplish the evacuation of Omsk. He contacted all commanders in the field and informed them of the decision. He wired the officials of Irkutsk to expect the Supreme Ruler and his government, which would establish itself in that city to plan a sweeping counterattack in the near future. He issued orders that all trains in the immediate vicinity be concentrated at Omsk and had the Russian gold reserves, six hundred and seventy-five million rubles in bullion, made ready to move with the government.

In the midst of this feverish activity one of Sakharov's aides kept after him with a request from a Czech pilot who wished to keep his aircraft and assist in the defense of Omsk.

"There is no defense, idiot!" the General said angrily.

"The French are asking him to give up his aeroplane."

"Tell him to go to Janin!"

"He has gone and had no satisfaction."

"No one is going to have satisfaction at a time like this. Clear him out!"

Sometime later the same aide brought the matter up again. Sakharov was beside himself with impatience. "Will you stop this nonsense, Igor! I said clear him out. You ought to know better. Let him do whatever he damned well pleases, but don't trouble me about it again."

"Yes, sir. I'll assign him to the rear guard, then."

"Assign him to hell, for all I care!"

And in this manner Count Albert Nojine received orders to act as air observer for the rear guard which would attempt to delay the Red entrance into the city of Omsk.

On November 10 the Irtysh froze and Kolchak's Second and Third Armies under General Kappel and General Voitsekhovsky were able to cross the river and screen the retreat.

On the night of November 14 Kolchak, his cabinet and their dependents crawled out of Omsk in seven trains, one of which contained the gold reserves.

General Janin had gone ahead with several echelons of Czechs to clear the track for the Kolchak government following in his wake.

The meager force pledged to delay the Red advance into Omsk stared dull-eyed across the frozen Irtysh and wondered what tokens of resistance would spare both their honor and their lives.

They wished the bullets, bayonets, lances and swords on both sides would turn to wax, that the artillery shells would burst as harmless jelly so they could make a spirited defense without being torn to bits. Yet their weariness was so great that given the choice of retreating or standing they would have chosen to stand. They wanted to sleep. The very thought of sleep drugged them, causing their pulses to slacken and their eyelids to droop. Only the fear of death kept them awake. Now and again a man in the line would be jerked up by the vision of himself being shattered into a howling, crimson blot on the snow, but beyond these somber considerations there was very little to hold their attention. They had long ago discovered that war was dull. Even in the height of an action it was the dullness spiked by occasionally witnessed horrors which was unforgettable.

They waited for the attack, humble, weary, already defeated, and the only relief they found from the dullness was the presence of an aeroplane in the pewter sky.

This aeroplane hung about their lines and the troops envied the pilot's detachment. A company of lancers standing beside their steaming horses looked aloft as the aeroplane passed overhead, then met each other's eyes and grinned in recognition of the unspoken wish that each of them could have such freedom. They longed to fly, to escape, to hear the whistle of the harmless wind in their ears, but the order came to mount and they rose to the saddle, calmed their chafing horses and stared down across the river at the Red forces massing there.

« 4 »

With a movement of his wrist the pilot tipped the earth and flew along examining its dirty surface. It was like a white porcelain plate which needed scrubbing, or a picnic plate left on the grass, with ants clustered around the particles of food trying to carry them off.

Ahead he saw the blur of his propeller and set the great white plate gently down to avoid cracking it. The heat of the engine blew back around the cockpit and the small pennants on the guy wires between the wings fluttered with a sound of their own.

The pilot loved his machine, its power, its frailty; above all he loved the superiority it gave him over all men and all women. For him, sex had become a long, strut-screaming dive broken at the last moment by the manipulation of those controls which, if the laws of aerodynamics prevailed, would result in a pull-out, and in this moment with the stick eased back against his thigh he frequently howled as his aircraft, straining to the last degree of tolerance, mushed beneath him, squirming, threatening to tear itself apart. And each time his beloved aircraft survived this maneuver the pilot felt a deep, perverse disappointment not unmixed with pride. He could never disentangle these contradictory emotions and each time he dove in this way he started higher, came down faster and pulled out closer to the ground as though there were some conjunction of altitude, speed and daring which would resolve these contradictions for him.

In the beginning he was annoyed at having fallen in love with an aeroplane — it was a Nieuport brought in through Odessa by the French when they assumed overall command of the Czechs — but ultimately he reached the conclusion that love of a machine was more dignified, more pure than human love could possibly be. With this understanding his aircraft had begun to live for him. The fabric covering its fuselage and wings was alive to the touch of his hand; the smell of fuel and warm oil was more vital than the fragrance of a woman's body and the engine spoke to him in all the variations of its speed. In time he learned the caprices of this individual aircraft, its tendency to nose over in a climb, the need to correct straight flight with a small amount of right rudder, the extra buoyancy of the left wings caused by the rotation of the prop, and all these things grew dear to him.

He could tell if his aircraft was out of sorts by the sound of the wind in guy wires. The machine expressed emotions entirely independent of his, eagerness when he felt dull, petulance when he was keen for the day in the air. He talked to it constantly, cheering or cajoling as the case required, and the aircraft talked to him, so that sometimes he laughed affectionately and caressed it. "My dear," he would cry tolerantly, "ah, my dear!" And they would go up after a cloud and do an exuberant loop.

At night while asleep he dreamed he was flying, so really there was no time when he and his craft were parted. When parachutes were issued he refused to take one, for he was too attached to his aeroplane to think of living beyond it.

As far as their service together in the war was concerned there was very little for them to do. They flew scouting missions and delivered messages from one Czech division to another, from Syrovy to Cecek, to Gaida. Once they flew from Ekaterinburg to the British in Archangel and from Archangel to Murmansk, then all the way back to Ufa. Sometimes they had difficulty relocating their lines because of the fluid situation on the ground and once, having landed in a field, they succeeded in begging fuel from a group of Red guards who were even so kind as to hold the tail while the engine revved up enough so they could clear the trees. That time he'd laughed aloud and the Nieuport had roared laughter too.

"Oh, my dear! My dear!"

They'd had so many narrow escapes, so many laughs!

The Reds made little use of aircraft. At least they didn't risk them in individual combat, which was a disappointment. They didn't seem to have the pilots. Flying wasn't a proletarian business. A factory worker from Petrograd might be good slogging on the ground with his rations and a rifle on his back, but he didn't have the gallantry to fly. Individual combat in the air hearkened back to knight-errantry, to the joust. It was aristocratic and there were no aristocrats among the Reds. This was a disappointment and they often spent the day hoping to see an enemy plane rise to meet them. But since this didn't happen they went after the trains.

They would drop out of the sky like an eagle toward a snake and when they were over the tender he'd drop a bomb from the rack by hand. He was pretty good at this and sometimes they'd feel the heat of the blast and looking back could see coal or wood or a human body rise in the air, spinning slowly like a cut paper doll. Then people would spill out of the train and stand about gabbling, pointing upward. They'd turn and come back along the length of the train, their machine gun raising splinters of wood from the roofs of the cars like sprouting corn. The passengers would scatter and howl under the knout of the chattering gun; dive for cover, some over the embankment, some under the cars, and if one of these contained explosives then there was a hot shaft of flame and boiling smoke.

But sometimes the bomb fell into the tender and failed to detonate, or he missed with all their bombs and the train didn't stop, so they flew along with the wheels nearly touching the tops of the cars, chewing at the engine with their gun until the engineer and fireman abandoned the cab and the train ran on uncontrolled.

Nothing they did really affected the course of the war; they had no illusions about this. What happened on the ground was immaterial as far as they were concerned. But sometimes the pilot, discovering a faithless need for human comradeship, would satisfy this by going to a club where officers gathered to drink and exchange views. In the fall when the Whites and Czechs were being driven back on Omsk these clubs were frequently no more than huts behind the lines or small train stations. The pilot would take a seat in the corner and listen to the men until he grew impatient with the discordant crosscurrent of tone, with the arguments and the expectations, then he would rise without a word and hurry back to the silent harmony of his aeroplane.

To those who knew his reputation the pilot was an object of curiosity. They thought him possessed, but they didn't know of what. Occasionally a staff officer coming forward from Vladivostok, Chita or Irkutsk would hail him across the noisy smoke-dim room and force his way through the crowd to shake his hand or embrace him. The pilot always accepted these demonstrations with a slight shudder and on one notable occasion just prior to the fall of Omsk he was met by a Czech lieutenant who appeared bent on getting himself killed. "Well, Albert," this officer said, "there you are."

"Yes, Raul," the pilot said, "here I am."

"May I sit down?"

"Please yourself."

They were in a building adjoining Kappel's headquarters. The guns of the Fifth Red Army could be heard in the distance and the incoming shells were already chopping craters in the snow beyond the river. The pilot kept a wary eye on his aeroplane, which could be seen through the frosted window standing on the ice-clad Irtysh a quarter of a mile away. "I see you owe the French an aeroplane."

"I'm keeping it for a souvenir," the pilot said.

"Then you're not going back by train."

"No."

"I'll tell Dubrovski. He'll want your place for someone else."

"I've already informed him."

"And Tatiana?"

"Dubrovski will tell her."

"What?"

"That I'll be delayed."

"Perhaps I'll be able to tell her myself."

"Do so."

They sat across the small table from each other, smiling. A victrola in one corner of the room was playing a reedy French song. Two Russian officers were playing billiards listlessly while waiting to be called to their stations.

"When can she expect you?" the lieutenant asked.

"I'll be with Kappel in the rear guard. When do you leave, Raul?"

"This evening, with luck."

They continued to smile. They did not drink or smoke but sat square on to each other smiling in a peculiarly challenging fashion.

"You haven't seen or written to her?"

"No."

"I should kill you."

The pilot shrugged.

"Tatiana and I have been lovers."

"I supposed you had been," the pilot said.

The lieutenant's face colored slightly. "I wanted to tell you."

"I see you did."

"It means nothing?"

"It means what it means to you, Raul."

"I did it because I despise you, Albert. I always have."

"Then that's what it means," the pilot said.

"I want to get at you in the worst possible way, Albert. I want to tie a knot in your soul."

"Well, I see you still believe in God, Raul."

They had not raised their voices and were to all outward appearances unperturbed. The billiard balls clicked over the table. The victrola record came to an end. General Kappel's rear guard artillery began snapping back at the Reds and a few officers left the room.

"I want satisfaction, Albert. I demand it!"

The pilot's smile broadened slightly. "Because you seduced my wife?"

"Don't ridicule me!"

"Then don't be ridiculous. What did you have in mind? That we blow each other's brains out? No one here would be impressed, Raul. You'd get more satisfaction and attract more attention by belching at officers' mess."

"I demand it," the lieutenant repeated. His smile began to tremble and he clenched one hand into a fist. "You owe it to me."

"There's nothing you can take from me, Raul, that I haven't been willing to give up from the first."

"Then what are you living for?"

"To observe."

The lieutenant glanced out the window at the aeroplane.

The pilot nodded. "That's what it's all about," he said. "The Bolsheviks know it."

For the first time the lieutenant detected a flicker of enthusiasm in the pilot's eyes; this gave him hope and eased his tension. "The aeroplane," he said.

"What else can we point to? It's the best example we have of technological progress."

"So you believe in that," the lieutenant said.

"What I believe doesn't matter. It's inevitable."

"Advancing technology, the machine, science?"

"Mankind serves these things, Raul."

The smile was back again on the lieutenant's face. "Do you still keep your mirrors, Albert, and the black circle?"

The pilot looked embarrassed and lowered his eyes for an instant. "Yes, that foolishness," he said. "A bit of bravado in an empty world."

The artillery fire on both sides died away and the officers playing billiards racked their cues. The lieutenant pushed himself up. "I have a car waiting outside," he said.

They didn't shake hands and when the door fell shut behind the lieutenant the pilot remained at the table listening for the automobile engine as he thought about what he had said. It was all very clear to him. Nations rose and fell like pistons in an internal-combustion engine. Humanity was the fuel. Stored intelligence was the carburetor. Emotion the fire, and the goal was greater speed and greater power.

At present the world was retooling. Old societies were being stripped down to their salvageable parts and reconstructed for a powerful thrust into the future. There was much waste in the process, but seen from above it was beautiful and in time mankind would make itself obsolescent. Then there would be purity, great purity in the absence of flesh and in the final unburdened assault on the unknown, but for now he and his aeroplane were riding the crest of the new wave. They were, for now, a unit, a blend of man and machine, but in time the machine would mature and man would wither away like the Marxist state.

The pilot did not hear the engine he had been expecting. He looked out the ice-glazed window and saw the lieutenant walking toward the Nieuport with a fire ax in his hand.

With a cry of horror the pilot leaped up and dashed to the door. The other officers in the room expecting an incoming shell clutched their heads and cowered, but when no explosion came they ran after the pilot.

"Raul!"

The lieutenant started to run.

The frenzied pilot plowed through the waist-deep snow in an effort to intercept the lieutenant before he could reach the aeroplane. "Saboteur!" he bellowed clawing for his pistol.

The lieutenant reached the aeroplane, ducked under its belly and swung his heavy ax at the fuselage. There was a ripping, splintering sound. The ax blade caught in some wires, but the lieutenant wrenched it free and struck again.

The pilot, bellowing, weeping, brandishing his pistol, fired a wild shot at the lieutenant, who ran to the tail assembly and hacked one of the ailerons away. The pilot fell to one knee as though he had himself been crippled by the ax, and as the lieutenant was about to strike again he fired.

The bullet caught the lieutenant in the shoulder and threw him down on the ice. The White officers rushed up and disarmed the pilot before he could kill the fallen lieutenant who, despite his wound, was laughing wildly.

"I've raped your god-damned aeroplane, Albert," he cried. "I've done for you at last, you heartless bastard!" And he stood up, laughing uproariously, then abruptly he fainted and two of the officers carried him up the hill between them.

A high-explosive shell slammed through the ice not a hundred yards away and sent a geyser of black water into the air. The officers around the aeroplane felt the ice tremble under their feet. The pilot, his face white as chalk, examined the damage to his aeroplane muttering: "It's all right, all right. It can be fixed." Like a frantic surgeon over a hopeless case, he smoothed the torn fabric tenderly and got a tool kit out of the cockpit.

Another shell punctured the ice and a wave of freezing water washed toward the aeroplane. "Leave it," one officer said.

The pilot set to work repairing the ruptured wires. His fingers worked nimbly. He would not listen.

The officers left him and went to their stations, for the Red bombardment was picking up, which indicated they would soon make their advance.

From their snow-topped breastworks along the river the men and officers watched the pilot work. "He'll never get it off."

"The Reds must have spotted the plane."

"What about that lieutenant he shot?"

"Patched up and on a train for Irkutsk."

"Lucky bastard."

The Reds adjusted their range and the shells started to bracket the line of defense. The men crouched in their cold earthworks, but between barrages they stood up to see if the pilot and his aircraft were still on the river.

"Still there."

"Crazy son of a bitch."

"Hope he makes it."

"Wish he'd take me with him."

Two hours later they heard the engine sputter, catch and roar to life. One of their own men had dashed out on the ice to spin the prop and now the aeroplane was turning upriver, a white patch on its side where the fabric had been repaired. The men cheered the pilot, then waited breathlessly to see if the craft would be airborne.

It bounced over the rough ice, straining into the wind. It careened to avoid a shell hole; then, as it began to lift, the men exerted all their willpower, pushing upward with it, and when the aeroplane settled into confident flight each of them felt partly responsible.

The pilot sighed with relief. He was free. They were free.

They circled higher, and at their maximum altitude with the engine

beating smoothly in the cold, rarefied air they could see the outline of the
battle which had now begun. Batteries of toy cannon flamed soundlessly
and dimpled craters appeared in the muddy snow. A sotnia of White
lancers charged and floundered in machine gun fire and their lances fell
interlaced like matches dropped from a box.

As the battle grew more intense some of the sounds rose to them over
the steady beat of the engine, the rude, blunt, clumsy sound of cannon and
chittering machine guns. To the east along the double line of rails and on
the trakt beside them, the city seemed to have sprouted a tail. Trains filled
with troops and civilian evacuees were moving away; people covered every
inch of space on the roofs of the cars while others, on foot, dragged their
possessions in sleighs.

From on high the city looked like a suppurating boil which had burst.
One could predict its collapse far ahead of the White generals on the
ground who were still, no doubt, encouraging their troops. The city,
however, had already fallen.

The pilot and his aeroplane circled all the points of the compass, resist-
ing an eastern heading, turning away from that direction as though there
were an invisible wall in the air. There was a line of commitment to those
on the ground which they could not cross. The aeroplane brought to this
line by the pilot as though testing it for a hidden desire to return by way of
Irkutsk to France would dip and circle and the pilot, pleased at this
confirmation of its wish to remain with him, would laugh fondly and yell
curses at the blockheads on the ground, at Dietrichs, Budburg, Kappel, Sakharov, General Janin who had requested the return of the Nieuport, and
most of all that bastard Markowitz who had attacked them with the ax.

Still there remained the decision what to do and the pilot trusted his
aircraft to make it. Letting go of the controls he waited a moment.

The doughty Nieuport faltered, then fell over on its right wing, toward
the west, and dropped into a steep dive. The pilot shouted with glee, seized
the controls and with the throttle wide open dove toward the ground at
such an angle that it seemed to him that the shadow of the tail section fell
across his wings. The white scarf at his throat streamed upward and his
voice joined the engine, the struts and guy wires in a prolonged howl. The
pilot hung in the air suspended by the belt around his waist and the ground
rose at more than a hundred miles an hour, not directly below, but a little
ahead of them as though they were about to twist under in an inverted loop.

Figures became distinct, batteries, horses, troops. Some raised their rifles
firing upward, others scurried for cover.

They came down on the Reds firing their machine gun, not for effect, just for the sound, and then, when there wasn't time enough, they tried to pull out.

The tail refused to drop. There was a shriek of ripping fabric and a terrible beating sound in the air close above. They skipped over a line of trees the top branches of which snagged a streamer of fabric from the lower wing and carried it away. The engine, panting convulsively, began to misfire and a gush of hot oil swept back into the pilot's face.

They made a dead stick landing in three feet of snow, six miles west of Omsk. The pilot was saturated with oil, made warm and comfortable by it. He felt newborn, free, astonished to be alive. He wiped the black oil from his goggles and saw a clean new world, white and silent as untouched paper. There were no human beings in sight. There were no tracks made by them, no betraying sign.

Laved in warm oil he had been delivered into the future life he had envisioned, the pure world of silent machines. He stood up to greet it. He raised one arm in fealty to it, then he saw the dark ciphers marching over the page toward him. He tried to make them out, to read this new language, but before he could do so a barrage of shots dropped him into the sweet cockpit of his aeroplane.

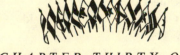

CHAPTER THIRTY-ONE

THE decision to evacuate Omsk sent a shock across the frozen landscape of Siberia and shattered the last remnants of political stability as Admiral Kolchak had known it would. All along the Trans-Siberian, generals, colonels, presidents of local government councils, Atamans Semenoff and Kalmykoff, partisan leaders and representatives of the interested foreign governments sprang into action, attempting to concentrate as much power in their hands as was possible. The Kolchak government during the year of its existence had at least provided a focus, a chain of command however nominal; now this was broken into hundreds of links and there was chaos.

This wave reached Vladivostok in the form of a putsch by General Rudolf Haidl Gaida, a Czech formerly in Kolchak's service who attempted on the night of November 18 to capture the city in his own behalf. He was opposed by General Rozanoff, Kolchak's representative in Eastern Siberia. The fighting centered around the railway depot where Gaida's armored train and three hundred of his supporters were surrounded by Rozanoff's troops.

The Allied commanders in Vlad had elected to remain neutral, but from his bedroom window General Graves could see the action. Down the street an unprotected machine gun was being manned repeatedly after the previous gunner had been killed. The stupidity of placing the gun in such an exposed position should have been obvious, but to continue manning it time and time again when it was apparent that the enemy had its range was almost more than Graves could stand. He wanted to open his window and order them to move the gun, but it was General Rozanoff's gun and they were Rozanoff's men and the Allied commanders were neutral.

The railway station where the Gaida forces were trapped was being bombarded by White destroyers in the harbor and by Rozanoff's artillery. A heavy orange glare hung in the sky over the station and there was a steady, almost rolling sound of explosions.

General Graves dressed and went to his headquarters, where he found Eichelberger and Robinson. "If it's this bad here, what must it be like up the line, Olie?"

"I haven't had any reports yet, General," Robinson replied.

"How much longer do they expect us to stay in this? Do we have communications to Verkhne-Udinsk?"

"Not at the moment, General," Eichelberger said.

"It's one hell of a mess."

"Yes, sir, that's what it is."

At four in the morning General Cecek, commander of the Czech forces then in Vlad, came to Graves' headquarters to say that Gaida and his men were being slaughtered by Rozanoff's forces. He asked General Graves to join him in an appeal that Gaida be paroled to the Czechs.

"I'm sorry, General, but you know I can't do that."

"Then I'll do what I can on my own authority," Cecek said and he left.

General Graves sat down at his desk, his face strained and gray. "Isn't that awful, Olie?" he said. "Isn't that one awful thing to have to say to a man?"

At dawn Gaida's supporters tried to break out of the railyards. A few succeeded. Eighteen who didn't were lined up in front of the station and offered an opportunity to join the Rozanoff forces. When they refused they were marched into the station and ordered down a circular stone staircase leading to the basement. As they began their descent they were shot.

Scattered firing continued all morning as men trying to break out of the railyard were sighted and chased through the streets by Rozanoff's troops and shot down in quivering heaps on the mud-stained snow.

General Gaida remained in his armored train; he was slightly wounded, but the train itself still had enough firepower to enable the General to treat for terms and at last it was decided that he would be allowed to go to asylum in Japan. This amnesty did not, however, extend to his men.

At nine o'clock Colonel Krakovetsky and four other Gaida supporters bowled past the sentry at the door to the American headquarters and begged for protection. They stood in the hallway, shuddering with exhaustion and fear, trying valiantly, however, to maintain their dignity.

Informed of their presence General Graves ordered the guard detail around his headquarters doubled and sent an inquiry to Washington asking if he could constitute his headquarters American territory and thus offer protection to the refugees.

"They've got to do it," he said to Robinson. "They've got to understand what's happening out here. I can't turn those men out to be killed!"

"I've handed them over to Colonel Bugbee for safekeeping," Robinson said.

"They wouldn't make me surrender those men, would they, Olie?"

"It's a ticklish legal question, General."

"Hang the legality! They're men!"

The reply to General Graves' request came the following morning: "Secretaries of State and War agree, not possible constitute your headquarters American territory."

General Graves studied these words on the flimsy sheet of cablegram paper. They hurt him deeply. He could not have imagined there was so much left in him to disappoint. He looked up at Colonel Robinson, who'd brought him the message. "There must be thousands of people dying and being killed all across this country right now," he said.

"Yes, sir."

"Men, women, and children."

Robinson nodded.

"Where are those men now, Olie?"

"Colonel Bugbee has them in custody."

"Have you seen them?"

"Yes, sir."

General Graves studied the cablegram again as though he could change the words by reading them. "Send for Colonel Bugbee," he said.

When Colonel Bugbee came into the office General Graves stood up and clasped his hand. The Colonel, gone a bit to fat, with serious brown eyes, was surprised by Graves' manner.

"It's about those men you have in protective custody, Colonel."

"Yes, General?"

"I've received the following cable from Washington."

Graves took the cablegram from his desk and gave it to Bugbee.

The Colonel read it and looked up, frowning. The two men remained for a long time staring at each other. "I see, sir," Colonel Bugbee said at last.

"It's damned unpleasant," Graves said.

"Yes, General, it is. I gave my men bloody hell for it, but the responsibility is all mine."

"What's that?"

"Those four men escaped, sir. I thought that's what you wanted to see me about."

"Damn it, Bugbee, how can four men escape in broad daylight?"

"I'm not sure, sir, but I intend to find out."

A grin spread across General Graves' broad face and in one of his rare demonstrations of emotion he threw an arm around Colonel Bugbee's shoulders and hugged him. "Do that, Bugbee," he said. "I want a full report for the State Department and the War Department."

When Bugbee had gone General Graves sat down at his desk and thanked God for decent men. Another colonel than Bugbee might have turned those men over without a qualm, saying he was following orders and that the responsibility for their death was not his, but General Rozanoff's. Graves picked up the cablegram again. He'd been on the verge of turning the four men out when Bugbee had saved him and them by his timely lie.

Yes, he'd been prepared to follow orders, to pass them along, to make the excuse that where thousands were dying four more could not matter.

Graves crumpled the cablegram into a tight ball and tossed it away. It was obscene. If it hadn't been for Bugbee four men would have died to preserve a legality.

On December 10, twenty days after the prisoners had "escaped" and the Gaida putsch was forgotten, General Graves received the following message: "State Department advises that you cause refugees to leave your headquarters as soon as consistent with general principles of humanity and before question of surrender arises."

Robinson and Eichelberger saw the blood drain from Graves' face and were alarmed. "Those slimy bastards!"

"Sir?"

"They make murderers of us, then squirm out of it with another cable. I can hear them: 'What! Killed by Rozanoff? Why, that was never our intention. Certainly not! See our cable of 10 December which clearly sets forth our policy in those circumstances.' Bastards!"

The General regained his composure and apologized. "When in hell are they going to let us out of this?" he asked. "Is the 27th ready to move, Olie?"

"Yes, sir."

"Where's Kolchak now?"

"At Marinsk, General," Colonel Eichelberger replied.

"Are we getting our people out of Irkutsk?"

"Yes, sir. They're being moved through as fast as trains can be made available."

General Graves shoved the latest cablegram over the desk. He considered it even more obscene than the first. "File that, Olie," he said.

« 2 »

Two thousand and eighty miles from Vladivostok the Allied High Commissioners held daily conferences in their private railway cars at Glaskov station across the Angara River from Irkutsk. Their primary mission was to evacuate their nationals in Siberia, but more perplexing military and political considerations frequently intruded as they tried, without appearing to do so, to take advantage of one another. General Janin represented the French; Ambassador Kato, the Japanese; Mr. Harris, the United States; Miles Lampton, Great Britain; also present were Monsieur Maugras of France and Mr. Glos of Czechoslovakia. There were no representatives of European Russia or of Siberia.

Behind this council of High Commissioners was another of equal importance, the Inter-Allied Railway Committee consisting of the chairman, Mr. Oustrougoff, a White Russian; General Dmitri Horvath, onetime Ruler of the All Russian Government of Siberia, General Manager of the Chinese Eastern Railroad, and currently Admiral Kolchak's plenipotentiary in the Far East; Charles H. Smith, of the United States; Monsieur Bourgeois, of France; Lioutsin Jen, of China; Sir Charles Elliot, of Great

Britain; Consul General Gasco of Italy; Mr. Matsudaira, of Japan; and Major Broz, of Czechoslovakia.

There were, beyond these two august bodies, thirty or forty more of varying importance and effectiveness. Irkutsk itself was governed by a coalition known as the Political Center which many suspected of being pro-Bolshevik. There was the Russian Railway Service Corps, mostly Americans, whose behavior was suspected by all the other factions as being calculated to help Americans to the exclusion of everyone else. There were half a dozen generals of armies, regiments and brigades who appeared and disappeared, cutting into the lines of communication with urgent demands. And above all there were the refugees, a constant stream of famished, disease-ridden, freezing humanity staggering along the trakt which paralleled the Trans-Siberian Railroad.

The goal of all these councils, committees, governments and military staffs was transportation. They struggled for possession of railway cars and engines, and questions of priority were often arbitrated in blood.

Since his arrival at Glaskov station Carlisle had been working with a kind of brute rage which was far more effective than rank or reason in cutting through red tape. He ignored orders of various councils and committees, ignored the paper work, ignored the contradictory requests of wrangling authorities and went after the trains. Day or night he was to be seen tramping through the marshaling yard at Glaskov seizing the trains as they arrived. He listened to no one, obeyed no one, and within a week had managed to hack order out of what had been total confusion. The method he initiated upon his arrival never changed. When a train came into the yard Carlisle hopped on the engine and told the engineer which siding to take. When the engine was shut down he told the engineer to report to a building near the roundhouse which was in fact a detention barracks. The first three engineers who protested this order he knocked cold and carried over his shoulder to the detention barracks and dumped them on cots.

Anyone who protested was told to shut up. If they blustered, threatened, or waved papers in his face Carlisle knocked them out with a sledgehammer blow of his fist and left them where they fell. Within a week four generals of various nationalities and seven lesser officers had been silenced in this fashion. The flow of paper work which previously had come down from the commissioners and committees on high was slowly reversed as complaints of Carlisle's behavior began to rise from below. There were forty court-martial actions against him and innumerable protests.

When the Allied High Commissioners sent him a sternly worded reprimand their emissary returned with a broken nose.

General Janin raved. Carlisle was mad! Arrest him!

A detail of Czechs sent to arrest Carlisle decided against doing so. Carlisle met them at the door of his boxcar with a forty-five in one fist and blazing sulphur in his eyes. "Tell that frog bastard I'm sending three hospital trains out tonight and that I haven't time to fuck around."

The Czechs were delighted to convey the message.

Three hospital trains? In the face of these tangible results General Janin swallowed his pride and sent Carlisle a private note consisting of one word and a signature: "Congratulations — FROG."

While authorities up and down the line were juggling railroad manifests, boxcar, carriage and engine numbers, Carlisle was coralling the key railroad personnel. He fed, paid and rested them and if they fought back he broke them.

Every evening he went to the barracks where the hulking railwaymen who'd fallen into his net were quartered under a guard of Americans. "Any complaints?" he'd bellow and he'd walk slowly down the line of cots waiting for a troublemaker. If one stood up Carlisle didn't listen to his words, but watched his eyes, and when he judged the time had come to settle the issue he'd chop the man down like a column of paste. Only once had a man stood up for a second helping and he promptly got it.

At the end of two weeks Carlisle was the undisputed master of the Glaskov marshaling yard and trains began to move in an orderly manner. All the manifests, requisitions and series of car numbers being flashed back and forth by committees lost their meaning because Carlisle was the only person who could assign a crew to a train.

The Allied High Commissioners bowed to Carlisle's fists and their results. He was appointed master of the yard and given a staff of four not too very gentlemen whose fists were capable of delivering Carlisle's messages secondhand, and for the first time in several weeks Carlisle was able to sleep six hours straight. He hadn't yet been across the river to Irkutsk, but he'd done a good job and he knew it. The only thing that troubled him was that he wouldn't find another violent task to absorb the bitterness he felt at being detached from his company. This worked in his blood and came out in the primitive rage with which he struck down those who opposed him. The bones in his hands, formerly so brittle, seemed to have turned to marble. Even when he struck to break them he could not do so. His damned white hands seemed to taunt him, to be superior to his raw Indian energy.

But beyond this was something worse, something deeper than even he had suspected. It was that in the naked center of his being he was still afraid. This was not physical fear or fear of death; he'd invited these too often in the marshaling yard with no sensation of fear at all. No, it was this other thing, this awful loneliness, this skin-crawling, shuddering recognition that he'd been shoved out of the pack.

He didn't know how to cure this. He didn't know what to do. He was afraid of his loneliness, afraid not to be alone. He was at war with himself and he saw no hope of victory, so he prowled the yard with his fists cocked and a growl in his throat and saw to it that the trains went through.

« 3 »

Because of the overcrowded conditions, the terrible cold, the shortage of food, the lack of transportation, the unreliability of news, in short the disruption and rapid disintegration of all the customary services of society, the refugees at Irkutsk drew into themselves.

Bundled in their clothing with their few belongings clutched in their arms they wandered about dulled by misery and half blinded by their own desperate needs and fears. They avoided meeting each other's eyes because there was nothing they could do for one another and if someone, starved or typhus-ridden, collapsed in the street everyone pretended not to notice.

Then one particularly still afternoon as the people shuffled about like golems a company of players appeared on Bolshava Street. These were led by a creature whose face was heavily powdered and rouged, wearing a fifteenth-century ball gown of green and gold lamé and carrying a beribboned shepherd's crook. There were about fifty persons in this company, dressed in every sort of costume, none of which appeared to offer any protection from the cold. But the players seemed to be unaffected. They pranced and caparisoned along the street behind their leader, who bowed and grinned bestowing gracious gestures on the huddled passers-by, who drew their coats closer around their shuddering bodies and stepped aside.

There were clowns and Harlequins, Columbines, pirates, knights in armor, all the figures of theatrical imagination. Caked with grease paint, perfumed, drunk, drugged or mad, this wild procession careened into the vast snow-covered square fronting the Angara River. They occupied the center of it and there proceeded to enact a pageant, a spectacle, or an orgy; no one was certain how it should be described.

In the center of the square, surrounded by the field of white, untrammeled snow they sang, declaimed, tumbled and built human pyramids under the direction of the courtesan with the shepherd's wand. Their colorful costumes were a sharp contrast to the drab buildings around the square. Their wild laughter and singing was the only sound of joy in the whole city. They had drums and musical instruments which they hammered and played with nerve-shattering intensity.

At first these players were ignored, but gradually their presence on the square drew a crowd which studied the players' senseless display of energy and wondered what it could mean. Here one spectator shook his head disapprovingly, another scowled and seeing the disapproval in his neighbor's expression he tapped his head to indicate he thought the players had escaped a lunatic asylum, whereupon both men smiled. Then, aware that the players had elicited this shared response, they looked at them again in bafflement.

Word of the players spread through the city and people drifted toward the square to see them. There was a great deal of conjecture as to where they had come from. Some said they were deserters who had broken into the wardrobe of the public theater and exchanged their uniforms for costumes to avoid being shot. Others thought they were lunatics or prisoners of war gone mad.

It was the first topic of conversation for months which provided any relief from the war. People seized upon it. Factions sprang up. There was criticism. There was defense. People met each other's eyes, coming out of their isolation to talk about the players. Society was being reborn.

For one whole day the players held the center of the square. Police and military authorities looked on and were uneasy because they didn't know what should be done. There was no edict against being a fool and clearly the players were fools, homosexuals rolling about in the snow under the prod of their fairy queen.

The police smirked and sometimes they laughed, but if their laughter was taken up by the crowd they scowled darkly and shook their heads in disgust. They listened closely to the players' speeches, but these were nonsense. If one phrase hung together in a meaningful way the player who uttered it was sure to receive a blow from the courtesan with the shepherd's crook. For saying "bread and jam," for instance, in an otherwise unintelligible stream of gibberish the clown was chased around the square and belabored by the courtesan. The spectators laughed, immensely pleased, and soon they were all cooperating with the courtesan, who was the only person allowed by the convention of this curious spectacle to say anything sensible. Her name was Nelya. Her face was paste white and her mouth was painted into a red smile of indefinable sweetness. The low bodice of her dress was loose in front and she wore a high powdered wig which fell off during her exertions, revealing short, soft blond hair.

Nelya was a great favorite at once. Even the children, undernourished, cold and fearful, clapped their hands and screamed with delight. "Nelya! Nelya! The Knight! Beat the Knight for 'dog and cat'! No, no, the Donkey! The Donkey said 'two and two'! We heard him!"

And Nelya chastised her players with the shepherd's crook, and the hearts of the people in the crowd were warmed when a player they had singled out was caught and thumped. It was ridiculous. It was glorious. For a few moments the war, the revolution, hunger, homelessness and the cold were forgotten. There was no fuel to be had, but for one day Nelya and her players provided a bit of laughter in the square.

As night drew on and the temperature dropped, people began to leave the square; a few of them left offerings behind, devaluated currencies, worn rugs and coats and also a meager supply of tinned food and bread. They asked Nelya if her players would return the following day and Nelya promised to return. The spectators applauded heartily, then went to their places for the night, to the public buildings which had been opened to them, or to makeshift shanties they had flung up to protect themselves from the elements. And that night many people consoled themselves and slept more easily because there was an event which they could anticipate with pleasure.

The authorities on the other hand didn't rest so easily. The city was at this time governed by a mixed bag of Social Revolutionaries ranging in sentiment from the far left to the far right who were, for the most part, ready to declare themselves in either direction once they ascertained the current balance of power. They had already accommodated themselves to so many influences that they were a bit dizzy. Unwilling to alienate any power group, they were courteous by turns to representatives of the Japanese, the Czech, the British, French, American, and Kolchak governments. They were even courteous to acknowledged monarchists on the chance that the Romanovs might rise again. They argued furiously over their differences of opinion, but they were pleased to find themselves united in fierce opposition to the players in the square. They could not agree about politics, economics, religion, military tactics or one of a hundred other things, but they were unanimously opposed to art and took immediate steps to save the community from it. Having done so they retired with a sense of accomplishment and the feeling that their fellows in office weren't so bad after all. Disputatious, yes; perhaps misguided, but about basic matters they were solid to a man.

The next day was clear and cold.

The weak sunlight christening the dirty ice in the gutters and glancing over the hardened surface of old snow, littered with paper, discolored with spittle and blood, brought to it, nevertheless, a morning freshness and new hope. People turning out of their wretched beds in close, foul-smelling quarters greeted each other and remarked on the change in the air. Crisp, but dry. Not so damaging to the bones.

They shook out their limbs and cleared their throats. Tea was brewed and shared around and conversation sprang up naturally and was frequently punctuated with laughter. Soon the whole city was buzzing and there was animation in the pinched faces of the people, which only the day before would have been impossible. They learned each other's names and where they had come from. They began to sort themselves out by districts and to discuss what they must do about the future.

Children, encouraged by the sound of their parents' voices, started to display their impatience to get to the square. And the adults, having regained a measure of social equilibrium, said there were more important things to do than visit the players, who were foolish in any case and a waste of valuable time. Having made this assertion to quiet the kids the adults hastened to support their thesis and soon were competing with each other to downgrade the players while the children stood about dumfounded.

At last, however, the people began to converge on the square. They came from all sections of the city, spilling into Bolshava and Amurskaya streets. Those who hadn't seen the players the day before questioned those who had and over the heads of the crowd there was a drone of conversation which might have sounded ominous to those who didn't know the subject of it.

Children ran ahead and finding the players already in the square they rushed back to their parents with joyous shouts and entreaties that they hurry to make a place for themselves in front rows. Some in the crowd began to run and their intermingling voices rose to a rumble.

Nelya and her players, encouraged by their reception the previous day, had expanded their presentation. They'd made a pavilion of rugs and blankets in the center of the square and surrounded it with colorful banners emblazoned with nonsense syllables and cutouts of hippogriffs, unicorns and centaurs. The number of players had increased by half to include

horses, giraffes and several characters from Greek mythology and they all
stood in a grand tableau with Nelya raised high on their shoulders as the
cheering mob filled the square.

The commissioner of police for Irkutsk and a captain in charge of an
unreliable band of mounted troops conferred nervously on a side street.
The captain was anxious to commit his troops before they disbanded of
their own accord. "I can't hold them idle, your excellency," he said.

"What's become of discipline!" the commissioner complained.

"Action is called for. These men are ready for it now, but a delay will be
fatal."

The commissioner looked at the motley collection of troops. There were
Lett and Mongol faces among them. Their ponies were shaggy and
unmatched in size or color. Their uniforms bore no markings and they had
volunteered for duty on the promise of being allowed to keep whatever
plunder fell into their hands.

"You've delayed too long already," the captain said. "We should have
attacked the actors before this mob came."

"It might not have come," the commissioner replied testily. "How could
I be sure of a thing like that?"

The captain stamped his feet with impatience and turned to his men with
a shrug. "Another time, boys," he said.

The commissioner caught his shoulder. "No, no," he cried, "send them
in. The actors must be dispersed. We have to prevent another occurrence at
all cost. Who knows what could develop?"

The captain gave a signal and went to his pony. The troopers started
down the narrow street toward the square, unsheathing their swords and
drawing their pistols as they jogged along. From their remarks and sidelong
grins it was clear that each of them hoped to bag someone with a cache of
unexpected wealth on his person. One never knew. Wealthy people and
corrupt officials trying to make their way out of the country often disguised
themselves in rags. A murdered Jewess, it was rumored, had tried to
swallow the contents of a small pouch containing diamonds in her death
agony. Jews were particularly known for this kind of trickery. They were
always concealing things and it was best to explore them thoroughly before
leaving their bodies. One poor chap, having stripped a Jewish corpse, was
much chagrined later to discover that he'd overlooked an emerald hidden
in the anus. One had to be thorough with Jews.

The captain trotted after his men trying to gain the lead, urging them to
remember that they were to attack the actors first. "Remember, boys," he

called, "first the actors. That's our promise. There's sure to be some Zhids among them. There always are. Then we clear the square of everyone who interferes. And be quick about it. That's the ticket. Over and done with in ten minutes."

« 4 »

Although the Angara River had not yet frozen, blocks of ice flushed out of Lake Baikal kept slamming against the pontoons of the floating bridge which connected Glaskov rail station to Irkutsk and ice floes were building up, giving the bridge a pronounced downriver curvature. Because he was responsible for the evacuation of American personnel, most of whom were housed on the Irkutsk side of the river, Carlisle had been watching the bridge with increasing concern. Normally it was withdrawn to the Irkutsk bank and ferries were put into service between the railyard and the town until the river froze solid enough that a road could be made across it, but the ferries were not in service and the bridge appeared dangerously close to being swept away by the weight of ice packing up against it.

On the morning of the second appearance of the players in Irkutsk, Carlisle rose early and walked across the bridge intending to demand that the officials in charge put the ferry boats in operation. It was a matter of extreme importance to him that the people he was to evacuate not be cut off from the trains when their orders came to move.

The wooden bridge groaned and swayed under his feet and was periodically shaken when a block of ice propelled by the racing current slammed into one of the pontoons. Halfway over Carlisle paused and looked down into the water on the upstream side trying to calculate how soon the river would freeze. The current was black and wild; chunks of ice which had formed along the banks during the night had been torn away and jammed against the bridge and the weight of this gathering ice made Carlisle wonder if he would gain the opposite bank before the bridge carried away. He hurried on determined now to withdraw the personnel for which he was responsible to Glaskov.

On the Irkutsk side of the river he paused to look back at the bridge. The downstream sway under the weight of impacted ice was even more pronounced than it had been the day before and the cables which anchored the bridge were strained. Carlisle went on, intending to warn his people not to use the bridge until other arrangements could be made.

As he came into the square and started toward the government buildings Carlisle saw a great crowd of people explode before his eyes. A geyser of color, red, white, gold, green and blue, erupted upward and people fled in all directions wailing like shrapnel.

Carlisle stopped. One hand went to the forty-five automatic in his coat pocket, but he was stunned to inaction by the scene.

A giraffe being pursued by a saber-swinging cavalryman lost its head and continued to gallop across the square.

Triton, in a flowing robe and beard, stabbed a horse in the flank with his three-pronged spear and was shot down by another passing rider.

In the center of the square an embattled group of clowns, Indians, animals and all manner of wildly becostumed people were trying to protect a woman in a green and gold ball gown who stood in their midst waving a banner which Carlisle couldn't read. Suddenly this nucleus was smashed by a charge of cavalry. Sabers flashed, shots stuttered through the howls, and blood welled up and splashed from the costumes into the snow.

Carlisle didn't believe it. He stood there as people fled toward the river and over the bridge. The heavy automatic dangled in his hand. A man clad in a vermilion tutu and white ballet tights staggered toward him and fell coughing blood. A gleefully howling rider with a big machine pistol swung toward Carlisle, who dropped to one knee and fired. The bullet fanned past the rider's face and sent him galloping off hugging his pony's neck.

In a matter of seconds the square was cleared. Here and there dark bodies lay where they had fallen. The cavalry had vanished as though exorcised by Carlisle's single shot. There was a heap of color in the center of the square and Carlisle jogged toward it keeping a wary lookout for a return of the cavalry. The first body he came to was dressed in a green and gold gown. There was a beribboned shepherd's crook clutched in one hand which moved faintly and Carlisle dropped on one knee to see if he could help, but there was blood spilling over the bodice of the gown and the eyes, grotesquely outlined in blue mascara, were already glassy. The pallor of imminent death was hidden under heavy white make-up, but the lips were moving and there was a painted smile on them which snagged Carlisle's memory like a barbed hook.

"My God!" he said. "Grachev!"

At the sound of Carlisle's voice the eyes seemed to struggle upward toward consciousness; they fastened a moment on his and the lips moved. "Nelya," they said faintly.

Carlisle's spine went cold. It was Lieutenant Grachev dressed as Nelya; he had been taken over by Nelya's soul, defeated and consumed by it. The hand holding the crook reached out toward him and Carlisle recoiled, but the fingers closed on the lapel of his coat and pulled him down with astonishing strength for a dying man. The painted lips were moving again and Carlisle heard the words, distantly spaced and painful: "What He was — He is not — what He will be — He was not — "

In his horror Carlisle was not certain he had heard properly and as the light died in Grachev's already sightless eyes he heard an awful wail through the square and he thought the cavalry had charged again. He jumped up and Grachev's lifeless hand fell from his coat. There was an American ambulance in the square but the wailing sound came from the direction of the river. Carlisle looked toward it and saw the pontoon bridge to Glaskov swinging downriver. Packed with humanity still fleeing the square, it had broken away on the Glaskov side.

Those in the forefront, seeing the chasm of water open before them, tried to stop but they were pressed forward into the icy river by the onrushing mob behind. Dozens were shoved screaming into the water, then all reversed course and ran back as they had come. At this, one whole section of the bridge broke away and careened downriver with people clinging to it. Some jumped and tried to swim to the section still attached to the Irkutsk side but the cold gripped them and they too were swept away.

Carlisle ran to the bridge.

Hysterical people were scrambling over each other to gain the bank. Those who fell were crushed beneath the feet of the mass. As the current drove the remaining section of the bridge closer to the bank many in the center of it jumped the railing and swam. Some of these reached the shallows and Carlisle pulled them up the ice-caked bank.

Children swarmed ashore like sopping rats and searched for their parents, calling aloud until they realized that their voices were lost in the general din, whereupon they fell silent and stood shuddering, their faces blue with fear.

Carlisle splashed about in the shallows doing what he could to help, but there were so many people; his mind was still in the grip of the mad scene on the square and nothing seemed real.

As he hauled bodies out of the water he kept thinking of Grachev. "Nelya? Christ, what a nightmare!"

Grachev's reappearance was like something in a dream. It was too bizarre, too disconnected, and as Carlisle splashed around, snatching people out of the current like huge fish and shoving them toward the bank, this too seemed like a dream. "I predicted the bridge would give way," he thought, "and it's happened."

But he looked toward the river to be sure the bridge was gone, and felt a twinge of guilt for not having given a warning. He stood waist deep in the freezing water, making an effort to wake up and find himself on his cot in the boxcar at the Glaskov marshaling yard.

By now relief had come. People who had been pulled out of the river were being carried to shelter. Two Red Cross trucks arrived with blankets, brandy and hot tea. Those who had been injured were being loaded into ambulances. Several women in gray skirts and jackets bearing an insignia which Carlisle did not recognize were trying to reunite children and their parents.

The two ferryboats which Carlisle had come to see about were headed downstream in pursuit of the section of the bridge which had been carried away. One of these was a side-wheeler. Smoke billowed from its lofty stack; its steam whistle blew piercingly and Carlisle, suddenly aware that he was in the water, waded out. A young man in a Y.M.C.A. uniform approached Carlisle with a steaming cup in his hand. He wore spectacles and there was a look of cheerful compassion on his sallow face as though he were thrilled at being of service in this emergency. Carlisle disliked him instantly, but took the cup of coffee.

"Quite a thing," the young Christian said.

"Yeah."

"We just got here ten minutes ago."

"Damned fast," Carlisle said.

"We were alerted by something over on the square," the young Christian said. "What was that all about?"

"Damned if I know."

"We passed three ambulances picking people up."

"That so?"

The young Christian sighed. "Never know what's going to happen around here," he said. "Bring the cup back to the truck, will you?"

"Sure," Carlisle said.

"We lose a lot of cups," the young Christian said and he went back to the truck looking for another act of mercy to perform.

Carlisle finished the coffee and began to worry about his wet feet, which were in danger of freezing. He worked his toes in his soggy boots and went to return the cup, but halfway to the truck he saw Tatiana.

She was helping some children into an ambulance; her back was half turned to him, but Carlisle recognized her instantly. He forgot his feet, forgot the cup in his hand, went toward her in a daze and stopped a few feet away, not knowing what to say.

She looked exhausted. Her large white hands were bare and gripped each child reassuringly as she helped them into the van. She didn't notice Carlisle until she shut the door and swatted it to send the driver on his way, then she turned and came face to face with him.

"You?" she said, then she smiled. "Of course it's you!" And she gave Carlisle her hand. "What are you doing here?" she asked.

"I came over from Glaskov and now I'm stranded."

"Were you on the bridge? You're wet through!"

"No. I came down to help."

"You've got to change out of those things." She looked around to find a place in one of the trucks for him, but they were filled.

"I'm all right," he said.

"Don't be a fool." She took his arm and pulled him down the line of vehicles which were now in motion. The young Christian rushed up to them. "Hey, what about that cup?" he yelled and he took it from Carlisle's hand.

"How about a lift?" Carlisle asked.

The young Christian glanced at Tatiana. "Where to?"

"The Metropole," Tatiana said. Then looking at Carlisle she said, "There's no place else. Major Ikachi has a room and fuel for his stove. You can dry your things there."

"All right," the young Christian said. "Let's get a move on."

They rode the Y.M.C.A. truck to the Metropole, but Ikachi wasn't in and his door was locked. "Down here, then," Tatiana said. "It's a great mess, but you must get dry."

She took Carlisle to the room she shared with the other volunteer nurses who had been called to the hospital in the emergency. "I've got to go there too," Tatiana said. She opened the door and thrust him into the room.

A young Russian woman gasped and bounded up from one of the beds on which she had been lying reading a newspaper.

"It's all right, Katya. This is a friend of mine, Captain Carlisle. This is Kayta Massakow who shares this room with me, Captain."

She was a dumpy woman in her early thirties with a round, rather handsome face. Carlisle acknowledged the introduction while Tatiana hurried around wadding up articles of female apparel and stuffing them out of sight.

The room was cluttered and smelled of creosote from the pans under the bed legs put there to discourage cockroaches. There were two beds, two chairs and a stove, and various boxes and suitcases stacked out of the way.

Tatiana spoke urgently to Katya, who took her coat from a hook behind the door and smiled oddly at Carlisle as she put it on. Tatiana came to him frowning. "Don't stand there! Off with your things and into bed. You're wet through and sure to catch pneumonia!"

Having never seen Tatiana in such a squalid setting Carlisle was amazed how different she seemed to him, not so far off and grand, almost common, and he was still expecting to wake up from this dream, but he couldn't account for Katya Massakow in it.

The skirt of his coat was dripping water on the floor. His pants legs were wet and clammy. He removed his coat and Tatiana took it from him and hung it over a chair near the stove. He couldn't remember anything which pleased him so much as that Tatiana had taken his wet coat and hung it over a chair to dry. She turned, and seeing him standing idly in the center of the room she clapped her hands. "Come along with your boots!" she said.

"Are you all right?" he asked.

"Of course I am. Don't be a goose! Katya and I have to go to the hospital. I don't know how long we'll be there, but you dry your things at once!"

"You'll be back?"

"Certainly! Now be quick!'

Tatiana went to the door with Katya but paused there and smiled. "I'll warn my nursing friends you're here so they won't burst in on you. Though who knows what might come into their minds in times like these? I'll say you're my special friend, my Captain of the Powder Room, and I'm certain they won't bother you. Meantime you get into bed and be warm."

When she'd gone Carlisle sat down on a chair near the stove. He was too weak to remove his boots. So much had happened since he'd crossed the pontoon bridge that his mind was spinning and he felt sick. Grachev's last words which he thought he had not heard at the time came back to him with sudden clarity: "What He was — He is not — what He will be — He was not — "

These words coursed through his mind, round and round, and he tried to understand them. Sometimes they referred to Grachev, sometimes to himself. What he was he is not. Yes, he was a company commander and was no longer. What he will be he was not. Yes, of course, whatever he was going to be would be different from what he was now.

But the words refused his analysis. Grachev had been Grachev and had become Nelya, but he was not Nelya and when a man dies he is no longer what he was.

Carlisle bent to unlace his boots and it was a great effort. He removed his trousers and wrung the water out of them into one of the pans of creosote under the bed legs. There were a few cockroaches struggling feebly in the sticky substance and Carlisle sympathized with them. He too had been caught in a quagmire on his way to Tatiana's bed.

At this he snorted. He hadn't been on the way there anyway; he hadn't expected to meet her, but of course the cockroach didn't expect to meet her either.

"What He was — He is not — what He will be — He was not —"

He remembered Grachev's dying whisper and Nelya's painted smile on his face. He remembered too the strong, clawlike tug on his coat lapel as Grachev pulled him down to hear those last words.

"Nonsense," Carlisle said aloud. "Damned nonsense!"

He hung his trousers over the other chair to dry and wondered which bed he should take. He preferred Tatiana's to Katya Massakow's. He chose the one with the cockroaches struggling in the creosote and pulled the blankets back. Something scuttled out of the sudden light and Carlisle grinned because the vanishing insect took with it all his remaining illusions about Tatiana. She was a human being, more beautiful than other humans, certainly, but human nevertheless.

Carlisle got into bed and pulled the blanket over himself hoping the insects which annoyed Tatiana would also annoy him. That much at least they could have in common.

"What He was — He is not —"

"Why, hell," he said aloud, "that could be anyone who changes. That's all it is."

He had been a half-breed Indian kid; she had been a wealthy Bohemian. Now they were both something different. And what they would be they were not.

And he fell asleep instantly.

« 5 »

As the commissioner of police toured the hospital with other representatives of the Irkutsk city government, dispensing encouraging words to victims of the bridge disaster, he was secretly pleased to find that everyone had forgotten about the players who had been driven from the square that morning. There was a great deal of indignation about the bridge. An investigation had been called for and promised. There were charges of criminal negligence, and plans for a permanent bridge across the Angara which had languished in the city files for many years were brought out and dusted off.

No one mentioned the players, but among the corpses brought in that day was one which had three bullet wounds in the chest and lay in a dim corridor with the other bodies which would be removed that night. There was a dirty sheet pulled up to the chin of the white face, which bore a painted smile, and Katya Massakow, passing down the corridor from surgery, was attracted to the whiteness in the gloom and paused to look closely at the face. At first she thought: "Poor girl!" assuming it was someone who had been drowned in the bridge disaster, but something about the face disturbed her, so she lifted the sheet and saw the naked, bullet-ridden chest. "A deserter," she thought then. "One of the players." For it had been established that most of the players were indeed deserters, young officers who had been ordered to serve in the ranks and who had refused.

Katya let the sheet fall and went on to find Tatiana so they could walk back to their room together. Katya was very tired; she, Tatiana and all the other volunteers had worked around the clock since the emergency. First it was the bridge; then trainloads of wounded had begun to arrive from Omsk.

Katya had no respect for deserters — her brother Boris was with General Kappel — but she always said a prayer for the dead, and the white-faced corpse had touched her and made her afraid for Boris' life. Somehow, despite the smile, there was an awful omen of death on that white face and Katya said an extra prayer for Boris, who was all the family she had left alive. But even as she prayed her fear of impending death increased and as she crossed the main floor ward to Tatiana's office in the far corner she could hardly keep from running.

She burst into the tiny office. "Oh, Tanya," she cried, "I'm so worried —" But she was stopped abruptly by Tatiana's appearance.

Tatiana looked up from her desk with a dead expression in her eyes. There was a telegram hanging forgotten in one limp hand.

Katya closed the flimsy door. "Tatiana," she said urgently, "what is it?"

"Albert has been killed," Tatiana said.

Katya took the telegram from Tatiana's unresisting hand and read the message: "It is with extreme regret to inform Count Albert Nojine killed in defense Omsk."

It was signed: Dubrovski.

Katya's reaction was one of immense relief because the telegram meant that her brother Boris was still alive. This was clearly an answer to her sense of impending death. In the next instant she was overcome with remorse and she fell to her knees and seized Tatiana about the waist. "Oh, Tatiana!" she cried. "I'm so sorry! Oh, my poor, dear Tatiana!"

"It's a whole life gone, Katya," Tatiana said softly. "It's a whole world gone, you see."

This was a life and a world which Katya Massakow had never seen. The cultured brilliance and sophistication of upper class prewar Prague were beyond her imagination, but she burst into tears and wept as though her heart were about to break, and Tatiana patted her shoulder comfortingly.

"There, there, Katya," she said. "You're just exhausted."

"Oh, Tatiana," Katya moaned. "What are we going to do?"

"I'm sure I don't know," Tatiana replied.

CHAPTER THIRTY-TWO

AT Verkhne-Udinsk, Colonel Boris Petrovich Sipialef was prepared to take advantage of the collapse of the Kolchak regime. The primary instrument of his policy was his armored train, the Invincible, and he poured money into its improvement knowing that in chaos the man who could move safely was master.

He improved the gun cars and added another engine. He organized a special force of Cossacks known as the Sipialefsky, who, besides being experts in the killing arts, were trained to lay rails and repair bridges ahead of the train while destroying the tracks, tunnels and bridges behind it. Twice a week exercises were conducted on the branch line to Kiatkha and the Invincible, painted in staggered patches of dirty white and green to blend with the trees and the snow, moved slowly down the tracks preceded and flanked by the Cossacks. In certain exercises they demolished bridges ahead of the Invincible and repaired them in time to allow the train to cross without slackening its average speed of twenty miles an hour. No track bed in Siberia could support such a heavy train at a higher speed.

Colonel Sipialef conducted these exercises himself with fanatical attention to detail. From his command car with its own wireless he was never out of touch with current developments. He spent hours over maps committing the Trans-Siberian and the Chinese Eastern to memory. Each officer on the train was required to know its operation thoroughly, to be able to act as engineer, fireman, oiler, to make repairs, to anticipate the slightest difficulty and to give unquestioning loyalty to Sipialef, who in turn paid the officers well and promised them great future rewards.

Sipialef sent out a network of spies whose particular mission was to report the condition of the broneviki held by Ataman Semenoff at Chita, the Mestatel, the Scourge, the Baikal; by the Czechs, the Orlik, the Masaryk, the Bohemia, and by all the other forces then in the Trans-Baikal. He gathered the specifications of these trains, their weight, their armament and firepower, and tried to plot their position day by day on the map in his command car.

There were forty-seven armored trains between Taiga and Chita, and Sipialef was satisfied that the Invincible was far superior to all of them, that he had devised a weapon which would serve his purpose. It annoyed him, however, that the more convinced he became of his power the more precautions he took for his own safety and the more ingratiating he tried to be toward those who still retained remnants of authority.

He had worked his way up through the ranks by knuckling his brow to those above him and visiting his rage at having to do so on those below. Every obeisance he made, every smile, every salute was paid for by the men under his command and his cruelty was known to be extreme in a military system where bobbing noses and ears was not considered an atrocity, but normal punishment for infractions of discipline.

He had been born in Kalgan of mixed parentage, abandoned at an early age and raised in a Methodist mission orphanage where he learned two things: Old Testament morality and the English language. These brought him an early preeminence, and at the time of General Bogoloff's death, though he was not yet thirty years of age, he had inherited the title of Kolchak's military commandant at Verkhne-Udinsk.

Not a day passed that Sipialef did not send a message to Kolchak assuring him of his loyalty, and to compensate his ego for this he usually executed one or more of his "Bolshevik" prisoners — personally, time permitting.

He logged the slow progress of Kolchak's seven trains toward Irkutsk with impatience and knew the situation day by day. The Kolchak entourage was currently at Krasnoyarsk, being held there by the Czechs. General Sakharov had been relieved as C.I.C. and arrested. General Kappel was now commander in chief and he had challenged the Czech General Syrovy by wireless to a duel because Syrovy was passing the Czech echelons down the line ahead of Kolchak's trains. General Zankevich, Kolchak's quartermaster general, sent urgent requests that Sipialef use his influence to expedite Kolchak's progress. Sipialef sent a wire to Kappel, expressing his loyalty to the new C.I.C. just as he had previously done to Sakharov and before that to Dietrichs. He knew these rapid shifts in command were the final contortions of a dying regime and he welcomed them. But Krasnoyarsk was still too far away and the Fifth Red Army was pressing. Of the three hundred evacuation trains crawling eastward from Omsk fewer than half had reached Krasnoyarsk; the rest had run out of fuel and frozen, they had broken down, or they had been intercepted by one of the roving partisan forces which preyed on the railroad.

Sipialef studied the maps and dispatches. He sent a message to the High Commissioners at Irkutsk beseeching them to allow the Kolchak trains to move and his anxiety increased with each passing day. But the Kolchak trains, particularly the seventh, which carried the Russian gold reserves, had to run the long gantlet from Krasnoyarsk and there was nothing Sipialef could do except wait.

He did not wait gracefully. The High Commissioners did not dignify him with replies to his wires. The movements of the Taseevo Partisan Army under Yakovenko troubled him greatly; this army had grown to three battalions of infantry and four regiments of cavalry with artillery and a machine gun detachment. Other partisan leaders, Kravchenko, Shchetinkin, Marmatov and Grandpa Karandashvili, ranged through the countryside capturing supplies and gathering willing recruits from the villages and the masses of deserters. The name Timokhin hung over the Baikal region like a mystical shroud and any one of these was capable of capturing the prize which Sipialef intended for his own — the Russian gold reserves.

With even part of this great hoard of gold he would never have to knuckle his brow again.

For four days Sipialef waited in vain for news that Kolchak's trains had been allowed to proceed. On the fifth day he made a sacrifice to appease his frustration, to warn the population of Verkhne-Udinsk what they could expect should they revolt and to intimidate the partisans.

At this time the temperature at Verkhne-Udinsk ranged from thirty to forty degrees below zero. The Selenga and Uda rivers were frozen, but the Chinese water carriers had cut several holes in the ice where they filled their water carts each morning. It was to one of these holes that Anitsky was brought just before dawn by a quartet of Sipialef's Cossack guards.

From the moment of his arrest through his final interrogation Anitsky had remained self-possessed and composed to a degree which exasperated Sipialef's most brutal inquisitors and finally even Sipialef himself.

Evidence of Anitsky's association with Maryenka Austin was irrefutable. They'd been seen together after dark walking along the river front. Some articles of Maryenka's clothing had been found in Anitsky's cabin and Dunia, in a vain attempt to save her own life, told Sipialef that Maryenka had been in her room prior to the fatal shooting.

Despite the evidence against him Anitsky steadfastly denied he had known Maryenka Austin. He was beaten. The bones of his hands were broken in a dreadfully methodical manner, but he did not confess.

Anitsky was accused of being an accomplice, of providing the murder weapon, of arranging the escape, but to these and all other accusations he simply shook his head and gasped when he was tortured. When asked to give the names of others involved in the plot his pale, pain-ridden eyes widened with astonishment and he shrugged.

After several days of this Anitsky was beyond pain or fear and life ceased to have any meaning for him. He could no longer respond to questions and it was clear to everyone that his mind was gone. For a time he lay forgotten in a cell, then Sipialef had him carried to the Chinese water hole.

At the edge of the ice hole two guards stripped Anitsky to his undergarments while the others, armed with an ax and a crowbar, broke through the cap of ice. Anitsky, blue and chattering in the subzero temperature, watched these men with curious interest, and looked into the faces of the guards who were supporting him. He smiled with his broken lips and looked up at the slate sky where the stars had begun to die in the morning light. There was an inch of clean frost on the boardwalk through the park and on the lacy branches of the barren trees. One of the guards laughed and spoke to him while the others tied a rope around his chest under his arms. Anitsky tried to understand what the guard was saying. He felt it was his duty to be obliging and listened attentively, but the words broke up in his mind.

The guard raised one arm pointing upward and laid his other hand over his heart. He looked very heroic. The other guard laughed softly and pulled Anitsky's arm upward and Anitsky understood they wanted him to mimic the pose. He did so awkwardly, self-consciously, and both guards nodded their approval.

Through the hole in the ice Anitsky saw the black water of the Selenga as the guards brought him to the edge and arranged his pose once more.

Then from behind one guard pushed him.

Anitsky went down with a cry of surprise and the cold water stopped his heart, but for a few seconds his mind returned to perfect clarity.

The current pulled him under the ice; the rope around his chest drew taut and in his final moments Anitsky sensed the presence of a great bone-plated beluga sturgeon lying deep in the river beneath him, a huge fish which would take him in as the whale had taken Jonah. Anitsky opened his mouth and blessed the sturgeon, knowing they would travel the great rivers of Siberia safe in God's infinite mercy and that he would pray continuously for the cessation of strife and sorrow. "Good sirs! Is God not watching? Oh, good sirs!"

The guards hauled Anitsky's corpse out of the river and arranged his stubborn limbs in the pose they had selected, one arm up, the other hand over his heart, but he looked more like a waiter bearing a tray of food than a hero. They stood his frozen body on the ice, packed snow around the feet to support it, and splashed him with water which froze at once, and when he was sheathed in ice they left him.

At daylight the Chinese water carriers found Anitsky's ice-ensculptured body and his eyes seemed to have life, to be staring solemnly at the park and city beyond.

The Chinese looked at each other in horror and did not fill their water carts at the hole where Anitsky had been immersed. And as they made their rounds that day they told about Anitsky's statue on the river and to avoid squeamishness on the part of their customers explained that they'd drawn their water from another place.

During the daylight hours silent crowds gathered to stare at Anitsky and were ashamed of their silence, but they dared not speak for fear of finding themselves beside him. They looked around cautiously, wondering who might be a police informer; the bolder men shook their heads in a noncommittal way and the women crossed themselves.

Those who had known Anitsky remembered his voice and many dreams were haunted by it. "Good sirs. Good sirs, why must it be so? Why can't we be good? Is God not watching?"

In the days which followed, Anitsky's frozen body gradually lost its shape. At first it grew larger by additional layers of frost which whitened the features and concealed the frozen eyes. Then the snow came. It was dry snow and blew powdery flurries over the ice-clad river which formed a drift around Anitsky's knees. With each succeeding snowfall this drift rose a bit and eventually only Anitsky's upraised hand showed above it; then, at last, this too disappeared.

People walking through the park invariably looked toward the white mound which entombed Anitsky and were relieved that he could no longer be seen. His naked presence had been a reproach to them, but now they liked to think he was comfortable under his blanket of snow. And for his part Colonel Sipialef was gratified to receive a dispatch informing him that Kolchak's trains had begun to move from Krasnoyarsk to Nizhne-Udinsk.

« 2 »

The American command at Verkhne-Udinsk was appalled by Anitsky's frozen body on the Selenga and even more by their own apathetic response to it. Colonel Spaeth sent a protest to Colonel Sipialef and in return received a transcript of Anitsky's trial which took Joe Silverman ten days to translate and by this time Anitsky was covered by the drifting snow.

The officers boycotted the Mulligan. The men referred to Anitsky as Sipialef's snowman and were ashamed of themselves for doing so. They were demoralized by the intense cold, by a deep sense of having been abandoned by their government, and by American policy which prevented them from interfering in the domestic affairs of Russia.

They moved about sluggishly performing the duties connected with protecting the railroad, but with no real belief that even this made sense. A few cracked under the strain of their depression and were invalided to Vladivostok. Seven men vanished — whether they had deserted or simply wandered off and been frozen no one knew.

Colonel Spaeth fought lethargy in himself and his command with all his strength, but every passing day left him more exhausted and he knew that he was spinning out his energy against the awful specter of nervous collapse.

Each morning he rose, studied his clean-shaven face in the mirror for a hopeful sign and told himself to hit it. "All right, you bastard," he'd say aloud, "hit it. Plaster a smile on your puss and hit it!"

But there was nothing to hit. There was no target. He began not to trust himself, to take extraordinary lengths of time to make common decisions and to doubt them after they had been made. He found himself delegating authority to Bentham and Cloak on the theory that it was a generosity on his part to give them more to do, then abruptly he snatched everything back to himself.

"I'm slipping," he thought, "slipping!"

Frequently an indefinable panic swept over him and he seized routine like a life line. He doubled the hours of close order drill and calisthenics and personally drilled the Headquarters Company, bellowing orders at them across the snow-caked field, watching his breath freeze in the air and trying to distinguish the shape of "To the reah, Harch!" from that of "By the right flank, Ho!"

He wrote long letters to Peg and the kids and sent them Siberian gifts in an effort to make up for another Christmas when he would not be home and he wondered if they really cared anymore and he swore at himself for wondering. "Maudlin, self-pitying bastard! Of course they do!"

But did they?

Well, they said they did in all their letters. He kept these in his desk drawer and though he'd stopped smoking, cut off his mustache to avoid twisting it and no longer fidgeted with his spectacles, he often found his hand in that drawer idly tapping an envelope containing one of Peg's letters. "Sexual fetishism," he groaned. "Jesus Christ!"

Joe Silverman came into the office.

Spaeth motioned him to a chair and he sat down with a weary sigh. It was nearly dark outside and snowing bleakly. "Did you read my translation of the Anitsky trial, Colonel?" Silverman asked.

"Didn't I tell you I had?" Spaeth asked.

Silverman frowned as though trying to remember. "I guess you did."

"I sent a copy to Graves for the record. What did you think of it, Joe?"

"A fabrication. Fiction. I thought the evidence against Leverett was whimsical as hell. Made him sound like the leader of the People's Liberation Army."

Spaeth nodded, but wasn't sure he'd read the transcript as thoroughly as he should have.

"I've got a problem, Colonel," Silverman said.

"Yes?"

Silverman pulled a thick envelope from his pocket and flipped it up and down on the palm of his big hand. "This came addressed to me. A Russian handed it to one of our sentries about an hour ago. It's from Leverett."

"Our Leverett?" Spaeth asked.

Joe Silverman smiled. "Is there another? Yes, ours."

"What's in it?"

"A couple of letters addressed to his family which he asks me to forward and a note to me."

"Where in hell is he?"

"He doesn't say."

Spaeth was annoyed. "Well, damn it, what does he say?"

"My problem, Colonel, is that I don't know whether I should mention this to you at all."

"You already have."

"Not officially."

"Oh, for Christ's sake, Joe!" Spaeth said disgustedly. "Then why did he write to you?"

"Because I'm a civilian, maybe. Maybe because I'm a Jew and a college boy. I don't know. Maybe to avoid embarrassing you."

"He's done a good job already."

Joe Silverman's expression set hard. He stood up and returned the envelope to his pocket. "Forget I mentioned it, Colonel," he said.

"Like hell!"

Silverman was on his way to the door, but Spaeth bounded up and intercepted him. "I can't let this go," he said.

"What?" Silverman asked.

"Leverett!"

"What about him?"

"That letter!"

"I asked one of the local news butchers to drop a copy of *Dalny Vostok* at the gate for me, that's all. There is no letter."

They stared at each other and Silverman's smile was easy but uncompromising.

"All right, Joe. We'll keep it unofficial. What does he say?"

"Leverett wants to come in when the coast is clear," Silverman said, "and he wants to bring Mrs. Austin with him. She's pregnant and he wants to get her to an American hospital, but he doesn't know what the official attitude of this command would be vis-à-vis Maryenka and the Bogoloff assassination."

"What in hell does he think it would be?" Spaeth demanded angrily.

"I don't think I've ever heard it expressed, Colonel," Silverman said.

"Well, for Christ's sake!"

"Mrs. Austin did kill General Bogoloff and Sipialef is the new military commander here."

"You think I'd turn her over to Sipialef?"

"You wouldn't want to," Silverman said calmly.

"I wouldn't do it, god damn it! What in hell do you take me for?"

"Well, sir," Silverman said, "I take you for a damned good colonel in the United States Army and sometimes colonels have to do things directly opposed to their own inclinations."

"There are limits, Silverman!"

"I don't think there are, sir. That's why this is just between you and me."

Spaeth walked back to his desk. He was angry because Silverman was right. Since the story of Sipialef's connection with the Pashkova massacre had spread through the regiment the men were aching for an excuse to attack the Sipialefsky. There had already been several encounters on the streets of Verkhne-Udinsk between Americans and Sipialef's Cossacks and if it was learned that Maryenka Austin had fallen into Sipialef's hands Spaeth doubted his men could be restrained from attempting to rescue her. On the other hand Maryenka had murdered the commanding general of the area and Spaeth was certain General Graves would be forced to honor a demand from the Whites that she be delivered for trial if she came into American custody. This raised the specter of further demoralization of his men and perhaps an open revolt which he would have to put down.

It all went back to his own stupidity for not having detached Sergeant Austin in Vladivostok after he'd married Maryenka without permission. The regulation was clear, but Spaeth had winked at it because he liked Austin and Maryenka and now the whole command was in jeopardy. Carlisle had been right all along. The damned Sioux was always right.

"Is it Harry Austin's child?" Spaeth asked abruptly.

Silverman met Spaeth's eyes and smiled slightly. "Would that make a difference, Colonel?" he asked softly.

"Damn you, Silverman!" Spaeth growled and he sat down. "All right, I was looking for an out, any out! You know as well as I do what might happen if she turns up here."

"Leverett says it's Austin's kid. For some reason he made a point of it."

"That doesn't make it any easier. We've just got to get them out, that's all. Where are they now?"

"He didn't say, Colonel. But I know where to drop an answer to him that'll be picked up."

"Here in Verkhne?"

"Yes, sir. But I don't know what to say."

"We'd have to get her across the Chinese border."

"I thought so too, sir."

"All right, handle it for me, Silverman. Tell Leverett he's being carried A.W.O.L. Tell him we'll get both of them out somehow. If he can get to one of our posts between Mysovaya and Tataurovo we'll get them out. You'll have to go down the line and tell the officers in charge, unofficially, how to deal with it. You make the arrangements."

"We might get them out on the Snorter, Colonel."

"That's a notion. We'll see how it works. And Joe, mail those letters to his family."

Silverman grinned. "I'll do that, Colonel," he said, and he flipped Spaeth one of his rare civilian-style salutes and left the office.

The following afternoon Major Bentham came into Spaeth's office and gave him a long dispatch. "The Czechs are moving out," he said.

Colonel Spaeth read it carefully:

The intolerable position in which our Army is placed forces us to address ourselves to the Allied Powers to ask them for counsel as to how the Czech Army can be assured of its own security and of a free return to its own country, which was decided with the assent of all the Allied Powers.

The Army was ready to protect the railway in the sector which was assigned to it and it has fulfilled its task conscientiously. But now the presence of our Army on the railway to protect it has become impossible because the activities of the Army are contrary to its aspirations in the cause of humanity and justice.

In protecting the railway and maintaining order in the country, our Army is forced to act contrary to its convictions when it supports and maintains an arbitrary, absolute power which at present rules.

The burning of villages, the murder of peaceable Russian inhabitants by the hundreds, and the shooting, without reason, of democratic men solely because they are suspected of holding political views are daily facts; and the responsibility for them, before the Courts of Nations of the entire world, will fall on us because, being an armed force, we have not prevented these injustices. This passiveness is the direct result of our neutrality and non-intervention in Russian internal affairs, and, thanks to our being loyal to this idea, we have become, in spite of ourselves, accomplices to a crime.

In communicating this fact to the representatives of the Allied Powers to whom the Czech Nation has been and will be a faithful ally, we deem it necessary to take every measure to inform the nations of the world in what a moral and tragic position the Czech Army is placed and what are the causes of it.

As to ourselves, we see no other way out of this situation than to evacuate immediately the sector which was given us to guard, or else to obtain the right to prevent the injustices and crimes cited above.

V. GIRSA

Spaeth looked up at Bentham. "Girsa?"

"The Czech plenipotentiary to the High Commissioners," Bentham said.

"General Graves would have given a year of his life to have been able to write this."

"It's our position too," Bentham said.

"But they're doing something about it. Has Graves seen this?"

"He would have by now, sir."

"I hope he fires a copy of it right down Woodrow Wilson's throat. This means they'll abandon the Baikal tunnels once all the Czech echelons are through. Get onto Carlisle at Irkutsk and be sure he's aware of this. Get me General Yoshie, I'll try to find out what Japanese intentions are. They may hold the tunnels, or we may have to do it. Do you know where Kolchak is now?"

"He should be close to Nizhne-Udinsk."

"O.K., Charlie, let's hit it. Let's see what we can do."

But when Bentham had gone a terrible lassitude clamped down on Spaeth. He was afraid that even this declaration by the Czechs would fail to break the log jam in which his regiment was trapped and he wondered how he would survive if this turned out to be the case.

He read the dispatch again: "— contrary to its aspirations in the cause of humanity and justice." He liked the phrase.

"This passiveness is the direct result of our neutrality and nonintervention in Russian internal affairs, and, thanks to our being loyal to this idea, we have become, in spite of ourselves, accomplices to a crime."

Spaeth set the dispatch aside. He thought of Anitsky and shuddered. He could never tell Peg and the kids about that, not about Anitsky. This much of him would remain frozen, sheathed in ice. Yes, in spite of himself he was an accomplice to a crime. He opened his desk drawer and touched one of Peg's letters. He said her name aloud and a bitter wave of self-pity broke up in his chest and brought stinging tears to his eyes. "We've got to get out," he said. "We've got to get out!"

CHAPTER THIRTY-THREE

IRA intended returning to his regiment when Maryenka was safe, but after having reached Timokhin's band in their caves on Lake Baikal he was determined not to go back without her.

He gave Maryenka several reasons for his delay. He was exhausted and had to recover. A way had to be found to guarantee his safe-conduct through Verkhne-Udinsk. The tactical situation was too unstable at this time to risk the trip.

"I'll have to wait for things to cool down."

"We've sixty degrees of frost," she said.

Ira grinned. "That's an American colloquialism — a slang expression."

She looked puzzled.

"A joke," he said.

"I've never been good at jokes."

"Well, it's hardly the time."

Maryenka considered each of his objections and found arguments against them. It was she who arranged to have Slavin deliver Ira's letters to Joe Silverman on one of Slavin's trips to Verkhne-Udinsk. And it was from Slavin that they learned Anitsky's fate.

Maryenka wept unconsolably over Anitsky's death and the men tried their best to comfort her. She was the only woman among them and her grief made them feel responsible for all the woes of Siberia.

Ira sat beside her through the night trying to staunch her tears. "It's all so senseless," she moaned. "So senseless, senseless!"

"No," he said.

"There's nothing but death all around."

"You'll be having Harry's baby."

She looked at him, her eyes deep black in the lamplight. "Do you know that?" she asked.

"Yes, I do."

"It's been ten months now," she said. "Ten months."

"That's not unusual for a first child," Ira said quietly. "Not unusual at all."

"But I don't know," Maryenka whispered helplessly. "I'm not even very large."

"That doesn't mean anything," Ira said and he stroked Maryenka's forehead until she lapsed into a fitful slumber, then he put his heavy coat over her, the coat Carlisle had given him, and went to the mouth of the cave, where he found Slavin on watch. They acknowledged each other and Slavin said something which Ira's Russian was inadequate to comprehend. He smiled and touched Slavin's shoulder and they stood together looking out over the snow-covered lake.

There was a crispness in the air, a fragrance beyond the chill neutrality of the falling snow. It was a growing thing, something clean, sweet and identifiable if only Ira could think what to call it. He wondered if this could emanate from Slavin, but no, the big Russian, bundled in his heavy coat, had a sour, unwashed smell. It was something else, something tugging at his memory.

The freezing air sliced through his clothing raising goose flesh on his arms and legs. He said good night to Slavin and went back inside through the double hangings which shielded the light of the cave and held the warmth inside. Six men occupied this cave and there were two other caves along the ice-packed path above the lake.

Ira rubbed his cold cheeks and the fragrance was there again.

It was Zelda! It was cucumbers, his Uncle Dave, Maryenka!

It was cucumbers from stroking Maryenka's forehead until she slept!

Ira looked at his hands in amazement. "My God," he thought, "I've fallen in love with her. I don't intend to leave without her. I never did. I've taken Austin's place."

An upsurge of happiness caught him and he nearly laughed aloud.

It was so obvious. So right!

He wished he had his Uncle Dave's letter to show Maryenka. "If you ever find a woman who smells like cucumbers, marry her."

That was it!

Yes, of course.

Ira moved past the sleeping partisans, bundled in their blankets, coats and robes, to Maryenka's side. In sleep her round, plain face was childlike and maternal at once. A strand of brown hair had escaped from the coil in which she wore it and fallen over her pale cheek. Ira felt a boundless, aching tenderness for her. He lay down at her side and adjusted the blankets, robe and coat so they were both covered. Maryenka stirred but did not waken and Ira took this for a sign that she accepted his presence and had grown accustomed to him. He didn't ask for more.

For a long time he lay awake staring upward into the flickering darkness of the lamplit cave with a contented smile on his face. At last he knew what it was about. He had a purpose. He'd take Maryenka to Vladivostok and marry her. Austin's child would be theirs. He'd have a family! Ruth and Uncle Dave would love her on sight. In time his mother would too and his father would give her a welcoming hug and scoop the child into his arms. If it was a boy they'd name it Harry Austin Leverett.

Ira grinned at this, imagining Harry's reaction. It was good. It wasn't bad.

His thoughts turned to the practical problems of getting Maryenka out of the country. He wondered about Joe Silverman. They'd only met one time at Headquarters and all it amounted to was an introduction and a handshake. Nevertheless, Ira trusted him. In his note he'd made a drop arrangement. Silverman was to leave his reply in a tobacco can at the base of a certain tree in the park where Slavin could pick it up without danger to himself. Slavin knew the place and Slavin was a good man.

He'd write another note to Silverman, but not until he'd had a reply. It would take a couple of weeks to arrange.

It was going to be all right.

Ira grew drowsy. He tucked one arm under Maryenka's head. She sighed and moved to him like a child.

It was going to be fine.

He closed his eyes. He was warm and close to Maryenka. He sensed the vast silence of Baikal, a lake bigger than the whole of Switzerland with tides of its own and black depths so cold that the water burned.

Yes, Ruth would love her at once. . . .

The partisans rose at dawn and since her arrival Maryenka had begun to cook and keep house for them. She went about her tasks, washing, cooking, sewing and airing their blankets and robes, with concentrated energy, complaining when they got in her way for she knew that what they longed to hear was a woman's complaints. She lost no opportunity to berate them. Brandishing a wooden ladle in their faces she called them louts and stupid good-for-nothings, lazybones, clods, pigs, and whatever else came into her mind. The men would scurry about to assist her, but those who had been left out of her stream of invective would take her aside. "My wife calls me dungheap," one said. "That's her way. You call me dungheap too." Another requested that he be called goatface and another cheapskate, so

Maryenka added these names to her list and until the necessary chores were done she moved from cave to cave muttering darkly, "Louts, dungheap, goatface, cheapskate, pigs!"

The men would roar with laughter and clutch their sides with delight, nodding happily to one another, for hearing Maryenka scold was as good as a message from home. When she did not do this a melancholy silence settled over the camp for they knew Maryenka was unhappy and they wondered how best to please her.

It was Timokhin's custom to eat privately with Slavin, Marrakof and Balashov, the three men still alive who had escaped with him from Dauria. They were his lieutenants and were not agreed about what the band should do with respect to the overtures by the partisan generals, Kravchenko and Marmatov. Timokhin continued to delay this decision, waiting, as he often said, for a sign.

His wound, though incapacitating, did not keep Timokhin off his feet. He walked about much as usual with the same listening attitude which so impressed the men, but now he seemed to be listening to his heart rather than to the exalted voice which spoke through him.

The only person he allowed to touch him was Maryenka, as though he sensed in her a wound as grave as his own. She wrapped his chest once a day in yards of clean bandage and washed the old one each night by the fire. She did not mention Timokhin's injury to anyone. She alone had seen it and knew the seriousness of it and that there was nothing to be done. There was not enough flesh on his flayed chest to close the bullet holes front and back and his heart could be seen through them like a bird in a cage, or an unborn infant. She kept all this to herself though it showed in her eyes that she believed Timokhin, with his heart exposed to the world like a panting redwing, to be a saint.

In the afternoon Ira found Maryenka alone, seated in her corner of the cave mending Balashov's sheepskin jacket. He sat down on the pallet they'd shared the night before and watched her sew. "I love you, Maryenka," he said after a moment. "I want to take you home with me, to marry and take you home with me."

She continued sewing, pulling the coarse thread through the skin with no sign of having heard him, no break or tremble in the smooth passage of her needle.

"I'm sure I can arrange it through my friend Silverman," Ira said. "We'll go to Vladivostok and then by ship to California. That's where I live. I haven't told you, but I'm a lawyer by profession. I have a sister, Ruth. You'll like her, I'm sure. My father and Uncle Dave are both from Russia, near Kiev. Our home is in Oakland. It's warm there most of the year. It'll be a whole new life."

Maryenka snapped the thread in her teeth and examined the seam she'd made to see if it was tight.

"What do you think, Maryenka?" he asked.

She looked up, meeting his eyes with a gentle impact. "Did you hear when I told you what happened to me?"

"On the train?"

"Yes, and after. Did I tell you about Glubov, who was killed fighting with Timokhin?"

"No."

"Ah, well, then you see, you do not know."

And she told him about Glubov's death while trying to free the labor conscripts and Ira knew almost at once that he had been on the other side in that fight, the one in which he'd killed the boy.

"But what has all that to do with us?" he asked. "We'll leave it behind, all of it. There'll be an ocean between all of this and us."

"You're very kind," Maryenka began, but Ira interrupted her.

"I'm not being kind! I love you; that's not charity. It's selfish as hell. I want you."

A blush rose to Maryenka's cheeks. She was ashamed of it and annoyed. "You're being foolish. There are pretty girls in California who don't have babies who will please you much better than I ever could."

"That has nothing to do with it, Maryenka. They don't smell like cucumbers. You do."

At this she laughed and Ira, overjoyed at having brought Maryenka this happiness, told her about his Uncle Dave's admonition not to let a girl who smelled of cucumbers get away. "California girls smell like oranges and limes. It's all right if you go for that sort of thing, but I'm a cucumber man myself and cucumbers are rare, very rare indeed. I'll never find another like you, so you can't refuse me, Maryenka. You mustn't. I'm sincere. I really am. I don't know why you hesitate. I'll love you all my life just as I do now. We'll name the baby after Harry, even Harriet if it's a girl. I thought about it last night. You make me afraid, Maryenka, that I'm not good enough for you, that's what I'm thinking. And I agree, I'm not much, but I'll try to make you happy. I promise you, I'll try the best I know how."

Earnestness cracked Ira's voice and to his dismay he thought he was going to burst into tears.

Maryenka caught his hand. Her own eyes were swimming. "Ira, please don't," she said.

It was the first time he'd heard his name on Maryenka's lips and it gave him such hope he thought his heart would break. He stretched out and put his head on her lap and they waited together for the ebb of their emotions so they could talk again, and Maryenka stroked his head as he had stroked hers the night before.

Presently he took her fingers and kissed them. "Cucumbers," he said. "My Uncle Dave will be proud of me."

"You don't understand," she said quietly.

"What?"

"Did you know I had been married — before Harry? Yes, to Petra Shulgin, who died."

"Yes, Harry told me."

"He died, Petra, I mean."

"Yes."

"And then Harry was killed."

"I know."

"And Glubov, and dear Anitsky."

Ira sat up and found Maryenka staring off with a look in her eyes which alarmed him because it was so despairing, so lost and dark. "What are you saying, Maryenka?" he whispered.

Her eyes came back from a distance to meet his. "But you see," she said, "these people all loved me and they're dead. Anitsky is dead and he loved me too. My father, my brother, even Rodion, in his way, Glubov, and my sweet Harry. All of them."

"Maryenka, that doesn't make sense," Ira said but he knew already where her thoughts had gone.

"If it hadn't been for Anitsky, perhaps," she said.

"People are dying all over. There's typhus, war, dislocation, famine."

"I only know my own."

Ira rose to his knees looking directly into her wounded eyes. "Maryenka, if you believe that by loving you I'll die, then so be it. It doesn't matter to me."

"Ah, yes," Maryenka said sadly, "but you see, it does matter to me. I can't stand any more. Even as little as I loved Glubov, and I loved him a little when I thought there was no hope of escape, it hurt me when he was killed. And when I learned about Harry I thought it was a punishment, but now, with Anitsky, I see it clearly. Don't love me, Ira. I can't be responsible. I can't return the feeling, not to you or anyone, I'm afraid. I'm a coward, you see."

"You don't know what a coward is!"

"Please, let's put it aside."

"It's my life!"

Maryenka smiled. "Today it is," she said and before he could protest she rose and told him she was going to return the jacket she'd mended to Balashov.

Ira did not press his case. He thought time and circumstances were on his side and that she would come to know he was sincere. They slept side by side on pallets of fir boughs, blankets and animal hides and though Ira never made a sexual overture more often than not they awakened in each other's arms, clinging together for warmth. Maryenka invariably sat up at once and looked around as though to say: What? How has this come about!

"Cucumbers," Ira said, and she would smile.

Sometimes it was his pallet which was vacant, sometimes it was hers. They gravitated toward one another in their sleep and Ira was pleased when it happened that she had come to him. "I'm attractive to cucumbers, you see."

"I smell like a owl!"

"Not to me."

"Well then, your nose has gone wrong," she'd say.

On his next trip to Verkhne-Udinsk, Slavin returned with a letter for Ira. It was from Silverman:

DEAR LEVERETT,

Thanks for picking me to share your tzorress. I feel honored though I don't know why unless it's because you're the only man in this outfit with guts enough to take positive action about anything.

Mazel tov!

I sent your letters on and spoke to the old man about what could be done for you and Mrs. Austin. He says come home, all is forgiven. You're being carried A.W.O.L. on the roster. All you have to do is get to one of our outposts between Mysovaya and Tataurovo where you'll be taken under guard and sent straight through to Vlad. With luck you could be home by Chanukah.

I'd like to buy your ticket, Maryenka's too.

In case you don't know it the general situation is disintegrating rapidly. The Kolchak government is in flight, the British, French and Czechs are pulling out, so if I were you I wouldn't let any grass grow under my feet. Come in and lie low. We'll be waiting.

Look forward to seeing you soon.

Best regards,
JOE

Ira read the letter carefully. The bantering tone annoyed him, but he read it again and decided Silverman had done his best under the circumstances. The letter wasn't as alarming as it might have been. In fact it was quite relaxed and he showed it to Maryenka.

"Read this," he said. "We could get to Mysovaya in one day."

Maryenka had great trouble with the written words; Silverman's handwriting was as casual as his note, but Ira let her take all the time she needed. When at last she understood it she looked up at him with a splendid smile of relief. "Then you're all right," she said. "You can go."

"We can both go," Ira said.

Maryenka shook her head. "I promised Timokhin to stay," she said.

"Him! You promised him?" Ira gasped. "What about me?"

"But you're free to go! It says right here," and she shook Silverman's letter in his face.

"Not without you," Ira declared. "I won't go unless you go with me."

"Timokhin will not allow it," she said, "and I don't want to go."

"What about the baby?"

Maryenka shook her head in a way which left no doubt in Ira's mind she intended to stay. "Nichevo," she said.

"But I've arranged the whole thing for us, together!"

"As long as I am here I don't think you would tell the Americans or the Whites where we are located."

Ira was insulted. "Do you think I'd do that?" he asked. "Do you, Maryenka?"

"No. Not if I stay."

"Even if you came with me do you think I'd inform on these men?"

"No, but Timokhin can't be sure. How can you expect him to trust you?"

"Why shouldn't he?"

"You fought him once. The Americans fought him when he tried to liberate the labor conscripts; the day Glubov was killed."

"He knows about that?" Ira asked dully.

"Timokhin knew when I told him how we'd escaped from Tataurovo. He recognized the engine. He knew the detachment had come from Tataurovo. I didn't tell him you commanded it."

"It was a mistake, Maryenka."

"But you did fight him?"

"Yes, I led the detachment, but it was an awful mistake."

"So," she said and she looked away.

Ira felt he'd lost her trust and searched desperately for a way to regain it. He'd suffered enough over killing that boy. It was wrong, unjust, and cruel that his action then should nullify Maryenka's trust in him now. "Maryenka, I love you," he said.

"Timokhin has allowed you to come here because of me. He has permitted you to send notes to the Americans because of me."

"Do you think I'd betray him?"

Her eyes flashed over his trying to catch the truth, hoping to be convinced, but she sighed miserably. "How can I be sure?"

"What can I do or say to make you sure?"

Maryenka shook her head helplessly. "I don't know, Ira," she said. "It's terrible not to be sure, but I'm not. I only know that if I bring death to this man who has helped and befriended me I shall kill myself. It would mean that I have brought death to everyone who has touched my heart. Who can live with that? Who could live knowing such a thing?"

"It's not true, Maryenka."

"Timokhin is the only exception I know," she said. "All the others, all of them, are dead."

"I must be an exception too."

Maryenka shook her head once more, almost angrily. "No," she said. "I will not permit it. I will not." She met his eyes resolutely. "Do you understand?" she demanded. "I cannot permit it. I will move my things to be near Timokhin. You must arrange to leave at once."

Ira tried to catch her shoulders, but Maryenka brushed his hands away and went to move her bed to the next cave, where Timokhin slept.

Ira put on his heavy coat and walked up the ice-paved trail to the hill where he could look across the lake. He stood with his back against a tree the bark of which was frozen hard as iron. The air was clear and there was a cap of gray-bellied clouds on the mountains as far as the eye could see.

He thought of death by freezing and felt it was coming to him as to the tree against which he rested. For the tree as for himself there was a time when the layers of bark and living wood could no longer stand the cold and the sap at the core would freeze. He felt the process. It was pitiless. No amount of intelligence could stay it, no song, no dance, no witticism could affect this cold, only human trust or love and sometimes not even these.

Maryenka was freezing too, but to protect him she would not love him; she did not trust him, soon his very presence would threaten her and at last in common decency he would leave to stop her suffering because of his presence and they would be frozen apart.

So?

He would return to California, to the oranges and limes, to the warm life. Time would pass. Picnics, baseball games, success in marriage and career, two or three children, a house with a view of the bay, a boat to sail and always the secret knowledge that he was living in expiation of crimes which up until now might be excused as misadventures, accidents, or the results of lack of experience. But this could not be excused.

No, to leave Maryenka and go out alone would poison his life. And he cared. Thank God he still cared enough to know that he could not go on stringing out this chain of expiations.

He decided to stay until the last line was drawn and Maryenka came with him or he died.

« 2 »

Reverence for Timokhin was undiminished by his delay in making a decision between Kravchenko and Marmatov. Only Marrakof, the giant half Kalmyk murderer whose lust for action made him tramp about in chafing impatience, seemed unsettled by it. Twice he had made impassioned appeals in full meeting that the question be settled by vote and that they get on with their business. He no longer cared whether they fell in with Marmatov or Kravchenko, he wanted to move, to fight the accursed White exploiters.

Twice Timokhin had firmly vetoed this suggestion. "There's no need for voting when each of us is free to go or stay as he wills, Marrakof," he said.

At this Marrakof grew sullen. He rolled himself up in skins at the back of the cave and tried to hibernate like a bear, but his limbs twitched and he moaned in his sleep, struggling, it seemed, to avoid waking up. He slept for three days with his heavy brown hair pulled forward into his beard so no one could see his face and some of the men began to worry about him. They stood about listening to Marrakof grumbling in his sleep, trying to make out the words as though these were more important from a sleeping man than from one who was fully awake.

At the end of the third day one of the men reported to Balashov that Marrakof was saying they must decide. "Come and listen," he said to Balashov. "We've all heard it three times now."

Balashov, seated near the fire honing a saber he'd taken in one of their early encounters with a trainload of Whites, bounded to his feet. His eyes glittered with anger as he went to the place where Marrakof lay surrounded by half a dozen men all listening intently. One of them cautioned Balashov to silence and they all bent closer to catch the words issuing through the mat of hair which covered Marrakof's face.

"We must decide, brothers," Marrakof said in a distinct but hollow whisper. "We can delay no longer, no longer."

The words were drawn out into a portentous, sibilant hiss which disturbed the hair over Marrakof's lips.

Balashov's face turned black and the men took this to mean that he too was shaken by the words. But to their consternation Balashov raised the saber he had been sharpening and held it with two fingers by the hilt with the gleaming point just a foot above Marrakof's hidden mouth. "I will now drop it," he whispered.

"He's asleep!" One of the men protested but Balashov dropped the heavy saber.

With a catlike twist Marrakof escaped the saber point which pierced the mattress of skins on which he lay. He leaped up bellowing curses and attacked Balashov in savage fury. He overwhelmed Balashov, threw him down and with his huge hands choked Balashov and beat his head on the floor of the cave and would have killed him if the men hadn't dragged him away.

It took six men to subdue Marrakof, who continued to roar like a beast.

"He was not asleep," was all Balashov said as he picked up his saber and left the cave.

The men knew then that Marrakof had tried to usurp Timokhin's position of leadership; and though they resented having been taken in by his method and thought it to be an affront to Timokhin's true voice, still they were willing to concede that if anything should happen to Timokhin they could do no better than to accept Marrakof for their leader. He had courage, initiative and a need for action which none of them possessed. Not even Slavin or Balashov.

So, although it appeared Marrakof had failed he had not, because an election occurred in the minds of the men which Marrakof won and this meant that faith in Timokhin's immortality had been shaken.

The men, even the most skeptical among them, who had only believed Timokhin would die in the distant future and that they would not witness his death, now believed he would die in their presence. To conceal this loss of faith and expunge the guilt it brought them they avoided Marrakof and gathered more closely around Timokhin. They listened eagerly when he spoke and tried to anticipate his wants. They expressed their love and respect for Timokhin in a hundred clumsy ways while Marrakof brooded in the darkness, alone.

But for all their kindness, their offerings of game, their attentiveness and their stalwart show of loyalty Timokhin knew. He knew what Marrakof did not know and he was undisturbed.

In fact he was relieved by the men's loss of faith in his earthly immortality. His wound, which heretofore had not troubled him greatly, began to be painful and though he concealed this from Maryenka he welcomed each mortal pain as a pledge from God that he would die. And with this assurance Timokhin found he was capable of making decisions once more.

He reconsidered the whole of his life. He'd always been a fighter, but had gained nothing by it. He could think of no one who had gained by it and he began to see that his choice was not between Marmatov and Kravchenko but whether to fight or to stop fighting. He considered this for some time and the men continued to wait for his decision.

Then one clear night with the moon striking such a hard blow off the frozen surface of Baikal that it bit the eyes with its brilliance Timokhin sat down near the fire and began searching for lice in the seams of a shirt he had worn. This was an occupation in which everyone engaged for although Maryenka scrubbed, cleaned and boiled she had no soap and the nits were in the furs on the floors and walls and there was no way to be rid of them short of burning every article of apparel and every animal skin in the caves.

Timokhin picked over his shirt with a look of enrapt concentration. His face, ordinarily red, was particularly bloody in the firelight and his broken profile pitched a giant shadow against the wall which bobbed and nodded as Timokhin searched the seams. The shadow appeared to have a life of its own and after watching it awhile Slavin went to the other caves and told the men to come.

When they were gathered Timokhin was studying a louse in the palm of his hand. The pale, waxy insect with its six single-hooked, crablike legs and fat bristle-studded body, which popped with a sound one felt rather than heard when it was squeezed, appeared magnified on the bare expanse of Timokhin's palm.

Timokhin gazed at the louse intently and presently he began to speak in those impressive, hollow tones which seemed to emanate from above and behind him. He glanced at Ira and smiled. "We must know what we are about," he said.

Ira was always deeply impressed by these oracular sessions of Timokhin's. Sometimes he didn't understand the words and Maryenka would whisper a translation to him, but most of the time he was swept into a deeper understanding than words conveyed and actually he knew more Russian than even he suspected.

But now, fascinated and a bit repelled by the louse in Timokhin's hand, Ira knew from inside what Timokhin was saying.

"We must know what we are about, brothers," Timokhin said, "because a time has come to men which is different from all others."

Here Timokhin raised his hand to display the louse; he nudged it with one finger and it scurried up on the heel of his hand and stopped there.

The men stared at the louse, their eyes tight in the effort to see it in the poor light as though they hadn't plucked thousands of them from their garments over the years, as though each one of them could not have produced the match of it from his own stale body at that moment. But for them the louse on the heel of Timokhin's palm was the emperor louse and nearly everyone there, having conquered his disgust of the insect through constant familiarity with it, remembered the long contemplative hours they had spent delousing themselves and realized what a great deal they owed the louse. Those who had been in prison were reprieved of their misery while searching for lice because each louse captured and crushed delivered with its extinguished life a small sense of accomplishment and triumph.

Among prisoners a man who had no lice to kill was a sorry case for he had no way to distinguish himself. He could not say he had killed ten, or fifty, or a hundred; he could not prove his excellence as a louse hunter or experience the triumph of the kill and he had no excuse to sit picking over his body and clothing. All he had was the terrible suspicion that lice found him inferior to all other men.

Such men could not survive prison life. Some died of shame, others went mad; others, despondent at having been rejected by such a low order of life, committed suicide.

They realized too as soldiers or impressed laborers, or even as farmers bound to the soil, that their deepest thoughts had very often come while crushing lice. The activity prompted them to considerations of the meaning of life and death. And sometimes, prior to crushing a louse between their thumbnail and forefinger, they paused a moment to wonder what it meant. What became of this bit of life after it was no more than a stain on their fingers, and what became of them? So their faith in God was tested by the existence of a louse, and those who had lived with lice for years found more solace in the finite louse than in the infinite God.

They stared at the emperor louse on the heel of Timokhin's hand and many of them smiled affectionately, remembering times when a louse prompting them to scratch and curse had reawakened in them the instinct for life, remembering too all the jokes about lice and volleys of booming laughter, remembering many things, but mostly that their life without the louse would be an infinitely poorer thing. The insect was their friend and their tormentor, a creature which gave in satisfaction more than it took in blood. Would that men were the same.

Timokhin turned his hand slowly so they could see the louse in the firelight and then satisfied it was fixed in their minds he rested his hand on his lap and looked down at it.

"My good brothers," he began solemnly, "last year near Boyarski Siding I came upon an old man in his death throes from the spotted fever. We have all seen such a thing. He died as I watched; and as I watched, the lice of his body, finding his blood grown cold, boiled up through his clothing like kernels of rice. It was a sight which brought tears and laughter. All those lice, having lost their world, scuttled about in the freezing air trying to decide what to do. Most of them carried the old man's disease, but they didn't know this. They didn't know what it was. They only knew that the world with its comforts and dangers, which had given them food, shelter, warmth and which had made it possible for them to have their children, was gone. Just gone.

"Imagine it, brothers! In the space of five minutes all their world was gone! How is such a thing possible? Generations of lice had known this world. They cultivated it, yes, you can believe they did, finding the safest place for their nits, the best places to feed, making plans for improvements, eh? The head lice marched about under the old man's fur cap, the body lice promenaded in the forests of the old man's chest, the crab lice held theatricals in the old man's crotch. Oh, yes! They had a society, brothers, believe me they did. Border patrols, no doubt. Improvement associations, eh? But all this had come to nothing because the world was dead. Yes, somewhere along the line their great world had come into contact with another and one louse, or two, maybe a dozen, had come aboard and they carried the spotted fever. They put it into the life streams of this other world and it died."

Timokhin sighed and shook his head sadly.

"Is God watching while such a thing can happen?" he asked. "We have all seen it, have we not? Not one world but many lying dead beside the tracks, in the fields and villages, and the lice, stunned by the catastrophe, bubbling up out of the clothing.

"Pause sometime to see them, brothers. At first they mill about clinging to the fading warmth, praying for the resurrection with all their being, praying for it, as you can well believe. But at last they are driven off by necessity.

"Ah, brothers, then you must draw close to see the caravans of lice leaving their corpse of a world, striking off into the snow in search of a new one. They abandon their homes, their fields, all the places they have known and march off into the unknown, heartsick and frightened, eh?, but wanting to live. Wanting? Can we doubt that a louse wants to live when we see such a thing? No, brothers, we cannot. They are even as you and I. A caravan of lice in the snow, perishing, falling by the wayside, with no destination.

"They must have a plan, eh? Yes, to seek another world. But where? What chance has a louse in a field of snow?"

Timokhin looked around at his listeners, his scarred face inexpressibly sad. He shuddered and grew pale as though his heart had stopped, then he continued speaking in a resonant, tender voice which was closer to the men than any they had known.

"And what do they carry? What do these poor lice carry as a gift to a new world, but death? So step back a little when you see them coming, eh? Step away because what they bring to you and to the lice of your body is death, which is something you already have in full supply. Do you doubt it? Come, brothers, are there any here who feel the need of more? A little bit will do, eh?

"Well, I have taken my share of death in small portions, but I feel no need of more. I'm satisfied with the amount I was given. I'm a louse in the snow, brothers, in search of another world. Yes, a louse in the snow.

"But brothers, what has happened to my home? Where is my warmth? Who has destroyed my fields? Which of all the lice around me in the snow is the guilty one? Let's settle with him now, eh? Let's be done with him."

Timokhin seized the louse on his palm between his thumb and forefinger and everyone heard it pop. They gasped and a few half rose in protest and horror as Timokhin wiped his fingers on his trousers.

"Justice, brothers," he said softly. "Justice, or mercy. Who can be sure? The hand of God, eh? One louse is gone, punished, or saved, but the rest struggle on through the snow. They too will die. Yes, all those poor, searching lice will die.

"But brothers, having observed these lice leaving the body of the old man, I passed on toward Mysovaya where Aunt Aglalia, whose kindness is known to us all, gave me a bowl of soup, a place by the stove and her blessing. I told her what I had seen and she wept, for she had known the old man, but about the lice she had this to say: 'Ah, Timokhin, by now someone without such a warm coat as yours has taken Pavel Stepanovitch's (for this was the dead man's name) and put it on, because what use had a dead man of a coat? Even now the heat of his body warms the nits which will soon hatch into lice, so there is no harm done. The mistake, Timokhin dear, is to go in search of a new world. If it is to come, it will come. We must cling to what we have and that is all.'"

Timokhin shrugged and looked around the cave at the men. He smiled and shook his head. "Women," he said, "do they always know best?

"In the morning I walked back to Boyarski Siding to see, but no one had taken Pavel Stepanovitch's coat, so I took it myself, hoping to make a new world for the lice. I succeeded, eh? Who can doubt it? So the message, brothers, is to wait for the world to come. Don't do as I have done and go in search of a new one. Stay where you are. There will be those who will say to you, 'This old world is dead, come move along to a new one, the Red one, the White one, this one that one,' but brothers, stay as you are until someone takes up the coat. Live in the seams, eh? Stay hidden away, waiting for the new warmth. If it does not come, so be it. A louse can't whistle a man to appear and a wise man doesn't whistle for God. The best we can do is to wait until someone picks up old Mother Russia's coat and puts it on. Don't try to guess who it will be, or for how long it will be worn. The coat is a heavy one, brothers, and even if the new owner has spotted fever, the nits which have not fed on that owner's blood will live to feast on another's. Mother Russia is dead, brothers, but the old coat has a lot of life in it, ready to come along given a little warmth."

Timokhin turned to gaze into the fire. There was a faraway smile on his lips and the firelight turned his eyes to embers. Behind him on the wall his shadow had lost its features. No one spoke. The men looked at one another, frowning a bit, then they rose one by one and left the cave through the skins over the doorway. Ira too felt the need to be alone and went out.

The moon, directly overhead, had lost its force and the ice on the lake was dull gray. It was very still, and far down the lake through miles and miles of silence Ira could hear a passing train.

Presently Maryenka came out and gave Ira his coat. He put it on feeling as though he were shouldering the world.

Maryenka looked away over the gray, dead lake. Her face was pale and very soft in the moonlight.

"We have to strike out for what we want, Maryenka," he said.

Maryenka tucked her hand under Ira's arm. The gesture was so rare that Ira wasn't sure what to make of it. He couldn't remember if she had ever touched him of her own accord. She had caressed him as one would comfort a domestic animal, but this was different. There was an acceptance in the way she held his arm which encouraged him. "Walk down with me a bit," she said, "the air was so close in there."

They walked down the path toward the lake picking their way carefully on the ashes the men scattered each day to make a footing and they came to the promontory which gave them a view of the lake in both directions. As they stood there they heard a thunderous report and the ice divided like white skin cleft by a saber, leaving an open wound ten miles long and half a mile wide with black water lapping the severed edges. A column of men crossing the lake at this place would have been engulfed without warning and would have died of cold shock within minutes.

By morning a skin of ice would have formed over the wound and if a snowfall hid the scar other travelers unused to the ways of the lake might fall through this crust and also die like lice in a field of snow.

The break in the ice was an obsidian dagger laid there by the hand of the moon. It pointed northeast toward the Lena, away from the lake, the cities, the road into the untamed Siberian plateau. It led the eye off into the north and with it the mind.

Maryenka's hand remained on Ira's arm and he felt himself thawing under the touch of it, but he was unable to say anything for fear of driving her away. It was Maryenka, however, who broke the silence. "Timokhin has given over fighting," she said.

"Given over?" he asked.

"He no longer believes in it. Those who do will go with Marrakof."

"What about him?"

"He will go off."

Ira frowned. He didn't understand.

Maryenka turned to face him directly and there was a softness in her eyes. "Timokhin is a holy man," she said. "Here we call them the startsy, not priests, but holy men who travel about sharing their experience of God. They are poor and beg their bread, but people often come for miles around, making pilgrimages to listen to such men, and Timokhin is one of these. I have faith in him. I believe. I would follow him to the ends of the earth."

"I see," Ira said hopelessly for he thought this was what she had decided to do.

"I told him so," Maryenka said. "I told him last night, but he said that you had taken up my coat. Now I know what he meant."

"You will go with me," Ira said.

"Yes."

"To my home. To California?"

"Yes."

This was so unexpected that Ira wasn't prepared. He had an urge to laugh and suddenly he did, a whooping, joyous shout of laughter which took him as much by surprise as Timokhin's trust in him. He caught Maryenka in his arms and tried to explain his laughter to her. "It's like getting all set to do something very hard and having it given to you, or like ice skating and suddenly falling down. It's a shock, you see. You sit there a minute to see if anything is broken, then you laugh in relief. I was going to try to make Timokhin understand and he's already done it without a word. We'll get a note to Silverman and tell him we're coming out. It shouldn't be too difficult."

He kissed Maryenka awkwardly. Her lips were cold and dry and she seemed very small in his arms.

"Don't be so solemn," he said. "It's going to be all right. I love you. Come on, let's get out of this cold."

The men around the fire looked up as they came inside and smiled. "I'll get your things from the other cave," Slavin said to Maryenka, who blushed but did not object.

CHAPTER THIRTY-FOUR

FROM the dingy room in the Hotel Metropole which she shared with Katya Massakow, Tatiana stared down into the snow-shrouded street at the people passing below. In the failing light their faces looked dark and featureless and their bulkily clothed bodies, distorted by the double panes of cheap glass in the window, seemed to shrink, swell and elongate like germ cultures under a microscope.

Tatiana felt dizzy and bleakly unattractive. Her nose was running and she daubed at it with a wretchedly soggy handkerchief.

"Sugar is thirty-five rubles a pound," she thought and the intrusion of this idle information brought tears to her eyes. "How can I think of sugar when Albert is dead!" But she thought of sugar and of a hundred other inconsequential things which scurried like night creatures through her mind. "I must make plans," she thought. "I have to come to a decision!"

She tried to think what alternatives she had. She must write to her mother in Prague and to Albert's parents too. Yes, at once. She would go home. Mrs. Custer-Farquart had written urging her once more to join them. She was desperately needed in the hospital here. The Bolsheviks were coming. Victims of typhus and exposure were crowding into the city. Major Ikachi and Captain Carlisle were in love with her. The hospital train carrying Raul Markowitz from Omsk had not reached Nizhne-Udinsk. Colonel Dubrovski expected to be in Irkutsk soon.

"Sugar is thirty-five rubles a pound."

Tatiana left the window and lay down on her bed. She was trembling. The paper on the ceiling was water-stained, threatening to fall down. The walls were infested with roaches. The room smelled of creosote from the pans in which the bed legs stood, moats of gummy creosote to trap the insects before they gained the bed. It was all dismal, dismal, dismal, and her nose was running horribly and was going to be red. She couldn't decide anything. She wanted to be cared for, needed to be.

Sugar, thirty-five rubles.

"My God," she moaned, "what do I care about that!"

She snuffled and rolled her head from side to side.

There came a soft rapping on the door.

Ikachi.

She could tell by his knuckles.

How odd.

She lay perfectly still knowing he knew she was there and this became a contest between her unsightly nose and his patience. She didn't want to be seen; he would not go away.

"I prefer Carlisle," she thought. "At least he knows to leave a person when he can't help."

"Countess?"

"Yes, Major."

"I've only just heard. Is there anything I can do?"

"No."

"Please call on me if I can be of any service."

He was going away. His voice through the flimsy wooden door had sounded formal and untouched. Katya wouldn't be back for at least an hour. She didn't want to be alone.

Tatiana rolled from the bed to her feet and pulled the door open. "Oh, Major!" she cried.

Major Ikachi supported her with one arm and helped her into the worn armchair. He closed the door, then faced her with a look of golden compassion. "My most humble and deepest regrets, Countess," he said.

Tatiana held the handkerchief over her nose and gazed at him. "I'm all right now," she said chokingly.

Subo Ikachi looked around the unremittingly shabby room and couldn't conceal his distaste. The setting was entirely improper for her. He could hardly speak because of it. "You must get out of this," he said.

Tatiana nodded, ashamed of the room in his presence when she hadn't been at all ashamed of it in Carlisle's. She swallowed convulsively, certain she was going to burst into tears. She had never felt so devastatingly poor and inferior.

"There must be a better place than this to put you up," Ikachi said. "If not, you can take my room."

"Oh, no."

"I insist. I could never be comfortable knowing you were in such circumstances. One must never let down, my dear Countess. That one must never do."

"I understand."

"I know what you must feel — please believe me, I do. I want to help you. Are you well enough, do you think, to come downstairs?"

Tatiana nodded obediently and Ikachi smiled. "You are a noble-woman," he said and bowing he let himself out, closing the door behind him.

Tatiana felt better at once. She had been complimented and of course it was necessary that she make an appearance. Albert would have said the same thing. One could not give way to emotions.

She rose, looked at herself in the mirror and began making the necessary repairs. The puffy exhaustion around her eyes and the redness of her nose would show through the powder, but not unattractively to those who knew her bereavement.

She elected to wear her blue-gray uniform in recognition that duty transcended personal grief, but with a blouse less severe than the usual shirtwaist, and her pearls as a mark of distinction for herself and of reverence for Albert. She combed and brushed her hair and arranged it in a large, rather severe bun at the nape of her neck and when she had finished she stood again in front of her mirror waiting for an appearance of that expression on her face which best suited her situation.

The figure in her mirror always seemed wonderfully sensitive and apart from her, and Tatiana was frequently surprised by the subtle play of emotion over its handsome, mobile face and in its large, expressive gray eyes. The mode or style into which it settled in any given circumstance was always right and seemed to require no effort on her part. Tatiana simply waited for a responsive chord to be struck between herself and her image, or between her image and herself. She was never sure of its genesis and it never seemed to matter. They were true friends.

She was extremely grateful that Ikachi had made this demand on them. The opportunity might have been lost. She could have continued for hours as she had been, sulking about, incapable of knowing what to do, but now it was simple once more. To appear. To make an appearance. To let people see.

There! In her mirrored eyes was exactly the proper expression.

Tatiana could never account for this miraculous aptness, she could only recognize it with a thrill of pleasure.

The face in her mirror wore a private grief too painful to admit being spoken of, but in that withdrawn and imposed silence it fairly howled for recognition. The eyes had gone darker by a shade; there was a slight tuck in the broad forehead; her wide mouth was beautiful in resignation and her chin, though firm, held the shadow of a tremble.

"Am I so false then?" she wondered and this thought enhanced her expression in the mirror. "Am I nothing but this reflection?" The tragic implication of substancelessness turned her dark brows up a bit as though to question the whole of existence.

A series of other mirrored images of herself flashed through her mind without in the least impairing the effectiveness of the one before which she stood. The tantalizing and mischievous child of nine, playful, radiant and adored. The slim, poised, leggy adolescent, bursting with such promise of beauty that people sometimes caught their breath. The nubile girl with such currents of life in her hands that young men often trembled by touching things she had only touched herself.

These images, all of them, thousands upon thousands of them, were stored in the mind of the creature in the mirror and could be called back, had been called back thousands upon thousands of times. Even the faces of childhood, of innocence and gaiety, of delight, coquettishness, those also of passion and abandon. What a store of faces it held! Millions! A variety and selection of perhaps hundreds of faces for each trifling incident and yet here was a new one as perfect as all the others had been for their occasion — the face of personal grief.

Tatiana turned from the mirror and put on her gloves, for the public rooms downstairs were always too cold for comfort now, and she hated to have her hands chilled. "Like a cat hates having its paws dipped in water," she thought. "I'm simulating," she thought. "I don't feel the grief, I just show it. It's all false and untrue, and simulated!"

But as she left she glanced once again into the mirror; the simulation was perfect and she was its prisoner. "How is one to break out?" she wondered and she went down to meet Ikachi. "But does one want to?" she wondered. "Aren't we all the same? Life is simulation after all."

Major Ikachi watched her approach with keen admiration, noting each delicate nuance on her face. "You have never been more beautiful, Countess," he said softly. "Never more gallant."

"I'm shamming, Major," Tatiana said.

"One cannot always give way to one's true feelings, Countess. There is self-control, discipline, to fall back on."

He took her arm and led her to a private booth in one corner of the dining room where tea had been served and was waiting for them.

"I feel nothing," Tatiana said as he seated her and took his place across the table.

"That is often true in cases of great personal loss," Ikachi said.

"To feel nothing?"

"Yes, to feel nothing at first."

"Then I can expect a reaction?"

"Yes," Ikachi said and he poured the tea and gave her a cup.

"I'll look forward to it," Tatiana said. "Albert doesn't seem real to me; I mean I can't think of him as being dead and it makes me think he was never real to me. I've known about it for days and still I've had no reaction."

"I'm sure you must have had, dear Countess."

"Are you?"

"I see it in your eyes."

"I was benumbed of course when the wire came from Dubrovski. I was shocked, let down. I really didn't know what to do. I haven't since then known what to do, but then I never really have known what to do. I've simply gone on, you know, doing as people have expected me to do and as

I expected myself to do in response to their expectations." Tatiana frowned and sipped her tea. "I really can't think of ever having done something out of my own desire to do it. That's strange, isn't it? I wonder if it's so."

Tatiana found Ikachi watching her attentively. "It will do you good to talk," he said.

"What about?"

"Anything you like," Ikachi said with a shrug.

"I must do something," she said. "I must do something of my own volition. I don't know what it is, but I can't go on like this."

"You have your work."

"Yes, but I was drawn into it by someone stronger than myself and I don't feel it. The reason I can continue is that I don't feel it, you see. I thought for a time in Omsk that I did, but everyone is a mirror. I hadn't thought of that before. Everyone is a mirror to me! I play out parts in front of them. I'm good at that. Do I look bereaved?"

Ikachi nodded. "Yes," he said.

"But I'm not. Not, at least, for Albert, but for myself. I'm a reflection. I've always been a reflection."

"And I am also a mirror?" Ikachi asked.

"Yes, you are," Tatiana said with increasing desperation. "You are a mirror. I've put on a face for you. You see it, but it's not true. I wish it were, but I don't know how to be true. I can't remember!" Tatiana put her tea aside and stood up. "I think I'd better leave," she said. "Please excuse me."

Ikachi came to her side and took her arm gently. "You're terribly upset, Countess," he said. "It's to be expected."

Tatiana wrenched her arm away. "Don't!" she cried. "You don't understand. You're very much like Albert, very polished. I hadn't realized. Please excuse me."

Tatiana hurried through the room clinging desperately to her self-control. Ikachi followed at her heels. "My room is at your disposal, Countess," he said urgently.

"No," she said. "No, it's not that! Please, I'm very sorry."

Tatiana ran up the stairs and along the hall to her room. She flung the door open and slammed it behind her and stood with her back against it, panting. Katya Massakow was there.

"Tatiana, what has happened!"

"Don't talk to me, Katya! Please don't. Not now."

Katya came toward her, sympathy glowing in her eyes, her hand out-stretched.

"Katya! I'm false, don't touch me!" Tatiana cried in anguish. She wrenched the closet open and took out her coat. "Please, leave me alone!"

"Tatiana!" Katya called in a hurt tone of voice.

But Tatiana was already fleeing as she had come. She passed Major Ikachi on the stairs and he tried once again to detain her.

"Let me go!"

"My dear —"

"No, I can't! I despise myself. All of us!"

She pushed Ikachi aside, nearly toppling him down the stairs, then she ran through the lobby into the street.

Once alone, she walked with no destination in mind.

The bitter cold stung her face. She buttoned her coat and from the pocket took a scarf and tied it around her head. "This is the reaction," she thought. "This grief is for Albert."

But it was false. Even now, alone, with no one to see, no mirrors, no eyes, she was lying to herself. "I must set out at once and *do* something!" she said aloud. But what?

How could she do something not for the mirror? What act of hers would shatter mirrors, all the mirrors, all the faces?

Suicide.

She turned toward the river.

It would be falsely interpreted. If her body was found they would say she had killed herself in grief over Albert's death.

What did it matter? She would be out of it. Free. Full of self-pity, bravely sacrificial. Yes, even suicide was self-dramatizing. She was too much a coward to do it.

Wasn't she?

She boarded the ferry and sat on one of the benches near the railing.

Wasn't she too much a coward to kill herself?

She had never considered this and she shuddered as snow collected on the collar of her coat. "I will do it," she said. "Yes, to destroy the mirrors."

She felt calm for a time.

Yes, it was self-dramatizing, self-pitying, all the rest of it, but such was her life; she knew nothing else.

She heard a bell in the bowels of the vessel. Two crew members cast off the ice-caked hawsers, which splashed into the black river and were drawn aboard. The engine began to throb and the dockside receded in a curtain of snow. She heard the current sweeping along the flank of the ferry and the crush of ice against the bow as it broke through headed for Glaskov.

"I shall do it," she said again and she looked around to see if anyone was nearby. "My God," she thought, "do I need an audience even for this?"

Very well, let it be so. But there was no audience. All the passengers had gone into the cabin. She stood up and looked over the railing into the coiling black water. "I commend my soul to Thee," she thought.

Yes, to the black onyx mirrors of God wherein she would see her soul as she had seen herself in its myriad faces and postures. The same, all the same!

Once again she looked around to see if there were any observers. None. No one to save her. No one to witness this final act.

"It's all too preposterously characteristic!" she thought. "I don't believe it. It's false, false as everything else I've done. God, who is watching, could not receive me and if Albert is watching there's a smile of contempt on his face."

And it was the thought of Albert watching, rather than of God, which caused Tatiana to hesitate. "I have not even the pride to do it. I am contemptible. I am a coward."

This at least seemed real and therefore satisfying.

She sat down and pressed her cheek against the freezing railing, commanding herself to weep in remorse, but no tears came.

The ferry beat on through the black ice-clogged water. Its lights were muffled in falling snow. The engine throbbed with rhythmic disinterest. A door slammed. The ferry from the Glaskov side passed by upriver like a stealthy ghost ship, soundless and phosphorescent through the snow. A crew member stumbled into her and went on without a word of apology much as to say she could jump over and over again for all he cared. How many, she wondered, had done so? Who cared?

Tatiana clenched her fists and beat them on her knees. "I must do something on my own!" she declared vehemently. "I must. I must! I must!"

Then she sighed despairingly and looked down again into the black water. "Narcissism," she thought. "Even suicide is narcissism! I must blind myself to live!"

Her nose was running again.

"Let it!" she declared and she refused to wipe it. "Let it run."

She sat bolt upright and mucus ran from her nose onto her upper lip.

Presently she could taste the saltiness of it, but she refused to move. "I will not surrender," she thought. "No, I will not!"

But at last with a violent, almost involuntary wrench of her arm Tatiana wiped her streaming nose on the rough sleeve of her coat and broke into a convulsion of tears and hysterical laughter.

She beat her head on her knees and hammered them with her fists, weeping and laughing at the same time. "Oh," she gasped. "Oh! Oh! I think to kill myself, but I can't prevent wiping my nose. Oh! Oh! How awful!"

She stood up, blinded by her shame, her rage and self-contempt. She put her hands on the railing fully intending to vault over it into the void, but the ferry bumped and careened, there was an outraged squeal of timbers, and when Tatiana opened her eyes the ferry had come into the Glaskov dock and people were pressing around her waiting for the gangplank and when the gate was opened she was thrust ashore by the crowd.

Tatiana let herself be pushed along through the ferry terminal to the street. Ahead she saw the lights of the Glaskov station, the roundhouses, shops and marshaling yard. She went toward these with no thought but that she must do something. "I must! I must come to some decision, any decision, this very night, or I'll live in this hell for the rest of my life!"

The station building was crowded with foul-smelling refugees and with wounded soldiers on stretchers waiting to be evacuated. In one dark corner she saw a man bandaging himself in yards of torn white sheeting and she knew without stopping to investigate that he was taking the place of one of the wounded who had died or been carried off to freeze. She thought nothing about this, but went downstairs to the platform and then out among the trains.

Yardmen with axes were going among the cars chopping away the heavy columns of ice from the urinals and kitchen cars which bound them to the roadbed. A guard patrol came along between the cars toward her. She thought they were Czechs at first, but then she recognized them as Americans. The soldier in charge of the detachment hailed her.

"Where you goin', lady?" he called.

"Can you tell me where I'll find Captain Carlisle?" she asked and she was astonished by the tone of authority in her voice, for until that second she hadn't known what she was going to say.

"Carlisle?"

"Yes."

The soldier pointed her the way. "Go to the end of this train, then four tracks over. You'll find his boxcar. It has an American flag on the side."

"Thank you very much," Tatiana said and she went on through the dark, cinder-strewn yard with a firm step but a wildly beating heart.

The Americans watched her out of sight, then moved on. "That Sioux has all the luck," one of them said.

« 2 »

After the official announcement by Girsa that the Czechs were pulling out of Siberia, trains bearing the Czech echelons had been hammering into Irkutsk at a great rate and there began a furious scramble for priorities from this point on through the Trans-Baikal tunnels to Verkhne-Udinsk.

Because the Czechs guarded the Trans-Baikal tunnels and would in all probability continue doing so until the last of their echelons passed through, it was important that priorities be issued to the Czechs in ratio to other Allied forces.

Carlisle was convinced the Czechs would abandon the Trans-Baikal tunnels when the last of their troops passed through, so he determined to keep enough Czech hostages in Irkutsk to insure continued protection of the tunnels. This brought him into direct conflict with General Syrovy and General Janin, whose primary interest was to save the Czechs. Janin was beside himself. "I would be most pleased to do all I am asked, if only not to be pestered night and day!"

Carlisle was the chief pest. He worked around the clock and didn't hesitate to ring Janin if things were not going to his satisfaction. In fact Carlisle felt a bit derelict in his duty if he didn't find at least one occasion each night to rouse the General or his aides from their slumber.

"This is Carlisle," he'd bellow.

"Have it your way," was the most frequent reply.

"Send a messenger to Czech train 4509 on Siding 8 that it is not to move until further orders and have the engineer report to the compound."

"Very well, Captain. In the morning."

"At once, if you please, sir."

"Oh, very well! Very well, at once!"

Carlisle's primary concern was for hospital evacuation trains. Working alone in his own teplushka furnished with stove, bed, table, gaslight and telephone he went over each manifest himself before passing it on to the division dispatcher for action. No train passed through Irkutsk without

Carlisle's signature. He'd won the grudging respect of all concerned though none of them were above trying to beat him out of a special privilege.

He was working thus at his table, going over a list of forty-four cars scheduled to leave in the morning, trying to pick out what was troubling him about it. There were thirty teplushkas with four hundred and forty-two patients and thirty-eight officers; five teplushkas with sixty-four clerks, druggists, workers, sanitars and twenty-four Russian nurses. Dr. Sweet was evacuation officer. The detachment commander was a Czech major. One mess officer. Dr. Judd, American. Dr. Nicolai. Dr. Pamonovora. Dr. Alfaroff in charge of heavy wounded. Dr. Diminsky, assistant surgeon.

"Diminsky?" Carlisle said aloud. "Diminsky again?"

He pulled the drawer of his desk open to go back through his files, certain that he'd seen the name Diminsky only last week, when there was a knock on the door.

"Yeah?" he grumbled.

He leafed through the manifests and the names swam under his eyes. "Damn," he mumbled, scowling at the lists, searching for Diminsky, Kominsky, no. There had been a Diminsky, he was sure. He took a sip of whiskey from the glass at his elbow, hoping it would clear his vision.

Again the timid rap on the door of the teplushka.

"Well, come in, damn it," he yelled.

There was an ineffectual tug at the heavy door, a kind of mouselike pawing which annoyed Carlisle. He stepped to the door and flung it open. "It slides!" he roared. "What is it?"

"Tatiana," the voice said.

He bent forward and saw a boyish, frightened face in the yellow light. At first he wasn't sure and the belligerent scowl remained, then it was transformed by a look of surprise. "It's you," he said just as she had said to him beside the river when they met. "Come in! What is it?"

He helped Tatiana inside and closed the door. He was sure there had been an insurrection in the city. He couldn't imagine what else would have brought her here. "What's happened?" he asked. "Here, sit down."

He pushed the only chair to the stove and sat her in it.

"What's gone wrong?" he asked urgently.

"I don't know," she said.

"But you're here!"

"I just came," she said.

Carlisle straightened up and looked around in total bewilderment. All his senses were alert. He was listening for gunfire, for artillery, for the sound of catastrophe, but there was nothing. Certainly by now someone would have phoned to alert him. He glanced at the phone to make sure it was connected.

"I just came on my own," Tatiana said humbly.

Carlisle looked at her once more in amazement. He hadn't seen Tatiana since she'd come back to the hotel with Katya something or other who told him Tatiana's husband had been killed. He'd been waiting in the lobby for her to return; his clothing was still damp, but he'd not wanted to remain too long in her bed. She'd gone straight up without a word to him, but her friend had explained it. Her husband was dead.

When he got back to Glaskov there were wires from everyone about the Czechs and from that hour to this he hadn't had a moment for himself. He hadn't even sent her a note, but now she was here, just here, seated beside his stove with melting snow from her scarf running in rivulets down her cheeks like tears.

He had but one cup, one glass, one spoon. He wanted to offer her something. He shook the coffeepot on the stove.

"Do you drink coffee?" he asked.

"Yes."

"Won't you take off your coat? You look cold."

She stood up and removed her scarf and coat as he poured the coffee into his chipped enamel cup, which was stained brown inside. His hand trembled and the cup ran over. He looked around for something to wipe it with and finally brushed the lip of it across the front of his blouse, hoping she wouldn't notice.

She hung her coat and scarf over the back of the chair and looked around the barren teplushka. It was poorly insulated and cold except near the stove. There was a narrow unmade bed in one corner with clothing hung on nails around it. She took the cup from his hand and sipped the black coffee.

"Do you take cream?"

"No, this is fine."

"Sugar?"

She shook her head mutely. Thirty-five rubles a pound.

There was nothing to say.

Outside there was a clash of couplings and the screel of cold wheels over the rails. Carlisle looked toward the sound knowing which train it was and on what track it was moving. He could tell this in his sleep. It was all right. He thought again of Diminsky, but it didn't matter now.

"I have to make a call," he said and he rang the dispatcher. "Carlisle, here," he said. "O.K. on 6240."

He hung up and stuffed the papers on his table into the drawer and rubbed his aching eyes trying to think what he must say. Her husband!

"I'm very sorry, Countess, about your husband——" he began, but she shook her head irritably and sat down once more on the chair.

"That's over," she said. "All of it. Prague. Home. Everything. It won't ever be again."

Having spoken of death Carlisle could think of no other subject. "I'm also sorry about your uncle," he said. "I still have his epaulet. I'll get it for you." He went to his pack, where the epaulet had remained since he'd brought it from Omsk.

"No, please," Tatiana said dully, "I don't want it."

Carlisle stopped beside his pack hanging on the wall, wondering if he should force her to accept the epaulet. "I was going to bring it to you," he said, "but I've been tied up."

"I really don't want it. I really don't want to think about it. That's all behind me now."

Carlisle remained where he was, feeling awkward. He looked about the dismal car wishing he could say something to make her feel less unhappy. "I'll keep it then," he said. "That's how we met."

"Yes, I remember."

"In the powder room."

"Yes."

"Captain of the Powder Room," he said and he smiled.

Tatiana put her elbows on her knees and stared toward the door over her cup. "What do you do here?" she asked presently.

"I'm helping to organize the evacuation. Getting the trains out."

"You look tired."

He nodded.

"I wish I could help."

"I can get you on a train to Vlad, if you like."

She frowned and shook her head. "That's not why I'm here. Did you think that's why I came? To get a train?"

"I don't know," Carlisle said, for it only just occurred to him that he could offer her this. He had the power to do it.

"I don't either," she said. "I hadn't really thought about it."

"There's a hospital train going out in the morning. I could add you to the nurses on it."

"I don't think so," she said.

Carlisle was at a loss what to do. He perched on the edge of the table and looked at her. She seemed to be deep in thought; her eyes were smoky and distant, almost asleep, though open. "Perhaps I did come for a train," she said. "Perhaps that was in the back of my mind, though I don't think so. How could it have been since I didn't know what you do?"

Again she looked at him, frowning this time, as though trying to discover why she had come.

"I didn't mean you'd come for that," Carlisle said.

"I'm certain I didn't."

"I just don't know," Carlisle said quietly.

"I think to break mirrors."

"What?"

"To break mirrors. I think you're the only person I know who could break all the mirrors," Tatiana said and she looked at him with dazzling candor.

"I don't understand."

Tatiana set her cup on the floor and stood up. She looked around once more and took a deep breath. "I must do something," she said. "I can't go back. Not to Irkutsk. Not to Prague. I'm in a terrible state. I know I am. I'm sorry to intrude, but I have and there must have been a reason. I came close to throwing myself into the river. I was too much a coward to do it, but I'm terribly, terribly sick of myself. I can't even say what I mean. This must be awful for you! Forgive me, Captain!"

She took her coat from the chair and moved toward the door, but Carlisle caught her arm.

"Countess!" he said.

They seemed to collide, to be thrust together by two opposing waves which carried them up to a precarious crest and suspended them. They stared at each other waiting for the collapse, for the descent, the fall, the dizzying slide. They closed their eyes and Carlisle's arm tightened across her shoulders. Tatiana let her coat drop and put her arms around him. Eyes clenched, mind tight, breathless they held each other knowing they could not stop this fall until they opened their eyes again, but they feared this impact as much as the falling.

"I must!" Tatiana thought. "I must!" It was suicide to do it, she know, but she did and their eyes struck together like garnets and diamonds.

"He will shatter me," she thought.

And her need to be shattered, to be broken like glass, transmitted itself to Carlisle, who trembled all over. His face went black and hard as granite. He let her go, latched the door and put out the light. In the darkness he found her hand.

"I can't speak," he said chokingly.

"Please don't," Tatiana said.

CHAPTER THIRTY-FIVE

AT this time there appeared a nameless prophet, a holy man, who walked the magistral against the tides of people fleeing toward Irkutsk. He was tall, with a fiery face and a shock of white hair which stood over his head like a banner. He wore a fur coat, felt boots, carried a pine branch for a staff and his rolling voice often mingled with the melancholy words of the "Charaban," which the refugees sang as they toiled over the frozen trakt pushing or hauling their belongings in sleighs. "Oh, my sweet lice," he said, "my dear ones; settle yourselves in the seams. Make camps where you stand. Build walls of snow and share what you have. There is nothing better further along."

But the people, their minds blinded by hope of what lay ahead, despairing, dislocated and dying in great numbers moved on singing the "Charaban" day and night. And the song was taken up by the soldiers and the trainmen, by deserters and prisoners of war, until it was heard all across the face of Siberia.

> *My wife is dead, my children are gone;*
> *All I have now is my little charaban,*
> *With the old chair on which my mother sat,*
> *The table where my father worked;*
> *My only home is my little charaban.*
> *Away, away, over the endless plain*
> *Seeking new shelter in a strange land,*
> *I set out with my charaban.*

It was a terrible lament, sorrowful as a summer wind at dusk, but it prolonged life in many who otherwise would have died. The voices of one group lost in the veiling snow marked the way for those who came behind but even so thousands died with its words on their lips. For every word thousands died, toppling beside their charabancs, which soon enough were shoved along by other refugees who needed them.

The "Charaban" was heard at night around cheerless fires where people watched their shadows on the snow hoping to see them move, but in those freezing temperatures people often died on their shadows.

"Dear lice, stop your scurrying. Childhood itself is dying. Where has it gone? You must stop and cling to childhood, nourish and preserve it. What is a country without nits?"

And the people, disturbed by this question, noticed that indeed there was no childhood. It had gone.

The children still alive had lost all notion of childhood. They marched along beside their elders, saw death, saw madness, murder, callousness and despair, and they too sang the mournful "Charaban."

"Find me a child," the prophet declared. "Bring one to me."

There was no child to be found.

All the children were old. Childhood had gone from the face of the nation.

In one place the people tried to teach childhood to a child, but they didn't succeed. They fell to arguing over the essence of it and the child thought them foolish. "What does it matter?" he asked and he marched on beside the tracks.

The Czech trains with their gaily painted teplushkas rattled eastward behind their fine engines. They were well provisioned, free of disease and well protected. Sometimes a sympathetic Czech soldier would throw some food out of the commissary car and there would be a race by those on the trakt to recover it. Snarling fights would ensue and the act of charity more often resulted in death than in relief.

The children never ran for these packets of food. They were too wise, too weary, too hopelessly old.

The holy man moved on against this stream of humanity, pausing often to look into the eyes of a child and never finding what he sought.

The trakt was strewn with corpses stripped of their boots and coats. Trains which had broken down lay along the embankment where they had been pitched over to make way for the trains still going through. Nearly all of these abandoned trains were inhabited by refugees who stayed until the wood, stripped from the boxcars, was burned and only the metal remained. The skeletal trains were mute and pitiable because each of them meant that hundreds of people had been added to the current of death and misery on the trakt.

Sometimes the holy man stopped at a vantage point and watched the refugees disappearing endlessly into the snow. A low, constant moan hung over their heads; it was the sum of their sighs, their anguish, their pain, and the only relief from it was their song, the "Charaban."

The holy man watched all this with tender eyes. He had forgiven his comrades who flayed him. Yes, at last. They were lice and it had been their destiny to suck his blood. His only concern now was to find a child and he went on, searching, with a dreadful fear growing in his exposed heart that childhood in all the world was dead.

« 2 »

There were no Christmas oranges from Mrs. Stern of Menlo Park, California, in 1919 as there had been the year before. The continued presence of American troops in Siberia was too much an embarrassment to warrant oranges. Old St. Nick himself did not appear. His reindeer would have been devoured by the starving populace and jolly St. Nick would have been shot by the Whites as a Red because of the costume he ordinarily wore. And since the Reds had given over such pagan nonsense and granted all power to the Soviets there was very little reason for St. Nick to make a landing west of Krasnoyarsk, which was in the hands of the Fifth Red Army.

Christmas was ashamed at having cropped up again. It was more like a sharp stick in the eye than a celebration of the birth of Jesus Christ who came to redeem the world. There were no feasts, no gifts of love to exchange, few prayers, few songs.

Bedraggled Russian priests made efforts to breathe spirit into the cathedrals, but there was frost on the ikons.

Members of the Y.M.C.A., the Knights of Columbus, the Red Cross and the Jewish Relief Committee gathered together for mutual self-protection; they plotted like anarchists, then sallied out on Christmas day to deliver their bombs of weary cakes, hard candy, cigarettes and cigars to the American servicemen. Some of them had the audacity to carol, but only when they knew there was a swift means of retreat. None of them were assaulted, which they took as a sign that God was not dead — their God, at least. Actually the men were too weary to raise their freezing feet and boot the chaplains and other purveyors of Christianity where it would have done them some good.

In Vladivostok it was twenty below, which was considered temperate by the natives. Further west it was colder, unimaginably colder. People could not be moving about in it, but they were; hundreds of thousands were moving, night and day.

Then, as Christmas folded its banners and crept off over the horizon, General Graves received a coded message from the War Department informing him that the State Department had at last come to a decision about the position of the United States in Siberia. It was bad. Since the British, French and Czechs were pulling out there seemed to be little reason for the Americans to remain.

General Graves gazed at the message for a long time. It was welcome. It would have been more welcome at Christmastime.

The only problem now was to get the men out.

General Graves glanced at the map, then rang for Robinson and Eichelberger.

"We're pulling out," he said.

"At last!" Robinson said.

Graves nodded tersely. "We'd better jump on it. The 31st is all right, but the 27th is going to be a long time getting here. How are communications to Spaeth?"

"Erratic," Eichelberger said.

"What's your estimate of the time they'll need to leave Verkhne, Olie?"

"At least two weeks, General."

"I want to give them a date they can comply with."

"The Allied High Commissioners are still in Irkutsk, General," Eichelberger said.

"They'll come out with the Czechs. I have no doubt on that score. They'll look after themselves. I want the 27th to fall back to Chita as soon as possible; at least from that point they have the option of two lines to Vlad, the Chinese Eastern through Harbin, or the Amur line through Khabarovsk. We'll hold the 31st in position until the 27th can link up. Give me a date, Olie. I want it hard."

"I'd say January 16, General."

"You think that's the best Spaeth can do?"

"He'll have to push like hell to make that, General," Robinson said.

"'All right, push him like hell. I want the 27th out of Verkhne and on their way by the sixteenth."

‹ 3 ›

On the twenty-ninth of December, Colonel Spaeth received a message informing him that he had two weeks to consolidate and entrain his regiment for Vladivostok. His elation at this was dampened by the enormity of

the task which lay ahead, and the clash of these feelings left him immobilized, filled with doubts, fears and indecision. He stood up and reread
the message, then paced about snapping it against his hand while Major
Bentham, who had brought it to him, waited.

"You're sure this is genuine, Charlie?" Spaeth said at last.

"What's that?" Bentham asked.

"This message! This order! Is it all right?"

"It was in code. I have no reason to doubt it."

"Let's signal for a confirmation."

"Very well, Colonel," Bentham said and he left the office saying he'd be
right back.

Captain Cloak came in and stood by the door with a clipboard in his
hand, leafing through the sheaf of papers on it.

"What is it, Ben?"

"We're going to have to find ourselves about eight trains, Colonel,"
Cloak said.

"Eight?"

"Yes, sir."

"I suppose so."

"Are you all right, sir?"

"What?"

"You don't look well, Colonel."

"I'm fine. What do you mean?"

"Well," Cloak said hesitantly, "you look, ah, abstracted."

"We're pulling out, Ben."

"That's right, sir."

"Isn't that something?"

Major Bentham returned to the office. "It'll take a couple of hours to get
a confirmation, Colonel."

Spaeth returned to his desk and sat down. "That long?" he asked, then
he read the order for a third time. "This appears to release us from our
obligation to protect the railway," he said.

Major Bentham and Captain Cloak exchanged a troubled look.

"Yes, sir, it does," Bentham said.

"I wonder who will take over?" Spaeth asked.

"The railroad?"

"Of course."

"I suppose the Japanese will keep order until the Reds move in,"
Bentham said.

Spaeth nodded.

"I'll draft an order for the company commanders," Bentham said.

"Has Silverman heard from Leverett?"

Since neither Bentham nor Cloak knew of Joe Silverman's arrangement to contact Leverett they were not only confused, they were alarmed. They had thirty-five hundred men and all their equipment to evacuate over seventeen hundred miles of uncertain track in weather which guaranteed a high factor of casualties from exposure alone and the Colonel was worried about a single man.

Major Bentham stepped to the edge of Spaeth's desk. "Bob," he said quietly, "what in hell are you talking about?"

"Send Joe Silverman in here."

"You think you're going to translate us out of here?" Bentham cried explosively.

Captain Cloak chuckled.

Colonel Spaeth looked at them both. "Well for Christ's sake," he said. "You think I've cracked."

"I think you're tired," Bentham said.

Spaeth jumped to his feet and hit the desk with the flat of his hand. "You're damned right I'm tired! Why shouldn't I be tired? But I'm not crazy. Now let's get cracking. Start rounding up trains, Ben. You can draft an order for the company commanders, Charlie, but I don't want this to get out until a confirmation comes through. There's a right way to do this and a wrong way. I don't want any mistakes."

"Why did you ask about Leverett?" Bentham asked.

"What about Leverett?"

"You asked if Silverman had heard from him."

"Another time, Charlie. I'd forgotten you didn't know about it. They're in contact with each other, that's all." Spaeth sat down again, frowning. "Oh, yes. We'd better inform Carlisle," he said.

"Now?" Bentham asked.

"Of course now. What in hell are we waiting for?"

"The confirmation."

"That's right. Send Joe in, will you."

Bentham and Cloak left the office. Spaeth pushed his glasses up on his nose, then scowled at his hands. There didn't seem to be any grip in them. He opened his desk drawer and took out a letter from Peg. Her Christmas letter. They'd gone to the Eberhardt's for Christmas. It had rained all day. Bobby had a cold, but in spite of it all they'd had a good time except, of course, they missed him.

The Eberhardts.

He couldn't remember any Eberhardts. Peg must have told him about the Eberhardts in another letter, perhaps in one that hadn't come through. He simply didn't know these people — Viola and Jack, Peg called them. Viola and Jack Eberhardt?

How in hell could people who'd never met him miss him?

Peg had made new friends. Well, of course she had! There was always a big turnover of people on a military base. They'd had a good time in spite of it all.

Joe Silverman came into the office. "You sent for me, Colonel?"

"What?"

"Bentham said you wanted to see me."

"That's right. Sit down, Joe."

Joe Silverman sat and Spaeth put his letter away. "So we're pulling out," Silverman said.

Spaeth slammed his desk drawer and looked at Joe, the light splintering in his glasses. "Who told you that?" he demanded. "Who in hell told you that?"

"I picked up a statement in *Asahi*."

"What statement?"

"The Japanese say that due to chaotic conditions they may find it necessary to maintain a small garrison in Vladivostok, Chita and at other points. They also pledge to remain in the Trans-Baikal and the Amur until the Czechs pass these points. I interpret that to mean we're pulling out."

"You're too damned smart, Silverman."

"So I've been told."

"It's not official."

"Facts never are."

"So the word is out."

"I'd say it was, Colonel. There'll be a lot of interested parties anxious to help us on our way back to Vlad. Bentham says you asked about Leverett."

"What?"

"About Leverett."

"Oh, yes. What about him?"

"He got the message we planted for him, that's all I know about it, Colonel. Or somebody got it."

"He won't know we're pulling out."

Silverman frowned and shook his head. "No, he won't."

Colonel Spaeth sighed and examined a space in the air above Silverman's head. There was something he wanted to say, but he wasn't quite in touch with it. He seemed incapable of coming to grips with things and this worried him. "Silverman," he said.

"Yes, sir?"

"Silverman?"

"Yes."

"I don't know," Spaeth whispered humbly. "I don't know what it is I want to say."

"Something about stray sheep, I think."

"Maybe so."

Joe Silverman got up and went to the door. He closed it, then turned to Spaeth, smiling easily. "You're all right, Colonel," he said. He lit a cigarette and came back to the desk, but he didn't sit down. "You can say any damned thing you want to. If Leverett doesn't come in he'll have to make his own way out. We can make a deal with the Japanese here to help him or with the Czechs."

"What about Maryenka?" Spaeth asked.

"Her too."

"I feel responsible as hell for them both. I don't want anything to happen to Leverett. I don't. I don't know why I feel so strongly about it, Joe. Maybe because I think he's the only man in this outfit who did something worthwhile. God, the people I've had to stomach!"

"Napoleon knew what he was talking about."

"What?"

"When he said an army travels on its stomach."

Colonel Spaeth smiled wanly. "I think Billy would have done the same thing," he said.

"Billy?"

"My son. I think he would have. I like to think he would have rescued the girl, carried her off to safety. My God, Joe, isn't it awful, how we build scenes in our minds! Billy would have rescued the girl. It was the only thing to do. It was the right thing and I've been thinking Billy would have done it because he's my son! I came in here to do the right thing and I haven't. I've done nothing. We're going out and it's all left up in the air. There's something left over, something incomplete. I don't even know what it is! A fight, a battle, some action, something to let me know the turning around point has come, but it's not there, Joe. We've come, we're going back. It's over, yet it's not. I don't even know where it is, what it is! There's a chunk missing, Joe. A piece of my life and I've got to leave it behind."

Joe came around the desk and dropped his big hand on Colonel Spaeth's shoulder. "There's a lot of that," he said quietly.

"But I've honed myself up, Joe. I've been ready to jump, to act, to settle something and it's all out of my hands! There's not going to be another time!"

"Let it go."

"For God's sake, Joe!"

Spaeth felt the big hand squeeze his shoulder. He caught his upper lip between his teeth and held on. It was over. He'd topped the hill and was headed down. The dramatic chance he'd waited for all his life hadn't come; it had passed him by and he still didn't know what it was, what it might have been, what he would have done. He'd never know. Tears filled his eyes and he shook his head. He trembled. The hand on his shoulder was reassuringly tender. He heard Joe Silverman's voice again, but couldn't make out the words because he was crying. He put his head down on his arms, ashamed and relieved.

"You're all right now, Bob," Joe Silverman said quietly. "Get it out. I'll make some arrangement for Leverett and the girl. You just let yourself unwind."

Spaeth heard the door shut behind Silverman. He tried to stop crying. He scolded himself. He was a god-damned baby. Sure, he'd been wound up like a dime store clock with his alarm set to go off, but the hands had never reached the hour. Well, Graves had warned him. He'd been told what neutrality meant. It was harder than fighting. One hell of a lot harder.

He'd just managed to gulp back a sob and was on the way to clearing up when he thought of Peg and Billy's bike in the garage. It was fixed!

"Oh, Christ!" he moaned as a fresh rush of emotion attacked him. "Oh, Christ! How stupid can a grown man be!"

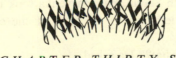

CHAPTER THIRTY-SIX

AT dawn a few days after Timokhin's discourse on lice the men of his partisan band awakened to find their leader had vanished. Like the very lice he had described they abandoned their caves and set out to find him except for Marrakof, who said Timokhin would not be found and ordered Maryenka to make breakfast.

Ira too remained behind. He'd explained the necessity of contacting Silverman to Maryenka and asked her to make arrangements with Marrakof to get a message to Verkhne-Udinsk, but to his consternation the burly Kalmyk refused to hear of it.

"But what's his reason for that?" Ira demanded.

Maryenka warned Ira to be calm. Marrakof's reason was that he would do nothing without prior orders from Kravchenko, whose force he'd decided to join.

"That could take days!"

"He doesn't trust you," Maryenka said quietly.

This was so. Ira could see it in the Kalmyk's truculent eyes. "Does he think he can keep us here?" Ira asked. "Does he think he can make prisoners of us?"

"I wouldn't trouble about that just now," Maryenka said.

Ira went outside to wait for the others. If Marrakof gave him any trouble he and Maryenka could slip out together. The guarantee of safe-conduct no longer seemed as important as it once had. That was stupid too, an excuse he'd made to delay his departure. C Company would protect Maryenka no matter what happened.

From his place in front of the caves Ira could see the men casting about for Timokhin's trail at the edge of the frozen lake. Another group had circled up the hill through the forest, but an hour later they all came back. They had found no sign, not so much as a footprint, and Timokhin's legend was enhanced by the saying that he could walk on new snow without leaving a mark just as Jesus was said to have walked on the water.

Marrakof assumed command of the group at once and no one questioned him. After they had eaten, Slavin rose, gathered his kit and left without a word.

"Where is he going?" Ira asked Maryenka.

"To make contact with General Kravchenko and get our orders."

Ira started out to catch Slavin, but Maryenka took his arm. "Come with me," she said and she led him to the back of the cave, where they sat down.

"Are we prisoners or what?" Ira asked.

"They won't let us go without clearing it through the General. Marrakof insists on it and the others have agreed. They're fond of me, but we mustn't do anything to displease them."

"But I'm an American!" Ira protested.

Maryenka smiled and took his hand. "It'll be all right," she said. "They won't harm us. They're just being official, you see. Now that they've joined a larger force, they want to make a correct impression."

"At our expense?"

"They've kept us here and protected us at theirs," she said.

"How long do you think this will take?"

"A week, maybe ten days. It depends on how soon Slavin finds Kravchenko and what he's told to do."

It was intolerable. Ira looked at the men in the cave and though none of them appeared interested in him they seemed to have changed into warders. "We could slip out tonight and follow the shore of the lake to Mysovaya."

"Even so, they'd miss us at once and I can't travel so well."

"Of course," Ira said. "I'm making more of a fool of myself each time I open my mouth. It's just that I'm anxious about Harry's baby."

It pleased Maryenka when Ira referred to her child as Harry's. It gave her hope that this was so, but with each passing day her doubt that it could be increased. Her pregnancy was already past its term and the child in her womb made only the feeblest signs of life and no indication that it was due.

To ease her doubt Ira wracked his memory for all he knew about pregnancies and found it woefully lacking, so he invented stories. That afternoon he hit upon the most successful one of all. They'd gone outside for some air and were standing on the promontory which overlooked the lake when it occurred to him.

"Did Harry tell you much about his childhood?" he asked.

"Oh, yes," Maryenka said.

"You know about his birthday, then."

"Yes, April 10. It was recorded on the license."

"No, I mean how that came about," Ira said, picking his way carefully.

"What do you mean?"

"Didn't he tell you?"

Maryenka frowned and shook her head.

"Well, maybe I shouldn't then."

"You must," Maryenka said. "How can you think not to tell me such a thing once you've started it."

Ira was pleased at this. He sighed. "Well, you know some people don't always wait until they're married to sleep together," he said. "It happened that way with Harry's mother. She was two months pregnant when his father consented to marry her. I think she caught him that way. Certain women aren't above such things. Not that she was bad, you know, but anyway that's how it came about. Harry told me this when we were in Harbin. He'd bought you a necklace of Chinese coins and was telling me."

"I know. He sent the necklace."

"So anyway his parents got married and his mother was determined that no one would ever know she'd made love before it was strictly proper to do so. Some women are like that. Very proper after marriage and she had two younger sisters to set an example for, you see."

"Harry didn't tell me about his mother's sisters," Maryenka said.

"He didn't think much of them, I suppose."

"His father was a mechanic and had two brothers," she said.

Ira nodded and went on quickly. "At any rate his mother refused to let it be known that she and Harry's father had sinned prior to marriage. Everybody counts their fingers in our country when a baby is born."

"It's the same here," Maryenka said.

"I suppose it is," Ira said. "There's a certain amount of disgrace attached if the baby comes early."

"It depends," Maryenka said. "In the city, yes. Not so much in the country."

"Harry's parents were city people," Ira said.

"That's true."

"So at any rate Harry's mother refused to have her baby until the time was right. Nine months after the wedding."

Maryenka looked dubious. "She refused? What do you mean refused?"

"I mean she refused to give birth until the time was right. Harry was an eleventh-month baby."

"It's not possible to refuse such a thing," Maryenka said and she shook her head.

"Harry weighed eighteen pounds and had a full head of hair."

Maryenka continued shaking her head and now she was giggling. "But one can't refuse!" she said. "Who ever heard such a thing? Nature is nature."

"Harry was born with two teeth," Ira insisted.

Maryenka burst into laughter. "But that's impossible! A woman can't just refuse out of stubbornness, or pride, to have her baby when it's due."

"You're right," Ira declared. "So it must be something in the genes, in the blood. Austin children are just naturally reticent about coming into this world."

"Reticent?"

"They take two months longer than anyone else to make up their minds to be born. That's all there is to it."

Maryenka pressed her face into Ira's chest and laughed happily while he held her. She was delighted and more than willing to believe his story. She looked up at him, her eyes shining with gratitude, and Ira kissed her on the forehead.

"I'm glad you told me," she said.

"I'm surprised Harry didn't tell you himself."

"He didn't know we were going to have a baby."

"He told me in Harbin he hoped you would have," Ira said and they went back to their cave.

For a few days Maryenka seemed lighter of heart, but one night she had a dream and whimpered like a lost pup and Ira knew the content of that dream as though he were having it himself. It was the horrible, visceral uncertainty about her child, the kind of uncertainty a man might experience if he thought he was losing his mind.

To take Maryenka out of this dream Ira closed one hand firmly over her breast and drew her close to his body. "It's all right," he whispered. "All right. All right. It's all right, Maryenka."

She stirred in his arms, then turned to see his face in the glow of the nearby embers. There was a moment always, when she awakened in his arms, that she hoped to see Austin. He saw this now and supposed it would always be so, but he didn't resent it. No, strangely enough, if there was any disappointment for him it was that he could not be Austin for her. If he could have changed himself into Austin he would have done so gladly.

"Was I dreaming?" she asked in a voice still hushed with sleep.

"A little," he said.

"It wasn't nice."

"Have you forgotten it?"

She nodded to please him. "Yes, already. It's gone."

"Good," he said and he kissed her eyes shut. "Go back to sleep."

He tucked the heavy greatcoat under which they slept closer around her and presently she was breathing easily once more, sound asleep and peaceful.

He thought of Carlisle, perhaps because of the coat. He wished now he'd sent Carlisle a note via Silverman. He should have. To say what? An apology? An explanation?

At least an acknowledgment of their friendship. A little note from the Jew to the Sioux.

Ira smiled into the dimness of the cave overhead. A feeling of completeness came over him again. A feeling of confidence.

Yes, it would all work out for the best. He grinned thinking how unprepared his mother would be to accept the role of grandmother. He could almost hear his family.

"Is it so bad after all, Rose?"

"Did I have any warning? Not a word! Not a whisper and poof I'm a grandma! At least a person should be on notice!"

"A soldier doesn't get a notice when he's shot."

"And that's how I feel. Shot! Yes, exactly! I'm a casualty of the Great War. A grandmother before my time!"

Whereupon she would take the infant and feed it portions of mashed peas more suitable to an elephant.

"Aunt Ruth," Ira whispered aloud. "And here is your Auntie Ruth."

He nearly laughed to think of it. It was going to work out for the best.

For a time he continued to watch the play of firelight over the distant roof of the cave, then he fell into a deep, contented sleep.

After an absence of four days, Slavin reappeared. He was bursting with information and a meeting was called which Maryenka and Ira were permitted to attend.

Marrakof presided with Slavin and Balashov seated beside him. He waited portentously for silence, then Slavin announced that Admiral Kolchak had resigned as Supreme Ruler of Russia and was on his way to Irkutsk, which was now under control of the Bolshevik Revolutionary Committee. Kolchak had appointed Ataman Semenoff of Chita supreme commander of all forces in Siberia and the far east and it was feared that Semenoff might attempt to rescue Kolchak and spirit him out of the country. "Our duty," Slavin continued, "is to prevent this. We will be reinforced and supplied by General Kravchenko in the next few days. Our task will be to destroy the railway bridges between Posolskaya and Verkhne-Udinsk to prevent Kolchak's escape."

Maryenka translated this for Ira, who was appalled. "But that will bring them into direct conflict with the Americans who guard those sectors!"

Marrakof demanded to know what Ira had said and when Maryenka told him he shrugged his massive shoulders. "So be it," he said.

Ira saw that Maryenka too was disturbed. There was no question now of getting a message to Silverman or to anyone. If Ira had not been a prisoner before, he was from this moment on.

"Tell him I understand," he said to Maryenka.

"He wants to know if you will give information about the defense of these bridges," Maryenka whispered anxiously.

"Say I can't."

"He wants to know if you will fight with him against the Americans if they try to let Kolchak escape."

"Tell him no."

Maryenka refused to translate; she knew Marrakof could not permit such a challenge to his newly assumed authority, but a translation wasn't necessary.

Ira's "Nyet" hung in the air and all the men with the possible exception of Slavin looked at him with sullen distrust. Then they turned to Marrakof waiting for his response.

Ira's arms and legs felt watery but he fastened his eyes on Marrakof's, thinking: "My God, is it going to end like this! In a lousy cave?"

It was all so different from the way he'd seen it the night before, so impossibly primitive, so trite. Marrakof's eyes skipped over the faces of his men, then settled again on Ira with furtive belligerence. He said something which Ira didn't even try to understand.

"Nyet," he responded.

Marrakof rose rumbling ominously and stepped over the fire pit.

Maryenka appealed to the men, to Marrakof, to Slavin, imploring them all to spare Ira, when suddenly he laughed.

Ira himself was astounded. For no apparent reason he'd suddenly remembered the exchange of blows between Austin and Carlisle in the barracks quad at Vlad. It seemed ludicrous for him to attempt such a thing, but with laughter still on his lips he jumped to his feet, stepped toward Marrakof and hit him straight on the nose.

It was Ira's ringing, almost hysterical laughter more than the effect of the blow which caused Marrakof to step back, lose his footing and sit down in the fire. Blood gushed from his nose. He gripped it with one hand and with the other fumbled for the pistol on his belt.

"He's going to kill me," Ira thought. "Why, certainly, you fool, what else?" And the lightning stupidity of his own thoughts, his apparent incapacity for understanding the dreadful seriousness of his situation, drove Ira to new heights of frenzied laughter. The black pistol appeared in Marrakof's fist and Ira kicked it so accurately that it flipped into the fire.

Marrakof bellowed. Smoke curled around his bottom and he tried to rise, but Ira sat him down again with a blow to the forehead. A shaft of blue flame ran up the oily surface of Marrakof's heavy fur coat. There was an awful smell of searing flesh, then Marrakof screamed and rolled out of the fire still smoldering.

Two men rushed to extinguish his burning clothing, but the shells in the pistol began to pop and they ducked for cover.

Ira, appalled now by what he had done, fell over Maryenka to protect her from the exploding pistol cartridges.

Blinded by pain, Marrakof staggered to his feet. Blood was still flowing from his nose into his beard. His eyes were blank white and his mouth was open in an unuttered howl of agony. He took several faltering steps, then with a roaring wail he smashed through the hangings at the mouth of the cave and disappeared.

The pistol stopped exploding. Ira sat up gasping for air like a man who has just been saved from drowning.

Slavin appeared at Maryenka's side and said something, then he, Balashov and the others went out to find Marrakof.

"You must go," Maryenka said urgently. "Go at once while they're out."

Ira shook his head dumbly. He was going to be sick.

Maryenka rose and hauled him to his feet. Ira allowed her to support him to the mouth of the cave, but when the cold air hit him he collapsed and vomited. The bilge of his stomach froze almost at once and the sight of it made him sicker still.

Maryenka tugged at his arm imploring him to get up.

Ira shook his head from side to side. "No," he gasped. "No, no. I'm done for."

He stood up nevertheless and leaned against the rocks at the mouth of the cave. He tried to smile reassuringly at Maryenka, but it went bad.

Until this moment he hadn't been frightened, now he could hardly stand. "They'll look after you," he croaked. "It'll all work —" but he couldn't go on for Slavin and Balashov came up the trail followed by the men.

Slavin said something to Maryenka, then went into the cave. Balashov glanced at Ira, then followed Slavin, and the men filed past Ira each fixing him with a look of curious respect.

"What is it?" Ira asked.

"Marrakof is done for," Maryenka said. "He fell over the embankment and broke his neck."

"What happens now?"

"I'm not sure," Maryenka said. "You'd better lie down." And she led him up the trail to the next cave, where Ira fell into the drugged, fearful sleep of a condemned man.

The first thing he saw when he opened his eyes was Maryenka's encouraging smile. He propped himself up on one elbow. "What?" he asked.

"They don't want to fight the Americans," Maryenka said quietly. "Slavin and Balashov have convinced them to wait."

"For what?" Ira asked.

"To wait," Maryenka said and she shrugged.

« 2 »

From his headquarters in Vladivostok, General Graves tried to maintain contact with Colonel Spaeth's command isolated at Verkhne-Udinsk but communications disintegrated after the collapse of the Kolchak regime. From Chita westward telegraph lines were being cut by partisans faster than they could be repaired. Messages piled up and were scrambled or lost, and Graves' concern for Spaeth's command grew with each passing hour. They were separated by seventeen hundred railroad miles and no one knew the current condition of the track. General Graves' last acknowledged order to Spaeth was that he move with all possible haste to Chita, which would give him the option of two lines to Vladivostok. There was still no word as to whether Spaeth had begun to move and the specter of his command disappearing in the icy vastness of Siberia began to assume real proportions.

Colonel Olie Robinson worked around the clock with Lieutenant Kirk, the chief signal officer, trying to piece together secondary communications routes to Spaeth's command. Eichelberger and Major Barrows of Intelligence scanned reports being received in Vlad by the British, French, Czechs and Japanese, but the picture they constructed from these was not encouraging.

The Czechs reported thirty or forty trainloads of Czech troops approaching the Baikal tunnels which were still intact at last report although one attempt to destroy them had been made by partisans blowing up a carload of explosives. The Kolchak government was en route to Irkutsk and had been offered the protection of the Allied flags. The Allied High Commissioners were still at Irkutsk.

General Graves paced back and forth in front of the big wall map of

Siberia glaring at it as though it were an offense to his common sense. The line representing the railroad looked like a lariat cast from Omsk with a loop beginning near Chita embracing Harbin, Vladivostok, Khabarovsk and back again to Chita. Graves scowled at the map, then went to the window and stared out blindly trying to estimate the number of men who were going to be lost during the withdrawal. A company? More? Less? He didn't know. "We'll never get them out by February," Graves said. "Not by February by a long shot. Not all of them."

"I'm figuring on March, sir," Robinson said quietly.

Graves turned from the window, his face drawn. "That long? Not that long, Olie!"

"We've got to think of the shipping too, General. We'll be lucky to get the bulk of them out by March."

"Bulk! Since when did we start talking about troops as bulk?" Graves demanded.

"With the auxiliary personnel we've got over twelve thousand people, General. Dr. Teusler has requested —"

"To hell with Teusler!" Graves exploded. "I suppose he wants to ship union suits to Washington!"

"There's a lot of Red Cross matériel."

"Stuff it!"

Major Barrows came in with a message in his hand. "From Colonel Spaeth, sir," he said. "They've cleared Verkhne-Udinsk. They're on their way!"

Eichelberger popped his hands together and let out a yip of relief.

Graves scowled at Eichelberger, then he too grinned. "Let General March know that we're on the move," he said. "I never thought I'd be so pleased to be commanding a retreat," he added. "It's one hell of a way to end a career."

‹ 3 ›

On January 8, the same day in which he had issued the order allowing Admiral Kolchak to proceed toward Irkutsk from Nizhne-Udinsk under the Allied flags, General Pierre Janin, commander of all the Russian and Czechoslovakian forces in Siberia, left Irkutsk in his private train headed for Vladivostok.

As might be expected a storm of protestations and accusations followed. He was accused of desertion, cowardice, treachery, and as his train sped toward the Baikal tunnels Janin fired telegrams of justification back along the line, some of them ten pages in length. For the most part these were carefully elucidated diplomatic imperatives which he said dictated his behavior, but in one telegram there was a reference to a "sacred trust" which necessitated his departure. When he dashed this off Janin was thinking of the three suitcases and a chest containing remnants of the Romanovs which were stacked with his private luggage in the next compartment.

They haunted him. He felt maligned, but he'd done all he could do. His agreement to deliver the Russian gold reserves to the Red authorities at Irkutsk had bought freedom for the Czechs and all the Allied personnel still west of the Trans-Baikal tunnels. His primary responsibility had always been to the Czechs. Let the others say what they liked.

Janin was tired. He was old. He'd been at war for six long years and he wanted to doze off, but each time he did so the Empress Alexandra's amputated ring finger appeared and beckoned him. It was a long, white finger which had no doubt been kissed by the Czar, by hundreds of ministers, duchesses, grand duchesses, by the Czarevitch and by Rasputin, a finger which had caressed the genitalia of an Empire.

And when he dozed off it beckoned to him.

Janin's head snapped up with a start and the finger vanished. He looked out the window at the stream of people headed overland toward Lake Baikal. They were leaving Irkutsk now, like lemmings.

What good was it, he wondered? What good was any of it? Human life was so cheap, so common, so easily reproducible, so troublesome by and large that all the struggling humanity in view of his train window was worth no more than the severed finger of an Empress. No doubt that finger had sent as many to their deaths with a persuasive tickle affecting the Czar's military tactics.

What was it all about?

La Gloire?

General Janin snorted a bit too contemptuously. He wiped his white mustaches with his hand and the palm of his hand on the knee of his breeches and he was disgusted to see a trail over the fine wool material like that left by a snail.

"La Gloire," he mumbled aloud. "La Gloire."

Snail trails on the leaves of history books. Moist and bright for a time they soon dried out, lost their luster and were forgotten. Heroism and sacrifice were forgotten. All he'd done was forgotten and he could see nothing ahead but recriminations.

The British were as responsible for Kolchak's safety as he was, but they'd skinned out. The Japanese could see Kolchak through if they chose, but they'd turned their backs and were already sucking up to the Reds. The Americans had refused to take sides.

"Canaille!" Janin muttered and the rumbling wheels of the train caused him to doze once more, and once more the Empress's ring finger beckoned.

Yes, he had in his possession the sacred relics of a regime. That was something at least; more than anyone else had come out with. He would deliver them to the Grand Duke Nicholas, senior surviving member of the Romanov family. They would be enshrined with a plaque, perhaps, a dedication to General Pierre Janin, a little footnote in history, a way to be remembered.

To be remembered.

Was it so important — to be remembered? The white finger hovered in Janin's mind. He sighed and his head fell forward. Yes, to be remembered. It was important. What else was more important than that?

Oh, my Empress! I kiss thy finger for its touch of immortality.

The pale finger vanished and General Pierre Janin slept.

CHAPTER THIRTY-SEVEN

In the first week of January, 1920, the Trans-Siberian Railroad and the trakt which paralleled it west of Irkutsk was a scene of unimaginable chaos. The Fifth Red Army advancing on the heels of the Russian echelons was capturing ten or twenty trains a day. Many of these, carrying women, children, wounded and ill, were stalled for lack of fuel; ice packed up around the wheels, and the railway personnel took to the trakt with the refugees to avoid being impressed by the Reds.

At Nizhne-Udinsk, Admiral Kolchak having announced his resignation in favor of General Denikin, Commander in Chief of the Armies of the South, made it clear that he would not sign a formal declaration of resignation until he and his entourage reached Verkhne-Udinsk and were thus safely through the Baikal tunnels. This offer to trade his signature for safety went unheeded by the High Commissioners at Irkutsk, whose chief anxiety now was to make their own getaway before the downline traffic engulfed them.

Raul Markowitz had lost two trains since leaving Omsk. The first came under a partisan attack at night, the second ran out of fuel and froze, but Raul, walking along the trakt, had managed to catch another Czech echelon as it rattled eastward. His arm was in a sling and because of his wound and his insignia the Czech rear guard pulled him aboard their train and so he reached Nizhne-Udinsk, where he found Colonel Dubrovski.

"Markowitz! By God you look awful!"

"So do you, Emil."

"I'd given you up weeks ago."

Markowitz fell into a chair in the little station office which Dubrovski was currently using to dispatch the Czech trains on the next leg of their journey, the three hundred miles to Irkutsk. "What's the situation?" he asked.

Dubrovski rubbed his weary eyes and tilted back on his chair. "Kolchak is still here. The 6th Regiment has his trains in preventive detention while the Allied High Commissioners shake him down. He's got seven trains and they've promised him safe passage if he reduces himself to one train and comes to Irkutsk under the protection of the flags of America, Britain, France, Japan and ours. We're waiting for his decision now. Do you happen to know where we can get an American flag?"

Markowitz shook his head.

"General Kappel is still fighting a good rear guard action. But the Reds are chewing up our tail. We lost our buffer force yesterday, a division of Poles we'd kept behind us. We're going to have to move fast to get out and we need those trains of Kolchak's to do it." Dubrovski took a bottle from his desk drawer and shoved it toward Markowitz. "You need a drink," he said.

Markowitz pulled the cork with his teeth and let it fall on the floor. He stood up and went to the window, coughing.

On a siding down the line he saw Kolchak's private car between two Czech armored trains. There were Czech guards all around; and as he watched, several Russian officers wearing the purple and white shoulder straps of Kolchak's household troops came down the track tearing these insignia off and talking excitedly. "Kolchak appears to have made his decision," Raul said. "His troops are tearing off their shoulder straps."

"There are more epaulets in the street than autumn leaves," Dubrovski said.

Major Hassek, the local Czech commander, came into the office. He was a slight man with a drooping black mustache and a pinched look about the eyes. He beat the tops of his boots with a swagger stick as he spoke. "The Supreme Ruler has accepted the Allied conditions," he said. "We'll remove all but four of his coaches and send him on tomorrow."

"The eighth," Dubrovski said and he made a note on his dispatch sheet.

"General Syrovy has ordered us to send train 6103 on at once," Hassek said. "Tonight."

Markowitz saw a look of surprise on Dubrovski's face.

"I will take personal command of the guard detachment and act as train commander. You're welcome to join us if you like, Dubrovski."

Dubrovski opened his desk drawer and began to empty its contents, including several bottles of liquor, into a valise which he pulled from under the desk with his feet. "Have you met Lieutenant Markowitz?" he asked. "Markowitz, Major Hassek. I've just made Raul my assistant. He may want to join us."

"He's welcome," Hassek said tersely, "but no more. Understood?"

"How far is 6103 going?" Dubrovski asked.

"General Janin has made an arrangement with Revkom at Irkutsk to surrender 6103 in exchange for unrestricted passage of the Legion to Vladivostok," Hassek said; then, with a nod to Markowitz, he turned on his heel and marched out.

Markowitz took another pull on the bottle and passed it to Dubrovski. "What's 6103?" he asked.

"Twenty-nine wagons containing the Russian gold reserves," Dubrovski said. "It means they've abandoned Kolchak and bribed the Bolsheviks to let them out of Siberia."

Markowitz smiled bitterly. "So we'll get to Irkutsk," he said. "From there we can ride out with General Janin."

"By the time we reach Irkutsk, my friend, General Janin will be gone. They'll all be gone, you can take my word on that." Dubrovski hoisted his valise and went to the door. "Are you coming?" he asked.

Through the window Markowitz saw Major Hassek walking along the track with a detachment of Czechs behind him. A Kolchak officer fell in beside him, talking and gesticulating earnestly, but Hassek waved him away.

Markowitz nodded to Dubrovski and followed him. "You've got the spirits, Dubrovski," he said.

« 2 »

One hour after the Kolchak train No. 6103 began to move eastward Colonel Sipialef's armored train, the Invincible, headed west toward Irkutsk with the announced intention of aiding the evacuation of Allied nationals still there. This offer was cordially received and he was given a clear track.

To ease his tense nerves Sipialef had resorted to cocaine and girls. He had an adequate supply of each in his armored coach as it beat westward through the night. The coach was warmed by two stoves and there were hangings on the walls to balk drafts from the closed gun ports. One end of the car was partitioned into a bedroom, in the center was the sitting room with a sideboard supplied with a variety of hot and cold food, wines and spirits. A cage of brightly plumaged cockatoos was suspended from the roof, swaying rhythmically to the action of the roadbed, and the sound of the wheels was muffled by heavy rugs which carpeted the floor.

This atmosphere of Oriental richness was spoiled, however, by four heavy machine guns on stanchions near the gun ports and by the austerity of the rear section of the car where Sipialef worked at a desk screened by potted rubber plants.

His attention at the moment was devoted to a railway map and in particular to a small station beyond Irkutsk called Polovina which marked the midway point between Moscow and Vladivostok. This symmetry pleased Sipialef, as did the tactical considerations. There were three sidings at this point. The local populace was demoralized and harmless. Most of the partisans in the area were converging on Irkutsk to report to Krasnoshchekov, who had emerged as the Soviet High Commissioner and taken over from the Political Center.

Sipialef sent for his train commander, a German prisoner of war, Captain Graetz, who had volunteered for this service and who had a genius for detail.

"Your excellency," Graetz said and he clicked his heels and bowed in the best Junker manner. His shaven head was bone white and there was a constantly alert glitter in his shallow blue eyes.

"Polovina," Sipialef said and he planted his finger on the station. "Can we be there in time, Graetz?"

Captain Graetz looked at the map, made a mental calculation and said yes.

"It suits our purpose," Sipialef said.

"Very nicely, your excellency. Three sidings. We divert the train, crop its tail and move on at once. The whole operation should not take more than twenty minutes."

"See that it doesn't, Graetz, and see that we're in position on time."

Graetz saluted and left the car. Presently Sipialef felt a slight difference in the beat of the train wheels and knew that Graetz had increased their speed.

Sipialef smiled; he felt a great surge of power and accomplishment. It was going so well. The whole operation was being so exquisitely timed by the decisions of others that it almost appeared they were in league with him. Consul General Harris and the British High Commissioner had left Irkutsk. The American troops east of Baikal had already pulled out of Verkhne-Udinsk. The Czechs were moving out as fast as possible. In ten days the Reds would move into the power vacuum, but by that time he would have reached the end of the branch line at Kiakhta with all the gold bullion they could possibly carry into the safe anonymity of Mongolia.

‹ 3 ›

When the High Commissioners had departed Irkutsk, the railway service personnel and certain guard detachments began to detect a slight relaxation in Captain Carlisle's hammer-handed grip over the marshaling yard at Glaskov. They accounted for this quite accurately by the frequent appearance of Countess Tatiana at his side. Those with quick minds and larcenous hearts began to take advantage of this situation. They watched Carlisle come and go and they watched Tatiana no less carefully and when these two signs were in conjunction there was great scurrying along the tracks and sidings of Glaskov. Certain loaded boxcars were thrown open, the contents disgorged and new merchandise installed, consisting more often than not of refugees who could pay the necessary bribes.

Carlisle was not entirely unaware of these arrangements, but he'd reached the limit of his power to control what went on in the yard and the attitude of most people and particularly of the intellectuals disgusted him. They didn't seem to understand what was happening. They resented the inconveniences and they talked. They talked interminably.

Temporarily sheltered by a dying establishment which for the most part they couldn't understand, the political aficionados continued their heated discussions, each faction offering grand schemes for the solution of current difficulties.

With a few bottles of vodka and some bread, butter and jam on the table, or even if there was only tea, these discussions grew heated to the point where people were insulted and huffed off with their partners into the frozen night still raving their particular variety of politics.

Then one night, the lights of Irkutsk went out. Exponents of political theories ranging from the far left to the far right were caught with their mouths open. "The lights!" they cried, Anarchist, Social Democrat, Bolshevik and Monarchist alike. "Dear God, the lights!"

There was much running about, switches were snapped, fuses checked, wiring examined. Some went off to telephone for information, some in search of policemen or militiamen, and there was unanimity as a result of all these examinations and excursions; it was that the lights of Irkutsk had gone out.

"Sabotage!" cried the Monarchists, Republicans, Social Revolutionaries and Moderates.

"Sabotage!" cried the Anarchists and Bolsheviks.

After years of strife and contention, of duplicity, violence and sacrifice, they had reached a consensus. The lights of Irkutsk had gone out! They could not see. It was dark, inside as well as out. There was no illumination!

"Ahhh!

Profound speculation!

Accusation and counteraccusation!

"Who took the vodka from the table?"

"A candle! Strike a match! Thief!"

"There was no vodka."

"Yes!"

"Take a vote! Vodka or not?"

"Who has their hand in my pocket?"

"On my thigh?"

"Lucky lady!"

"Boor!"

Darkness reigned and fear mushroomed.

Because the lights were out they wondered about the trains, the telegraph, the mail, the currency exchange. As disrupted as these services had been, the prospect that they could stop altogether was terrifying. Among these city-dwelling intellectual, revolutionary theorists, not one in ten had ever considered the effect of an electrical failure, not one in a hundred. Oh, there had been temporary blackouts caused by a faulty generator or a broken line, but these had been greeted with laughter and candles and the confidence that someone, somewhere, was doing whatever had to be done to reestablish the service. But after the first hour of darkness on this night people huddled in their hotel rooms began to notice the profound silence which had fallen over the city. They could hear the falling snow and strained their senses hoping also to hear the crunching boots of a repair crew coming with tape and pliers to fix the lines.

No crew came.

There was no power for the lights, the electric heaters, curling irons and hot plates. Conversation about politics, ethics, economics and warfare stopped as though these too had lost their source of power. The intellectuals in Irkutsk felt they had been thrown back a hundred years when it became apparent that no one was going to fix the electricity.

A minor official of the defunct city government at Omsk who had been expatiating on the necessity of enlisting the support of the muzhik and the laboring classes for the re-creation of Russia was caught in midflight by the darkness and waited irritably to continue his thesis. "How long is this to go on?" he grumbled.

"The hotel manager is out of candles."

"Fools!"

"Make a wick of something and we'll burn oil."

"There is no oil."

"Well, something! Good Lord, there's something!"

The host fumbled about in the darkness trying to manufacture a light, with poor success. Presently the guests left in search of a place where candles were burning. The Omsk official, deprived of his audience, lost interest in his thesis and felt that he had been betrayed by the very class he'd been defending. "Incompetents!" he growled. "Ought to be shot."

"Who?"

"Why, whoever it is who does for the lights," the official replied and in the darkness he began to imagine this person as a murderous brute who was at that very moment taking advantage of the darkness to rape and plunder. He became frightened and began to tremble. "Are you there?" he asked.

But the host had also left the room and the official, paralyzed by fear, cringed in the darkness, shuddering like a prehistoric man lost from his tribe. "Are you there?" he squeaked.

And if there had been an answer out of the darkness he would have died.

‹ 4 ›

Carlisle and Tatiana had come to the Metropole to pick up her things and Katya Massakow was helping Tatiana pack a suitcase.

"I'll only take one," Tatiana said.

"But you still have so many lovely dresses," Katya protested.

"They're yours if you like, or you may give them away."

Carlisle sat in a chair near the window feeling depressed. He wished Katya had not been there. He felt comfortable with Tatiana only when they were alone. There had been that look in Katya's eyes as they came which Carlisle had found unbearable, a look which said: Can this be so? Tatiana and this man, together? What can she see in him? What hold does he have over her?

What hold? He had none and in the presence of others he experienced a terrible uncertainty which made him feel as though he were dreaming. The main thing was to get her out, away from Irkutsk to a place where they'd have time to understand one another.

The two women at the bed were black against the lantern light and their shadows fell toward him. "Jack gave me these in Vladivostok," Tatiana said.

Carlisle, always surprised to hear his name on Tatiana's lips, saw Katya take one of the silver lieutenant bars from Tatiana's palm.

"He'd just been made a captain," Tatiana said and she went on to relate how they'd met. "Do you remember, Jack?"

"Yes," he said, but it seemed to him that Tatiana was trying to justify herself to Katya by making it appear that their friendship was one of long standing. She spoke as though their brief acquaintance in Vladivostok made their present relationship inevitable. She spoke as if they'd known each other for years.

Katya glanced in his direction and smiled. She was being won over and Carlisle was annoyed that Tatiana found this so important. He stood up. "I'll wait downstairs, Tatiana," he said. "There's someone I want to see."

"Do you remember this, Jack?"

Tatiana held up her autograph book and the sight of it caused a flash of anger in Carlisle. She was going to read Katya the page he'd written. For some reason she had to do that too. He nodded. "I'll be downstairs," he said. "Don't be long. We've got to get back."

There was a kerosene lamp on the floor at the end of the corridor which threw shadows upward on the ceiling. An old woman whose duty it was to tend the lamp was snoozing on a chair beside it. Her toothless mouth was collapsed inward and her swollen hands lay in her lap like driftwood snags.

Seeing her, Carlisle thought of his mother and for the first time understood what she must have felt when she married Hinky Carlisle. A sense of achievement.

He paused beside the old woman and looked down on her unprotected head of sparse gray hair. "I love Tatiana," he thought, "so it's not the same!"

But his sense of achievement was undeniable. He felt cheapened by it. He didn't want to think about it and his anger fanned up in his eyes.

He went down quickly into the drafty shadow-crowded lobby. There were kerosene lamps in each corner of the room and one was gushing black smoke, threatening to burst into flame. Carlisle crossed the lobby to trim the wick and there he met Major Ikachi, who put out the lamp and smiled at him. "It seems we share the same impulses in times of emergency, Captain," he said. "Were you about to trim the lamp?"

"Yes."

"It's better to put it out and save the oil for those who stay behind."

"You going out?" Carlisle asked.

"Yes, I'm going down and have a chat with Ataman Semenoff. He's very important now that Kolchak is finished."

Major Ikachi glanced at his watch, then invited Carlisle to join him for a drink. He had a bottle at the bar and saw no reason to leave it. "Better for those who remain to keep their wits about them," he said.

They found an unoccupied corner with a view of the lobby so Carlisle wouldn't miss Tatiana. Ikachi brought his bottle and two glasses. He filled them and raised his own. "To a lucky man," he said.

"Me?"

"You have the prize, my friend. Countess Tatiana is a very complex, beautiful woman. I was attracted to her in Vladivostok just as you were, just as we were both attracted to the smoldering lamp. I wouldn't have minded having my wings singed."

Carlisle's face tightened and Ikachi noticed. He raised his hand. "Please," he said, "we can't quarrel. We're on the way out. Gentlemen never quarrel on the way out."

"I don't get you," Carlisle said.

"It stems from a conversation I had with your friend Leverett. I'd better not describe the setting. I see you're angry about something. How is Leverett, by the way?"

"He's missing."

"Missing?"

"I said missing," Carlisle retorted. "Lost. Over the hill."

"Ah, yes," Ikachi said thoughtfully. Then to avoid difficulty he changed the subject. "When are you going out?" he asked.

"In the morning."

"The last train from Irkutsk."

"The last American train," Carlisle said.

"Well, I wish you the best. I sincerely do."

Carlisle glanced at Ikachi, saw he was sincere and relented. "Thanks, Major," he said.

"It's been an interesting experience all around," Ikachi said. "Something of an experiment."

"One I could have done without."

"There'll be others," Ikachi said. He drained his glass and filled it again.

"None for me," Carlisle said.

"You make me feel unwelcome."

"One then. I'm waiting for Tatiana."

"I've always found waiting a pleasure," Ikachi said.

When Carlisle left the room Tatiana and Katya fell silent as though their conversation had indeed been for his benefit. They finished packing with smooth efficiency, then closed and locked the leather suitcase. For a moment they stood facing each other in the dim lamplight, then Katya took Tatiana's hand in her own and they sat down on the bed side by side.

"What is it, Tatiana? You must tell someone."

Tatiana sighed and shook her head.

"You went off without a word. You've been gone for days and I've been worried half to death."

"I'm sorry for that, Katya."

"I thought you'd thrown yourself into the river."

"I couldn't."

Katya caressed Tatiana's cold white hand trying to judge her state of mind by the feel of it. "You'll be going off with this man then," she said.

"Yes."

"To America?"

"Yes, I think so."

Katya was troubled by Tatiana's spiritless tone. "I don't understand it," she said.

"He's unique," Tatiana said and she removed her hand from Katya's and brushed her hair back from her brow. "I admire his uniqueness."

"Everyone is different," Katya said.

"No. No, most people are the same. The underlying sameness of them has always disgusted me. I don't know why. I don't know what I expected of life or how I came to expect it, but people are the same for the most part. All the same. I know it's an offensive thing to say to another person, Katya. Forgive me for it."

"I don't mind being common," Katya said. "It comforts me to be so. Being common lets me understand the others, I suppose. To feel with them."

"Yes, there's that."

"I wouldn't understand uniqueness."

"I don't understand the other. It all seems such a cheat to me, this pretense at speciality, everybody's claim to individual preciousness. It's all rot. It's a lie, a terrible lie. It's nothing but our isolation and fear of what others might do to us that makes us say the human individual is sacred. Hundreds of thousands of them have been killed or died in the last few years and perhaps one or two of them were unique. There may have been a Mozart among them, but then there were Mozarts who made their music on bone whistles thousands of years ago. It's not the loss of life we regret, it's the shattering of society."

"Your husband —"

"Albert was society," Tatiana said.

"I don't understand at all," Katya said and she shook her head in perplexity.

Tatiana rose and crossed into the darkness near the window. "Nor do I," she said. "The city is lying in wait," she said. "It'll spring up again. It'll always be here."

"So you love this man," Katya said.

Tatiana turned toward Katya and smiled. "Oh, Katya. You are so good. You're so very, very good! What can I say to make you happy?"

"That you are happy," Katya replied.

"Then I am happy," Tatiana said and raising her arms she turned clear around like a schoolgirl.

Katya's expression brightened hopefully. "And I suppose you'll be married in Vladivostok."

"Yes."

"I wish I could be there," Katya said. "It would be so grand! You must send me a picture. And you'll sail at once for America. Oh, Tatiana! You must be excited. Imagine such a wedding trip!"

"I'll send you a picture, of course."

"And a letter when you reach America."

"Yes, of course."

They fell silent again. Katya's enthusiasm faded and she studied her own blocky hands in her lap. "I have someone also," she said presently.

Tatiana returned to the bed and sat down beside Katya. "I'm glad of that, Katya."

"Since my brother was killed I've felt so alone," Katya said.

"And you've met someone."

"Oh, Tatiana, I'm so frightened and happy. I don't know what to do!"

Katya burst into tears and hid her face in her hands. Tatiana put her arm around Katya's shoulders and hugged her.

"It won't last," Katya said. "It can't! It's too awful! I mean I'm afraid all the time he won't come back, or that he won't want me and I've given myself to him and now I'm more afraid than ever for having done wrong. He says I haven't but I know better than he does. He's a Bolshevik, Tatiana! I didn't know it before. He's so big and amiable, so kind that I didn't know."

Tatiana laughed. "You are a goose, Katya," she said.

"I know. I know. I know!"

"I'm sure he's as good a person as you are even though he is a Bolshevik."

"Oh, he is! He's better than I am! He's so courageous!"

"Then what are you fussing about?"

"I don't know what he must think! What do men think, Tatiana? I'm so stupid and ugly! I've known him only two weeks and he said he had to go off on a mission of some kind and because I thought you weren't coming back I invited him up here. I just told him to come right along with me and spend the night!"

Katya was blushing so furiously that she had to wipe her face to cool it.

"What did he say when he left you?"

"That he would be back, but all men say that, I think."

"Many don't."

"I'm such a fool! I don't know anything about love-making. I don't know if I did right."

"Were you frightened?"

"He made it possible for me not to be. He was so good and warm. I wish I knew what to think. I wish you could tell me, Tatiana. You know and I don't."

Tatiana withdrew her arm and asked the man's name.

"Boris Ivanovitch Berezkin. It was because of his given name I made his acquaintance. He'd come to visit a comrade in the hospital, Sergei Kodor, you know, the boy who lost his foot. I'd told Sergei about my brother, and when Boris Ivanovitch came to visit, Sergei told him I had a brother of the same name. So that's how we met, you see. But oh, Tatiana, I'm so unclear about it, so anxious. He couldn't tell me where he was going, or how long he would be gone, only that I should wait and trust him to return."

"Ah, yes," Tatiana said.

"And I do!" Katya cried. "I do! I do! I may be making a fool of myself, but I do trust him and I will wait and if he never comes I'll go right on waiting and waiting and that will be my punishment for having done wrong. I'll go on living and be dead and not know it. Oh, Tatiana, isn't that awful!"

"He'll come back," Tatiana whispered. "He will." And she pressed Katya's hands reassuringly. "Your Boris will come back," she said. "You've done nothing wrong, nothing to be punished for. I must go now, he's waiting."

She rose and kissed Katya, then she put on her coat. Katya helped her and offered to carry the suitcase down.

"No," Tatiana said. "I must do that."

"I'll never see you again," Katya said and tears filled her eyes.

"No," Tatiana said. "But we can write."

They embraced, then Tatiana took her suitcase and went out. "God bless you, Katya," she said and she closed the door.

"And you," Katya replied.

The suitcase was heavier than Tatiana had expected. The old woman guarding the lamp at the end of the corridor looked up at her with eyes the color of ashes.

"That love lasts longest which has the most to consume."

Tatiana remembered it was her uncle who had said this to her when she'd married Albert. "Some love is like wood and some is like coal. The variety of a wood flame is greater, but for myself I prefer coal when it is to be found."

Tatiana gave the old woman a ten ruble note and received her blessing, then she went down the stairs with the suitcase bumping on the step behind her. She thought it curious that she remembered so many things now that she had no use for them. Her memory was coming back and she'd kept no diary. Perhaps it was because she'd broken the mirror image of herself or because appearances no longer mattered.

She reached the lobby and Carlisle came to her from the bar with Major Ikachi at his side. He took the suitcase from her hand without a word. Ikachi, smiling softly, bowed. "I'm sorry we won't be going out together, Countess," he said, then hastily he amended this. "The three of us."

"Perhaps we'll meet in Vladivostok, Major," she said.

"In any case I've taken the liberty, after our meeting in Omsk, to attempt what I'd hoped to be a preliminary sketch." From his inside breast pocket Major Ikachi withdrew a folded square of silk and shook it out. On the silk in delicately brushed strokes was a rising flight of sandpipers. "Your laughter on silk," Ikachi said. "I hope you'll accept it?"

Tatiana took the portrait of her laughter and thanked Ikachi. "In times ahead perhaps I'll be able to reproduce it," she said, "thanks to you, Major."

"I'll have done the world a service to remind you how it was," Ikachi said, then he offered Carlisle his hand. "I'm reasonably certain we'll meet again, Captain," he said.

"Well, fine," Carlisle said, not certain at all.

"I plan a trip to your country in ten or fifteen years if all goes well."

Carlisle grinned flashingly. "You plan a long way ahead, Major."

"These things take time. Good luck and happiness to you both."

Ikachi bobbed once more and went out.

Carlisle took Tatiana's arm and they found a battered horse-drawn sleigh at the curb. Carlisle looked around for something better, grumbling that Ikachi might have offered to drive them to Glaskov.

"I don't mind," Tatiana said. "I'd just as soon walk."

"You're not thinking, Tatiana. It must be thirty below."

"I don't feel it."

Carlisle helped Tatiana into the sleigh and wrapped her in the lap robe.

The runners clattered over the ice-rutted street, but when they reached the frozen river the ride softened and grew silent except for the horse's hooves. The sky was clear, with stars snapping in the blackness of it. Carlisle and Tatiana were silent. They watched as the cold stars laughed and chattered in the crisp black sky over them, and in their finitude they clasped hands under the lap robe. Their silence was eloquent; they were close together in it, closer even than when they were nakedly locked against each other.

"I love you, Tatiana," Carlisle said.

"I know, Jack. And I love you."

But the words, like the stars, shattered in the cold air and they each wished they hadn't spoken as they crossed the broad white, frozen river and clattered up the common road to Glaskov.

They skirted the depot into the marshaling yard, where Carlisle heard the rumbling snuffle of a heavy train heading west toward Nizhne-Udinsk. This was unusual and he stopped their driver at the dispatcher's office and got out.

"You go on," he said to Tatiana. "I want to check on that train."

"Will you be long?"

"No," he said. "Ten minutes."

He stood a moment watching the sleigh jolt over the tracks toward the car he and Tatiana shared, then he went up the wooden steps to the dispatcher's office located in a tower at one side of the yard.

The dispatcher on duty, a paunchy Nebraskan of fifty, stood at the window gazing down into the yard with the stub of a dead cigar in his mouth. He wore a fur-lined overcoat and there was a suitcase on the floor at his feet. His name was Jud Conners and he'd been with the Russian Railway Service Corps since its inception. He greeted Carlisle as he entered.

"Evening, Sioux. What brings you up?"

"I heard a train going west," Carlisle said and he looked at the clipboard which recorded traffic through the yard.

"Yeah, it was a big armored job. Went through here like a phantom."

"Whose was it?"

"I don't know. Don't care. I'm off, Jack. I was hoping you were my relief. I was giving him two more minutes to show."

"What the hell."

Conners grinned around his cigar and shook his big, homely head. "Don't start, Sioux. Us old union men stop work on the clock."

"I'm not running a union shop, Jud," Carlisle said.

"We'd better be out of here before Kolchak arrives," Conners said. "There's going to be a snarl about that."

"Maybe."

"They've sent the gold train ahead — 6103. It should come in tomorrow night. What in hell are we waiting for anyway, Sioux?"

"I'd rather travel in daylight."

"Crap. You want the dubious honor of being the last man out."

"You'll be with me, so will the others."

Conners grinned. "Have I got a choice?"

They were both tough and they liked each other. Carlisle shook his head. "Our train made up?" he asked.

"Flagged, fueled and ready to go. Two coaches and enough American flags on her to be seen a mile. I want to get home to my grandchildren."

"Only two coaches?"

"You and your lady still have the compartment."

"Thanks."

"Don't mention it. There are only a dozen of us left. I'd be happier if we had a larger armed guard."

"You're timid, Jud. I've got four good men and some firepower."

"I'd be happier with a company of good men."

"So would I," Carlisle said, then he frowned and tossed the clipboard down.

The door opened and two young Russians in leather jackets came in. They seemed surprised to find anyone in the tower and looked at each other uncertainly.

"Bolshies," Conners said to Carlisle.

The young Russians smiled and one produced a paper from his jacket pocket and offered it to both Carlisle and Conners in turn.

Conners took it and glanced at the heading. "An order from Revkom," he said. "Yeah, they're Bolshies. Well, dosfidania, buddy." He thrust the paper back at the Russian, picked up his suitcase and headed for the door. "You coming?" he asked Carlisle.

Carlisle nodded and followed Conners down the steps.

"Well, that's it," Conners said when they reached the ground. "The Reds have it, lock, stock and barrel."

"They can have it."

"You coming?"

"In a minute."

Conners said good night and walked toward their train on the siding. The last train of the American Siberian Expeditionary Force.

Carlisle stuffed his hands into his coat pockets and looked around. The yard wasn't his anymore. All the High Commissioners and Americans were gone and the Czechs held Glaskov under the uneasy terms of an agreement with the Reds across the river.

Tatiana was waiting in their compartment. They'd moved into it three nights ago. They didn't like it there as much as they had in the boxcar. There were too many people around: four infantrymen from Headquarters

Company who'd been sent in to guard the consular offices and the six Russian Railway Service Corps men who would operate the train.

Carlisle crossed the yard to his train. The American flags painted on the coaches and the engine were so large that it almost looked like a circus train.

He went up the steps and along the corridor to the door, where he knocked.

Tatiana asked who it was.

"It's Jack," he called.

She locked the door behind him and Carlisle took off his coat. "We'll go out tomorrow," he said.

Tatiana's suitcase lay on the table, unopened. She stayed by the door with her back against it. Major Ikachi's silk portrait of her laughter was around her neck and her hair flowed over it like black amber. Her independent stance made Carlisle remember a steel-blue Apaloosa with a patterned rump and chocolate eyes which had bruised his heart because the horse was beyond his attainment; it made him think of the shacks of Khailar and of all the green sprouts of his own yearning frozen black in the bud until his heart was crusted like a pine cone. The blood deepened in his eyes as they met Tatiana's, which were sea gray.

"This is impossible, Jack," she said quietly. "I've been thinking about it."

"Don't," he said.

"One must."

"Why?"

"Katya needs me. I've decided to go back."

Carlisle shook his head. "No."

"I'm torturing you."

"No," he said again.

"All the same," she said and she took her coat from the wall hook, but Carlisle snatched it away and she slapped his face.

The flat sound of the blow caused them to draw their breaths. Carlisle's hand came up to retaliate and she looked at it, then at him. "Is it this way with us, then?" she asked.

Carlisle seized her roughly and she tried to twist away. "Oh, Jack," she said and there was a note of irritation in her voice which was almost patronizing.

Tatiana was not frightened, she was angry. She'd felt many things in her life, but never such anger and she was strengthened by it. In comparison with this freshening rage all her previous emotions seemed petty — petty frustrations, petty fears, petty enjoyments, none of which could be expressed except in petty ways.

Afraid he would hurt her Carlisle let Tatiana go. She started again to the door, but he caught her by the shoulders and shook her so furiously that her head snapped back and forth like a machine gun bolt.

"We'll have it out," he growled. "This time," he said. "This time we'll see!"

"There's something left yet to consume," Tatiana thought. "Wood fire or coal, what does it matter?"

Carlisle stopped shaking her and looked into her dazed eyes. "Katya doesn't need you," he said.

"No one does. Least of all you, Jack."

"What in hell do you want from me?"

"I don't know! I'm not sure! Perhaps I've had what I wanted, to be put in touch with myself, to be made to feel something —"

"To be made to feel common. Is that it?" he demanded.

"Perhaps so," she declared. "Perhaps I've wanted to be common all my life, would that be so strange? What can you know about my life? What do you know about me after all? We're as different as water and fire!"

Carlisle pulled Tatiana up and kissed her brutally. "I know what's common," he said. "That's one thing I know damned well," and he crushed the breath from her body as he bore her down.

CHAPTER THIRTY-EIGHT

As train 6103 began moving through the yard at Nizhne-Udinsk, Colonel Dubrovski, his rotund face flushed and cheery, came into the compartment he shared with Raul Markowitz and gestured out the window with a bottle of brandy he'd just taken from his valise. "We're leaving Kolchak and company, Lieutenant," he said loudly, then he dropped into his seat and began to worry the brandy cork with his teeth.

Markowitz looked out the window at the trains on the siding. One coach with drawn curtains was being decorated with British, French, Czech, American and Japanese flags and the green and white pennants of the Kolchak government were being removed.

Czech guards, posted at intervals along the track, stamped their feet against the caked snow and watched enviously as 6103 moved slowly through the switching yard. Now and again one of them would wave, but mostly they beat their arms with their mittened fists to drive out the cold.

"I've just heard the Russian garrison has revolted," Dubrovski said around his cork. "They revolted at Krasnoyarsk too." He clamped his heavy teeth into the cork once more and pulled on the bottle with no effect. "Do you have a knife?"

Markowitz shook his head.

"Hell of a thing," Dubrovski grumbled and he looked out the window once more at Kolchak's train. "They held him six days at Krasnoyarsk. Probably hold him longer here while our echelons go through. Come down to the next car with me. Everyone's there. You look in the need of company. There's a game going, plenty to drink and singing."

"I'm fine," Markowitz said.

"He's fine. He's fine," Dubrovski said and he bit into the cork and twisted the bottle in his paws like a bear. The cork came out of the bottle with a stubborn pop and some of the brandy splashed over Dubrovski's blouse. He looked surprised, removed the cork from his teeth and examined it as though seeking a way of punishing it for this offense. "Bad cork," he said, then he smiled and without asking filled Markowitz' glass on the table. "To Vladivostok!" he said and drank from the bottle. Markowitz nodded, but did not drink.

Dubrovski peered out the windows, squinting his eyes against the snow glare. "They're peeling Kolchak down," he said. "From seven trains to one and who knows how far that one will get? Ministers and officials popping out of his trains like fleas off a burning dog. Here's an example!"

Dubrovski tugged at Markowitz' sleeve insistently. Markowitz jerked his arm away, but he saw a portly man in a fur coat running toward their slowly moving train waving a fistful of ruble notes. He was yelling, but his words were lost and two Czech sentries were plodding after him, the bayonets on their rifles gleaming like icicles.

"Poor bastards," Dubrovski said when the man could no longer be seen. "There's no joy in Christ for them today," and he drank from the bottle again. "To Vladivostok," he said.

"To Vladivostok," Markowitz replied irritably and he hoped Colonel Dubrovski would hasten to drink himself insensible. He was annoyed by the man's familiarity.

Beyond the Nizhne-Udinsk marshaling yard the train settled into a steady pace and Dubrovski closed his eyes, letting his head roll against the cushioned back of his seat. "I love trains," he said. "I feel them. I feel safe in them. By the sound of the wheels I can count the rails and the ties and the spikes, and I can judge the condition of the roadbed by the squeal of the flanges on the metal. We're lucky to have a damned good American engine on this one, I can tell you. If we had any kind of track under us we could clip along. Clip, clip along." He opened his eyes lazily and looked at Markowitz, who was gazing out the window at frozen landscape. "Drink up your brandy, Markowitz," he said.

Markowitz glanced up disdainfully and Dubrovski closed his eyes again with a contented smile. "Too refined, eh?" he said. "Too elevated to share a little joy with an old foundry mechanic like me. Well, I expect all those distinctions will come into play again when this is over, but for now it's Colonel Dubrovski and Lieutenant Markowitz, eh? Have a good time, my boy, drink your brandy and that's an order." Dubrovski opened one eye to see if Markowitz had taken his brandy. He had not. Dubrovski sighed and closed his eye. "Hassek was right," he said. "The Austrian Army was riddled with Schweiks and we got every damned one of them in the Czech Legion, including Hassek. Schweiks from top to bottom. I'm a Schweik, you're a Schweik. Good soldiers all, but it's God-awful on discipline. You might say we've malingered a new nation into being. Czechoslovakia borne on the shoulders of its malingering Schweiks."

Markowitz shifted his position and cursed under his breath as he bumped his wounded arm against the sill. "Why don't you join the others?" he said.

Dubrovski was gazing at him contentedly. "You're a man of few words, Lieutenant," he said. "You keep mum and exude contempt like buttery salve and how can anyone criticize you for it? What have you said? What have you done? A perfect gentleman in all respects, but oh, the greasy contempt that rolls off! It's something they don't teach old factory hands like me. It's the slipperiness that keeps us at the bottom of the hill except when there's hard work to be done at the top, whereupon you sprinkle a little cordial sand, enough for us to get traction and poke our heads up where the bullets fly. But when the danger's gone you all get to work exuding contempt and down we slide again."

Dubrovski made a sweeping gesture with his brandy glass, scattering an arc of brandy across the table. Markowitz looked at him. "You're being a bore, Colonel," he said.

Dubrovski laughed heartily. "Of course I am! It's bores makes the wheels go around, my boy. If this train broke down you'd find me captivating! Oh yes! There's not enough social grease to slide this train from here to Irkutsk, but it's building up, I can tell you. When we board ship at Vladivostok we'll all be dripping in lard, you can bet, and most of it will be coming from classy young lieutenants. But if that steam engine up ahead broke down, my conversation would be fascinating enough, you can bet."

"We all have our expertise, Colonel."

"Well now, what is yours?" Dubrovski asked with attempted sarcasm. "I like you well enough, but I've failed thus far to perceive it. I'm a bit dense, you see, a bit common in the head."

"You're a bit drunk, if I may say so."

"You may say so!" Dubrovski responded gleefully. "You have said so. It must be for this extraordinary perspicacity that they made you rub shoulders with the Allied high command while the rest of the boys boiled tea water on machine gun barrels. You have an observing eye, Markowitz. Insight. Intelligence. Thank God for it. You also give off lard."

Markowitz, irritated beyond endurance, sat forward. "I don't know what's got into you, Colonel, but I warn you not to provoke me."

"Ah, a duel!" Dubrovski thundered. "Good, good! Maybe that's the secret of my failure as a gentleman. In the corridor, or shall we have to leave this comfortable train?"

"It can be arranged when we're on home soil once again," Markowitz said.

"There's going to be more gunfire when we get home than a little bit, Lieutenant. There must be thousands of duels promised when we've been repatriated. Thousands, tens of thousands. It's a very popular thing. We'll have to book time in the parks there'll be so many in line to shoot."

"I'm perfectly in earnest."

"Of course, my boy. But since dueling grounds are apt to be at a premium immediately we get home, suppose we devise a way to settle this thing without a long, tedious wait."

"Certainly."

"And since I'm challenged I have the choice of weapons, isn't that the form?"

"Yes."

Dubrovski nodded gravely and appeared to be considering the matter. "Ah!" he cried. "I have it!" And he fixed Markowitz with a crafty grin and tipped his brandy bottle into his mouth, smacking his lips. "Just the thing."

"Well," Markowitz said.

"Lunch pails at arm's length," Dubrovski said, and convulsed by his own humor he doubled over, laughing uproariously. "Lunch pails!" he bellowed. "It's the only weapon we have in my flat, assuming my old woman has kept mine in condition. Fine heavy tin it is, with a wire bail and wooden handle. Why, we could thrash away at each other with lunch pails, first one down the loser. We could mash each other's noses and collect a couple of respectable scars on our cheeks like Heidelberg saber enthusiasts!" Tears streamed from Dubrovski's eyes. Markowitz' face was white as candle wax. "Now all that remains is to judge the gravity of the case and decide whether your offended honor requires us to fill the pails or leave them empty. What do you say? Full pails, of course, will do more damage."

"You're an idiot, Dubrovski," Markowitz declared, but he couldn't resist smiling.

Dubrovski drew a deep breath and composed his features. "Full pails it is, then," he said. "I'll charge mine with liver sausage, sauerkraut, a piece of Prague ham and maybe a liter of good beer soup. But I think we should stick to the conventions of civilized warfare and outlaw gas-producing foods!"

Once again Dubrovski was convulsed. Tears appeared in his eyes; he gasped for breath and his face flushed almost purple. "It's too ridiculous, Markowitz!" he cried. "Too ridiculous!"

"What in hell's got into you?" Markowitz asked.

"Why, here I am! Here I am rolling through the Siberian landscape in a train full of gold, drinking brandy, warm as toast, and all I can think of is my lunch pail on the mantelshelf. The point is I'm too old to change. The point is that my tastes are set. If I had all the gold in those wagons behind us I'd still be the same, still longing for the old woman and the lunch pail on the mantelshelf."

"How old are you?" Markowitz asked.

"Forty-eight, I think. Yes, forty-eight and I still don't quite believe I'm alive. I've been waiting all my life for something to happen to prove it, you know. And here I am almost done and I haven't given it a thought. If I did I wouldn't know what to think, but I'm a great talker."

"Yes, you are."

"I surprise myself sometimes with the things I say. I'm sure if I could be selective at all people would think me a very clever fellow; as it is, I babble whenever a chance arises. I went back to have a look at the gold in the wagons before we pulled away. That's where I was. Have you seen anything like it? Very common, it is. Like blocks of gilded pig iron. Doesn't look real, until you heft it and look at the markings. It's real enough. Gold and social lard is what makes the world go around. Yes, I believe it does. One greases the skids for the other. If you've got the manners you get the gold and vice versa, unless you're too set in your ways like me. Yes, sir, we've been fighting all these years for gold and the manners of kings. They both float on a sea of blood, my friend. A sea of blood."

Dubrovski poured another dose of brandy down his throat, then shook his head sadly at Markowitz. "You won't drink with me," he said.

Markowitz raised his glass and drained it. "You're a clever fellow, Dubrovski, but you talk too much."

"Just what I tell myself!" Dubrovski cried. "But I don't miss much. I'm too stupid to be a liar as most people are. So you fought Count Albert, is that it?"

"I chopped up his aeroplane with an ax."

"Did you now!"

"And he shot me for it."

"Well, if you'd done a better job you might have saved his life."

"Oh!"

"He's dead."

"I didn't know."

"Yes, crashed right into the lap of the Red Army and they shot him."

"Well," Markowitz said and he felt ill. The skin of his face seemed to shrink, making his eyes appear larger.

"You look bad," Dubrovski said and he tipped another jot of brandy into Markowitz' glass.

"He was my greatest friend," Markowitz whispered hoarsely. "My greatest friend."

"That's a hard thing," Dubrovski said.

"I hated him," Markowitz groaned. "Oh, God how I hated that man!" Tears welled into his eyes and flowed down his cheeks like spring water. He turned his face to the window and bit his underlip, trying not to sob.

Dubrovski sat for a moment, entirely confused, then he got up and excused himself.

When the compartment door shut Raul Markowitz folded forward, hugging his bandaged arm in its sling like a baby, and wept. He was lost. He saw no reason to go on. There was nothing. Tatiana would not feel such grief as this. No, she had not loved Albert so deeply.

Raul put his forehead against the windowpane. "You didn't love him as I did," he whispered through his trembling tear-dampened lips. "No, you did not. No. No." And rolling his head against the cold glass Raul Markowitz continued to weep as the heavy, gold-laden train lumbered on through the icy darkness.

« 2 »

At Polovina station the Invincible was hardly visible against the embankment of stained snow bordering the right of way. Tense with silence it seemed about to scurry away, to take alarm and squirm off seeking another hiding place into which to scuttle and lie there testing subtle changes in the atmosphere with its antenna and watching with invisible eyes. The snouts of its two cannon were leveled at the siding beyond the main tracks; machine gun barrels protruded slightly from the gun ports and occasionally these moved slightly, like sockets from which a limb had been torn away. It smelled of cold metal and lubricants and gave off a sense of awesome intelligence.

Sipialef's Cossacks occupied the depot and were monitoring telegraphic transmissions. The villagers had been driven into their homes and the local Russian guard imprisoned. The streets were empty and silent except for a detachment of black-clad Cossacks on their dark, impatient horses.

Up the line toward Nizhne-Udinsk another Cossack detachment watched for a train to appear while Captain Graetz cursed under his breath as two men attempted to thaw a frozen switch with blowtorches.

Two others with crowbars chipped ice away from the stock rail and switch rail which would send the gold train onto the siding across from the Invincible. The signals had been altered, so the engineer would not expect his train to leave the main track and would barely have time to stop before he hit the abutment.

Captain Graetz threw his weight against the switching lever, but it was still jammed. He could see failure because of this jammed switch and he began to perspire. The men with the crowbars having freed the rails came over and beat on the switch to shake it loose. The clang of metal on metal sang off through the cold air; the blowtorches threw grotesque shadows and roared with a keen, blue flame. They tried the switch again. This time it moved. The switching rails grated over the chipped ice and came into place.

Graetz sighed, inspected the connection, then signaled his work crew back to the train.

"It's good," he said to himself as he followed them. "It's good."

Half an hour later 6103 came down the slight grade and entered the level stretch toward Polovina. The train was making good time. The engineer estimated he was four hours from Irkutsk. Through his side window he saw the signal block which gave him the right of way and relaxed on his seat.

Markowitz felt the train lurch to the right. He stood up, but a sharp braking action threw him down on the seat again. He could hear the heavy gold wagons crashing against one another and the ear-piercing sound of locked wheels scraping over the rails.

Dubrovski, who had been sleeping, was instantly alert. "The damned fool!" he roared. "She'll derail!"

Their car swayed, then held the track, but behind them they could hear others jackknifing, the sound of splintering wood and screaming metal. Dubrovski looked out the window.

Explosions tore the air, followed by machine gun fire.

The window burst in Dubrovski's face and he fell into a sitting position clutching his head. Blood flowed between his fingers. He staggered to his feet and the traversing machine guns caught him a second time through the window. He fell writhing at Markowitz' feet yelling something Markowitz couldn't make out.

Two shells hit the train in rapid succession. Men were howling. There was a fire. Machine gun bullets washed along the side of the cars.

Markowitz fell to the floor and crawled into the corridor. Someone stepped on him, cursed, then ran half the length of the car, trying to stay ahead of the bullets, but they caught him.

Markowitz reached the door, but he couldn't open it without standing up and he couldn't stand up without being hit by the machine guns.

He lay huddled in the door well. The car pitched under the impact of a shell which exploded with a blinding, slapping sound, tearing a great hole in the side. Shrapnel, glass and wood ricocheted through the car. Markowitz' wounded arm was shrieking and there was something else in the vicinity of his legs, but he had no time to consider this.

He dragged himself toward the gap left by the shell, closed his eyes and pitched out. He fell and continued to fall through space leaving a streamer of sound behind him, an iridescent strand which at first he couldn't identify, then he knew it for a spider web being spun from his gut; and he saw himself as a spider on it, a little black ball which would continue falling until there was nothing left to spin out.

The Invincible continued firing at the gold train. Shellfire had already reduced the engine to a steaming mass of metallic viscera and the machine guns traversed the coaches, seeking members of the Czech train guard who lay face down on the far embankment trying to collect their wits.

In his private armored coach Colonel Sipialef, wearing a long robe of yellow Chinese silk, fired one machine gun through the port; the second gun on his side of the car was manned by two girls, both naked to the waist. One was Chinese and she fed the long cartridge belt into the gun. The second was Eurasian; her breasts quivered under the stuttering recoil of the gun and there was an expression of intense satisfaction on her face. Their bodies glistened with excitement. Hot cartridges ejected from the gun fell unnoticed on their naked feet and flames from the burning train danced in their dark eyes.

Major Hassek rallied the surviving members of his guard and made a dash for the gold cars at the end of the train. Sipialef saw them and emptied his machine gun; he dashed to the next one, struck the girls away from it with one swipe of his arm and continued firing at the legs of the scampering Czechs.

A cannon shell burst and caught Hassek; he stood a moment silhouetted in the glare of the explosion, then he vanished, atomized.

Captain Graetz and the Cossacks meantime were uncoupling the last four gold wagons, which had not been derailed. The Cossacks roped horses to the cars, pulled them back on the main track, then switched them to the siding where the Invincible lay.

Graetz shot the lock away from one wagon door and climbed up to inspect the cargo. For a moment he thought the car was empty, then the floor shifted beneath his feet; he pulled a canvas cover back and discovered he was standing on a floor of gold bars, four inches thick. The wagon had been loaded to its weight capacity, but the precious cargo took up very little cubic space. Graetz caught his breath, touched one of the blocks lovingly, then went to inspect the other three cars. In one he found a great collection of specie the value of which he could not determine. The other two cars held a mixed cargo of gold, silver and platinum in ingot blocks.

Having shot the locks away Graetz was now perplexed about how to seal the cars again, but he decided to settle this after they were moving and he went to report to Sipialef.

Colonel Sipialef turned from his smoking machine gun and wiped his hands on the front of his robe. "How many, Graetz?" he demanded.

"Four, Colonel. The rest were derailed."

"Good cargo?"

"All you could expect, Colonel," Graetz said with an enthusiastic grin. "They're coupled and we're ready to go." He looked at his wristwatch. "Ten minutes to the second," he said.

Sipialef went to his desk and gave the signal to start and the Invincible, still firing, began to slide away.

A few Cossacks too laggard to get their horses aboard had to leave them and four men who had been wounded were left behind to add their groans to those of the maimed and dying Czechs.

Sipialef opened a bottle of champagne, poured half of it down his throat, then tossed the bottle to Captain Graetz, who caught it neatly by the neck. "Which one suits you, Captain?" Sipialef asked. "I feel generous tonight."

Graetz looked at the girls. Their bodies were smudged and they smelled of cordite and flame. The cannon and machine guns fell silent as their train picked up speed. The Chinese girl's eyes traversed Graetz' face obliquely, leaving him with a sensation of having been cut. "That one," he said.

The cockatoos in their swaying cage squawked and fluttered. The Invincible settled into a smooth flow over the rails.

Sipialef pulled his robe around him, closed the two gun ports and pulled the draperies.

He ordered the Eurasian girl to sweep the spent machine gun cartridges from the carpet. "Take her," he said to Graetz," "but you'd better be prepared for Glaskov."

"I will be, Colonel," Graetz said as he led the Chinese girl away. "No one will stop us at Glaskov, or anywhere else," he said.

« 3 »

In that cold hour just before dawn when sound itself seems to have frozen, the Invincible came to a stop on the siding at Innokentievskaia a few miles short of Glaskov and a picked patrol of seven Cossacks led their horses down the specially constructed drop ramps to the ground. When raised again these drawbridge ramps made doors for the horse wagons, which, like the troop carriages, were sheathed in iron.

The Cossack patrol rode off to scout the situation at Glaskov and the rest of the troops spilled out to make their train ready for the run through the marshaling yard.

Captain Graetz supervised the work. The two engines were fueled and checked for operating efficiency. The gun ports were opened and the cannon turrets cranked around to free the mechanism of collected ice.

Ammunition was distributed to the machine gunners. The cargo of gold in the four wagons taken from 6103 was transferred to the main section of the train, much of it going into Sipialef's private car and those immediately adjacent to it. The four emptied wagons were uncoupled and the switches thrown to put the Invincible back on the main track.

A connection from the telegraph line was carried to Sipialef's communication car and the messages were deciphered. Since the lines had been cut at Polovina after the attack, telegraph traffic should have been light. Breakdowns in communication had become a usual thing and did not ordinarily cause alarm, but in this case there was a repeated and urgent attempt being made from Irkutsk to raise the operator at Polovina. It was transmitted every few minutes and Colonel Sipialef's assumption was that someone had reached Irkutsk by wireless to alert them that the gold train was coming through.

Sipialef called for Graetz and they decided to move through Glaskov at once before the Reds blew up the tracks or gathered a force sufficient to stop them.

As was his custom Carlisle was up before sunrise. There weren't many cars in the dark yard. Seven trains had gone out of Glaskov the night before. But he knew the Czech rear guard was due and after that Kolchak and the remnants of Kappel's shattered army, which would, in all likelihood, skirt northward around Irkutsk and pass east over Lake Baikal.

With his hands rammed into his pockets Carlisle walked east to set the switches which would put his train on the main line. Hoar frost stood like white fur on the outer edge of the rails and the fresh glaze of new ice cracked under his feet.

As usual he sensed the coming light and paused to greet it, wishing it would enlighten him.

Ateyapi kin
Maka owancya
Lowan nisipe-lo
Heya-po —

"Thus the father sayeth; Lo, he now commandeth all on earth to sing."
But he had no song.
There was a chipped stone in his throat.
He had not believed that a man could love a woman, could make love to her and never take possession. But this was so.

He had pitched his pennies and lost. But perhaps there had never been anything to win. Perhaps love was a monstrous joke, a twitch, an ecstatic little spasm of nothing.

Perhaps he'd run the wrong way at Binidayan.

Perhaps all his life he had run against his own nature, trying to be something other than was in him to be. He didn't know. The only thing he was sure of was that he was an army man. A soldier.

Yes, an army man, like Hinky Carlisle.

The rest didn't matter. It couldn't matter anymore. He was a captain and he'd done a good job evacuating Irkutsk, a damned good job that should earn him a citation. His white hands were unimportant, Indian roots and love were unimportant. He'd done his duty.

A line of brain-gray light appeared and in that motionless moment Carlisle saw seven riders rising black against the lighter background. They seemed immense, each poised in an alert attitude; then as the light broadened they began to move. Their dark horses picked delicately over the ties and through the morning ice.

Carlisle went toward them and as the light plucked him out of the darkness the riders stopped.

They were Cossacks dressed in elegant uniforms which Carlisle did not recognize. He thought they might be an advance guard of Kolchak's personal troops, or a special detachment assigned to the gold train, which meant in either case that these trains were ahead of schedule. They seemed unhurried and not a bit disturbed by his presence. They stood hard etched, gathering detail with the light, and appeared to be taking stock of the number of cars and the defenses of the yard.

Their leader rode out ahead along the main line, then stopped and looked back. The legs of his horse planted on the ties appeared to tremble, then the vibration reached Carlisle and he knew that a heavy train was coming fast. He put one foot on a rail and it sang under his heel. The Cossacks whirled their horses and galloped back as they had come, hugging the necks of their horses.

Carlisle dashed forward to the switch and threw his weight against the lever. Ice cracked from the grease-insulated gears and he hit the lever again. The block signals up the line raised their warning slowly and the switch rails came into place. Then Carlisle ran toward the tower across the yard.

As he ran the cold air was like a shark loose in his lungs. He heard the train itself now and looking back saw it come out of the light with the seven Cossacks galloping along its flank trying to swing aboard. Four of them made it, one fell and the other two were left behind.

Apprehension jumped up in Carlisle. "It doesn't intend stopping," he thought. "It's going to blast through!"

Across the yard he saw the Czechs tumbling into their sandbagged emplacements. A company of Reds came out of the depot with guns.

The big train came into the yard, its whistle screaming as the engineer saw the block signal and ordered his brakemen out. Carlisle recognized the Invincible. He saw a contingent of Japanese troops take position. "Christ, there'll be a pitched battle," he thought as the Invincible hit the switch and was shunted off the main track, almost derailing.

Its gun ports were open and the two turret guns swung menacingly toward the Czech troops on the tower side of the yard.

At the foot of the tower steps Carlisle was met by a gaggle of officers, all babbling at once. One Czech captain who spoke English caught his arm. "That's Sipialef!" he said.

"I know who it is," Carlisle retorted.

The two young Reds who'd taken over the tower came down the steps armed with machine pistols.

"There's going to be a fight," the Czech said.

"There's not going to be any fight. What are the Reds saying?"

"They intend to attack."

"Tell them to hold their fire. I'll go out and talk."

The Czech captain spoke to the Reds, who looked anxious, and Carlisle headed for the Invincible, which had come to a stop.

"They suspect Sipialef has contraband gold aboard his train," the Czech called after him.

"Tough," Carlisle shot back. "You just tell them to hold their fire. This yard is still under American protection."

As he approached the Invincible, Carlisle saw Jud Conners trotting toward him.

"That damned train has a gun poking into my window," he said as he fell in beside Carlisle. His face was gray and he was puffing.

"Don't worry about it."

"Don't worry about it! What in hell do you mean? The muzzle is ten feet away."

"There's not going to be any trouble."

"What in hell are you going to do?"

"Shut up, Jud, and get back to our train and tell our people not to get excited."

"It's a lousy way to start a day," Conners said, but he went back to the American train, which was one track away from the Invincible.

Carlisle hammered on the door of the coach he knew Colonel Sipialef occupied. Presently it was opened and a Kraut with a shaven head appeared.

"I want to talk to Sipialef," Carlisle growled. "Tell him it's Captain Carlisle."

The Kraut disappeared and Carlisle tried to recall the times he'd met Sipialef. He hated the man without really knowing why and this was dangerous. There was Pashkova of course, but that fell into the category of Russian domestic affairs toward which Carlisle had pledged his neutrality. Because of Maryenka, Austin and Leverett he could be personally involved if he allowed himself to be, but this was no time for personal involvement. Perhaps there was no time for personal involvement.

His only clear impression of Sipialef was from the day the Cossacks had entrained at Tataurovo. He remembered thinking that Sipialef always looked ready to spring. He had a coiled, snakelike quality which made Carlisle's heels itch to stamp down and grind. But this was not the time to antagonize Sipialef, not when his machine guns could rip through the American coaches where Tatiana lay sleeping.

The key phrase of the American proclamation with respect to traffic on the Trans-Siberian flashed into Carlisle's mind: "All will be equally benefited, and all shall be treated alike by our forces irrespective of persons, nationality, religion or politics."

When Captain Graetz reappeared and beckoned him inside Carlisle knew exactly where his duty lay.

Graetz opened a door and motioned him in with a courtly gesture.

"Ah, Captain!" Colonel Sipialef said as Carlisle entered. "I'm surprised to find any Americans still here."

Sipialef was wearing a white, fur-trimmed dolman and there was a glazed look in his eyes. Carlisle noticed bars of gold stacked on the floor and the smell of opium in the air. A girl lay on a bed at the far end of the car, watching him indolently.

"You made quite a racket coming in, Colonel," he said.

"We hadn't intended to stop," Sipialef replied lazily and he smiled.

"There are a lot of excited people out there."

Sipialef shrugged. "It's the times," he said.

"You going to Verkhne?"

"Yes, that's our intention."

"I'll pilot you down," Carlisle said abruptly.

"What's that?"

"I said I'd pilot you down. My train is on the next track over. We're going out too."

Sipialef looked at Captain Graetz incredulously, then he smiled once more and his voice rose musically. "I have no intention of shooting up your train, Captain," he said. "I didn't know you were here."

"You'd better not. You'd better not shoot up anything. The Reds have artillery across the river, enough to blow this yard out, and by now they're ranged in. I told them not to fire and I'm telling you the same thing. If you don't they won't. My orders are specific in this respect. Anyone can use the road. You give me your word not to fire and I'll go talk to them."

"You'll arbitrate?" Sipialef asked.

"I'll tell them by God not to fire because they'll hit my train and anyone who fires on an American train is going to have the whole god-damned American Army down their throats. That includes you."

"How many troops do you have here, Captain?"

"Enough," Carlisle retorted. "Do I have your word?"

It was so preposterous that Colonel Sipialef almost laughed. He was a bit drugged, but not so much that Carlisle's offer didn't impress him. It was bizarre, still the Reds did have artillery and Carlisle could have troops. Obviously it would cost him nothing to wait and if the American was willing to pilot him out it would make passage through the Trans-Baikal tunnels easier. "You have my word of course, Captain," he said.

"Good enough," Carlisle said. "I'll put my train ahead of yours."

When Carlisle had gone Colonel Sipialef turned to Graetz. "These Americans," he said wonderingly. "They're God's gift to Asia!"

Carlisle went to his train and told Conners to switch it ahead of the Invincible and prepare to move out, then he walked back to the tower where the officers were waiting for him. Their number had been increased by several Bolshevik officials whose faces were like padlocks.

Carlisle used the Czech captain as an interpreter and when the Red officials heard the message they began to threaten and wave their arms about.

Carlisle did not listen. He was adamant and kept making the Czech, who by now was quite frightened, repeat what he had to say over and over again.

"Tell them," Carlisle said, "that it is the policy of the United States government to protect railway property and insure the passage of passenger and freight trains without obstruction or interruption."

"But they say this train has Russian gold reserves aboard it which are consigned to this station," the Czech captain said.

"Tell them that the policy of the United States government is to protect the railway and insure the passage of trains without obstruction or interruption."

"They say that Sipialef's train isn't a passenger train or a freight train," the worried Czech captain said.

Carlisle's face, hard as basalt, did not change. "Tell them," he said, "that it is the policy of the United States government that trains will pass through this sector without obstruction or interruption. And if the sons of bitches want to tangle with me, I'm ready. My troops are ready. The United States is ready."

The Czech put an artificial smile on his face and relayed the message. Across the yard the American train pulled ahead of Sipialef's and switched onto the same track.

"They want to know if you saw any gold on that train," the Czech captain asked.

"Tell them the United States policy with regard to the internal affairs of the Russian government is one of strict neutrality," Carlisle said.

"But they have information that a train delivering the Russian gold reserves was attacked at Polovina," the Captain said.

"Tell them," Carlisle said, "that our aim is to be of real assistance to all Russians in protecting the necessary traffic movements on the railroad and all shall be treated alike by our forces irrespective of persons, nationality, religion or politics."

By now the Czech captain would have given all he possessed not to be in this unenviable position. His voice had dropped to a pleading whisper. "They ask what religion has to do with it," he said.

"Tell them not a fucking thing," Carlisle said.

The conciliatory smile withered on the Czech captain's face. "I can't translate that, sir," he said.

"Fucking. Screwing. Fornicating. Don't they have a word in Russian for that?"

"Several," the Czech said.

"Then take your pick and tell them that if they start anything with me they'll have the whole United States Army camped here and that our

President, Woodrow Wilson, will spend his summer vacations fishing in Lake Baikal."

Curiously enough the mention of Wilson's name had an effect. Two of the Red officials began arguing with each other. The Japanese officer said his troops would not fire unless fired upon. The Czech captain said that his forces were also neutral, of course. The Reds continued to argue.

"Tell them I've got the train to promise not to fire, that I accept their word also not to fire, and that I'm going out."

Carlisle walked across the yard toward his train without a backward glance.

The Czechs, Japanese and Reds fell silent and watched him go. They saw him signal the Sipialef train. They saw him board his own engine and pull the whistle lanyard three short blasts; then the American train began to move and the Invincible crawled along slowly behind it.

The Red officials looked at each other accusingly, wondering which of them had given the promise not to fire.

Colonel Sipialef and Captain Graetz watched the tower as they passed it; the officers and officials there appeared stunned. They passed the depot where Red troops lay behind their sandbagged emplacements, but not a shot was fired; then they passed out of the Glaskov yard and were on the main line headed toward the Trans-Baikal tunnels with the American pilot train running ahead of them. Sipialef and Graetz turned from the machine gun ports and grinned at each other. "Let's drink to America," Graetz said.

"Does he really intend to pilot us through, Graetz?" Sipialef asked.

"You can depend on it, Colonel."

"But why?"

"Because he conceives it to be his duty," Graetz said. "I know the type very well."

"I'll be interested," Sipialef said.

Carlisle hung on the step of the American engine looking back toward the Invincible. Jud Conners was at the throttle. "They keeping up, Sioux?" he called.

"Yeah. They're riding about two hundred yards behind us."

Carlisle swung into the cab and Conners frowned at him. "I don't like it, Sioux," he said. "I feel like someone has a gun in my back."

"A lot of guns, Jud. Just remember we're neutral."

"That's crap!"

"You have any suggestions?"

"We might try to outrun them."

Carlisle grinned. "You know this track bed, Jud, and they've got two engines as good as ours. And with all the traffic ahead of us we'll be lucky to get twenty miles of clear track at a time."

"Just a suggestion," Conners said. "A bad one."

"I said we're going to pilot them through and that's what we'll do. We'll take them as far as Verkhne-Udinsk."

"I guess there's nothing else to do," Conners said.

"If you think of anything, let me know. I'm open. How far you going to take her?"

"Through the tunnels, then Sawyer is going to spell me."

"All right, I'm going back to get something to eat."

"She's got it waiting for you."

"What?"

"I said she's got your breakfast waiting," Conners yelled. "The Countess."

Carlisle nodded and worked his way back along the tender to the first coach. He slammed the door behind him and beat the cold air out of his coat, then he paused at the first compartment to speak to his American guard.

"You men figure a way to make yourselves look like a full platoon," he said. "I don't care how you do it, but I want you all over this train when we stop. Keep moving, switch around, keep the shades drawn and make some dummies with blankets and your coats. I'll tell the R.R.S.C. men to help you out. And I want a man on the back coach to watch that armored train on our tail. If it moves up on us let me know."

"That's the Invincible, isn't it, Captain?" one of the men asked.

"Right, but don't get any notions."

"Colonel Sipialef's train?" another asked. "The bastard who sacked Pashkova?"

"I don't want any trouble," Carlisle said. "Is that clear? We're on our way home and I don't need any heroes."

Carlisle stopped in the next coach to speak to the Russian Railway Service Corps men who were playing poker in one compartment. He told them to draw the shades when they stopped and to cooperate with the guard detail to make it appear they had more men on board.

"A fat-looking lot of soldiers we'll make," one of the railroad men said.

Carlisle smiled. "Stick out your chins and hold your breath. We'll be in the clear once we get through Verkhne-Udinsk."

When he came into the compartment he shared with Tatiana she had a breakfast of army rations and hot coffee on the table for him. She was seated by the window watching the landscape with a pensive expression and she didn't look around as he sat down.

Carlisle poured himself a cup of coffee. "Have you eaten, Tatiana?" he asked.

"Yes, I have, thank you."

"We're on our way," he said.

"I thought you handled it very well. One of the machine guns was just across from this window."

"I hope you weren't frightened."

She turned from the window, smiling slightly, and shook her head. "I didn't care," she said.

A feeling of terrible frustration balled up in the pit of Carlisle's stomach. He wanted to roar and his cup chattered as he put it down on the table. "I'm sorry about last night," he said.

"You needn't be. I asked for it."

Carlisle's face hardened and took on its mahogany hue. He tried to eat, but couldn't. Tatiana continued to stare out the window. "I wish to hell," Carlisle began, but then his mouth clamped shut.

She turned to him again. "Yes, Jack?"

The cool tone of her voice raised blood in Carlisle's eyes. "I hope to hell I knocked you up," he blurted.

Tatiana frowned at the unfamiliar expression. "What?"

"Made you pregnant!"

"Because you were angry?"

"To keep you, god damn it!"

"Oh," she said and for a time she appeared to consider this. Presently she turned to him and smiled. "I wouldn't mind," she said. "Did you think I would? I've never taken precautions about it, so perhaps it isn't possible. I don't know." She frowned slightly and shook her head. "I really know very little about myself after all. But it's not surprising because I've always been a representative, you see, a representative of my family, of my class, of a certain style of life and I think that's what attracts you to me. Isn't it so, Jack? Will you tell me the truth?"

"I want you," Carlisle growled.

"But how more than you've had me already?"

"I want you with me!"

"In what way with you? I really don't understand."

"As my wife."

"To bear your children, do your clothes, keep your house?"

"Yes, that."

"You'd be in the army, I suppose."

"Of course."

"Then you'd be away a lot."

"That would depend on conditions."

Tatiana nodded and was thoughtful for a time. The sound of the train filled the compartment and Carlisle grew uneasy. "Tatiana," he said humbly, "I love you."

She met his eyes warmly, but her voice was distant and quiet. "I think you love what I represented, Jack, but that's behind me now. You loved it without really knowing what it was. I was something far off in a fairy story; it seems that way to me also. Now, I hardly remember what I was; it depended so much on Albert. But you can't have that person, Jack, because she's gone and I won't cheat you by pretending to be her. Isn't she the one you wanted, Jack? Countess Tatiana Nojine?"

"Yes," he said.

"Wasn't she the one you thought of last night?"

"Yes."

"Could you ever forget her?"

Carlisle frowned, not sure how to answer. In his heart he knew he would never forget Countess Tatiana Nojine as she had come down the staircase of the Aleksander Hotel in Vladivostok, but he sensed the danger of admitting this. To marry her would be an achievement which seemed now to depend on his answer to this question. She didn't want gallantry, she wanted the truth, but he was afraid of it. "I want you as you are, Tatiana," he said. "Just as you are."

She held his eyes, trying to satisfy herself that he meant this. "Not the old Tatiana, but me," she said, "for bedmate, laundrywoman and housekeeper?"

Carlisle grinned flashingly. "You make it sound pretty rough," he said.

"I don't mind, if you mean it."

"I do."

"All right then," she said. "If we get to Vladivostok we can arrange when to marry."

Carlisle went to her side and Tatiana took his hand. "I'll get us to Vlad if I have to harness myself to the coach," he said.

CHAPTER THIRTY-NINE

MARRAKOF's body had been buried in the snow at the base of the cliff over which he'd fallen and for several days thereafter the men were depressed. Slavin and Balashov grew wary of one another. They took opposite sides about common things and if one came over to the other's point of view the other felt tricked and took the side he'd previously opposed.

They tried to cooperate; they meant to agree with one another, but in the search for what was best to do all the variables appeared to bear equal weight. They were used to presenting alternatives and having someone else make the final decision; now it was different. Until Marrakof's death they had not realized how impotent they were without a leader.

They couldn't agree, for instance, what to do with Ira, whether to let him go, hold him hostage, ransom him to the Americans or send him to Kravchenko for trial and punishment, and this disagreement made it impossible for them to act. They conferred endlessly and did nothing.

Then one morning two men were missing. They'd gone off during the night taking a quantity of food and weapons in a sledge. Slavin sent a party of four men to recapture them. This party also failed to return and Balashov blamed Slavin for this. "They were unreliable," he said. "You should have known."

That night the men around the campfires looked at each other with distrust. They were no longer an effective partisan band, but they didn't know how to break it off. No one had the courage to stand up and say, "Brothers we're finished. Let's pack up and go home."

The others might not agree and who knows then what they would do?

They held their tongues. No one was certain which way he'd jump if someone suggested they disband. He would look around quickly to read the faces of the others before he spoke. He'd try to stay in with the majority. No use to risk one's neck for nothing, and it dismayed them to find how afraid and distrustful of each other they had become. This was a new and terrible thing, this silent watchfulness.

Then one afternoon a party of seven mounted men were spotted crossing the ice from Olkhon Island. The partisans snatched their weapons and ran to their prepared positions. They were delighted. They winked congratulations at each other for the alacrity with which they'd responded to the alarm. It was like old times. They laid their cartridges out and sighted their rifles on the distant figures, which they assumed were a White patrol. They would have just as soon had an army marching toward them; anything was better than the demoralizing inactivity which they'd suffered.

Balashov and Slavin lay side by side in their ice trench observing the riders through field glasses.

"Czechs, I think," Balashov said.

"No, wait."

"Damn your eyes, I know Czechs! Only Czechs have such fine horses as that."

"Let them come."

"Of course let them come! We'd need cannon to hit them at this distance! Have you lost your mind, or what?"

Ira and Maryenka had been ordered to remain in their cave, but pulling the hanging aside they could see the patrol trotting over the ice. They were well outfitted and rode in good formation and Ira asked himself what he would do if they turned out to be Americans.

"Their horses are ice-clad," Maryenka whispered.

Ira nodded. The men were coming in rifle range and he still couldn't identify them.

"If they're Americans — " he said.

Maryenka read his thought and clutched his arm, but before she could speak a shot rang out. The patrol broke formation and scattered. Slavin was on his feet roaring and waving his arms.

"They're Kravchenko men," Maryenka said. "Slavin has recognized them," and she sat down abruptly, looking pale.

"Are you feeling all right, Maryenka?" Ira asked and he knelt beside her.

"Yes," she said. But she was heavy and weak. The infant kicked in her belly and she closed her eyes. "Will the time ever come?" she thought. "Will it ever, ever come?" But she wasn't sure what time she wanted to come.

The patrol from Kravchenko led their warm-smelling, chuffing horses up the trail to the caves and grumbled curses at the partisans for firing on them.

The patrol leader went into a cave to confer with Slavin and Balashov, the rest came into the cave Maryenka and Ira occupied and helped themselves to tea and bread. Maryenka listened to them and translated what they said for Ira.

"They're demolitions men," she said. "They've been ordered to take a position on the track this side of Verkhne-Udinsk. We're ordered to help."

Then she went very pale and clutched her abdomen. Ira took her in his arms.

"When?" he asked.

"At once," she said. "We're to go into position tonight."

"Where?"

"They don't say. It hasn't been chosen."

"Come with me to Slavin," Ira said. "I know the track well. I know how they can avoid the Americans."

Maryenka resisted, but he pulled her along to the next cave and burst in on the meeting of the three men there. Balashov rose, his expression angry, and waved them out, but Ira would not be intimidated. "I've come to help you," he said. "Tell them, Maryenka."

Maryenka hesitated and Ira shook her shoulder. "Tell them! Tell them I know all the American positions and how to avoid them. Tell them I'll do whatever I can, but in exchange they've got to let us get out. Make them understand, Maryenka."

Slavin and Balashov in the meantime had identified Ira to the Kravchenko leader, who was looking at Ira in a curious, not unfriendly way. Maryenka began to speak, but the Kravchenko man interrupted her. Again she looked distressed and turned to Ira.

"What is it?" he asked.

"The Americans have gone," she said.

"Gone?"

"They're gone from Verkhne-Udinsk. He says there are no American guards on the railroad anymore."

"He must be mistaken!" Ira said.

Maryenka spoke again at length to the leader, whose name was Berezkin; he was a captain and had a round, tolerant face and city manners. He listened to Maryenka patiently, nodding to encourage her, then he took a notebook from his jacket pocket and read from it to her.

"What does he say?" Ira asked.

"The Americans left Verkhne-Udinsk last week. All the interventionist forces are leaving. He plans to occupy the American position at Tataurovo."

"Tell him I know Tataurovo, that I was in command of the troops there, and can help him. Convince him to carry us along, Maryenka. If we can get to Verkhne we'll still be able to get out."

Berezkin listened attentively and often smiled when he looked at Ira. He had a pug nose and mild gray eyes and there was something boyish about him which appealed to Ira and raised his hopes.

When Maryenka had concluded Berezkin nodded, then Slavin took him aside and the two men spoke quietly at great length. Berezkin frequently looked at Maryenka as he listened to Slavin, then without warning he came to Maryenka, embraced her heartily and kissed her on both cheeks. He shook Ira's hand, rattling on at a great pace, and Maryenka explained that they were being congratulated for Bogoloff's death.

"He'll take us along, then," Ira said.

"Yes," Maryenka said. "He thinks we're Bolsheviks."

That night the partisans, reinforced by Berezkin and his men, set out down the lake toward Mysovaya. Because of her condition Maryenka rode a sled behind one of the horses and Ira walked along beside her.

He felt free and good and sometimes he rode the runners behind Maryenka, who was wrapped in furs so just the tip of her nose and her eyes were showing. Her presence warmed Ira like a charcoal fire and made him think of upland summers in California with the heavy scent of golden grass where one could lie staring into the measureless sky with the sun beating into one's face and the tang of salt water on the breeze from the bay. He thought: "My God! All that hospitable, harmless landscape, where we can roam for hours unhindered, half naked, nut brown, happy."

He tried to tell Maryenka some of it. They'd carry a bottle of warm red wine, cheese and French bread, oil and garlic dressing, pimentos and olives. Their fingers and mouths would be stained with wine and oil and their baby would sleep nearby in a bower of grass.

"And the sea there is warm," she said.

"Oh, yes. With miles of sandy beach and tide pools filled with sea anemones, kelp, little fish, small crabs and kids with sticks poking at them."

Maryenka laughed happily, but Ira liked the uplands better, where they could be alone and make love in the sun.

To the partisans what Berezkin told them meant that the conflict was coming to an end. They could afford now to look ahead to peaceful times, to being reunited with their families. They would take up their lives once more and now with ice in their beards they dreamed of summer days. Like Ira they felt the sun in their hearts. They thought of berry hunts and children and loafy wives and of somnambulant afternoons in the forests bordering Lake Baikal. It was good. The winter war was over.

Berezkin, having given his horse to pull Maryenka's sled, led the column on foot with Slavin at his side. A patrol on horseback had gone ahead with Balashov, who knew the country well. Others rode protectively on the flanks.

"There may be a midwife at Tataurovo," Slavin was saying, for the subject had turned to Maryenka.

Berezkin thought not. Anyone with any medical knowledge had been pulled into service. Doctors, imprisoned by their calling, were kept under guard and worked around the clock. Veterinarians had been raised to surgeons and while their shaking hands fumbled the unfamiliar instruments they dreamed of escape. There were too many refugees, too many wounded and ill. It was all a bloody incompetent business and in the midst of so much death a new life would be meaningless. "There's a good hospital in Irkutsk," Berezkin said. "I have a special friend there who would look after her."

"The American wants to take her with him."

"He can't take her all the way to Vladivostok if she's overdue," Berezkin said.

"You can't expect him to go with her to Irkutsk."

"What kind of man is he, then?"

"There's a hospital in Verkhne-Udinsk if it comes to that," Slavin said.

Berezkin looked glum and shook his head. He wanted to send Maryenka to Irkutsk as a way of getting a message to a nurse he'd met and fallen in love with there. "She'd be well looked after in Irkutsk," he said.

"It's her business after all."

"We'll see."

They reached Mysovaya at dawn and there were no Americans there. When Ira actually saw their abandoned encampment he realized that he'd been clinging to the hope that not all of them had gone. D Company headquarters had been at Mysovaya. There had been three line officers, one medical officer, one dental officer, and a hundred and seventy enlisted men housed in boxcars, but they were gone.

Ira still hoped there would be some Americans in Verkhne-Udinsk, a rear guard detachment, somebody who could help them through. Perhaps he was worrying about nothing. All the same he wished there were some Americans.

With several armed men at his back Berezkin marched into the Mysovaya depot to see if he could make contact with his commander in Irkutsk. Slavin came out presently with a mug of hot tea and a piece of bread for Maryenka. "They're well fixed in there," he said. "Captain Berezkin is onto Irkutsk by telegraph."

Before Maryenka could drink her tea Berezkin burst out of the depot. He looked excited and barked a peremptory order which brought the men running.

Berezkin came to Slavin unfolding a map and the two men conferred over it anxiously. Slavin turned and spoke to Maryenka urgently.

"They want to know are you familiar with the bridges at Tataurovo," Maryenka said to Ira.

"Tell them yes."

"And the defensive positions there."

"Yes, all that."

Berezkin and Slavin both spoke at once and Maryenka's eyes widened with apprehension.

"What is it?" Ira demanded.

"Colonel Sipialef," she said. "His train, the Invincible, has to be stopped. It's coming from Irkutsk, having stolen the Russian gold reserve."

The first thing which struck Ira was that Sipialef was west of them and not at Verkhne-Udinsk. "Who has control of Verkhne?" he demanded.

Maryenka asked Berezkin, then told Ira that the Japanese were in military control and that a provisional government held the city.

"Are they Reds?" he asked. "If so, they wouldn't bother you. The Japanese have a hospital there."

Maryenka shook her head obstinately. "I won't go without you," she said, for she already knew what Ira was thinking.

Ira took her face in his hands and tried to keep his voice light. "Don't be a fool. I know the bridge at Tataurovo. I can help with that and join you in Verkhne. I'm sure as hell not going to let Sipialef and that gang disrupt things while you're there. Now you must be reasonable, Maryenka. Please, for your sake and mine, and Harry's kid, tell them."

Her resistance weakened slightly and Ira kissed her on the forehead. "Ira, please —"

"No, no, no," he said soothingly. "You know I'm right, now please make it clear to them. I want Slavin to take you to Verkhne and in exchange for that I'll help at the bridge."

"Why can't you take me?"

"Because I know all about the bridge and because I'm selfish. I want a chance to get back at Sipialef."

Berezkin grew impatient and started away, but Slavin caught his arm and asked Maryenka what Ira wanted. When she told him Slavin looked at Ira and nodded. How much he had agreed to Ira did not know, but enough. So they started toward Tataurovo.

When they reached the bridge Maryenka was exhausted and, though she still objected to leaving, it had become increasingly clear that her child was due.

"There's a hospital there," Ira said, "so you're going for Harry's kid, understand?"

"Yes," she said, but her eyes were troubled.

"That's the thing to keep in mind. You'll be safe and looked after there"

"And you'll come soon?"

"All we have to do is mine the bridge. Two days, maybe three, and I'll be there. Slavin will look after you. Now go along because they're waiting for me."

"In three days," she said.

"Yes, because I love you and Harry or Harriet, as the case may be, and I'm anxious to get you home to sunny California."

She smiled from her place on the sled, then he kissed her cold face and signaled Slavin to go on. Maryenka looked back as Slavin led the horse and sled toward Verkhne-Udinsk and at the last minute she waved, then she was gone through the black stand of trees.

Ira felt the tug of her leaving and to make it endurable he turned at once to the task at hand. He showed Berezkin over the defenses which he'd helped lay out for C Company and was pleased when Berezkin nodded his approval. Together with two of Berezkin's demolitions men they inspected the bridge and Berezkin issued instructions that the river was to be mined so no force could attack across the ice.

The partisans and Berezkin's men set to work at once. Berezkin spoke too rapidly for Ira to understand him but he could tell by the activities of the men what was going on. Berezkin's demolitions men planted dynamite charges on the bridge and the river ice, concealing them expertly. Three Czech trains carrying troops came down the line that day and though these slowed warily at the bridge and sent a walking patrol ahead there was not so much as a footprint to alarm them.

By midafternoon both the bridge and the river had been mined and there was nothing to do but wait in their concealed positions for the Invincible.

The teplushkas which had housed C Company were gone. So was the Snorter. All that remained to commemorate the American presence at Tataurovo was the toilet pits, which had been filled, and the machine gun pits, which had not been. Even Dunc Ferber's sacred barbed wire had been rolled up and accounted for.

Ira took Berezkin and Balashov to a dugout on the hillside above the river which gave them a good view of the bridge. He indicated this was where his company had positioned one of their 37 mm cannon. Berezkin seemed to understand. Balashov didn't seem to care; he sat down in one corner and pulled his coat collar up around his ears and was soon fast asleep. The demolitions men installed three detonators in the dugout, one for the bridge and two for the river charges.

It began to snow lazily. Berezkin looked at his watch. Ira looked at his own and wondered how soon he should begin worrying in earnest about Slavin's return. It was forty-six miles to Verkhne-Udinsk and back. Slavin had been gone nearly five hours.

Ira forced his thoughts in another direction. It was growing dark, but from his place on the hill he could see over the river to the snow-laden meadow from which the Cossacks had entrained. He smiled remembering Carson and the mixers and he thought of Carlisle, wondering if they'd meet in Vlad and how that meeting would go. He wanted to see Carlisle's reaction to Harry and Maryenka's baby. It made him smile to think what it might be, one of those big raw grins or a sudden, face-crabbing scowl of bewilderment. But this wouldn't matter because when he told the Sioux that Maryenka and he were getting married it would sure set him back. Ira almost laughed imagining Carlisle's big face twisting out a reaction to this news. It would damned near kill Carlisle to think he'd stepped into Austin's shoes, but he had. That's exactly what he'd done and Carlisle was just going to have to concede the point.

It surprised Ira to find how important Carlisle's reaction to all this was to him, more important even than his family's would be, but of course they didn't know what had gone into it. They'd never know. "The damned Sioux is almost like a brother to me," he thought. "Maybe we'll name the next one Jack."

It was dark and the snow was falling thickly now. "Going to make it hard to hide our footprints," Ira thought; then he dozed off, sleeping deeply with his chin on his chest. He was jarred awake by another presence in the dugout. He didn't know how long he'd slept. He reached for the pistol Berezkin had given him, but a face loomed up, close by. It was Slavin.

"What is it?" Ira demanded.

Slavin struck a light and put it down against the dugout wall.

Balashov was gone. Slavin and Berezkin looked at Ira, then grinned at each other.

"Tell me!" Ira said.

Berezkin made a cradle of his arms and rocked it.

"The baby!" Ira shouted. "When? Is it born already? What happened?"

Slavin held up his hand and shook it.

"Not yet?"

"Nyet."

"When?" Ira demanded. "Is she in the hospital? Nurse? Nurse? Doctor?"

"Da," Berezkin said and he nodded his head vigorously.

Ira wanted to dance. He jumped up, banging his head on the ceiling of the shallow dugout. "Christ, that's great!" he yelped and clutched his ringing head. "That's great!" And tears of pain filled his eyes.

Slavin had a note from Maryenka which he thrust into Ira's hand.

Ira huddled down in one corner of the dugout, pulled his overcoat over his head to make a tent and snapped a match to read Maryenka's note. His fingers were awkward as he unfolded the paper and the match went out before he could read the first words. He struck another after the paper was open and read quickly:

DEAR FRIEND IRA,
Slavin has brought me to the Japanese military hospital where they have kindly taken me in as my labor started almost at once we reached Verkhne-Udinsk. They know me here and instructions have been left for us by Mr. Silverman. Please hurry to me.

                                        MARYENKA AUSTIN

The match burned out in Ira's fingertips. Her handwriting appeared to shake with pain. He could feel her suffering in it.

Ira trembled in the darkness under his coat and prayed for Harry Austin's kid. For his kid and Harry's and Maryenka's. They were all in it together, the three of them. He felt Austin's close presence in the sheltering darkness of the coat. "It's going to be Harry's kid," he said aloud as though this would make it so. "Yes," he said, "it is."

He heard Berezkin talking urgently to Slavin and came out from under the coat.

A messenger had come from Mysovaya to say that the Invincible had cleared the Trans-Baikal tunnels, but was preceded by a pilot train bearing American flags.

Berezkin wanted to know if this could be true. He rattled away at Ira, who did his best to understand.

"An American train?" he asked.

Slavin pantomimed the position of the trains on the track.

"Amerikanski!" Berezkin declared.

Ira shook his head adamantly. "Nyet! Nyet Amerikanski!" His mind was racing. The Americans were gone. It was a ruse. They wouldn't have pulled out of Verkhne leaving someone behind them. Sipialef was using the flags to bull his way past the Czechs. But Ira wasn't certain. He was damned uncertain. Perhaps there was an American train coming down the line, but it sure as hell had nothing to do with Sipialef. He kept shaking his head and Berezkin glared at him. Ira wondered about the note Silverman had left and what the instructions were. Perhaps they said something about this last train coming out. "Nyet Sipialef!" he said and he drew his finger across his throat to indicate he sure as hell wasn't going to let Sipialef get across the Tataurovo bridge while Maryenka was in Verkhne-Udinsk. "Nyet!"

Berezkin and Slavin scowled at him uncertainly, then Berezkin shrugged and sat down to wait.

« 2 »

When Maryenka's own belief that her child could be Austin's had gone she had clung desperately to Ira's. His assurances and his faith had become more important to her than what her own body told her.

Now she was alone.

She stared up at the paste-gray ceiling of the delivery room trying desperately to believe what common sense denied and the identity of her child seemed to depend more on Ira's existence than on her own. By his faith he was more its father than any other man could have been.

In the flashes, when the pains came, she knew Ira was right, that the pains were Austin's child, but when there was no pain she knew it could not be as she hoped. For hours she swung from one conviction to the other, condemning her own weakness for endangering her child. It was Harry's. It was Ira's. It was theirs.

As the pain increased Maryenka found relief in opening her eyes and gulping draughts of light as though it was air, and in these moments she saw the huddled figures of the Japanese doctor and old Senya, a midwife who was there to attend her. She began to breathe light through her eyes, catching and holding it in ever faster gasps until there came a flash so pure that she closed her eyes, her mouth, her ears and all her senses in an attempt to hold it, but something terrible broke and she cried out and the light vanished in a wail from her open mouth.

When at last she opened her eyes Maryenka was very weak. It was dark in the room, but there was a crack of light through the partially open door. She stared at this for a time, trying to understand what it was. It was a chill yellow light from the hospital corridor. The smells and sounds of the overcrowded place came into being for her and Maryenka knew she had given birth.

At first she was afraid and denied this, but her body in flat lassitude, exhaustion and dull pain told her it was true. For a time she considered this.

Somewhere there was her child; somewhere this new being, this answer to all her months of desperation existed.

She did not want it.

No.

Maryenka closed her eyes and tears flowed down her cheeks.

Then she was struck by a thought which caused her to gasp and sit up. The child was dead! She'd killed it with her denial! It had been stillborn! They were keeping this from her! It did not exist!

Maryenka called out: "Is anyone there, please!"

There was no answer.

The child was dead! It didn't matter whose child it was! What could be more terrible?

"Please! Is anyone there?"

The anguish of her own voice terrified her. "Oh, it must be alive!" she thought.

"Please."

Then old Senya came to the door. There was a smile on her face and she carried a bundle in her arms. She came through the gloom to the side of the bed, chirking and smacking her lips, her gray eyes gazing fondly at the infant which she pressed into Maryenka's arms.

Maryenka took the weight and knew it to be alive. She lay back and waves of emotion broke in her eyes. She couldn't stop crying. She couldn't see, but there was a smile on her face to tell the old woman it was all right.

"I'm all right," she said at last.

"Of course you are, my dear," old Senya replied.

Maryenka asked that the door be opened to give more light, then she looked at the child's face with no thought as to who might have fathered it, and the pinched knot of human features, the wide mouth, tiny nose and clenched eyes, gave her no clue.

From her place by the door old Senya watched Maryenka meet her child and was as pleased as if she herself had made it. When Maryenka looked toward her Senya smiled and made the sign of the cross. "A boy, may God preserve him," she whispered.

Maryenka looked again at her baby. "His name is Ira Austin," she said quietly. Then she bared her full breast and after a moment the groping infant began to suck.

CHAPTER FORTY

THE trains which transported the 27th Infantry Regiment and its collateral units out of Siberia had fallen into line with the other evacuation trains for the tedious journey to Vladivostok. It was not simply a matter of boarding a train and chugging down the line. There were priorities. There were breakdowns. There were problems of food and fuel and these, though not as desperate as they were west of Baikal, were great.

It was rare indeed to cover a distance of two hundred miles in a twenty-four-hour period and when this happened it usually meant that the train would be shunted off on a siding and left standing for one or two days as though to punish its occupants for the heady speed they had previously enjoyed.

Colonel Spaeth and his staff tried to estimate their arrival in Vladivostok, but these estimates were revised daily. Their initial assumption that the distance could be covered in two weeks rose to three, then four.

"We should reach Vlad about the twentieth of February," Major Bentham said as he scowled down at the much-scratched-over travel schedule on his knees.

"All right, Charlie, see if you can get that through to Graves," Colonel Spaeth said wearily.

In the beginning they'd tried to hold their trains in a group along the line, but this proved to be unfeasible. The American trains occupied so much of the line that if a priority train came through, a hospital train, for instance, it meant that the whole American contingent would be left on a siding then have to buck its way back into the line, which meant endless telegrams, demands, threats and sometimes bribes to the assortment of Japanese, Czechs and Russians who controlled the traffic.

To minimize these frustrations Major Bentham suggested they leap-frog the command down the line, taking advantage of as much track space as appeared, with the units going ahead waiting for those in the rear to catch up before proceeding.

Colonel Spaeth accepted the suggestion and while there was no way of knowing if this increased their speed it gave an illusion of movement. Each of the trains was made as self-sufficient as possible. Flatcars were sand-bagged and 37 mm guns placed on them. The water-cooled Browning machine guns froze if they were exposed to the air, so they mounted Vickers machine guns on top of the coaches and stood half-hour watches around the clock.

When they stopped at a siding they ran defensive exercises and train drills to keep the men alert. A motorcycle patrol was organized to carry messages from one train to another and these men, who always traveled in pairs along the trakt, came back with harrowing stories of what they'd witnessed there.

Engine breakdowns, derailments and wrecks constantly put trains out of service leaving the passengers to find another way out and there was no other way except the trakt, which was lined with frozen corpses.

At first the passengers of a stalled train would sit waiting for relief, praying it would come, that repairs would be made or that their cars would be attached to another train. They would stay by their cars for days until the need for food would drive them out and they'd walk down the line begging to be taken in.

Officers' wives with infants in their arms passed down the track with tears frozen to their cheeks.

Frost bitten, half-starved soldiers roamed the right of way too apathetic to draw their weapons and kill for what they needed, not knowing whom, in fact, to kill.

There was violence, particularly when a useless engine had to be removed from the track to clear the way for those behind. This operation was performed by one of several armored engines protected by troops whose one instruction was to fire into any group which opposed clearing the track. It was a ruthlessly surgical business.

The troops, armed with machine guns, had learned through experience to begin firing at the first voiced objection. It was no good temporizing, no good listening to pleas for mercy. The machine guns spoke to clear a passage for those who came behind. In that alone they were being merciful, splattering a hot arc of blood, flesh and bone over the snow.

All down the line the people on trains, who knew what was in store for them if their engine failed, did not pray to God; they prayed to their locomotives.

At the watering stations, which were more often frozen than not, with ice extruding from the pipes and the pumps burst, dark, muffled figures could be seen passing buckets of snow up to the locomotive boiler, working urgently like men bailing a leaky ship. Their lives depended on a balance of fire and water. If the engine went dry the heat would burst the pipes and they would be stranded. If the fire went out the boilers would freeze. They worked and prayed to keep their locomotives going and through the frosted ice on the windows of their trains they could see the trakt and what would become of them if they failed.

The sluggish parade on the trakt moved eastward over the trampled snow on sledges, horseback and on foot. Skeleton regiments numbed by the cold, their feet wrapped in wads of dead men's clothing, passed over the trakt as in a dream and always there was the plaintive song, the "Charaban."

Artillerymen dragging their dismantled guns were too weak to reassemble and fire them had they been asked to do so and they were too habit-ridden to cut them loose. They clustered around the sledges like pall-bearers, so intent on saving the guns that possibly they could not have gone on without them.

Convoys of freed prisoners, deserters, peasants, officials, men, women and children, too weak to whine or prey upon one another, shuffled eastward in the vague hope that somewhere relief would appear.

A Cossack officer, bolt upright in the saddle, failed to clear the ice from the nostrils of his horse. Suddenly the animal began to shudder. The Cossack slid from the saddle but his horse reared and broke away, shaking its head, pawing the air until it fell, furrowing a trail in the deep snow as it kicked and suffocated its way toward one of the American trains stopped on a siding.

The Cossack stood at the edge of the trakt. He saw the train and started toward it, wading waist deep in the untrammeled snow. When he reached his dead horse the Cossack stripped off the saddle and bridle, threw them over his shoulder, and after studying the train a moment he retraced his steps to the trakt.

From the windows of their trains the American troops witnessed this panoramic tragedy and tried to alleviate it. They gave their rations away and took children into the cars. In a short time there were over sixty children ranging in age from three months to sixteen years on the American trains. Women slipped aboard at night when the trains were on sidings and offered themselves in exchange for passage down the line. Men tried to hide on the rods and axles and between the cars.

Major Bentham issued a strict order putting a stop to this. He could not turn out the children without a mutiny, but he concentrated them in two cars and prohibited any more coming aboard.

All adults found on the train were put off at the nearest village and court-martial action was threatened for anyone bringing refugees aboard. The men hardened themselves. In some coaches they blanketed the windows, or drew the shades if they still existed. In others they avoided looking out the windows, or if they did so they thought of the people as images on film being projected from a booth by a mechanism they didn't fully understand, black and white images flickering past their windows to while away the tedious hours.

Colonel Spaeth sat in his compartment with a book open on his lap. He didn't know the title of it. There were several to choose from and it didn't matter. Nothing he could do would improve the situation or hasten their progress toward Vladivostok. He couldn't mend communications or force priorities. They were measuring motion and resources against the weather and he couldn't change the weather.

But it hurt him all the same. It hurt him to know that every decent human impulse was a threat to their survival and to know that this was the lesson being taught his men. A man caught sharing food from their stores was to be tried and imprisoned, so also a man who brought a starving refugee aboard.

One car had been set aside as a jail and there were seventeen American soldiers in it, all but one of them for attempted acts of charity. The other, Private Carson of C Company, had to be held separately after being surprised in a boxcar having unnatural sex relations with a Kazak girl. Carson's defense was that he wasn't a "mixer."

"I ain't goin' to have no brats by them Greasers. Not me! Not like some of these guys done! I ain't leavin' none of mine here, not a bit! She wanted a ride and I promised her a ride. She's the one wanted it! There's a lot of mixers on this son of a bitch train, but I ain't one of them!"

When they put the girl off at the next village Carson grew violent. "You bastards makin' a liar out of a white man!" he bellowed. "I promised her a ride. You all makin' a liar of a white man!"

Colonel Spaeth turned the unread page of his book. The train was grinding along at four or five miles an hour. He wondered how many illegitimate children his troops might have left behind. He wondered how many of these would survive, how many bastard American, Czech, Japanese, Chinese, British, French, Polish, Austrian, German, Italian, Canadian kids left behind in Siberia would survive. If he looked out the window he wondered if he might not see Peg and Billy and Alice stumbling along the trakt.

He didn't look out. The shade was drawn.

Words from the open book on his knees swam up mistily into his vision:

He was forthwith conveyed to the nearest hospital, and there pronounced to be still living, although in an asphyctic condition. After some hours he revived, recognized individuals of his acquaintance, and, in broken sentences, spoke of his agonies in the grave.

Spaeth looked at the spine of the book, then cast it aside. *The Tales of Edgar Allan Poe,* for Christ's sake.

Some men in the car ahead were singing:

There's a long, long trail a-winding
Into the land of my dreams,
Where the nightingale is singing
And the white moon beams . . .

They'd gone through their whole long repertoire and had begun to repeat it. "Sweet Rosie O'Grady," "A Bicycle Built for Two," "The Bowery," "Red Wing," "Keep the Home Fires Burning," "Over There," "I Didn't Raise My Boy to Be a Soldier."

Just a song at twilight
When the lights are low
And the flickering shadows
Softly come and go . . .

Yes, they sang to avoid the flickering shadows, to avoid the looks on the faces of those in the snow beyond, the large imploring eyes, the awful recognition by persons on foot and freezing that their lives were of no consequence to whose who were riding and warm.

And mostly they sang to avoid the mournful "Charaban."

The regiment passed through Chita without incident and took the Amur line. Several Americans of the Russian Railway Service Corps and some Red Cross people were taken aboard.

Captain Cloak picked up a file of dispatches which had collected at this point. He came into Spaeth's compartment after supper. "Here's a piece of luck, Colonel," he said. "R.R.S.C. says Carlisle has cleared Irkutsk. He's on the last train out."

"Good, Ben," Spaeth said. "Any news from Verkhne?"

"No, sir. Sorry."

"Well, that's good about the Sioux."

"He'll make it out, sir," Cloak said.

"Sure he will."

"I mean Leverett, sir."

"I hope you're right, Ben," Spaeth said.

« 2 »

Two days after Carlisle left Irkutsk, Admiral Kolchak's coach arrived in Glaskov station under the protection of the Allied flags.

A detachment of one hundred Red guards was drawn up at the station to receive him.

Admiral Kolchak, the few remaining members of his staff, and Madame Timireva had been confined to their coach for over two months since leaving Omsk. Food and fuel to heat the coach had always been in short supply. The quarters were cramped and each day brought news of fresh defections and delays. Now they were defenseless and all that stood between them and the Red guards was the flimsy directive left behind by the Allied High Commissioners:

"The Allied High Commissioners declare that all measures must be taken to ensure, as far as it is humanly possible to do so, the personal safety of Admiral Kolchak."

The occupants of the coach stared out the windows at the dismal yard. One hour passed. Then another. Their meager detachment of Czech guards were posted around the coach. Darkness fell, but with it came a rising hope that this delay like all the others was only temporary, that they would be allowed to proceed.

Admiral Kolchak smiled encouragingly at Madame Timireva, who was dressed in the uniform of the Volunteer Nurses Corps. "They are going to let us pass," he said quietly.

"Yes, of course," she said.

Then, at six p.m. Colonel Rakatin, of Kolchak's personal staff, came into the compartment. He was pale and his voice trembled as he spoke. "Your excellency," he said, "the Czech guard is about to stand down. Orders have come, through headquarters of the Czechoslovak Army Corps, to turn your excellency over to the local authorities."

Admiral Kolchak's expression did not change. "So, the Allies have betrayed me," he said calmly.

Colonel Rakatin glanced toward Madame Timireva.

"I will accompany you, Aleksandr," she said.

"Have you informed Papelyaev?"

"I'll do so at once, your excellency," Rakatin replied.

"Tell the others they are released. And thank you, Colonel."

Rakatin saluted and left the compartment with tears in his eyes. Minutes later there was a minor panic as the officers released by Kolchak ripped off their epaulets and jumped from the windows and doors of the coach in a final attempt to flee before the Red guards closed in. Others remained in their seats, too proud, too weary or too fatalistic to avoid arrest. Among these was Colonel Rakatin.

Victor Pepelyaev joined Admiral Kolchak and Madame Timireva in their compartment. The officer in charge of the detachment of Czech guards appeared at the door and when Kolchak insisted he repeat General Janin's order he did so in a faltering, shamefaced way. Admiral Kolchak took Timireva's arm and they left the coach with Pepelyaev and were met outside by an escort of Red guards.

Kolchak glanced at the Allied flags which decorated the side of his coach; a slightly sardonic smile twisted the corners of his lips, then he fell in with the escort, which guided the prisoners through the yard.

They crossed the frozen Angara River on foot. The torches of the escorting Red guards cast long shadows on the pale ice. Halfway across, Admiral Kolchak's boot went through a weak place in the ice and one of the Red guards steadied him.

"Merci," Kolchak said and once again he smiled.

On the opposite bank a staff car and a lorry with a cavalry escort received them. Admiral Kolchak and his Prime Minister were put in the staff car while Timireva shared the cab of the lorry with the driver. Twenty minutes later they entered the Irkutsk jail, a vast stone building on the bank of the frozen Ushakovka River in the northeastern section of the city.

At Glaskov the banners of nations whose representatives had promised to protect Aleksandr Kolchak were stripped from the sides of the empty coach and used as the railroad yardmen saw fit. Some were cut into strips for foot wrappings; others found their way into the waste bins, where they were used by mechanics to wipe their greasy hands, and in a matter of hours one could not have distinguished these rags from any other.

‹ 3 ›

The Czech guards on the Trans-Baikal tunnels saw the American flags on the engine and waved Conners through without hesitation. If they had doubts about the Invincible these remained unexpressed.

There had been frantic wires from Irkutsk demanding the Invincible be sidetracked until an investigating committee could ascertain whether or not it had been involved in the piracy of the Russian gold reserves, but Carlisle had stopped at Port Baikal and again at Kultuk to wire ahead for a free track and the Czechs, whose last troop trains had gone through that day, weren't interested in provoking a fight. Their orders were to wait on station for the arrival of a Major Hassek and the Czech rear guard still at Irkutsk and then to pull out. Only the Red Cross and hospital evacuation trains had priority over the traffic then on the line.

When they had cleared the tunnels Dave Sawyer relieved Conners, who joined Carlisle and Tatiana in their compartment. The two men were teaching Tatiana the finer points of draw poker, a game which Conners insisted every woman should know, when their train was flagged off the track at Murinskaya. Carlisle snatched his coat and went out to see why they had been stopped. The Invincible, its two heavy engines panting, came onto the siding behind them and Captain Graetz ran across the main track to the depot where Carlisle was conferring with the local railroad guards.

From the compartment window Tatiana and Conners watched the men on the station platform. Graetz waved his arms about and seemed to be objecting violently to the delay. Carlisle turned on him suddenly and appeared to bark into his face. Graetz fell back a step; one hand dropped to his holster, at which Carlisle advanced firing volleys of words into his face with such force that Graetz continued backing away until he reached the end of the platform and dropped to the ground trying desperately to maintain his balance and his dignity.

This action, silent through their window, was so comic that Tatiana and Conners laughed. "The Sioux has more firepower in his mouth than Graetz has in that holster," Conners said.

"Have you known Jack long, Mr. Conners?" she asked.

Conners shuffled the cards as he spoke. "Just while he was in Irkutsk, but I've worked with men like him all my life, railroad men."

Tatiana asked what distinguished railroad men from others and a twinkle appeared in Conners' eyes. He shuffled the cards once more, then dealt them off the top of the pack in perfect order from ace to deuce. "Well, for one thing they can't get off the track," he said. "They're married to it and they love it. They're tough. They're loners. They know one thing and that's all they'll ever know. They're a narrow gauge group, by and large. You can kill them, but you can't hurt them. They're happiest when they've got a problem they can handle with their fists. That's a railroad man and a soldier too, I guess."

Conners laid out the rest of the cards, then began to shuffle again.

"I'm not a problem that can be solved with firsts," Tatiana said presently.

"I thought not," Conners said.

"But I fear I am a problem," Tatiana said with a sigh.

"We're all jigsaw puzzles," Conners said. "You know those pictures all cut up that you put together again."

"Oh, yes."

"And there's always one or two pieces missing."

"Inevitably."

"Annoying," Conners said.

They saw Carlisle crossing the track toward their train and presently he came in, removed his coat and hung it up.

Conners recognized the look of belligerent accomplishment in Carlisle's eyes. "What's happening?" he asked.

"A hospital express coming from Polovina," he said. "It has priority, so we'll have to wait until it goes through."

"Graetz didn't like it."

"No, he didn't," Carlisle said.

"But you put him in his place."

Carlisle nodded and sat down.

"What happened at Polovina?"

"They say the gold train was attacked."

"I'll bet you four bits I know who did it," Conners said.

"Somebody will catch up with him someday," Carlisle said.

"I suppose you're right."

To pass the time they played cards, but with no particular interest. The shades on the empty compartment windows were drawn and the guards rotated themselves around trying to make it appear there was a strong detachment on the train, but after four hours this attempted ruse wore thin and one of the guards came to Carlisle. "I think they've got us counted by now, Captain," he said. "We've done everything but come out in black-face and those damned Cossacks are beginning to laugh."

"All right," Carlisle said. "You'd better stop it. Just keep one man on watch."

The three engines idling on the siding clanked and sighed. The waiting grew oppressive and Carlisle checked his watch wondering if they'd reach Tataurovo while there was still daylight. He wanted to see the place one last time.

Then they heard a train coming down the line, moving fast. Carlisle got into his coat. "That must be her," he said. "I'll go forward and help Sawyer get us back on the track."

The big train thundered through, shaking the compartment window, its cars booming as they went by. The coaches were marked with red crosses but these were covered with frozen mud and hardly visible.

Conners looked at Tatiana and his eyes narrowed with a glint of good-natured shrewdness. "I bet you'd like to be on that one," he said.

"Why do you say that?" Tatiana demanded.

Conners' smile broadened. "Oh, because I'd rather be on it myself and the way you watched it go by made me think you would too."

"Perhaps because I'd be more useful on a hospital train than I am here," she said.

"Maybe that's it," Conners said.

Carlisle and Dave Sawyer, a gaunt, pipe-chewing man of fifty, whose favorite subject was the virtues of San Antonio, Texas, stood beside their engine as the hospital train cleared through. "You ought to settle there, Sioux," Sawyer yelled over the clattering sound of the wheels. "It's your kind of place! I know you'd like it!"

The last car on the hospital train went by, leaving Sawyer's words suspended in relative quiet.

"I've seen it," Carlisle said.

"Friendly people, nice climate. Plenty of opportunity."

"You're a one-man Chamber of Commerce, Dave."

"Nothing wrong with that, is there?"

"I'll check the switch. When you get to the bridge at Tataurovo slow down, will you? In fact I'll ride down with you if you can give San Antone a rest."

"Glad to have your company, Sioux. But I can't make any promises. A man is where his heart is."

"I suppose."

Five minutes later they were once again on the main track headed toward Verkhne-Udinsk with the Invincible trailing them two hundred yards behind.

‹ 4 ›

Berezkin knew that the best way to stop a train with the fighting capacity of the Invincible was to catch it dead center on the bridge and drop it in the river. It had to be done properly or not at all.

But he could not anticipate how the Invincible would behave. If it was alarmed and stopped short of the bridge it could back away, fighting. The Sipialefsky could abandon it, load the gold on sledges and make off down the Selenga Valley and over the Mongolian border. Berezkin couldn't blow the bridge before the Invincible arrived because that would stop all traffic on the line.

He sat in the dugout with Slavin and Ira, straining to see over the bridge in the gathering gloom. The Invincible should have come through long before this. Berezkin's hand rested lightly on the detonator plunger and his fingers tingled with nervous anticipation.

He and Slavin had gone over possible reasons for the delay time and again and what they feared most was that the Invincible had already stopped, perhaps at Mysovaya, that the gold had been transferred to sleds and was already on its way overland to Mongolia.

"He'll come through and take the branch line to Kiakhta," Slavin said for perhaps the fiftieth time.

"God be willing," Berezkin said though it was very un-Bolshevik to appeal to authority higher than the party. "Do you think they'll send a scouting party forward?" he asked again.

"Not with the pilot train, I think."

"That's good then. Are the men in position?"

"Balashov has them in dugouts along our bank," Slavin said.

They waited.

Ira was possibly more tense than the other two men. By now Maryenka had had her child, Ira was sure, and he wanted to get to Verkhne-Udinsk. Waiting was as painful as childbirth. He was certain of this too. Every sound caused him to ache trying to identify it. And the possibility that there was still an American train this far west kept him in an agony of suspense. It could be their transportation to Vlad. Obviously Silverman had made some arrangement for them. He had to make sure their train crossed the bridge before Berezkin pushed the plunger. He had tried to make this understood, but neither Berezkin nor Slavin seemed to know what he was talking about.

"Amerikanski cross over bridge —" this with pantomime, "Sipialef boom, boom!"

Slavin and Berezkin nodded agreeably, but they thought him a little mad.

"Sipialef boom, boom! Amerikanski nyet, boom, boom."

"O.K." Slavin said irritably, "O.K. O.K.!"

It was his only Americanism and it gave Ira no feeling of confidence.

The snow had stopped as the temperature fell but it was getting dark. Visibility was poor and their eyes smarted with the effort of holding the light. Suddenly all three men at once stopped breathing.

They heard a train. A big one. Heavy. Coming fast.

Slavin raised his binoculars, straining to see the train at the first possible instant.

Berezkin tightened his hand on the plunger of the detonator. "Let it come through," he thought. "Let it come straight on."

He squirmed closer into the moist earth of the dugout and tucked the detonator between his knees. The train sounded immense. A cold sweat burst out on his skin.

Berezkin saw it. He saw the engine and it told him nothing. His hand shook on the plunger handle.

How could he be sure? How could he know?

"That's not it!" Ira said. "Nyet!"

Berezkin looked at the American. How could the American know? His hand started to press the plunger down.

"Czech!" Slavin yelled.

The train came onto the bridge, fast. There was only a second now.

"Czech!" Slavin yelled again.

Then Berezkin saw the cars clearly marked with crosses. He jerked his hand off the plunger as though it had given him a shock. A hospital train! Katya could have been on it! He trembled and let out his breath, which made a cloud in front of his eyes.

They listened to the hospital train hammering over the tracks toward Verkhne-Udinsk. They felt good having let it go. They were grateful having been spared such a mistake. Berezkin smiled at Ira and made a gesture expressing his relief, then he trembled again.

They listened to the hospital train thinking that none on board it knew how narrowly they had escaped death and while thus occupied they failed to hear the slower approach of the second train, or of the third.

Ira saw it first. He spotted the American flags painted on the engine and snatched Slavin's binoculars. It was an American train all right, moving slowly, drawing almost to a stop as it approached the bridge. Ira could see the engineer. He adjusted the focus, and as the engine poked onto the bridge and started over, another figure swung out onto the step of the cab.

"Good Christ! It's the Sioux!" Ira cried.

He looked at Slavin and Berezkin, but they didn't understand the reason for his astonishment.

"It's Carlisle," he said.

"Amerikanski?" Slavin asked.

Ira nodded vigorously. "As American as they come," he said but at that moment they all heard the deeper rumble of another train coming down the slight grade through the village of Tataurovo.

Berezkin silenced Ira with a gesture. They all listened for what seemed an eternity, but the American train had only crossed the first span of the bridge. They could sense the bigger train; they could almost smell the menace of it. "Sipialef," Berezkin whispered.

Slavin picked up his rifle.

Ira dropped the binoculars, lunged out of the dugout and was running, sliding, half falling down the hill toward the bridge even before he knew what he intended to do. He expected to be shot at, then knew he would not be. The partisans couldn't risk a shot at him because it would alarm the crew of the Invincible. He reached level ground and sprinted toward the bridge. He had to get Carlisle's train clear of it before Sipialef's train hit the center span.

Carlisle hung by the side bar and gazed at the frozen Selenga and at the hills around the river. He had a deep attachment to the place. He remembered the Tataurovoan girls splashing in the water around the caissons, remembered the winter hunts with Yakushef, the loneliness, the growing sense of his own identity. He remembered the good things and as the train came onto the second span of the bridge Dave Sawyer called to him and the engine began to brake, throwing clouds of steam into Carlisle's face.

"What's wrong, Dave?" Carlisle yelled, then he saw the man at the far end of the bridge waving his arms. "Son of a bitch!" he said aloud. "I'll be a son of a bitch!"

They came abreast of Ira on the last span of the bridge and stopped.

"Leverett, what the hell you doing here?" Carlisle bellowed.

"For Christ's sake don't stop!" Ira yelled back. "Keep rolling! Get the hell off this bridge, Sioux. It's mined! Come on, move! Move!"

Carlisle dropped off the step and grabbed Ira's arm. Sawyer started his engine forward intending to clear the last span of the bridge. "Hold it, Sawyer," Carlisle roared.

"Hold it hell!" Ira yelled wildly. "Get over! This thing is going sky high in about five seconds!"

Sawyer hung out the cab window uncertain whom to obey.

Ira wrenched away from Carlisle and started to board the engine, but Carlisle caught him again.

"You dumb Sioux bastard! Don't you understand what I'm telling you?"

"They can't blow this bridge," Carlisle declared. "There's a train behind me."

"That's the one we're after!"

Ira fumbled for the pistol in his coat pocket while at the same time trying to ward Carlisle off. He got the pistol out, but Carlisle grabbed it. They struggled briefly and Ira kept yelling: "Sioux! Sioux! Listen to me! Listen!"

Carlisle wrenched the pistol from Ira's grasp and jammed it into his stomach. "You listen!" he growled. "I'm going through!"

"That's what I'm trying to get you to do!"

"But I'm not delivering my train to your Bolshevik friends, Leverett! How many men do you have?"

"They don't want your train! They're after Sipialef."

Carlisle raised the pistol and fired three quick shots. The sound slapped over the river ice and reverberated off through the hills.

Ira's face went white.

The four American guards on Carlisle's train swung out of their cars and ran forward with their rifles at the ready. "We've got a fight up ahead," Carlisle said.

"You warned Sipialef," Ira groaned. "You stopped him!"

Carlisle shoved Ira roughly. "Turn around and walk, Leverett. Follow us over slow, Dave. If they open fire highball it."

They started across the last span of the bridge. The guards hugged the shadows, ready to take cover and fire. Carlisle, with Leverett in front of him, walked in the beam of the engine headlamp and their combined shadows were thrown forward like giants.

Ira listened and knew that the Invincible had stopped short of the bridge. He wondered how long the partisans were going to hold their fire. He expected to be cut down at any moment, but perhaps Berezkin still hoped the Invincible would come onto the bridge after the American train cleared it. That was their best chance after all. "You're a damned fool, Carlisle," he said.

"At least I'm no Bolshevik."

"You're a fucking hero, you are."

"We're supposed to protect this line, not blow it up."

"You sound like a Sunday-school marm."

"Stop right here, Leverett," Carlisle said.

They stopped where the bridge met the bank and Carlisle stood in the headlamp beam holding Ira at gunpoint. "Tell your Bolshie comrades we're going through," he said.

Ira turned to face Carlisle. He smiled. He almost laughed because the Sioux didn't know what was going on and it struck him as ludicrous. The light from the headlamp was blinding and he raised one hand to shield his eyes and see Carlisle's face. "Maryenka Austin is at the Japanese hospital in Verkhne," he said. "She's having Austin's kid."

"Tell your partisans, or whatever, that we're going through."

"I want to get to Verkhne myself," Ira said.

"Are you going to do what I tell you?" Carlisle demanded.

"No," Ira said. "No, I'm not."

The planes of Carlisle's jaw hardened. "Jesus, you are a stubborn bastard!"

"You're one hell of a lot better off with us than with Sipialef."

"He's going my way. That's all there is to it."

"I'm going to marry Maryenka," Ira said.

"You're what?"

Ira laughed. Carlisle's expression was just what he had expected it would be. His laughter filled the tense silence around the idling train and rolled off downriver. Ira slapped his thigh and roared with laughter.

Balashov, about to drop his hand to signal his men to open fire, was arrested by the sound of it.

Berezkin and Slavin, nervous perspiration breaking out like diamonds on their foreheads, couldn't have been more shocked by a live bomb rolling into their dugout than they were by Ira's burst of laughter.

But through this laughter they heard another sound. It was the In-vincible coming on with both engines at full throttle. Sipialef, warned by the shots, had stopped long enough to detrain his Cossacks; he'd waited until he saw the American train pass over the bridge, then ordered Graetz to take their train through, all guns firing.

"They're still on the far side, Colonel," Graetz had objected.

"Get us through, Graetz," Sipialef roared. "One bridge! Brush them aside!"

Graetz uncoupled the lead engine and sent it ahead to ram Carlisle's train if it still blocked the line, then Graetz himself took the throttle of the Invincible.

Carlisle heard the oncoming train. "Highball it, Dave!" he yelled. "Clear out!" Then he pulled Ira off the tracks.

Sawyer slammed the throttle full open. The drive wheels burned the rails, throwing a shower of sparks; then the engine began to move.

"Take her through to Verkhne!" Carlisle bellowed. "You men go on!"

The four guards caught the side bars of the passing coaches and swung up.

Bullets rattled through the steel girders of the bridge. Carlisle and Ira dropped to the deck.

"Your friends?" Carlisle asked.

"I don't know."

They felt the bridge pounding beneath them and saw the headlamp of the oncoming Sipialef engine careening toward them.

As the big engine reached the center span Carlisle saw the engineer bail out, flip over the guard rail, and drop to the ice like an ejected cartridge.

"Oh, good Christ!" Carlisle thought. "It's wild!"

In his dugout Berezkin, trembling from head to foot, nearly pushed the plunger, but Slavin caught his hand as he saw the Invincible enter the bridge all guns firing. Berezkin waited, counted, prayed. His lungs seemed to have turned into blocks of ice, but his head was on fire.

Carlisle leaped for the Sipialef engine as it went by. He caught the side bar in one hand and was snapped off his feet. He hung on but all the tendons in his arm seemed to have snapped. He was slammed about, then he got one foot down on the step. His other hand groped for a hold and he hauled himself into the cab, staggered up and jerked the throttle down, then pulled the brake lever with all his strength. The big engine seemed to nose down; it began a kind of slow spin like a waltzing elephant and as it started to topple Carlisle jumped.

Ira heard gunfire all around him and saw Sipialef's Cossacks charge over the ice, brandishing their sabers and howling. They were like a picture, every man poised, the horses straining and eager. They reached the center of the river, and the ice blew up in heaving sheets like wind-blown paper. The Cossacks spilled into the water and were swept around in the conflicting current. Machine gun fire ran over the black water like hail. Horses screamed and went down with their riders clinging to them.

Then Ira saw the Invincible charge the bridge with its guns blazing. "The damned fool son of a bitch," he thought. "He's going to make it!" But there was a deep explosion which flattened the turbulent water and the center span buckled upward and collapsed. One, two, three cars dropped into the river with a metal-tearing roar. The engine tore loose, careened over the next span, then plunged into the river. Horses, men and machines were screaming. Machine gun and rifle fire raked the air and stitched the ground.

The rear gun car of Sipialef's train was still on the bridge firing rapidly, the shells blossoming like huge poppies among the trees.

Ira pulled his coat close around him as though it were armor, then he scrambled back toward the partisan dugouts. He kept crouched and threw himself down twice and another time he was thrown down, but he rose again with a quick, burning exhilaration. He felt that his eyes were filled with light; they seemed to illuminate everything they touched with a glow of silver purity. He tried to laugh again, but he didn't hear any sound and his knees gave out. "Wait'll I tell Uncle Dave," he thought and he stared at the patch of snow in front of his knees. It was untouched, like a clean pillowcase, and he fell forward into it with a feeling of cool relief.

The partisans swarmed over the disabled train killing the Sipialefsky who did not surrender. Slavin and Berezkin forced their way into Sipialef's armored coach and found the Colonel alone, seated on the high-backed chair. His face was pale, flaky as half-dried calcimine; his mouth trembled and his hands flopped about like sick birds in his lap. The derailed coach was canted at a fifteen-degree angle and the cockatoos were squawking. Sipialef was clad in a white dolman trimmed with fur at the collar and hem. There was an assortment of weapons within his reach, but he made no move toward them.

Berezkin shot him hastily. The heavy bullet cleaved a furrow across the top of Sipialef's skull. Blood welled up and ran down the sides of his head and began to drip on the shoulders of his dolman.

He continued to stare at Berezkin, who steadied his hand and was about to fire again, but the glazed expression in Sipialef's eyes told him the man was dead.

Carlisle limped back toward the river searching for Ira. One of his arms was badly sprained and he'd twisted his leg jumping from the engine. He saw the armored gun car on the bridge and Sipialef's private coach which hadn't gone into the river. They weren't firing any more and the partisans were swarming over it from the twisted girders of the bridge which still protruded above the racing black water of the Selenga.

Carlisle came to the place where he'd left Ira, but he wasn't there. He searched around and called a couple of times, then he saw a dark patch against the snow and knew, even in the failing light, that it was Ira. He ran to him, dropped on his knees and rolled Ira over on his back. Ira sighed like a man who hates being wakened up in the morning. "What is it?" he grumbled. "What do ya want?"

"Ira," Carlisle said. "It's me, the Sioux."

"O.K. Sioux," Ira said.

"I'll take you to Verkhne."

"O.K."

Carlisle tried to open the coat, Austin's coat, but he saw a gaping hole in it just over the shoulder and he was afraid.

"Maryenka," Ira said.

"What?"

Ira made an effort to go back to sleep, but his hands were cold and he couldn't hear his own voice, just a distant sound in his head. "She's a cucumber," he said, then he opened his eyes.

Ira saw the Sioux and he wanted to laugh again. He felt light and good. The Sioux's heavy face was blurred, warm brown, indistinct and solemn. "What is it, Sioux?" he thought. "It's going to be all right."

The partisans were still firing, but Carlisle didn't hear the guns. He was holding Ira's eyes in his own, trying to keep the light in them, trying to hold Ira's life together in Harry Austin's bullet-torn coat, but after a moment he knew Ira was dead.

Carlisle looked up at the hills and remembered that this was the place where he'd rediscovered his mother's song. He heard the Selenga and remembered the words once more: "Thus the father sayeth/ Lo, he now commandeth/ All on earth to sing/ to sing now. Thus he hath spoken/ Thus he hath spoken/ Tell afar his message."

He tried to say them in his Indian tongue:

Ateyapi kin
Maka owancya
Lowan nisipe-lo—

But he got no farther because something hard closed his throat and he was afraid of weeping and Ira wouldn't understand the song anyway because he was a Jew, not a Sioux. And Carlisle wished now that he'd told Ira about it, but it was too late for that.

He brushed Ira's eyes shut and the lashes under his fingertips sent a shudder through his body. He wrapped Ira more closely in Austin's coat. "At least I can take him out with me," he thought.

Then he lifted Ira and carried him down the track toward Verkhne-Udinsk.

CHAPTER FORTY-ONE

BEFORE dawn on February 7, 1920, a lone truck with a chain drive and solid rubber tires jolted its way uneasily down a rutted, ice-armored road toward the frozen Ushakovka River. The beams of its headlights, made sulphurous by the mist, pitched up and down and finally came to a stop, leaving a corridor of light which ended at a black hole in the ice.

A firing squad dropped from the truck bed to the frozen ground and took positions on either side of the headlights. Their hands and their rifles were cold and they shuddered inwardly at the hour and at the task which lay ahead.

The Red Military Commandant of Irkutsk beckoned his guards to bring the prisoners forward. Chairman Chudnovsky of the Extraordinary Investigating Commission which had been interrogating Admiral Kolchak for the past weeks stood by as Pepelyaev and Kolchak were guided toward the hole. The Prime Minister fell once and had to be helped to his feet. Both men were handcuffed. Admiral Kolchak marched forward resolutely and turned to face the headlights, his pale face set in what he knew to be his last effort at self-control. Pepelyaev was placed beside him and fell again, for his knees would no longer hold him up.

Kolchak shook his head when offered a blindfold.

Chudnovsky admired him. "Is there anything I can do?" he asked.

A look of resentment crossed the Admiral's face as though he would have preferred not having been delayed. Then his expression softened. The waters of the Ushakovka whispered at the heels of his boots. "If you would be so good as to get a message to my wife in Paris to say that I bless my son."

"I didn't know you had a son."

"Yes, I have."

Their eyes met in a moment of recognition and regret, then Chudnovsky stepped back to make way for the priest.

Both men said their prayers aloud. The priest bowed and retired to the truck.

The condemned men heard the cold rattle of rifle bolts and stiffened their bodies.

The squad fired a stuttering volley which threw the two men back into the black pool of water. The squad fired another volley, then a soldier with a board poked the two bodies down until they were seized by the current.

Thus the man whom the British and French had inspired, supported and betrayed died; a small man in whose name countless atrocities had been committed and for whose government thousands upon thousands had lost their lives. He died without flinching, gazing calmly into the muzzles of the guns which snuffed him out.

Chudnovsky looked toward the jail knowing that Madame Timireva, awake in her cell, had heard the shots and he supposed she was weeping now.

A third prisoner, Cheng Ting-fan, a Chinese sadist employed by the Kolchak government to extract information from its prisoners, was frog-marched to the edge of the ice and shot unceremoniously; then Chairman Chudnovsky got into the cab of the truck. The tunnel of light had vanished with the coming dawn. "Well," he thought, "it's over. Let Kappel and Voitsekhovsky share the blame. If they hadn't tried to rescue Kolchak we would have sent him to Moscow."

But General Kappel was dead of frostbite. Having refused to give up command of his troops in their desperate drive toward Irkutsk, he died on the trakt in a sledge. General Voitsekhovsky had pressed the attack to the last station before Glaskov.

To stop this rescue attempt the Reds had mined the Angara River and declared siege law in Irkutsk, and as a last resort they killed Admiral Kolchak, the object of the Voitsekhovsky drive.

"Yes, let them all share the blame," Chudnovsky thought. "The interventionists too. Kolchak was in many ways an admirable man. Well, so are we all.''

The driver got into the cab and turned off the lights. No one spoke on the way back, but there was a sense of historical finality in the chill morning air and a feeling among them that their lives would always be blighted by their share in this shabby execution.

It was unnaturally silent, dark and cold as Carlisle plodded toward Verkhne-Udinsk with Ira in his arms. He tried to measure his stride to the ties, but his twisted leg made walking painfully slow. He stopped at Mostovoi and Divizionnaya Post to rest, laying Ira's body down on the siding platforms there. He hadn't seen a human being since leaving Tataurovo. He hadn't even seen a dog. The only movement in all that darkness seemed to be his own. At this point the trakt was farther north and he wondered about the pilgrims there, wondered how many, like himself, bore their dead in their arms.

His breath crackled in front of his face and the rails gleamed with frost. It was wolf-hunting weather and he remembered the long, silent waits with Yakushef, remembered the bewildered wolves staring at him over the line of flags, their legs tense, their nostrils quivering. There would be no one ringing the wolves with flags now. There were too many corpses in the forest, too many dead horses with crows perched on them. The wolves would be glutted in their lairs.

Carlisle sensed them there, healthy wolves settling down to sleep through the coming day with their powerful muzzles buried in their own deep fur.

Had he told Ira about the wolves? No, not all of it. He had never been able to come out of his own lair of silence.

"I meant to tell you about the wolves, Ira," he said, then he picked Ira's body up and started on once again.

"They're handicapped," he said, "by their intelligence. They can't go over flags. No, they can't do it. They die.''

Ira's corpse had frozen. His legs, bent at the knees, hung down over Carlisle's arm. His head, turned a bit to one side, was rigid on the neck and his arms were crossed over his chest. His whole body was stiff and unyielding in Carlisle's aching arms, but there was nothing to be done about it.

Carlisle spoke aloud now and again for the comfort of his own voice. It gave him strength though he hardly knew what he said. He told about the shacks at Khailar, about the battle of Binidayan, about his uncle, Henry Buckeye, and whatever else came into his mind.

It occurred to him that he knew very little about Ira. "I hardly know you," he said one time. And he thought about this until he reached Verkhne-Udinsk.

The few people on the streets who saw Carlisle didn't offer to help him. He was just another man with a load of grief in his arms. No one met him. He went to the train depot and eased Ira's body down on the floor and looked away quickly because the cocked legs held it up in such an awful way.

He found the officer in charge of the Japanese guard but the man, though courteous, spoke no English. Carlisle thought of Ikachi and mentioned his name. "Ikachi," he said. "Major Subo Ikachi, Chita."

This had an effect and the officer told him to wait. Twenty minutes later he returned with a translator and instructions wired by Major Ikachi from Chita to give Captain Carlisle and his party all possible assistance.

Carlisle asked if his train had come through and was told which siding it was on. The Japanese translator offered to have Ira looked after — "encoffined" was the word he used with some pride.

"Yes, all right," Carlisle said gruffly and he went down to find his train.

When they saw him coming Jud Conners, Sawyer and the rest of the men spilled out of their coaches, hammered Carlisle on the back and helped him inside. Conners shoved a cup of coffee in his hand.

"Where's Tatiana?" Carlisle asked.

"At the Japanese hospital," Conners said.

"What's she doing there?"

"Helping out."

Carlisle lay down on the berth and sleep swept over him like a black wave. He tried to fight it, but someone put a blanket over him. "I'll go up there in a little bit," he said.

"We'll tell her," Conners said.

In the main ward of the Japanese hospital Tatiana sat beside the bed where a patient lay sleeping; he'd lost one leg at the knee and the Japanese surgeon said he'd probably never regain the full use of his wounded arm.

Tatiana untied the scarf around her neck and studied the laughter Major Ikachi had painted on it. It seemed so long ago. She smoothed the silk scarf on her knees and the man on the bed beside her stirred. "Tatiana?"

"Yes, Raul?"

"Are you there?"

Tatiana took Raul's hand and smiled. "I'm here, Raul," she said.

"We'll go back to Prague together," Markowitz said.

"As soon as you're able to travel, Raul."

Markowitz looked at the vacant place in the bed which should have been occupied by his lower leg and felt a perverse jubilation. He was skewed. By the absence of this leg he was sufficiently different from other men to hold Tatiana's affection. She had always needed a man who was in some way crippled and now he qualified. Raul loved Tatiana helplessly and he smiled thinking: "I've given my leg for a wife and Adam only gave his rib." Then he gripped Tatiana's hand tightly and looked into her eyes.

"I know what's going to happen, Tatiana," he said quietly. "We're going to go through it all over again. We're going to repeat it all."

Tatiana was already imagining their life together in Prague. They would be a handsome couple, touched by suffering, not so brilliant as before, not so cynical, but leaders of the new society all the same.

"Yes, all over again," Markowitz said.

"But perhaps this time it will be different," Tatiana said. "Perhaps this time it will be better, Raul."

"Let's hope it will be," Markowitz said. "I'll try to make it be."

He was heavily sedated and presently his grip on her hand relaxed. Tatiana tucked his arm under the blanket and stood a moment looking down at his pale, handsome face which was more dear to her now than she would have thought possible. He'd been on the hospital train which had passed them at Murinskaya. Fate, it seemed, had decreed that they were to be together. They knew each other well enough to make a worthwhile life. Yes, perhaps she could re-create Ikachi's portrait of her laughter.

Tatiana draped the silk scarf around her neck and went to the window which looked down over the park toward the river. It was a mild day. The sun, through an overcast of clouds, seemed to be laboring mightily to bring some warmth to the desolate city. There was an icebreaker on the river crushing its way upstream toward the confluence of the Uda, leaving blocks of ice in its wake; and as she watched, a mound of frozen snow separated from the bank of the park and was carried away, turning slowly in the current.

Soon the river traffic would begin, commerce would be restored; she and Raul would witness another spring in Prague.

"What a thing to have lived through," she thought. "What a thing to remember."

Jud Conners had telephoned from the depot to say Carlisle had arrived and was sleeping. What could she tell him? What need was there to tell him anything, after all? Wouldn't he see it?

She smiled thinking of Carlisle once again as her Captain of the Powder Room. Surely he would understand when he learned Raul was alive.

Tatiana returned to Raul's bedside, made sure he was sleeping easily, then she went into the corridor. She'd asked Mr. Conners to have her luggage sent to the hospital and she wondered if it had arrived.

As she came down the stairs she saw Carlisle talking to the nurse at the desk. Her suitcase was at his feet. She hesitated on the steps, wondering if he'd brought her things, wondering again what she was going to say. Her figure was dark against the pale light of the window; the desk nurse looked toward her and smiled, then Carlisle also looked up.

Tatiana came down the last flight of stairs. She was very erect, smiling graciously, and the silk scarf at her throat set her face off above the drab Volunteer Nurses uniform she was wearing. She crossed the footworn linoleum floor with her hand extended and Carlisle came to meet her, limping slightly. He caught her hand in both his own. "Hello," he said.

"Are you hurt, Jack?"

"Twisted my leg. It's nothing."

That was all.

They sought each other's eyes expecting to find again the wordless intimacy of that moment in front of the hotel in Omsk, but it wasn't there. Not in his eyes, nor in hers.

Instead they saw the insurmountable barrier of their past lives; her need for the society of Prague, his need for achievement. There was respect in their recognition and there was regret.

"Raul Markowitz is here," Tatiana said.

"I brought your things. Conners said you'd asked for them."

"Yes, I did."

They did not flinch from each other's eyes and gradually the pain went out of them.

"We'll always love each other in a way," she said.

"I suppose that's so."

"There are just too many pieces missing."

He nodded as though he knew exactly what she meant and they were able to look away. He turned her hand in his and Tatiana thought he was going to kiss it, but he let it slide out of his own.

"I came to see the wife of one of my men," he said. "Maryenka Austin."

"You can ask at the desk."

"I have. She's upstairs."

"Can I show you?"

"I'd rather go alone."

"Jack?"

"Yes?"

"You do understand?"

Once more he nodded, then his face darkened and he caught Tatiana in his arms and pressed her to him. "Goodbye," he said. He brushed her forehead with his lips, released her abruptly and went up the stairs to find Maryenka.

Tatiana watched him out of sight, then went to the desk, picked up her suitcase and carried it to her room in the nurses' quarters. She thought it best not to see him again, never again. It was so final that it hurt, but she knew it would not have worked out. Raul would tell her so. She would depend on Raul's telling her because he knew her life almost as well as Albert had known it. Raul would remember. Raul always remembered everything, so she could forget.

It was best, after all, to forget.

The moment Carlisle appeared at the foot of her bed Maryenka knew that Ira would never come. She didn't want the Captain to tell her so and tried to hush his first words, but they came out brokenly and the Captain sat down on a nearby chair as though it had cost him more to say the words than it had for her to hear them.

"I'm sorry," he stammered. "Terribly sorry."

"Don't, please," Maryenka said.

"Perhaps I'd better come back another time."

"No," she said. "It isn't necessary."

"You'll want to come with us."

"No."

"We can help you and the child," he said.

"No, please go. I'm sorry."

He rose awkwardly. "I'll come back," he said.

"No, please. I don't want you to. I'll be all right."

He nodded as though he hadn't heard and started away, but he paused at the door "Is it a boy?" he asked.

"Yes."

"I'll come back," he said.

When he'd gone Maryenka lay perfectly still for a long time waiting for the crushing seizure of grief which she was sure would come. At feeding time the maternity nurse brought her infant and put it down at her side. "Are you all right, dear?" she asked.

"Oh, yes," Maryenka said.

She gave her breast to her child and felt its urgent mouth, but even then the grief she'd expected did not come.

"It will never come," she thought. "I'll carry it inside me always."

She looked down at the small, tight face of her child. It no longer mattered who had fathered it. Perhaps the grief locked inside her would prevent her from loving too much. She had to be careful about this because everyone she had loved died — except Timokhin.

Maryenka closed her eyes and thought of Timokhin stalking across Siberia exhorting the people to settle in the seams and wait. Perhaps he was an exception. Perhaps there was still hope, but she must be cautious, nevertheless.

When the nurse came for her child Maryenka asked if there was an American captain in the hospital.

"No, he's gone. He waited for a time, then said he'd come back in the morning."

"Do you know where he can be reached?"

"If it's important I'll find out."

"I'd like to send him a note," Maryenka said.

« 3 »

Jud Conners arranged for their train to clear Verkhne-Udinsk the following morning at ten a.m. Dave Sawyer was in the cab waiting for Carlisle to return from the depot where he'd gone to make a call. He saw Carlisle crossing the yard now, but his head was down and he didn't respond to Dave's highball signal.

When Carlisle came into his compartment Conners was lying on the berth. He sat up and smiled, but the expression on Carlisle's face sobered him.

Carlisle tossed his coat down and took a seat at the window.

"Anyone else?" Conners asked.

"No," Carlisle said.

Conners stood up and checked his big railroad watch. "Well, we'll be right on time," he said. "I'll go tell Dave."

"I forgot," Carlisle said hollowly.

Conners left and Carlisle was glad to be alone. There was nothing to talk about. The note from Maryenka, written in a neat but curiously Russian script, told him it was her intention to remain in Siberia where all her loved ones were buried. But Ira was in the compartment behind; riding out in a Japanese coffin, and Maryenka would not know that.

She said she would return to Pashkova and raise her child, Ira Austin Shulgin, and that if Carlisle wanted to do so he could write her there. He'd gone to the depot to call Maryenka, to be sure she hadn't changed her mind. The nurse said Maryenka couldn't come to the phone, but that she thanked him and said goodbye.

He'd thought about calling Tatiana but he wouldn't have known what to say.

The train jerked noisily and began to move through the dismal yard. There was dirty snow packed against the base of the buildings, but most of the ground was cinder-strewn and bare. As they worked through the switches to the main line a familiar sight caught the corner of Carlisle's eye. It was the Snorter abandoned on a siding across the yard. The big golden bell was gone, only the frame which had supported it remained. Its gay red trim and the American flags were covered with grime and had begun to flake away.

Carlisle turned his head to keep it in sight but as it passed from his window tears stung Carlisle's eyes, dampening the customary fires in them.

"Christ, how I loved that engine!" he thought.

And as the train gathered speed he knew that the Snorter was a sad but fitting monument to the whole expedition.

« 4 »

The last section of the 27th Infantry Regiment pulled into Vladivostok station February 25, 1920, and went into barracks to wait for the ships which would carry them home. Thirty-seven men were hospitalized for frostbite and exposure, twelve for other diseases including typhus. The sick list was amazingly short considering the conditions through which they had traveled. One man, Private Carson, had died of despondency. Two were lost carrying messages between trains and though reported missing they were presumed to be dead.

Colonel Spaeth reported to General Graves at once, but they found very little to say to each other. Spaeth was exhausted and General Graves was relieved to have his whole force in one place again. They shook hands and Spaeth handed the General his report.

"Thanks, Bob. What else can I say?"

"Nothing's necessary."

"Well, relax. We'll handle it from here on out," Graves said.

Captain Carlisle arrived in Vladivostok on March 15. He didn't announce his presence at once. Instead he went to the Aleksander Hotel and roved the place like a dark ghost. It was shabby, dusty, squalid. The staircase which he remembered as having bannisters of alabaster was narrow, with a torn carpet and a railing of common oak. The hall formerly inhabited by the now defunct Russian Officers' Club looked like a place which might be hired by a regional convention of hardware salesmen. The flags were gone. No bells rang.

He went into the women's powder room. It smelled of urine and perfume. The mirror in which he'd seen his face and Tatiana's was cracked and dusty.

He thought again of General Bogoloff's epaulet still in the bottom of his pack; it flashed gold beside the garnet necklace in the mirror and was gone. He tried to recall tactile impressions of Tatiana's body, but they would not come. All he could visualize was her disembodied face like a cameo set in red and gold and he knew she would never have been real to him, that she would have always been a countess from Prague. He saw his reflection in the dusty mirror, the heavy-shouldered torso, the massive jaw, the nose a bit off to one side and the eyes devoid of any whiteness. They too were rose and gold and perhaps it was only this that she had been staring at as they stood facing each other in Omsk. But no, there had been complete acceptance on her part then and because of it he could accept his own limitations now. He was an old army man, duty bound, and he couldn't jump the flags.

That evening he reported to Colonel Spaeth and told him about Leverett and Maryenka.

The Colonel listened in silence and when Carlisle was finished he nodded. "Well, that's it," he said.

"Yes, sir," Carlisle said.

"Take C Company, Captain," Spaeth said.

"Thank you, sir."

On the last parade Carlisle marched at the head of his company, down Svetlandskaya Street, past the depot, toward the docks. He searched the crowd along the way hoping to see a familiar face. He saw one. A woman with bad teeth and a yellow pallor. It took him a while to remember that she was the girl he had nearly taken with him the night of the Armistice ball. He averted his eyes, straightened his back and marched on.

The American troops boarded the transport *Great Northern* on the morning of April 1, 1920. It was a clear day in Vladivostok. The sun was shining and there was a white moon like a tissue paper disc hardly visible in the pale sky.

During this last week General Graves had attended various military functions honoring his service in Siberia and, parenthetically, his departure from it. He'd been decorated with the Order of the Rising Sun (Second Class), the Order of Wen Hu (the Striped Tiger of China), the Czech War Cross and sundry other baubles. But these occasions were so trying to a man of his temperament that he had begun to despair of shaking himself free of Siberia and it was not until he felt the deck of the American ship under his feet that he permitted himself a sigh of relief.

The Japanese commander, General Oi, had sent a military band to play the American troops aboard their ship and when Graves stepped out on deck to watch the 27th Infantry file up the gangway he found Colonel Spaeth leaning on the rail.

Spaeth looked around, then straightened up. "Good morning, General," he said.

Graves smiled. "I want you to know I didn't pick this date on purpose," he said.

Spaeth looked puzzled.

"April Fools' Day," Graves said. "That's what it is."

Spaeth nodded. "The thought had crossed my mind," he said.

They stood side by side watching the troops come aboard. The men paused at the foot of the gangplank to have their names checked off the roster, then they came up, moving slowly with full packs on their backs. Salt-water smells rose between the ship and the dock and a breeze raised a ruff of whitecaps on the Bay of the Golden Horn.

"Eichelberger will bring the last of them out on the sixteenth," Graves said.

"Yes."

"The whole episode will probably have been forgotten by then."

"Yes, I suppose so," Spaeth said.

The Japanese band played a medley of tunes one of which was repeated frequently and Graves was annoyed because he couldn't recall its name. "What's that tune, Bob?" he asked.

"That one? Darned if I know."

Spaeth cupped his hands and called to the lieutenant at the foot of the gangplank. "Ryan, can you give me the name of the tune the band is playing?"

Lieutenant Ryan asked if anyone in the line knew what the Japanese band was playing. The question ran down the line of men and the answer came back to Ryan, who cupped his hands and called up to Colonel Spaeth. "They say it's 'Hard Times Come Again No More,' Colonel."

"That's right," General Graves said. " 'Hard Times Come Again No More.' " Then he grinned and went to his cabin to write General Oi a note of appreciation.

Two hours later a pair of tugboats pulled the *Great Northern* away from the dock and gave her a heading toward the harbor entrance. The big propeller began to churn and Carlisle, standing on the afterdeck, gazed back at the city waiting and listening for the bells.

Epilogue

THE American Siberian Expedition was hastily forgotten. Those who took part in it were always regarded with mild astonishment when they mentioned that the United States had sent troops into Russia in World War I. What for? they were asked. And to this they never had a satisfactory answer.

The debris of the Romanov dynasty was carried to France by General Janin, but the Grand Duke Nicholas, senior surviving member of the Romanov family, refused to accept it. The box and suitcases containing relics of the Romanovs were sent to Baron Wrangel, the last White general, but they were lost, somewhere in the Crimea.

Of the fifteen flags which had hung in the ballroom of the Aleksander Hotel seven no longer exist as national emblems and the flag of the Japanese Imperial Marines is rarely unfurled.

Nations have come and gone.

General William S. Graves was retired in 1928. He wrote a book about his experiences, and died at the age of seventy-five in 1940.

Robert L. Eichelberger lived to fight the Japanese and to write his account of that contest in a book called *Our Jungle Road to Tokyo.*

Subo Ikachi made two visits to the United States and toured California with a copy of Homer Lea's book, *The Valor of Ignorance,* in his hand. He was in command of the landing at Cavite when Japan took the Philippines, and narrowly missed meeting Colonel Jack Carlisle, who was flown to Pearl Harbor before the surrender of Corregidor.

When Carlisle returned with MacArthur two years later General Ikachi had been killed in the bombing.

Mrs. Raul Markowitz lived through the Second World War in Prague and saw much of her city reduced to rubble. She was a beautiful woman always, but sometimes a bit confused, and her husband often said to her, "Tatiana, you really must begin a diary."

"No, it's much too late, Raul. Much, much too late."

In October, 1942, a small gray-haired woman, the schoolmistress of Pashkova, was informed that her son, Ira Austin Shulgin, had been killed at Stalingrad and this confirmed what she had always known, that her love was a curse. She tried to conceal and withhold it, but the children in her classroom understood and though she was often impatient with them they were devoted to her.

After the Second World War the United States persisted in the course which Subo Ikachi had anticipated and the westward thrust to dominate the Asian mainland went on year after year.

Half a century after President Wilson wrote his Aide-Mémoire authorizing the American intervention in Siberia a Catholic archbishop speaking from his pulpit in the San Fernando Cathedral, San Antonio, Texas, concluded his sermon by saying: "Such intervention is not merely allowed and lawful; it is a sad and heavy obligation imposed by the mandate of love."

The archbishop was referring to the American intervention in Vietnam and the President of the United States, seated in the audience, looked properly solemn; he alone, with the uncontestable power granted him by the Constitution, had committed his nation to a war on the Asian mainland. He had the Constitution, he had the consensus and now he had a mandate of love.

Outside the sun was shining. Local San Antonio boosters had organized a fete for the President's guests, a party of Latin American ambassadors. A barge on the San Antonio River had taken these diplomats past a series of entertainments on shore, a flamenco dancer, two go-go girls dancing in cages, a Dixieland Jazz group and a hillbilly band.

Now the bunting and the flags were being removed and Colonel Jack Carlisle, U.S. Army, retired, sat in the sun watching the activity. He was eighty-seven years old, still erect, but his eyes had gone bad from years of close writing in a diary which no one had read. "What flags are those, Austin?" he asked.

Austin Carlisle, one of his four grandchildren, looked to see what the old man meant. "That's just decorations, Grandpa," he said.

"They're all around us, Austin," the old man said.

"Yes, sir, they are."

The old man studied the flags. He stood up and turned around, seeing the pennants dimly wherever he looked. "I'll go over now," he thought. "Yes, now I'll go over." And that night he died peacefully in his sleep.